# THE TRUTHS WE HIDE

Kathy ♡ Lockheart

# THE TRUTHS WE HIDE

KATHY LOCKHEART

Cover design © By Hang Le

978-1-955017-19-0 e-book
978-1-955017-20-6 Paperback
978-1-955017-21-3 Hardcover

Published by Rosewood Literary Press

# THE TRUTHS WE HIDE

This collection includes two full-length, tension-filled romances in the Secrets and the City series: Lethal Justice and Grave Deception. Both are stand-alone romances with no cliffhangers.

# LETHAL JUSTICE

# LETHAL JUSTICE BLURB

A hostage isn't supposed to develop feelings for her captor—a man who's the antithesis of everything I stand for. And my captor isn't supposed to see me in a way no one else ever has, let alone want to protect me from the other men who plan to end my life...

Surrendering to our unexpected feelings could spell death for us both. Especially when Easton is given a direct order: Kill me, or they'll kill him and his brother.

**Soon, our lives, along with the lives of everyone we love, are in danger. And time is running out...**

*For my mom, my role model in unconditional love.*

# AUTHOR'S NOTE

Lethal Justice is a tension-filled romance that contains violence and other content that may be triggering for some readers. I prefer you go into a story without spoilers, but if you would like a **list of detailed triggers**, you can find it posted on my website at Kathy-Lockheart dot com.

## 1

No one ever expects to be held captive by three men who intend to murder them. No. They go about their lives, oblivious to the imminent danger around the corner—even when it's only a few hours away.

Just like I was doing right now while Dad watched the evening news, the anchor's voice piercing through our townhouse.

"Another brazen robbery last night, this one in the River North neighborhood. Where police say two armed men broke into a home and stole over $20,000 worth of valuables."

Twenty grand. Jeez, Louise. *I wish I had that kind of money*. I glared at my latest utilities bill, which had been haunting my countertop for the past five days, as if a contagious plague would sicken me the moment I opened it.

Which was stupid. I'd turned off the air conditioner despite the sweltering summer heat, so I bet it was under a hundred. Maybe even below ninety. It had to be. Anything beyond that, I was screwed, even with my upcoming paycheck.

I tore a tiny corner open with my nail and then slowly ripped a line down the envelope, taking a deep breath before I unfolded the paper and looked at the amount owed.

*$154.12.*

*Ugh.*

Maybe by some miracle, another bill hadn't cleared yet, and I could do that magic juggling thing, where this bill got paid while another was in limboland. I opened the banking app on my phone and checked my balance.

Nope. A whopping $25.57 sat in my checking account, pre-grocery shopping. *Pre.*

*Deep breath. You made a fantastic case to Michael, and he was supportive of your ask.*

For two years, the company I worked for had not given raises to anyone, citing pressures from the economy. While I didn't think I was above others, I'd watched a TED Talk that inspired me to put a business case together and be brave enough to ask for one. To advocate for myself. As a marketing analyst, my work this past year had brought in $1,500,000 in advertising fees to our company, which was $350,000 over my target. I'd worked my butt off to accomplish that, and I was mega proud of it. And yet, when it came time for my performance review? I got a pat on the back instead of a raise.

*Again.*

This time, I decided to stand up and ask for what I felt was fair— something I did professionally with a lot of financials to back up my request. And the great news? My boss, Michael, was taking it to HR yesterday, who had the final say.

He probably hadn't emailed yet because he was trying stupendously hard to get a yes. Or maybe he was able to secure more than the five percent I'd asked for and wanted to share the good news in person.

I checked my phone anyway.

*Holy crap.*

*There's his email.*

My heart spasmed as I opened it.

*RE: RAISE REQUEST*

. . .

*Zoey,*

*As discussed, I spoke with HR about your request for a raise. Unfortunately, they will not make exceptions to the company-wide policy of no annual adjustments this year. I'm sorry it wasn't the answer we were hoping for, but please know your hard work is very much valued in this company, and hopefully, next year might be a different answer.*

*Sincerely,*

*Michael*

Damn.

The company withholding raises for all employees sucked, but what sucked even more was that this put me back to ground zero with solving our financial problems.

My eyes stung.

"Everything okay?" Dad asked.

I cleared my throat and smiled. "Fine," I lied.

Dad hadn't been able to work since his accident, and as it turned out, my marketing job wasn't enough to pay for everything my dad needed. His prescriptions alone were seven hundred dollars a month.

Seven. Hundred. Dollars. My older brother, Anthony—who lived on the other side of the country and was desperate to help after the accident—sent us more money each month than he could probably afford. It covered half of Dad's meds, and I was immensely grateful for that, but there was still the other half. And that didn't include medical bills, physical therapy, and all the other stuff he needed if he had any hope of recovering.

Lesson learned: Don't fall victim to an accident. It could screw you *and* your family.

But I guess that wasn't entirely fair. If it had happened when Dad was still employed with health insurance, our financial situation wouldn't be in a complete tailspin right now.

*Whatever.* I couldn't let this setback stop me from focusing on my goals: help my father recover and regain his independence, so we could both get our lives back and get justice for him against the son of a bitch who hit Dad with their car and then sped off without even checking if he was alive.

Justice that hadn't come in the eight months since it happened.

Dad resumed staring at the news story and said, "I don't want you going anywhere near that neighborhood." As if I were a teenager and not a twenty-six-year-old woman.

"We have nothing to worry about."

Not as far as robberies went, anyway—those felons only targeted rich people, and we were anything but rich. Our rented townhouse that hugged the outskirts of Chicago was long overdue for a renovation. Its cherry wood doors, cabinets, and trim had suffered so much damage in the forty years since it'd been installed that in some places, baseboards had turned black with water damage, which came with the added bonus of omitting a faint smell of mold. The matching hardwood floors weren't much better, chipped and scratched in more places than it wasn't, and the kitchen and bathroom countertops were police-caution-tape yellow. I'd often wondered if the person who'd picked them was color blind. Point being, we didn't have to worry about burglars.

Money, on the other hand, was another story.

Case in point? I knew what Alex—a family friend and Dad's current physical therapist—was probably coming over to talk to me about, and it had kept me up half the night, worrying about it. That email from my boss? Was basically my nail in the coffin.

What in the world was I going to tell Alex now?

As if my anxiety had summoned him, a knock at the front door came.

"Look through the peephole," Dad said.

I refrained from rolling my eyes. *Armed burglars don't knock.* But whatever. I appeased him, confirming it was Alex before opening the door.

"Hey, Zoey."

With blond hair and green eyes, Alex stood six inches taller than me. He had a lean body with broad shoulders and very thin legs, but the most prominent part of him was the freckles speckled over his nose and cheeks.

I'd first seen those freckles when he and his parents moved into the house across the street from ours right before our high school freshman year. He used to come over for dinners at our house a lot and had been like a brother to me, a friend to our entire family, really. So, after getting his college degree in physical therapy, he'd heard about the accident and offered to help.

Alex nodded a hello to my dad, then returned his gaze to me, shoved his hands into his pockets, and nodded toward the front yard. "Can we talk out here?"

*Crap.*

I stepped into the summer air, noting the pastel purples drifting through the pinks with the setting sun.

Summer had always been my favorite time in Chicago. I loved the warm weather and how the bright blue skies canopied the skyscrapers with happiness. I loved the tourists who traveled from all around the world, reminding us not to take our remarkable museums, historic architecture, and gorgeous landmarks for granted. And I loved how there was an endless list of things to do.

I'd get to enjoy all of it again. I totally would, just as soon as Dad got back on his feet.

We stood on my front porch, which sat on a street with rows of identical townhouses, many with rusted chain-link fences. The narrow buildings sat so close together that only a few feet separated them, and the two-lane road in front of us was a favorite for teenagers blasting loud music from their cars while the smell of weed wafted out of them.

I stared at the porch's cedar planks, noting a fresh crack splintering near the steps that led to the sidewalk. I bet the board never saw that crack coming, probably thought it would exist forever without problems.

"Listen, I wanted to talk to you about something." Alex wouldn't meet my eyes. He kept his gaze pinned to his shoes, as if they'd give him the courage to say whatever uncomfortable thing he was about to say.

"I'm going to keep helping you guys," he caveated. Which was bad. Caveats were very bad. "But, uh…" Alex grabbed the back of his neck. "The thing is, my landlord just upped my rent, and, uh…well, there's a new client that wants to take your dad's spot."

*No. No. No.*

After eight months of hell, things were finally on the cusp of turning around. Dad's physical therapy had gotten him from being bedridden to wheelchair-mobile, and last week, Dad had a major breakthrough, standing up and getting a couple of steps in with a walker. He was, as doctors put it, at a precipice in his rehabilitation. A fork in the road. Keep pushing forward? He'd regain his ability to walk and live a normal life. Scale back, and his body would regress.

Physical therapy was the only tool that would make or break the most pivotal point in his recovery, and if Alex stopped giving it to him, it would throw almost all of Dad's progress down the drain.

"I was going to turn him down," Alex said, his tone laced with apology. "But…"

But I owed Alex $2,200 and counting. No matter how good a family friend he was, no matter how much he wanted to help us, that was a lot of freaking money and time to be spending not getting paid. Especially if his rent just went up.

For a long time, Alex had done Dad's PT for free, but when I realized we were in this for a much longer haul than expected, I insisted on paying him *something*. He'd given me a mega discount, and even then, I was behind.

"I can still come at least a couple days a week," Alex offered. "Hopefully more."

But anything less than five wouldn't progress Dad; it might simply slow his regression.

My voice was a near whisper on account of choking back tears; I swallowed them down, so I wouldn't make Alex feel even worse by crying in front of him. I could cry later, alone in my room.

"Please," I said. "You're the only person who's willing to work with us on this, and if Dad doesn't keep his current therapy, he might never get out of that wheelchair or get his independence back."

*And I'll never get my life back.*

What a selfish thought to have when Dad couldn't even walk and Alex was getting screwed right now. It wasn't fair to ask him this.

I felt like a terrible person, like I was taking advantage of him when he had his own bills to pay. I mean, honestly, how could I ask Alex for an extension when I already owed him for three months of unpaid work? But this wasn't just about me. It was about Dad and his quality of life.

Alex studied my eyes, a crease in his forehead appearing, as if my desperation had caught him off guard. I wondered if Alex wasn't as hopeful as I was that Dad would have more breakthroughs. And fully recover. The thought of him doubting it made a rock drop in my stomach.

"You know what?" Alex offered a smile and waved his hand. Guilt etched through his words as if *he* were the one being selfish for having even entertained the idea of getting paid for his time after eight months of favors. "Never mind. I can figure this out."

"No," I insisted. "I'll get you your money." I'd find a way…

I knew this financial breaking point was coming. It was a juggling act I'd avoided for nearly a year. Robbing Peter to pay Paul—charging groceries on my credit cards, things like that. But now, my credit cards were maxed out, and I had no more financial tricks up my sleeve.

But I did have one option left. A painful option, but I would do anything to keep Dad's rehabilitation going and not take advantage of Alex in the process.

"I have a ring," I said. A special ring Dad had given to me the Christmas before I left for college. "It's worth a lot, and I can pawn it."

I'd have to get it from Dad's old place, but that was totally doable; it hadn't sold yet, and I still had Dad's spare key.

"Zoey." Alex's voice dropped low. "I don't want you to do that."

"I'm doing it whether you like it or not," I decided. Maybe after I paid Alex, I'd have some money left over to put toward other bills.

"Zoey..."

"I don't want other people having to bail us out, and I know what it's like, trying to make ends meet." I didn't want to see Alex struggle the way we had; I didn't want to drag him down like that. "It's no big deal," I claimed.

Alex sighed, the same exacerbated breath he used to do when we were teens. And then his gaze fell across my face, flickering in curiosity. "I don't understand why you're doing so much for him after what he did to you."

I kept my face neutral, as if his words hadn't detonated inside me, blasting shrapnel throughout my chest.

"I can't thank you enough for all that you've done for us," I said. "I'll pawn the ring, and I'll have cash in your hand tomorrow."

Alex looked at the ground and shook his head in frustration. "Your dad had to be making, what, multi-six figures as that corporate strategy executive? He should've had enough money for a lifetime or, at the very least, for any medical crisis. But his negligence becomes your problem? It's bull."

On top of losing his physical health, Dad had lost his money and his old home—a high-end condo, where he'd lived for the past several years. Any day, it would sell, and he wouldn't even profit from it or break even. Not with all the money owed to the banks and hospital bills. No, that money would go to creditors.

Not that I said any of that; I preferred not to feed Alex's resentment toward my father. Truth be told, I hadn't resolved my own frustrations over my dad's financial negligence, but I needed to stay focused on the hurdle before me—securing continuity in Dad's therapy.

Alex put his hands back into his pockets. "You know I'd do anything for you, right?"

"Is that a yes?" I balled up on my tiptoes.

Alex nodded.

I reached up and hugged him, catching him off guard. He wobbled back a couple inches and returned the embrace before I released him.

Selling the ring was a stopgap. One that wouldn't last for long, but these days, my life was so chaotic, I could only focus on one hurdle at a time.

And this was a gigantic hurdle that had moved out of my way.

"I will make this up to you!" I didn't know how, but I would. Someday, I'd pay him interest on all this overdue money, and in the meantime, I could do little things, at least. "Do you want to stay for dinner? I'm making tacos."

Alex looked at his watch. "I'm running late for my last appointment."

I nodded, and when he stepped off my porch, I said, "I'll have your money tomorrow."

He pulled his lips up on one side, sadness still pulsing through his gaze before he began to amble away. "I'll see you later, Zoey."

"Alex?"

He turned around.

"Thank you."

After getting a lopsided smile from Alex, I went back inside, struggling to contain my glee.

"Everything okay?" Dad asked.

"Yeah," I said.

Because now, everything might just be okay. The fear of losing Dad's therapy had been suffocating me for weeks, but I'd been lucky to get this reprieve. And while it didn't solve all of our problems, it was a huge win, and I hadn't felt this light in forever.

I'd go to ten pawn shops if I had to, maybe even jewelry stores, to get the absolute best price for that ring, but by this time tomorrow? So help me, Alex would have that money in his hands.

Thank God.

I hummed as I loaded the dishwasher and cooked tacos, and when they were done, my dad wheeled himself over to the kitchen table.

At six feet tall, Dad once had broad shoulders, thick black hair, and a commanding aura that demanded respect. But now, his shoulder bones poked out of his shirt, his hair had thinned enough to see the scalp, and his legs were like skeletons with skin. It was scary how quickly a human body could go from being healthy to withering away to almost nothing.

Dad glanced at the television, which was on another news station about the robbery—this one focused on the manhunt.

"Speaking of criminals," I said as I sprinkled shredded cheddar onto my taco, "I'm thinking of asking for a new detective to be assigned to your case."

Dad frowned as he picked up his water glass, which was already frosted in condensation, thanks to the ice cubes battling it out with this summer heat. Even with the windows open, a bead of sweat trickled down his temple. "Maybe it's time to let this go."

My jaw almost bounced off the floor. "And let him get away with what he did to you? Fat chance."

"We need to accept that it's improbable the case will get solved at this point. It's not healthy to be this obsessed over it."

"How can you say that?" It would be bad enough if Dad had been jaywalking, but he'd had the pedestrian green light. "A person hit you and drove off like it meant nothing. They left you dying in the street. They took everything from you."

"But not my life."

"And that means you let them off the hook? Because you happened to survive? Seriously?"

"I'm not defending them. I'm just saying you've been fixated on this for too long. I want you to be happy and live your life."

"And I want the lowlife that hit you to rot in prison for the rest of their life."

"You're twenty-six, Zo. You should go out with friends. Date. Not obsess over some cold case."

"Some cold case? It's not a case; it's our life."

"Zo..."

"Let's just drop it," I said. Because I was downright blissful for once, and this was about to burst my bubble.

We finished dinner in silence. I ate and pretended not to notice

Dad's troubled glances my way. Honestly, he didn't need to worry about me so much. Did this situation drag on longer than we expected? Yes. But it was temporary. For now, the best thing I could do was ensure Dad made all his appointments and I got Alex his money.

"Will you be okay if I head out after I get you settled tonight?" I asked.

This piqued Dad's interest. Which, I had to admit, was a little pathetic in terms of a twenty-something's social life. I didn't see my friends very often because Dad was home alone all day, every day, and while he *could* be alone, I felt bad, leaving him longer than I needed to. Even though Dad tried many times to get me to go out.

"Where are you going?" he asked.

"To meet up with some friends."

Dad smiled. "Really?"

I hated lying to him, but if he found out that finances were so bad that I needed to pawn my ring, he would try to stop me. And this wasn't up for debate; it needed to get done and get done fast.

"I won't be long," I said.

I cleaned up the kitchen, got Dad situated, made sure he had his phone, water, and the remote control easily within reach, and then headed out to run my secret errand.

I walked several blocks to the "L" station and cringed; I wanted to enjoy my little bliss bubble, but no. When I walked across the platform, three guys locked eyes on me.

"Helloooooo…"

*Here we go.*

These guys harassed every woman at this "L" stop, and it was getting old. Didn't they have anything better to do with their time than make people uncomfortable?

Sometimes, they made sexual innuendos about my wavy black hair, chocolate eyes, caramel-colored skin, or thick lips. But most of the time, they were far more explicit than that, reciting what they'd like to do to me if they got me alone.

The taller guy followed me, looking at me up and down like a piece of meat, and then had the audacity to position himself a mere two feet away.

I clenched my hands into balls.

"You have a beautiful mouth," he said, licking his teeth. "Know what would make it prettier?" He grabbed his crotch. "Seeing it wrapped around this."

"How are you out in society right now?" I asked. "Did someone leave your cage open?"

His two buddies let out a burst of laughter, punching each other in the shoulders as I stood on the platform, watching the train approaching.

Unfortunately, my quip didn't shut the guy up.

"You know when I saw you tonight," he said suggestively, "a thought crossed my mind."

"Poor thought. Must have been a long, lonely journey."

His friends let out more laughs as the "L" rounded the final bend with a metallic wail and came to a rest, opening its doors. I stepped onto the train, grateful they didn't follow me. They never had before, but I always worried one of these days, they might escalate their harassment.

In any case, I enjoyed the ride into the heart of the city, where I got off and began walking the rest of the way.

Tonight, Chicago looked mythical. Seventy-story skyscrapers glistened against a thin layer of fog, stretching toward low-hanging clouds that swallowed their top floors. I could taste the hangover from this morning's thunderstorm, the air muggy, causing a bead of sweat to roll down my back. The smell of wet concrete blended with the scent of fried potatoes funneling from nearby restaurants while a rumble of engines echoed off the buildings as vehicles chugged along the roads.

When I reached my dad's old building, I took the elevator up and entered his condo.

As soon as I stepped inside, though, the skin on the back of my neck prickled with an unsettling feeling. I scanned the space, trying to isolate why my sixth sense's alarm bells were sounding, but there was nothing to explain it. The lights were off, and the only sound was the ticking clock above the fireplace.

I flipped the lights on and looked around again. The condo was like entering a time machine, back to when Dad was in the prime of his life. The blue and gray furniture, picked by some decorator, complementing white cabinets in the oversize kitchen—the kind that closed gently and had organizers galore. Wood flooring, high-end artwork, and even higher-end electronics.

But the pride and joy of my dad's old place was his sports memorabilia collection. Two dozen white baseballs with red stitching and black signatures proudly sat in a six-foot-tall mahogany case with custom lighting. Some of them were worth a few hundred. Some a few thousand, maybe more. All were a point of contention in the bankruptcy case.

None of his assets had been sold yet, but they would be soon to pay off Dad's creditors.

With only a couple of exceptions. Like the ring. Since it was a gift to me, I was the legal owner, thus I could sell it. I just needed to retrieve it from the safe in Dad's office.

My dad's ex-wife, Holly, had put it there after I'd thrown it in my dad's face.

But that was a whole other story I didn't need to think about right now.

I went into the office and walked around the L-shaped mahogany desk that sat between shelves stacked with books, organized by height and color. On the far wall, a painting of the Chicago River winding through buildings—its primary color an unnaturally greenish teal— hung in front of the concealed safe. I carefully lifted it up and off its hanger, set it on the ground, and started on the combination Dad had shared with me when I'd become responsible for helping with the sale of this condo. Frankly, I should have cleared the safe of any personal effects we had by now, but other priorities kept delaying me.

When the dial clicked on eighty-eight, my vision went black, something pressed against my mouth, and I was pulled until my back pressed into something hard. It took my brain a fraction of a second to realize my screams were silenced by a leather-gloved hand. My sight blocked with another.

"Don't move," a man's voice growled.

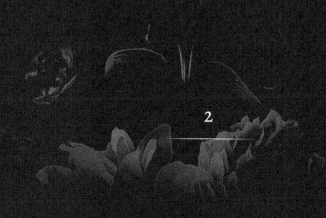

2

My nose's breath whistled against the smoky smell of the leather glove clamping my mouth, and my heart thumped in my ears while needles of adrenaline shot through my fingertips.

"Keep your eyes closed," he said. "Did you hear me? Keep 'em closed."

I nodded, and when he took his hand away, I obeyed, clenching my eyes shut. His chest peeled away from my back, and then something soft draped over my eyes and knotted behind my head. Among the sea of my long black waves, one hair howled in pain, getting plucked out in the process.

"Will you keep quiet? Or do I need to gag you?" he asked.

"I'll be quiet," I whispered.

His cold gloves gripped my upper arms, traced them down to my wrists, and pulled my hands behind my back, wrapping a similar silky fabric around them.

The bondage pinched my skin and tugged three times with each knot formed. Which might as well have been a one-two-three punch, for in this moment, I knew I'd done all the wrong things. I should have run. I should have kicked. I should never have let myself become bound and blindfolded because now, I had no way to fight against whatever horrors this guy might unleash upon me.

My odds of fighting him off might not be great—at five foot four, I was only a hundred and fifteen pounds. But any chance would have been better than none.

"Come here." He took me by the arm and guided me a few steps.

It was disorienting, trying to move without sight, trying to think coherently with fear suffocating the blood flow to my brain. Something pressed into the back of my thighs, and one of his hands pressed down on my shoulder while the other wrapped completely around my bicep as he gently lowered me into the chair.

I opened my eyes, grateful for a small strip of light near the brim of my nose, where the fabric didn't meet my cheek. I could only see a bit of his feet, but it was something, and if I tilted my head, I saw more.

*He's wearing black combat boots.*

Was he a squatter? Or here to rob the place? Or worse...had he followed me—his real target—in here to...to...

I couldn't even finish the sickening thought.

Through the crack in my blindfold, I saw his knees appear.

*He's squatting in front of me.*

"What's your name?" he asked.

"Zoey."

"What are you doing here, Zoey?"

It was eerie, hearing my name roll off his tongue, but at least I didn't seem to be his primary target.

That didn't mean I was out of danger, though. Even if I wasn't the original purpose of him being here, he might certainly adapt his agenda. Make me his primary focus...

No. I needed to stop letting fear take control here. I was fine. This was fine. I would absolutely get out of this. I mean, if the guy wanted me dead, he could have done it right away, before I even knew he was here, and the fact that he tied me up? Was probably a good thing, to make him feel like he was in control, so he'd just get the hell out of here.

But evidently, my nerves weren't completely sold on my safety because when I spoke, my voice quivered. "This is my dad's condo. I came tonight to get a ring that I left here."

He was quiet for a moment. "A ring."

I nodded, conscious of the way my body twisted backward, recoiling as far away from him as possible.

"This house has been empty for months."

*How does he know that?*

I wasn't sure, but I'd file that clue away to tell the police when I got out of here, so the cops could find this guy and put him away forever. Hell, I'd gather as many clues as possible.

"We were waiting to clear it out until it sold," I explained.

"Shit." He stood up and, based on the clunk of his steps along the wooden floors, began to pace. "Why did you have to show up tonight of all nights?"

The anxiety in his voice made my mouth run dry. A hostage expert I was not, but that level of nervousness couldn't be good. There was a reason the expression, *Wrong time, wrong place,* was so widely known.

*Focus, Zoey. Focus on information. Tonight of all nights.*

That meant he was only here for the night, so he wasn't a homeless squatter. He had to be a burglar, then. *Right?*

"I haven't seen anything," I said. "Just let me go, and I'll never tell anyone."

I held my breath, waiting for an answer as his feet stilled, angled toward me.

He didn't answer my plea for release, though. Instead, notes of confusion braided around his frustrated tone when he finally spoke. "Were you hanging around this building a couple weeks ago?"

*Was I...what?* "No," I said. "Why?"

I felt his gaze on me. "You look familiar."

I evaluated his voice with a fresh level of scrutiny, trying to match it to anyone I knew. His voice was rough and deep, like something you'd hear from a radio host, but no one in my life sounded like him.

"Do I know you?" I asked.

Nerves prickled my skin.

*One Mississippi.*

*Two Mississippi.*

*Three Mississippi.*

"No," he said.

Which had to be true. If someone in my life was a secret villain, they'd recognize me, not fish around, trying to place me.

Might he know my dad?

Dad...

Oh God, right now, he was home, assuming I'd be there in the morning to cook his breakfast and help with the bill collectors and bankruptcy attorneys and everything else. I was the only person he had, so I couldn't let this guy do something to me.

Who the hell was this guy, anyway?

*What if he's a killer? Or a guy who's already served two stints in prison, one strike away from being sent away for life? Prepared to kill any witness that could jeopardize his freedom?*

No. That was fear talking. There was no need to blindfold someone you're going to kill; dead people can't rat on you.

But just when hope flickered, another sound extinguished it.

A clomp-clomp echoed down the hallway's planks, yet this guy's shoes remained frozen in place.

"Shit!" A scratchy voice sent ice through my veins.

Through the sliver my blindfold didn't block, I saw his brown boots as he came into the room, followed by a third set, wearing blue Converse.

*Brown boots. Blue Converse.*

"The hell, Green? *This* was the sound?"

*Green must be the original guy's last name.* The guy that tied me up.

"She hasn't seen anything," Green said in an authoritative tone.

"You don't know that," Brown Boots snapped in a condescending voice.

When I sensed him walk toward me, my body instinctively shrank into the chair.

"I haven't seen anything, I swear." I hated that my voice sounded high-pitched and wobbly.

"Shut up," the guy in brown boots yelled just before he slapped me. It stung so badly, a handprint probably reddened on my cheek.

"Brown," Green cautioned in a sharp tone.

*The name of the guy that hit me is Brown?*

Pathetically, my entire body shook like an animal left in the cold. At least the first guy hadn't been rough with me. This guy was clearly dangerous, but worse, he was irate and flustered, too.

I discreetly yanked at my makeshift handcuffs, the cool fabric assaulting my skin with rug-like burns. But it didn't deter me. I needed to get my wrists free, so I could make a run for it, or fight, or hide, or do something other than just sit here like a caged animal.

"Now, what are we gonna do?" the guy in Converse asked. I hated that he sounded nervous; nervousness couldn't be good right now.

"She didn't see anything, Orange," Green said in a calming voice.

*Orange? No way the guy's last name is Orange. It has to be some sort of code name, just like Green and Brown must be, too—each man assigned a color as another layer of protection, just like those criminals in that movie.*

When the three guys stepped into the hallway, my hope swelled that they might leave, but they stopped just outside the office and had some sort of huddle. I could only make out part of what they were saying, but I tried to unravel every word.

"...she'll call the cops..."

"...might've seen..."

"...recognize our voices..."

I perched at the edge of my seat, trying to convert my ears into satellite dishes.

"...no other option..."

"...not going to prison for the rest of my life..."

The anxiety in their voices had settled into a resolve that made my palms sweat.

"...no choice..."

"...have to kill her."

And then silence.

A chill cooled the air around me as ice frosted around my lungs, making me tremble.

I wasn't going to make it out of here. I wasn't going to go back to our apartment, slide under my covers, and forget this day ever existed. I wouldn't help Dad regain independence.

*I'll never see him again. I'll never have the chance to apologize for what I'd done.*

*I would give anything to have just five more minutes with everyone I love. To feel their arms around me and tell them I love them one last time. Because suddenly, all the other times I've said it before doesn't feel like enough.*

A sequence of events flashed through my mind.

*I see my ratty teddy bear's head bobbling in the corner of a cardinal-red wagon as my dad pulls me through the zoo.*

*I see the black hairs below my dad's knuckles as he grips my bicycle's handlebar while he runs alongside me, cheering, "You're doing it!"*

*I smell cinnamon cookies while Mom pats her daisy apron with its sunshine-yellow tie, leaving white handprints on her lower tummy.*

*I smell wet leaves as my brother and I race through a field of red and orange trees sheening with dew.*

*I'm eight, swaying in Dad's arms in my elementary school's gymnasium at the annual father-daughter dance.*

*I'm thirteen, picking a piece of food out of my front tooth's braces.*

*I'm three, running from the front door to my dad's car and jumping into his arms.*

*I'm twenty-six with my arms tied behind my back, about to experience the moment of death.*

I heard two sets of footsteps clomp down the hallway, their sounds getting quieter the farther they got from the office, but the third set took a couple of steps closer and stopped.

I leaned my head, seeing a set of black combat boots standing ominously in the doorway. Green—the original man—stood with his feet slightly apart.

Here to end my life.

3

"You really screwed things up by being here tonight," Green snarled.

*Evidently, criminals don't like having to murder people unexpectedly. They must prefer to plan it out.*

This wasn't fair, dying just because I'd interrupted a robbery. If these guys thought I was just going to sit here and accept their death sentence, they had it wrong. I might not survive, but I'd go down swinging—that was for damn sure.

Aside from the slice of light near the brim of my nose, blackness extinguished my vision, so my other senses completed an urgent inventory. The faint thumping of footsteps confirmed the other guys were on the far end of my dad's place, and louder steps disclosed only Green was near me.

If I wanted to make a run for it, it was now or never.

Adrenaline surged needles into my legs, and my lungs drew in a large gust of oxygen as my heart thundered in anticipation. I shot up like a missile, blasting my body through the office and into the hallway.

Where I didn't make it far.

My captor's arm shot around my stomach, the other just beneath my breasts as he pulled my back against his iron chest, my feet now dangling in the air. The calmness of his grip screamed of a man in power, his arms a cage around me while my hands remained helpless balls, pressed between my back and his stomach.

Which was rock hard, skin stretched over firm ridges.

*Shit. He's built like an athlete with a broad chest and lean body, so it'll be seriously hard to get away from him.*

But not impossible...

"Let me go!" I screamed, provoking the leather glove to trap my voice.

He pressed his cheek against my jaw as his lips brushed against my right earlobe. "If you don't stay quiet, I'm going to have to gag you."

He shifted his hand over my belly button and pressed up, lifting me higher off the ground.

*He's tall.* Though how tall, I couldn't be sure.

I kicked my legs wildly, trying to land a blow to his shin, but missed. Instead, my body spun, and simultaneously, I flew higher off the ground, something slammed into my stomach, and a bar squeezed behind my knees.

*He's carrying me in a fireman's hold.* My body now draped over a blanket of muscles, covering a gargantuan body.

I jerked my legs, trying to break from his grip, but I didn't feel him flinch.

Or sound fazed, for that matter, when he said, "Calm down."

My belly button squished further into his shoulder with each of his steps as he carried my irritatingly small body.

Once we were back inside the office, he slid his hands up the backs of my legs, and when one reached my thigh and the other my upper back, my body twisted through the air, and something soft slammed into my back and butt. His hand was on my shoulder now—thumb on my collarbone—forcing me to sit while the other reclaimed its position over my mouth.

The leather cool against my lips.

"Are you done?" he asked.

I used his voice as a guide, kicking my foot straight toward the sound, hoping to pulverize his nose, but he captured my ankle in his rigid grip. I threw my other foot forward, but like the first, it missed its mark, and he pinned my thigh down with his knee.

I sensed him hovering over me, the heat of his breath bouncing off my cheek.

*His face is only inches from mine.*

I jerked my head forward, but my headbutt missed.

"*Now*, are you done?" he asked.

The amusement in his tone made me even more frustrated with my failure.

*He isn't even out of breath. I fought with everything I had, and it wasn't even a challenge for him.*

After almost a minute, Green released me and walked to some other part of this room.

"Who knows you're here?" he asked. His deep voice drifted through my skin like an arctic blast and sent a shiver down my spine.

*Lie. Tell him someone knows you're here.*

*No, don't lie. If he thinks people are looking for you, he'll kill you faster. As hopeless as this situation feels, you can't give up yet. You have to find another chance to escape.*

"No one," I admitted.

"You didn't tell anyone that you were coming here tonight?" he clarified.

"No one else will walk in that door and become a witness. No matter how much I wish they would."

"That's not why I'm asking." His tone was lower, as if he was... unsettled by something.

Which got my attention. If he wasn't vetting potential complications, where was he going with this?

"Why'd you come *tonight*, specifically?" Tension wove through his words.

Beneath the cloth that felt like a silky tie, I blinked, confused by his line of questioning. Wasn't the only relevant fact a potential second witness showing up?

"I owe someone money. Why?"

The clock on my dad's desk ticked four times.

"It doesn't matter."

But it did matter. I could tell. I just couldn't imagine why.

I tilted my head, so I could see through the gap beneath my blindfold, noting he was now blocking the doorway. Facing me, based on the position of his boots.

Holding a knife perhaps. Or a gun.

Desperation flooded my veins like an animal waiting in line at the slaughterhouse, smelling death coming.

It's tragic how confronting your own mortality makes you realize the value of your life isn't exclusively defined by your lost experiences, but also in the devastation your death will have on others.

Like Dad.

Fight and flight had failed, but I had to keep trying, if not physically, verbally.

*Maybe I can convince him to let me go. Get him to see me as human, help him to understand what's at stake tonight.*

"It's not just my life on the line if you kill me." I felt beads of sweat drip down my back. "My dad's disabled. He lives with me, and I take care of him, and if I don't return—"

The clock in my dad's office ticked on.

Tick. Tock. Tick. Tock.

"Facing your demise and your first thought is about a family member." His low tone made me wonder if this had at least given him pause, if only for a moment.

"He needs me."

Tick. Tock.

"What happened to him?"

"He was in an accident."

Tick, tock.

"What kind of accident?"

The memory of that day made me wince. "A hit-and-run of a pedestrian. He can't live by himself, so he moved in with me."

"And you take care of him." His voice was almost a growl.

"Someone has to help him recover."

Judging by the sounds of his footsteps, Green walked to my right several steps and then stopped. "Who's the woman?"

I blinked. "What?"

"There's a picture on the desk. Of a guy—assume he's your dad, based on the age—and some woman. Who is she?"

"She *was* my stepmom." Lord, I hated that term, even when she'd made my dad happy.

"And she can't help him?"

My animosity for Holly billowed in my chest. Could she? Yes. Would she? No. She was too busy, being an awful excuse of a human.

"She won't even return his calls."

*How do you go from marrying someone to not caring about them?*

"I'm all he has," I repeated. "So, please. I haven't seen anything. You came at me from behind and immediately blindfolded me."

"Maybe you saw something before that happened."

I tightened my fists behind my back.

Maybe this was some sort of game to him. Foreplay that he got off on before the actual murder. I wanted to tell him off, tell him to go screw himself. But as he paced on the other side of the room, I forced myself to remain calm. To refrain from antagonizing my captor and would-be killer.

"Please, just let me go."

"Afraid that ship has sailed."

I clamped my jaw shut. How could he be so callous? Especially after everything I'd told him. "I won't tell anyone what happened."

"Can't take that chance."

I scraped my nail into my palm, and this time, when I spoke, I couldn't suppress the anger from my tone. "You *know* I didn't see anything. You know I can't identify you or your friends even if I wanted to."

"I don't know that," he said in a monotone voice, like he didn't care about having to end my life.

"You do. So, you have nothing to lose by letting me go. But if you don't? And you do something to me? You'll be running from the police forever. There's no statute of limitations on murder. You want that chasing you every day for the rest of your life?"

"Stop talking."

"Think about that. A month from now. A year from now. Five years from now. Twenty-five years from now. You could be caught and get life with no parole."

"Stop. Talking."

"I. Haven't. Seen. Anything. I have no clue what you look like. Who you are. You'd be killing me for absolutely no reason."

I waited for him to say something, to give me any indication I was getting through to him, but as the seconds passed, despair dumped a rock into my stomach.

"There's nothing I can say to convince you to let me go"—my shoulders sank—"is there?"

*Tick.*

*Tock.*

"Afraid not."

Afraid not. Two words that, strung together, never created a more sinister meaning. Will you help rehabilitate Dad until he's finally back on his feet? *Afraid not.* Will you live past the age of twenty-six, have the chance of finding love again? *Afraid not.*

He was going to kill me. No matter what I did or said, he was going to kill me.

It's crazy how, in a single moment, your entire life can change. That summarized my life as of late. Every time I turned around, the landscape of my future repainted into something darker.

Almost three years ago, my boyfriend died. It was shocking. Violent. And tragic.

He was murdered.

There one day, gone the next. Not because of some accident or unfortunate illness. Because some vile human being willingly and purposely ended his life. As if it meant nothing.

And one of the things that had gutted me the most? Was that when my boyfriend was being brutally killed... when he was suffering unimaginable pain and terror, I was mad at him. I was mad because he wasn't answering my calls. I was mad that he hadn't come home yet and didn't have the courtesy to at least text me back. I was mad because I'd jumped to the conclusion that someone who claimed to love me hadn't made me their priority.

As my boyfriend fought for his life, as he took his last breath, I'd been angry with him.

I don't know anyone who can come back from that kind of guilt.

And I don't know anyone who could stop the torturous questions that came next. How scared did he feel? How long, exactly, did he know he was going to die? What were his final moments on this earth like? How badly did he suffer? The questions had infected my mind like a disease.

Now, facing a similar fate, I knew the answers to some of those questions. And that knowledge was unbearable.

I tried to combat those thoughts by forcing myself to think about the good memories I'd had with him.

One memory in particular flashed through my heart.

*"Tell me something you've always wanted to do, but haven't done yet," my boyfriend says.*

*I'm lying with my head on his lap while he looks down at me, running his fingers delicately through my hair. Each stroke concludes with his fingertips dancing along the skin on my neck, warming my chest.*

*I feel so peaceful in his arms.*

*"I've had a dream since I was a little girl to watch the sun set over the Grand Canyon. To see its 270-mile-wide rock formations, while the blue water of the Colorado River snakes along its bottom." I smile. "I want to hike to the South Rim, take off my socks, and feel the red rock beneath my feet while I watch the clouds turn pastel purple as the sun dips below the canyon. Casting birds into silhouettes."*

*His tone is soft. "Why haven't you done it yet?"*

*I shrug. "It's expensive, I guess? Spending money on that when I have so many other bills seems irresponsible."*

*His eyes turn reflective. "When my parents were suffering through the grief of my sister's death, they let years pass without doing the things that* made them happy." He brushes his knuckles along my temple. "Life is short, Zoey. No matter what happens, you have to prioritize living."

This is something I absolutely love about him. He's full of wisdom far beyond his years.

"I want you to promise me something," he says. "Promise me that you'll go there. Soon. And that you'll never let anything stop you from being happy."

This had to be hard for him—witnessing his parents' grief had manifested into worry for those closest to him. I want to make him feel as good as he makes me.

So I bring his palm to my cheek and say, "I promise."

With our future stretched out in front of us, it was an easy promise to make.

Until he died a week later.

At first, his death didn't feel real. I kept expecting him to call me or walk through the door. One night I'd even woken up, and texted him, **I love you and can't wait to see you tomorrow**. And then the brutal reality came crashing back and shattered me once again.

It was shocking to know he'd never be at Thanksgiving dinner again, skimping on the mashed potatoes to save room for his mother's home-made apple pie. Heartbreaking to picture his chair empty, uncaring that its void would suck all the happiness from every celebration.

It wasn't fair that he had to die. If life had to take someone, why did it have to be him? Why couldn't it be someone else? Which was an insensitive thought, but that's what grief does to your mind.

The finality of him being gone hit me like a dial on the radio, turning up slowly, and as it did, I no longer wanted to be happy.

Pain was the only thing I had left of him, and I held onto it like a toxic security blanket, scared that once the pain left, it would mean he was gone. For good.

But then I'd feel ashamed of myself, because I was breaking my promise to him, and he'd be devastated if I let this destroy my life.

So eventually, for his sake, I put myself back out there. I tried to construct some semblance of normalcy. But even when I thought I was starting to make progress, grief would hit me out of nowhere. I'd see someone that looked like him. I'd see apple pie on a menu. Or a song would come on the radio, and my heart would rip in half again, spilling carnage everywhere.

And in the rare times I caught myself having fun or smiling, guilt would immediately shock me like a dog's electric collar as it ran from the yard. How dare I smile. How dare I feel happy when my boyfriend never would.

And thus began my seesaw of guilt. Guilt for allowing the pain to swallow me, which felt disrespectful to his life. Guilt for having any moments of joy when he was dead.

Every day felt more exhausting than the last.

Losing someone you love is like being sliced in half with a chainsaw. Your body will never go back to the way it was before the chainsaw cut it. Your tissue will regrow differently, and you must learn to live with the scar tissue left in its wake.

Instead of fighting the grief, I finally surrendered to it. Accepting that I couldn't make it go away. I needed to learn how to wrap my life around it and weave in happy times wherever possible.

Praying that one day the happy moments would begin to outweigh the sad ones.

So, after a tremendous amount of counseling, I finally started living my life again. I spent time with my friends, took long walks in the fresh air, and began to welcome joy back into my life. And you know what? It felt good.

Did Dad's accident disrupt that a bit? Of course. And of course it brought back some pangs of grief after almost losing my father, but I was proud of how far I'd come. It was like I'd sunken to the bottom of a lake and had swum all the way to the surface. And I knew that my boyfriend would be proud of me, too.

The stresses I now coped with were the stresses of life, not the grief of losing him.

But as proud as I was that I'd overcome grief—as much as anyone can, that is—I still hadn't fulfilled my promise to him. So even though I didn't have the money yet, I'd started planning the Grand Canyon trip.

But I would never see the sunset at the Grand Canyon or anything else because this thief was about to rob me of my future.

And for who knew what reason, he was dragging it out, torturing me by waiting for the reality to slowly sink in.

"I heard what you were planning in the hallway. Why haven't you done it already?"

No answer, but when I peeked through the sliver of sight below my blindfold, I saw his feet still there. Doing nothing. Was he having second thoughts? Could he be getting cold feet?

But as quickly as hope came, sorrow snatched it away when I realized what must be going on.

"You're going to wait," I deduced in a sick voice. "You guys are going to wait to kill me until you're done robbing the place, in case the cops show."

*One one thousand.*

*Two one thousand.*

*Three one thousand.*

"Yes," he said in a near whisper.

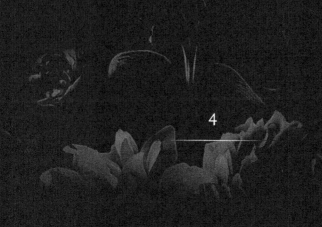

4

Of course they'd wait to kill me until the robbery was done. Who'd want to risk having a freshly murdered body on their hands if the cops showed?

Why was I upset about this? I should have been elated since it afforded me more time to try to get away, but I was praying he'd change his mind. That today wasn't really my last day.

"And you have to stay here and babysit me, so I don't get away."

He didn't answer.

Which wasn't just unsettling; it was unacceptable. This guy viewed my life as a disposable inconvenience. A complication of his criminal acts, stealing from hardworking people. People who spent *their* entire life working their ass off to pay their bills, pay their taxes, and be a contributing member of society.

"Shit, this night is spinning out of control." Green's tone rose in pitch, and he started pacing again. "Why couldn't you get your damn ring yesterday? Or wear it like a normal rich chick?"

How dare he. Break into our home, tie me up, vow to murder me, and then, on top of that, try to *blame* me? *Me* for having interrupted his burglary?

*This guy has some balls.*

Maybe the smart thing to do was play nice, but it was getting harder to bite my tongue, and that was what he expected, wasn't it? For me to sit here and keep quiet until they killed me. I was not about to do that; I'd make another run for it, and the only realistic chance to succeed was if this guy left the room or lost his focus. Keeping quiet wouldn't achieve either of those things, but maybe if I irritated him and got under his skin, he'd want to take a break and leave the hostage alone. Or at the very least, take his eyes off me long enough, so I could bolt out of this room.

I raised my chin. "Listen, you moronic waste of space."

Green stopped pacing. "Did you just call me a *moronic waste of space?*" His casual tone didn't sound irritated yet; if anything, it was surprise, mixed with enjoyment.

"I'm the opposite of rich," I said.

"Swear you did, but that can't be the case."

"This house isn't ours; it belongs to the bank."

"Because you seem halfway intelligent."

"I sold our only car to pay for food and medicine."

"So, I'd expect you not to anger someone in my position."

Speaking of position, I leaned my head back to confirm what the sound of his voice made me suspect—he was now standing only a couple feet in front of me.

I kicked my foot toward him, hoping to slam the heel of my foot into his dick. But he blocked that one, too. I tried to yank away from his grip, but doing so rocked the chair and tilted one side of it into the air. Before I could correct the center of gravity, the chair tipped over, sending me into a free fall, my nose on a collision course with the wooden planks.

But he grabbed me before I hit—one arm around my stomach, his other hand gripping my upper arm.

He pulled me into a standing position as if I weighed nothing and set me back on my feet.

"Careful," he said, a blend of irritation and enjoyment seeping from his tone. "I'd hate to see you hurt that beautiful face of yours."

"Because you prefer to do it yourself?"

I heard him huff a laugh-breath.

*Why isn't he letting go of me?*

He stood there, his hands on my body, doing what? Staring at me? Smelling like burnt sugar.

*Strange. I'd have expected him to smell like chemically rotting feet, not delicious and inviting.*

"So, this is what you do?" I said, heat pooling beneath my cheeks. "Break into people's homes and then murder them if they happen to come inside?"

No answer.

"What an exemplary member of society we have here," I snarled.

"Let me give you some advice." His tone was low and even.

"This ought to be good. Advice from a criminal. I'm waiting with bated breath."

He tightened his grip around my waist until my breasts pushed into his chest. "You're bound and blindfolded and at my mercy. Provoking the very person who holds your life in his hands is unwise."

"You've made it clear that there's nothing I can do to stop you from killing me, so if you're looking for some docile hostage, you picked the wrong girl."

A breath of air huffed out of Green's nose. Like he'd…*chuckled?*

"Your attitude is unnecessary." He sounded like a father reprimanding a child.

"Your existence is unnecessary."

He chuckled. Again.

*Dammit.*

I wanted to tear him apart psychologically until he left this room, whimpering with his tail between his legs.

I was going to escape. I was. It was that simple. I had however the hell long a robbery took to do so, and by God, I was going to succeed. And if I failed? Well, I'd scratch and bite and claw DNA from him, so he'd for sure get caught.

Speaking of biting…

I opened my mouth and chomped down on the skin in front of me, but his hand pressed against my forehead and jerked it back.

"Did you just *bite* me?" Amusement and shock battled for first place in his voice.

Not hard enough. Probably didn't even leave a mark, let alone lose a chunk of his body.

I twisted my head, trying to gain access to his wrist so I could tear open his radial artery with my front teeth, but he held it out of my reach.

*Have it your way.* I'd have to settle for my original target.

I bucked my knee fast and hard, but he twisted his hip, so I missed his groin.

Green tsked. "You're a feisty one, aren't you?"

"Untie me and see how feisty I really am."

He laughed—laughed!—and released his hand from my face. Based on his leaning and the subsequent metallic squeak, he picked up the chair and rolled it over to me.

"You're trying to be a lion." He pressed down on my shoulder until I flopped back into his chair. "But you're a kitten."

If ever there was justification for pulling a Lorena Bobbitt on his ass...

A chime sounded from across the room, and magically, Green's footsteps receded away. Not far enough to make a run for it, though.

I could hear him rifle through the backpack I'd arrived with.

Because he hadn't invaded my privacy enough by breaking in here and holding me hostage.

"If you're looking for money, you won't find any in there," I snapped.

I heard my cell phone clunk onto the desk as he shook my bag upside down.

"I'm not looking for money," he said flatly. "I heard a chime."

I bit down on my teeth.

"It's the alarm on my phone to remind Dad to take his pills," I snarled. "Why don't you make yourself useful and dial 911?"

I heard a small breath of air, as if he'd laughed.

*Great. I show a brave act of defiance, and he's merely amused by it.*

Through the crack in my blindfold, I leaned my head back to see his fingers power off the cell phone. Right. Wouldn't want cell towers picking up the location of wherever he dumped my body and belongings.

As soon as that thought came, another crashed right behind it.

If these guys were willing to commit murder, what if they were also willing to hurt me in other ways? What if death itself wasn't the only thing I needed to fear tonight?

My heart started to race so quickly, it felt like it was going to explode from my chest, and dizziness performed a hostile takeover of my mind. I felt like I was going to be sick.

If they were going to do that, part of me didn't want to know because knowing would be mental torture, listening to every footstep with sickening dread—wondering when they would violate me. But I couldn't stop myself from asking.

"Are you going to…" I swallowed, my throat so dry that my voice was a whisper. "Are you going to rape me?"

"What?" he snarled. "God, no."

The resolve in his voice made me believe him, but he was one of three.

"Will they?"

Green let out an angry breath. "No."

"How can you be sure?"

"They're thieves, not rapists."

"And if you're wrong?" My chin trembled.

"If they even tried it, I'd kill 'em."

My muscles relaxed slightly.

If he cared enough to stop me from being violated, maybe there was still hope to make him see me as human, to convince him to let me go. It failed before, but I had nothing to lose by trying again.

And meanwhile, I'd work a parallel play of wrestling my hands free from these bindings.

Later, he might leave the room to check on his accomplices or go to the bathroom, so there might be an opening to run.

There had to be.

And when it came? I'd be ready.

I pulled at the makeshift handcuffs, assessing them in more detail. A loop wrapped around each wrist individually and then another loop around them together. The fabric—a tie, I presumed—was silky, so maybe I could slide my hand out.

Trying to conceal my arm movements, I pulled my right wrist, but couldn't wiggle my thumb bone through the opening. I confronted the same failure with my left hand. In fact, he'd tied them so tightly that each time I pulled, the tie dug deeper into my skin.

I twisted my hands and wrists in every direction, stretching my fingers to try to reach the binding's knot. My right middle finger touched the lump, but the angle was off, so I couldn't pinch the fabric, let alone loosen it.

I bit back angry tears.

"Why do you need the ring so bad?" His tone was ambivalent, as if merely asking the question to satisfy his own boredom.

As much as I hated this criminal with every fiber of my being, I forced myself to clear the animosity out of my throat and answered his question. "We need the money."

"Anyone who lives in a place like this has money."

Had. Past tense.

"I told you, this is my dad's place, not mine. And we don't live here; we live in a six-hundred-square-foot townhouse. Rented."

I churned my hands behind my back, the skin on my wrists getting so raw that I wondered if it would start to bleed.

"Why?" Curiosity danced through his voice.

I didn't want to answer Green's question; talking about our precarious financial situation wasn't something I liked to discuss with anyone, let alone this guy. But I couldn't let my ego block any avenue of possible escape.

"My dad defaulted on his mortgage, so the bank is doing a short sale. Even that won't fill the financial hole we're in, though, so I need to sell that ring to pay bills."

Green spoke, but this time, his voice was completely different. He sounded...empathetic. "Why haven't you pawned some of this furniture? Or TVs? This place is loaded."

"I've pawned what we're allowed to." I shrugged. "But the rest is tangled up in my dad's bankruptcy."

"Except the ring?"

"It's the only thing left that's legally mine."

Speaking of the ring, he'd walked in on me about to open the safe. Why hadn't he asked me what was inside it or tried to open it?

As he took another step forward, I noticed his footsteps had changed. Before, they'd been forceful. Now, they were soft.

"Didn't he have medical insurance?"

"He'd been laid off shortly before the accident. Failed to line up continuity insurance. Guess he assumed he'd have another job before there was a gap in coverage."

He assumed wrong.

When I met with a lawyer who tried to help me sort out my dad's paperwork, he told me you'd be surprised how many people making crazy-high incomes live paycheck to paycheck. You'd assume they'd squirrel away that extra income, but nope. A lot of them just increased their lifestyle with mortgages, and vacations, and toys, presuming the income will last forever.

"And now, you're supporting both of you," Green realized. Almost as if...this bothered him. "How long've you been doing that?"

"Eight months."

The sound of skin grating over skin made me wonder if he was scrubbing his face, and when he eventually spoke again, his voice was a whisper, as if he was speaking more to himself than me. "You had to step up and take care of someone, too."

*Too?* Too, as in he had taken or was currently taking care of someone?

Who was this guy? Was he just some guy who had stumbled onto a house for sale and saw it as an easy target? It made sense. Lots of people were hard up these days, and if I was a burglar—which I'd never be—I guess I might try to target houses that were vacant. Was that why he chose this place? Because he knew no one lived here?

My shoulders felt taut with my arms bound behind my back, and as I continued to twist and turn my hands as discreetly as I could, it stung like hell, and the pressure against my bone seemed on the verge of breaking it.

A new grim sound from the main area stole my attention—a drawer being opened in the kitchen, metal clanking against each other. I'd spent so much time talking with Green, I hadn't given much thought to how they'd kill me. But hearing what had to be knives clanking sent my heart into convulsions. Of all the ways to die, I didn't want to be stabbed.

Green sighed, and in a soft voice, he asked, "Are you cold?"

I blinked. "What?"

"You're shivering."

"I'm not cold. I'm scared." Admitting that left an awful taste in my mouth.

The taste lingered for five seconds before Green came over to me. I heard a zipper, followed by the rustling of fabric. Something warm draped over my shoulders. A jacket, I realized.

Beneath his coat, I could smell the faint hint of his sugary scent again. I tried to tell myself it didn't smell good or sexy for that matter because only a crackpot would think such a thing.

It sounded like Green walked back to the other side of the room while my mind—probably just looking for an escape from worrying about being stabbed to death—analyzed him. Trying to measure the undercurrents of his temperament, trying to figure out why he'd put the jacket on me.

What did it mean? Had I won him over?

"I'm sorry about the restraints," he said. "It's a precaution."

"They're tight." I was careful to keep my tone pleasant. "Too tight. They're hurting me. Is there any way you could loosen them a little?"

Silence eclipsed the beating of my heart.

"I can't do that, Zoey."

And just like that, I realized again there was nothing I could say to get him to help me. He hadn't given me his jacket because he was being nice, warming up to me. He put it on me to make my last moments on earth bearable. A small act of mercy.

I was sitting in my future coffin. Green knew it. I knew it. The only person who didn't know it yet was Dad.

The pain came at me like a wildfire washing over my body, as I pictured my dad sitting in his wheelchair tomorrow, looking out our front window, worrying what might have happened to me.

I bet these guys would move my body, and no one would ever find it. Not for a long time, at least. What if Dad thought I took off? Cracked under the weight of the never-ending responsibility of taking care of him?

Tears marched down my cheeks, and whimpers escaped my throat.

Green's feet advanced toward me in soft, slow strides, and beneath the sliver of sight my blindfold allotted, I saw his shins, then his knees. He squatted directly in front of my chair, close enough to feel the heat from his body.

"Hey," Green said, his tone adding, *"Don't cry."*

"I'm the only person my dad has to take care of him," I repeated, words tumbling out of my mouth at rapid speed. "He needs me. Please, don't kill me. Don't do this to my dad. Even after what he did to me, I'd never wish this on him, so please. Just let me go."

My tears left a salty river down my cheeks, my mind exhausted. During the ensuing silence, my breath caught in my throat as he removed his glove, revealing tan and smooth skin on his hand.

When he brought his arm up, the flash of sudden movement caused me to flinch, shrinking my neck back under my shoulders. Which wasn't ideal since it divulged I could at least partially see.

But Green didn't hit me. Instead, he pressed his finger lightly against my cheek and brushed upward, toward my eye, wiping the line of tears away—a tender gesture he repeated on the other side. But what was even stranger than what he was doing was how it made me feel.

His touch felt...nice.

Did he feel this energy shift, too? Because he stilled, and we both existed in the silent space of quiet breathing.

The clock on my dad's desk ticked ten times before Green stood up, walked away, and crossed one boot over the other—presumably leaning against the desk.

What just happened? Was he feeling upset, finally understanding the extent of the damage he was going to cause when he killed me?

Minutes passed with silence. Minutes that felt like hours while I heard the other guys moving around in the living room. Were they almost done? Were they making enough unusual sounds to spark any questions from a neighbor? Because now that I thought about it, this place was always empty. Surely, that would tip someone off, would it not?

"I'm going to ask you something." Green's words flooded with authority. "And you're going to be honest with me."

I waited.

"Did you see anything tonight?"

I pursed my lips. "You mean when I was trying to open the safe and you accosted me from behind? No. I didn't see you. I would have kicked you in the groin and then broken your nose if I had."

The fact that he chuckled surprised me and gave me hope that maybe he didn't hate me as much as he did a bit ago. "There's no way you could do any real damage. You look like an overgrown porcelain doll."

Maybe he even liked this banter. "Then, untie me and see how small I really am."

The breath of air sounded like he'd laughed lightly, but whatever moment we'd just shared came to an abrupt halt with the appearance of another voice in the office.

"Orange needs your help with the surround system. Having trouble with the wires."

Green paused. "Can't he just yank them out?"

"And ruin 'em? We'd never get full price for it if he did that," Brown snapped. "Get over there and help him. I'll watch her until you get back."

The goose bumps came fast, the hairs on the back of my neck standing on end. Especially since it took Green several seconds to finally exit the office.

As if he didn't want to leave me alone with this guy.

5

Having time with Brown could be a positive thing, though. While I felt like I was getting somewhere with Green, I couldn't be sure that was true, and having a chance to plead my case with someone else doubled my chances of getting out of this nightmare.

"You really screwed things up." The irritation in Brown's voice blended with superiority.

"I haven't seen anything. Please, just let me go."

He laughed, a careless disregard for my life echoing through its tempo.

A blizzard of fear blew through my chest, gusting snow through the oxygen.

"My dad needs me."

"Like I give a shit. Where're the valuables?"

I paused. "What?"

Through the void beneath my blindfold, I saw his brown boots stalk closer. The chair jolted from his hands, which slammed into the armrests, his breath a putrid mix of cigarettes and menace.

"We haven't found any jewels or cash. Where are they?"

"My stepmom's the one that kept jewelry, but she took it with her when she left."

"Place like this always has stacks of emergency cash and jewels." The chair tilted when he leaned so close, the heat of his breath invaded my throat like vapor. "Tell. Me," he snarled, "Where. They. Are."

Frustration tangled my chest. "I am telling you. There's no—"

But I never finished my sentence. A blow thrust my head to the side, and a stinging pain soared through my cheekbone.

Instinctively, I recoiled, as if the extra inch of space between me and the guy who'd just slapped me afforded me some layer of protection.

"Tell me!" he yelled.

"We lost all our money. We don't have anything." I didn't know why I was lumping Dad and me into a we. We didn't lose our money; he lost his money, but those kinds of details weren't relevant right now. What was relevant was this guy expecting a mountain of cash.

"You're lying," he growled. "Tell me where the jewelry is, or I'll make your death slow and painful."

My heart attempted to jump through my ribs. "The money went to medical bills."

"Bullshit." He seized my neck. I gasped as his fingers stretched around my windpipe and tightened. "Tell me."

But I couldn't tell him anything because he was cutting off my air supply.

Something hit my temple with enough force to knock the chair over, spilling me onto the floor. My left ear rang with a high-pitched chime, and my right cheek pressed against the cold hardwood as pressure mounted in my ears.

Disoriented, I tasted metal, warm blood dripping from my nose, pooling over my lips and onto my chin. Something squeezed my upper arm and yanked so hard, a sharp pain tore through my shoulder as my body was tugged into a sitting position.

"The jewels and cash," he barked. "It's in the safe?"

I wanted the boat to stop rocking, or I might throw up. "Just one ring."

"You're lying." He grabbed my jaw.

It took me a moment to answer; my thoughts weren't coming quickly. "Open it," I said and told him the combination. Praying that when he discovered I was being honest, he wouldn't hurt anymore.

He released his claws and, based on his footsteps, advanced toward the other side of the room. While the safe's dial clicked, I yanked my wrists with more desperate jerks, the fabric biting at my raw skin.

"What the..." Another voice emerged near me.

I pressed my hands against the ground behind me, using my feet to scoot on my butt until my back hit a wall, where I curled into a semi-ball, my knees up for protection.

Brown's demonic laugh bathed the space in misery as I cowered away from the new man, who squatted before me.

When his hand rose, I jerked my face away.

"What'd you do?" the man snapped.

That voice. I tilted my head until I could see his combat boots.

*Green.*

"She won't tell me where the jewels are."

"You didn't have to hurt her."

I could only guess a look was exchanged because the room grew silent. It was a full thirty seconds before the safe's wheel started to click again.

Green's fingertip lightly pressed beneath my jaw, guiding my face up toward the light, and then an angry breath rushed from his nose.

"There's no cash!" Brown sounded furious. "Only one fucking ring that looks like maybe a grand or two."

It made no rational sense that his anger made me even more nervous. Why would anyone feel even more afraid when they'd already signed my death warrant?

I suppose it was human nature—adrenaline reacting as the promise of death ticked closer with each second of the clock.

I needed to try something different; begging and trying to win Green over wasn't happening fast enough.

*I'm going to make another run for it.*

I'd have to time it right, and it was a long shot. No doubt. I could trip and fall on the way or stumble onto one of the burglars, and that didn't even include figuring out how I'd get to be alone in the first place. But so help me, I was going to run.

It quite literally might be the last thing I did.

"What a waste of time. Hold this," Brown snapped. I heard the clank of the ring hitting wood and saw Green's feet move toward the desk. "Watch her. I'm goin' back to help."

Brown stormed away, leaving me alone with Green, a bloody nose, a stinging cheek, and wrists as raw as uncooked meat.

## 6

Brown had quite the right hook. He damn near knocked me out with that punch, leaving my head on an imaginary Tilt-A-Whirl. Why was the room cold all of a sudden? *Oh.* Green's jacket came off me during my fall.

"Here." Green's palm brushed along the skin of my arm and squeezed gently.

You'd think me recoiling from his hand would've frustrated him, but he held my upper arm, quietly waiting for me to accept his help.

An uncomfortable taste of iron lingered in my throat. I hated how blood tasted. How it smelled. How it felt. The sensation was disgusting, the flow slowing as it trickled over my lips and onto my chin.

"I'm not going to hurt you." He wrapped his other hand around my waist and pulled me to my feet.

When I wobbled, Green's arm tightened around me, pulling me firmly against his rock-hard torso. His muscular chest rose and fell against my cheek with each breath he took, and snuggled against him, protected in his grip, I stopped shivering.

His body felt dangerously sweet, pressed against mine, peaceful after what just happened. A warm fire crackling near your skin after escaping a frigid rainstorm. His chest a sanctuary, his grip comforting as his fingers spread over my hip.

Strange how, when you're going through hell, you latch on to any sense of security because, right now, I longed to stay in his tranquil embrace just a little longer. To listen to the tempo of his heart beating beneath my ear and savor his sweet scent.

Rationally, I knew he was still my captor, holding me hostage. But right now, his tender touch reminded me more of a friend than an enemy, and in my desperation to extend this reprieve from fear, I nuzzled my face deeper into his chest.

Green's other hand came up to the side of my head, holding me, as if sensing I needed comfort, no matter who it came from.

I closed my eyes and pictured the staggered rocks of the Grand Canyon blanketed in orange, etched in shadows as gradients of blue and purple clouds stretched into the horizon. I could feel the warmth of the setting sun on my face and smell the fresh pine from nearby trees. I could even hear a lone bird singing as it soared above the valley.

"Come on," he whispered. "I'm going to clean you up."

If he took me out of this room, maybe I'd have a legitimate chance to escape. If I could wiggle my blindfold up another inch to see, I could make a run for the front door.

Green guided me forward carefully, his arm wrapped securely around me so I wouldn't fall.

Still, I was unsure of my steps and shuffled at an agonizingly slow speed. Green didn't rush me or yank me along, though. Instead, he was patient, adjusting his grip when he sensed I needed reassurance with my footing.

Beneath my blindfold, I saw that we exited the office, crossed the hallway, and went into the guest bathroom.

When Green released me, he took the fire's heat with him, sentencing my skin to a prison of ice. The striking temperature shift wasn't merely from the absence of his body's heat, however, but more so from the compassion of his caress. As if tenderness radiated from his skin.

How could I long for his embrace to return?

*Because being in his arms was the only time you haven't felt terrified tonight.*

I shut my eyes, willing the uninvited, inappropriate feeling to go away.

*I must be delirious from shock.* In the face of death, plagued with fear, grasping on to any semblance of compassion and humanity in my final moments of life.

*Green isn't your ally, Zoey. Don't be fooled by his chivalrous act. He's lethal, and he's going to kill you.*

A threat that transformed this place into an eerie set of a horror movie. Normally, this bathroom looked gorgeous with beige tumbled stone blanketing the floors and walls, black faucets, granite counter-tops, and a claw-foot tub against the far wall. But with my sight obstructed, the room was a hallway of darkness, cold and damp. The faucet drip, drip, dripped, its tiny splash echoing like a countdown to my death. In here, the only warmth came from my captor's body, which was so close that I could sense it towering over me. With my arms bound behind my back, I remained at his mercy, vulnerable to whatever he decided to do.

*The living room is only fifteen feet away.* Maybe I could kick Green between his legs and make it to the front door before he could stop me. My stomach came alive with flutters, and as the faucet turned on, I tried to block its noise, so I could listen to where the other guys were.

But when I heard them, my heart sank.

Brown's and Orange's voices permeated down the hall from the living room—the very room I needed to run through to escape. Getting away from Green was already a long shot, and making it past both of them was undoubtedly a death sentence.

My eyes stung from frustration.

"Hold still." Green softly gripped my chin between his thumb and finger and tilted my face up slightly.

A warm, wet towel brushed against the skin just below my nose. It smelled like the pomegranate soap Dad kept in this bathroom—sweet with a trace of cinnamon. I had to admit, it felt nice. The water washed away the tacky, iron-scented blood while Green—being as gentle as if he was treating a burn—glided the cloth back and forth until the skin no longer felt soiled.

As he brushed my face lightly, carefully working the blood off, I felt confused by his touch, for the very hands that would later end my life were being caring and tender. Even harder to comprehend, however, was the unexplainable desire that worked its way into my head. His strokes against my skin didn't feel like a simple act of cleaning. The way he caressed me somehow felt sensual, my lack of sight making me more sensitive to his touch.

A touch that stunned me. Not just because of *who* had sparked this reaction, but also because it was making me feel something I shouldn't.

"I'm sorry he hit you." Green's voice brimmed with…sorrow?

"That makes two of us."

"He needs to learn self-control."

"What he needs is a psychiatrist who isn't deterred by a lost cause."

I liked that I heard Green chuckle.

I swore his strokes lightened into a more suggestive, rhythmic manner, and his deep breaths slowed, his face mere inches from my own.

His cleansing ceased, and I breathed in and out two times before Green spoke again, his tone low and raspy. "Can you part your lips?"

After a small hesitation, I opened my mouth slightly.

The wet fabric caressed the corner of my mouth—an intimate spot few had ever touched. It ignited a blaze of fire that spread from my lips to my throat and down to my stomach. He took his time, gliding the wetness over my crevice, and as he did, I wondered what he was thinking right now because my thoughts jumbled into confusion.

I should've been appalled by his touch rather than liking it. I should've hated him standing this close to me rather than savoring it, and I should not have compared his gentle strokes to that of an artist painting a canvas. The fact that this moment felt seductive made me wonder if I was having some sort of mental breakdown.

The towel returned to my face, this time dry, soaking up the left-over water droplets. The cloth calmed my nerves like a massage, and when it abandoned my skin, my breaths hitched as I anticipated his next touch.

As the faucet dripped with each passing second, I wondered what he was thinking. Why was he just standing here, not doing anything? I could feel him looking at me. Did he feel this irrational flicker of chemistry, too?

The energy coming off his body was like a magnet drawing me to him, and I craved being nestled against his chest with his arms wrapped around me.

After an eternity of waiting, I felt his finger, gloveless, on my lower lip, gently eliminating the last water droplet. His skin was soft, warm, just like when he'd wiped away my tears, and I closed my eyes to appreciate this moment.

Surely, everything going on in my head was all some warped survival-denial thing that was happening to me, like an alternate reality to help me cope with imminent death. I never believed in those people who claimed temporary insanity as a defense. But for the first time, I sort of understood what it meant because his touch...

*Lord, his touch.*

There was absolutely no reason to revel in physical contact, let alone like the guy. So what if he was nice enough to clean the blood off? He was responsible for the blood being there in the first place even if he hadn't been the one to hit me. Any compassion I felt for him was a misdirected coping mechanism. Period.

And as for the empathy he was showing me? Probably fake. Probably just something to keep me from screaming. Make me less of a liability; that was probably his real job—to keep me quiet.

But if that were true...why did I have to keep reminding myself of it? As if my rationale was fighting to overpower the energy between us.

"That's why you look so familiar." Green sounded as if he had solved a mystery that had been bothering him this whole time. "We've met before."

I blinked, stunned. "We have?"

He hesitated. Admitting that he'd met me was a bad idea if he wanted to keep his identity hidden.

I quickly flipped through my mental Rolodex of people I had met in my life, wondering if I could place his face among the sea of Dad's health care workers, waiters, or who knew what else.

He'd said I'd looked familiar, but he must not have placed me until now, when he stood only inches away, studying every curve of my face as he cleaned it off.

"You remember walking along the lakefront three months ago? A guy on Rollerblades crashed into another guy?"

I did remember that...

*SPRING TEMPERATURES CAME EARLY THIS YEAR. MELTED THE SNOW AND ICE into puddles of mud and water standing on the grass near the lake that stretches out to the horizon. The air is still cold, but when you live in Chicago, you learn cold is relative. Fifty degrees in August is something people complain about. But that same fifty degrees in April? You'd think the city was having a national holiday or something, what with all the people swarming near the lakefront.*

*I hate it. I'd rather it be ice cold right now, so I could walk along the lake and think in peace. Clear my head in my favorite place. But no. People taking selfies, jogging, walking their dogs. They're everywhere.*

*Case in point? Some dude in Rollerblades is on his phone—who the hell blades and texts?—and crashes into a guy walking eight feet ahead of me, nearly knocking him over.*

*"Watch where the hell you're going," the guy snaps.*

*I can't help but smile, grateful I'm not the only one in the city annoyed by people.*

*The Rollerblader stares at the guy for a second before frowning and rolling away.*

*But Angry Guy continues walking, obviously not realizing that in the crash, his wallet fell to the ground. I know it's his because I happened to be looking at his butt when the wallet became dislodged. I wasn't gawking. It was just a split second of appreciating something that gorgeous right in my line of sight.*

*In my defense, his backside belongs in a museum, to be admired for generations to come.*

*I pick up the wallet and jog a few feet forward. "Excuse me!"*

*He doesn't turn around.*

*I tap his shoulder. "Sir?"*

*He turns around, and holy crap, my icy mood instantly melts. This guy is level-ten gorgeous. He's over six feet tall with tan skin and brown hair that's short on the sides and several inches longer on the top with caramel highlights. Same darker color as his eyebrows and facial stubble, framing piercing blue eyes that stare at me like they can see through my skull.*

He has to be a model.

*That would explain why it takes me several seconds to remember what the hell I was about to say, hypnotized not only by his beauty, but also by this sense of mystery radiating off him—coming from the intensity in his face and the long silence he allows to pass, staring at me while I struggle to act human in his energy field.*

*"Is this yours?" I hold the wallet toward him.*

*He looks down at it. Stacks of hundreds shuffled in the fall, so they stick out slightly.*

*"It fell out of your pocket when that guy crashed into you."*

*He eyes me skeptically for a second. "You see a wallet full of cash lying on the ground, and you give it back to the owner?"*

Lord, even his voice is unfairly beautiful. He could do voice-over work and make panties melt with it.

*"Of course."*

*His lips twitch slightly, and his dazzling eyes soften.*

*"I'd like to believe most people would give it back, too," I claim even though I don't fully believe it myself. Truth be told, my life has turned me into quite a cynic lately.*

*"I'd argue most people wouldn't," he says.*

*"If more people chose to do the right thing, it'd make life more bearable for the rest of us."*

*He raises his eyebrows slightly, which makes him even sexier.*

*My hormones seriously need to simmer. But no. They are F-ers, warming my inner thighs with each second I stare at his flawless face and body. Because, yeah, with his jacket open, I can tell he's ripped beneath that long-sleeved shirt. His muscles bulge against the fabric.*

*"And life isn't bearable?" he asks in a tone that's not playful or antagonistic. More like a deep curiosity, his gaze somehow stabbing even deeper into my brain.*

*"Not lately." I chew the inside of my cheek.*

*He studies me. Left eye, then my right, and he looks at my lips as he parts his own. This energy buzzing between us makes no sense. I've heard of strong chemical attractions to someone, which must be what this is, but Lord to hell, no one warns you it's as strong as the suction of an F3 tornado. And they don't warn you it goes beyond physical and into full-on curiosity zone, wondering who this guy is.*

*Where is he heading? Does he live in Chicago, or is he a tourist, visiting? And—shamefully—does he have a girlfriend?*

*I raise his wallet a little higher—has he forgotten I'm holding it?*

*He looks down at it again, but when he moves to take it, he halts his arm mid-swing, his eyes cutting to my hand. Which is wrapped in gauze.*

*His jaw moves to the side, and he licks his teeth in displeasure before his sapphire gaze snaps back to mine.*

*My cheeks warm under the heat of his sudden irritation. Irritation that I can tell isn't directed at me, but oddly, at the injury to my palm.*

*Last night, Dad had knocked his wheelchair into the end table, and his water glass had broken on the floor. I was careless enough to think I could pick up the bigger pieces without slicing my skin open. A one-inch gash in my palm proved me wrong.*

*The guy's gaze becomes so intense, it's like the entire city vanishes around us.*

*"Did someone hurt you?" he growls, and his gaze borders on a glare.*

Of all the ways one could injure themselves, why would he assume that?

*"Not my hand." My heart? Hell yes.*

*Based on the tightening of his jaw, he doesn't like my answer.*

*It looks like he's debating grilling me on this, so I wiggle the wallet again to change the subject.*

*When he reaches for it, his finger brushes mine. The warmth of his skin against the frosty air sends a wave of heat up my arm and into my lower belly, and I swear he feels it, too, because he stills for a moment. Stares at me before shoving the wallet into his back pocket.*

*He glances down at my bandage again. "Your hand is bleeding," he says, the edge still punching through his words.*

*I look. Sure enough, blood has breached the gauze on my palm. Just barely, though.* How did he see that before me?

*"How deep is the cut?" His tone is full of authority and concern.*

*I shrug. "I've had to change the bandage a few times."*

*"You should go to urgent care."*

*I purse my lips. "Yeah, maybe I will," I lie.*

*I swear, he must sense my deceit because he studies me, seemingly trying to unravel the hidden meaning behind why I won't go.*

*I'm thankful he doesn't press me on it because the reason is embarrassing.*

*"If you won't get it stitched up," he says, putting a hand into his pocket, "can I at least buy you a cup of coffee?"*

*I try not to smile. "You want to get me coffee?"*

*His tone borders on playful. "There's no need for you to be thirsty and bleeding."*

*I want to go with him and learn about him and see if his magnetic field ever weakens, but my life is so complicated right now, and I barely get five minutes to myself each week. Let alone have time to date.*

*Plus, I haven't felt butterflies like this in a very long time. I don't think I've ever had them this strong before, and their power intimidates me. Everything in my life feels out of control lately, and the prospect of adding gasoline to this pull overwhelms me. I'm not sure if I'm ready for that right now. Especially when Dad needs me so much.*

*So, I don't take him up on his offer. I don't even ask his name or offer him mine. I simply say, "Sorry. I can't."*

*I give him an apologetic smile and turn to walk away but quickly pivot to face him one more time before I do.*

*"You should be more careful." I don't know why I said it—protective*

*instincts maybe—but the words came tumbling out of my mouth. "You shouldn't keep so much cash on you. This city can be dangerous."*

*To this, the corner of his mouth tugs up as if he's fighting back a grin, and cripes, the flutter Gods make him look even sexier for it.*

*He stares at me as I walk away.*

*After a few seconds, I look back over my shoulder, wondering if he's resumed walking. He hasn't. He's still staring at me. Only now, a hunger consumes his eyes, as if he wants to march over and claim me as his own.*

*It takes every ounce of willpower to turn around and leave him behind.*

*Later, when I go to bed, I find myself thinking of him. Of his spellbinding eyes and magnetic charm. There was something about the guy that pulled me in, leaving me gasping for more. It felt different from other guys. Other guys are easy to forget about, yet here I am, tossing and turning, wishing I hadn't turned down his offer to get coffee.*

*After thinking about it, I can't help but wonder if I'd panicked a little when he asked me out. I mean, maybe I was worried that it wasn't just one cup of coffee. Maybe I presumed it could easily lead to two or three. And maybe that scared me a little, letting myself get invested in someone. Especially since I hadn't dated anyone seriously since the death of my boyfriend.*

*Because now? I can't think of a single good reason to have said no. In fact, yes is the only answer that makes any sense, and I find myself wishing I could go back in time and change my decision.*

*As days pass, disappointment fills me that I have no way to reach him. My eyes search for him on the streets. I even walk back by the lake, hoping to see him like a junior high school girl with a crush.*

*I try to tell myself that's all this is. A crush.*

*And crushes fade fast.*

BUT MINE DIDN'T. I NEVER GOT THAT WALLET GUY OUT OF MY MIND. Was that guy Green? Or was he the Rollerblader? Or one of the other onlookers who'd seen it?

"Couldn't believe you didn't take any money for yourself," he said.

I heard a soft noise, as if Green was rubbing part of his face.

"Was that you?" I asked. "The guy that lost his wallet?"

That was the only way he would know there was no missing money, right?

Unless another guy was watching me when I picked up the wallet and returned it...

Green didn't answer right away. "Lotta people were there. Saw what happened."

*Translation; he's not stupid enough to reveal what he looked like that day.*

"I can't believe I didn't recognize you sooner." Any trace of anger or animosity from our earlier fighting had faded behind reverence. "Because I've thought of you every day since." His voice was like velvet, gliding over my skin.

"Why?" I whispered, surprised by how much I cared about his answer.

Green's tone lowered into a rumble. "You had this...mix of sweetness and salt that I'd never seen in anyone before. Kind enough to return a stranger's money, but you still had this edge to you. This... anger toward the world."

My belly came alive with flutters.

"I found it to be quite...intoxicating," he said.

Whoa. No matter who this guy was, this had to be good.

*Work with this, Zoey.*

Maybe he wouldn't reveal his ID, but he *had* revealed we'd met, and that was a big give. It gave me the chance to figure out who he was. Plus, he'd had the compassion to clean my face, had scolded Brown for hitting me, and evidently, had thought of me every day since.

*Could I win him over now?*

There was one way to test it, I decided, before blowing my last chance at begging for his mercy. I could ask him something that had been gnawing at me, forced to the back burner of my mind while the front burner had been focused on surviving. And see if he answered.

"Why'd you keep asking who knew I was coming tonight?"

Because when I'd assumed it was to cover his own ass, to learn what other hostages might be on their way, he'd said, "That's not why I'm asking."

So, why then?

Green ran the sink—rinsing the towel, I presumed—and then I lifted my chin and saw him grip the edge of the counter. Looking down or at himself in the mirror, I didn't know, but his knuckles whitened as he stood there for several seconds before pivoting his feet to face me.

"Zoey..." Green cleared his throat, and I heard his body move, running a hand through his hair perhaps. "Someone sent us to rob the place tonight. Someone who knew this place."

## 7

Beneath my blindfold, I blinked. "What are you talking about?"
He hesitated. "We shouldn't talk in here."

I was about to demand he answer me, but the bathroom was closer to the living room than the office, so his colleagues might overhear. If I had any hope of getting the truth, we needed to be somewhere farther away.

Green wrapped his arm around my waist, his fingers pressing into my hip as he pulled my body against his torso again. Even through the fabric between us, I could feel the firmness of his bicep and forearm and the heat radiating from his skin.

With a gentle nudge, he guided my feet forward, and like the last time, I moved slowly. I saw the tile give way to wood as we entered the hallway, and despite having a little bit of vision, my foot caught on the doorframe.

But Green's arm tightened around my hip and righted me before I could fall.

"You okay?" he asked softly.

I nodded, relieved by how much he really sounded as if he cared.

We slowly crossed through the hallway and back into the office, where his warm body vanished from my side. A squeak, followed by a light rumble, told me he'd picked up the chair from its fallen position and rolled it behind my legs, his hands gripping my shoulders, ensuring I didn't fall when I sat back down.

"Comfortable?" He slid his hands to my upper arms.

I released an exasperated breath.

"What?" he asked.

"I'm tied up with my arms yanked behind my back, and you're asking if I'm comfortable?"

A small pause.

"Do your arms hurt?" His tone was deep with seeds of sympathy sprouting.

"Yes."

He was silent for four breaths. "If I retie your hands in front of you, would that be more comfortable?"

My heartbeat spiked; I hadn't anticipated him giving me this option. With my hands in front, I'd have a much better chance at escaping. I could move my blindfold easily, defend myself, and open doors quickly. *This might be the moment that saves me.* "Yes."

Another pause.

"I'm trusting you not to run, Zoey." His tone seemed to add, *If you do, you won't like the consequences.*

But I had to run.

The second my hands were untied...

He pulled me by my shoulders back into a standing position, then seized my hips and twisted me around so my back faced his chest. The heat of his breath tickled the back of my neck, and his fingertips brushed my wrists as he worked the binding's knots, the fabric tugging at my pained skin as it loosened. Then vanished completely.

The relief was better than I'd expected. The cool air soothing what must be significant rug-like burns. Plus, my arms no longer ached from being pinned behind me.

I moaned, my shoulders rejoicing at their new freedom, the muscles aching from having pulled on them so hard earlier. I rubbed my wrists but regretted it immediately; the skin was raw, and when I touched it, the salt from my fingers made it sting.

*My hands are free.*

He grabbed my hips and turned me back around to face him.

*This is it.*

I'd only have *one* move before he caught on and reacted, so what would it be? Run? Or move the blindfold?

Run, I decided. Once I made it a few steps away from him, I'd remove the blindfold.

But that meant I needed a seriously good assessment of where he stood in relation to the door. Based on the number and direction of our steps from the hallway, I'd ballpark the door at ten feet forward, to my left, but I could be wrong.

I never realized how hard it was to lose your vision. How crippling it could be. Aside from the crevice at the bottom of my blindfold, all I could see was blackness.

With my heart pounding, my breathing quickened, drawing in Green's aroma of burnt sugar, a scent that—should I be asked later—I'd deny smelled sexy.

Right before my legs sprinted, something soft danced along my skin.

His fingertips, I realized. Tracing my wounded wrists.

"Does it hurt?" His voice was a near whisper.

I paused. "Yes."

He trailed a finger down my hand, over my knuckle. "I'm sorry. I wish I didn't have to put this back on."

Something told me to keep working this angle, that I was winning him over, but with a decent chance to flee, fear took control. Because what if I never had another chance like this? This whole night felt like a fatal version of chess with me having to anticipate all the scenarios that could play out, calculating my best odds of survival.

Green draped the fabric beneath my arms.

But I moved faster.

I jumped to my left like a quarterback avoiding a tackle and broke into a sprint.

But I hit a wall, my body jerking to a stop.

My palms flattened against pectorals, and my stomach pressed against his as Green caged me in with his arms.

"Zoey." His whisper glided across my skin. "You run out there, they'll kill you on the spot."

"I stay in here, I'm dead anyway."

"Zoey…"

"Give me a chance to live."

If it was possible for a heart to stop beating, I swore mine did, waiting for his verdict. I wanted to rip my blindfold off and look him in the eyes to plead with him, but if I did that, he'd have an even bigger reason to kill me.

A reason I couldn't take back.

I was in enough trouble already; he'd warned me not to run, and now that I'd broken that promise, I had no idea what horrible consequences he'd inflict.

I braced myself for a blow or a hand around my throat, but as he held me prisoner in his arms, nothing came.

*He's not hurting me.*

*I broke my vow to him, and even then, he refuses to hurt me.*

Did that mean the only true threat was from the other men?

Fear melted away, softening my muscles, and a warmth buzzed beneath my skin as I became conscious of his body. His broad chest, rising and falling beneath my palms, his heated breaths rolling across my face, his steely grip around my waist, and the contours of his tight stomach pushing into mine.

But mostly, I sensed him staring at me, his face mere inches from my own.

Even blinded, I was sucked into his gaze.

And then his fingertips skimmed my cheek as he tucked a fallen hair behind my ear. The gesture was tender, igniting a firestorm of flutters in my stomach.

Sixth senses couldn't be trusted evidently because, right now, mine was telling me the way he was holding me, staring at me, was as if he wanted to kiss me. Which was ludicrous. He must be furious with me for lying to him, for trying to escape. But even more absurd was the small part of me that wondered what his mouth would feel like.

*I'm definitely having a mental breakdown. It's the only way to explain this insanity in my head.*

"I'm going to sit you back down," Green whispered, the energy crackling between us. "And you're going to hold still while I tie your hands. Understand?"

Maybe the survivalist in me wanted to sense his kindness, to fool me into believing I still had a chance to survive. Maybe that was all this was.

Green walked me backward and lowered me into the chair.

On my left arm, he slid his grip down to my hand and turned my wrist until the palm was face up. His thumb brushed along the scar from where that glass had cut me.

"This doesn't look like it healed properly." Disapproval wrapped around his words.

That had to mean he was wallet guy, right? Then again, there had been plenty of people nearby who could have witnessed the bandage on my hand. Maybe even overheard wallet guy's suspicion that someone had hurt me.

"I couldn't afford stitches." While I had medical insurance for myself, my deductible meant I was on the hook for the first three grand of medical bills. Stitches would run me a few hundred, at least.

"You get hurt, and you couldn't even afford medical treatment." Green seemed to say it more to himself than me. "And yet you hand back a wallet full of cash."

Was that...admiration in his tone?

Green didn't say anything else for a minute, his thumb trailing up and down the white scar on my skin. And when he finally spoke, a growl of vengeance dragged through his voice. "Did someone do this to you, Zoey?"

I was surprised by his reaction. "No."

"Tell me the truth."

"What difference does it make?"

"A big one."

"And if someone did do this to me, what would you do?" *Let me go? Because you feel sorry for me?*

"I would ensure the culprit who hurt you regretted it. Immensely."

What. In the actual. Hell?

"And why would you do that?"

No answer.

"Is this a last wish sort of thing? Because need I remind you what your buddies are going to do to me?" It was far worse than damage to a palm.

I wished I could see his face. Gauge his temperament with something other than sound and touch.

"Give me a name." His voice scorched with anger.

"There is no name. I hurt it, cleaning up a broken glass."

He hesitated. "That true?"

"Yes. If you want to do something for me, let me go."

He sighed.

But he didn't say no...

Was it possible he was reconsidering? Maybe even starting to brainstorm ideas of how to help me out of here? Even if we couldn't act now, even if we had to wait until the coast was clear, might he help me?

After another long pause, the fabric wrapped back around my wrists and tightened into knots. But he made sure it didn't rub the sore spots.

Was I reading too much into the small act of kindness?

He draped his coat over my shoulders again, the warmth of the fabric eliminating my chills. In the crack of my blindfold, I saw Green's feet walk to the other side of the room and cross, as if leaning against the table.

I imagined I had been here for about twenty minutes now, but I couldn't be sure. It could have been an hour. Either way, Dad wouldn't be calling the police yet to report me missing. He had no idea I was being held hostage or that my captor had just admitted someone had orchestrated this robbery.

"Who ordered the job?" I clenched my fingers.

Green kept his voice low. "I don't know."

"What do you mean, you don't know? You said someone hired you guys to do this, so who was it?"

"Didn't meet the person. They used a middleman, who introduced them to a...colleague of mine."

"A middleman?"

"Person on the streets who knows how to get in touch with us," Green said.

"How would anyone even know they could do that?"

"Our group is...well known in Chicago." Green's tone sounded matter-of-fact. A professor educating a student.

"What in the hell does the tipster get out of it?"

"A cut of the take."

"Of course." I shook my head. "It's always about money."

"It's not uncommon to get tipped off about places. Most places are insured, so the homeowners don't lose any money." His patience gave way to worry. "Anyone you can think of that might've organized this?"

Organized a heist? Seriously? "No." I didn't even know that was a thing until a few seconds ago.

"Who would know this place was empty?"

"I don't know. Our realtor?" I shrugged.

Green cleared his throat. "Whoever it was knew details of what we'd find inside."

"They tell you you'd find cash and jewels?"

"No."

*That's why Green wasn't going after the safe.*

"Then, why was Brown such an asshole when I told him that?"

Green's voice wound with tension. "He's not part of my crew."

Green's crew. As in he was a leader?

"Well, I don't know then. I hate to say it, but maybe it was my dad's ex-wife. She left him as soon as the money train dried up, so she doesn't strike me as the most moral person."

"Would she still have a key to this place?" Green sounded bitter.

"They gave you a key?"

No answer.

"If it wasn't her, maybe a neighbor, a friend of my dad's. I have no clue who'd want to or know how to hire someone to rob the place. My dad's friends are all rich-ish, so I can't imagine them doing something like this, but then I can't imagine anyone doing it, so I have no idea."

"Who knew you'd be coming tonight?" Green growled.

"I already told you. No one."

"Not a single person?"

"Not really."

"Elaborate on *not really*."

Where was he going with this?

"A family friend knows I needed to get cash quickly. He knows I was planning to sell a ring, but I never told him that I'd be coming here to retrieve it."

"What's his name?"

"I'm not handing his name over to you."

"I'm trying to help you. Figure out if someone set you up."

*Set me up?* That was a stretch.

But *help* me? My hope grasped on to that word like a drowning person clinging to a life raft.

Was this guy capable of changing sides?

Who was Green? Based on what he'd told me, he was the leader of his own crew, which did not include Brown, who he clearly didn't like.

As if the org structure of his criminal enterprise wasn't confusing enough, Green implied he'd had to take care of someone, too. Who? Was he still taking care of them? And if he was responsible for caring for someone, why would he risk his freedom by robbing places?

"Can I ask you a question?" I tilted my body forward slightly.

"Depends on the question," he said.

"Why'd you become a burglar?"

## 8

"What difference does it make?" Green sounded confused. "I'm curious."

"Why?"

"You seem…" *Nice?* "Not abysmal."

Green chuckled. "Well, if that's not a ringing endorsement."

"You're part of that gang they talk about on the news, aren't you? The ones they call the Robin Hood Thieves because, after each heist, anonymous donations appear to homeless shelters."

"Veto," Green said.

"What the hell does *veto* mean?"

"Means I'm not answering that."

"That's a yes."

"You'd be wise to stop trying to guess our identity."

*Our.* So, at least one of those guys out there was a member of his crew.

"Do you really make donations to homeless shelters after each burglary?" I couldn't hide my high-pitched surprise.

"Why?"

I shrugged. "Seems odd."

"Yeah? Why's that?" he asked dryly.

"Criminals don't help other people."

"Because we're too busy plotting evilness in our lair?" He sounded amused.

"Or holding unsuspecting women hostage."

I wondered if he rolled his eyes.

"So, if criminals did anything nice for someone," he said, "it would surprise you?"

"Surprise me? I'd be less surprised if a black hole sucked me out of the atmosphere at a thousand miles an hour."

A gust of air burst from his nose. And when he spoke, his tone flooded with amusement. "It's confusing you, isn't it?"

"What is?"

"That a *bad guy* might be capable of doing something good, too."

"People's actions speak volumes."

"Like your father's."

My lips curled. "What?"

"You said *even after what he did to you, you'd never wish this on him.* What did he do?"

I'd said that to him?

*Right.* When verbal diarrhea exploded from my mouth, begging for my life.

"You're changing the subject, so you don't have to answer my questions," I said sternly.

"Maybe," he said. "What did he do to you?"

"Veto."

"Did he hurt you?" A protective edge sliced through his words.

"Why do you care?" I tightened my forehead.

"I want to know about you."

Hope took flight in my chest. While I didn't want to talk about what went down with my dad, my captor had just expressed interest in me, which meant he was seeing me as a human being, not just his hostage. A human being that he cared enough about to scold his colleague for hitting, clean the blood off my face, and warm me with his jacket.

Telling him I was a caregiver hadn't been enough to sway him because, clearly, he was interested in *me*, not in whoever depended on me.

Perhaps opening up to him would finally make him let me go, but if I was going to run this play, I needed to do it now; the robbery would be done soon. And if I hadn't won Green over by then, I'd be dead.

Of all subjects to get into, I wished he hadn't pressed for such a painful one. But in the fight for my life and my dad's life, I would pull out all the stops to stay alive.

So, I sucked in a deep pull of oxygen and steadied my quivering heart.

"It started a few years ago."

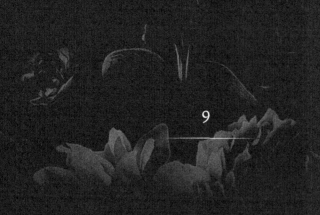

## 9

I suppose the darker times wouldn't make sense without some context of what life was like before it all went to hell.

"I grew up in Illinois," I started. "With my brother, Anthony, two stable parents, and a white picket fence. The life where you think everything will stay peaceful forever..."

"MERRY CHRISTMAS." DAD SMILES AS HE HANDS ME A THREE-INCH CUBE *wrapped in silver.*

*We're in our living room in Oak Brook. Outside the eight-foot window, snowflakes drift from the gray sky, joining the four inches of snow already blanketing the ground. Inside, the fireplace's logs crack, spitting embers as we sit around the Christmas tree, sipping hot chocolate with whipped cream, its sticky sweetness lingering above my lip.*

*I set my mug down and take the gift from my father, who slings an arm around his crooked knee, and smiles. Joy dancing through a father's heart as he waits for his only daughter to open his gift.*

*I tear open the paper and open a black jewelry box. And not just any jewelry box. It's from L&B Fine Jewelry, the fanciest jewelry store in town, the one that sells one-of-a-kind pieces to rich people. We don't wear jewelry like this in our family—we wear stuff from Target—so I look up at him, wide-eyed.*

*His grin reminds me of a kid. "Open it."*

*I comply and see the most gorgeous ring I've ever seen. A pear-shaped ruby, surrounded by diamonds, in a rose gold band.*

*"Dad..." I bring my hand to my chest.*

*"This is our last Christmas together before you leave for college, so I wanted to get you something special. Something you'll have for the rest of your life, to remind you of how much I love you."*

*My eyes sting.*

*"I'm incredibly proud of you, Zoey. Straight A's. Getting accepted into the University of Illinois. I don't know what I did to deserve a daughter like you."*

*It would be hard, leaving the only home I've ever known next fall. To no longer have breakfast every day with Dad—eggs, blueberries, and a bagel. Extra cream cheese. I cherish our mornings together. It's when we talk about life. I'm closer to my dad than I am to my mom, not that I don't have a bond with my mom. I do. She's fantastic. There's just something...magical between me and my dad. Pixie dust that's been there since I was a toddler, running into his arms when he'd gotten home from work.*

*"Love you, Zo," he says. "Never forget that."*

*He hugs me.*

I DID NOT KNOW THAT, SOON, OUR HAPPY FAMILY WOULD BREAK APART.

The first fracture wasn't a fracture at all. It was an earthquake. Magnitude eight, at least, when I got that phone call in college.

I was particularly vulnerable at that time, not only because I was new to college and struggling to find my confidence, but also because my best friend from high school had basically stopped returning my calls and texts. We hadn't had a fight. She'd moved to Arizona for college, and we went from seeing each other daily in high school to talking every day, then every week, then texting only, and then, well...my texts went unanswered. Calls went straight to voice mail.

She'd been my best friend since fifth grade, and all of a sudden, it was like I didn't matter to her anymore. Like she'd found new friends and I was in her rearview mirror.

How could our friendship not matter to her as much as it did to me? Each text that went unreturned sliced another gash in my chest.

That was when Dad called me up one day, out of the blue, his voice foreboding.

*"I NEED TO TALK TO YOU." HIS TONE IS OFF. AND WRONG. AND SCARING ME, and I can't go to school or focus, worrying about what's wrong.*

Is he sick? Is Mom sick? Is Anthony okay?

*I ask him all these things, of course, but all he says is, "We should wait to talk in person."*

*"Tell me now," I plead.*

*"Zoey."*

*"Are you dying?"*

*"No, it's nothing like that," he assures.*

*"But it's something terrible. Please, just say it."*

*"This isn't something to be discussed over the phone. How about I drive over on Friday—"*

*"Friday! You think I can go through classes until then? I won't be able to focus."*

*I've never heard him like this. Sad. Afraid even. He's never been afraid to tell me anything.*

*"I'll drive over. We can have dinner."*

*He's covering something up. Mom must be sick, or he's sick, or someone's dying. He's playing word games to avoid telling me the truth because whatever it is, it's so bad, he thinks I can only handle it in person.*

*"I don't want dinner. I want you to tell me what the hell is going on."*

*"And I will, on Friday."*

*"Tell me now, Dad."*

*"Zoey."*

*"Tell me, or I'll leave right now and come home, so we can talk. I'm not waiting until Friday."*

*A weird hesitation passes.*

"You can't come to the house right now, Zoey."

Can't? "Why?" I start pacing.

"I'll explain when I see you."

Suddenly, my best friend abandoning me loses its significance because if someone in my family is dying, nothing else matters.

"I'm packing a bag." I grab my travel suitcase from my closet and throw it onto the floor.

"Zoey."

Desperation comes out like the blunt tip of a sharp knife. "I'm not waiting to talk, Dad, so last chance. Spit it out, or I'm on my way."

I can hear Dad sigh like he does when something isn't going the way he wanted it to.

I'm silent during the next several seconds until, finally, he says, "Zoey, I've...well..." Dad clears his throat. "The thing is...I've met someone."

I've. Met. Someone. Three words that thrust a sword into my heart, puncturing it deeper with each stab.

"I didn't mean for this to happen," he claims. "But we have a lot in common, and we fell in love."

"What exactly are you saying?" I demand, clenching my fists so tightly that my fingernails sting my palms.

"Zoey...I've moved out of your mother's house."

"So, it's Mom's house now? Not our house?"

"Zoey—"

"Who is she?"

"I...she's someone I met at work."

"Does she know you're married?"

He sighs. "She knows everything."

"What kind of person dates a guy who's married? With kids? And is willing to break up a family?"

"Zoey...it's not like that."

"That's exactly what it's like! How could you do this to Mom? To us?"

"I understand you're upset—"

"Upset? More like betrayed and disgusted! The father I know would never cheat on his wife and leave his family for some other woman!"

The dad that I know is the rock of the family, the man who lifts us up when we fall, and the person I turn to anytime I feel lost or overwhelmed. After talking with him, I'm always clear in the direction that I want to head with whatever I'm facing. To put it plainly, he is my North Star, and even though I love my mom and my brother, I suppose we all have that one person in our life that is the most influential with guiding us. And Dad is that special person to me, not only because of his wisdom, but because I look up to him as a human being. That is the dad that I know.

"I'm going to let you go, so you can calm down. I'm coming up on Friday. We'll talk about it then."

"So, you're going to drop a bomb like this and just hang up on me?"

"This conversation isn't productive. You're too upset to talk right now."

"More like you destroy our family and can't face the heat of our broken hearts."

"I'll be up on Friday." He tries to make his voice sound loving, but it sounds dismissive. And then he hangs up.

This has to be a sick joke. This cannot be real. Dad gave no hint that anything was wrong with their marriage, let alone something big enough to leave Mom. Maybe he got catfished online, and he's a victim of some swindler that's brainwashed him. Or worse, maybe he has a brain tumor—something causing a sudden personality shift. Because the man that would do everything for his family would never do any of this to us. To me.

And if he would? Then, that would mean the father that I thought I knew for all these years wasn't real. That he was a completely different person. Not the hero who I looked up to, but a villain willingly hurting those he supposedly loved the most.

Which is too painful to endure. It's pathetic, I know. People face far worse heartaches in their lives. Death of a child. Famine. Abuse. And here I am, pathetically unable to cope with Dad leaving his family.

I put my hand over my aching stomach.

This is like a mudslide. Standing on what you thought was a solid foundation, only to have it go out beneath you.

Days pass in a fog. Days when I call my mom and brother. Mom tries to hide the hurt in her voice, and she's being diplomatic about the whole thing, reminding me he's a great father even if he's not being the best husband right *now. Her having the grace to take the high road when he's ripping her heart out makes me even angrier at my father.*

He doesn't deserve Mom.

*I can't wait until he comes because I have so many questions: How long has this been going on? What does she have that we don't? And so many other things to get off my chest.*

*The day before Dad's visit, I'm a nervous wreck. I feel like our entire relationship hangs in the balance of this weekend because I don't think I can ever get past this. I desperately need him to say something to help me understand, or I'll lose my father forever.*

*When my cell rings with his number, I assume he just wants to confirm that I'm actually going to show up.*

*But as soon as I answer, I can tell something's wrong based on his tone.*

*"Zoey"—his voice has notes of apology and assertiveness—"I'm afraid I'm going to have to reschedule."*

*I laugh, my body rigid with anger and disbelief. "You're kidding me, right?"*

*"She didn't know I'd made plans with you and surprised me with a trip."*

*"You're going on a trip? With that woman?"*

*"Zoey."*

*I close my eyes and grab the lifeline to my father. Tugging as hard as I can. "Dad, we need to talk right away." If we don't, this anger will fester until it's spread through my entire heart, damaging it beyond repair. Our only hope is to talk now.*

*And I shouldn't have to beg him to make the right decision. This is my father, someone who's supposed to prioritize me above the entire world.*

*I can't believe he's hesitating on the other end. Each beat of my heart that passes in silence widens the chasm between a father and daughter.*

*Which is selfish of my feelings—to grab the wheel and take over like this. The headline here is him leaving Mom for another woman, not how badly he's breaking my heart. And yet, my emotions grip the wheel tighter, putting his decision to come here on center stage because right now, it feels like the most defining moment of our relationship.*

*"You need to make a choice about what's more important this weekend, Dad. Her. Or me."*

"This isn't about who's more important."

"It is now."

"And we will talk," Dad said, his voice bordering on aggravation. "Just not tomorrow. The tickets she bought are nonrefundable. It's just a few more days, and then I'll come over, okay?"

I hope he realizes what he just said has taken that sword he'd placed in my heart and twisted it. Then sliced until it hemorrhaged.

"Well, I guess you made your choice then."

"Zoey."

"No, you've made your priorities clear, Dad."

I hang up and can't stop myself from cracking in half and falling to my bed in a heap of sobs. I'm angry that I'm crying. He doesn't even care enough about me to come when he said he would. He's more worried about some nonrefundable ticket, a trip with his new girlfriend, than salvaging a relationship with his only daughter. And I'm angry that I'm so fixated on this stupid visit when I should only be focused on how he's hurting the entire family.

But I guess it's hard enough when your parents are splitting, but a thousand times more hurtful when your dad is rejecting you in the process.

I'm pathetic because I stare at my phone, willing it to ring. He's my dad, and he should fight with every breath in his body to talk to me, to beg me for forgiveness, no matter how angry I am. Of course I'm angry! He's married, and he's just walking out on Mom!

But five minutes pass, and my phone doesn't ring.

He must be pacing, thinking about what he wants to say.

Ten minutes pass.

He realizes how badly he's hurt me, and it means so much that he's taking the time to gather his thoughts.

Fifteen minutes pass.

He's telling his girlfriend that he's not going on that trip. He's packing a bag and coming straight here. Now.

Thirty minutes pass. Then an hour. Three hours later, I throw my phone across the room and bury my face in my pillow.

He's not calling back.

*As it turns out, the blade of the sword cuts much deeper when the person wielding it is supposed to be your protector.*

A CHILD WAS SUPPOSED TO BE THE FIRST PRIORITY OF THEIR PARENTS. From the moment I was born, Dad loved me with an unspoken promise that my importance to him would never diminish. But it did diminish. Severely.

After he never showed up that weekend, the next time we spoke, there was an undercurrent of frustration in my dad's tone. Which made me even angrier. It was like, even though he was the one in the wrong, he expected me to revert back to being a five-year-old and just accept his decision as final, no questions asked. Which led to even more distance between us, and the more distance there was, the less he tried to fix things.

I guess my pain was too much of a handful to bother with.

That's when I discovered a shattered heart can crumble into even smaller pieces until the only thing left is dust.

When you have the unconditional love of your father, the world is a sanctuary of optimism and peace, but when that love is revoked, when you become insignificant to the person who's supposed to love you above all others, your foundation cracks.

And you question if his love was ever there for you in the first place. And if his love could go away, how could I ever trust anyone else's love again?

Mom and Dad got a quick divorce, which Mom didn't fight him on. She was probably too humiliated to beg him to love her the way he'd promised he always would. Especially when he hired some big-shot lawyer and left Mom with nothing—nothing, not even child support since Anthony and I were of age.

As if that weren't bad enough, right before my last year in college, I got an email from my father, letting me know I was on my own finan-cially for my senior year tuition. Which was due a month later. I almost had to drop out of college because of it. Thankfully, I scram-bled with loans and two jobs. But the thing that hurt the worst was that it felt like a penalty, like his promise as a father was contingent upon me approving of his life choices. And if I didn't? He was willing to risk my college degree to punish me.

In the years that followed, I became blinded in life, unsure of my footing, particularly in my relationships. I was skeptical anyone actually cared about me. Convinced it was only a matter of time before they would hurt me, too.

I almost didn't even allow myself to build a new friendship with my college roommate, Jenna, but I supposed we had something big in common—she and I shared in the betrayal of a father leaving his family.

But even with that friendship and a slow build of others, my foundation never mended.

After Dad married that woman—I didn't attend the wedding—he started calling me and reaching out again, but I doubted it had anything to do with his love for me and more about him wanting me to meet my new *stepmom*.

Fat chance.

I refused repeatedly until, one day, Anthony guilt-tripped me into attending Thanksgiving with him. After my big brother graduated college, he took a job in Oregon—pretty much as far away from Chicago as you could get. He used to fly home every holiday, though, and was hard at work, trying to make a peace treaty between me and Dad. But it was easier for him to encourage a reconciliation; Anthony had earned a full ride to college with his grades and soccer, so he dodged the bullet of having a tuition crisis with Dad.

A tuition crisis with a brand-new development.

Two months before Thanksgiving, I'd discovered the first three years of college tuition—the tuition that Dad *had* covered—hadn't been paid off like Dad had told me it would be. Instead, the "temporary" student loans that he'd cosigned with me—the ones that were supposed to be paid off when I graduated college—had recently defaulted, destroying my credit score and leaving me with over $53,000 in loans I hadn't been expecting. Without so much as a heads-up.

Did I expect my parents to fund my college? No. In fact, I offered to pay for it myself by getting jobs, but Dad insisted —*insisted*—on funding my education. It was something he'd wanted to do my whole life, and even though we had fallen out, I guess I'd let him pay for two reasons. One, maybe part of it was an FU. You want to ditch me, destroy Mom, and ruin all our lives for some woman? Least you can do is fulfill the promise you'd made to me. And two, maybe the little weakling in me grasped on to the only proof I had that he still cared...until he stopped funding senior year, that is.

In any case, paperwork had been filed. With both our names on it. Loan paperwork, so Dad had a little flexibility with cash flow, given the timing of his bonuses each year. At least, that was what he told me.

But as it turned out, those monthly statements he'd arranged to only go to him had been ignored. He hadn't paid them and never bothered to tell me they'd been sent to collection.

My credit rating tanked, and I was sacked with the unexpected debt, which had accrued interest and penalties.

What a slap in the face.

To drag my credit score down without even telling me.

Not surprisingly, finding an apartment in Chicago willing to rent to a tenant with horrible credit was nearly impossible. Not to mention, drowning under unexpected financial weight was beyond stressful.

So, when my brother pushed me into Thanksgiving, I rolled up my sleeves, ready to confront my father about it all.

*I ARRIVE AT DAD'S PLACE. A LUXURY CONDO THAT MAKES ME SEETHE WITH anger.*

*Mom and Dad graduated college together without a penny to their name, and Dad worked his ass off, climbing the ranks of a sales executive until he finally made some serious bank. Just in time for this new woman to invade our lives and live in the lap of luxury.*

*It's not that I wanted the money or the lifestyle. It's just that it feels like another slap in the face. Another thing she took from Mom that was right-fully hers.*

*"Zoey." Dad smiles when we enter. "I'm so glad you came."*

*He must've practiced that fake-ass smile in the mirror. Like he gave a crap if I came. Like he gave a crap about me at all.*

*I twist the ring on my finger. The one he gave me that fateful Christmas Day, the last one we spent as a family before he let his dick make all his deci-sions. I don't know why I still wear it. Probably some last tiny string of hope that my dad will come back to me.*

*"This is Holly."*

*He ushers a tall woman, wearing a bright red dress, toward me. Her black hair looks like it has a thousand products in it to keep every strand in perfect waves, her makeup thick and elegant. Like a bride on her wedding day.*

*I, on the other hand, am wearing jeans and a black sweater. I chose black on purpose. Like,* FU, Dad. I've been in mourning since the day you left.

*But any thoughts of our outfits quickly fade when I see what's on her hand. Not her left hand—although her wedding ring is ten times nicer than the one Dad gave Mom. Another FU to our family. But her other hand. Because on it is the identical ring I am wearing.*

*Rose gold. Pear-shaped ruby. Diamonds.*

*Dad sees my gaze cut to it, and his eyes widen.*

*"You were screwing her back then?" I snap.*

*The handful of people at Thanksgiving stop talking and stare at the scene.*

*"Zoey."*

*"You gave her this ring, too?" I'm crying, and I'm furious that I'm crying because he doesn't deserve my tears. Back when he gifted me that ring, I was special to him, and that time in my life was all I had left of my dad.*

*But it, too, is gone. He'd been cheating on my mom back then. He'd given this woman the same ring he claimed was special, just for me. A tender moment between us ruined. A ring he claimed he wanted to remind me of his love.*

*What a crock of shit.*

*The ring once symbolized his unending love for me, but now, it symbol-izes betrayal.*

*I take off the ring, and I throw it at my father's face.*
*I run out of his condo and out of his life.*

I COULDN'T BRING MYSELF TO TALK ABOUT WHAT HAPPENED NEXT; IT was so painful, it made me feel sick to my stomach.

As the silence ticked on, Green said nothing. In fact, he'd barely moved or made a noise.

"Are you still there?" I pretended I couldn't see his combat boots.

"Yes." His voice had changed. It was lower, as if pain anchored it down.

Another pause.

"Has something happened?" I bent my neck. "You went all quiet."

"No."

"You sound different." I wrinkled my forehead. And he did. He sounded like…sad or something…

He didn't respond.

"Are you okay?" I asked, my pitch higher.

"I'm fine."

"You don't sound fine."

He cleared his throat and seemed to take a second to calibrate his response. "You were mistreated by someone you trusted. Someone who should've protected you," he snarled. "At least what happened to me wasn't done to me by my own flesh and blood."

There was a lot to unpack there. What happened to him? And by whom? And more importantly, was this the moment I'd been hoping for, when his allegiance shifted to me?

But before I could ask, Green spoke again. "How'd you get stuck taking care of your dad? And why'd you bother after he'd treated you like that?"

It took me a second to stop wondering what Green's past was. "That's an even longer story," I hedged.

As much as I hated everything my dad did to me, nothing topped what I'd done to him.

"How long ago did he leave your family?" Green asked.

I squirmed. "Six and a half years ago. My sophomore year of college."

"So, you graduated, what, four years ago?"

I nodded.

The clock ticked three times.

"But the bank didn't tell you about the loans defaulting until now?"

"I found out about it last year. I can only assume minimum payments were made for a while before they finally stopped completely."

"And now, you're on the hook for them? Isn't he still on the hook, too?"

"Legally, he might be, but the reality is, my name is on them, and he can't pay. Most likely will never be able to. He was already in financial distress before the accident, and now, the hospital bills killed any hope of him avoiding bankruptcy. We started the process a couple months ago."

What an overwhelming crash course in how personal bankruptcy works. The different versions you can file, each with pros and cons. It didn't release the burden of the student loans, though.

"And your dad's ex won't help?"

"She left him right after the accident. Before he was even discharged from the hospital."

"That's why he came to your place when he was released?"

"She wasn't going to take care of him, and my brother lives too far away."

Green's voice lowered another octave and let out a huge sigh. "Taking care of someone's an expensive burden," he said. "And yet, you had that wallet in your hands, stuffed with money. And you didn't take any of it."

The admiration in his voice wrapped around my skin like silk.

"Stealing won't change what that guy did to my dad."

"You said it was a hit-and-run?"

I had to clench my eyes shut from the memories of not just how badly Dad had been injured, but also, everything else that came before it. "He left my dad without even checking if he was alive."

"Maybe he panicked."

To this, I tilted my head, both in offense and scrutiny. Because why would he say that?

"Did *you* hit someone?"

"No," Green assured. "And I don't know anyone that did, either. I'm just saying..." He was silent for a minute, and when he finally spoke, his voice was vulnerable. "Sometimes, good people are capable of bad things, Zoey."

Good people doing bad things, meaning what—something happened that caused him to become a thief?

"You never answered my question before." I leaned forward slightly.

"What question?"

"Why did you choose a life of crime?"

Green sighed in a way someone does when they're preparing to give a long answer.

But before Green said anything, I heard a thump.

Then another and another, in quick succession, and as Green's ankles stiffened, I realized someone was on their way down the hall.

*Thump. Thump.* Angry boots slamming against the wooden floor.

Green moved to the doorway, and the way he positioned his feet— half-forward, angled toward me—if I didn't know better, I'd swear he was frazzled. The footsteps grew louder, closer to me, and with Green blocking the doorway, I had nowhere to run.

There was only one reason a man would be coming toward us, and Green would be rigid.

The robbery was done, and it was time to kill me.

## 10

M y body trembled, ready to take all one hundred fifteen pounds and turn it into a lethal weapon. With my hands in front, I could punch and claw and open the front door hella easier than when they'd been behind my back. It'd be easier if I could free them, though. As I twisted my right wrist, trying to pull it through the loop of confinement, Green's breathing quickened. Another step echoed through the hallway.

I'd have to act now. Jump up, move the blindfold, bulldoze my way past whoever was in the hall, and make it to the front door. Not ideal. Not probable I'd succeed, but what other choice did I have?

I braced my feet on the ground and prepared to strike.

But when the person took their next step, they were on a different surface. The carpet in the master bedroom, I realized.

Whoever it was wasn't coming into the office.

Not yet, anyway. But if they were finished with the main area already, it wouldn't be much longer until they were done.

I wasn't going to sit here and wait for a perfect shot because one wasn't coming. When Green shifted his position to come back near the desk, I decided it was now or never.

My heart pounded in my chest so hard, I felt dizzy as I assessed my senses. I could hear the padding of one set of footsteps in the master, which was twenty feet away, but I couldn't hear the other. Was he in the living room? Or maybe already starting to haul away stolen goods?

*They must have a getaway van in the garage, which meant they might— probably did—have lookouts.* I'd have to avoid the lobby in case they had them there, too.

Green stood to my right, fifteen feet from me, and the doorway was to my left. Maybe eight feet away.

*Screw it.*

I shot up out of the chair like a jack-in-the-box, sprinting to the doorway as I yanked the blindfold up and off my head.

Sight. A sense I'd taken for granted my whole life, but now that it was back, it afforded me the ability to see the hallway as I rounded the doorframe to the left and bolted four steps into the hall.

"The hell you think you're doing?!" Brown yelled. I recognized his growly voice behind me.

I hadn't seen him yet—hadn't seen anyone—and I didn't dare risk a glance behind me to give him another reason to kill me. I needed to stay focused on what lay ahead—the living room, which was only ten feet away.

But arms slammed around me like steel bars, squeezing my waist as he lifted me off the ground, pulling me back into the office, back into the nightmare. My hands flailed wildly for an anchor, finding the office door handle.

I held on to it with everything I had, kicking my feet, trying to break free of his grip. His smell—stale cigarettes smoldering in an ashtray—made my stomach roll.

"Brown." Green's voice was behind me now, too.

"Stupid bitch was trying to escape!" Brown snapped.

My ribs threatened to crack under the pressure of his arms, but I focused on the handle. On the only thing that kept me from going back into that prison.

Brown shifted his focus to my fingers, trying to pry them off. As it turned out, the groaning I heard was my own, my body crying in pain from Brown's death grip.

The wolf had caught his rabbit, but I'd try to thrash my way out of his trap.

He grabbed my fingertips and pulled backward, and though I fought it, my middle finger slid over the handle, and the rest of them followed suit.

Just like that, I was robbed of my escape, trapped back in my cage with a killer.

The vise around my body released, and my body flew like a rag doll until my head smashed into something. A sharp pain channeled up my spine as I crumpled to the ground while things pelted me from above. I threw my still-tied hands above my head out of instinct, protecting my head from further blows as something rained down on me. Books, I realized. Brown had thrown me against the office's bookshelf.

My sense of up or down had been compromised by the blow to my head, the room waving as if on a boat. Two more books hit my shoulder and my thigh, and then the noise stopped, and something smashed into my ribs with a searing burn. I shrieked, the sound almost inhuman, like an animal. Another blow slammed into my back. I buried my head into my arms even deeper, protecting it, when a third strike whacked my hip. My scream was bloodcurdling this time.

"Enough!" Green shouted.

The strikes stopped, but I remained cowering in the fetal position, arms covering my head, eyes still clenched shut. My body ached. My head was pounding, and my lower back was on fire from Brown's kicks.

The blindfold snaked around my eyes before I had a chance to see them—pain having a way of clamping your eyes shut. It took only a second, and I suspected it was Green who'd covered my eyes. If it were Brown, he'd have been rougher.

"Move," Brown ordered.

Peeking beneath the gap, I noticed Green's boots standing in front of me, facing Brown's feet.

"Go back down the hall," Green insisted.

"Move aside," Brown snarled.

A high-pitched metallic shrill pierced through the silence. It reminded me of silverware scraping together.

"What are you doing?" Green's voice rose in anger.

"Killing her," Brown explained in a resolute voice. "Before she has the chance to get away."

My stomach twisted. That was what that sound was—a knife, pulled from its sheath.

Green remained in what appeared to be a protective stance. "No."

"Move," Brown ordered.

"Finish the job first."

"She just tried to escape. Not gonna let that happen again. She dies now."

"I'm not going to get life in prison because you're impatient." Green took a step closer to him. "You kill her now, then we *leave now.*"

"News flash: you don't call the shots. Move the hell out of my way," Brown said, his voice sinister. "Move."

At the sound of his footsteps advancing, I collapsed into my body again, my muscles clenching at the thought of the knife tearing into my flesh. I heard a crack and waited for the pain. When I heard another snap, I still didn't feel pain, and then the sounds of grunting and thuds gave me the courage to peek through the crevice of my blindfold again.

It took me a second to realize why their feet patterns were tangled and irregular—Brown and Green were fighting. Punches flying, they moved all over the room. Had they not been blocking my path to the door, I would have tried to jump up, no matter how badly Brown's beating had hurt. But I didn't dare get closer to the knife meant for me...

"Break it up!" Orange shouted, standing between the two men. "Green's right. We need to finish the job first."

The two men breathed heavy.

"Big mistake, attacking me like that, Green," Brown snarled.

So, it was Green that had thrown the first punch...

"Here," Orange said. I heard a small thump, as if something had been thrown and landed in someone's hand. "Tape her up, so she don't escape again. We're almost done. Let's just finish the damn job, and then we'll deal with her."

For a moment, things were silent.

"Fine," Brown finally agreed. "But I'm the one that tapes her up."

He marched past Green, who didn't stop him this time. My hair yanked back so hard, I was confident blood came with it, my hands instinctively grabbing Brown's wrists as he dragged me and shoved me into the chair.

The unmistakable sound of duct tape unwrapping from its spool preceded my ankles being slammed together. I could feel the anger coming through the tape, wrapping roughly around my feet. Over. And over. And over. Round and round the tape went, enough to go around the freaking Empire State Building. Brown shoved my shoulders back, wrapping tape around my torso a dozen times, binding me to the chair.

This tape—and my failed escape attempt—signed my death warrant. If I couldn't save myself, I refused to give him the satisfaction of seeing me cry.

"There," Brown snarled. "You ain't goin' anywhere now. Gonna come back for you, sweetheart." He made a kissing sound. "We'll have some fun before I kill you."

"Well then, it's a match made in heaven," I snapped. " 'Cause the only thing I'd want to do after sleeping with you is die."

Someone chuckled, and Brown slapped me, severely stinging my cheek.

A tearing sound preceded duct tape slamming over my lips.

"She gets away," Brown said in a warning tone, presumably to Green, "I'm holding you responsible."

His threat hung in the air for several moments before he and Orange left.

After a few seconds, Green's feet slowly advanced toward me. He must have been pissed that I tried to get away. That I got him in trouble with his accomplices. That I risked him going to prison by trying to escape…

When he squatted in front of me, I slinked my neck between my shoulders, waiting for his blow, for his revenge.

"Hold still." Green pulled the corner of the tape off my cheek, then gently peeled the rest of it off my mouth.

"I thought you said they were thieves, not rapists." I could taste the disgust in my throat.

"Brown's a loose cannon, but I've never heard of him touching a girl. He's probably just flexing."

"*Probably?* Well, let's file that under *not comforting at all.*"

"I won't let him touch you." Green's voice rumbled with protection. "But you really didn't need to provoke him."

"Yeah, well, he really didn't need to rob my house."

"Does your head hurt?" He pressed his fingers in my hair now. "You hit it pretty hard."

When his fingertips landed on a soft spot, I gasped.

"You're bleeding," he said, pulling his hand away.

He left, returned to the room, and pressed a towel to my head. I didn't mean to hiss, but the pain overcame my lips.

"Sorry." He applied pressure, his body close to me.

I didn't like being taped to this chair. Even if I couldn't get away, I felt like that girl on the railroad tracks in those old movies. Tied down, waiting for the train to run her over. I'd just rather it be over already.

"You need to be quiet," Green urged. "If you scream, they'll kill you, and there will be nothing I can do to stop them."

*They.*

Not him.

That one word shifted everything. It drew battle lines, them against me, with Green caught somewhere in the middle. When he'd saved me from being killed a moment ago, when he'd fought Brown, I couldn't be sure if it was for my sake or for Green's. If he'd done it because he wanted to wait until the end of the burglary to kill the hostage for his own protection. But that word. *Them.* Told me the fight was something more.

Or maybe I was wrong.

All he'd said was that if I screamed, there was nothing he could do to stop them from killing me. So, really, it was more of a threat than a warning.

Not to mention, he'd told them that they had to wait to kill me until the robbery was finished. Wait. That was all he'd pushed for. Waiting made sense, for his sake. You don't stick around a place with a murder victim inside. Maybe his saving me hadn't been a display of battle lines. Maybe it was self-preservation.

He was just trying to control me. Keep the hostage calm, so I didn't screw things up for them.

He probably didn't care at all if I lived or died.

If he did, he'd have helped me get out of here by now. He could see. He knew his colleagues and would know how long it took them to clear each room. If he really wanted to, he probably could have come up with some way to let me run without his colleagues knowing he'd let me escape. Yet he hadn't even tried.

The only thing he'd done was delay my killing.

"You're shivering again," Green said. As if he cared. As if it bothered him.

"Leave me alone, Green," I whispered over the lump in my throat. "Or whatever the hell your name is."

I wasn't going to talk to him anymore. I'd lost my chance at escape. I ruined everything by not timing this right, and now, I was screwed, and by default, my dad was screwed, too.

"Easton," he said in a quiet voice. His fingertips grazed gently along my forehead, sweeping a fallen patch of hair back into place.

I blinked. "What?"

"My name is Easton."

## 11

My adrenaline dispatched needles throughout my limbs. He'd told me information that I could use against him.

And when he spoke again, he kept his voice low to shield the sound from the other guys.

"This…new life, I guess you could call it, started when I was thirteen," Green—or, I guess *Easton*—said. "My brother and I returned home after having dinner at a friend's house. When we walked in the door, first thing I noticed was the glass tumbler broken on the kitchen floor and how its ice cubes were melting into little puddles. Like they were bleeding. Should've pulled my brother back outside and gone to a neighbor's, but my feet just…"

Apprehension spread over my skin.

"They were in the master bedroom. Both of my parents. Shot to death." He hesitated. "Dad still had the gun in his hand."

*Oh God.*

*Why is he telling me this? Is he trying to keep me calm by distracting me? And why am I so interested that I'm tilting my head forward?*

*It must be morbid curiosity, same as a person who looks at a car accident as they drive by.*

After all, finding out what makes a person rob houses is a captivating mystery, and I was a moth to its flame.

"Later, they ruled it a murder-suicide. Pieced together that they must've had an argument, and my dad was drunk when he shot my mom. Whether it was intentional or he was just trying to scare her and the gun went off, we'll never know. But once he shot her, he turned the gun on himself."

Easton stayed silent for ten heartbeats, and when he spoke, his voice darkened. "I've often wondered why I was sentenced to survive their deaths. What had I done that deserved the punishment of staying alive after that?"

My throat clenched.

"My little brother was ten at the time. I walked into the house before him, and I just...froze. If I hadn't, maybe I could've shielded him from seeing..."

I couldn't even imagine. Seeing your parents in a pool of blood and then the shock, realizing your life would never be the same.

"Both sets of grandparents were already dead, so they tried to locate an aunt on my mom's side and a distant uncle on my dad's. They told us they couldn't get in touch with them, but I suspect my relatives weren't willing to take on the burden of two kids. Neither relative was close to my parents, and that's a lot to take on."

A pang hit my chest. "Did they find anyone to take you in?"

"We went into the foster care system. First homes we went to, we got split up. Brother went to one family; I went to another. I stayed with a guy who was an alcoholic and liked to use my face as his punching bag when he'd had too much to drink. One night, he got so drunk, he burned the only things I had left of my parents in the firepit as a punishment."

Easton paused, his tone becoming even more somber. "I remember the way the flames seemed to grab the cloth and the pictures and pull them to the center of the heat. Eat them until they were ash."

When a stretch of silence elapsed, I wondered if he was fighting tears—especially when he had to clear his throat before speaking again.

"Anyway, didn't take long before someone noticed bruises, and I was taken out of that place. Second home I went to was worse. They fostered two other kids, who were a year older than me and had been through hell, so I was getting it from both the parents and the other kids. Beatings mostly."

Jeez. All while trying to process the sudden deaths of his parents.

A rush of unease skated up my spine as I listened to the predator's transformation back into prey.

"Then, finally, we got our first stroke of good luck, and my brother and I got put in the same home. Was the first time I felt hope since my parents died. At first, things felt almost too good to be true. Home-cooked dinners every night. Warm beds, trips to the Lego Store. The foster dad even bought us our very own bikes. But the way he looked at my brother, gave him more attention and treats than the other kids staying there...couldn't put my finger on it, but it gave me the creeps. Thought maybe I was just being paranoid, like after having so much shit happen, I was too messed up in the head to accept that we were safe and well cared for.

"But one night, I heard another foster kid's bedroom door squeak open and then latch shut. Kid was only ten or eleven, so I thought maybe he was having a bad night, missing his parents or something. Didn't want him to feel alone, so I went to check on him. His door was locked, and when I knocked, the kid told me to go away. But his voice sounded more scared than sad. I refused to go away, kept knocking, and eventually, the door opened. Out walked the foster dad, at two o'clock in the morning with his fly still open. Took a while to get it out of the kid, but he confirmed that the foster dad...*liked* little boys, if you know what I mean. And my ten-year-old brother was his favorite age."

Bile swirled in my gut.

"I wanted to tell our case worker, but if I did, we'd be separated again, and I wouldn't be able to protect my little brother. And that was assuming they'd get him away from that pedophile immediately, before it was too late. Decided our best option was to run away. Life on the streets was better than any other alternative we had at that point, and even though I didn't have a plan past escaping that house, I'd do whatever it took to keep my brother safe. I wasn't going to let that son of a bitch keep hurting other kids, though, so I reported him to the cops before I left."

The bile crept up my throat, threatening to erupt. "Where did you go?"

"The foster family lived in a condo on the east side, and luckily, it was relatively warm at the time. Above fifty. So, that first night, we found an awning in an alley, hidden from the main road behind a dumpster." Easton's voice darkened. "My brother wept for hours that night as I held him. Sounded like a puppy whimpering for his mother."

This was hard to listen to. I wasn't sure I could endure any more of it, picturing two children so hopeless and lost that sleeping behind a dumpster in an alley was the only place they felt safe. Yet I needed to hear what happened next.

This time, when Easton spoke, I could hear him fighting off an emotion. "My brother kept crying that all he wanted was Mom and Dad. Wanted to go home and finish building his Mandalorian Starfighter Lego with Dad and draw Chewbacca using sidewalk chalk with Mom."

*Damn.* Here I was, feeling sorry for myself for Dad's medical bills and how hard it was to take care of him, and these kids had endured hell on earth.

"After that first night, everything just turned into survival. And evasion. If cops or anyone found us, they would turn us back over to the foster care system. We didn't feel safe, going to a homeless shelter or anything. Figured they'd turn us in."

"And you started...robbing people to stay alive."

Easton cleared his throat.

"I got good at pickpocketing. Would get some cash to buy food that way. Last for a day or two, and I'd do it again. The first time I broke into someone's place was when I was sixteen. We were still living on the streets, but we'd managed to find the best places to stay, where it didn't seem so bad anymore." Easton's reflective tone became weighed down with sadness. "It's strange. When you're in a dire situation, how you get used to it, so it doesn't feel so dire anymore."

He let a small silence elapse.

"So, one day, I walked past this townhouse, and the guy left in such a hurry that when he slammed the door behind him, it bounced open. But he didn't turn back; he walked down the street and got into an Uber. Figured there must be someone inside, but out of curiosity, I went up and rang the doorbell. When no one answered, I looked around and realized I could get more than just a few bucks. Found a stash of cash in his sock drawer. Enough for a month of food. Found a couple of watches that I later pawned. And that night, I was able to buy a cheap hotel room for me and my brother. It was the first time we'd slept in a bed in years."

Years of sleeping on a dirty concrete floor. Outside. On the streets of Chicago, where violent beatings and killings unfortunately happened daily. Not to mention, the unforgiving winters with snow and ice.

"That's why you make donations to homeless shelters." My posture slouched. Because he knew how it felt to be vulnerable with no one there to help him.

The snake had gained his venom and used it to help unsuspecting prey.

"I didn't want my brother to have to go back to sleeping on asphalt, in subzero temperatures, so I came up with a plan. To rob my first house. I targeted the wealthy because I didn't want to take something from someone who really needed it."

*I didn't want to take something from someone who really needed it.*

I never expected to feel this rush of compassion.

"And you got away with it."

"With enough money to last three months," Easton said. "Rest is kind of history. Got it to the point where I could usually get a few hundred bucks to survive on in just a few minutes. Everything just escalated from there. I figured if I could do that, I could save and get our own place. Started putting crews together to help me."

What an awful way to live. Now, I understood why this guy had been drawn into a life of crime because, yes, these were things I took for granted: having food, a warm bed, safety. Even though my life had dealt a few tough blows, I didn't spend my childhood worrying about starving. Afraid of being abused. Terrified of dying on the dangerous streets. I didn't have to spend my youth plotting ways to get money just to survive. That was too much for an adult to handle, let alone a kid.

"Funny, what I was capable of doing once my brother's life was on the line. Before my parents died, I never broke rules."

It was in this moment that my feelings for Easton transcended beyond pity. Would I have had those same street skills to keep myself alive at that young age? Would I have had the balls to do what he did? Grow the fangs needed to survive?

"It's hard to imagine you as a rule follower."

I heard a burst of air from his nose.

"Yeah, when I was a kid, I never would've imagined my life going this way."

"What did you imagine?" I couldn't hide my curiosity. "Before everything happened with your family, what did you want to be when you grew up?"

"What does every young boy want to be? A professional baseball player."

I smiled.

"Wanted to play for the Cubs, of course. Starting pitcher. Future Hall of Famer."

"Naturally."

"What about you?" His pitch increased with interest. "What do you do for a living?"

"Marketing analyst. I do analytics to identify the most profitable ROIs on our clients' advertising campaigns and work with them to scale up their most effective ads." Which generated revenue for our company.

"You like it?"

"Honestly? No. I wish I had done something with animals. When I was a kid, I wanted to be an animal rescuer or something."

"Why didn't you?"

I shrugged. "I let myself get coached by my parents on the practicalities of life. Getting a degree in something that could earn decent money to support a future family. And now, I'm kind of stuck because I can't afford to give up the paycheck." Especially with the huge student loan debt and Dad's medical bills.

He grew silent, and I wondered if it was because he felt guilty that I wouldn't have a future family to support. Why did he want to know about me, anyway? And why did he share what had to be the most intimate moments of his life with a stranger?

"Why did you tell me all this?" I wondered.

"You asked why I became a thief."

True, but he could've just said he was homeless and needed the money. He didn't have to tell me about being abused and running away, trying to care for his brother.

He chose to share this with me. The lion wanting the lamb to understand the reason for her fate. A fate that might end in death, but didn't need to include torture.

"Is that why you saved me from Brown?" I shifted in my seat. "You feel bad for targeting someone who couldn't afford to lose stuff?"

A rubbing sound of skin on whiskers told me Easton must be scrubbing his jaw for several long seconds. "I'm sorry about this. If I could take it all back, I would. I'm sorry about your belongings, your dad's health, about everything. I wish we'd never come here tonight. You don't deserve this."

This. As in the end.

The rattlesnake raised his tail and began shaking it, offering a warning of what came next.

It still didn't feel real, the prospect of death—and I wasn't giving up on going home, no matter how abysmal it might seem—but I needed to cover my bases. Just in case.

"If tonight doesn't end well..."

Dad would suffer more pain than I'd wish on my worst enemy. But there was one pain even worse than your daughter dying—having her disappear and never knowing what happened to her. He'd spend the rest of his life hunting, holding on to a shred of hope that I was out there somewhere, alive. Or worse, he might think I'd left him, just like he'd left me.

"If I don't make it out of here"—I tried to hide the cracking in my voice—"will you please make sure my dad knows what happened to me?"

I was fully aware of how insanely bizarre this was—asking my captor to help ensure my body was found. Even contemplating the aftermath of my death felt akin to preparing a will. You don't want to think about your death, but you also feel a sense of responsibility to make sure those around you are protected from the subsequent fallout.

Easton remained silent, and then he blew out an angry huff. "I'll be right back."

He was gone in an instant. He must have been standing outside the doorway because Easton's voice was still loud when he commanded, "Orange. A word."

*I'm alone.*

I began jerking my body, trying to pry a crack in the layers of duct tape. Most likely a fruitless effort, but I had to at least try, so I twisted, and stretched, and jerked, and thrust my torso.

Orange's steps joined Easton's as they shuffled a few feet away from the doorway, but I could still hear the discussion.

"Listen to me." Easton kept his voice low. "I need you to distract Brown. Keep him occupied on the other end of this place."

"Why?"

Easton said nothing.

"No fucking way," Orange said in angry disbelief.

"He's going to kill her."

"I'm not going against Brown," Orange whispered in a high-octave panic. "You know what he'd do to us?"

"That's exactly why I never wanted to work with him! He's a fucking lunatic," Easton snarled. "An unpredictable loose cannon."

"You want to save the witness, talk to him. Not me."

"I don't trust him." Anger thrashed through each word.

"You don't trust anyone."

"Least of all him. I trusted *you*, though. You knew I refused to work with him," he barked. "And you blindsided me by bringing him anyway! Why?"

"He agreed to let me in on another heist if I let him in on this one. I didn't tell you because I knew you'd say no."

"So, what, you're going to work with *him* now?"

"He's forming a bigger crew. Plans on doing bigger heists. Tonight's a trial run. If he's pleased with how it goes, I have a chance to work my way into a leadership position in his organization. You know how much cash that would bring in?"

"That guy'll get you killed. I've spent every day of the last decade keeping you safe, and I'm not going to watch you throw it all away."

"Not your call." Orange sounded ambivalent about my death. "And I don't have time for this shit. We're already ten minutes past our end time."

Ten minutes *past* their estimated end time. I would have thought a robbery was a lot faster than this. A grab-and-go, frenzied type of thing. But this was methodical, calm. They clearly knew the house was empty, knew no one else would be showing up, and used that to their advantage.

"Let's just finish this job." Exasperation pulled Orange's tone lower.

Three footsteps clanked on the hardwood before Easton spoke again.

"Are you really going to go along with this? *Killing* someone?"

Orange said nothing back.

Just walked down the hall.

When Easton's steps returned into the room, I felt dizzy.

"They're really going to kill me, aren't they?" I clenched my stomach.

Why did this continue to feel shocking? I guess facing your own mortality comes in waves. You think you'll die. You hope you'll live. You plan in case you don't, but you still hope. And then you get another confirmation. *It's over.*

*There's no way I'm making it out of here.* I'd never watch another sunset. Or hear the birds sing to each other. I'd never feel the ocean's surf lapping at my feet. And I'd never get to tell Dad I was sorry for what I'd done to him.

I expected to start sobbing uncontrollably, like I had before, but all I felt was numb. Maybe it was exhaustion or the realization and acceptance that I couldn't change the outcome.

Not for *me*, at least. But Easton, on the other hand...

"You should leave," I said, defeated. "Put as much distance between what's about to happen and you as possible."

He squatted down and rested his hands on my armrests, his face, undoubtedly, only inches from mine.

"You want me to leave you alone? With *them*?"

"If you stay, you're going to get caught and spend the rest of your life in prison. Walk away while you still have the chance. I'm doomed, but you don't have to be."

Another loud noise made me jump.

It was a clap, followed by, "That's it," from one of the guys.

They were really done this time. No doubt about it, no more false alarms. The robbery had been completed.

Which meant, there was only one thing left to do.

Kill me...

## 12

"Go, Easton."

A huff escaped his nose.

"You shouldn't want to help someone like me, Zoey." The tone of his voice turned sullen and reflective with undercurrents of pain. "Trust me, I'm not a good person."

A metal scrape sliced through the room from what I presumed to be the blade of a knife drawn from its sheath.

Trembling, I cringed, clamping my eyes shut so I wouldn't see even a sliver of the coming carnage.

*I love you, Dad. I wish I'd said I'm sorry when I still had the chance.*

A tearing sound—like wet fabric ripping—preceded my torso loosening from the chair, then my legs.

"You know about the back staircase?" Easton whispered.

The emergency exit was next to the master bedroom, at the end of the hall.

"It's always locked," I said, crinkling my forehead. With a separate key I didn't bring. If I had, I'd have tried to make a run for it to that door already.

"We unlocked it when we got here." Of course they did. Methodical burglars would want a second escape route, just in case. "You've got fifty-five flights ahead of you. Go. I'll hold them off as long as I can."

My mind raced. I couldn't believe this was happening. As Easton cut away the rest of the duct tape and my wrists' bindings, I prepared myself to take the last chance I had to stay alive.

"You understand?"

I nodded. "What will they do to you if they realize you let me escape?"

He didn't answer. Instead, he lifted my wrists, and I felt his lips gently press against my injured skin.

I sucked in a breath because his kiss unleashed a wave of pleasure that surged up my arm and became a tsunami in my chest.

"I'm going to take your blindfold off, Zoey."

His hands moved to the back of my head, and his knuckles brushed my scalp as he loosened the knots.

And then the fabric lifted from my eyes.

I clenched them shut and lowered my head, assuming he'd want to disappear into another room before I could see him, but Easton's thumb and finger pressed my chin up until my face aligned with his.

*He wants me to look at him.*

I waited another second, just in case I was wrong, before slowly opening my eyes.

*Holy crap.* It was him. Wallet guy. Sexy, stunningly gorgeous, and seductive.

He still had dark brown hair with caramel highlights, longer on the top by several inches and so short on the sides that it was nearly a buzz cut. Matching facial stubble stretched down his jaw and around his pouty lips, which sat beneath a perfectly sculpted nose. But most distinguishing were his spellbinding eyes, which were the color of the Caribbean Sea.

Those same eyes had popped up in more than one fantasy since I'd seen them last...

He kept them locked on me as I quickly took in the rest of his appearance. His frame was even more muscular than I'd remembered, trying to break out of his long-sleeved ivory shirt, his jeans.

Inappropriately, my lower belly warmed just as it'd done the day I'd first met him. Especially now that he stared at my lips with an insatiable hunger.

And then never breaking that gaze, Easton lowered his face and gently pressed his mouth against mine.

A sane person wouldn't have a wave of sensual heat rush through her body when her captor's lips seized hers. She wouldn't find his lips warm, and gentle, and...utterly perfect. And her skin wouldn't erupt into thrilling goose bumps when the palm of his hand cupped her cheek.

It felt like time froze, and I existed in the confusing space of unexpected desire.

And then Easton pulled back, leaving me reeling.

He cupped both sides of my face with his hands. "I've been wanting to do that since the first moment I laid eyes on you."

That day at the lake, I'd wanted him to do that, too. Even though I wouldn't admit it to myself at the time.

He helped me stand up, grabbed my cell phone from the desk, handed it back to me, and watched me shove it into my back pocket.

*He wants to ensure I can call for help.*

When he spoke next, he tilted his head slightly to compensate for his height. "I'll keep them back as long as I can," he whispered. "But if they catch you..."

I nodded.

"When I give you the signal, you run, Zoey."

His eyes glided down my face, and then he went to the door, where he looked up and down the hallway. I could hear his colleagues in the living room, checking for anything they might have missed. The emergency exit, located by the master bedroom, would be to the right, in the opposite direction.

But I still had to go into the hallway and expose myself.

Easton looked at me again—his eyes swimming with trepidation— and then he stepped outside the office. His broad shoulders and tall frame provided some cover, allowing me to quietly step outside behind him. I could see the tension radiating across his muscles as he cast his azure eyes back to me.

Looking into his eyes was like looking into his soul, an intimate moment between the man who was risking everything—his freedom, retaliation from his colleagues—to save me.

Adrenaline surged through my muscles.

Easton nodded his head.

I kept my footsteps light, trying to shield their sound as I ran toward the end of the hall. It only stretched fifteen feet in front of me, yet it felt like one of those dreams where you're running and it keeps extending beyond your reach.

"The fuck!" a voice shouted.

I risked a quick glance over my shoulder and witnessed Easton tackle a guy to the ground. Orange, based on his Converse. As Easton and Orange exchanged blows, the third guy—a bald, tattoo-covered dude with a nose ring—locked his merciless eyes on mine. And charged me.

I opened the door and threw myself into an outside hallway, hearing the *thwap, thwap* of blows. I wanted to see if Easton was okay, hoping they were his punches, but I couldn't slow down.

I hurled myself through another door, into a stairwell, and down the first flight of steps. The beige stairwell was silent, only wide enough for three people, and I was going so fast, I lost my footing and missed the last step, having to grab the cold banister to save myself from falling. I spun to make the next fourteen steps when the door slammed open behind me.

As if someone had kicked it in.

And then thundered down the steps behind me.

My legs began to tremble with each step. I tried not to look back, but Brown was right there, taking two steps at a time, using the railing to balance himself.

*He's only ten feet back. And gaining on me.*

My dad's condo was on the 55th floor of this building. There was no way I could make it down another fifty floors without him catching me.

But every floor had its own emergency escape door leading to the other condominiums. With people. Witnesses. People who could hear my cries.

When I landed on the next platform, I threw open the door and launched myself into the hallway.

I screamed for help.

But I was too late.

My neck snapped back as he yanked a fistful of my hair and then kicked me to the ground. I rolled onto my back and tried to get up, but he jumped on top of me and pinned me down, straddling me with knees on each side of my hips. He pulled a knife from its holster and raised it above his head.

His eyes were dark, soulless, as he thrust the blade toward my body to stop my beating heart.

I threw my hands up and held his wrists, slowing the knife's descent.

The hair on his arms twisted beneath my fingers. His nostrils flared, and a drop of sweat pooled around his titanium nose ring as his tattooed muscles swelled with strain.

He growled. He wanted me dead, but I wanted to live more.

With the knife heading right for my throat, I bucked with all my might and managed to throw Brown off-balance.

It was enough to roll out from underneath him.

I kicked him right in his nose ring and then took off running.

Screaming.

"Help me! Help!"

Fifteen feet ahead, a door opened, and a middle-aged man emerged, his face contorted in confusion as he saw me running toward him.

I charged past him, and as I entered the guy's open apartment, I turned around and spotted my attacker's figure running in the opposite direction.

13

Sitting in the back of the open ambulance, I second-guessed my refusal to go to the hospital because dozens of pedestrians stood outside, staring at me. Or maybe it wasn't so much at me as it was the chaotic scene.

Six police cars hugged the curb. Uniformed officers came and went from the building's front entrance while an EMT treated a cut on the back of my head. He wore purple latex gloves that looked so tight around his knuckles, I wondered if they would tear.

The smell of disinfectant and the lingering taste of blood in my throat angered my already-unstable stomach, no matter how many deep breaths of fresh air I took. Earlier, it had been muggy out, but now, a chill draped around my shoulders, as if the nightmare refused to release its grip on my goose bump–lined skin while Dad's sixty-story building towered over me, looking down on me and my omissions.

All I wanted to do was get home, take a shower, and crawl under my covers.

But right now, a detective was interviewing me, taking notes in a royal-blue miniature notebook. He'd introduced himself as Detective

Shane Hernandez of the Chicago Police Department and looked to be in his late twenties with black hair and thick eyebrows.

"I'm going to see if we can get you in with a sketch artist tomorrow." He scratched the side of his face while he looked at his notes. "In the meantime, can you think of any other details?" His eyes implored me to come up with something. "Anything at all that might help us identify these guys?"

His stare penetrated my body like he could see through my lies, uncovering my hidden deceits.

I twisted my hands together.

Why did this feel so confusing? It shouldn't be confusing. I was furious at myself for allowing apprehension to choke my words. I had told him every single detail that I could think of. How one of the burglars wasn't as aggressive as the others, the description of the man who had attacked me as I ran away. The timing, the weapons I had witnessed, the number of men, how they seemed to know that the place was going to be empty and seemed to be aware of what was inside.

I even told him how I'd heard one of them say they'd been tipped off to the heist.

I told him everything, except for a couple critical details—Easton's name and description, claiming I'd only gotten a good look at Brown. I also left out that Easton had kissed me—*because how the hell do you explain something like that to a trained interrogator when you don't even understand it yourself?*—and that Easton helped me escape. Worried it would make the detective suspicious that I was holding back.

Which, of course, I was.

What was wrong with me?

Yes, Easton had saved my life. Yes, he seemed different than the other ones, and something told me deep down that he was never going to participate or allow my death. But I couldn't be sure of that. My adrenaline was high, my thoughts incapable of being trusted.

I was being interviewed by an official law enforcement officer, who was here to help me and my dad. I needed to give them everything I could, so they could track down these sons of bitches and put them behind bars before they could hurt anybody else. That was what a good, moral person would do. And I, of all people, was on the extreme end of that moral scale of holding people accountable.

*Tell him Easton's name.* It was an unusual name—surely not a lot of Eastons in the city. Maybe he'd been arrested in the past, and they'd pick him up within the hour. And he'd spend the rest of his life behind bars. No matter what his circumstances were in the past, that was where he belonged, I reminded myself.

Why was I having to remind myself? Was this some sort of shock? Because I definitely felt like I was in shock. Traumatized, relieved to be alive. All of those things. But also uncertain what to do. Once I gave him Easton's name, I could never undo it.

"I think it might be the same group on the news." I watched his expression for any kind of reaction. "The one that's been robbing houses."

Hernandez kept his face neutral, but I swore a flare of newfound interest flickered in his eyes. "What makes you say that?"

"The guy that had to babysit me. I asked him, and he didn't deny it."

"Did he confirm it?" The detective licked his bottom lip.

"No. But he'd mentioned being homeless at one point in his life, and the news said homeless shelters get donations after the robberies, so I figured..." I shrugged.

The detective held his unblinking eyes on me. "He told you he'd been homeless." His tone contained undercurrents of...skepticism? "He tell you any other personal information?"

I bit my lip, trying to remember. Because honestly, with my head spinning, I couldn't think of anything. Except his name. Which just kept echoing in my mind like it was trying to break free.

"It's okay," Detective Hernandez assured. "You did good."

*No, you didn't. Tell him, Zoey. Tell him now before it's too late. Before he walks away and you've left your interview, having withheld information from a police officer.*

"If you think of anything else." The detective handed me a business card.

It was blue with a raised Chicago Police logo on the right side, Detective Hernandez's name on the left, embossed in white letters.

"I'm glad you're okay, Zoey." Detective Hernandez offered a sad smile.

"Detective," a cop with a stocky torso called out. "Condo's empty."

I tried not to flinch; I could feel the detective's eyes on me, gauging my reaction to this news. Cops were trained to detect liars, and I wasn't very practiced in the art of deceit.

But this meant Easton had survived the scuffle with his colleague, and somehow, they'd all made it out.

*But is Easton hurt? Could they have killed him in the getaway car?*

Worry pitted in my stomach, recalling the thump I'd heard when I ran. Easton had committed a cardinal sin; he'd sided with a hostage, and I could only assume that warranted a harsh punishment. A punishment that might have gotten interrupted in order to escape. But certainly, they'd resume carrying it out, right? Easton had to be in danger.

"It *was* the Robin Hood Thieves, wasn't it?"

Hernandez said nothing.

"The MO fits what I've seen on the news," I pressed. No denial. "Have you worked other burglaries by them?"

"More than I'd like to count," Hernandez said with an edge. "Nothing would give me greater satisfaction than taking them down."

"So, you *do* think it's them." I bent my head toward his.

"Too early to say." Hernandez rubbed his jaw. "But if they are? You're the first person who's seen their faces."

My mouth ran dry. "That a good thing or a bad thing?"

Hernandez tightened his lips. "I'd keep your doors locked if I were you. Just to be safe."

## 14

The EMT finished cleaning me up, and then one of the uniformed officers drove me home. Walked me to the front door to make sure I got in safely and locked it.

Sitting in the living room in his wheelchair was Dad. Watching TV.

*If I hadn't made it out, how long would he have sat here, waiting, before he realized I was never coming back?*

"Dad."

I rushed to him, knelt, and wrapped my arms around his fragile shoulders, relishing the warmth of his hand on my back. He smelled like his spicy aftershave and like home.

*I'd prayed for just five more minutes with him, and now, I'm holding him.*

We hadn't held each other since before he'd left Mom. His accident had warned me not to take this for granted, and yet I had. I'd been selfish. At the time, I told myself it was only human to rebuild our fractured relationship slowly. But tonight? When I thought I was going to die? I realized that the larger truth was that I was afraid; letting myself feel his love for me this way made me vulnerable.

"What's going on?" he asked.

But the words failed to come. If I started talking about it, I might start sobbing, and then I wouldn't be able to stop. What I needed was a hug, a shower, and a good night's sleep because I was exhausted.

"Zoey?"

"I'm fine," I assured. Even though I felt anything but fine. It felt like my world had opened some sort of portal to another universe, one where you can walk through a wrong door and have your life taken. One where you can be robbed of the chance to apologize to your father for the terrible things you'd said to him.

If I had an ounce of energy left, I'd start having that long-overdue conversation now. But Dad deserved a thoughtful, deep apology from me. Not the ten percent version when he'd only be half-listening, trying to figure out what in the world happened tonight.

Dad pushed my shoulders back and scanned my bruised face with wide eyes. "What the hell happened to you?"

"I'm fine," I repeated.

"The hell you are."

I tried to pull away, but Dad held on to my arms. Firmly. "Tell me what the hell is going on."

I was so exhausted, I felt like I was about to fall over. The physical aspect of my ordeal was only part of it; the emotional toll it took was like swallowing an entire bottle of sleeping pills. The only thing prying my eyes open had been the last micro surge of adrenaline from seeing my father, but now, it was waning.

He wouldn't let me go to bed without at least a partial explanation, though.

"Why did a police officer walk you to the door?"

When he let me stand up, I looked down at him, wishing I didn't have to tell him something so upsetting. "Tonight, I went to your condo, and it got robbed."

"What?"

"Some guys held me hostage, but I escaped."

Dad's eyes were so wide, I could see the whites above his irises, and he gripped the wheels of his wheelchair so tightly, his knuckles turned white.

"What did they do to you?" Dad scanned my face.

"Turns out, burglars don't like to be interrupted. They prefer to have the place to themselves."

Dad licked his teeth, his voice seething. "Did they...Zoey, were you—"

"No."

A momentary relief relaxed his shoulders. But he kept his eyes on me, rage funneling through his thin body. Somewhere in the back of my mind, behind my exhaustion and shock, there was a piece of my heart that appreciated his protective edge. Because it reminded me of my dad before he had broken my heart.

"Who are they?" Dad demanded.

"Police are trying to figure it out."

"Why did you go to the condo?"

"To get my ring," I said, walking into the bathroom.

"Your ring? Why the hell..."

"Dad, I love you. I do. But please, I can't even keep my eyes open."

He looked like he was about to let it go for now and let me get some rest, but instead, he said, "Tell me everything that happened."

I pinched the bridge of my nose, blinking back exhausted tears. "Please, Dad?"

Dad pursed his lips and studied the bags under my eyes. And evidently decided my physical needs outweighed his emotional ones in this moment. Because rather than fire off his million questions, he sighed and thankfully allowed me to shower and climb into my bed without further interrogation.

I couldn't sleep, though. My mind flashing through memories of the night, no matter how hard I tried to stop it.

Not to mention, the weight of what almost happened invading every cell of my body.

I almost died before I'd resolved things with Dad.

After his accident, all our unresolved feelings had been swept under the carpet, daily survival taking center stage. Getting Dad well enough to get out of the ICU, then a normal hospital room, then home with me. Juggling the medical appointments, bills, and bankruptcy in addition to the paperwork for his divorce. All of it had taken priority, pushing our unspoken pain regarding our relationship deeper into the cracks of our foundation.

But now, I was again reminded we didn't have forever. Dad and I needed to have a conversation soon—to lift up the carpet and work through our pain. If we had any hope to reseal our bond, we needed to talk.

I pressed my fingers against my eyes. My head was spinning. I needed to stop my brain.

I couldn't though—until I took one of Dad's sleeping pills.

I closed my eyes and drifted to sleep like welcoming a current, floating through the silent waters of detachment, pulled deeper into the sea from the meds.

Suddenly, I sat up in my bed, acutely aware of footsteps headed toward my room, which was blanketed in candles, whose flames flickered against the shadows like they were dancing.

The footsteps grew louder, but I didn't tremble; I clenched the covers and leaned forward, watching the doorframe. Knowing who was coming for me.

Easton stalked into my bedroom like he owned it. Like he owned me.

He wore the same ivory shirt and pants from the robbery, only this time, they seemed to encase his body tighter, showcasing his rugged muscles.

"What are you doing here?" I whispered.

The soft glow of candlelight wrapped around him as he closed the distance between us and sat next to my hip, the bed shifting with his weight.

Easton's sapphire eyes stared into mine as he brought his hand up and cupped my chin.

I tilted my head, ready to surrender my lips to his, the heat of his breath rolling across my skin as he whispered, "Forgive me for stealing one more kiss."

My heart fluttered as he trailed his fingers down my neck, goose bumps erupting all over my body. He looked at my mouth and drew his body closer, inch by inch. I closed my eyes and felt his lips brush against mine so lightly, it tickled.

He didn't hold it there for long enough. He didn't deepen the kiss or let me taste his tongue, instead pulling away far too soon, leaving me silently begging for more.

When I opened my eyes, he was gone. The candles were gone. My phone's alarm singing a lovely melody.

I sat up in my bed and touched my fingers to my lips.

*It was a dream.*

Easton coming into my bedroom was a dream. But it had felt so real.

His touch, his fingertips, his lips. And most of all, how badly I'd craved him.

I shut off my alarm and sat there for a minute, stunned.

The dream meant nothing. It didn't mean I wanted Easton. It was probably nothing more than my brain's warped way of processing this entire situation. I mean, seriously, how many people were held hostage and kissed by their captor? It was only human for that to plant a seed deep in your psyche and mind-F you.

Not to mention, I'd taken sleeping pills, which could probably give you seriously weird dreams.

I probably dreamed about him because I was hella worried about what might have happened to him after he'd betrayed his colleagues.

*Is he okay?*

Sweat broke across my palms at the memory of him fighting Orange, wondering what happened after they'd left. I would never find out, would I? Unless Easton was arrested and his name made it into the news, I'd never know if he was alive. I swallowed over the lump in my throat, unsure how I'd endure the day, let alone the rest of my life, without knowing.

I forced myself to stand up, hissing when I stretched my body. The aftermath of being kicked and hit last night was no longer dulled by adrenaline, so my ribs, my back, even my neck ached. The paramedic didn't "think" my rib was broken, but all my bruises still hurt, so I'd need some Advil to get through the day.

I shuffled over to the window and opened the blinds. Light assaulted my eyes so severely, I had to turn away from it, and when I did, I noticed the sunlight reflecting off something shiny on my nightstand.

Something that hadn't been there yesterday.

I stepped closer to get a better look, and what I saw made me grin with my hand over my mouth.

My ring. The very ring I'd been hell-bent on getting last night.

There was only one person who had access to that ring, knew how much it meant to me, and had the skills to quietly sneak into my house and leave it here—Easton.

*Easton* was *in my room last night.* And while I knew the rest of it was just a dream—candles don't magically appear and disappear on romantic command—I wondered if any part of it had been real.

Had his fingertips touched me? Had he whispered in my ear? Had he grazed my lips with his? I wasn't sure, but one thing was certain— the ring meant he'd gotten away last night.

My smile widened.

He must have followed me home or something.

Where was he right now? I looked out the window, up and down the block, but saw nothing. I wondered how long he'd been here last night and if I would have heard him had I not taken sleeping pills.

Placing the ring on my nightstand meant he'd been only two feet from me.

A warmth rushed through my veins.

Followed by ice.

Because someone had gotten into my place and I didn't even wake up. If Easton managed to get inside, did Brown and Orange know where I lived, too?

No. Orange and Brown were on the other end of the condo—too far to hear—when I'd given information to Easton, and Easton had protected me. Saved me, so he wouldn't be reckless enough to lead those men to my front door. They probably scattered from that building like the roaches they were.

I'd take precautions just in case—locking all the doors and

windows, turning on the air conditioner against the oppressive heat, costs be damned. But deep in my soul, I trusted Easton to keep me safe.

No matter how irrational it sounded.

I hid the ring in my underwear drawer and emerged from my bedroom to get caffeine.

"Morning," Dad said. He rolled his wheelchair from the living room to the kitchen, where I began making coffee. "How'd you sleep?"

I hated the worried look on his face. Was that the way I'd looked at him when he'd first come home from the hospital?

"Fine," I lied.

Exhaustion weighed my body down like lead, and I had to keep snapping my eyes open. Ironic that when you want to sleep, you can't, and when you want to stay awake, your body wants to sleep.

It was going to take a seriously strong cup of coffee to get me through this day. Maybe a hundred.

I avoided his incredulous stare by starting the coffeepot and rooting around the cabinets, looking for anti-inflammatories, but as luck would have it, no Advil to be found.

*Great.*

I watched the machine start to spit its brew. It gurgled out dark liquid into an amber-stained pot, puddling the way my blood had last night on the hardwood.

"I think we should go down to the police station today," Dad announced.

"Why?"

"I want to find out if they've arrested the guys."

"I'm sure the police will keep us informed." And call me in when that sketch artist was ready.

"Zoey..."

I pressed my finger above my eyebrow, pinching off a growing migraine. "Dad, I spent forever talking to that detective last night. I'm sure they're doing everything in their power to find the guys, and by us monopolizing their time, we're taking them away from the investigation."

"Nonetheless, I want to know where they're at with it and, if they haven't arrested the guys, what they're doing to catch them."

My eyes stung.

Dad hadn't acted like my protective father in a long time. I'd almost forgotten what it felt like—to feel him fight for me like this. Demanding justice for me. That he wanted to ensure whoever had laid a finger on me would be put in prison.

Tragedy had a way of flipping things around sometimes.

"Maybe after work," I said.

"Work?" Dad choked. "You're thinking of going to work?"

"What I need and want more than anything is to have a normal day. To work and do my best to completely forget about last night by staying busy."

I yanked the coffeepot out long enough to pour myself a cup.

"Your face is bruised."

So was my body. My body, I could hide with clothes. My face…

"I have concealer." If I couldn't conceal my bruises well enough, I'd consider staying home, if only to avoid questions. But I hoped I could go. I needed last night to stop playing on repeat in my head.

I took a sip of bitter caffeine.

My dad's chest inflated slowly and then collapsed. I felt bad for him. I was sure it was gut-wrenching for a parent to sit back and not be able to actively fix what happened to your kid. And I was again warmed by his desire to help me, just like he would've done before he left our family.

"Why did you go there in the first place?" Dad rolled his wheel-chair closer to me. "Why did you want your ring all of a sudden?"

A knock at the door thwarted my ability to answer. Thank God. I didn't want to get into our dire financial situation right now.

I looked through the peephole and opened the door, surprised to find him here.

"Alex?"

He wore his usual physical therapy polo and khaki pants, his trimmed blond hair polished with hair product that smelled like the ocean.

His grin quickly vanished. "What the hell happened to you?"

His eyes widened as he scanned my face, then my wrists.

"Are you okay?" he demanded.

"Yeah."

"What happened?"

"Long story." I motioned for him to come inside. "What are you doing here so early?"

Alex stepped into the living room and crossed his lean arms over his chest. I could tell he wasn't going to let the bruises go—he couldn't take his eyes off of them.

But he begrudgingly answered, "I had a client that requested the night spot, so I figured I'd come before my workday started."

This was the first time he'd ever come before work. Was it really because of a client's schedule? Or did he know that the robbery took place last night and wanted to check in?

I mentally chided myself. Alex had done nothing but help us in our time of need. What I'd just experienced was making me look at people and suspect the worst, and it wasn't fair to look at him with even an ounce of suspicion.

Was this what it was going to feel like from now on? Looking at everyone in my life with a skeptical eye, paranoia infecting my relationships?

No. I was just exhausted and overwhelmed. This would all go away.

It had to.

And in the meantime, I didn't have the energy to recount it again.

"My dad can fill you in." I slammed a giant chug of coffee and headed for my bedroom. "I have to get ready for work."

I escaped more questions, took a shower, and managed to cover up my bruised face fairly well. I changed into my favorite outfit—hoping it would incite confidence in addition to covering up my other injuries—and came back into the living room.

"You sure I can't talk you into staying home?" Worry etched into the crease between Dad's brows.

"Positive. Have a good day, boys." I made my way to the door.

"Zoey?" Dad called after me.

I turned around.

"I know you don't want to talk about this, but when your mom calls, I'd answer."

I pursed my lips. "You told her?"

He offered me a silent apology. Dad and Mom didn't talk to each other often. For him to make the effort to fill her in meant he was even more worried about me than he was letting on. Plus, it meant another person wanting to talk about the one subject I wanted to avoid.

"And Anthony?" I tensed.

"They're worried about you." Dad tugged his ear.

Ugh.

At the "L" platform by my house, I passed the usual group of guys who harassed women, but today, I looked at them and wondered, *Who do they work for?*

If people on the street knew how to hire Easton's crew, could these guys be associated with Easton? Oh God…what if they knew Brown? What if they were like his eyes and ears on the streets or something?

My heartbeat turned into a racehorse. I took a seat on the "L" and stared at them out the window. Surely, if they were part of Brown's crew, they'd follow me, right?

As I sat on the "L," I answered Mom's call. Her voice was high-pitched, and I could hear her pacing in her kitchen.

"This is all too much stress for you, honey. Let me make some calls. The last thing you need is to take care of Dad right now."

"I like him being here." I was surprised that I said it and even more surprised that I meant it. Because it meant I wouldn't be alone each night.

"I'm fine," I assured. "But I'm on my way to work right now. Maybe we can talk tomorrow?"

She sighed. "You're really okay?"

Mom wouldn't have anything to do with the burglary.

*I know I'm going crazy when those ridiculous thoughts pop into my head.*

"I'm okay, I promise."

I shut my eyes with relief when I hung up, but two seconds later, my phone rang again. This time from my brother.

"Anthony."

Now that he was married and had a baby, I barely saw him.

"You were held hostage?" His voice was as high-pitched as Mom's. It was only five thirty in the morning on the West Coast.

"How early did Dad call you?"

"I'm getting on the next flight."

"Don't."

"My little sister was robbed, and you think I'm not coming?"

"I appreciate it, but there's nothing left to do, except catch the guys. What I want right now more than anything is normalcy. My routine."

"Zoey..."

"Anthony, I swear I'm fine. You have a family you need to focus on. If you spend the money to fly all the way here, there's nothing you can do but stare at me. Let's save the trip for another time—when I'm up for a visit, okay?"

Anthony was silent for ten seconds. "When they catch those guys, I want five minutes alone in a room with them."

Anthony had always been a good brother. Caring and protective. When someone stole my inline skates from our driveway when I was twelve, he scoured the neighborhood and found the girl who took them—a stranger two blocks over. Had it been a boy who'd stolen them, he'd have probably gotten a black eye out of it, too. When Dad left us, Anthony flew home and spent a few days with Mom and me. Truly, I was lucky to have him.

"Do they, uh," he started, "have any suspects?"

I crinkled my forehead. "Suspects?"

"Dad said there weren't any arrests last night."

*Oh.* "Not that I know of," I said.

"Did they know the place was empty or something?"

There was something in his question that made me pause.

Did he already know the answer to this?

*Am I reading too much into his question?*

"Yeah. They were definitely surprised to see me."

In the background, a baby cried, and my heart ached, wishing I were there with my brother, doting on my new niece.

Among the many sacrifices we'd made financially, one of the hardest was that I hadn't gotten to meet my brother's baby yet. I always thought that when Anthony had children, I would be one of the first to the hospital. And while living on the other side of the country didn't make getting there that fast realistic, I hadn't expected this many weeks to pass without getting to meet his daughter. But leaving Dad wasn't feasible, nor were airline fees. It was another joyful experience withheld because of all of this.

"How's the baby?"

Anthony hesitated. I could picture him picking at his thumbnail, looking down at the floor. "She's good. We're good. I just...worry about you."

"It's over," I assured.

"Not just about the robbery." Anthony sighed. "I worry about everything you have on your shoulders with Dad. I wish I lived closer."

After the hit-and-run, Anthony kept asking if there was more he could do to help. But what could he do? He couldn't physically be here to help without quitting his job.

There were times I felt resentment toward him for being so far away, like, somehow, he left me holding the bag by taking care of Dad while he lived freely. Which wasn't fair. No one *expected* me to take care of Dad. Not even Dad himself.

"You're raising your family, Anthony, and no one ever makes decisions to move away, thinking their parent might get hit by a car."

"It's too much for you to handle alone. I wish I could do more."

"You send money every month. It helps more than you can imagine." Without it, we'd have probably been homeless already.

I didn't have the energy to get into all this again. When Anthony's guilt for living far away reared up, it normally took thirty minutes to talk him out of moving back. Moving back meant losing the job he loved, moving away from his wife's family, who provided free child-care. As much as I'd love to have him closer, Anthony deserved the little slice of heaven he'd carved out for himself.

Besides, like we'd talked about last time, by the time he sold his house, moved here, and found another job, Dad would be back on his feet. He'd have given up everything for nothing.

Was Dad's recovery going longer than originally planned? Yes. But he *was* recovering, and there was no point in allowing the damage from this whole situation to spread.

"I'll call you later, okay?" I smiled.

"Zoey?"

"Yeah?"

"I love you."

My throat swelled.

"I love you, too, Anthony."

As I walked the rest of the way to work, it surprised me how ordinary the city felt today. The steel buildings stretched so high, they cast me in their shadow, but even in the shade, the sweltering heat was as relentless as it had been the last few days. The businessman walking ahead of me already had a dark spot on the back of his blue shirt, and his iced coffee was sweating, a single drop splatting onto the sidewalk. The morning traffic jam on Wacker Drive was in full swing with bumper-to-bumper vehicles casting a symphony of impatient horns, infecting the space with the smell of car fumes. The routine of it all was almost eerie. How mundane any day can seem until it takes a tragic turn.

I kept walking and was suddenly overwhelmed by an ominous feeling of being watched. I looked around at the pedestrians, at the cars. The doors of the buildings opening and closing as people entered and exited, but nothing explained the chill skating across my skin.

I hustled quicker, and once I was safely inside my office building, I'd hoped I could put it all out of my mind and have a normal day. But as soon as I walked to my desk, my friend Emily—a gorgeous redhead with a curvy figure—saw me, and her eyes grew wide.

"Holy crap! What happened?" She grabbed my arms and scanned me head to toe.

Clearly, I hadn't covered up the bruises well enough, and I couldn't escape yet another interrogation.

As I sidestepped her questions, only revealing the bare minimum, I twisted my hands together so forcefully that it became painful. The only way I could get her to stand down was to promise to do drinks "soon" and tell her everything then.

"Did you call Jenna?"

I shook my head. "I'm not going to call her when she's home with a newborn."

My best friend had been through a lot, and the last thing I was going to do was steal her joy during her maternity leave with her second baby.

"If you need anything..." Emily's voice trailed off.

And then, thankfully, she walked away from my desk and let me work.

By the end of the day, she returned. "Do you want me to walk you home?"

"No." She'd ask me a thousand questions, and the "L" was safely public. "I'm fine. I promise."

And I *was* feeling better. It helped, getting lost in work. Taking phone calls, building spreadsheets, presentations. It was good for me to focus on anything other than the memories that kept flashing through my mind.

Some of them were disturbing. The violence. The promise of death.

Some of them were of Easton. The touch of his finger in the corner of my lip as he washed the blood away. The sound of his voice, rough, like life's hardships had manifested into sandpaper in his throat. And the look in his sapphire eyes after he'd gently removed my blindfold.

I felt like I was a prisoner trapped in my own thoughts, incapable of controlling them.

As I left work and walked toward the "L" station, I rounded the building's corner, and something prickled my spine.

*I'm being watched.*

I looked around at the city, crowded with bodies, trying to place where this sensation was coming from. Until my eyes landed on the source.

Standing on the other side of the road, staring directly at me, was Easton.

## 15

E aston stood with his hands in his jean pockets, a gray T-shirt strangling his lean muscles and flat stomach, his gaze firmly locked on me. His stillness—a statue among a stream of pedestrians—stood out like a rainbow in a black-and-white photo.

The gentle breeze blowing in this sticky weather seemed to penetrate my stomach's walls and swirled around inside. Jazz music from a nearby saxophone blended with the groans of vehicles crawling along Wacker Drive, flanked by seventy-story buildings, and the overheated asphalt smelled like fresh tar.

A smarter person would take off running in the opposite direction or call the police. But evidently, I wasn't very intelligent because after a few seconds of staring at him, I ambled through the crosswalk and closed the distance between us.

Based on the stern look on his face, I couldn't tell if the Easton standing before me was the captor who had held me hostage or the savior who had helped me get away.

He looked down at me with those ocean-colored gems, darkness locking his jaw and tightening his lips—a lip which was split, the only indication of his scuffle from last night. The peppering of caramel highlights in his hair looked brighter in the sun than they had in the condo, the texture richer with the deeper tones underneath.

It was impossible not to notice how incredibly sexy he was, his olive skin glistening with sweat beneath the base of his throat, his athletic frame standing nearly a foot above mine so he had to tilt his chin down to look at me. Even with a drop of sweat journeying down his temple and the ends of his hair damp against his forehead, Easton looked unfairly gorgeous. Like sweat was an accessory.

Easton tightened his lips when his eyes landed on my bruised cheek. It had been dark in my bedroom last night, so clearly, he hadn't seen it until now. And in the sun, the concealer didn't block it fully. He raised his hand and touched the skin just beneath the mark, tilting his head to get a better look.

"What did he do to you?" he growled.

I swallowed. "He caught up to me in the hallway and took me down. I got away, though." Obviously. What a stupid fact to clarify.

"Is it your ribs or your back?" His eyes snapped to my waist, then my shoulders.

"Is what my ribs or my back?"

"You were wincing in pain when you walked over."

*He misses nothing.*

"I'm fine. I just ran out of Advil," I hedged. There were more pressing issues than listing my injuries. Most notably, "Why are you here?"

And why did he feel so distant, compared to last night? Why did hostility seem to pulse outward from his body?

Easton ran a hand through his thick locks. Looked off to the sidewalk and furrowed his brows, then returned his attention to me.

He motioned with his chin to follow him into an alley, presumably where we could talk in private.

I froze. Yes, Easton had saved me, but he'd also held me hostage, broken into my house last night, and had clearly been following me. Isolating myself with him wasn't wise, no matter how much my heart claimed he'd never hurt me.

I glanced around at the pedestrians, at the busy traffic.

It didn't feel safe to talk out here, where police or Brown's crew might spot us. But I wouldn't go too deep into the alley with him; I'd stay close enough, where people could see what was happening.

Just in case.

The narrow passage—which felt like a tunnel burrowing through steel skyscrapers—was a welcome ten degrees cooler than the sidewalk, thanks to the buildings blocking the sun, but I had to watch where I stepped. The asphalt ground was a spiderweb of cracks, so deep that they threatened to twist my ankle with one wrong move. As we stopped walking, I noticed an army of ants carrying off what appeared to be crumbs of food, marching in organized lines with their loot.

"Why didn't you give the police my name?" He tilted his head to the side.

"How do you know I didn't give them your name?"

"If you had, I'd be in jail by now."

"So, they know you, then."

"Petty theft. And Easton's not a common name."

When his gaze tightened and a crease cemented between his brows, I wondered, *Has anyone ever shown kindness to him before?*

"You saved me," I answered. "Didn't feel right to sic the cops on you for that."

He said nothing, as if still struggling to understand why I'd protect him.

"Is that why you're here?" I grabbed my elbow, holding my arms over my body. "To find out why I didn't turn you in?"

To this, Easton finally broke eye contact. Widened his stance as he looked down.

"My colleagues are furious I let you get away. In their eyes, you're a liability. A big one."

I gulped. That term, *liability,* was a thinly veiled threat. One that I couldn't tell if Easton was on board with. Was his rigid posture from being upset about what his colleagues had said? Or because they'd changed his mind and he now agreed with them?

"Do you see me as a liability?"

Easton's eyes cast over my face, and he took a deep breath.

"Brown's crew runs different than mine," he hedged. "You're an innocent. But to him, you're nothing more than a risk."

Brown had people on the street, too, didn't he? People that worked for him?

"Do you think Brown might've sent someone to find me?" I held my breath, waiting for his verdict.

Easton furrowed his brows. "What makes you ask that?"

"There were these guys hanging at the "L" stop by my house."

"What guys?"

"They're there every day, and they always give me a hard time, but, today, I wondered if maybe—"

"Give you a hard time how?"

"Like, what if they're part of his crew or something?"

"What do they look like?"

I shrugged. "Tattoos covering their arms, with, like, lightning or something extending down their hands? One of them wears a cross earring, and another has a missing lower tooth, like he's been in a fight or something."

"No," Easton said. "They're not Brown's crew."

"How can you be sure?"

"No one in his crew has tattoos like that. Or looks like that."

"And they aren't on your crew? The…middleman who someone contacted to arrange the heist?"

Easton's shoulders relaxed two inches. "No, not part of mine."

I let out a relieved breath.

Easton licked his teeth. "They give you a hard time?"

I shrugged. "They do it to every girl that walks past them."

"Do what?"

"Wolf whistle. Say crude things. Grab their crotch while they follow me for a few steps. The first few weeks it happened, I was terrified they were rapists. Started getting off at a different stop and taking a taxi the rest of the way, but I couldn't afford it, so I had to go back to walking past them."

Easton's glare became so intense, it could crack me open.

"They've never attacked, though," I assured.

But his expression didn't soften; the way he scrubbed his temple with an unfocused gaze looked like he was mentally trying to identify who they were.

"You're sure they're not part of Brown's crew?"

His jaw ticced. "No. But he's got a lot of dangerous minions at his disposal, ready to kill on command."

*Well, that's comforting.*

"So what, you're here to…convince me to retract my statement? So he never gets caught? Because he deserves to be in a prison cell for the rest of his life."

"But I don't?" Easton towered over me, his frame screaming power.

I looked down at my hands. "I owe you my life, Easton. If you hadn't helped me escape, I'd be dead right now. And I can't even think about what that would mean for my dad. Plus, I promised that if you let me go, I wouldn't turn you in."

If I were being honest, some other part of ratting him out felt wrong, too. Maybe it was some sort of chemical reaction. With the threat of death hanging over my head, he had been the warm comfort in the midst of it, the man who'd saved my life. That was what I tried to tell myself last night. But seeing him now, I knew that was a lie. It was something deeper. It wasn't rational, but something lured me into his intoxicating presence, and now, I wanted more. I wanted to know everything about him.

It felt like the second he walked out of this alley, he'd vanish forever.

"I was worried something happened to you last night," I admitted. "I couldn't fall asleep."

"You looked to be sleeping soundly when I saw you."

I snapped my eyes to his. I couldn't believe he'd just admitted to being in my room, but he couldn't deny it, could he? "How do you know where I live?"

"I followed you."

"Did you see me sitting in the ambulance?"

He nodded.

He was good; neither I nor the cop noticed him.

"How did you get in?"

To this, the corner of his mouth curled up slightly, like he found my innocence amusing. "You do know what I do for a living?"

*Right.*

I was consumed with disappointment because if I'd known he was there, I could have talked to him. Spent time with him without fear of Orange or Brown interrupting. And it stung that I'd been robbed of that opportunity.

"Why didn't you wake me?"

Easton moved a stray piece of hair away from my cheek, his fingertip leaving a blazing fire in its path. "You looked peaceful."

But I would have stayed up all night if I'd known he was there.

"I wish you had woken me," I managed.

Easton sucked me into his gaze, the city around us vanishing until nothing else existed, except me and him.

"You should stay as far away from me as you can, Zoey."

"Why?" I'd already lied to the police. What harm could it do if we spent time together and got to know each other?

Silence.

"I know you're a burglar, but…"

He pursed his lips, a profound depression casting his features in disdain. "If only that's all it was."

A panic settled into my bones, manifesting in anger. "If this is the last time we can ever talk to each other, at least tell me why."

More infuriating silence.

I lifted my chin. "I deserve to know what's going on."

To this, he looked down as he nodded and rubbed his cheek, some sort of internal debate waging in his head. It felt like an eternity before he finally looked back up at me, tucked his hands into his pockets, and cleared his throat.

"No good way to say this."

"So, just tell me."

His chest inflated. "I've been sent to kill you, Zoey."

His hardened voice grated across my skin and squeezed air out of my lungs.

Easton ran a thumb along his jawline. "They've given me one chance to make this right. Eliminate the witness that got away. Or I'll pay the price."

Instantly, I felt sick.

"If I don't do it soon, they'll send someone else for you."

Easton kept his eyes locked on me, like he was worried I'd faint.

Maybe I'd been wrong about him. Maybe when he was backed into a corner, he'd make a very different choice than the one he'd made last night.

After all, keeping a girl from being killed was one thing. But giving up your life to protect her was another.

Maybe he'd even think he was doing me a favor, being the one to end me so it would be as painless as possible.

His eyes stretched past me to the nearby pedestrians. Was he searching for a member of Brown's crew? Or possible witnesses to whatever he was about to do?

Instinctively, I took a couple steps back until my back hit the alley's wall, suppressing the hiss from bumping my bruise in the process.

Easton furrowed his brows and stalked closer until he was only a few inches away. "I'm not going to kill you, Zoey."

But he could. He very much could. He was a body carved of chiseled stone, and I had no doubt his fighting skills were crazy high for him to have survived on the streets as long as he had.

The hint of danger wrapped around me like a dark embrace.

"Why?" My words tripped over my dry throat. "Why would you risk your life for some girl you barely know?"

His spellbinding eyes warmed. "You saved my life"—his voice rumbled over my skin—"when you returned that wallet."

I blinked. "What are you talking about?"

Easton swiped his nose with this thumb. "My brother and I approach this lifestyle differently. I'm more, I guess you could say, methodical. Planning. Careful. He's more a wild card—after the easy cash, spending it faster than he can earn it. Whenever he gets money from a heist, he blows through it like water, which is not only risky—that kind of shit'll get you busted by the cops. It's also unsustainable. You still have to pay your rent and bills, but when you save nothing for that?"

Easton licked his lips. "Kept bailing his ass out of financial holes until I had nothing left in my own reserve. Once that happened, my brother went to a loan shark. The kind that collects in blood if you don't pay it back. He was going to get killed because he didn't have their money. So, I talked the guy into giving me one more week to come up with it, but to do it, I had to vouch for the debt. Which meant, if I didn't pay it, they'd kill my brother. *And* me."

My jaw fell open slightly.

"I barely scraped it together in time. I was on my way to pay it off when you found my wallet. And returned every dollar to me. If you hadn't…"

He didn't finish the sentence.

He didn't have to.

"That's why you protected me last night? Why you saved me?"

He placed his palms on the wall next to my head, tight lines of muscles twisting around his forearms, as if blocking himself from coming any closer.

"Even if you hadn't returned my wallet, I was never going to hurt you, Zoey. I was standing watch to figure out how to get you out of there."

Which had to feel impossible with how adamant Brown had been about killing me and his failed plea to Orange to let me go.

Orange. Easton had spoken to him in a familiar tone and had said he'd spent a decade protecting him.

"The other man, Orange, he's your brother, isn't he?"

Easton's lips pursed, but eventually, he gave a soft nod.

Why did I feel so safe around a man confessing he'd been ordered to kill me? Denial? Temporary insanity? Or a sixth sense that told me he would never harm a hair on my head?

That he was telling me the truth?

"Thank you"—I placed my palms on his chest—"for protecting me."

The muscles blanketing his torso rose and fell while his Caribbean eyes looked from my left eye to my right. Easton's Adam's apple bobbed, and his breaths grew quicker as he shifted his gaze to my mouth, studying it, as if fighting against urges that wouldn't lead to anything good. Kissing me would make this even more complicated and painful than it already was.

This crazy pull we had toward each other might be wrong, yet nothing ever felt so right.

I studied his mouth, remembering how it had felt on mine last night, but it had been so unexpected when it happened that I hadn't been able to savor it. His full lips taking mine between them.

I wanted to feel his warmth against me now, his hands in my hair. I wanted to taste his tongue, and I could tell he wanted it, too. Even if he was fighting the urge not to.

Unable to take it anymore, I reached up on tiptoe and gently brushed my lips against his.

That was all it took.

Easton groaned and crashed his mouth against mine. His tongue pressed through my lips, and I welcomed it, licking it, weaving my hands around his neck. Feeling it tighten as he pressed his body up against me.

Our kiss deepened, and I ran my hands down his shoulders, down his tight bicep muscles, and back up again. His body was smooth and rock hard, ridges upon ridges of lean muscles bulging beneath his shirt. I traced my fingertips down his back, and my every touch incited a growl from him.

I wanted him. I wanted to feel his hands all over my body.

"Zoey," Easton managed.

He pressed his forehead against mine and panted, his hot breath bouncing off my lips. I tried to reach up, to feel our lips unite again, but he stepped back.

Balling both hands into fists as he stared at the ground.

"We can't be seen together." Despair washed through his tone. "It's not safe."

How could it hurt this much, him stopping anything before it even started? Him making it clear that he'd come here to tell me good-bye?

I shouldn't care.

At all.

And yet...my heart burned. Why?

Whatever the reason, I wanted to lose myself in the feeling even if only for a little while.

My cell phone interrupted my thoughts, though, ringing with a number I'd pre-saved into my Contacts.

It took me a second to digest what I was looking at, to break from the sensual fog and back into the crisp reality.

"It's the detective." I held the phone toward him. "He must want to ask me more questions." Maybe put me with that sketch artist. But what if I could give him something better than a description? "Do you know Brown's real name?"

He scratched his temple. "Yes."

"Let me give it to the police."

"You ratting him out will only put you in more danger."

"He already has a hit out on me. What more danger could there be?"

"You don't want to know."

I shivered.

"I'm going to give Brown a day or two to cool off." Easton stretched his fingers straight, then balled them into a fist again. "And then I'm going to talk to him. Try to convince him that hurting you will just bring more heat on him. Heat he doesn't need right now."

"But if you show up to that meeting without having"—killed me— "taken care of me already," I said, "will you walk out of that meeting alive?"

## 16

I stepped onto my front porch to catch the Lyft to the police station for my scheduled meeting with Detective Hernandez and almost tripped over a blue bag.

I froze in my tracks.

The mysterious plastic gift bag was the size of an index card.

*What if it's a bomb?*

It had been a day since I found out there was a hit on my life. In that time, I went through life shell-shocked, processing it, trying to figure out what to do about it.

Today, I called in sick to work. Dad assumed it was because I was tired, but after hearing about the threat, I didn't want to risk leaving the house. I drew all the blinds closed. I checked the locks on the windows and doors no less than thirty times, and I wanted to stay inside forever.

But Hernandez insisted on meeting today. *Insisted.*

And if Brown didn't listen to Easton, the only other thing that would eliminate the threat to my life was if Hernandez locked up Brown. ASAP. So, here I was, rushing out my front door toward a waiting Lyft.

A ride I couldn't even afford, but I was too scared to venture farther outside to get to the "L" or walk. The car was parked ten feet away, just a few steps from this possibly deadly bag at my feet.

With my heart galloping, I pulled up Hernandez's number, but just before I clicked the Call button, something else caught my eye—the tag on the handle.

It had a handwritten note and, on the bottom, a signature.

*E.*

I inched closer until I could read the rest.

*Take four with food. Then another two when that wears off.*

I moved even closer and pressed the tip of my finger on the edge, opening it slightly.

Inside was a bottle of Advil.

I let out a huge breath of relief that the bag wasn't some ploy by Brown to hurt me and looked around. Was Easton out there somewhere? Watching me? When did he leave this here? Didn't he realize how dangerous this was? Dad could have seen him or found the bag, or a million other things could've happened.

I scrubbed a hand over my face, reminding myself I needed to hurry. I quickly ripped the note into a million pieces so Dad would never be able to read it, shoved the Advil into my pocket, and discarded the bag and note remnants in my neighbor's trash can before getting into the waiting ride.

Fifteen minutes later, I arrived at the police station, praying Hernandez might have some good news about the investigation. But equally worrying he might have information on the one person I didn't want locked up. Because if they locked Easton up, I had no doubt Brown would hire someone else to kill me—someone who would never hesitate.

It was wrong to withhold information from the cops. I knew that. And I hated that I was doing this—again—because it went against every moral fiber in my being. But my first priority right now was to do what I needed to do in order to stay alive. Because it wasn't just me who'd pay the price if I was executed; Dad would, too.

The lobby of the police station had become all too familiar to me, from the many times I'd come here to press the detective assigned to my dad's case to keep searching for the criminal who had run him down. I'd always tried to be strong, coming here during those times, pretending my heart wasn't a hot mess, shuffling through haunting images of my dad's mangled body after the accident. The way doctors gave us that look of uncertainty about his future.

I walked up to the mahogany desk and gave the gray-haired woman my name, and then I stood back and waited in the open area, where a handful of chairs—all occupied—hugged the exterior wall. Blue-and-tan tiled flooring stretched beneath my tapping foot with the Chicago Police logo at its center. To my right, a staircase wide enough to fit a compact car led up to a landing, where a bulletin board housed perfectly aligned papers, before the stairs twisted to the right and ascended to the second floor. Above my head, lights illuminated the space in a soft white glow, and the air conditioner hummed, blasting cool air throughout the space. It smelled like rubber in here. And crime. Crime and rubber.

"Zoey." Detective Hernandez came from the first-floor hallway and motioned for me to follow him. "I appreciate you coming in today."

He led me to a conference room that was so small that when I pulled the chair from the wooden table, it hit the wall. I had to slide into it like someone had parked their car too close to me.

"I'm going to grab a water. Would you like one?" he asked.

"Sure." I hoped it would help wash down all this trepidation of what he was going to tell me.

My cell phone buzzed in my pocket. Maybe Dad needed me to pick up something on the way home.

But it wasn't Dad texting me; it was from an unknown number.

**Be careful what you say at the station.**

Ice surged through my limbs.

**Me: Who is this?**

**We talked in the alley.**

*Easton.*

My muscles relaxed.

**Me: How did you get my number?**

**Looked it up on your Settings when you were…subdued.**

**Me: Why?**

**Because I couldn't imagine never getting to talk to you again.**

My heart pathetically melted into a puddle of goo, but my army of suspicion quickly slapped my heart, warning against possible manipulation. After all, how convenient to have the phone number of the only witness who could land you in prison.

**Me: If the police search your phone, they'll think you're trying to intimidate a witness.**

**I'm not trying to intimidate you, Zoey. I'm trying to protect you. And this is a burner.**

*I bit my nail.*

**Don't give him anything that will put you in more danger. Not until I can make sure you're safe.**

**Me: If he shows me a photo lineup and I recognize HIM, I'm going to point him out.**

Then again…if I did that, would he turn Easton and his brother in, too? Surely, Brown wouldn't take the fall by himself.

Even so, the only way to protect myself was if Brown was locked up, right?

"Sorry about that," Detective Hernandez said.

A badge hung from the belt of his black pants, a navy button-down clung to his shoulders, and his dark hair complemented his eyebrows. Which sat atop blue eyes that looked at me as if he could see right through me.

He set down two bottles of water on the table, shut the door, and then—much more gracefully than I'd managed—took a seat opposite of me. Pen and paper in front of him.

"How are you holding up?" He scratched his eyebrow.

I shrugged and started to pick at my nail, watching my phone. The chess pieces on the table had moved while he was gone, and I was trying to decide where to position my pawn.

"Have you made any headway on the case?"

"Nothing I'm at liberty to talk about." He frowned. "I'd like you to work with a sketch artist. She'll be here in a minute."

I nodded, the disappointment of not hearing, *We got him, Zoey. You're safe*, making my posture slump.

"You okay?"

My stomach felt like an empty pit.

"I think my life is in danger."

Detective Hernandez kept a poker face. He folded his hands on his lap and leaned back in his chair, studying me. "Has someone threatened you?"

I clenched my toes.

"Zoey?" Detective Hernandez pressed.

I forced myself to clear my throat. "They threatened me that night," I reminded him. "I saw that one guy's face, so he wanted me dead. He chased me down and attacked me, and I know he's going to come after me again. And if he does, what if my dad is there? If he won't leave one witness alive, surely, he won't leave another, and my dad's in a wheelchair and can't even fight back."

Hernandez said nothing. He studied me with tight eyes, as if he was cataloging my every word, analyzing it even. Maybe he sensed something had changed.

"This group"—I clenched my eyes shut for a moment before opening them again—"have they killed people before?"

He regarded me. "We're still trying to identify who 'they' are."

"I saw the news about that gang robbing wealthy houses. If it's them, have they killed before?"

"A lot of wealthy residences are targets. Unfortunately, they're not the only crew out there, hitting them."

"You're not answering my question."

"You're scared."

Maybe I could get something useful out of this meeting. Something to keep us safe. "Can you put a protective detail on my house?"

He leaned forward, picked up the pen, and twisted it around. "I can send a car to drive past your house every so often, but we don't have the manpower to put protective details on people. You only see that kind of thing in the movies."

I frowned.

"I'd like to go over your statement again." Hernandez glanced down at the paper in front of him.

"Why?"

"Standard procedure. After a couple days, you might've remembered something that you didn't at first."

My neck broke out into an instant sweat. Was that true? Or did he sense I'd lied?

I shifted in my seat, wincing from the back pain, where Brown had kicked me.

"You mentioned three men. Is that correct?" he asked.

"Yes. One guy, Brown, seemed to be the mastermind."

Hernandez nodded.

"I described the tattoos." I motioned toward his paper. "Wouldn't those be on file if he'd ever been arrested?"

"We're still working on that," Hernandez said flatly. "But it's possible he hasn't been apprehended. Or the tattoos are new."

Translation: It hadn't led to Brown's identity. So, either the tattoos took place after his last police bust, or maybe he'd never been busted. Maybe he wasn't in the system. Maybe he was scary good at evading cops because he'd do anything to not get caught.

"And you believe someone tipped them off to the heist." Hernandez raised his brows.

I nodded. "Someone who knew the place."

Hernandez stared at me and narrowed his lips, as if…what? He thought I was the one who'd tipped them off?

A flicker of panic sparked in my bones.

"It wasn't me," I clarified. "If I knew the place was getting robbed, I never would've gone there that night."

Hernandez nodded, but I couldn't tell if it was because he believed me. He then went through his routine follow-up questions. I told him everything all over again with the exception of the things I'd omitted before—Easton's name, the kiss, him helping me escape.

He didn't ask me if my captor broke into my house to return my ring or if he'd kissed me after warning me I was in danger. So, at least that was one less outright lie.

Funny how thin a moral fiber I was clinging to these days.

Throughout it all, Hernandez prodded me along with more detailed questions and follow-ups. His attention to detail gave me renewed hope that maybe, just maybe, the detective would be able to solve this case quickly. Maybe Brown could be locked up without risking our lives.

A redhead with her hair slicked back into a bun walked in. She smiled at me. "Ready?"

"Think I got all I need for now," Hernandez said. "But if you think of anything else, anything at all that can help us identify these guys... nothing would make me happier than getting you justice."

Justice. Would I get justice? It felt much more possible than it ever had with Dad's hit-and-run case because Hernandez was good. Thorough. Nothing like the detective currently working Dad's case.

Which gave me an idea.

Even though I was obsessed right now about the robbery case, I had an opportunity here—an opportunity that might close as soon as I walked out that door. Who knew if I'd be back here, talking to Hernandez again?

I cleared my throat. "I was wondering if you would consider taking over the investigation of my dad's hit-and-run."

Detective Hernandez stared at me.

"Someone hit my dad and got away with it, and I'm sure the detective assigned to his case is doing the best he can, but I think it's time for a fresh set of eyes to look at it."

"That's not how things work around here," the detective said tightly.

"Could you at least make some calls? See if you think that they've done everything they possibly can?"

Detective Hernandez rubbed his chin. He was silent for what felt like an eternity before offering me an empathetic hint of a smile. "I'll see what I can do."

Sweet optimism etched its way into my soul.

He left me alone with the sketch artist, and when I finished, I walked outside the building, staring at the app that warned me the nearest ride was forty-three minutes away. That long of a wait didn't happen often, but sometimes, the city traffic became so jammed, cars were trapped on the roads.

I looked up and down the street for a taxi, disappointed that none were in sight. I rubbed my arms and looked up at the "L" train platform a half-block away. It didn't feel safe, taking it. But it felt less safe, walking home.

I debated going back inside the station. Waiting for the ride there. But the ride was going to be another fifteen dollars I shouldn't spend, and what was I going to do? Spend thirty dollars a day or more to get to work or anywhere else I needed to go? The "L" was public, always packed with witnesses.

And a train was approaching.

*F it.*

I ran like a girl being chased in a bad horror movie—more than a few eyebrows arched at me, I was sure—and hopped on the thankfully crowded train.

I felt like I was in a fog on the ride home. So much so that when I reached my stop, I almost didn't notice the punks that normally harassed me. But this time, they didn't wolf whistle. They didn't shout profanities or say obscene things.

Instead, when I walked past them, their cocky grins fell, and their eyes rounded to the point of looking...afraid?

All three of them had black eyes. Fat lips. Not to mention, other bruises along their faces and necks. One of them had a white bandage where his forehead met his hairline, blood seeping through.

They only looked at me for a couple of seconds before turning around and putting as much distance between me and them as possible.

## 17

I pulled out my phone and texted the same phone number Easton had used earlier. I quickly added his name to it so I wouldn't do something stupid like accidentally text someone else something meant for him.

**Me: I have a question for you.**

His text back was swift.

**Easton: Can't talk right now. On my way to meet...a *friend*.**

I felt ill, worried about Easton walking into a dangerous conversation. Because I knew he was referring to Brown.

**Me: Be careful.**

**Easton: Are you alone?**

**Me: Almost home. Why?**

**Easton: Because I don't want you to be alone until I know how this goes.**

I held my hand to my stomach.

**Me: Will you text me when you're done?**

**Easton: Yes.**

**Me: Promise?**

**Easton: Yes. I'll text you the second I'm able.**

After jogging from the station to my house, I walked inside, needing to think in complete silence because the thought of Easton talking to Brown fired my nerves on all cylinders, and I seriously needed them to calm down before coping with normal life. But Dad didn't even wait for me to get my shoes off. He wheeled himself over to me, studying my face with such scrutiny that I wondered if he could see right through all my falsehoods.

"How'd it go?" he asked.

My shoulders slumped. "Fine."

"Did they have suspects for you to look at?"

*I don't have it in me to go into this right now. Right now, Easton's life hangs in the balance of a conversation.*

"No. But now, they have a sketch of one of them." I tried to do Orange, too, but I didn't recall enough details to make the sketch useful. I was hopeful that if I ever saw him again, I'd recognize him. I just didn't have a strong enough memory to create a sketch like I had with Brown.

"Have they had a development in the case?"

*Please, Dad. Sense my need for space, allow me to talk about this later.*

"If they have, they're not saying anything."

"What *did* they say?"

I pinched the bridge of my nose. I so did not have the energy to go through a play-by-play of all of this. I knew Dad meant well, and before, I'd appreciated his worry. But right now...couldn't anyone just give me five minutes without having to talk about it? Could I take my shoes off first? Could I have that one minute of sanity to myself?

How was anyone supposed to get over something traumatic when the police and your dad insist you go over it and over it? Making it feel like your entire life now centered around one awful night.

"We just went over the details again."

Based on my dad's tightened lips, that was unacceptable.

"Tell me everything they said," Dad insisted.

"There's nothing more to say." I didn't mean for the edge to slice through my words. Maybe my mood shift wasn't just from exhaustion; maybe it was from worry over Easton.

All I wanted to do was have some peace and quiet until I knew he was okay. But no. The universe wouldn't let that happen, would it?

"Zoey."

"Dad, even if I felt like getting into all this, Alex is on his way over."

My dad looked confused. "I already had my physical therapy this morning."

"I know." But he left while I was still in the shower, before we could chat. "I need to talk to him about something."

"About what?"

I took a deep breath, trying to calm my growing frustration. I didn't have the time or patience to get into this because I needed to focus on the task ahead of me—telling Alex that I didn't have the money I'd promised, hoping he'd still give Dad PT while I figured out a new plan.

It was selfish of me to beg him for another extension, but I was so desperate, I didn't know what else to do.

In the midst of all this drama with the robbery, life still moved forward. Bills still had to be paid, and Dad had to keep progressing with his PT and his medical appointments or else he would never get better.

The problem was, if I couldn't sell the ring Easton had returned— it was flagged as stolen by police, who were probably watching for it to turn up—I was running out of ideas on how to get extra money. The only thing I could think of was to try to get a second job. It would mean leaving Dad alone at night to wait tables or tend bar. That I'd have to figure out, but the bigger problem was that finding a job and getting paid would take time, so I prayed Alex would work with me.

It felt like a group of rubber bands had wrapped around my ribs, like everything in normal life was at the mercy of this upcoming conversation.

Normal life. Excluding a group of criminals who intended to end my life.

"Our bill," I said, and before he could ask another layer of questions, I cut him off at the pass. "I'm going to lie down for a minute because I'm beyond drained."

Then, after I got Alex's verdict and Easton's—God willing—good news, I'd take a warm bath and slip into bed to get some sleep. Because I didn't trust myself in this life-or-death game of chess when my mental gas tank was running on fumes.

I tried to walk into the hall, but Dad rolled in front of me.

I gritted my teeth at yet another blockage between me and what I needed.

How did Dad's concern go from feeling loving to suffocating?

"Where are they with the investigation?" Dad pushed.

I curled my fists tighter until my nails dug into my palms.

"If you're this curious, why don't you call them yourself?" I tried to massage the frustration out of my temples.

Dad flinched at my tone. "I did. They're not telling me anything, but you, they should tell you."

"I think they're not telling you anything because there's nothing to tell. They haven't caught whoever's done it yet."

"Which is bull. Why aren't they behind bars?"

"Why are you so angry?"

"Three violent criminals held my daughter hostage, beat her, and threatened her life, and you're asking me why am so angry?"

So, now, he was going to act like a good dad? The protective one?

I was pathetic because part of me relished him being the protective dad, the one extending affection that I'd desperately craved after he left us. But I was also angry because he lost the right to act like a good father—a good father doesn't leave you for another woman and doesn't subsequently blow you off at every turn, making it clear you are no longer a priority in his life. Sabotaging your finances in the process while he lived in the lap of luxury.

"I'm starting dinner." I walked around him.

"Those cops aren't doing enough," Dad growled.

"I really don't want to talk about this anymore."

"Do you know if they got any fingerprints or anything?"

"I don't know! If you wanna think about anything, maybe you should think about who all has a key to your condo."

"What?"

"They got into the condo, Dad. Maybe you should think about who could've gotten them in."

"What the hell is that supposed to mean?"

"It means, maybe the person had a key to get inside the condo."

"They think this is an inside job?"

"I swear they're even looking at me like I might've had something to do with it."

"That's preposterous," Dad said. "You'd never do anything like that." But then he stared at me with this look that I swore said...*Would you?*

*Wow.*

"Does Holly still have a key to the condo?" I tried to sound curious and not accusatory.

"Zoey..."

"If someone did set this up, it had to be her."

"I know you never liked her but—"

"She's always been obsessed with money, and when you got hit by that car, her lifestyle went up in smoke. She didn't get anything in the divorce. She's bitter, angry, and always acted entitled to your money. Stealing the last of your stuff fits her to a T."

"I know you didn't care for your stepmom—"

"Do *not* call her that."

"But she wouldn't rob me."

"So, in all your years together, you're telling me she never did anything that made you second-guess her character?"

His silence was all I needed to hear.

"Do not call her my stepmom. Ever again."

Dad studied me, picking up on the deeper meaning behind my words. "Do you have something you want to get off your chest? Because it certainly feels like you do. And we've never talked about everything."

"And you want to have that talk? Right *now*?" I crossed my arms over my chest.

Dad seemed to consider this and scrubbed his face. "No," he decided. "Talking things out is exceedingly overdue, but you and I have a long conversation ahead of us, and I'd prefer to wait a bit. You've been through a significant trauma and need time to heal from that first."

My eyes watered. Making me remember how desperate I'd been to work through our hurts when I was tied up. Shame on me for being mean to him. A lot of this anger probably wasn't even because of *him* right now. I was scared, and exhausted, and taking my frustrations out on my dad.

"I'm sorry for snapping at you," I said. "I'm overwhelmed with… this entire situation, and I'm exhausted."

"It's okay," Dad said gently. "Why don't you get some rest?"

"I will. As soon as I'm done talking to Alex."

## 18

"Hey," Alex said when I opened the door. Then, he noted the look on my face, and he looked past me toward my dad before returning his gaze to me. "You okay?"

"Yeah." I forced a smile. I checked my phone for the millionth time, willing Easton's call or text to arrive to let me know he was safe.

Alex looked from me to my dad again, perhaps sensing the tension. "Want to step outside for a second? Get some fresh air?"

My mouth ran dry. Getting fresh air and a moment to breathe from my father sounded like heaven. But I couldn't afford something as simple as stepping outside for some fresh air anymore, could I?

I clenched my teeth, looking at the glorious summer sky that I was missing out on.

"Are you afraid to come outside?" A crease formed between his brows.

I shrugged.

Alex's mouth curled into a line of frustration, no doubt because he could tell the robbery had stolen my sense of peace. "We could go inside?"

I didn't want to have this conversation about money in front of Dad.

"I have been staying inside," I said. "But even that doesn't make me feel safer. I keep thinking someone could just set fire to the place or shoot me through the window even if the blinds are closed. Or ignite a bomb or something. Staying in hasn't made me feel safe; it just makes me feel like a prisoner again."

Only this time, I was confined to my townhouse instead of that chair. This time, Brown didn't just inflict fear during the span of one burglary. Now, he'd infected every safe haven in my life—my home, my work, my bedroom.

And the problem was, even if it was safer to hide in my house, it wasn't sustainable. I couldn't miss another day of work without losing pay. We were out of groceries, Dad couldn't physically do the shopping, and I couldn't afford the hike in fees to have them delivered. Plus, I had to get to the pharmacy to get Dad's medication. Staying inside indefinitely wasn't an option. I had to figure out how to live my normal life amid this chaos.

"We could go around back?" Alex offered.

"No," I decided.

If I had to come out of hiding, then I just wanted to get the first time over with. I looked up and down the block twice before finally stepping my right foot outside. And then my left.

I took a huge breath of air.

Nothing bad happened.

I took another step.

And another.

No gunshot. No man appearing from around the corner or parked car.

I walked farther outside into the summer evening air and savored the way a light breeze danced across my cheeks. It was twilight, the sun having set not long ago, and in the near distance, the city's skyscrapers were aglow against darkening lavender clouds. Here, the beat of a rock song drifted from a few houses away, and the delicious scent of barbeque ribs puffed out of a neighbor's grill, making my stomach growl and my mouth water. I could almost taste the sweet mesquite flavor.

Alex's concern for my mental health was obvious through his tone. "You okay?"

*No. But I need to be.* Because I needed this conversation to go well. I needed a win. Without it, I felt like I would just crumple, and once I did, I wasn't sure I would get back up this time.

"Honestly?" I ran a hand through my hair. "I've been better."

Alex tucked his hands into his khaki pants pockets, his white polo shifting around his biceps. The freckles on his face had darkened in the summer's sun.

"I can't imagine what you must be going through. You talk about it with anyone yet?"

I shook my head.

Alex frowned. "You need to talk about it with someone, so you can process this. What about a therapist?"

"Can't afford one."

"Jenna?"

"Maternity leave."

"So, she's home then," Alex said.

"Not sleeping. Up all night with a newborn. Breastfeeding. I'm not dumping on her right now."

"Emily."

I sighed. He wasn't wrong; I could feel a level of tension winding inside me, ready to snap. Maybe I did need to talk about this with someone. And of all the people in my life, Emily was certainly the best candidate. I trusted Emily. I could be completely honest with her, including details I hadn't even told the police.

"Yeah," I allowed. "Maybe I'll talk to Emily."

But right now, I needed to focus on Alex.

"Listen, the reason I asked you over was to talk about the money."

"Zoey—"

"The ring I was planning to sell was in my dad's condo."

Alex tensed. The veins on his forearms bulged like little snakes beneath his skin, and his eyes tightened as they stared at me, unblinking.

"You were at the condo that night for the *ring?*" he asked. His angry tone cut through the air.

"I've been thinking a lot about this. And I think if I get, like, a second job, waiting tables or bartending, I can have the money to you within the month," I said. "Two at most."

"You kept that ring at your dad's place?" he asked.

"I feel awful, putting you in this position, asking for another extension, but I feel like I don't have any other option."

"*I'm* the reason you were there that night?"

I blinked. "What? No. I just mean, I have to figure out a different way to get the money."

Alex flexed his fingers straight, then tightened them into balls, and for some reason, the breeze that had been dancing across my skin chilled my shoulders until goose bumps erupted.

"Don't get a job," Alex said. Now, his voice was soft and low, and his shoulders sagged.

"Alex, the only way—"

"Let's not focus on the money right now. We'll figure that out later. For now, the important thing is that you're okay."

"But your rent—"

"I'll figure that out."

I opened my mouth to protest, but he held up his palm.

"I'm going to keep coming pro bono until we figure something out, together. Okay? You're not alone in this, Zoey."

I couldn't stop my lips from quivering. Relief—sweet relief washed over me like cold water putting out a fire. When Alex saw the look on my face, he reached out and pulled me against his chest and held me.

I leaned into his embrace, the sanctuary of his body calming my nerves.

"Why are you doing all this for me?" I asked.

"We're friends."

"Yeah, but this is a lot. Even for friends."

Alex was silent for a minute, and then he cleared his throat, his tone low and riddled with pain. "You remember junior year of high school," he said, "when things went to hell with me and my parents?"

Of course I did. I remembered the very first day I noticed something off—when his mom pulled into the driveway and didn't even look at Alex as she walked into the house. Same thing with his dad. At first, I'd figured Alex had gotten into trouble and they were pissed—normal teenage stuff—but it quickly became apparent there was something deeper going on. After that day, Alex's demeanor became sullen at school, and I'd see him climb out his second-story window onto the roof of his house and lie there for hours, looking at the stars, as if needing an escape.

Whatever was going on in that house was clearly painful, so my family and I stepped up and started to invite Alex over. A lot. He had dinners with us and even spent some holidays with us, but he never told us what was going on with his parents.

"You became my family, Zoey," Alex said, "when I didn't have one. And I've never forgotten it."

He hugged me tighter.

Would he ever tell me what went down with his family? He never mentioned them, so I could only assume they'd never repaired whatever fallout had happened.

My cell phone rang, and when I saw the number, I pulled away from the hug and walked a few feet away.

"Hello?"

"Zoey," Easton said.

I could tell by his tone that whatever he was about to say was bad.

"He's not letting you off the hook," I deduced.

"No. He's added some…motivation."

"Meaning?"

"If I don't follow through, it won't be just me who pays the price." Easton sounded exhausted. "My brother will, too."

## 19

"Holy crap." Emily perched at the edge of her seat, leaning her elbows on the small circular table, looking as gorgeous as ever with her auburn hair flowing around her unfairly perfect porcelain skin and wearing tight jeans and a red top that accentuated her curvy body. Around us, the bar was in full swing with a scattering of people ordering drinks from two bartenders, wearing teal polos, while rock music blasted through the speakers so loudly, the bass vibrated in my bones.

The entire space was lit up in blue lighting, making the walls look like ice, people's skin look purple—as if we were having drinks inside an ice castle. The salt along the edge of my margarita looked like snow, the liquid's sharp lime scent pricking my nose.

"Why did you leave your house tonight if there's a threat on your life?" Emily glanced around the place. "Should we leave?"

"No."

"Zoey—"

"Cowering in my bedroom for the rest of my life isn't an option."

"Coming to a club *is*. We could go to my place?"

"Your roommate won't leave."

"Your place, then."

"My dad's there. He keeps staring at me like I might crack, and I seriously need a break from that. Besides, I don't want him to hear any of this."

"We can sit on your front porch."

Two girls at night, alone?

"Out in the open? This place is safer. It's public, with a lot of witnesses."

Emily's lips pulled into a worried line. "That's a lot of deliberation just to have a drink with a friend. I can't even, like, fathom how stressful this is. Are you okay? Like, mentally?"

I laughed. "Probably not."

Maybe I *was* being reckless.

But I was done letting Brown control my life. How dare he threaten both Easton and his brother if Easton didn't obey his commands?

Hell, maybe this was my FU to him. I spent most of the robbery convinced I was going to die, and then I got lucky enough to escape, and he thought he could send me back into that chair, tied up, terrified?

*No way, mother-F-er.*

Tonight, I wanted to talk to my friend.

I *needed* to talk to my friend, so here I was, spilling everything to Emily.

*Everything.*

"I can't believe you kissed that guy."

"He rescued me."

"Still." Emily crinkled her nose. "He's, like, a criminal."

*Criminal.* Why did that word feel like a betrayal to Easton?

"He's not just a criminal."

To this, Emily sat back in her chair, head tilted.

"What?"

Emily took a long sip of her margarita before finally spitting it out. "Okay, so first of all, I don't think you're processing the robbery itself or even the almost-dying part. I think there's something else that you're working through that's even deeper than that."

I raised my eyebrows.

"If you think about it"—she traced her glass's rim with her glossy red fingernail—"this is, like, the first time that you've paused to consider someone's reasons behind their bad choices."

I blinked.

"This Easton guy opened that up for you."

Hearing his name roll off her tongue made me tense. I trusted Emily completely. But was it a mistake, telling her his name? A betrayal?

"Before this," she continued, "everything was, like, black and white. Like when your dad left your family, there was no explanation that could justify it."

"It wasn't just that he left," I reminded her. "It was *how* he left."

"I know. I'm just saying that you—understandably—only look at people's *actions* when you're forming an opinion of them. Easton is the first person that shifted that. He made you pause and wonder *why* he was doing the things he did. Part of you empathized with why he became a burglar. You started to see him as a flawed human, not just a list of choices he made."

Easton's words echoed through my ears. *"Sometimes, good people are capable of bad things, Zoey."*

"Most people probably would have just sat there and been victimized," I said. "But he took actions that most people wouldn't have the courage to take. What kid lives in an alley in Chicago when winters get below freezing and takes care of his little brother?"

Emily looked at me like I'd just admitted to eating caterpillars for protein. "When you said you guys kissed, I assumed it was like a momentary sexual-tension thing," she accused, her jaw dropping open. "But you *like* him."

"What? No, I don't."

*I can't.*

"You *do*." Her eyes grew so wide, her eyelashes nearly hit the roof of her forehead, and horror rolled across her features.

I took a sip of my drink.

"You can't like him. He's a *burglar*. He held you hostage and has been ordered to kill you."

"I'm aware."

"He might've helped you escape, but that does not mean he's a good person."

I said nothing.

"Any feelings you have for him is probably, like, that kidnapping disorder. What's it called? Stoke ham?"

Emily looked it up on her phone, then read from the screen. "Stockholm syndrome. When hostage victims have positive feelings toward an abuser or captor." She put her phone down. "That's got to be what this is."

"Yeah. Probably," I lied.

*That's not all it is. I can't stop thinking about him, wondering where he is. How he's doing. Worried how much he's sacrificing just to keep me alive.*

I took an uncomfortable sip of my margarita, avoiding Emily's accusing stare by glancing around the club, and when I did, my eyes landed on a familiar face. Who appeared to spot me the same moment I'd spotted her.

"Is that Willow?" Emily squinted.

Willow was a friend that I'd made at the University of Illinois. Jenna was friends with her, too. I just happened to be a lot closer to Jenna than anyone else in my life, but when Willow moved to Chicago, she came around our friendship circle enough to get to know Emily as well.

Willow waved at us and then started walking toward our table.

I plastered a smile onto my face and shot Emily a warning look that the conversation about the robbery was paused until we were alone. It wasn't that I didn't trust Willow; I could only stomach unraveling all this chaos to one person right now, and that person was currently Emily.

"I didn't know you girls were coming out tonight." Willow gave me a quick hug, then Emily.

"Last-minute thing," I hedged, not wanting Willow to feel excluded.

"Want to join us?" Emily motioned to one of two empty seats at our table.

"I was just leaving, actually." Willow waved to a friend who was standing by the door, in full flirtation mode with the bouncer. "Maybe we could get together soon? For dinner or something?"

I smiled, relieved. "Sounds great."

"Have a great night, ladies!" Willow walked off.

And thankfully, it was just Emily and me again. To resume Operation Dissect My Crisis.

"So, you think the person who hired the robbers was your step-hag?" Emily leaned forward.

I shrugged. "She's the only one with the motive and the means to do it."

"Do you think you're letting your hatred for her cloud your judgment?"

"She texted my dad." I curled my lips. "The day after the robbery. Claimed she heard about it from the detectives who'd been by to see her. Guess they were following up with anyone who might've had a key to the place. Or a reason to rob it."

"And his cell phone caught fire?"

I smiled. See? This was why I was out tonight. Emily could pull me out of the heaviness and we could laugh at ourselves.

"She asked if I was okay and then got to the real reason for her text. She asked if, by any chance, I'd grabbed her necklace before escaping."

Emily's jaw almost bounced off the table. "She did not."

"I didn't even know she had a necklace there. Evidently, she'd kept it in the master bedroom."

"Why? I thought she moved out a while ago?"

"She did. Convenient, isn't it? She probably didn't leave it behind; if she did, she could've gotten it at any time. I bet she put it there, so she'd have something to lose in the robbery, too, so she'd be a victim. Diverting suspicion away from her."

"Or she could be lying about there even being a necklace, hoping to collect the insurance money," Emily added.

Also possible.

"She's just the gift that keeps on giving, isn't she?" Emily arched a brow.

I smiled. "Thank you for talking about all this with me. I feel a lot better."

"You sure you don't want to go?" Emily bit her lip.

"Positive." I nodded.

Alex was right. Getting all this off my chest to Emily made me feel lighter, and now, I wanted to try and feel like a normal person, if only for an hour or two.

"Let's just have some fun?" I suggested.

Her grin widened. "How about we find some cute guys to talk to?"

That was Emily's version of fun, not mine. "I'm not in the mood."

"Oh, come on. It's been forever since I've been kissed."

"I find that hard to believe."

Emily's dating life was active. She was a redheaded fox, and the only thing that kept guys away was intimidation by her beauty.

"Look." She nodded her chin toward the bar. "There're two super-cute guys staring at us."

"Let them stare. How about we dance?"

"With them?"

"With each other." I rolled my eyes. "Guys are the last thing I want to deal with right now."

"Well, that's too bad because they're walking over here." She grinned.

I groaned.

"That tall guy is so cute. At least let me talk to him for, like, a few minutes, okay?"

"Emily..."

"Please? I haven't had a date in over two months, and it's totally making me insecure."

I frowned at her puppy-dog eyes. Emily had been a really good friend to me tonight. The least I could do was give her a few minutes to see if she'd hit it off with this guy.

The two men sauntered over to our table like they were in a

hottest-men-in-the-club competition. Spoiler alert: they'd probably win, but that made me like them even less. Hot guys weren't hot when they acted like their beauty was a gift to civilization.

"Good evening, ladies," the tall, thin guy said with a grin.

Even his grin was arrogant.

"I'm Henry," he said, flashing his super-white teeth to Emily.

"Emily." Emily nodded, already folding her shoulders into a flirtatious pose.

"I'm Thomas," the other guy said to me.

I forced myself to smile. "Zoey."

Thomas nodded with his chin to the dance floor. "Would you like to dance, Zoey?"

*I'd rather go to my high school reunion, wearing my bra outside of my shirt.*

"She'd love to!" Emily chirped.

I threw her a death glare, and she shot me a *pretty please* look. I sighed and reminded myself—again—that she'd been a good friend, coming out with me tonight despite all my baggage.

One dance. I could do one dance—for her.

"Stay where I can see you!" Emily insisted.

Thomas chuckled, probably thinking it was a sexual inuendo, but the look she flashed me said, *If you leave my sight, I'm going to assume you're being murdered and call the FBI.*

I followed Casanova to the dance floor.

The beat of the music vibrated my bones as overhead lights transformed the room to a shade of purple. The air smelled like sweat from young couples wearing outfits that showed off their bodies—girls in dresses so short that their underwear was nearly exposed and guys in tight shirts with the top two buttons undone. Eyes raking over their partner's body, hands wandering, fingers touching. Sexual tension radiated through the club.

Thomas moved closer to me.

I glanced over at Emily and saw the huge smile on her face as she ran her fingers flirtatiously through her hair and then leaned forward on the table.

*She likes him.*

I wasn't going to ruin that; I'd give her a few minutes of fun—enough time to exchange numbers—before I politely sent Thomas on his way.

Dancing like a horny college boy, Thomas stepped into my personal space.

I took a step back, trying to keep a minimum of three feet between our bodies, but he didn't get the hint. Instead, he circled me, his eyes wandering over my body as he did a lap like some sort of mating ceremony. The dude reminded me of a peacock flaunting his feathers, like his mad dancing skills were supposed to make me want to drop my panties right here on the dance floor.

And he clearly flunked the course in reading someone's body language. Because mine was saying, *Back up, buddy,* but he didn't back up. He put his hands on my hips. I winced, less from the pain from where Brown had kicked me—my injuries were starting to feel better, and I'd taken Advil before coming here. It was more that his fingers felt like paws, grabbing at my torso like he had a right to me.

I was about to push him off and tell him that if he liked having unbroken fingers, he wouldn't lay a hand on me again without my permission.

But if I were being honest, my seriously foul mood had little to do with this guy. I think the whole situation just reminded me that Easton and I could never date, let alone anything past that.

And the guy was just dancing, for heaven's sake. Maybe spending time with another guy wasn't a horrible idea. My hormones had evidently imprinted onto Easton, and I needed to train them to become attracted to someone else—anyone else.

I put my hands on Thomas's shoulders and let him pull me to the beat of the music. I willed myself to feel a spark—any spark—with him. If ever there were a guy hot enough to feel a spark for, Thomas would be it with a tall frame and chocolate eyes that reminded me of Hershey's Kisses.

But nothing flickered between us, not even when he moved his hands up my back.

Suddenly, a tall figure appeared near my left shoulder.

"I'd like to cut in." He didn't state it like a question; his broody voice made it sound like an order that bordered on a warning, causing Thomas to look at me and then slink away.

He positioned himself in front of me. Dammit if he didn't look sexy as hell in a black T-shirt that showed off his muscles and flat stomach and jeans that stretched around his legs.

I crossed my arms over my chest. "What are you doing here?"

## 20

"What are *you* doing here?" Easton demanded. "You should be at home."

His voice was raised, but I couldn't tell if he was actually yelling at me or if it was just to compensate for the loud music, which, thankfully, provided a privacy shield around us. Around everyone. You were lucky to hear the person standing right in front of you, but that was about all you could hear over its beat.

"And what, wait in my tower until you tell me it's safe to let down my hair?"

"There's a hit on your life. You're being reckless."

"*I'm* being reckless? You're standing out in the open with the woman you've been ordered to kill. Pot. Kettle." I pointed with my finger between us. "How did you even know I was here? Are you stalking me?"

"*Stalking* is an unkind word."

"That's a yes."

"You shouldn't be here," he repeated.

"I'm just having a drink with a friend."

"Do you not understand the danger you're in? Honest to God, Zoey." Easton ran a hand through his hair. "Do you have a death wish? How the hell am I supposed to keep you alive if you're this careless?"

"So, the hit man's going to lecture his target on staying alive?"

"I'm not a hit man." Easton stepped into my space. "You keep acting like this? I'm going to throw you over my shoulder and take you somewhere. Keep you there until I know you're safe."

Shame on my hormones for squealing, for acting like kids begging their parents for ice cream. *Please?*

"And when will we know I'm safe, Easton?"

"It's only been three days."

"It feels like a decade."

"I'm working on this," Easton said.

"Working on this? Didn't he threaten your brother?"

"He did. And you should know, I don't respond well to threats. Especially when it comes to those I care about."

I tightened my lips. "How are you going to convince him to not murder me?"

How peculiar my life had become for those words to make sense.

"Last time I talked to him, I made it all about you. About killing an innocent unnecessarily, on my heist. Next time, I'm going to make it all about him."

"What the hell does that mean?"

"Right now, the cops haven't made any arrests for the heist. So, there's a chance it'll blow over. But they kill the only living witness? All of a sudden, homicide's involved and up their ass so deep, they can't conduct business as usual. Financials suffer. People start getting pulled in for questioning. Risk people talking."

"And you think that'll change his mind?"

"Brown has his eye on a huge heist coming up, so he might focus on his new toy and let this go. But only if he doesn't feel the heat from the condo. Best thing we can do right now is let things cool down. Let the investigation fizzle out."

I didn't know why Emily's words suddenly echoed in my head. *"He might've helped you escape, but that does not mean he's a good person."* But they began to mind-F me, making me question my judgment, question if I'd read this wrong, if Easton was the good person I thought he was.

"How can I be sure you're not actually working with Brown now? Trying to scare me? Maybe what you're really trying to do is intimidate me into not telling the cops your name."

Easton took a step closer to me. I held my ground and looked up into his angry eyes.

"If all I'm trying to do is manipulate and intimidate you, then why would I have returned the ring? Why would I have left you Advil on your front porch? Why would I be here tonight, watching over you? To keep you safe?"

I bit my lip, watching his eyes snap to my teeth.

"Let's say, for argument's sake, you can't convince Brown to let me live. What will you do?"

To this, Easton's eyebrows crunched in a disgusted line. "I would never hurt you, Zoey. And I *will* figure a way out of this—a way to keep both you and my brother safe. I'm asking you to trust me."

Trust him. Could I let go of my lingering reservations and trust Easton?

*I'm scared the good side of you isn't the real you.*

I studied his face, looking for any sign of deceit.

"You didn't have to scare off my dance partner to keep me safe," I reasoned.

Easton flexed his fingers at his sides, his jaw ticcing as he looked away before returning his gaze to me. "I can't stomach another man touching you."

I tried not to smile, and after a moment, the fast song ended, and a slow song started.

A sultry song.

*Because the universe likes to torture my hormones.*

Without taking his eyes off me, Easton stepped forward and gently grabbed my hips. And instantly, I no longer wanted to escape the dance floor. I drew my hands up, placing them on his rock-hard shoulders, and began to sway with him as his piercing blue eyes remained fixed on mine. That facial stubble framed his perfectly kissable lips, as if calling attention to how amazing they would feel, pressed against mine.

I was grateful the volume of this song was much lower than the last, so we didn't have to shout anymore. In fact, with us dancing this closely, we could talk much softer and still hear each other.

His eyes scanned my body. "Are you still sore?" His tone was full of angry concern, like he hated imagining me in pain.

"The Advil helped," I said. "Thank you."

He nodded, relief not fully consuming his features. He still had an edge of anger that I'd been hurt, but something else washed over him, too. Desire.

"So, this doesn't bother you?" He tightened his grip on my hips.

I shook my head, loving the way he was looking at me right now. Loving the feeling of his hands on my body.

"I keep reminding myself to stay away from you," Easton said. "But I can't seem to listen."

Could he see the flush in my cheeks?

"Why?"

"I tell myself it's to keep you safe."

"But that's not the only reason?"

"No." His gaze drifted to my lips. "That's not the only reason."

I had to focus on my next breath. "Weren't you just lecturing me on irresponsibility?"

He licked his bottom lip and then pulled it into his teeth.

*I'm officially jealous of teeth.*

"What if I told you I can't get you out of my head?" he growled. "That I haven't been able to get you out of my head since the moment I first laid eyes on you?"

I cherished the feeling of his knuckles brushing my temple.

"That day by the lake," Easton said, "the wallet wasn't the only thing you gave me."

I waited for him to explain.

He hesitated, though, like he was second-guessing going into whatever it was, but after a few moments, resolve cascaded over his features.

"The last decade of my life, my only purpose has been raising my brother, but now, he's a grown man. And while I'll still protect him, having that chapter of my life end..." Easton chewed on the inside of his cheek. "I'd been so fixated on raising him that I never built a full life of my own. Found myself feeling like there was something missing in my life."

Human connection.

"And then, that day by the lake, there you were. I'd never been so drawn to anyone before."

He cleared his throat.

"And the more I got to know you during the heist, the more captivated I was by you."

Easton pulled me closer until our chests were touching. I could feel the rise and fall of my breasts pressed against him, and the sexual haze he cast around me made me wonder if Emily was right.

If Easton was affecting me more than I wanted to admit.

"Emily thinks you're changing me."

Easton's delicious mouth curled up on one side, and he ran the backs of his knuckles down my neck, leaving a spark in their wake. "How so?"

It was hard to focus with him looking at me like I was the only person in this club, the only thing that deserved his attention.

"Making me rethink my point of view on some things," I managed.

Easton's gaze glided down to my lips. "Elaborate."

I took a deep breath and tried to think of how to explain this. "Ever since my dad left, I've believed that people's actions tell you everything you need to know about them."

"Actions speak louder than words," Easton said.

"Especially if those actions hurt you."

Easton's jaw tightened. "Like your father?"

"We're going to finally talk things out."

Easton evaluated me. "You don't look happy about it."

"I am." I scrunched my shoulders.

He waited, staring at me until I revealed the rest of the answer.

"But I'm also scared." I bit my lip. "Forgiving someone who's hurt you is like handing them back the loaded gun they shot you with. They've already shown what they will do with it."

He trailed his thumb along my collarbone. "So, you shut them out to protect yourself."

I tightened my grip on his shoulders, trying to focus on our words rather than my lower belly, which was warming. Begging me to kiss him. "Just like you left that home to protect you and your brother from being hurt."

Easton stared at me silently, our bodies swaying to the music.

"I think there's a difference, though." Easton brought his hand to my cheek, cupping the side of my head, inciting another riot from my hormones. The burnt-sugar smell of cologne on his wrist wasn't helping.

His touch, his smell, the way he looked at me—it was like he was flooding my body with an aphrodisiac.

"I left people who didn't give a shit about me." Easton's voice was low. "Some of the people you're pushing away are people you care about."

I ran my palms down his shoulders a few inches, my fingers falling into the folds of his arm muscles. "When someone's done something that hurt you, why would you give them another chance to hurt you again?"

"Because"—he stroked my cheek with his thumb—"you wouldn't worry about getting hurt if you didn't still love them. And if you love them, that's all that matters." Easton studied me. "It's easier to give up on people. It's harder to love them despite what they've done to hurt you. But some people are worth fighting for."

I thought about how Easton's brother had been pulling away from him, and I wondered how badly that hurt and how vulnerable Easton must feel, never giving up on him.

"And here I thought you despised my dad for what he did to me." I slid my hands back up his shoulders.

"I despise anyone who causes you an ounce of pain," Easton said, his voice pulsing with vengeance. "But I also want what's best for you."

He traced his thumb down my jaw. "And living in an ocean of isolation will only make you miserable."

I wrapped my arms around his neck, which pulled our bodies even tighter together. "You think I should forgive *your* actions?" I raised my brows.

To this, Easton looked at me carefully. "No." He frowned. "But I'd be lying if I said I didn't *want* you to."

I bit my bottom lip. A gesture that didn't go unnoticed by him. Easton glared at my mouth like it was the enemy he was trying to fight, a temptation he was trying to resist.

But I didn't want him to resist it. His kiss was something I hadn't been able to shake from my thoughts since he'd first pressed his mouth to mine.

Easton took my chin in his hand. "You should walk away from me," he said in a tone that implied he lacked the strength.

"Is that what you want?" I kept my lips parted.

Why did my heart feel like it was slowly being poisoned every moment it wasn't with him, the only relief coming in the moments we were together?

All the while, it felt like Easton was about to disappear, and I'd never see him again.

Easton studied my eyes, then my lips for three breaths. "What I want is you."

His gaze pinned my mouth, and it felt like my heart stopped beating as he slowly drew his face closer. And brushed his lips against mine.

Surrendering to our kiss, all the complications outside evaporated, if only in this moment.

Easton's tongue connected with mine, delicately at first, then with urgency. If we couldn't be together, it was like this kiss was his goodbye. And like the waves of the ocean, it started gently, then crashed to the shore more forcefully as the sea's waters darkened with the coming storm of us being separated.

I raked my hands through his hair. Silk tickling my fingers as I opened my mouth wider, pulled his neck so he kissed me harder, greedily taking the kiss he felt he didn't deserve. Easton put his hands in my hair, gently scratching my scalp with his nails. It sent a rush of goose bumps throughout my body, my lower belly pulsing with his touch.

In a sea of people, it was as if we were the only ones that existed. The only things that mattered right now were his hands on my body and his tongue dancing with mine. I ran my palms down his chest, feeling the ridges of his strength.

Easton growled against my mouth as I nibbled his bottom lip.

I could've kissed him forever, but every moment the kiss continued, my desire soared to have more of him. To do things we could never do with each other, let alone in this club. I sensed Easton struggling with the same urges when he pulled away from me, as if hoping it would curb his hormones.

Panting, he pressed his forehead against mine. "How will I ever endure the pain of seeing you in another man's arms?"

My stomach clenched. There was no way Easton and I would ever be free to date like two normal people, but for a fleeting moment, we'd existed in a heaven, pretending we could. Until he burst the bubble, the cold reality of our forced separation freezing every organ in my body. Did his comment imply he'd always be in the shadows, watching over me?

"I wish this wasn't so complicated," I said, clutching his arms tightly.

Easton separated his forehead from mine, and every inch of space was a raft floating farther out to sea. Threatening to never return.

"I should let you get back to your *date*."

I could tell that was the last thing Easton wanted, that he was once again trying to be noble after his jealousy had overcome him.

"He isn't my date. He's a guy I just met here."

I'd have thought Thomas's ego would be too bruised to want anything more to do with me, but he lingered by my table, obviously waiting for my return.

Easton glanced over at him, and instantly, all the romance evaporated from his eyes, his jaw tightening in disgusted anger.

"What?" I studied his face, puzzled.

His chest ballooned.

"What's wrong?" My voice hitched.

"They're a team." Easton's lips tightened.

"What? Who's a team?"

Never taking his eyes off Thomas, Easton let me go. "Don't drink anything. Tell your friend not to, either."

"What? Why? Where are you going?"

Easton kept his eyes fixed on Thomas as he marched across the bar toward him. As soon as Thomas spotted him, he pivoted and slithered away to the back of the club.

Easton didn't give up that easily; he pursued Thomas like a hunter locked on his prey.

I jogged over to Emily and whispered in her ear, "Don't drink anything."

Emily looked at me, confused. "What?"

I glared at her date, who put his hands in his pockets as he watched his "friend" vanish into the back hallway of the bar, followed by Easton. The fact that Henry asked no questions sealed my suspicion.

I now understood what Easton meant when he said they were a team.

"You guys work together," I accused.

Emily flashed me a puzzled look.

"The two of you separate the girls, so it's easier to spike the drinks. Easier to let the effects of the roofie kick in, and the longer you keep them apart, the easier it is for the girls to assume it's alcohol affecting their friend. Especially if that girl's drugged, too."

"The hell are you talking about?" Henry snarled.

"As soon as you and your buddy came over, you immediately split us up. Thomas took me to the dance floor while you stayed with Emily. Then, we were conveniently separated, so you guys could roofie us easier."

The guy's eyes hardened. "You're crazy."

I made eye contact with the bouncer and motioned for him to come over.

"Then, you'd have no problem drinking Emily's margarita." I held her glass up to him.

His lips curled. He did not take the glass or drink.

"That big a dose, eh? It'll knock you on your ass?"

"Everything okay?" The bouncer looked from Henry to us.

"No. This guy's drugging your female patrons."

The bouncer's eyes cut to the guy, then the glass in my hand. Took it. Sniffed it. "Empty your pockets."

"Go to hell," Henry snapped.

The bouncer shoved Henry against a nearby wall and searched his pants until he produced a baggie of capsules.

I looked at the back hallway, where Easton had disappeared, and as much as I wanted to witness this guy getting escorted out by his face, every second I stood here, Easton got farther away.

"I'll be right back," I said to Emily.

"What? Where are you going?"

"I think a friend of mine is about to do something reckless."

"After everything you just said, I'm not going to leave you alone."

"This place is packed, and I won't be alone. I can't explain this right now. I'll be right back." My tone was firm, leaving no room for arguments.

Emily pursed her lips and glanced around the very public, theoretically safe bar. "If you're not back soon…"

"I know." I nodded.

I offered her a reassuring smile and then made a beeline for the back of the bar, the last place I'd seen Thomas and Easton, but the hallway was empty.

The back door to the club was ajar.

I pushed it open.

The warmth of the outside air cascaded over my skin as I entered the alley. Twenty feet wide, it stretched a hundred feet long and swallowed everything in its shadows. The only lighting came from a single overhead bulb on the opposite building and from the reflections of headlights and taillights as they scurried past either side of it. But even with minimal lighting, I could make out a very distinct shape fifteen feet from me.

A man was hunched over another, fists swinging. Each strike landed with a thwap and a groan from the man on the ground, who tossed his arms up in a failed attempt to defend himself. The man on top, however, was in a primal predatory position. He threw another blow, and this time, it cracked the guy's face.

And he stopped moving.

This was the moment the assailant turned his head and spotted me. He was still nothing more than a silhouette, the only light coming from behind him.

"Easton." I marched up to him.

Clenching his fists, he looked nothing like the man who had rescued me from a hostage situation. This Easton looked dark. Dangerous with a tightened face and rigid muscles. Rage pumping through his eyes as he glared at the man on the ground.

Nearby car engines rumbled as the metallic squeak of the "L" train echoed off the buildings.

"You beat up those other guys, too," I said. "Didn't you?"

*One Mississippi.*

*Two Mississippi.*

*Three Mississippi.*

"You'll have to be more specific."

"The guys at the "L" station by my house. I told you they were giving me a hard time, and the next time I saw them, someone had beaten them up."

"You said they harass a lot of women. Probably make enemies out of a lot of men."

Why wouldn't he give me a direct answer? It made no sense...unless...

"You're denying it, so I have no knowledge of that crime," I accused. So, if I was ever questioned about it, I couldn't get into trouble for knowing about it.

Easton raised an impressed eyebrow. Looked down at the guy groaning on the ground. "Didn't intend for you to see this one, either."

"So, that's a yes."

"Whatever happened to them? Sounds like they had it coming. I'm sure they won't be bothering you anymore."

And something in the air shifted in that moment. All remnants of skepticism dissipated like the clouds after a storm, and the rainbow that came out was a moment of pure honesty.

Easton would never hurt me.

His every action had been one of protection. Helping me escape. Warning me about the hit. Risking his safety to try and talk Brown out of it and planning to do so again. Protecting me from the guy that'd slipped something into my drink. Roughing up the guys on the "L" who'd been harassing me.

His actions backed up his words.

Easton was my dark protector, hiding in the shadows of the city.

The ordered killer, risking his life to keep his target safe.

His eyes stabbed mine, then speared the man who was stumbling back up.

"Go back inside, Zoey." He gritted his teeth. "You don't want to see what I'm going to do to him."

## 21

"What's going on?" I froze.

Because when I walked into my townhouse, I'd clearly interrupted something. Something that I could tell Alex and Dad had not meant for me to see, based on their rounded eyes. I'd told Dad I'd be out later because I hadn't expected for Easton to show up at the bar.

Or beat up a guy who'd tried to hurt me.

*Only* beat up. I hadn't left that alley until Easton walked away from the man before killing him. Only then did I rejoin Emily and call it a night.

Alex stood by the kitchen table, where Dad sat in his wheelchair with papers splayed out in front of him. Copies of police reports, photos of my injuries from the night of the robbery. In the middle of it all was Dad's cell phone, currently on speaker.

"I'm gonna have to call you back." Dad's finger hovered over the End Call button.

"I have enough information to get started," the man on the other end of the line said in a voice so gruff, he might have been a smoker. "I'll be in touch."

"What's going on?" I repeated, unable to hide the alarm in my voice.

"Didn't expect you home so soon." Dad's mouth curled down slightly.

"Who was that guy?" I motioned to the phone.

"Did you and Emily have a nice time?"

I looked at the table. "Where did you get all these police reports? And these photos? Do police hand these out to anyone who asks?" Wasn't there some sort of privacy protection for something like this?

"I'm not anyone. I'm your father and the owner of the condo that was robbed."

"Who was that on the phone? Because it didn't sound like the police."

"Zoey."

"It was a private investigator." Alex turned his lips down, as if he knew I wouldn't like the answer.

Dad shot him a glower.

"A private investigator?" I put my hand over my stomach. "Why were you talking to a private investigator?"

Alex crossed his arms over his chest and couldn't hide the frustration in his tone. "We hired him to help find the assholes who hurt you."

"What?" I looked at Dad. Expecting him to tell me that Alex was wrong.

But Dad didn't say that. Instead, he just offered me an empathetic look.

"Why would you hire a private investigator? The Chicago Police Department is working this case."

"They've failed to arrest anyone."

I threw my hand in the air. "It's only been three days!"

"Most crimes need to be solved within forty-eight hours, or they go cold."

"I think that's for homicides, Dad."

"They're not moving fast enough. The longer this goes on, the harder it is to get justice."

"Dad," I started.

He slammed his fist onto the table. "Three men held you hostage and beat the hell out of you. And I'm not going to rest until they're behind bars."

This couldn't be happening. Easton was right; the best way for me to stay alive was if this entire investigation fizzled out. Because even if I could miraculously get Brown behind bars, I had no doubt that Brown would order his crew to eliminate the witness. No witness, no testimony, and he'd go free.

"Dad, having some guy poke around in an active investigation is probably going to get in the *way* of the police."

"This guy has come highly recommended to us. He's solved more crimes than most police detectives have in their entire careers."

My heart pounded so hard, I wondered if he could hear it. "How are you even paying for him?"

"I'm funding it." Alex scrubbed the side of his face.

I snapped my eyes to him. "Why?"

"Because you're like family to me, Zoey." Alex's voice was soft, as if it hurt him, that the answer wasn't obvious to me. "And someone hurt you."

My eyes stung. Alex had no idea how much it meant to me, him going this far out of his way to try and help. If only he'd put his big heart into something that wouldn't get me killed.

But as soon as that feeling came, a chill erupted through my ribs. Why would Alex take this big of an interest in the investigation? PIs couldn't be cheap, and he told me he was short on cash—his rent sucking him dry.

"I thought you needed money for rent," I said.

Alex crossed his arms over his chest again. "My Mastercard isn't maxed out yet."

"And when the bill comes?"

"You let me worry about that," Alex said.

I could see in his eyes there was no changing his mind, no matter how financially irresponsible he was being, so I returned my attention to my father.

"Dad, please don't do this."

"Why do you care if we hire a PI?" Dad looked at me with...suspicion?

Really? Did he seriously think I'd orchestrate the heist? And be stupid enough to show up when it went down? How insulting.

"These guys are dangerous." My legs felt weak. "If they find out you're poking around, trying to get them arrested? They might hurt you."

"They tied my daughter up, beat her, and planned to kill her. So long as there's a breath in my body, I'll hunt them down. And make them pay."

And in that instant, my fairy tale and nightmare collided. The fairy tale of Dad finally loving me so much that he put me above all else, to the point he'd risk his own life for me. And the nightmare that his good intention might cost me my life.

## 22

As flattering as it was that Dad was finally showing me the kind of love I'd been craving for years, why'd he have to pick now of all times to finally do it? Why couldn't he have done something when I was in college, pleading for him to come talk to me to salvage our relationship?

I had no right to be mad. I should only feel flattered and appreciative that he loved me this much. And I had no right to be angry because what I had said to him was far worse than anything he'd done to me. But there it was. Anger. Bubbling in my veins until it boiled over the surface.

"Dad, can I talk to you for a second?"

At the tone of my voice, Alex exchanged a look with my father. "I'll step outside for a minute."

I waited until Alex left and crossed my arms over my chest. "Maybe instead of solving who the strangers were involved in this robbery, you should look at your inner circle and figure out who set all of this in motion."

My dad's head tipped back. "What's that supposed to mean?"

"Someone hired these burglars, and *they* need to be found, too."

"If anyone else was involved, the PI will figure it out. But in the meantime, those three criminals need to be locked up, and I will not rest until that happens."

If only the yellow countertops could somehow disperse cheer into the room. Because right now, all the hurts that I had swallowed over the past few years unraveled in my chest, firing a mixture of anger and resentment through my veins.

Where was *this* dad—this protective, loving dad—all those years he'd basically abandoned us? Why did he show up now all of a sudden? And why so dramatically?

Was this whole thing because I'd taken him in and he felt some sort of obligation because of that? Or was this his way of pacifying his guilt for having been a bad father to me?

"Solving this robbery isn't going to undo everything that you did to me, Dad."

I could tell by the jerk of his head that my comment had taken him by surprise.

It took me by surprise, too, especially since we agreed to wait to air our grievances until this robbery was behind us.

But that's the thing about emotions. Sometimes, they escape when you least want them to.

Dad folded his thin hands on his lap. "I know that, Zoey."

"No, you don't."

He couldn't expect this Band-Aid would heal his third-degree burns.

"Leaving Mom was bad enough, but you abandoned *me*."

"You were angry. I was trying to respect that and give you your space."

I didn't appreciate his tone of voice. He should be begging for forgiveness, not annoyed with me right now.

"And when I thought I'd given you enough time, I did try." Dad's cheeks reddened. "But you wouldn't let me in."

"Because it was too late! You broke my heart, and you broke my trust, not just in you, but in humanity. Because when the foundation of your world crumbles beneath you and your dad is the one holding the bulldozer that destroyed it, the rest of the world feels like a pretty unsafe place. And after that, you look at everybody with a skeptical eye, looking for any clue that they might hurt you, just like your dad did. And if you see any red flags, you immediately walk away."

I hated that I was crying. I hated that I was standing here, looking down at the father I had once looked up to, and I hated that I was finally having this out at a time when his body was physically so vulnerable. The whole thing made me feel like an awful human being, unworthy of his or anyone else's love. And yet, I couldn't stop the waterfall of words from finally breaking from their dam.

"You're the reason that when somebody does something wrong, I walk away from them and write them off. You're the reason I don't know how much slack to give people for their mistakes or their bad choices. The only thing I've learned from you is to protect my heart because you broke it so badly, it can't withstand another break."

Dad ran both hands over his face. His shoulder bones rose and fell with a deep breath, and his long fingers interlocked again on his lap as he regarded me. "I'm glad you're finally being honest with me."

"I'm finally being honest? You never gave me an opportunity to be honest! You left us without so much as a single conversation with me face-to-face. You went off with that woman on your trip and your holidays, and you left me like I was disposable. It's one thing for you to stop loving Mom, but when did you decide to stop loving me?"

"I never stopped loving you."

"Your actions said otherwise. We were your disposable family. The second some new, shiny car came along, you threw us in the junkyard and never looked back."

Dad shook his head. "There are some things I've never told you, Zoey. If you understood the circumstances around everything, I think you would be less critical of me."

"I wanted to understand. Desperately. With every fiber of my being, the only thing I wanted to hear was some words that would make sense out of nonsense, that would have the power to unbreak my heart. But you no-showed. Again and again. And that's when I decided it didn't matter what you said. The only thing that mattered was what you did."

And that was why I'd judged everyone based on their actions, never listening to their justifications.

"I'm not saying I didn't make mistakes," Dad replied. "I did. Gigantic ones. I should never have gone on that trip the weekend I was supposed to come to your college to talk, and I realize now that space was the opposite of what you needed. That lapse in judgment is something that I can never forgive myself for. But as far as leaving your mother for this other woman, you need to trust me that there was more to it than meets the eye."

"So, this is the part where you tell me Mom was a bad wife or you were unhappy in your marriage or she wasn't giving you enough attention or whatever? Because none of that is going to fly with me. You took an oath for better or for worse, so long as you both shall live, and you tossed it aside."

"Why did you take me in then?" Dad snapped. It was the first time he had shown anger toward me since his accident. "If I'm such an awful human being, why are you helping me?"

"Because you're still my dad!" I wiped a tear. "What am I supposed to do? Anthony's raising his own family on the other side of the country, so he's not here to help. You destroyed Mom and left her, so she's not going to help you. And the woman that you broke all our hearts to marry? Left you the second times got tough. So, what am I supposed to do, Dad? Leave you to rot in some homeless shelter? I could never turn my back on you—on family—regardless of how much I've been hurt. I'd like to think I'm better than that"—*than you*—"even if you don't deserve it."

Dad stared at me as his body slowly deflated, drained of every morsel of energy in its cells. His mouth turned down as he gave a slow, disbelieving head shake.

"And here I thought it was because I was getting a second chance with you."

Dad turned his wheelchair around, rolled into his bedroom, and slammed the door.

And all my anger burst, replaced with suffocating guilt that I'd just broken my dad's heart.

## 23

I slammed the door and stepped outside our townhouse, into the dark summer night, wiping tears from my cheeks. The sticky humidity had cooled slightly with a gentle breeze frosting the bands of sweat on my neck. The front porch's wooden planks vibrated to the bass of music—a party nearby in full swing with laughter cracking through a hum of voices. What did that feel like, to be young and carefree? How had my life become so complicated?

My cell phone buzzed with a text.

**Easton: You okay?**

I scanned my street, looking for Easton, wondering where he was.

**Me: No. I just had a huge fight with my dad.**

**Easton: Did he hurt you again? Because if he did, so help me…**

**Me: No. But we have a problem with the case.**

**Easton: I don't care about the case right now, Zoey. I care about you.**

Tension began to loosen in my muscles, and my heart warmed.

**Easton: Do you want me to pick you up?**

My insides quivered.

I wanted Easton to pick me up. I wanted to talk to him about all of this. I wanted to spend time with him, just me and him without a bar full of people, without anything around us. Without distractions or complications. But if I left right now, I'd probably hurt Dad even worse than I just did.

Yet I did need to talk to Easton. It felt like every second that this private investigator had a head start risked Dad's life exponentially. Dad and Alex were sticking their necks out with this private investigator, and if they ID'd Brown and Brown found out Dad and Alex were responsible for putting him behind bars? Revenge city. I needed to protect them.

Maybe Easton would know how to ensure the PI didn't find anything that could make Brown do something reckless.

Three dots appeared on my screen, indicating Easton was texting me again.

Before he finished, though, Alex appeared.

"Hey."

I looked out at the street, at the shadowed row of townhouses, at the road, with its trickle of traffic lumbering along, at the sidewalks. Blue-and-silver beer cans pooled along the base of my neighbor's broken chain-link fence, and the smell of freshly cut grass floated through the air.

"You're crying." Alex placed his hand on my upper arm.

"I appreciate you checking on me, but I just want to be alone." I looked down at my cell. The three dots had vanished.

"What happened?"

"I don't want to talk about it."

Alex rubbed his jaw, evaluated me. I recognized that stubborn look in his eyes. He'd had it many times in the past when everything had gone down with my dad and I'd come home from college for visits. Alex would sometimes sit silently next to me on the front porch of my home for hours. And I could tell he was gearing up to do the same thing when he took a seat on the stairs, inches from my hip.

"I don't mean to be rude." I pinched the bridge of my nose. "But I really do want to be by myself."

"I'm not going to leave you alone when you're upset."

He rested his elbows on his thighs and stared at my tears, as if debating wiping them away. I did it myself before he had the chance.

"Everything will be okay," Alex cooed.

Somehow, his empty promise made me cry harder. Because it was starting to feel like nothing would ever be okay again. Each time I found a glimmer of hope that things might get better in my life, it got obliterated. Finally carving a path of independence after college? Boom. Dad gets hit by a car. Finally have a way to pay off the physical therapy? Boom. We get robbed. Finally escape the robbery? Boom. A hit's put on your life. Easton comes up with a solid plan to appeal to Brown's goals—a plan that'll only work if the investigation stays quiet? Boom. PI enters the picture.

But worse than all of that combined? Was that look on my dad's face as he'd rolled away from me.

My lips quivered. "I broke my dad's heart."

As it turned out, being the person wielding the sword hurt worse than suffering its sharp blade.

Alex rubbed my back. "He broke yours first."

I looked at my phone again, but it was still empty of texts.

"That doesn't make it okay." I wiped my dripping nose. "Plus, as it turns out, I'm a judgmental hag."

Alex tried to cough back a laugh. "You are not."

"I am. I never listen to people's words. I just write them off the second I disagree with something they did. Like I'm so perfect."

"You're being too hard on yourself."

"You wouldn't be saying that if you knew what I did to him," I said.

Alex regarded me. "What did you do?"

I wiped a tear. "I said the worst thing a person can say to someone."

He looked at me. "Which was?"

I let out a huge breath. "It's so bad, I can't even repeat it." I still couldn't believe I'd ever said it in the first place. "I feel like…like I used to be a good person. But when my dad and I fell out, I became this bitter, resentful version of myself." I pushed down the pain. "I feel like I became a bad person."

"You're the furthest thing from a bad person, Zoey."

That wasn't true. Alex didn't know that bubbling beneath the stress of taking care of Dad, resentment had planted its seeds and spread its roots over everything that was on my shoulders. A good daughter would never feel resentful, no matter how overwhelmed she might feel. She'd only feel grateful that he'd survived and gotten a second chance at life.

And that didn't even include how critical I was of people now.

"I changed into someone I don't like." I bit my lip. "I just want to be the good person I was before everything happened." A person I was proud of.

"You are a good person, Zoey. It's only human to put your guard up after someone hurts you."

I thought cutting people out of my life would hurt less than handing them the knife and waiting for their slash. But years of hardening my skin into an impenetrable shield had done nothing more than pump loneliness through my blood, poisoning my happiness.

"Why did you team up with him?" I asked. "I thought you were angry at him for what he'd done to us?"

Helping him learn to walk again was one thing, but becoming his BFF detective buddy was another.

"I told you, you're like family to me, Zoey, and whoever did this needs to pay. That trumps anything I had against your dad."

Alex put his arm over my shoulders, and when he pulled me in for a hug, an ominous question echoed through my ears. What if Alex had organized the robbery as a way to get back at my dad for hurting me? And what if the real reason Alex had inserted himself was to stay close to the investigation? If he was the one funding the PI, maybe he could push the PI in certain directions? Away from himself?

Or at the very least, get a heads-up if any suspicion was about to fall onto his shoulders from the police.

*You're being paranoid again. You know who did this.* Holly, not Alex, who'd been nothing but kind and generous to us.

Yes, we owed him a lot of money, and he knew about Dad's stuff—
like his collector's items. And, yes, someone else in his position might
feel entitled to get some of that money before Dad's things were sold
and we had nothing left to pay him. But still, this was Alex.

I trusted him, and even if I didn't, Alex didn't have a key to Dad's
old place and couldn't root around for one without Dad noticing.

Besides, Alex was like family to me, too, and not just because he'd
been there for me through hard times; we'd bonded when the mystery
drama went down with him in high school.

"Can I ask you a question?" I said.

Alex waited.

"Is the reason you never told me what happened with you and
your parents because you thought I'd judge your family?"

Alex picked at a crack in the wooden plank. "No," he said. "I didn't
tell you because it's freaking embarrassing."

"I thought maybe you didn't feel close enough to tell me."

He'd only lived across the street from us for what, two years before
it went down? At the time, him not telling me wasn't shocking, but I
was curious why he'd never told me in the years that followed.

"If anything," Alex said, "what happened with my family made me
feel even closer to you. Because I know what it feels like to have a
parent choose someone over you."

I scrunched my face in confusion because, as far as I knew, his
parents were still married. So, his dad didn't walk out on them the
way my dad did. Did he?

"When I was seventeen," Alex started, obviously seeing the questions in my eyes, "I walked home from school early because I'd gotten
hit with the stomach flu right before lunch. I walked in on my mom
with another guy."

My jaw fell open.

"She begged me not to tell my father, said it would break up the
family, but I couldn't live in a house of lies. My dad deserved to know
what was going on, and I wasn't going to get sucked into her affair.
Especially when I'd lost all respect for her. So, I told him, and we had

this huge family blowout over it, and I lost my cool. Called her some names that I shouldn't have and tossed all her shit into suitcases and told her to get the hell out. Told her she was the biggest freaking hypocrite, going to church and holding everyone else to a high standard when, the whole time, she was banging some guy. My dad was furious with her, but he told me not to disrespect my mother like that. Said this was between him and his wife and I was to honor my mother. I told him I'd never honor her again after what she'd done."

Alex chipped a dry piece of wood off the plank and kept his eyes down.

"Things just escalated after that. I wasn't speaking to my mom, and she stopped speaking to me. Dad started drinking, and of course, he and my mom were fighting every night, but he still tucked away enough anger at me for falling out with her." Alex cleared his throat. "Shit just became toxic."

"I thought they were still married," I said.

"They are." Alex shook his head. "He decided to stick it out and work through it, but it was years before we started to talk like normal again."

"You guys are talking now?"

"A little," Alex said. "It's a work in progress, but we're finally trying, and it's headed in the right direction."

I nodded. "I'm sorry you went through that."

He shrugged. "Felt like she chose that other dude over us, you know? That's the part that hurt the worst, so when your dad left, I knew what it felt like."

That was why he felt so close to us. First because we'd taken him under our wing when he was evidently in a toxic home and then when we went through something similar.

We sat in silence with the wind breezing through my hair, understanding settling around us.

"You've always been there for me, Zoey, more than anyone in my life, and I'm not going to stop until I find who hurt you."

My stomach dropped.

Alex shifted his gaze down to my face. "You're like a sister to me, you know that?"

He leaned down and kissed my cheek.

And when he did, I heard the cracking of a tree branch from across the street.

## 24

I t had been four days since Alex kissed my cheek. A kiss that Easton must've witnessed and misunderstood, given his abrupt drop-off in communication. I knew it probably looked romantic, but if Easton would talk to me, I could explain that Alex was like a sibling, not a love interest. I almost tried to explain that via text since he wasn't answering my calls, but I got paranoid that maybe I was full of myself or wrong that the kiss had anything to do with him blowing me off. And then I got angry that he wouldn't tell me *why* he cut me off.

He didn't completely ghost me. Doing so would make me think something bad had happened to him, and I guess he cared enough to not put me through that. But with each unanswered communication, I felt Easton drifting further away from me.

I stared at our string of texts.

Four days ago, when I wanted to tell him about the PI.

**Me: I need to talk to you about something.**

**Easton: I can't today.**

His abrupt change in tone alarmed me. And hurt. From *did your dad hurt you* to *I don't have time for you.*

**Me: It's important.**

No response.

**Me: I'd rather not do this over text. Can we meet?**

No response.

**Me: Easton?**

No response.

**Me: There's something you need to be aware of.**

No response.

Then, three days ago.

**Me: Are you okay? Because you're starting to scare me.**

Easton: I'm fine. Just busy.

**Me: Can we talk?**

No answer.

**Me: Are you there?**

No answer.

Two days ago.

**Me: Are you safe? I'm getting worried.**

Easton: I'm safe.

**Me: Why are you avoiding me?**

It took him ten minutes to answer.

**Easton: I'm sorry, Zoey. I don't think it's a good idea for us to talk anymore.**

My stomach caved in on itself in pain. I put my hand over it, pacing as I tried to call him.

But he didn't answer.

**Me: Can you tell me why?**

No answer.

The hurt from his rejection consumed me, but I didn't bother texting him yesterday; my pride took the steering wheel. If he wanted nothing to do with me, I wasn't going to chase him. I wished I could tell him Alex's kiss on the cheek meant nothing, but if he wouldn't listen to me, if he'd write me off this easily, then maybe he didn't care as much about me as I thought.

And if that was true...if he wanted nothing to do with me anymore, did that mean his oath to keep me alive was also broken?

A growing pit had implanted itself into my stomach walls, and now, its tentacles reached into my chest and pulled.

My silent suffering was disrupted by my cell phone's ring, which, pathetically, I hoped was Easton.

"Hello?"

"Zoey, it's Detective Hernandez. Catch you at a bad time?"

My heart deflated. And then it galloped as I wondered if the detective was about to tell me they'd locked up Brown. After all, it was late —Dad was already in bed—so why call at such an odd hour?

I began pacing. "No. Not at all. What's up?"

"I just wanted to keep you posted. I might have something on your dad's hit-and-run."

Adrenaline tingled my fingers. *This isn't about the robbery.*

"You do?"

"I *might*," he caveated. "Made some calls. Day of the accident, a witness got a partial plate number. At the time, it didn't yield anything, but I bounced it against traffic violations that've taken place since the accident and got several new hits."

"You did?"

"Doesn't mean any of them will be the car that hit your father, but I wanted to keep you posted. Might be a step forward."

I nodded even though he couldn't see me. "Thank you, Detective Hernandez. Seriously. Thank you."

Finally, some good news.

I opened my phone and was about to text Easton about it.

It's funny how for a split second, you can forget someone's rejection.

Whatever his reasons, Easton was pulling away from me just like Dad had when I was in college. And Easton wouldn't even explain why.

*What is it about me that makes it so easy for people to walk away?*

Maybe I repelled them. Everyone had flaws, but maybe mine were so off-putting, people couldn't stand to be around me after a while.

No. I would not let my self-esteem spiral; I was stronger than this.

I shouldn't even care about Easton's aloofness. It was stupid, this ache in my chest.

I set my phone on the counter with more force than necessary.

Maybe cleaning would help my mind from spinning about Easton. It was late; I'd have to be quiet.

I padded into the kitchen and unloaded the dishwasher, straightened the counters, and stared at the holy-mother-of-God-that-stinks trash. I'd forgotten to take it out after dinner, and now, the smell of decomposing food was going through some sort of biological transformation, infecting every ounce of air with its exponentially stinky smell.

I pulled the trash bag out of the bin—gagging in the process—and tied knots as tightly as possible, setting it by the back door. Hopefully, it would contain most of the smell until morning. I moved into the living room, straightening the pillows, picking up our water glasses and fallen food crumbs Dad had dropped.

But that damn trash. The smell had already doubled in the span of five minutes, and even though the outside can was only a few feet from the back door, I wasn't about to go outside at ten thirty at night. Not when there was a hit on my life and my protector had abandoned me.

Maybe even turned on me.

My traitorous lips quivered. I shut it down by scrubbing the bathroom counters, the sink, the back of the toilet.

By the time I went back into the main area, a nuclear bomb of a smell had blown up.

I gagged and noticed the bag had a small tear in it, and a teaspoon of liquid oozed out of the bottom.

*Son of a...*

I considered attempting to tape it, but the smell would just get worse with each passing hour. Dad was going to be stuck inside all day tomorrow, and I wasn't about to let him open windows when I wasn't here to protect him.

This was infuriating. I was sick and tired of overanalyzing something as benign as quickly throwing a trash bag outside.

I grabbed the bag and looked out the back window. The trash can was nestled against the exterior wall, resting on a concrete passage, riddled with two-inch-wide cracks and black engine oil stains—which you could sometimes still smell on particularly hot days. I studied the space for several beats, making sure there was no sign of activity.

Then, I unlatched the lock and swung the door open. It betrayed me by squeaking hella loud, and when I stepped outside, the city traffic seemed suspiciously quiet, too, like the universe was making my footsteps as loud as humanly possible.

It only took two seconds to make it to the exterior can and pry the lid open.

The attack came from the front.

It was so sudden; all I saw was a flash of dark lunge toward me and hit my chest. The asphalt drive slammed into my back, and the next thing I knew, screams echoed off the building's bricks. My screams, I realized. Bloodcurdling as my mind raced to process what was happening.

The person attacking me was small.

And…fuzzy?

"Zoey!" a deep voice bellowed from a distance.

When the assailant jumped off my chest, I shot up to my feet, my eyes straining in the dark to see my attacker.

And when it scuffled back up into the trash, I stopped screaming.

Because as it turned out, my murderer was a freaking raccoon.

"Zoey?"

The silhouette of a man appeared between me and the porch light. A man whose hands clenched my shoulders as he tilted his head down, staring at me, chest chugging like a train picking up steam.

"Easton?" I jerked my head back.

"I thought someone was fucking killing you!" He let go of my shoulders and shoved an angry hand through his hair.

"What are you doing here?"

"Do you always scream like that when you see a damn animal?"

"You just cut me off!"

"You're lucky I didn't pull my gun!"

"Stopped returning my texts."

"One shot, and I could've blown your head off!"

"Without even explaining why!" I hated that my voice was shaking.

"Over what? A fucking rat?" Easton extended his arm toward the trash can.

"It was a raccoon." I gestured toward the scene of the attack.

Glowering at my unwelcome correction, Easton put his hands on his hips and began to pace, a pair of dark shorts hanging beneath perfectly sculpted abs.

Exposed abs, because he had no shirt on.

*Where would he even put a gun?*

"Have you been here the whole night?"

"Zoey?" Dad shouted.

I held up a finger. "So help me, if you run off, I will go off into the dark and roam around, looking for you."

Easton stopped pacing and glared at me.

I glared right back.

I jogged inside and explained to my dad that a raccoon had scared me and I was cleaning up a garbage mess. I told him it was a big mess to buy myself some time to talk to Easton. Thankfully, Dad appeared to buy it, his eyelids already heavy again as I left his bedroom.

When I went back outside, I half-expected Easton would be gone, but I guess he believed me that I would go hunting for him, so he stood there. Looking as pissed as ever.

"You've been here all along, haven't you?" I accused. "Watching me."

"Protecting you."

"Blowing me off." I pointed at him.

"We can't be friends, Zoey. You know that."

My traitorous heart burst into flames. If that was how he felt, he could have acted like that from day one instead of inviting me in, dancing with me, making me feel something for him, just to yank it away.

Making me question his motives.

"When you refused to talk to me, I thought maybe you turned on me. Maybe you changed your mind and you were going to follow through with your order."

I'd never seen such an intense mixture of disgust and anger contort someone's face like this.

"I told you, I would never hurt you, Zoey," he snarled.

"You did hurt me. You shut me out, just like my dad when he left me."

Easton's eyes rounded slightly, and the line between his brows deepened.

I tried to storm past him, but he grabbed my arm. I looked at his hand and then up into his sapphire eyes, a foot from my own.

"I'm sorry," he whispered. "I never meant to abandon you." He searched my gaze for understanding. "I'm trying to do right by you, Zoey. Whatever's going on between us can't continue."

"If that's how you feel, why are you out here right now?"

"You know why."

"If you want nothing to do with me? Then, no, I don't understand why you'd watch me at all hours to ensure Brown doesn't send someone else for me."

Easton flexed the fingers of his free hand and then balled them into a fist. "You think just because I won't allow myself to be with you, I'm going to stand back and let you get killed?"

Allow himself.

*Allow.*

That one word redefined this whole argument. My anger washed from my veins, replaced with the longing I could see him fighting as his eyes stole glances at my lips.

"I'm not going to let anything happen to you," he growled.

"Alex didn't kiss my cheek in a romantic way," I said. "I'm like a sister to him. And he's like a brother to me."

Relief extinguished the jealousy in his eyes. But pain followed. Because it obviously didn't change his stance.

"We can't be together, Zoey."

Easton needed to understand that my feelings for him wasn't just some survival thing with the robbery. That even if Alex, or anyone, *had* kissed me romantically, it wouldn't change how I felt.

Standing inches from me, his eyes hardened as they roamed over my face, and he licked his lip with a greedy want he wouldn't allow himself to have.

"When this blows over—" I started.

"You deserve someone better. Someone uncomplicated. Who doesn't have colleagues who want you dead."

"What about what I want?"

He released my arm. "I won't let you throw away your life on me."

My eyes burned. "That's what this is about. You think you don't deserve me."

"You don't know the things I've done."

Goose bumps erupted on my arms.

No, I didn't. But I wanted to know every detail of his life's story.

"Have you killed before?" My heart caught in my throat, seemingly stilling until he finally answered.

"No." He looked from my left eye to my right. "But I would in a heartbeat, if anyone ever hurt you."

The air chilled over my skin. A good person would feel appalled by that confession. Disgusted maybe. But I felt the opposite.

"You're a good person." My chin quivered.

"I'm not." His gaze lowered to the ground. "I haven't been for a very long time."

"Easton…"

"You paint me as a good monster, but there is no such thing. After I'd lived on the streets for a few years, I could have tried to go mainstream. Get a normal job. I didn't."

"You were trying to survive the only way you knew how."

"Maybe I liked who I became. From victim to ruler. Powerless to powerful." He stared at my mouth, his breathing near panting, as if his willpower had begun to fray at the edges. "You deserve the prince, Zoey. Not the villain."

Was that how he saw Alex? A better fit for me?

I stared at Easton's mouth, remembering how his tongue had played so perfectly with mine.

"Want to know what I think?" I turned my body, so I faced him head-on, watching his eyes for any sign he'd stop me. I placed my hands on his bare chest. "I think you haven't felt unconditional love since you were a kid. I think you focused on money because money made you feel safe. And powerful. But deep down, those don't fulfill you. They never will. Not the way love will."

He hadn't let anyone in since he was a kid. And it scared the hell out of him.

In the distance, the "L" train cast its high-pitched metallic screech as it roared nearby, and a fire truck's wail pierced the air. The summer heat caused sweat to dampen my lower back and gloss the skin across Easton's chest, making his muscles look even more defined.

"You should avoid me." Easton's jaw shifted.

*Should.* I was making progress.

I stepped even closer.

The exterior auburn light draped over Easton's shirtless body like an artwork's spotlight, highlighting the curves of his chest and arms—ripped muscles clenching one another like bands of iron. His body was exquisite, perfection, save for scars that peppered his skin in various shades and shapes.

"I believe you," I whispered. "That you're protecting me. That you'd never hurt me."

"That doesn't mean I'm a safe person to be around, Zoey."

The threat of danger when I was near him—danger from his associates, his lifestyle—glided across my bones.

Maybe a smart person would heed his warnings and never talk to him again, but all the rational reasons I should never talk to him evaporated in his presence, and the only thing that existed was this persistent fear that he would walk away and I would never see him again.

That I would never get to learn every part of his life's story, like where all these scars came from. I wanted to inventory them, catalog them, uncover every piece of his puzzle.

Visible imperfections—a symbol to remind us no one is perfect.

I watched his eyes as I reached up and touched a six-inch jagged white line with my fingertip. "What's it from?"

He was silent at first, but in a low growl, he said, "Foster dad number two. Broken beer bottle."

He had three others just like it. I traced each one—on his right shoulder, along the base of his abs, and the one on his ribs.

"Same?" I whispered.

Easton gave a nod.

My eyes prickled, and I wondered how many times he'd been hurt before being removed from that home.

No wonder he'd assumed the cut on my palm was from someone hurting me.

I moved my hand to his bicep, where three crimson dots peppered his skin.

"And this?"

"Foster dad number one. Cigarettes."

I swallowed. I wouldn't cry in front of him.

"And this?" I traced what looked like a clean surgery scar.

"Foster dad number three. Box cutter."

I swallowed. There were probably thousands of excellent foster parents in this country. What were the odds that this one kid would get the exception multiple times? No wonder he was so desperate to save his brother from what must have felt like certain hell. And that didn't even include that new abuse his brother was about to endure...

I wouldn't go as far as saying I forgave Easton for choosing to rob the condo, but I would say I understood how he'd fallen into an unsavory lifestyle. And that despite his choices, something in my heart had opened up to him.

I respected his fierce protectiveness. To know that all this time, he'd been steps away from me. Keeping me safe, even when he thought I was asleep in my bed.

Tracing my hand up his iron torso, I locked eyes with him as I slowly reached up on tiptoe.

A war raged inside his eyes as I inched closer to his mouth. I could tell by the quickening of his breaths that he wanted to kiss me, but he grasped on to the thread of resistance.

Six inches separated us. Then four.

His warm breath bounced off my skin, my heart pumping against my ribs as the summer night seemed to vanish around me. The only thing that existed was him and me.

Two inches.

Easton's brows pulled together as his resolve unraveled.

One inch.

And then…I grazed my lips against his like a whisper, and the dark notes of his primal instincts unraveled. He groaned and crashed his lips against mine.

Hard.

Easton grabbed my waist and pushed my back up against the wall, just as he slipped his tongue into my mouth. I accepted it with a moan of my own, my hands roaming up his arms, his rounded shoulders.

I nibbled at his lip.

He growled and slipped his hand under the hem of my shirt, cupping my chest.

I wanted his hands all over me. I wanted him to pin me against this wall and rip my clothes off.

Like his mouth, his hand was rough, full of pent-up sexual frustration that clenched my skin until I moaned.

"When you stopped answering my texts, I thought maybe…" I panted, my lips still hostage to his. "I thought you didn't want me."

Easton pressed his waist against me, silently proving me wrong. "I've never wanted a woman more in my life."

He moved his hips back a couple of inches to give his hand room to slide down my stomach, beneath the fabric of my cotton shorts, lower and lower until…

I grabbed his shoulders as he kissed me and moved his hand with perfection. He knew my body. Knew the spots to caress. If this felt incredible, what would it feel like with him on top of me?

Easton slipped his tongue into my mouth again, and my muscles began to tense. Feeling the rise from his hand's magic.

"I've wanted you since the moment I first saw you." Easton licked my lower lip.

That was all it took. My release consumed me, and he pressed his mouth tighter against mine, like he wanted to eat my moan. Swallow it. Devour it. And only when my last tremble subsided did he pull his hand back and stop his kiss.

But it wasn't enough. I needed more. Wanted more. Had to have more.

He cupped my cheek, stroking my lower lip with this thumb.

"Good night, Zoey," he whispered.

He offered one last kiss—a soft, gentle movement—before staring at me for three more seconds and turning to walk away.

"Wait," I said.

I couldn't let him leave without telling him why I'd been so desperate to get ahold of him these last few days.

"A private investigator is looking into the heist."

Easton said nothing. Didn't move.

"I can't imagine he'll be able to find anything that cops won't." I fidgeted my footing. "But another person poking around, trying to solve it, isn't going to help Brown calm down."

Easton ran a hand along the back of his neck. "No." He pursed his lips. "Especially since he's planning something big. Last thing he'll tolerate is someone poking around."

## 25

A week had passed since that kiss with Easton outside my townhouse with no complications developing.

Nothing had come of the case yet. No updates from the PI or cops, and while that might have been bad news to Dad, it was good news to me. No update meant leads might be dwindling, and that was my best shot at staying alive, the best shot for Brown to give up and move on. The best shot at finally getting my life back.

I was about to start making dinner for Dad and Alex when a knock came. I looked through the peephole and seriously considered not answering, but her incessant knocking drew Dad's attention.

I opened the door and found my dad's ex staring back at me.

"Holly," I said with a clipped tone. "I didn't know you had our address."

"Holly?" Dad wheeled himself closer, the shock of her unprecedented pop-in written all over his face.

"What are you doing here?" I demanded.

I looked over her shoulder, across the street, where Easton stepped out into the early evening light, hands shoved into jean pockets, watching me, his hackles raised from the distress in my tone.

"May I come in?" Holly smiled.

I licked my bottom teeth when she walked past me, as though my nonanswer held no weight.

As soon as she came inside, she noticed the dining room table, which was blanketed with papers and photographs and notebooks filled with little scribbles. Alex and Dad had been at it every night this week, working the case.

Which I totally didn't understand. I mean, why hire a private investigator if you're just gonna turn into an amateur sleuth? What a waste of money. I tried to tell them that repeatedly, but they wouldn't listen.

"What's all this?" Holly arched one of her penciled-in eyebrows.

I still stood in the doorway with it wide open, and Easton stared at me with guarded eyes.

He mouthed something to me, which I was pretty sure was, *Are you okay?*

I nodded.

And reluctantly shut the door.

"We're trying to find the guys that hurt Zoey." Sitting at the table, Alex fidgeted with a pen, glancing from the awful woman to me, then back to her.

"It was such a shock to hear about the robbery," she claimed.

"Was it?" I crossed my arms over my chest.

I wanted to tell Holly off and tell her what a repulsive human being she was. But I tried to calm myself down because, hell, if I'd learned anything from Easton, it was that even if she had orchestrated the burglary, maybe she had a story of her own—a desperate reason for having done it.

But what I could not get past was how awful she treated my father.

Holly put her hand on her collarbone. "To think, I was just at the condo the week before. It could've been me in there!"

"Why were you in the condo the week before? It's Dad's condo, not yours."

"Zoey," Dad said. Outwardly, he appeared respectable—expecting me to act that way, too, I guess—but I could see from the way he clutched his wheelchair tightly that he didn't want her here either.

"No, it's fine." Holly smiled, but it didn't reach her eyes. "When I moved out, I had forgotten that I had stored some of my Manolo Blahniks in your father's closet."

Because Holly's closet—the master suite had his and her closets—was overflowing with her crap.

"Why did you stop by, Holly?" Dad cocked his head.

Seriously, why? I'd rather sit on a beehive than have this woman in our home. And clearly, she wasn't here out of the goodness of her heart; she'd never checked up on my father in the eight months since the accident.

"Just say whatever the hell it is you came to say and leave." I gestured for her to get on with it.

"Zoey." Dad flashed me a *be polite* look.

"No, it's okay." Holly held up her palm to him, as if she was going to be the bigger person here and deal with the unruly toddler in front of her. "I guess I'll get right to the point." She raised her blood-red lipstick-stained lips up in the corners.

Alex leaned forward in his seat, studying her.

"I'm waiting." I tossed my palm in the air.

"I'm afraid I left a necklace behind in the condo."

"You already texted Dad that," I said. "Pretty odd that you made sure you got every last thing you could get your hands on, and yet you left behind some expensive necklace."

She traced her collarbone with her perfectly manicured crimson nail. "I don't know what you're insinuating."

"I think you do."

Holly's lips pursed into a bitchy line. "As I told the police, I had no involvement in that awful burglary."

*Yeah, right.*

Even if Easton had taught me to consider why someone might have robbed Dad's place, she had some balls, coming here like this. Putting Dad's emotions through the wringer. For what? One of her bazillion pieces of jewelry?

"We don't have your necklace," I spat. "So, if that's why you came here, there's the door."

"Zoey," Dad said.

"What? She never even checked on you once after you were almost killed!"

Alex looked from Holly, to Dad, then back to me.

"I didn't come here to get into all this," Holly said. "I came here to ask if the police are letting you inside the condo. Because they won't let me inside and I want to know if the thieves got the necklace. If they didn't, I would really appreciate getting it back."

A chuckle of disbelief erupted from my throat.

"You have some nerve." I went to the front door and opened it, noting Easton was gone. "Get out."

"Zoey!" Dad chided.

"This is my townhouse, and you are officially trespassing. Leave, or I'll call the cops."

Holly glared at me.

Seriously? Getting her precious jewelry back was more important to her than asking a single question about how Dad was recovering? This was the first time she had seen him since the accident, and she didn't even seem to notice, let alone care, that he was in a wheelchair and had lost almost half his body weight. I bet the police wouldn't let her inside the condo because they suspected her and didn't want her fingerprints to get inside and destroy evidence that could be used against her.

Once she stormed out and I shut the door, I turned to my dad.

"You know she wasn't just coming here to ask about a necklace, right? She was trying to establish her alibi for having been in the apartment days before the heist. I bet her fingerprints are all over things that they shouldn't be."

*I bet she cataloged everything of value in that apartment.*

"Zoey, Holly's made a lot of mistakes, but—"

"Don't tell me she's not capable of it, Dad."

Before my dad could argue further, his cell phone rang.

"It's the PI." Dad's surprised eyes met Alex's.

I immediately tensed.

"Hello?" Dad answered it on speaker, probably so Alex could hear, too.

"Turn on the television right now. NBC. Evening news," the PI said.

Dad and Alex exchanged a look, and then Alex jumped up and dashed to the TV in the living room. Turning it on. Dad ended the call and rolled his wheelchair in front of it as Alex flipped around until he got to the top story on the evening news.

Curiosity lured my steps closer, and my eyes landed on the news anchor sporting a blonde bob with not a hair out of place.

"Two weeks ago, a robbery took place in the Loop. Police say three men broke into a home, where a young woman interrupted the robbery."

An electric volt shocked my limbs.

"Live with the latest is our own James McGey."

The shot cut to a young blond man. "That's right, Jules. It was here"—the reporter pointed toward Dad's old building—"that police say three armed men broke into a luxury condominium, and now, law enforcement is looking for tips that will lead to their arrests."

The shot cut over to a prerecorded message by Detective Hernandez. "We encourage anyone with information to call the police hotline. The number is on your screen."

Ten digits appeared in the lower part of the television.

Hernandez looked right into the camera. "We are offering a twenty-thousand-dollar reward for any tip that leads to the arrests and subsequent prosecution of these suspects."

The electric shock ran through the rest of my body while my head took on the characteristics of a helium balloon.

Dad's worried eyes remained locked on me, as if he was waiting for me to say something.

Incapable of calming my erratic heartbeat, I managed to utter some syllables that sounded like words. "It's been two weeks. Why put it on the news now?"

"The PI said he put pressure on them."

"Police didn't need pressure, Dad. They have every motivation to solve cases without someone else pounding their fist on their desk."

"Two weeks. No arrests. Someone needed to turn up the heat on the investigation before it grows even colder, and now, anyone who has any information will be motivated to turn in that band of thieves."

Nausea swirled in my stomach.

My life depended on the investigation fizzling out, but now, it was front-page news with a bounty on Brown's head.

## 26

I pried open my heavy eyelids and looked at the digital numbers on my iPhone—1:53 AM. I sighed, wishing I'd slept a lot longer. After that news story last night, the only way I'd silenced my inner anxiety was by, once again, taking a sleeping pill. But evidently, it wasn't enough because here I was, already waking up with a bundle of nerves.

I rolled onto my left side and tucked my hands in a prayer position beneath my ear.

And froze.

*I'm not alone.*

The shadowed figure of a man sat in the corner chair, his head tilted at an awkward angle to his side.

Instantly, adrenaline became my caffeine, pumping energy through my heart and my muscles.

*He isn't moving.*

*Is he asleep?*

Could it be Easton? He'd gotten into my room before to return the ring. It had to be him, right?

But the shape didn't look like him. Easton was bigger. And the angle of the nose looked different.

Then again, it was dark, so maybe his size and angle did match Easton?

No. Easton wouldn't scare the shit out of me by breaking into my home. He'd call, or text, or even knock. He wouldn't just break into my bedroom like this and not wake me up.

Even if he'd seen the news story and assumed I'd be scared.

That news story...

Whoever this was must have come with a mission to hurt me.

Why did he sit down so long that he fell asleep? Was it because Dad had been staying up late these days, reading police reports, and the hired killer was quietly waiting for Dad to fall asleep, so he didn't get caught? Why wouldn't he have just killed Dad outright?

I wasn't sure, but thank God it meant Dad must still be alive.

*For now.* I needed to act before this intruder woke up.

I looked at my nightstand for any kind of a weapon. My cell phone, a lamp, and a book. The lamp was plugged into the wall behind the nightstand, which I'd have to move to unplug it. Too noisy. My only weapons were my cell phone and my library book.

A hardcover, at least.

I kept my eye on the guy as I slowly reached out and lifted the book. My shaking hand held it tightly, sweating as I watched the criminal.

The man made no move, no sound, his head still at that awkward angle over his shoulder.

I dangled my feet off the side of the bed and pushed up on my elbow an inch at a time until I was finally sitting. I grabbed my phone and looked at him again.

*He still hasn't moved.*

I scooted forward onto my tiptoes, then the balls of my feet, then they fully met the carpet, and I quietly began shifting my weight onto them.

The figure didn't flinch.

*What if he's faking being asleep? Knowing I have to walk by him, no matter which route I take?*

*What is my best escape route? The window? No. The blinds would make too much noise. I need to get out the door, go into Dad's room, and call 911.*

*I wish I didn't have to get within strangling distance to get past him.*

I took the first step on the ball of my foot, and I swore my lungs squished into a tiny knot in my ribs. I gripped the hardcover book tighter, its glossy cover cool against my now-sweating skin.

I took a second, then a third step, rounding the corner of my bed.

Now only four feet from him, I strained to get a closer look at the guy, but the only light came from the moon's glow via a cracked blind. Nothing to illuminate his face—*is it Brown?*—or his eyes to warn me if they were open or closed.

My mouth ran dry as I tiptoed through the three-foot gap between him and the bed. If he opened his eyes, I was standing right in front of him within punching distance. He could reach up and choke me before I could ever make a sound.

A creak on the floorboard beneath the carpet sounded like a cannon.

I froze, and his head moved.

*He's awake.*

As he tilted his chin up, I slammed the hardcover down onto his head as hard as I could. Corner first.

His head snapped back, and I ran for the door.

"Motherfuck!" he said, bringing his hand to his head.

I stilled. *I know that voice.*

"Easton?" I whispered.

He groaned and sat up straighter in the chair. Hand still clutching where I'd smashed him with my weapon of mass destruction.

"What the hell did you hit me with?" he asked.

I flipped on the light switch.

*It is Easton.*

"What the hell are you doing here?" I whisper-shouted.

"Why the hell did you hit me?"

"Why the hell are you in my bedroom? You can't keep breaking into my house in the middle of the night. What if my dad caught you breaking in and called the police?"

"I think you dented my skull." He pulled his hand away, which now had blood on it.

*Who knew a book could do so much damage?*

"Did you climb in through the window?"

"You're going to need to get me a towel or something, or I'll bleed all over your chair."

I hesitated. "Don't move," I demanded.

I tiptoed out into the hallway and risked opening Dad's door a crack.

*He's still asleep.* Thank the Lord.

I went into our tiny bathroom, retrieved hydrogen peroxide and a washcloth, but I couldn't find our Band-Aids. Not without rifling through the drawers at a decibel level of one thousand.

I returned to the bedroom and shut the door, so Dad wouldn't spot Easton if he woke up.

Easton still sat in the chair, one elbow on his knee, the other holding the side of his head that I had bashed. He wore black running shorts with a black T-shirt that stretched around his muscular arms. His hair looked tousled, like he'd been stressed and running his hands through it, but his eyes were still slightly puffy—still half-asleep.

"Here." I drizzled some hydrogen peroxide onto the washcloth and brought it up to the side of his head.

He hissed.

Luckily, it wasn't bleeding that bad.

"Why are you here?" My shock made my voice almost sound shrill.

"We need to talk."

"Normal people knock at the front door, between the hours of eight in the morning and nine at night. Or call. Or text."

"We have a problem." Easton's eyes darkened.

"No shit."

"You saw the news story?"

"Pretty sure half of Chicago saw the news story."

"This changes everything. Brown's not going to listen to reason now. He's not going to risk his freedom over one witness. He wants you dead now more than ever."

"Feeling's mutual."

I pulled the washcloth away, folded it in half, and put some more hydrogen peroxide on it. I pressed it against his head, and Easton looked up at me.

"Is that why you're here? To watch over me?" I dabbed his wound.

A sadness etched into Easton's eyes, and his tone strained with anguish, as if he knew I wouldn't like this. "Zoey, I need you to tell me exactly what you told the police. Word for word."

I pulled the washcloth away from his head and didn't like the look in his eyes.

"Why?"

"Because we need to get our story straight."

"Our *story*?"

He pursed his lips. "You withheld my name. You lied to the police about an ongoing investigation. You've aided a wanted felon. I need to know what you told them so that I can align my facts to what you said. So that I don't get you into trouble."

"Meaning what? You're going to talk to the police?"

"I won't contradict anything you've said."

"You're going to turn Brown in," I realized.

"No." Easton touched his head, pulled his fingers back to see if there was any blood on them. There wasn't. "You are. So he'll get locked up and you can collect the twenty thousand dollar reward."

"What?"

"First thing in the morning, you're going to tell them the news story sparked a memory. That you'd heard one guy call out *Easton*. You're going to play it off like you're not sure if it's a real name. They have no reason to doubt you, a witness who barely escaped with her life. They'll bring me in. I'll flip on Brown, and you'll collect the money. You can use it to get back on your feet."

"You'd go to prison." My jaw went slack in horror. "Possibly for good, if they add on kidnapping or other charges."

He said nothing.

My eyes watered. "I don't want you to go to prison."

"Keeping you safe is the only thing that matters."

"No." I shook my head.

"Tell me what you told them in the initial reports."

"No." I walked away.

"Zoey, if you don't turn me in, I will. Only difference is, no one will get the twenty grand."

"You said if you were in jail, he'd get to me faster."

"Not if I put him in jail, too. And not if I become a bigger problem to him."

"Why won't you just give me Brown's name? I'll come up with an explanation for knowing his name and turn him in."

"I'm not going to have you be the person who *names* Brown and gets him locked up."

"Me going to the cops will lead to his arrest anyway, so what's the difference?"

"A big one in his eyes. The person that actually *names* him is a hell of a lot different than moving the investigation in a direction that finds him. I'm not going to let you do that."

"If you snitch on him, he'll kill *you*."

"If he does, he'll face a murder charge."

"No! That's not an acceptable solution," I said. "And it wouldn't work anyway. He would probably just hire some minion to take me out."

"If you're the key witness against an organized crime ring, you could get protective custody."

"You don't know that for sure, and what about your brother? If you turn Brown in and yourself, there's no way your brother won't get tangled up and arrested. You've spent your whole life protecting him. Are you really okay with him being behind bars?"

"If I don't do something, my brother's going to cross the line and become an accomplice to murder. That's not a line he can uncross. Ever. Maybe some time away will be the pause he needs to find himself again. But even if it's not, I can't stand by and let him turn into a killer."

"I'm not turning you in."

"Zoey."

"They wouldn't give me the money anyway; I lied to the police."

"There's a reason they say *anyone* with information is eligible for that reward money. They start cherry-picking who they think *deserves* the reward money? The incentive system crumbles. Next time they need help, no one would come forward, and they know that. You'd be surprised what kind of people land rewards, Zoey. Trust me. They have to follow through; you'll get the reward money."

"Answer's still no."

Easton walked up to me. I could feel the heat coming off his body as he stared down at me for several long seconds before bringing his hand up to my face. He brushed the backs of his knuckles along my cheekbone.

"This isn't just about you. You have to keep your dad safe, too."

My lips trembled, and my eyes watered. I pressed my forehead against Easton's chest and allowed his arms to wrap around me. There had to be another way out of this nightmare. One that kept us all safe and didn't include Easton sitting behind bars when it might not even lead to anything good.

But there was no other option, was there? He was probably right, no matter how much I wanted him to be wrong.

My heart felt like it wept in my chest.

*How come every time I find happiness, it gets taken away?*

I shouldn't be focused on my feelings right now, though; I should focus on how badly this would hurt Easton and what I could do to make things right.

"If I go there," I whispered, "I'm going to tell them everything. Including how I lied to the police."

"Zoey—"

I looked up into his sapphire eyes. "I'm not going to rat you out for the stuff you did wrong without coming clean myself."

He tucked a hair behind my ear.

"You withheld my name to protect me." The corners of his mouth turned down. I wasn't sure if it was the lighting or if his eyes were growing glassy, but when he spoke again, his voice sounded almost hoarse. "No one has protected me for a very long time."

On top of everything he'd been through—abuse, homelessness, running from police—he'd never had anyone in his corner, watching out for him. Making him feel loved and safe. Easton was the big brother, but no one had done that for him.

What did it feel like to have your sanctuary ripped from you at such a young age? To know no one would ever fight for you again? I couldn't imagine how hollow and alone Easton must have felt all these years. Living in the outskirts of society like an unwanted stain.

He stroked my cheek with his thumb, his skin brushing against it so gently that it was like the whisper of a breeze before a storm. Charged with electricity.

"If ever there was a person worth sacrificing the rest of my life for, you are that person, Zoey."

I wiped a tear from my cheek. Easton had a way of making me feel like I was his everything, that I was all that mattered to him. His heart was bigger than most people's I'd ever met, and this whole thing didn't seem right.

"I don't want you to go to prison."

"It's where I belong."

But it didn't feel that way.

Yes, factually speaking, he was a criminal. And perhaps an honorable person wouldn't feel like her heart was collapsing into itself at the thought of him in an eight-foot cell. But he'd opened my damaged heart up like a flower's petals, and the thought of him rotting in a jail made me sick.

"In the morning, I'll escort you to the police station," Easton said. "I'll watch to make sure you get in the building safely, but I won't walk inside with you. Doing so would get you in a lot of trouble."

"And then?" If I went along with his crazy plan?

His tone dropped a painful octave. "It'll be the last time you'll ever see me."

My eyes stung like they'd been hit with a hostile cloud of tear gas.

Easton going to prison would mean him leaving me, too, that he was choosing to leave me, just like my dad had.

"No."

"Zoey."

"I won't do it."

"There's no other way."

"There has to be. We just have to think about it."

"You have to take care of your dad. You can't do that if you're dead."

I was full-on crying now. There had to be an out we weren't thinking of. "Maybe an anonymous tip."

Easton wiped a tear from my cheek. "With no proof, it'll just give them his name from someone who isn't a witness and can't corroborate he's the burglar. And if cops start watching him, Brown will move quicker to remove you from the equation."

"We'll think of something."

"Zoey"—Easton stepped even closer to me—"this is the best way to keep you and your dad alive, and deep down, you know it. Even if you won't admit it to yourself yet."

There had to be another way to get Brown locked up without risking my dad becoming collateral damage. How did it even come to this anyway? Feeling like I had to choose between Easton's life or Dad's?

Easton going to prison didn't feel fair. He'd lived in a form of prison since he was a child, and he deserved to feel free for the first time, not have life deteriorate even further, forced to live like a caged animal, confined to a concrete cell for decades. The little boy who'd once dreamed of becoming a baseball player deserved to feel some semblance of happiness.

To get his happily ever after.

But as I stood there, staring up into his eyes, I could see his resolve. He was going to do this whether I helped him or not. He was going to turn himself in and accept the consequences of his actions, and there was nothing I could do to stop it.

Maybe it was time to realize that I couldn't control Easton's choices—or anyone's for that matter. The only thing I could control was how I reacted to their actions and how I would deal with the fallout.

Clearly, I couldn't talk him out of taking responsibility for his crimes. But if he thought I was going to walk away from him, he had another thing coming.

"I'm not giving up on you, Easton."

Because that was what this was about, too, wasn't it? Him not being worthy of my affection.

I placed my hand on his chest. "So long as your heart is beating, I'll fight for you. Even if you do wind up in jail, this won't be the last time you see me."

Easton brushed his knuckles down my jaw, staring at me like I was the eighth wonder of the world.

*I wish the kindness I've shown him weren't so foreign to him.*

Easton's forehead crinkled as he brushed his fingers down my jaw, my neck, and then he traced my collarbone with his thumb. His touch was a match, igniting the flames of desire now pumping through my veins. I licked my lower lip, watching his pupils dilate with my movement.

Far too slowly for my greedy desire, he inched his face closer to mine. I parted my lips, anticipating the fullness of his, the taste of his tongue. And then, finally, he brushed his mouth against mine.

For this one glorious moment, I wanted to live in the present with just me and him, alone. Our bodies touching, our lips connecting. After this moment would be tears and heartbreak and sadness. But not right now.

Right now, I pulled his face harder against mine, willing our burning passion to create a rainbow from this hurricane.

Easton brought his hand to the back of my head and twisted his fingers in my hair, opening his mouth to invite my tongue inside. I accepted his invitation and slipped my tongue past his teeth, treasuring his moan. His left hand cupped my cheek as our kiss deepened, our mouths opening and closing in perfect rhythm.

A greedy need pulsed in my lower belly as our kiss gained momentum.

But a kiss was not going to satisfy me. Not tonight. Not if this was the last night I might ever have with Easton. The last night of his freedom.

I still couldn't process everything he'd said to me, especially now that my body was exclusively focused on only one thing—needing him to touch me everywhere.

I let my hands roam down his shoulders, down his arms, feeling the ridges of power beneath his skin. I traced my hand down his stomach.

His hands began to roam, too, and when he briefly pulled his mouth from mine, his eyes raked over my sleeping attire—a white T-shirt and a pair of pink lace panties.

Easton tugged at the hem of my shirt. I lifted up my arms as the fabric glided up my skin and over my head, a whisper of cooler air dancing across my chest, which instantly perked under the weight of Easton's eyes.

His gaze continued its journey down my stomach, my legs, and back up to my face.

"You're even more gorgeous than I imagined," he whispered.

*Imagined. He's thought of me like this.*

Everything warmed. I wished we were somewhere else, where we didn't have to worry about time or the need to be quiet.

I tugged his shirt up and marveled at how effortlessly he pulled it off over his head.

Damn, he was sexy. Skin wrapped tightly over lean bands of muscles. Arched shoulders cut into rounded biceps. Wide chest, narrowing to a flat, washboard stomach. And on top of it all, the scars that spoke of his strength. Survival.

I grazed my hands along his chest until he kissed me again, licking my tongue, opening his mouth wider and wider. But it wasn't enough. Nothing would ever be enough. I needed him now. All of him. Every inch of his body.

Easton walked me backward until my legs hit the bed, and then he gently lowered me down and climbed on top of me. His weight sank gloriously into my thighs as his lips trailed along my neck and down my chest.

Where he cupped me so hard, it made me gasp. I ran my hand through his hair, feeling the air dance across my freshly wet skin, where his tongue had licked me—across my chest, down my stomach, and then to my thighs. His fingers skimmed beneath my panties and slowly pulled them off.

Followed by his own shorts.

A while back, when I'd had a love life, I'd kept supplies. Supplies that, when I'd recently cleaned out my drawers, I'd discovered hadn't expired yet. I reached over, pulled one out, and handed it to him.

Easton kept his eyes locked on mine as he ripped open the foil packet and slowly shielded himself—agonizingly slow. How a man could make something like that seductive was beyond me, but I loved every second of it.

Every. Single. Second.

I worshipped the wanton look in his eyes—him knowing what he was about to do. The way he seemed to drag it out and make me wait for it, heightening the anticipation.

And then, finally, he leaned back down.

I arched my back as he trailed kisses up my stomach, my chest, up my neck, and back to my mouth. And then I felt him positioning himself between my thighs.

He pressed his hips down one inch at a time.

I grabbed the back of his shoulders as he filled me more and more. When his hips had completed their journey, he crushed his lips to mine, slipping his tongue past my teeth while his hand cupped my chest.

And then he began to move.

*Oh my word.* Never in my life had I felt something this...sensual. The weight of his body, his desire filling me, his greedy mouth roaming all over my skin. I wanted to explore every inch of him forever.

I wrapped my legs around his waist, linking my ankles together.

And, man, he knew how to move. He knew how to hit my pleasure points, varying his pressure as he moved his body, his lips wandering down my throat to my chest again. His every touch was magic, radiating sensual energy throughout my body, making me curl my toes in pleasure.

As our bodies worked against each other, I could tell he was trying to be quiet, but it was becoming exceedingly difficult for both of us. I began to move my hips with the rhythm of his, and the only way to silence my cries was to bite his shoulder.

Inciting a soft groan from his lips.

He sensed my rising wave and watched my eyes as he moved methodically until, finally, I tightened my legs around his waist and gripped his arms.

"Zoey," he growled.

And then he really began to move.

I had held my breath through my release, and just as I took my first pull of oxygen, Easton moaned into my neck. And stilled on top of me.

## 27

When my morning alarm played on my phone, something felt different. My pillow was warmer and firmer than usual, and some sort of rhythmic metronome beat beneath my ear. The soft sunlight that warmed my eyelids meant it was after sunrise, after five thirty in the morning.

I slowly stretched out my legs and arched my back, groaning as I tried to free myself from the grip of deep sleep.

"Morning," a gruff voice said.

My eyes snapped open. Easton was lying on my bed, the covers draped over his nude body, and I was lying next to him, my head on his chest. Last night came flooding back to me. The news story, Easton, our talk, our...lovemaking.

I bolted to a sitting position and shut off the alarm.

"Crap." I flung the covers off of me. "Get up!"

"What's the matter?" Easton asked.

I grabbed the T-shirt and panties I'd been wearing before Easton and his magnetism had stripped them from my body and began to throw them back on.

"My dad gets up soon," I whispered. "And you need to be gone before he does because if we go along with your plan…" And that was a big freaking *if*. I seriously needed at least three cups of coffee and a hella lot more consideration before I could commit. Not to mention, I had some things to say to him before it was too late. "There'd be no way to explain how or why the guy in the defendant's chair had been in my bed."

Lord, what had I turned into? A liar, rushing around to cover her tracks?

I'd own up to all of this. I would. I needed to come clean to the police about withholding information, but right now? Dad was seething with rage against the men who'd held me captive. Letting him see the very man he was hunting walk out of my bedroom? Was like pulling the pin of a grenade and waiting for it to explode.

"Get dressed!" I demanded.

I wished we'd woken up sooner and had time to talk because it felt like we had so much to say to each other, but right now, I had to focus on getting him out of my bedroom without being spotted.

Maybe he should go out the window. I opened up the blinds and peeked outside.

"Shit," I whispered.

Parked out front of our house was a police cruiser with an officer inside. A cruiser with a full view of my bedroom window. Seeing a man climb out of it? That'd be pretty damn suspicious. Inviting him to come investigate.

"Why is there a cop here?"

Of course there was a cop here. Was it here when I'd *wanted* one to keep me and my dad safe? When I'd stayed in like a hermit, convinced someone was outside, waiting to get me? Oh no. *Let's wait until your captor-slash-lover is trying to sneak out of your bedroom. Then, we'll put a cop outside.*

I seriously deserved this level of karma, but I was too flustered to soak up the irony.

Easton risked a glance outside the window. "Probably doing extra patrols now that the news story broke."

I let out a huge sigh of stress. "Maybe we should just go outside together," I said. "If the whole goal is to identify you as the burglar, what difference does it make?"

"It's the difference of you turning from a witness to an accomplice."

"I *am* an accomplice," I said. "I withheld your name from the police."

"We both know that's not how this is going to look," Easton said. "If you come clean about withholding my name, you do it the right way. In an interview with the detective. Not getting caught red-handed, helping a burglar sneak out of your house."

He was right. That would look a thousand times worse in the police's eyes, and it was already pretty bad. I was ashamed of myself for being the type of person that was dodging police right now.

"Besides, the point is to protect you from Brown."

I wanted to argue, but we had no time.

"I'll take you out the back door." I'd have to figure out the rest later. "Come on. We need to be quiet."

Easton threw his clothes on, and I opened my bedroom door, looking across the hall. Thankfully, Dad's bedroom door was still closed.

I put my finger over my lips and motioned for Easton to follow me. Quietly. We walked down the hallway, and just as I entered the common area—the kitchen to my right, dining room table in front, living room to my left—I saw movement.

Too late to do anything about it.

Dad was wheeling himself from the living room toward the kitchen when he stopped abruptly, eyes narrowing as the grenade's pin came out.

*Boom. We're dead.*

*Forget Brown. I'll be murdered by my own father, right after he slaugh-ters Easton.*

"Zoey?" Dad's lips narrowed as he glared at Easton. "Who's this?"

*No worries, Dad. He's just the guy you've been hunting day and night. He broke into our house last night and made sweet, sweet love to me.*

"Uh…" I risked a glance at Easton, who silently implored me to not answer the question. "This is my friend."

And then, because this wasn't awkward enough, Alex stepped out of the living room. As he looked from me to Easton, his eyes narrowed like a protective older brother who'd caught a man banging his little sister.

I hadn't had sex in forever. Of course the first time I do, I have not one, but *two* witnesses to catch me. The worst two.

"Alex"—my voice quivered slightly—"what are you doing here so early?"

Very early. Before Dad even normally got up in the morning.

Alex didn't answer me. He was too busy condemning Easton with his eyes.

Something Easton obviously didn't appreciate, what with the way he was now glaring at Alex and flexing his fingers at his sides.

I needed to get Easton out. Now.

"He was just leaving," I explained and tried to take a step.

But Dad didn't move out of our way.

Just past his shoulder, on the dining room table, was a stack of police reports and photographs of my injuries and whatever the hell else he and Alex had accumulated in their investigation.

I willed Easton's eyes to not look over there because, if he did, I wasn't sure how he'd react.

I tried to pretend like my breathing hadn't become erratic. I tried to look as innocent as possible because while the truth would come out eventually, now was not the time.

"Detective Hernandez called." Dad's gaze hardened. "He wants us to come down to the station."

My mouth ran dry. "Right now?"

"Right now. Was just about to wake you up."

*Holy handbags, that would have been a thousand times more awkward than this already is. If awkward were a bomb, that would be the nuclear one.*

"Why does he want us to come down to the station?" I asked.

Dad glowered at Easton, then looked back at me. "Because he has somebody in custody."

Instantly, I felt dizzy. But I couldn't faint; I couldn't leave the boys unsupervised.

Did the cops lock up Brown? Orange?

"And he wants me to do a lineup?" I clarified.

"He didn't say, but I can only assume so," Dad said.

"Why'd he call you and not me?"

No answer.

Either way, that news story clearly worked. It only took a few hours before $20,000 had motivated someone to turn one of the burglars in.

"Is that why Alex is here?"

"I invited him to come along." Right. Co–armchair detective and all. "Say good-bye to your *friend* and get dressed," Dad demanded. "You're coming with us."

I didn't appreciate the authoritative animosity in his tone—I was a grown woman, and he was staying at my house, not the other way around—but I wasn't about to pick a fight with him right now.

Dad wheeled out of the way, so I could walk Easton to the front door. Which felt like a terrible idea with that cop parked outside, but there was no way to explain taking him to the back door at this point.

"Remember what we discussed," Easton whispered. He gave me a severe gaze, and then he slipped outside and walked down the side-walk with his back to the police cruiser.

While I got ready to face Hernandez and whoever he had in custody.

## 28

It took forty-five minutes to get to the police station. Twenty minutes getting ready, calling off work, and waiting for the wheelchair-accessible van to show up, so my dad could come. Another twenty-five minutes battling rush-hour traffic.

When the van pulled into the parking lot of the police station, I forced myself to focus on the bigger priority—the robbery investigation and the possibility that whoever they had in custody might not be the only one sleeping in a jail cell tonight.

I might be as well, for having lied to the police in an active investigation. No matter what Easton said, I had to take accountability for my mistakes.

I double-checked that my license and credit card hadn't fallen out during the ride—I'd shoved them in my back pocket because I wanted to travel light in case I got arrested. I opened the van door, helped roll Dad up the concrete walkway, and as I turned him around to pull the back wheels of his chair over the slight lip of the doorjamb, a chill crawled up my ribs.

I looked around, trying to identify the source of my internal red flag going up.

This police station—Chicago had several peppered in and around the city—was on the west side, blocks away from the skyscrapers. Here, buildings stood only a few stories tall, and the station sat at an intersection managed with a traffic light. A parking lot wrapped around the building on all sides, and police cruisers lined up like a white-and-blue barricade along the left side of the building while out front, a row of identical buildings nestled across the street with a café a half-block down —likely the source of the coffee smell that floated through the sunny air. A gray pigeon sat on top of a steel pole, where an American flag fluttered against the morning's breeze. Aside from a Boston cream donut twenty feet away that had fallen victim to a tire, nothing seemed out of place.

"Zoey?" Dad's tone became worried.

I didn't realize I had frozen.

"Sorry." I jerked the wheelchair backward while Alex held the door open. And as I glided the wheels over the lip, my eyesight's radar finally hit its target.

Across the street—tucked between two buildings—a man leaned against the exterior wall with his shoulder, his right hand in his jean pocket, his left drawing a cigarette from his mouth.

*He's staring right at me.*

The guy threw his cigarette to the ground and watched me as he stubbed it out, then disappeared behind the building.

If he wanted to watch me, he wouldn't have walked away, though.

*Right?*

Alex must have misconstrued my delay as a lack of upper body strength because his hands replaced mine, pulling the wheelchair backward into the lobby.

Where Hernandez was already waiting for us. Wearing black trousers and a gray button-down, his badge hanging from his belt, he said his hellos, introducing himself to Alex, and motioned for us to follow him down a hallway, up an elevator, down another hallway, and into some sort of conference room.

He gestured for us to sit down.

Alex rolled Dad's legs under the table and let me have the chair directly across from Hernandez.

As the detective leaned back in his seat and pressed his fingers into a steeple, I wondered if he could smell my guilt like a canine could sniff drugs—if it would overpower the scent of stale coffee and bagels. I wondered if he had already pieced everything together and had called me in here to arrest me.

He gave nothing away. Not with his sapphire eyes, not in the way he carried his tall, muscular frame that stretched his wrinkle-free shirt.

"As I explained to Zoey," Hernandez started, "day of the accident, we obtained a partial license plate from the vehicle that struck you, Mr. Williams. And while it didn't help us find the vehicle at the time, we bounced that partial against traffic violations that took place *after* the accident."

I blinked. "This is about my dad's hit-and-run?"

Hernandez looked from me to Dad. "That's why I called your father."

"After that news conference last night, I assumed this was about the robbery," I said.

"So did I," Dad agreed, annoyance ringing through his words.

"I should've been clear when I called. I know this has been a long road, Mr. Williams, looking for justice. I thought you'd want to come in and see the person responsible."

"You have him?" I asked.

"Yes."

"Here?"

"Yes."

"And you're sure he's the one that hit my dad?"

Hernandez rubbed his jaw. "After bringing him in for questioning, the guy confessed."

Finally, something was going right for the first time in forever! For months, I had dreamed of the day that I would walk into this police station and look at the person who had done this to my dad. And finally have justice tip in our favor.

"Can we see him?"

"It would be helpful if Mr. Williams could identify him," Hernandez said.

"I don't really remember what the driver looks like," Dad reminded him. Dad didn't remember much about the accident, courtesy of his concussion.

"It might be a long shot. But sometimes, a witness's memories can get triggered when they see the perpetrator in a lineup. Witness identification would help, just in case he withdraws his confession."

Hernandez spent the next couple of minutes walking my dad through the process and then led us into another room with a large two-way glass. On the other side of it, six men stood beneath the numbers one through six. All of them looked similar. Thin, short, jet-black hair. And young.

Younger than I expected.

Dad was able to see through the glass despite his lower height in the wheelchair. His eyes swept through the men, one by one, and then they landed on man number five. Dad gripped the armrests of his wheelchair tightly.

"Take your time." Hernandez stood next to my father while Alex and I stood in the corner of the room.

"Number five," Dad said. "I can't be sure. But I think it's number five."

Hernandez's lips curled up on one side.

*That's the guy that confessed.*

I stepped closer to the glass and studied the suspect's chubby cheeks and round, childlike eyes.

This whole time, I had no idea what the person looked like who had destroyed my father's life. I didn't know what I expected, but as I stared at the face of the boogeyman that had haunted our lives, he looked nothing like the evil monster I imagined him to be.

"He's just a kid," I said in disbelief.

He couldn't be more than sixteen.

"Texting and driving," Hernandez said. "That's why he didn't slow down. He wasn't paying attention, and once he realized he hit somebody, he panicked."

That was all this was? I never truly believed that what happened to my dad was some diabolical murder for hire or anything, but somehow, this explanation was incredibly empty. Unsatisfying even.

When someone has taken almost everything from you, I guess you expect the explanation behind it to match the size of its damage.

But he was just a kid. A human being who made a horrendous split-second error in judgment.

"What's going to happen to him?" I asked.

"He'll be tried as an adult. Face a jury on multiple felony counts."

"So, he'll go to prison."

"Most likely," Hernandez said.

Why did I feel so hollow inside? This was everything I ever wanted. Finding the person that hurt my dad and putting him behind bars. Here the guy was, wrapped up in a red bow, in the express lane for justice.

I didn't expect to feel this…emptiness, where I thought only celebration would be.

I thought this moment would feel different, but when we left here, nothing would change for my dad. He'd still be in his wheelchair, fighting to regain his mobility, fighting to reclaim his financial independence. Arresting this guy didn't magically give my dad his old life back.

I paused to examine the kid for another moment. "Does intention get taken into account during sentencing?"

Hernandez regarded me. "What do you mean?"

I shrugged. "I don't know. He's just a kid who panicked."

"He almost killed a man and never turned himself in."

True. But who was I to judge him? Look at my behavior. Over the past couple of weeks, I had lied to my dad and Alex. I committed a crime by withholding information from the police, and I protected a wanted criminal. I had my reasons, but if I were friends with someone like me during all this? I would have left her.

Before, I would've judged her actions and cast her out of my life.

But today? After everything that had transpired over the past couple of weeks? Maybe I would have stopped and listened to her before shutting her out. Because, yes, some people were probably inherently bad. Some people made inherently bad decisions with a callous disregard to the trauma they caused others. Like Brown, who'd gladly murder an innocent person to save his own ass. But he was the exception. The rest of us? We were flawed humans.

Maybe that was why I met Easton—to pull me out of my judgmental funk and force me to see people past their missteps.

"You guys are free to go." Hernandez gestured toward the door.

But I couldn't go.

I needed to tell him everything. And come clean about all the mistakes I had made in the process. I didn't want Easton to go to prison, but that was out of my hands. We had all made our mistakes, and we all had to answer for them, just like this kid had to answer for his.

I followed Alex and Dad down the hallway, down the elevator, and to the lobby.

"You guys go ahead." I opened the door for them. "I'm gonna stay and talk to Detective Hernandez."

"About the burglary?" A crease appeared between Dad's eyebrows.

I nodded. "I feel like we should talk after that news story."

"I can stay." Dad's expression softened.

"Me, too," Alex said.

"No," I said. "That's not necessary. I won't be too much longer."

*Unless I wind up in handcuffs.*

Dad pressed his lips together. "You'll come right home when you're done?"

"Right home," I assured.

"You'll get a taxi, not walk alone?"

"No walking."

"Good. Because I have some questions about your *friend.*"

Alex flashed me a look that said, *So do I.*

With one last glance, Alex wheeled Dad down the ramp and into the waiting van. I watched to make sure he got loaded safely, and then when the van drove away, I walked back into the lobby and asked to see Detective Hernandez again.

It didn't take him long to greet me.

"Zoey?" He furrowed his brows. "Everything okay?"

"Can we talk?"

Hernandez looked at his watch. "Is it quick?"

I shook my head.

"I'm running late to a few meetings."

We were supposed to be here twenty minutes earlier, but traffic. Mobility van waiting.

"Why don't we schedule something for tomorrow?"

"It can't wait until tomorrow."

Hernandez hesitated, and then he pulled out his phone, glancing at the screen. "How about six o'clock?"

"Can you do it any sooner?"

He studied me, must've measured the severity of my gaze.

"I can line up another officer if you—"

"No." I picked at my nail. "I prefer to talk to you."

"Is it an emergency? Because I can—"

"No," I assured. It wasn't, was it? It was urgent. But not an emergency. "I just...what's the soonest you can meet?"

Hernandez stared at me, then frowned at his phone. "I can move some things around and make four o'clock work. Can you come back then?"

It wasn't even seven thirty in the morning. I guess that would give me a few hours to talk things out with Easton and say our good-byes.

"Four o'clock," I agreed.

I turned to walk out the door.

"Wait." Hernandez's tone had a sense of worried urgency to it.

I pivoted and looked at him.

He sighed. And motioned for me to follow him.

## 29

The interrogation room was dark, save for one light centered above a rectangle table, with two metal chairs on opposing sides. The mossy-green walls showcased no artwork—only two mirrors on each side of the room, undoubtedly two-way glass, and a door occupying the third wall. The space, which smelled like stale coffee, was eerily quiet, tucked in the back of the hallway so the person left here would be alone with their thoughts.

I rubbed my hands along the outsides of my arms, willing the goose bumps to die down as Hernandez stared at me with those knowing eyes, like he could see past all my lies.

"I'd like to make a deal." I folded my hands, trying to look confident.

He leaned back. Held a pen between his fingers. "Have you done something wrong?"

"Yes. But the deal isn't for me. I have some important information about the burglary that can lead to the identities of the burglars you're looking for. Before we get started, I need some assurances."

Hernandez kept his eyes guarded. "Assurances." He folded his hands together and placed them on the table, his eyes revealing nothing about his mood. "What kind of assurances?"

I swallowed and tried to muster the confidence of someone capable of striking a deal.

"I know the name of one of the burglars."

Hernandez held perfectly still for several seconds, as if he knew my heartbeat needed time to come back down. "How do you know the name of one of the burglars?"

"I'll explain all of that, but before I say anything, I need a pledge that he won't be charged."

Hernandez kept his face completely neutral. "You want one of the burglars to get immunity?"

I nodded.

Hernandez leaned back in his chair and steepled his fingers together, staring at me for several seconds. "You know the name of one of the people that robbed your father's condo. Held you hostage. And you want to protect that person," he clarified.

I nodded.

"Why?"

"Like I said, I'll get into that, but first…"

"*When* did you uncover the guy's name?" Hernandez asked sharply.

"I'll explain all of that, but I need to know—"

"Zoey, were you involved in the burglary?"

I blanched. "What? No."

"Then, do you care to explain to me why you withheld the name of a wanted criminal who supposedly held you hostage?"

*Shit.*

"He saved my life. If I give you his name without assurances, he'll go to jail, probably forever, for doing the right thing. I can't sentence him to that."

"That's not how this works. This is an active criminal investigation, and you're required to be transparent about the facts of the case."

I couldn't rat on Easton, not without protecting him. No matter what Easton said, it didn't feel right. I needed to take responsibility for my mistakes, but I couldn't look at myself in the mirror if I took down the one person who'd saved my life in the process.

"Zoey…" Hernandez cleared his throat. I sensed him swallowing down his frustration as he kept his voice low and steady. "If you have knowledge of someone who has committed a crime and withhold that information with intent to help that person avoid arrest or punishment, you can be charged with accessory after the fact. Meaning you could face charges related to that robbery, maybe even the other string of robberies that took place after, if they prove they're connected. You have to tell me his name."

I opened my mouth, but words failed me. I should've thought through this better. We had come here in such a rush, and it just felt like everything was spiraling out of control.

"Did you lie to me, Zoey?" Hernandez pressed his fingers together tighter. "When I asked you if you had any other information that could help with the robbery, were you withholding something?"

I bit my lip. And nodded.

"Lying to a police officer during an ongoing investigation is a crime. You could be charged with obstruction of justice."

"I'm sorry."

Hernandez ran a hand through his hair. "Why did you protect him?"

"He saved my life. I told you everything I knew about the other two men, I swear. I just didn't tell you the name and description of the man who saved my life. He risked his own to do it, and I guess I was scared that in the eyes of the law, he'd be treated equal to the other two. It didn't seem fair."

"That wasn't your place to sort out. I specifically asked you if there was anything else you knew."

"I know."

"And you lied."

"I'm sorry. But I want to state for the record that he risked his own life to save mine."

Hernandez frowned.

"Look, my goal of coming here today was to give you his name. So, I'm not intending to help him avoid arrest. I just don't think he should be treated like the other two burglars who beat me and intended to kill me."

"What's his name?"

How could something so right feel so wrong? No matter what Easton said, this felt like betraying him.

"Easton," I said. "I just know his first name is Easton."

I guess it would have been too suspicious for Easton to tell me his last name.

Hernandez scrutinized me. "You had nothing to do with the robbery?"

"I would never do that. And I would never put myself in a position where I might get killed. My dad needs me."

I couldn't tell if Hernandez believed me or not, but all the fight inside of me evaporated.

In hindsight, this whole time, I'd been trying to control the outcome of everything. Control the outcome for Easton, for me, for Dad. But I had let things spin out of control, and now, whatever happened was completely out of my hands.

"Are you going to arrest me?" I deserved it.

Hernandez scrubbed his hands over his face and let out a huge breath. When he looked at me, his chest inflated, and I got the sense that he believed me.

"Do you know how many man hours we've spent on this case?"

I hadn't thought about that, all that time and money.

"I wasn't sure only a first name would help." I lowered my head and stared at my hands. "But I was probably just trying to rationalize away my bad decision."

Hernandez rubbed his fingers along his upper lip, tugged his ear, and then straightened his chair.

"Are you going to arrest me?"

He cleared his throat, looking as though part of him really *wanted* to put me in cuffs. Maybe all of him did, actually. "Unfortunately, it's not uncommon for victims to be less than forthcoming after suffering a traumatic ordeal. Arresting victims anytime they aren't entirely forthcoming would widely reduce the rate at which they report. And that rate is already damn low."

I twisted my hands together.

"Don't pull that crap again, Zoey," Hernandez said. "This Easton guy might've saved your life, but he's a dangerous criminal."

"He's the only person that can give the names of the other burglars."

Based on the hardening of his eyes, this seriously seemed to annoy Hernandez.

"I can't speak to what the prosecution might be willing to do for him."

I bounced my leg under the table, feeling like I'd failed Easton. I'd screwed this up, giving up his name without a written agreement stating that he wouldn't be charged. And while I trusted Hernandez would try, there was no assurance he'd protect Easton at all.

"You know any other details that could lead me to the names of the other burglars?"

"One of them is Easton's brother." I hoped Easton was okay that I'd said that.

A pause.

"Anything else?"

I shook my head, feeling like a child in a principal's office, who'd been caught cheating.

Hernandez stared at me. "He's dangerous, Zoey."

My cheeks warmed.

The detective stood up so slowly, he almost made a show of it. "You're free to leave."

I blinked. "I am?"

"Like I said, don't pull that crap again."

I wanted to ask him how long it would be before he might have Easton in cuffs. But I seriously didn't want to piss him off further.

What I wanted to do was talk to Easton one last time. Because I had some things to say to him that I might never get the chance to again. Not without being able to hug him after, at least. From this day forward, we might be separated by bars or plexiglass.

I needed to find him.

Fast.

## 30

Hernandez escorted me through the lobby and out the front door of the police station. It was there, as Hernandez was about to walk away, that ice prickled the back of my neck and flashed down my spine. I looked across the street, searching for the source of my sudden unease, and spotted a man.

*That's the same guy who was staring at me earlier.*

His grim gaze fastened onto me, and then he shook his head. Like I'd just made a lethal mistake.

"That guy"—I pointed—"I saw him out here earlier."

But the guy was crazy fast; he dipped behind the building before Hernandez's eyes drifted across the street.

"Where?" Hernandez asked.

"He was just there." I pointed again. "I saw him before I came into the police station, and I just saw him again. I think he's following me."

"Did you recognize him?"

"No. But he was staring right at me with this...*look*. Like I just made a mistake, coming to the police station."

Hernandez squinted, scanning across the street for any indication of a person. Then, he hollered, "Deputy."

A thin police officer with a mustache diverted his original path to the front door to join us.

"I need you to take Ms. Williams home."

"Sure." The officer's tone was like a student wanting approval from a teacher.

"I'll be right back," Hernandez said.

I followed the deputy as he led me to his car, but my eyes stayed fixed on Hernandez as he jogged across the street and looked around.

I sat down in the passenger seat of the cruiser, and as the police officer started the engine, Hernandez jogged back over and leaned into the now-open window.

"Whoever it was is gone."

"What if he follows me home?"

Hernandez shifted his gaze to the officer. "Keep your eyes open. If you see anything suspicious, bring her back here."

The officer nodded.

With nerves twisting my stomach into knots, I watched Hernandez grow smaller as the cruiser pulled away. With no further sign of the mysterious guy.

I looked at the cruiser's dashboard with its computer screen and keyboard positioned directly below it. Right now, the screen illuminated a digital map, but with the click of a button, it would undoubtedly have access to names and addresses and all sorts of information. So much information and so much power, harnessed in this mobile vehicle, and yet the people that you really wanted to find felt like they could hide from that screen.

"Do you think it's safe for me to go home?" I asked the officer.

"If I know Hernandez, he'll send officers to perform a more thorough sweep. If someone's out there, they'll find him."

I wished I shared the same confidence that the officer did, but any fragment of hope that the bad guys were not actively hunting me just went up in flames. It felt like it was just a matter of time before they unearthed my identity, my location, or both.

In the race between the bad guys and the good guys, I could feel the hourglass's sand draining faster and faster to the bottom with no clarity on who would win.

I had no clue how any of this would unfold, and worse, it felt like there was nothing more I could do to influence the outcome. I had laid all the cards on the table for the police, and now, all I could do was wait.

It was overwhelming. And beneath my nervousness and my fear was guilt. Guilt for lying to Dad about Easton. Guilt for all the things that came before that—most notably, the massive fight Dad and I had gotten into the day of the accident.

The guilt over what I'd said to him had been lurking in the shadows of my heart ever since, veiled behind judgment and criticism of others, infecting my body like a cancerous growth. And now, my time to apologize might be running out.

Time was running out even faster to talk to Easton. Any second, he'd get arrested and locked in some jail cell, possibly forever.

I worried he might give up mentally—what hope did he have, facing decades in prison?—and without his physical freedom, his mind and heart were all he'd have in his hollow concrete cell. In the decades he'd spend there, he might sink deeper into the abyss of self-hatred. Easton saw himself as a villain, doing nothing but bad things in this world. A cancer to our society that I, and everyone, would be better off without. And without hope of ever breaking free physically, without seeing anything good about himself, he might eventually lose the desire to keep himself safe from other violent prisoners. Because he'd think he deserved whatever came to him.

But he needed to know that he'd done a tremendous amount of good in my life, that he was my prince, rescuing me from my own demons. And that he wasn't a monster; he was a beautiful human being.

And he needed to hear it now; otherwise, he might think I was just trying to cheer him up when the undercurrent of depression dragged him down in prison. This would be the last time I could get through to him.

As the police officer silently pulled onto another road, methodically scanning the side and rearview mirrors for any sign of trouble, I pulled out my cell phone and texted Easton.

**Me: Where are you?**

His response was immediate. Thank goodness. That meant he probably wasn't in custody yet.

**Easton: At home. Making it easy for the cops to find me and arrest me. The sooner the cops get me, the sooner I can give them Brown's name, and the sooner he's behind bars. Are you okay?**

**Me: No. I need to talk to you before that happens. And now, I'm not even sure you sacrificing yourself will help to protect me.**

**Easton: What are you talking about?**

**Me: There was this creepy guy staring at me. I can only assume he's part of Brown's crew, and if I'm right, he probably thinks I just gave some important information to the cops.**

**Easton: Where was he? What did he look like?**

**Me: He was standing across the street from the police station.**

**Easton: Fuck. Brown must've assigned a detail to watch the station. Are you still there?**

**Me: No. A police officer is escorting me home, making sure we're not being followed.**

**Easton: When you get there, lock all the doors and windows. I'm going to head to the station and look for him.**

*What?*

**Me: No! He could be dangerous. And the police are canvassing that area right now, looking for the guy. If you go there, they'll arrest you right now, and I need to talk to you before that happens. Can we meet?**

Easton didn't text back for five seconds.

**Easton: Lock the doors. Stay inside. Do NOT open the door until I'm on the other side of it. I'm coming right over.**

## 31

The officer walked me to the door and waited to leave until I'd gone inside and locked up.

I double-checked all the window and door locks and drew the blinds closed. Just to be safe.

*I'm sure that guy didn't follow me here.*

The officer had kept his guard up. Looked around. Hernandez had probably found him already, had him at the station.

Still, I rubbed my arms, praying these walls wouldn't become my and Dad's tomb.

"We need to talk." Dad appeared out of his bedroom.

"Dad, I know you have a lot of questions about the guy staying over—"

"I did." Dad wheeled himself into the living room and folded his pale, bony hands onto his lap. "I was going to give you the third degree over that guy, but then I reminded myself about something."

Dad's expression was firm—tight lips, resolute eyes.

"It's none of my business. You're a young woman, Zoey, in the prime of your life. And you shouldn't have to worry about your dad intruding on your personal business."

Why did this feel like something deeper than letting me off the hook with an explanation about Easton? It was in his eyes, I thought, in the way Dad stared at me, alerting me that he was about to say something important.

"I called your mother." Dad brushed nonexistent wrinkles out of his pants. "She's going to make up the couch for me."

"What? Why?" And why now?

"I should never have stayed as long as I did. It was selfish of me."

"It's not selfish. You were in a horrible accident and need help."

"But I should never have put you in the position of being the person to help me. Candidly, a lot of these decisions were made when I was still in extensive pain. Maybe if I hadn't been, I wouldn't have burdened you with this. But if I'm being honest with myself, I think the reason I let you take me in was because I wanted to reconcile with you. All that time we'd spent apart had broken me, and the opportunity to be with you? Every day? Was something I didn't have the strength to turn down."

My eyes stung so badly; Dad's face blurred with my tears.

"But you and Mom are divorced. She shouldn't—"

"We might be divorced, but we both agree on one thing—the priority right now is giving you your life back. Your mother wants to take me in because it will help you. I don't like the thought of leaving you right now because I want to protect you, but being wheelchair-bound makes me more of a liability than a help."

"Dad, I swear I did not mean to make you feel like a burden. I'm sorry." I wiped a tear from my cheek.

"Zoey, you've gone far above and beyond anything that I deserved, ensuring I made all of my doctor's appointments, arranging physical therapy, working with bill collectors and the bankruptcy attorneys. You're a young woman; you shouldn't have to deal with any of this."

I wiped the stream of tears from my face.

"But I've seen the toll it's taking on you. I know the reason you went to the house that night was to get a ring. To pay bills that you can't afford."

I looked down, ashamed I hadn't been able to keep that secret from him. "How did you find out?"

"I know which drawer you hide the bills in. And I know how expensive health care is. It wasn't hard to piece together." Dad's voice sounded like it was being stabbed in self-loathing. "That burglary, the reason you were there, was like shining a big spotlight on the damage I'm causing to your life. And it's all I've been able to think about since."

"Dad, it wasn't your fault."

"It's time that I move out. It'll take a couple weeks, and I'll want to work with police to tighten up the locks of this place, put a game plan together to keep you safe, but it's time for me to go." Dad squared his shoulders, resolute in his decision. "This is something that I should've done a long time ago."

I knew he was trying to be noble, but it didn't lessen the throbbing from his blade.

"So, that's it?" My lips trembled. "You're just going to leave me? *Again?*"

He sighed. Wiped his face with his palm. "Zoey, it's long overdue for us to discuss what I did to you in college."

"I'm not just talking about that." I stepped closer. "On Thanksgiving, you almost left me forever."

Before he got hit by the car, I took for granted that my dad was there and that whenever I was finally ready to reconcile with him, I'd have that chance.

But with the squealing of tires and a thump that had since haunted my dreams, I was nearly robbed of that opportunity. And then it turned into life-saving measures, conversations with the ICU team, working to get him healthy enough for a regular room, then rehab, then home, then medical bills and paperwork and finances, and now, here we were.

Having never worked through our pain.

"On Thanksgiving, you almost left me again. Forever," I repeated. My eyes burned, and tears cascaded down my cheeks. "If you had died, we wouldn't have had the chance to fix things. I'd have been so angry; there would have been no way to move past that. I would have hated you forever for taking that chance from me! I would have hated myself!"

Dad's shoulders shrank three inches, and his eyes shimmered, heartbreaking understanding washing over him. He tugged my arm and pulled me onto his lap.

"I don't want to hurt you," I whispered, realizing I meant more than just the weight of my body on his frail legs.

"And I never meant to hurt *you*, Zoey."

He held me for a minute as I cried on his shoulder. I could feel him crying, too, with the jerking of his chest and the sound of his sniffles.

"I have something I need to say to you," Dad said.

I lifted my head up, and Dad motioned with his hand toward the couch. Whatever it was, it must be too long for me to continue cutting off the blood supply to his legs.

I looked at the front door, wondering how long I had before Easton would show up. I wanted to come clean with Dad about Easton, about my lies, about it all, and I wanted to give Dad the time he needed to get whatever he was about to say off his chest.

I walked over, took a seat, and watched Dad position himself in front of me.

Taking several seconds before finally speaking.

"We never had that talk when you were at college." Dad folded his hands together. "The day I told you I'd left your mother."

My scalp prickled, and my stomach grew queasy. I could tell by looking into Dad's chocolate eyes that he was about to finally unveil all his ugly truths as to why my family had unraveled.

The old me would never sit here and willingly listen to explanations, would write them off as nothing more than excuses. But Easton had shown me I should listen to people fully, to hear everything Dad was about to say to me.

Even though it was long overdue, I wasn't sure I was strong enough to hear it, though. It was like having a deep, festering wound, and the doctor informs you he needs to open it and scrape it out. You know the pain will be unimaginable, but you also know you can't heal if he doesn't do it. You dread the experience in front of you.

Plus, hearing him out, in a strange way, scared me because once we broke the last shackles of resentment, once I allowed him back into my heart fully, I'd have even more to lose if something ever happened to him.

Six feet separated our bodies, yet the space between our hearts was the length of a football field. My heart, at least. I twisted my hands on my lap—a gesture that did not go unnoticed by my father, who looked at my fingers and then looked up at my face.

"I've been thinking a lot about what you said the other day." Dad folded his hands in his lap. "I should've had this conversation with you a long time ago. But the truth is, the more time that passed, the angrier you were, and the harder it became for me to get the courage to talk to you."

He scratched his jaw.

"I suppose the first place to start is back before I left your mother. There's something that we kept from you kids because we didn't want to worry you. I'd had a bit of a"—Dad stretched his fingers—"medical scare. I'll spare you the graphic details, but I'll just say, many men of a certain age have uncomfortable preventative exams, and sometimes, those exams uncover things that need to be looked at closer. The doctor that had done the procedure sent the samples off for testing, but he warned me that based on the appearance and his experience, it was most likely cancer."

My breathing quickened.

"It took about three weeks for the test results to return. Three weeks of staring down the barrel of a terminal illness, you can't help but take a step back and examine your life. I had this remarkable family and comfortable home."

I stared at his lips, eager for his next words.

"But I also saw all the unfulfilled dreams I'd had for my life. When I was a kid, we struggled financially. I had this dream to build a high-end executive career with the financial windfall that came with it. The beautiful condo in downtown Chicago, luxury cars, charity function invitations. But most of all, I vowed to create a new family legacy. When I was a kid, it felt like everyone was running a race in the game of life, and for some of us, the starting line was a lot further back than others. I wanted to set you and your brother up with a starting line that was much more advanced than mine so that you and your kids would have a better head start than I did."

I didn't know his career aspirations stemmed from that.

"Then, I met your mom. And I fell madly in love, and I became what a lot of people become. A father, a husband, and I never pursued my dream because it came with a price tag of long hours and relocations—things that didn't fit in with our family. I don't regret it," he clarified. "But when that doctor told me that I might be dying, instead of focusing on everything that I *did* accomplish, I became fixated on what I *hadn't* accomplished for my family."

Dad leaned his head back and looked up at the ceiling. "For three weeks, this was all I could think about, and then I got the news—it was a false alarm. The lab tests confirmed there was no cancer. And I felt like I had been given a second chance. This cancer scare was a wake-up call that life was short and I needed to go after these dreams. That's when I started buckling down and getting much more serious about my career and the dream for my family that I'd pushed aside."

I remembered Dad working longer hours. I remembered him starting to miss family functions. In hindsight, they were the first cracks in the facade of our perfect family.

"Your mom was understanding at first, but at the time, I don't think I understood that going after my dreams meant changing hers. She was completely fulfilled with her family and had no desire for it to change."

Mom had been so happy back then. I missed the way her smile used to reach her eyes.

"So, when I started to work longer hours, reaching for my aspirations, it started to cause friction between us. She said this was nothing more than a midlife crisis that would pass, and I thought she was trying to hold me back from building the life that I really wanted. She thought I was being selfish and putting my career ahead of our family.

I thought she was being naive, not understanding that I was doing this for our family."

I'd always wondered what happened between Mom and Dad before he left us; it wasn't something I dared to ask Mom, and Anthony and I could never figure it out, no matter how hard we tried to speculate. Hearing about the start of their problems was surprising in a way. Because it was so…understandable.

"You can see the back-and-forth snowball that began as a result of all of this," Dad continued. "Your mom and I became distant, emotionally separated, even though around you guys, we made it seem like we weren't."

They did a good job; I had no idea.

"I think if we had worked at it," Dad said, "maybe gone to counseling, we might've been okay, but I don't think either of us realized just how big the crack between us had grown."

This was hard to hear because maybe there was a chance our family's destruction could have been avoided if we'd seen the signs the same way that doctors saw red flags for cancer.

Dad stared at his hands, locking his fingers together. "It was around that time that Holly started in our office. And a friendship started. She was encouraging of my career, encouraging of all my dreams."

And yet, she didn't care about him giving up his biggest dream of all—his happy family.

"As time went on, subconsciously, I felt Holly had become the supportive good guy and your mom had become the unsupportive bad guy, who was trying to hold me back."

What a perfect role for Holly to play. The encouraging "friend."

Dad scrubbed his face. "When I got a promotion, Holly came in with a gift bag, a thoughtful card, and a congratulations. Your mother crossed her arms over her chest and asked how many more hours this would mean in the office."

Of course Mom would feel like that. She'd gotten her happily ever after, and he was changing that. Maybe she even sensed something was going on at the office.

"Things just escalated from there. Our marriage fell apart, and I fell into the arms of Holly."

I tightened my stomach muscles to fend off the ache. I understood better what had happened behind the scenes. I did, but it still hurt, hearing about when he'd left us all.

"You and Anthony were out of the house by that time, so I told myself what was happening was just between me and your mother. Clearly, I underestimated how this would make you and your brother feel, walking out on your mom. I wasn't just walking out on her. I just didn't realize that until a couple years later. I think that's one of the reasons I didn't come visit you in college that weekend. If I'm being honest, when I called you on the phone and heard how hurt you were, I was nervous to see you face-to-face."

"You should have made more of an effort," I said.

He rubbed his forehead. "I know. I kept telling myself to give you just a few more days to cool down because you and I couldn't seem to get through a phone call without—"

"Fighting," I said.

And we couldn't stop fighting long enough to have a meaningful conversation.

As much as I blamed him for leaving and as much as I still believed he should have tried harder, I couldn't discount how hard I'd made it for him to talk to me back then.

Dad shook his head. "There's no excuse for my not coming. You deserved better. Your mom deserved better, too."

The tentacles of resentment began to unwind in my ribs.

When someone has hurt you deeply, having them acknowledge that hurt and acknowledge that you deserved better is incredibly healing.

"It took a while before I realized Holly wasn't the ride-or-die wife I thought she'd be. Holly chose to stay at home to free me up, so I could focus on my career. So, she took care of everything—cooking, shopping, errands. Even our finances. I was relieved to have the help, so I could focus on my career goals without distractions."

Dad rubbed the side of his face. "At first, it was incredible. She'd have a hot dinner waiting for me every night, kept the fridge stocked with my favorite foods. Took care of the administrative part of paying all our bills. It wasn't until years later that I discovered she was terrible with money. I would have noticed a lot sooner if I hadn't handed everything over to her with no oversight, but I'd been too blindly trusting."

Now, I felt guilty for how many times in those early days I'd hoped Dad's relationship with Holly would combust. Because hearing the beginning of its end made me realize that Dad was someone looking for happiness.

Like we all do.

Even if he looked for it in the wrong person.

Like many of us do.

"Holly spent money faster than it came in, and by the time I figured it out, my savings was gone. And that wasn't the worst of it. Those student loans were supposed to be paid off in full from my bonuses. But when Holly got control of the bills, it turns out, she didn't pay them off. Worse, she dug us in such a bad financial hole that she stopped making payments on them altogether. She's the one that sent you an email from my account about not paying for senior year. I didn't find out until shortly before that Thanksgiving when…well, you know."

He didn't cut off my college money? She did? He didn't even know?

"This was the last straw. I already knew I'd made a mistake, being with her, but I could no longer allow Holly to destroy more of my life. We had a huge fight about it. She claimed it was her poor financial skills that got us into that mess, but I started to wonder if there was more to it. She'd always been insecure about my relationship with you kids. In particular with you since you and I were struggling."

He scratched his cheek. "I wondered if she'd intentionally not paid that bill. And hidden it from me to drive a wedge between us. Finding out she'd sent that email to you made it pretty damn clear she didn't care about my relationship with you."

And that she'd stolen my college money. And if she was capable of doing that, she was certainly capable of stealing from Dad's condo.

He shook his head. "I held on to that relationship longer than I should have because if we didn't work out, I felt like I'd blown up our family for nothing."

I clenched my eyes shut for a moment, so tears wouldn't spill, at the thought of Dad forcing himself to stay with someone who made him miserable.

"I'd made a huge mistake in marrying Holly," Dad whispered. The tone of his voice made a rope twist around the inside of my rib cage. "I'd taken my family for granted, hurt my relationships with my children, I had broken your mom's heart, and I was ashamed of myself."

Dad played with the bare spot on his ring finger, where his wedding band once sat. "All I wanted was my family back, in whatever capacity you guys would allow. I didn't deserve you. But I was prepared to do whatever it took to make amends. That's why I begged Anthony to bring you to Thanksgiving. I wanted to apologize for it all and finally beg for your forgiveness."

Dad stopped fiddling with his finger and rested his hands on his chair's wheels. "Humans are capable of making mistakes," he said. "Enormous ones. But it's not because they're evil. Sometimes, we just...don't make good decisions."

My heart immediately thought of Easton.

"Mistakes can become learning moments, though. They can remind us of who we are and inspire us to be a better person."

Dad rolled his wheelchair forward, closer to me. "How I treated you was unacceptable. I was your father. Nothing and no one should have come between me and my daughter, and I allowed my panic over a health scare to cloud my judgment. I convinced myself I was doing this for a greater good, but I wasn't. All I was doing was neglecting the family that had loved me and supported me."

He looked down for a moment. "After the accident, it was weeks before I was well enough to have the conversation with you I needed to have, and by then, you were taking care of me, and I didn't want you to think I was only apologizing because you were helping me. I needed you to know it was sincere.

"I'm sorry it took me this long to apologize to you, Zoey. I don't expect you to forgive me. But you deserve an apology. I swear to you, throughout all of this, I never stopped loving you, not even a little. I love you more than you can imagine."

I reached out and hugged my dad, putting my chin atop his bony shoulder as I cried. His chest shook just as intensely as mine as we mourned the loss of the life we could have had together.

I now realized why I had been so nervous about hearing his explanation. Hating the version of Dad that made his bad decisions was easier, keeping that part of our relationship black and white. In that version of Dad, he was the villain, and all my nasty behavior that followed—the years of treating him with disdain and disgust—wasn't just understandable; it was justifiable. Because he *deserved* it.

But if Dad explained his actions in a way that made me understand, it wouldn't be black and white anymore. It would be gray, and that would mean all my awful, hurtful behavior wasn't defensible at all. The moment I'd accepted that as reality, I'd feel every ounce of pain I'd inflicted on him, and that hurt would be a hundred times worse than any pain anyone could ever cause me.

This whole time, I thought I needed to forgive my father. But the real person I needed to forgive was myself. No matter what he did, no matter how hurt I might have been, I had a choice in how I treated him, and I was the one that had turned into the awful person. I was the one that threw the ring in his face and said things I could never take back.

"I forgive you, Dad." I wept. "But I'm the one who should be asking for *your* forgiveness. I'm really, really sorry for what I said to you that day…"

Those words were forever lodged in my heart.

I could still picture the door flinging open as I ran through it.

· · ·

"ZOEY, WAIT! IT'S NOT WHAT YOU THINK!" HIGH-PITCHED PANIC PIERCES Dad's voice.

But I don't listen. If I'd wanted to talk to him, I wouldn't have thrown that damn ring in his face and stormed out of his condo's building and into the city's congestion.

He made his choices. He gave her that ring when it was supposedly some heartfelt gift for his only daughter. A special gift, the last Christmas before I left for college. How dare he rob me of that memory, too!

No, not just a memory. A version of my father that wasn't real. The version that made me feel special and wanted, like I mattered. He had no right to become the selfish, lying, cheating scumbag that he is.

"Zoey!"

"Leave me the hell alone!"

"Zoey, do not walk away from me!"

I turn around, so I can look at his face, so he can for sure hear what the hell I'm about to say. "You don't care at all about me!"

"That's not true."

"Six years!" I shouted. "You've had six years to make things right, and now that your life is perfect, now that the life you left us for is satisfactory, now, you make time for me by inviting me to Thanksgiving? Fuck off! I'll make this really easy for you. You don't have to make time for me because I will never make time for you again."

"I know you're angry."

"Angry? No. I'm not angry." I sweep my arms up. "I don't care anymore, Dad. I give up on you. I give up on wanting you to be the man I thought you were because you're not. You're a pathetic asshole excuse of a father who chose another woman over his family. Don't bother inviting me to anything else because I won't show up. I won't even come to your funeral."

In that instant, I know I don't mean what I said. I know what I said is the worst, most hurtful thing you can say to someone, let alone your own father. The man who gave you life. The man you should respect. But my pain didn't care about any of that. It had been bottled up, poisoning me from the inside out until it finally exploded.

I guess sometimes, when people are hurting, they can say terrible things that they don't mean.

*The difference? Most of us get the chance to apologize and take it back.*

*But when I run through a crosswalk and hear the awful thump behind me, I turn to see my father lying on the ground, bleeding.*

*Our chance to make amends hemorrhaging.*

*I scream and run to his side, looking into my father's terrified eyes.*

*I'm about to say,* I'm sorry. I didn't mean it. I love you.

*But his eyes close before I can utter a syllable.*

*A thin trail of crimson streams away from his head and pools into the uneven asphalt, like it's forging its own creek, while a screech of tires slices through the gathering crowd of voices.*

*"Dad," I cry. "Don't leave me yet."* Not until I can apologize. Not until we've made up. I can't spend the rest of my life having this fight be the last thing we ever have together. *"Please," I beg. "Please don't leave me."*

*And I sit there, sobbing, wishing I could take it all back. Wishing I had another chance with him.*

"I'm so sorry, Dad. For the way I treated you and the awful things I said to you that day."

"I forgave you the second those words left your mouth." Dad tried to hide the quivering of his chin.

"I've always felt the accident was my fault," I whispered.

Dad's brows furrowed in shock. "It was never your fault."

If only that were true.

His eyes glistened. "I've always felt like I deserved to be hit."

His confession made my breath catch, my throat swelling.

"That's why you never pushed harder to find the driver," I realized.

Because he felt the man responsible for it all was sitting in a wheelchair in this townhouse.

"You never deserved it, Dad."

When he rubbed the side of his face, I couldn't tell if he agreed with me or not.

"There's one more thing I want you to know," he said.

I waited.

"The ring was special, Zoey. I never gave it to Holly."

I felt the air still in my lungs.

"She saw the ring in a picture of you one time. Told me she wanted one, and I explained that it was a special gift from me to you. Which seemed to only make her want it more. When she pressed me on it three more times, I got angry and made it clear there was only one person in my life who would wear that ring. And that person was you."

Dad bit his lip angrily. "That was the first time I saw how nasty she could be. You would think that anyone who had seen the love a man had for his daughter would be viewed as a good thing, but she took it as a threat. To her existence maybe? Her position in my life? I'm not quite sure, but it was the first time I actually saw her true colors come out, and I started to question if she was the person I thought she was."

It was sad that so much damage had been done to his family by then.

"At Thanksgiving, when you showed up," Dad said, "you saw that ring at the same time I did; Holly must have gone to the jeweler and bought it herself."

My jaw went slack.

"By that point, to say our marriage was on the rocks was an understatement, so I can't help but wonder if she thought causing a huge fight between me and you would send me running back into her arms." Dad pinched the bridge of his nose. "Who knows, but her buying that ring? I can't imagine a more self-centered, narcissistic thing to do."

That was why Dad looked shocked when he saw the ring; that was why he kept begging me to let him explain as he ran after me that day. All the way out of his apartment and into the crosswalk.

If I'd listened to him, he'd never have been in that intersection, too focused on me to spot the car coming.

I hugged my father's brittle shoulders as we both cried our shared guilt for that fateful day. It felt good to cry it out, a river of tears cleansing our past and washing a path to our future.

I was grateful for the fresh start that we now had. I felt like I had grown internally more in the past few weeks than the last several years combined. I wanted to tell him that I truly did not want him to move out, that I wanted to take care of him for as long as he needed. And I needed to tell him about Easton, his role in the robbery, before he got arrested. But before I could start, a knock came at the front door.

I reluctantly let go of my father—savoring one last look we shared between us—and ambled toward the front door, emotionally shell-shocked from what I had just gone through. And yet, I knew I had another deep conversation ahead of me with Easton.

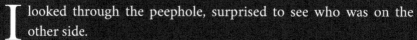

32

I looked through the peephole, surprised to see who was on the other side.

"It's Alex," I said.

"He ran out to get us bagels and coffee," Dad said.

Alex had accompanied us to the police station, but…

"Doesn't he have to get to work?"

I grabbed the latch of the door lock and hesitated. Easton said not to open the door for *anyone* but him, and for reasons I couldn't pinpoint, having Alex here didn't provide the comfort I expected.

"Zoey, open the door."

"I don't know if that's such a good idea to let *anyone* in." Except Easton. How would I explain that?

Dad pulled his head back. "You don't trust Alex all of a sudden?"

"I…I just…"

"Alex has been a family friend for years, Zoey. He's just trying to help."

I pulled my lips between my teeth and shut my eyes as my fingers clenched the silver lock, the two-inch piece of metal that protected us. And then I flipped it and opened the door.

Alex gave me a crooked smile and walked inside, carrying breakfast into the dining room, where Dad and his empty stomach followed.

A few seconds later, another knock at the front door, this time Easton.

I opened the door long enough for Easton to slip inside.

Easton's eyes were wide with worry, his rough palms brushing my upper arms as he studied my eyes and asked the question that had clearly haunted him the entire drive over. "Are you okay?"

"I'm fine."

"What did—" Easton stopped when he realized we weren't alone.

Dad abandoned his bagel in favor of wheeling over and staring at Easton. He was trying to hide the glower, but I could see it in Dad's eyes; I might be a grown woman, but this was still a guy who'd slept with his daughter.

"Sir." Easton nodded a hello to my father and quickly returned his attention to me, a silent question pulsing through his eyes. *Does he know?*

I shook my head.

"Can I steal you for a minute?" Easton asked, nodding his chin toward the front door.

I was surprised he'd want to step outside, but when he turned slightly, I noticed a subtle line sticking out of his waistband. I wanted to hurry and tell Dad who Easton was before he got arrested, but I didn't want to do it with Easton here. I didn't know what Dad might be capable of with all his pent-up anger toward my captors.

After a brief pause, I followed Easton toward the door, feeling awful for, once again, delaying coming clean with my father. And also feeling awful for leaving my dad's side, however briefly, when there might be some stalker out there somewhere.

"Will you stay with my dad until I come back?" I asked Alex. "Make sure the doors are locked."

Alex thinned his lips. "Sure, Zoey."

I didn't have time to deal with his big-brother-like disapproval— no man would ever be good enough for me in Alex's eyes and certainly not one who spent the night before even meeting my dad.

"Thank you." I offered a weak smile and waited until I heard the front door lock behind me before following Easton across the street and into the black BMW.

The inside was pristine, like it had just been driven off the car dealership's lot. The white-and-blue BMW logo shining in the center of the steering wheel, cream-colored leather seats, digital screen so crisp that I wondered if it was 4K, a shiny gearshift, and what looked to be a high-end speaker system. It still had the new-car smell.

"Please tell me this car isn't stolen."

Easton furrowed his brows. And smirked. "No. It's not stolen. But the funds used to acquire it weren't from legal sources."

I frowned.

"I need to talk to you about something." I picked at my nail.

"You can talk on the way."

"On the way to where? I thought we were just going to sit in here and talk?"

"Put your seat belt on," he demanded.

"What?"

Easton started the engine and pulled out into traffic. He darted in and out of cars, and when a green light turned yellow, he gunned it, blazing through the intersection, narrowly escaping getting clipped.

"Seat belt. On," he repeated.

"What are you doing?" I gripped the edge of my seat tightly.

Without taking his eyes off the road, Easton reached all the way across my shoulders, yanked the belt down, and poked around until it clicked into place.

"You said he was standing across the street?"

I blinked. "You're going to the police station?"

Easton snapped his eyes to me. "Some guy was stalking you, and you think I'm not going to find out who it was?"

"There's no way the guy would've stuck around. The cop told me Hernandez was probably canvassing the place, so best case, the guy is gone; worst case, the place is crawling with cops, and they'll arrest you before I can ever talk to you."

"If the guy is part of Brown's crew, I need to find out what he knows. Because if he already has your name, we're screwed."

"Screwed as in…"

He flashed me a look.

*As in I'll be killed.*

## 33

"Turn around." A flush of adrenaline rushed through my body. Easton's knuckles whitened with his grip on the wheel, his eyes fixed on the road in front of us as our vehicle careened through traffic.

"What good can come of confronting this guy?"

"I need to find out if they've figured out who you are." His chest inflated. "Because I'm not turning myself in until I ensure you're safe."

"That place is across from the police station," I reminded him. "If they've put your face with your name by now and you go there, a cop will see you."

"Not if I'm careful."

"Unless you've summoned the power of invisibility, you're playing with fire."

Easton glowered at me.

"You're not thinking this through."

But he kept driving. Racing, really. A red Toyota Camry with a dented right fender blazed its horn when Easton gunned it through a yellow light. As we tunneled through the six-story buildings, I gripped the edge of the seat for balance, rocking from side to side as Easton wove in and out of traffic, the groaning of the engine rising in pitch as he accelerated.

"We don't know who this guy is or what he's capable of. If you confront him, it's just gonna make things so much worse! You could get hurt, and if he sees you with me? Brown's crew will figure out you've been helping me all along."

Easton pressed the accelerator harder.

"He might not even be alone! He could have buddies nearby."

"I don't care about *me*, Zoey," Easton growled. "I care about you. Only you."

The thought of Easton rotting in prison cut me open and left my soul bleeding, but the thought of him getting killed obliterated the remaining fragments of my heart into dust.

*This can't be happening.* Would the landscape of my life once again repaint, this time with Easton in a coffin?

No. That couldn't be how this ended.

And yet, there was clearly no way to talk him out of this. I'd never seen anyone's eyes like that before. Rounded with a hardened edge of vengeance that demanded reckoning.

And as if this weren't bad enough, there was no way to have the deeply personal conversation with him that I'd desperately longed for. I could tell he'd never truly listen to *anything* I had to say, no matter how hard I tried. It would be like talking to someone with earphones in, where the music was cranked up so high that it would drown it all out.

All too soon, Easton parked a block away from the police station, out of view.

Theoretically.

"Please don't do this." I put my hand on his knee.

But he got out of the car, opened my door, and grabbed my hand.

I got up only because I didn't want him to go into the alley alone. But I didn't cease my pleas to stop this, even as he began walking toward the row of buildings across from the station.

"One cop sees you, and it's over." I looked around.

But I could see my words were bouncing right off of him; his eyes darted around the pedestrians, looking for any sign of danger.

Danger that dripped through the musk-scented air with the humidity of a coming storm. Bands of charcoal streaks crawled beneath dense clouds, cloaking the six-story buildings in its shadow, motivating many vehicles to turn on their headlights.

"Show me where you saw him."

"I don't remember," I claimed. "Please, let's just go back to the car—"

"Show me," Easton demanded.

I licked my lips.

I nodded my chin toward the building, and Easton tugged me by my hand as he walked across the street, down a half-block, and into the pedestrian path behind the building. All out of eyesight from the police station.

Again, in theory.

I thought for sure we would stumble across the police, but they must have already completed canvassing the area. Because when we emerged between the two buildings where I had seen the man standing, there was no one. Not a single person.

*Maybe the police picked him up already.*

"You sure this is where he was?"

I nodded, relieved. I didn't want Easton to confront this guy, and it looked like the universe had finally tipped the scales in my favor to keep him safe from himself.

"Can we go?"

"What did he look like?"

"Dark hair, jeans, black T-shirt. I was too far away to get his eye color or height."

Easton frowned. "Let's look around," he said, tugging me by the hand to move.

"Easton—"

"I can't leave you in the car, unprotected."

"Let's just go. He's not here so—"

But my words were immediately cut off because when we made a right turn down the pedestrian walk, a man blocked our path.

Not just any man.

*The* man.

The one that had been staring at me.

## 34

Tendrils of fear coiled around my muscles, urging me to run, but caught in the headlights of a villain, I became a doe. Frozen in place, staring at the man who'd evaded police earlier.

His dark eyes felt like weapons as they assessed me and then Easton, whose hand tightened protectively around mine.

"Easton." The guy's raspy tone rang through the air with echoes of warning.

I didn't like how Easton's body tensed. I didn't like how Easton's gaze fell to the man's waistband, as if looking for a gun, or the way Easton's fingers twitched toward his weapon. I didn't like that my sixth sense said whoever this guy was, he was powerful.

He wasn't the guy who had chased me the night of the burglary, but everything about him fired off sinister shots. The ghost of a smirk on his thin lips, as if he'd caught his prey. The callous indifference in his too-relaxed posture when facing a man more muscular than him. And the way he flicked the nail of his middle finger with his thumb, flick, flick, flicking a countdown to something.

"Why the hell are you here?" Easton demanded.

The guy scrutinized Easton.

"Assumed it was 'cause *you* couldn't find the witness." His eyes fell to our clasped hands. "Clearly, that was a lie."

*His use of the word* witness *must mean they don't know my name yet. Right?*

"How did you know she would be here?" Easton's eyes didn't blink.

"At the police station?" he asked as if it were a stupid question. "The day after the police put that parade on the news? Call it a hunch that they'd bring her in for questions."

So, he was watching the place then. A spider waiting in his web for the unsuspecting insect to walk into his trap.

"You're going to have to come with me, sweetheart," he said firmly, like his command was final.

"Over my dead body." Easton stood in front of me. "You so much as lay a finger on her, I'll end you."

Again, Easton's fingers flexed toward his waistband.

"You brought her here." The guy smirked. "What did you think was going to happen?"

Before Easton had the chance to pull his own pistol, the guy yanked a gun from the back of his waistband and pointed it at Easton's forehead.

"Come with me." He nodded his chin. "You and I need to go for a little drive."

I quickly assessed my options. Running was out. I couldn't make it around the corner fast enough when Easton's life was a squeeze away from ending. If I tried to pull Easton's gun and failed, Easton would die, too. If I screamed, would he pull the trigger? Or would police get here fast enough to stop what was happening?

"Now!" the guy snapped.

But when he grabbed my arm, everything changed.

Easton slammed his left palm into the assailant's wrist, knocking the aim of the barrel to the side, then grabbed the weapon with his right hand and kneed the guy in the balls. Even in obvious pain, the guy tried to fight for control over the gun, but Easton spun around, grabbed the guy's arm, and cracked it over his shoulder.

The snapping of the bone preceded his howl.

Easton smothered the guy's scream with his hand.

"Take this," he said, putting the weapon into my hand.

I was relieved that he handed me the gun because I assumed it meant the fight wouldn't escalate to death. But then I realized the gun was simply too loud to use this close to the police station.

Easton locked eyes with me for a heartbeat, his infuriated gaze plagued with the same warning he gave when he beat up that guy in the alley. The one that said, *Don't look, Zoey. I don't want you to see what I'm going to do to him.*

Easton had told me a few days ago that he would kill for me. In that moment, I knew with the cascading freeze to my bones that Easton was about to honor that promise. He was my dark protector, an unimaginable blend of kindness and danger, a man capable of violence, yet I knew with certainty that he'd never harm a hair on my head. Only those that wished me harm had reason to fear his form of justice.

Justice that could turn lethal.

"Let's just go," I pleaded.

But it was too late. Easton unleashed his tsunami of rage with his clenched fists against the man's face. Over and over. Cracks and thwaps echoed off the building's walls as blood splattered across Easton's face with each blow.

If I didn't stop him, he was going to kill him.

I wedged myself between Easton and the man, causing Easton's arm to halt mid-swing.

Panting, Easton stared into my eyes as I pressed my palm against his massive chest, feeling the thumping of his erratic heartbeat.

Knowing each beat was for me.

Easton was powerful, but with that one gentle move, I halted all the power coming from him and silently convinced him to stop. He looked down at the guy, who was unconscious but still breathing.

Easton clenched his jaw. Spat on the man's torso, took the guy's gun back—shoving it into his waistband next to the other—and led me by my hand down the abandoned alley toward the car.

## 35

"**E**aston," I whispered as we walked toward the sidewalk peppered with people.

He stopped walking and followed my gaze to his bloodstained shirt.

No way we could get to his car without someone seeing that. Not if we left the protection of the alley.

"You need to wipe your face, too."

Easton's jaw ticced, but he acted swiftly. Releasing my hand, he yanked the shirt up and over his head, turned it inside out, and wiped his face clean.

As clean as he could, anyway. Traces of blood still lingered in the hairs of his eyebrows, in the crevice of his right ear. He wadded the shirt into a ball, jogged to a dumpster, and threw the shirt inside.

Only then did he take my hand and lead me all the way back to the car.

"I can see the tops of the gun handles sticking out of your waist-band," I warned.

Easton shoved them down further, protecting the exposed parts with his arm. Once we were safely inside, he stuck them in the center console.

"Who was that guy?"

Easton rumbled the engine to a start and pulled out into traffic. "Brown's right-hand man."

"He saw you holding my hand."

Easton blew through a yellow light so fast, I thought he was going to clip a red pickup truck.

"I'm taking you home," Easton declared. "What I just did will enrage Brown. I'm not leaving you alone, unprotected, until I can think of a way to keep you safe."

With that one violent episode, the pendulum of danger swung away from me and over to Easton. A witness was one thing—a risk of operations, so to speak. But another crew member betraying Brown like this? Surely wouldn't go without severe repercussions.

It felt like the air became trapped in the lower part of my lungs, and I had to focus on my breaths, so I wouldn't pass out. I couldn't lose Easton. Not now.

"We need to stick with the original plan now more than ever," I disagreed. "We need to get Brown behind bars because after what you just did? They're going to come after you."

"I don't care about me."

"Well, I do." But I could see I needed to appeal to what Easton cared about. "If they go after you, how are you gonna protect me then?"

Easton clenched the steering wheel.

"Turning yourself in is the best chance we have to stay alive, and you know it. You're a pivotal witness to an important prosecution, so maybe they'll have protective custody or something."

Guaranteed safety didn't exist. All we could do was evaluate the options in front of us and pick the safest bet.

"They could get to you while I'm being interviewed," he said.

I was making progress.

"So, I'll go in with you, then. I'll sit in the safety of the police station the entire time you're being interviewed."

As lightning began to flash in the distance, Easton gripped the steering wheel tighter, staring out the windshield, clearly willing a better scenario to present itself. But what other choice did we have? Even if I had the financial means to run, it physically wasn't a possibility with Dad's medical situation. Dad said it would take a couple weeks or so before he'd be able to move in with Mom, and even then, they might identify his name and come after him. I wasn't about to leave my dad behind and risk him becoming collateral damage. Plus, Easton would be a wanted criminal wherever he went. Now that the police had his name, it was only a question of *when* he would be brought in. Not if.

We could either try to get in front of this with the police or give Brown and his crew another advantage.

Easton was silent for several seconds. I could see the wheels spinning in his mind as the sky darkened even more, warning of the perilous storm brewing.

While our own hurricane intensified in strength.

"I need to get cleaned up first," Easton allowed.

Ten minutes later, Easton parked in an underground parking structure and held my hand so tightly, he cut off blood supply to my fingers, his eyes darting around the empty space as he pulled me into an elevator, then into a hallway.

He unlocked a door, ushered me inside, and immediately relocked it, glancing out the peephole for any sign that we'd been followed.

I took in my new surroundings. An open space with a kitchenette only three steps from a living room/bedroom containing a two-seater couch, a bed, and a dresser. Along the far wall, a six-foot window's white blinds were drawn closed, the sounds of the city—the roar of car engines, the high-pitched metal scraping of the "L" train, a distant fire truck's wail, and the rumbling thunder of the coming storm— muffled through their panes of glass. And in here, the air conditioner sputtered through rattling vents, flooding the cool air with the scent of someone's laundry soap.

In the midst of surreal chaos, it was remarkable, getting to see a piece of him like this.

"Is this where you live?" I wondered aloud.

Easton flipped a light switch on in the next room, the only other room in this small space—a bathroom.

"No," he said as he yanked off his jeans. "It's a studio apartment I keep off the books. Use it to hide out when things get too hot."

Stripping to a pair of boxers, Easton turned the shower's water on.

"So, we're safe here?" I touched my throat. "Brown doesn't know where it is?"

"Brown doesn't know where it is, but, no," Easton said, dropping his boxers, "I don't feel you're safe anywhere right now. Give me two minutes to rinse off, and then we'll head to the station."

Easton stepped into the shower and vanished behind a black curtain.

I was overwhelmed with a cascading sequence of emotions radiating through me. Anytime now, Brown would find out what Easton had just done, and though I talked a good game to Easton, deep down, I was terrified that the police might not be able to protect Easton from Brown's vengeance. It was Easton's best shot at staying alive, but it was by no means foolproof.

Nor was it foolproof that Easton would be able to get leniency from the DA.

How long would he be facing in prison?

I quickly googled *prison time for armed robbery*, and when the search results appeared, I felt sick. Up to twenty-five years in prison. And that didn't include the other charges on the table, charges they might slap on everyone involved that night—kidnapping, assault and battery. Easton might really spend the rest of his life in prison.

My stomach clenched.

A smarter person would stay focused and not let this heartbreak consume her right now. There were much bigger priorities, but my heart didn't seem to care about any of that. It was too busy crumbling, imagining the next thirty years without Easton.

Without the man who, after all my years imprisoned in judgment, had freed me. Had saved me, both physically and emotionally. I needed to tell him the impact he'd had on my life.

When the shower's water stopped, Easton emerged from the bathroom, wearing nothing but a towel fastened around his hips.

He locked his eyes on me and walked up to me with urgency, as if he'd worried something might've happened to me while I was out of his sight.

"You okay?" He planted his warm palm against my cheek.

I nodded and leaned into his touch. He released it far too soon and threw on a pair of fresh boxer shorts he retrieved from the dresser.

"I need to tell you something." Butterflies took flight in my stomach.

Easton pulled a new pair of jeans from his drawer but paused at my tone.

I swallowed. I had so much to say, yet my words jumbled in my head.

An avalanche of sadness swallowed every other emotion and its path.

"This might be the last time we see each other for a long time," I realized.

And this time, it wasn't hypothetical or in the future. It was right now. In a matter of minutes, we'd be driving to the police station, and then we'd have no control over when or if we could see each other.

Easton stepped closer and traced my cheek with his thumb. I could see in the curve of his lips that as he stared at me, he was trying to memorize every inch of my face, perhaps so he could call it up at will in his darkest days in prison. And then a hurt washed through his gaze.

"It *will* be the last time we see each other," he said. "*Ever.*"

I stilled from shock.

"I won't let you throw your life away, waiting for me."

My eyes stung. "That's not your call to make."

"We both know I'm going away for a long time."

"You could get a deal."

"Even if I do, I'm looking at years behind bars, Zoey. I'm not going to ruin your life even more than I already have."

"You didn't ruin my life." My eyes welled, and my lips quivered at him seeing himself as nothing but destructive to me. He needed to see that he wasn't the hurricane; he was the rainbow. "You saved it."

The crease between his brows deepened.

"Before I met you, I'd write anyone off that did something I didn't agree with. I've been so closed off, particularly after my dad left us, but you opened my eyes. You made me realize that behind every action lies a motivation, and it's equally important to understand both, to never presume to know why someone is making the choices they are.

"You changed me, Easton. Emily was right; you're the first person who made me stop and listen to *why* someone is making the choices they make. Before you came along, I never listened, but now, I'm trying to hear people out instead of jumping to my own conclusions. It helped me have a better conversation with my father than I would have before, but this won't stop with my father. It'll strengthen every relationship I have with people from now on. You've made me into a better person, and I don't ever want you to forget that."

Easton stood before me, wearing nothing but a pair of boxers, the jeans still clutched in his hand. His skin smelled of fresh soap, his hair still wet after being towel-dried. He looked at me beneath thick eyebrows as I placed both of my hands on his chest and looked up into his eyes.

Easton traced my cheek with this fingertip. With the slow breath escaping his lungs, I could see the battle raging in his heart, his feelings for me wanting to take the steering wheel, wanting to embrace my love, but his honor fighting it.

"You would pick me, even after everything I've done?"

"Without question."

Something shifted in his eyes, and instantly, I needed to know something.

*Does he feel as strongly for me as I do him?*

"If you weren't facing prison…what is it you'd want, Easton?"

Easton stroked my cheekbone with the backs of his fingers, his touch igniting sparks in my heart.

He pierced me with his gaze and was silent for several agonizing seconds.

"I want you," he said in a low rumble.

I allowed myself to have a silent gasp, savoring his answer. Relishing that in this moment, I got to hear what he really longed for even if it could never come true.

"If I weren't going away, I'd want to give you every desire you could possibly imagine. You want ecstasy? I'd sink to my knees to pleasure you. You want protection? I'd annihilate anyone who ever hurts you. You want to be worshipped? You'd be my altar."

I swallowed as he cupped my chin in his hand.

"I've lived the last decade in a prison of my own making, but you broke me out, Zoey. You gave me purpose, and now, every drop of blood in my body belongs to you. You asked me what I'd want if I wasn't going away." He pinned me with those piercing blue eyes and held the side of my face. "I'd want to be anything to you that you'd allow me to be."

A hungry desire pulsed in my lower belly, and the need to feel him overwhelmed me. He stared at me as if needing to memorize my every feature while my hands tried to memorize the contours of his skin.

Every other rational thought faded along with every sound, every smell. He was the only thing in my world right now.

His profession wrapped around my heart like a warm blanket after a thunderstorm, and the need to make a profession of my own surged up my chest, to the tip of my tongue.

"I know this sounds crazy, illogical, and much too soon," I said. But after everything that happened in my life, including the robbery, I learned that life is too short to hold back from saying something that's truly in your heart. "But I'm falling in love with you."

Easton's lips curled as if my declaration healed the last remnants of his wounded soul. "I think I've already fallen."

My heart hiccuped at his words, watching his lips as he lowered his face.

When his lips finally grazed mine, I groaned and wrapped my

arms around his neck as his tongue swept into my mouth. There was no way I could spend the next thirty years without being with him one last time. I let my hands roam down his chest, down his stomach.

"Zoey—" he warned.

"Once we walk out that door, we might never get to touch each other again."

I skimmed my fingertips down the ridges of his abs, sensing his resolve wavering with the quickening of his breaths.

"I need one more memory of us to cling to," I said. "Every night you're not in my bed."

As I skimmed my palm along his stomach, Easton's body remained frozen, but with each inch of skin I touched, his breathing quickened until one tug of his waistband made him lose all control.

He yanked my shirt over my head and almost tore my bra, taking it off. Then my pants. Feverish movements as he walked me backward, kissing my jaw. My neck.

And then he shoved me down.

I landed on his bed with a bounce, staring up at him as he stood over me, pulling his boxers off.

"If this is the last time I get to touch you..." He grabbed my legs, yanked me to the bottom of his bed, pulled my panties off. And knelt. "I'm going to make it memorable," Easton promised.

He trailed kisses up along my inner thigh, repeating the same agonizing tease on the other side until he pressed his tongue to my center. I gasped. When I moved my hips, he held down my thighs so forcefully, his hands pinched my skin.

I existed in a slice of ecstasy that I never wanted to end. He kissed me like a hungry man, like he'd been fantasizing about this moment since he'd first laid eyes on me, and now that it was here, he couldn't get enough. I'd never felt anything this sensual, this intimate before, and with him, I didn't feel shy at all. He was a sensual extension of my body, someone with whom I could live out my wildest desires without feeling self-conscious. When I began to squirm, feeling the rise, he held my thighs tighter. Until I called out his name.

He waited until every last aftershock rippled through my body before he stood up and grabbed a small plastic wrapper from his wallet.

"Turn over," he growled as he ripped a foil packet and slipped on protection.

I gladly obeyed and crawled up higher on the bed, feeling it sink behind me with the weight of his knees as he positioned himself behind me.

And then joined our bodies.

I bit his pillow as he began to move.

I loved every growl that escaped his throat. Every whimper that came from mine. He moved with perfect rhythm, as if knowing my body's tempo. And then, never breaking our bodies, he pulled my torso back, resting on his heels.

He grabbed my chest as he twisted my head around so he could kiss me. Slipped his tongue against mine as I rocked my hips on top of him, feeling another release coming. And when his hand found my center, it triggered my collapse, my mouth gaping.

"Easton," I cried out.

Once every tremble subsided, he pulled away, flipped me onto my back, and sank his body back to mine.

How was it possible that every position felt better than the last? As good as it felt with him behind me, there was nothing like the weight of his hips pressing into my thighs, his arms on either side of my head, his lips trailing kisses along my jaw. There was nothing like getting to grab his shoulder muscles as he controlled his body in perfect sync with my own.

He kissed me again and moved his body with mine harder and harder until he felt another rise of mine coming. I grabbed his back.

"Don't stop," I whimpered.

I looked up into his azure eyes as he worked his body against mine, and he watched my release.

"Easton..."

Easton growled and slammed his body into mine until he stilled on top of me, cupping my face. His majestic blue eyes searched mine for the happiness we both wished we could hold on to forever, but I watched as his happiness receded behind a curtain of despair.

"I *have* fallen in love with you," he said.

I didn't like the hurt in his voice or the way his shoulders sagged slightly. Nor did I like how he traced my lip with his finger, pain radiating from his eyes as he gathered himself to say what came next.

"But I meant what I said, Zoey. I don't want you to wait for me."

It felt like my heart burst into flames, spreading its inferno to my bones.

"You spent the last year putting your life on hold to take care of your dad." He shook his head. "I'm not going to allow you to put your life on hold for me."

Instantly, the oxygen didn't come fast enough; my lungs inflated at a rapid pace, searching for relief that wouldn't come.

"You are my life." I clasped his arms tightly, as if holding on to him could make him stay here with me.

But with the distress on his face and his gaze falling from my eyes, I could feel him slipping through my grasp as he climbed off the bed and put his pants on.

I didn't know what to say, how to shift the cold front that had moved through the room so fast that I didn't see it coming.

He wouldn't look at me anymore.

I sat up and pulled the covers up to my chest, too raw to feel this hurt in the nude. I rocked slightly, clutching my knees, my mind racing.

I didn't know a lot about prisons, but I was fairly certain that if an inmate refused to see someone, there would be nothing I could do. And as painful as the years ahead of me would feel without him by my side, that pain was nothing compared to never getting to see him again. Feeling him cut himself out of my life like a cancerous tumor, unaware that doing so sliced my heart open, causing it to hemorrhage.

I couldn't let him walk in the police station without him promising me he'd never turn me away.

I opened my mouth to plead my case, but suddenly, the front door burst open.

A dark-haired guy, wearing a black T-shirt and jeans with tattoos of skulls wrapping up both arms, stormed inside and cut his eyes to me.

I tightened the bedsheet across my chest and stared into the dark eyes that made my body tremble. The guy's chest inflated, his fists clenched, as he turned his attention to Easton, who glared at the intruder.

"You fucking kidding me?" The guy gestured to me.

And that was when the ice in my bones chilled into an arctic freeze because I recognized that voice, and I remembered that face from the brief glimpse I caught on the night of the robbery.

It was Orange.

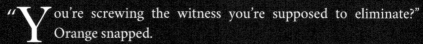

## 36

"Y ou're screwing the witness you're supposed to eliminate?"
Orange snapped.

Wearing nothing but a pair of jeans, Easton walked to the door, poked his head out, and looked up and down the hall before shutting and locking it.

"Thought Victor's guy had to be mistaken, that you were with some other chick, not her," Orange snarled.

"How did you find me?" Easton asked over a tightened jaw.

Orange looked at me with disgust, his face pinched, as if my very presence sickened him. "Weren't at your place, so I figured after what you did to Victor's guy, you might be here."

"Is anyone else with you?" Easton demanded.

"No." Orange glared at me. "Thought you'd be alone, too, after the stunt you pulled." He reached into his waistband and pulled a gun out. Pointed it at me.

I tensed.

Easton jumped between the barrel and me.

"Gavin." Easton's vein bulged from his neck.

"You know what Victor's going to do to you when he finds out about this?"

"You take your orders from Victor now?"

"He's making sure we don't get busted."

"He's reckless and violent," Easton barked.

"He's protecting himself and his crew. Including me."

The night of the robbery, Orange/Gavin said the heist was a test, that if it went well, Brown/Victor would offer him a job. The heist went sideways, so why invite him to the team? Was Gavin really in as good of graces as he thought?

Or was Victor using him?

"You think he gives two shits about you?" Easton snapped. "I'm your brother. I've always protected you and had your back."

"I know you have." Gavin dropped his arm slightly, the gun now angled lower, but by no means were we out of danger. "That's why I want you in on this opportunity. Victor has a bigger crew, bigger heists. We can be kings in this city. You always told me, 'We have enough cash. No one owns us.' He's offering us more money than we ever dreamed of."

"He's going to kill you, Gavin. He told me if I don't find the witness, he'll kill me and then you."

"Victor wouldn't kill me."

"Have I ever lied to you?"

"Yeah. When you left out that you're screwing the one person who can put us behind bars."

Gavin stepped to his right and raised the aim of the barrel again, but Easton matched his movement, taking up a protective stance, shielding me.

"Gavin, don't do this," Easton said.

"Step aside."

"You want to kill her, you'll have to kill me first."

"You fucking crazy?" Gavin demanded.

"Put the gun down."

"She's just some girl!"

"You're not a killer, Gavin."

Easton had a lot more faith in his brother than I did because the tone in Gavin's voice seemed pretty damn murderous to me.

I wanted to run, but exposing myself past Easton would get me killed.

"Look, it don't have to go down this way." Gavin's voice lowered with sympathy. "You come with me now, I'll tell him you lured her here, okay? That you were the one that took care of her."

The silence was earsplitting.

"You really plan to kill her," Easton said in disbelief, as if only now, it was finally sinking in.

"She could put us in prison for the rest of our lives." Gavin's face pinched.

Easton took a step closer to his brother. "If you spend the next however many years pulling off heists, you think you won't stumble across other witnesses? You gonna kill them all, too?"

Gavin said nothing.

"This isn't who you are," Easton insisted.

"And who am I?" His voice lowered.

But the thing was, Gavin didn't ask it in a biting, win-an-argument tone. He asked it as if truly seeking the answer.

The old me would see him as nothing more than an awful human, but like Easton, Gavin had a story, a reason for how he was acting, and my heart bled for him. For this human who'd been plucked from happiness, lost his parents to violence, and lived on the dangerous streets with none of the usual connections and guidance the rest of us had. Teachers. Structure. Friends. Sleepovers. Birthday parties. He probably didn't even remember what living in a non-fight-or-flight moment felt like. Knowing if he'd be able to eat again or if a gang would kill his brother, leaving him completely alone.

What is a human capable of when suffering from that much trauma?

He might be making terrible choices right now, but if Easton could change, maybe Gavin could, too.

"You're my brother," Easton said. "Who I would do anything for. I mean, shit, Gavin! What's this all been for if you go off the deep end and turn into some lowlife who'll kill people? I did all this to try to save you."

"You thought a life of crime on the streets would save me? You raised me in an alley! You ripped me from heat and food and a warm bed and made me sleep on concrete."

Easton's body tensed. "I yanked you out before a pedophile got his hands on you. I sacrificed everything for you, and this is how you repay me? Going against me for some guy who's willing to kill us and anyone else who gets in his way?"

"We've been stealing and lying since we were kids, and now, you grow some conscience and draw a line in the sand of what's an acceptable crime and what's not?"

Easton grabbed the back of his neck.

"We could rule this city," Gavin repeated. "Take whatever the hell we want, when we want it, and no one'll be able to do anything about it."

With his every word, I could see in the sag of his shoulders that Easton's heart was closing in on itself.

That was what this was about to Gavin; it wasn't the money. Like Easton, this life of crime was about the power. Going from powerless to powerful. Feeling afraid for years must be a heavy burden that leaves behind battle scars. And the desire to never feel vulnerable again clearly was a drug too tempting to pass up.

"I can't let you do this, Gavin."

"You've always protected me." Gavin flexed his fingers on his free hand. "Why won't you do it now?"

"I *am* protecting you," Easton said, his tone a mixture of anger and disappointment. "Even if you can't see it."

Easton charged Gavin, causing the gun to drop from his grip. Gavin grunted as he fell to the floor. He lay there for a few seconds before charging Easton's knees.

As Easton and his brother rolled around, swinging fists at each other, I hopped up with a bedsheet around my body and grabbed the weapon.

"Get off him." I pointed the gun at Gavin.

The men froze, eyeing me. But after a few seconds, Gavin and Easton both stood up.

"Get out," I ordered.

I held my arm out as intimidatingly as possible, unsure if I would have the courage to pull the trigger even if he came at me. Gavin looked from me to his brother in absolute disgust and then began straightening his shirt.

As if unfazed by my threat.

"You made a big mistake, brother." Gavin's face flushed red.

"I said, get out!"

Easton stepped closer to me in a protective stance while Gavin picked up his wallet, which must have fallen out of his jean pocket in the scuffle.

"Victor's going to come for you," Gavin warned.

And then his eyes caught something else on the ground. Something that clearly sparked his interest based on the slight widening of his eyes. My driver's license poking out of my jean pocket.

*No.*

Easton lunged for it, but Gavin kicked him in the ribs, sending Easton to the floor as he grabbed it.

"*Zoey Williams,*" Gavin read.

My blood thinned.

"This your current address?"

Easton wobbled, holding the side of his ribs, but by the time he stood up, it was too late.

Gavin was in the doorway. "We'll be seeing you soon, Zoey."

And then he was gone.

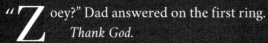

## 37

"Zoey?" Dad answered on the first ring.

*Thank God.*

Easton made a left turn so fast, my body pressed into the passenger door. After Gavin left with my ID, Easton ran after him, but Gavin had vanished. I threw my clothes on, and Easton and I ran to his car, where I quickly pulled out my cell.

I was glad the storm wasn't producing rain yet; rain would make it harder to drive fast.

"Where the hell have you been?" Dad demanded. "I thought you stepped out to talk to your boyfriend, and you just vanished! Do you know how worried I've been?"

"Dad," I said, "listen to me very carefully. Do not open the door for anybody. I'm calling the cops, and I'm coming to pick you up."

"What's going on?"

"I'll explain everything as soon as I get there, but right now, I need to call the police. Do not answer the door. Do you understand me? And if you hear or see anything, call 911."

Easton wove in and out of traffic so quickly, I feared we'd crash.

"Are you okay? Are you in danger?" Dad's words fired as fast as bullets.

"The burglars have our address."

Easton turned right and nearly clipped a blue Ford pickup.

"What? How did they find out—"

"I'll explain everything, I promise. But right now, do not answer the door."

The light in front of us turned from green to yellow, but Easton pressed the accelerator, grinding the engine as we launched into the intersection seconds after the light had turned red. A cement truck coming eastbound nearly crashed into Easton's side, both vehicles swerving to avoid a collision.

Our back tires lost traction and fishtailed, but Easton regained control and changed lanes to get around a slow sedan in front of us.

His apartment was only a few minutes from mine, but with the men who wanted me dead now having my address, it might as well have been light years away.

"I'll be there in a couple of minutes," I said.

"Zoey," Dad started.

"I love you, Dad. Don't open the door. I'll be there in a minute."

I hated ending it with him like that, but I needed to call the police. They needed to send the full cavalry to my apartment to protect my dad. I quickly looked up Hernandez's phone number and dialed his extension. It rang three agonizing times before he picked up.

"Hernandez."

"Detective Hernandez!"

"Zoey?" His voice was tense. "What's wrong?"

"One of the burglars took my ID, which means he has my name and address."

"What makes you think he has your ID?"

"I saw him. He could be on his way to my house right now!"

"You saw him?" Hernandez echoed with angry confusion.

"Yes."

"Where?"

"And now, my dad could be in danger. He's home all alone with no way to defend himself."

"Zoey, I need you to calm down. Come to the station, and we'll discuss this further."

"I'm not leaving my dad at my townhouse alone! Not when they could come looking for me there at any time now. I'm going home. Can you send some of your men right away?"

"If one of them has your address, your house is the last place you should go. Come to the station."

"I'm not coming there until I get my dad! Can't you send a car?"

"Manpower's light at the moment. It'll take longer than usual for them to get to your place, so you need to come straight here."

"Why is manpower light?"

"Anonymous call about a robbery in progress."

"You think it's real?"

"I don't have confirmation one way or the other yet." Hernandez didn't hide the skepticism in his tone. Or the worry. "Worst case, it could be a diversion to lure manpower elsewhere while they try to come after you. So, you need to come to the station right now."

"And what about my dad?" I yelled.

"I'll send someone for him, but *you're* the witness. You're the one that's in danger."

"Right now, my dad's a sitting duck. I'm not risking my dad's life. I'm going to pick him up and bring him with me."

How I'd do that with Dad in a wheelchair, I wasn't sure. But I'd carry him myself if I had to.

"I'll be there as soon as I can." I ended the call.

Easton rounded the last corner and slammed the car into park so fast, I jolted forward.

With our eyes darting around the neighborhood—at the sedans parked along both sides of the road, one littered with orange tickets beneath its windshield wiper; at the passages between townhouses that could easily conceal someone's hiding position—we jumped out. I kicked an empty beer bottle out of my way as we rushed to the front door, Easton keeping a protective hand on my lower back.

I fished the key out of my pocket, unlocked the dead bolt, slipped inside with Easton, and immediately locked up again.

Inside, Dad and Alex were at the dining room table. My relief that they were okay lasted for only a moment before I saw what was splayed out on the table in front of them. Case files, police reports, and enlarged photographs.

They must have been working the case after breakfast since the lineup hadn't been about the robbery.

"What's going on?" Dad demanded of me.

Like a moth to the flame, Easton approached the table.

"You've been trying to solve the case?" An anchor dragged Easton's voice down.

Alex puffed up his chest, offense washing over him, like anyone that truly cared about me would be trying to solve this mystery. "Those scumbags won't get away with what they did to Zoey."

As Dad rolled himself closer to me, I was about to tell him to grab his stuff, that we needed to hustle into Easton's car and get the hell out of here.

But Easton eyed the pictures splayed across the table. Pictures of my mutilated wrists. Close-up shots of my bruises and scrapes, mascara dripping down my puffy eyes. And as he did, his lips curled down into a sickened expression.

Outside, a storm that had been brewing intensified with blowing winds and lightning.

Inside, a different storm raged on. One where Easton looked at Alex, then my dad. And after seeing the photos of what his life of crime had caused me, he must have decided jail or death by Brown wasn't enough punishment. Evidently, he felt like he also deserved a father's wrath, too.

Because he looked at Dad dead in the eyes and said, "I'm one of the men you're looking for, sir. I robbed your condo."

"You what?" Dad snapped. I thought he was going to jump out of his chair and strangle Easton.

Alex beat him to it, lunging and punching Easton across the face so hard that he wobbled back a step.

"Stop!" I shrieked, but Alex pounded his fists into Easton's face repeatedly, pushing Easton deeper into the living room with each hit —but Easton didn't even attempt to fight back. His hair bounced with each undefended jab.

Dad watched the brawl from the confines of his chair, making no effort to tell them to stop. If anything, I wondered if he was living vicariously through Alex's fists as Alex tackled Easton to the ground.

"Stop!" I climbed onto Alex's back, but he flung me off and continued to hit Easton's stomach, chest, and face.

I tried again to pull Alex off, but one of his blows accidentally landed on my ribs, knocking me to the ground with a sharp stab of pain to my right hip.

This was the only time I saw Easton's arm move. With one swift motion, he nailed Alex in the head, sending him flying backward into the couch.

"You ever touch her again…" Easton warned.

Finally, I was able to wedge myself between them, palms on each of their chests. I could feel their thundering hearts pulsing beneath my hands.

Easton clenched his hands into balls, glaring at Alex, who glared right back.

"We don't have time for this." I gave them both a gentle shove. "We have to go. Now."

Alex and Easton breathed heavily, perhaps contemplating fighting to the death. Alex wiped a drop of blood from the corner of his mouth while Easton looked…well, a little disheveled but otherwise fine.

"I'm not going anywhere until you explain what in the hell is going on," Dad snarled.

"I'll explain on the way to the station, but right now, we have to go. One of the other burglars got my ID. They know my name and address and could be headed here right now!"

"Zoey, tell me what the hell is going on!" Dad demanded.

"Dad!"

"Did you try to kill my daughter?" Dad growled at Easton.

"No, sir."

"Easton saved me that night, and he's been trying to protect me ever since."

Dad's accusing eyes met mine, full of anger that I lied to him, that I'd slept with one of my captors.

"Look, we *have* to get to the station, so we're safe. Once we're there, I'll answer any other questions you have, but if we don't leave right now, they'll kill me, Dad, and they might kill you, too."

Finally, the stubbornness in Dad's face took a backseat to his concern for my safety.

"Fine." Dad rolled his wheelchair a few inches closer. "But this conversation is *not* over."

Animosity wrapped around us as Alex and Dad followed me and Easton out the front door.

Easton held a protective hand around my waist while he looked up and down the street, scrutinizing all the cars and pedestrians, looking for any sign of trouble. Once he was satisfied we could make it the forty feet to his car, he ushered me forward, and Alex wheeled my dad behind us.

It was clunky, thumping his wheelchair down the first curb, crossing the road, and jerking it up the second curb to reach Easton's passenger door.

To most people, transferring someone from a wheelchair to another chair probably sounded simple, but the angle was off. The door didn't open wide enough for the chair to pull up alongside the seat, and Dad didn't have enough strength to move himself.

"I'll grab his shoulders," Alex offered.

"I can try to stand." Dad pushed his arms up on his armrests.

I wanted to help but felt it was safer with two strong men helping my father. I held the wheelchair steady as Alex grabbed my dad underneath his armpits from behind and Easton grabbed my dad's waist. They pulled my dad into a standing position, and while they began to shift him toward the seat, I quickly wheeled the chair to the back and opened the trunk.

As I folded and lifted the chair, tires screeched to my left.

A pop exploded in my ears and left them ringing.

It took my brain what felt like an eternity to process the scene unfolding around me. Easton had dropped my father and now stood hunched over, both hands grabbing his stomach, which leaked crimson. Alex must have tried to catch my dad's fall because both he and Dad were lying on the sidewalk with Alex's arm pinned beneath my father's back. A white van with a cartoon cockroach logo on the side stopped right next to us, and two men grabbed Easton while another grabbed me. Smothered my mouth and dragged us inside.

Where three men dressed in black threw us to the ground, slammed the van's side door shut, and then a fourth man gunned the engine, squealing away.

## 39

The back of the van had no seats, just a metal floor with a tarp that smelled like bug spray. The air was stale and hot, like neither air-conditioning nor an open window had seen the inside of this place for months.

"Easton!" I shrieked. "Are you okay?"

Easton slumped along the far corner of the van, his hand pressing against his bleeding abdomen. His muscles drooped, and as one guy held him down to take the gun from Easton's waistband, he groaned in pain.

Before Easton could answer me, one of the guys—who had a gap in his teeth wide enough to stick a pencil through—duct-taped my hands together and then did the same to Easton, who growled in pain from the movement. I didn't recognize Tooth-Gap Guy or the one with a tattoo of a spiderweb on his cheek. But the other guy…

The other guy was Gavin, Easton's brother.

Gavin shoved his fingers through his hair, staring at Easton's bullet wound with wild eyes. "Look what you made me do," Gavin said. "This is all your fault. If you had gotten rid of the girl like Victor told you to, it'd have never come to this."

"You don't have to do this," Easton mumbled through gritted teeth.

"Don't you get it?" Gavin snapped. Anger mixed with heartbreak in his tone, his voice trailing off as he said, "It's already done."

The finality thickened the oxygen in the van until it was almost unbreathable.

I glanced at Easton, whose grimaced face stared at his only blood relative with a look of betrayal. Knowing the very brother that he had sacrificed everything to protect was going to become his executioner.

Gavin scrubbed his face for several seconds before glaring at Easton with a fresh question.

"What the hell was that wheelchair dude doing with her?" Gavin snapped. "You never told me you talked to him."

I exchanged a look with Easton, whose narrowed eyes looked just as confused as mine.

The van made a sharp turn, sliding me into one of my captors' thighs.

"Answer me!" he demanded.

But Easton didn't answer him; instead, he grunted words through his pain. "Gavin, don't do this."

"Answer me!" Gavin kicked me in the ribs. "Or I'll beat the shit out of your girlfriend."

Easton tried to crawl to me, but one of the guys held him down.

"I'm calling Victor." Gavin jerked his phone from his pocket.

Gavin turned his body toward the side of the van as it careened through traffic, taking us God knew where. He punched a button, and after a few seconds, he said, "Hey, it's me. Yeah, we got 'em, but, dude, I think we have a problem. Remember that guy I told you about? The one in the wheelchair? He was with them." Silence. "I don't know, man. We grabbed them and drove off."

Gavin must have met my father at some point, but when? Had he come to the house after the robbery, trying to find me, and Dad had answered the door? If that were true, he would've known my address before he got my ID, and he wouldn't be so confused as to how I knew him.

I had no idea how he seemed to know my dad, but I didn't have time to speculate; I needed to tear my bindings, so I had a chance to protect Easton.

I pulled at my wrists. The duct tape had been wrapped twice around it.

"You want us to do it, or you want—" Gavin stopped talking. Nodded. "Okay, we'll bring 'em to you."

Gavin ended the call and shouted to the driver, "Change of plans. We're bringing 'em to the tunnels first."

*First...*

Gavin leaned in so close, I could smell the cigarettes and rage on his breath. He grabbed my jaw and looked at Easton. "You two love-birds are going to answer all our questions, or we're going to cut each of her fingers off, one by one. Keep going until she's nothing but a stack of flesh."

Easton looked sickened by his brother's vile threat.

I quivered, but the guy didn't ask me anything, obviously waiting until we were at the new location.

Even though the bumpy drive only lasted a few minutes, it felt like a year because the entire time, I was tugging at the duct tape, trying to free myself while simultaneously evaluating my options. Assessing the threat levels, trying to gauge who was armed with what. And if I managed to break free, how I'd ensure Easton was saved, too.

The van stopped, and the driver jumped out while one of my captors opened the van door and yanked me out. Then Easton. The bloodstain on his shirt was now the size of a softball, and his shoulders sagged, his body droopy.

I tried to get my bearings as to our location. If I could figure out where we were, maybe I could remember where the closest hospital was. We were parked in an alley littered with empty beer bottles, only wide enough to fit the van, the surrounding buildings at least thirty stories high.

Still in Chicago, then. But what area?

They pushed us, forcing us to walk down a small concrete staircase and through a metal door, where more stairs took us deeper underneath the city.

It was only after descending all the steps that I realized where we were—the underground tunnels of Chicago. Many school kids in Chicago knew about these tunnels because we had to study them in tenth grade.

Constructed in the late 1800s and early 1900s, the rails were constructed for hauling large spools of cables and other supplies through the city, but by 1909, the construction costs had bankrupted the Illinois Tunnel Company. By 1959, the tunnels were abandoned and closed off to the public.

But here we were, walking through them.

Tooth-Gap Guy held me by my elbow while the other three walked us deeper into the abyss. Portable lights broke up the darkness of the twenty-foot-high arched concrete ceilings, which rested above a cylindrical-shaped passage with two iron tracks. It smelled like water had once accumulated and then slowly dripped away from its stained concrete, leaving mildew and mold behind—along with a metallic taste pricking my tongue. And the place was cold. With no air circulation, the chill of being underground blanketed my skin and penetrated my muscles, making me shiver as our footsteps echoed off the hollow chambers.

I glanced at Easton, who didn't even have the strength to walk by himself; two men—Spiderweb Tattoo Face and the van's driver with long, oily hair—had an arm under each of Easton's armpits, pulling him forward as his semi-limp body sagged more with each step. He locked remorseful eyes with me as our captors drew us closer to our doom.

*I love you,* I mouthed. No matter what happened, I wanted him to know that.

*I love you*, he mouthed back.

But I knew that if I didn't do something drastic, that'd be the last time he could ever say those words to me.

The tunnel forked into two different directions, and we were pulled right.

*Right*, I repeated in my head. I needed to memorize our path, so I could find my way back to the door if we broke free.

But we didn't have much time. Easton was barely able to walk; he didn't look like he'd be conscious much longer.

After walking for a couple of minutes, we came to a clearing that must have been where the city had once stored extra train cars. Two tracks were covered with engine-sized wooden boxes that appeared to be man-made, and standing in front of them, staring at his phone, was the man who'd chased me the night of the burglary.

Brown. Also known as Victor.

He looked up from his screen, and when he saw us approach, he crossed his arms.

He regarded us with a sinister smirk. "We meet again."

I gritted my teeth. A smarter person would probably sink to her knees and beg for his mercy, but I knew there was nothing I could say to convince him to let us go. Our only hope was to escape. And that evil little smirk incited a rage inside of me. He stared at me like I was a pathetic weakling, one who was obviously stupid to ever think she could outsmart him.

"Victor—" Easton started, his voice weak.

"Shut the fuck up." Victor looked at Gavin. "You sure it was him?"

"Positive."

"Couldn't have mistaken him for some other cripple?"

*Cripple.* So help me, if I had the chance, I would knee him in the balls for using that offensive word.

"It was him," Gavin declared.

As Victor began to pace and his goons spaced out from us, I locked eyes with Easton, who stood ten feet to my left. His stomach was bleeding even more, causing his body to sway, as if about to fall at any second.

I looked past Victor. Where the tunnel extended into nothing but blackness, no lights illuminating the path. Could I run past him? And make it?

Not with Easton in his condition.

"The man in the wheelchair"—Victor's arm twitched—"how do you know him?"

Again, Easton flashed me a confused look.

I had no clue who they thought my dad was, but I could tell this string of questions was the only thing keeping us alive.

"How do you know him?" Victor repeated with an impatient edge.

And in that instant, something changed inside of me. It was my turn to protect Easton.

I was done with Brown/Victor making me feel afraid. For once, I wanted to make him feel afraid while I waited for my opening to get out of this mess. Bonus if I got to mind-F the hell out of him in the process.

A fresh rush of adrenaline coursed through my veins and sparked my mind to work on overdrive, firing on all cylinders. It was as if the adrenaline acted as a focal drug, my mind flooding with ideas—clear, crisp, and coming together with something that might rattle him enough to get us out of this mess.

"I'm an undercover, moron," I started. "We set you up, let you take me. It was a trap. So they could follow you to your stupid lair and take you down. Right now? Three dozen of Chicago's finest are surrounding all exits of this tunnel. You're screwed, asshole."

I relished that flinch in his face.

Victor stopped pacing.

"You do anything to me or him," I said, "you'll have a rock-solid murder charge to add to the mix. And you can spend the rest of your life getting raped in the showers."

"You ain't no cop."

"No? Why do you think the cops put a twenty-thousand-dollar bounty on your head? For an average civilian?"

Victor's dark eyes darted to his minions, then back to me. "You're lying."

"Why do you think you went to that condo?" I asked. "Kind of odd, don't you think? That someone set up that heist where an undercover agent just happened to walk in?"

"If you were undercover, you would've arrested us that night."

"You ran away like a little bitch out of a different exit than we'd anticipated. But we learned our lesson. Case in point, here we are." I looked around. "Fitting that you run your operation in this sewer."

"This isn't a sewer," Oily Hair said in offense.

"Shut up!" Victor snapped at him.

"I'm guessing we'll find a lot of stolen goods in those crates." I curled my lip slightly. "So, like I said, game. Set. Match."

"I'll kill you and any other cop that gets in my way." Victor tried to sound confident, but his breathing had quickened.

I couldn't contain my smirk. "You're outgunned. You kill even one of us? You'll be locked up before breakfast for the rest of your life. And the DA? Doesn't take too kindly to cop killers. He'll pull his weight to send you to a prison that makes Alcatraz look like a kindergarten camp."

Victor stomped up to me.

"Your choice. You let us go, I put in a good word for you with the DA. You kill us? You'll be in rat-infested solitary for the rest of your days." I looked at the hired guns. "Your buddies, too."

His subordinates looked at their leader with an obvious question in their eyes. *She telling the truth?*

"Look outside." Victor took a few angry steps away and began pacing. "See if you can spot any cops."

"Please do." I raised a brow. "Make sure you *don't* put your hands up. I want to hear what your brain sounds like, splatting against the wall."

Oily Hair looked nervously to Victor.

"Go! Look!" Victor demanded.

My mouth ran dry.

Oily Hair jogged down the tunnel, the clomp-clomp-clomp of his echoing footsteps growing quieter the farther he ran.

As he waited, Victor walked over to Gavin and grabbed a fistful of his shirt. "I find out the guy that hired you to rob the condo was a cop? I'll fucking kill you."

My blood ran cold, and vile pulsed through my stomach, inching up my esophagus at the shock of what he'd just said.

I couldn't have heard that right—*the guy that hired you.* There was no way it could be true.

Victor had to be either lying or mistaken. Dad would never have any contact with these people, let alone arrange for anyone to rob his condo.

After all, what did he have to gain? Money? There was no way Dad was that desperate. I mean, yeah, as it turned out, he'd seen the financial undercurrent that was pulling us under, he saw how much I was struggling to make ends meet. But he would never cross the line and do something illegal.

*Right?*

But why make up a story? These guys didn't even know how I was connected to Dad. Or maybe they did. Maybe *he* was playing mind games with me?

Why bother if their goal was to kill us?

None of it made sense.

My mind raced, looking for the missing piece to the puzzle that felt like it was just within my grasp. I quickly replayed our abduction and Gavin's confusion, seeing my dad. His nervousness over it.

When nothing clicked, I went back in time, sifting through the last few months to prove they were lying. But as I did, a sickening new lens came into focus.

I thought about the time Dad found out Anthony was helping pay for medication and how Dad had said, "If I could just get my hands on some money to help…"

And then some of his other words flashed back to me.

"I'd do anything to help, Zoey. Anything. This isn't fair to you, the burden I've become."

And…

"Why did you go to the condo?" he'd asked in a tone that bordered on panic.

My stomach twisted into knot after knot, growing sicker with each layer of realization. That it wasn't as impossible as I wanted to believe.

Dad knew everything that would be in that condo, save for Holly's necklace and the ring since Holly had put the ring in the safe *after* the accident—when Dad had been in the hospital. Dad knew the place was empty. He'd been watching those news stories religiously about the robberies and how they helped homeless shelters after. Perhaps willing to gamble on trusting them to help him. Dad was alone all day, every day while I was at work and had the means to roll up and down the blocks, getting to know people that worked the streets. People who could introduce him to Gavin. Dad had insisted we pay the insurance premium that recently came due on that condo despite how financially underwater we were.

All of it lined up to one sickening conclusion.

Dad must have been the one that hired them.

## 40

I t didn't seem real. Felt like my world's foundation rocked beneath me, the landscape before me once again repainting a different reality. A different father figure.

If he'd done such a thing, why wouldn't he have come clean with me about it when we'd had our big talk? We'd put everything else on the table, and he kept this?

My chest tightened, wanting, demanding all the answers to my questions. But those answers would have to wait. Right now, I needed to focus on staying alive and figure out how in the hell to get Easton and me out of here.

I quickly assessed my surroundings, trying to identify any other paths out of here than the one behind us. One that might take them off guard. The arched concrete tunnel was thirty feet wide, twenty feet tall, with no doorways or staircases within view. Two iron tracks rounded a bend and came to rest behind Victor, where a flat man-made-looking train car stored ten wooden barrels. Far too big to pick up, but if I could get behind one, if they weren't filled with anything, maybe I'd have the strength to kick one and send it rolling over Victor. Or maybe I could turn the lights into a weapon. Three light bulbs with blue cables, connected to a car battery, rested on tripods, casting a wide spotlight in the otherwise blackened space, which smelled of stale water. Maybe there was a puddle out of sight, something I could use to electrocute these douchebags.

No. All of that was too far-fetched. My best shot was to run. And figure out how to take Easton with me, who was fading by the second. His eyes were barely open now, making my heart flutter in panicked beats.

But the goons. Tooth-Gap Guy was off to the left, leaning against the wall, Spiderweb Tattoo Face to my right, arms crossed over his chest. While Gavin—who stood in front—gave one last look of apprehension to his brother before facing Victor.

"No cops," Oily Hair declared, jogging back into sight after checking outside.

My heart became a racehorse.

Victor smirked at me.

"They're there," I claimed.

But I could tell by the narrowing of his eyes that he suspected I was lying. And judging by the clenching of his jaw, he was pissed he'd been tricked.

He picked dirt out of his thumbnail, then glared at Gavin. "The guy in the wheelchair. Why didn't you bring him?"

Gavin snapped his head back. "Why would I?"

Victor stopped picking his nail. "A witness who could *identify* you, and you're asking me why?"

"You told me to get her and Easton, and that's exactly what I did."

"I sent you to pick up the witness and the traitor. People who could turn us in. And you didn't think to grab the cripple? You fucking stupid?"

"I'm the one that got her ID. I found her and Easton."

Victor took two steps forward. "And you left a loose end behind."

"We had seconds to grab two people without being seen. That guy wasn't moving; if we'd grabbed him, these two mighta gotten away, or the cops mighta seen us."

"You're filled with excuses. Have a PhD in 'em. You never leave a witness behind. You grab them. It's not rocket science."

Gavin's fingers flexed. *"I'm* the one that found that heist in the first place. *I'm* the one that organized it. Easton is the one that screwed this up, not me."

I cringed. Even with death hanging over our heads, it still had to hurt Easton, having his brother turn on him like this. Not even caring that Easton was dying. The only indication Easton was still coherent was his fingernail scraping at the tape on his wrists.

My throat burned, seeing him so helpless. He didn't deserve to die like this, handed over by his very own brother to his executioner.

I needed to save him.

"You never had what it took to be part of my crew," Victor declared. "Let alone one of my commanders."

Victor raised his hand and fired a shot, making me jump. In the condensed space of concrete, the blast was so loud, my eardrums rang. Gavin stood with his eyes wide, a crimson hole appearing in his stomach, before his body thumped to the ground.

"No!" Easton growled.

"Dump him in the sewer." Victor didn't even look at his fallen frame. "Let the rats feed on him."

Easton's eyes darkened as he stared at Victor.

"I'm going to take care of the cripple," Victor announced, ambling back the way we came in. "Kill them both and dump them in the sewer, too."

Victor's figure got swallowed by the tunnel's shadows.

Spiderweb Tattoo Face walked up to me and pulled the weapon from his waistband, but I slammed my leg into his crotch. He collapsed to his knees, but he didn't drop the weapon. I grabbed the gun, fighting to push his finger off the trigger and replace it with my own.

He was stronger than me; I couldn't get the shot lined up to his head, but I did manage to thrust it toward his torso.

I pulled the trigger.

But it missed him and fired into the wall, sending a chip of stone splintering through the air, backlit by one of the portable lights. It stunned the guy for a moment, though, affording me time to line up another shot.

Meanwhile, Easton bolted to his feet. He'd managed to free his hands, and now, with Tooth-Gap Guy raising a semiautomatic, Easton charged him. And knocked him to the ground.

As Easton wrestled with the guy on the concrete, Oily Hair walked toward me. I pressed my finger on the trigger and aimed my barrel at him, but it wasn't easy. Especially with Spiderweb Tattoo Face still fighting for the weapon, but I didn't need to be precise. I just needed to maim.

When Oily Hair took another step and raised his arm, I pulled my trigger.

Oily Hair jerked, his hip spewing blood as he screamed.

"Zoey!" Easton shouted.

Spiderweb Tattoo Face knocked me down, jumped on top of me, wrapped his hands around my neck, and squeezed.

I pressed against his wrists, thrashed my body. Wiggling it, twisting it. I tried to bring my knees up, my ankles, but it was fruitless. The guy's lips curled over his teeth as he looked down at me and squeezed my neck tighter, pressure mounting in my head.

As I stared into the eyes of my killer, my only hope was that everyone else would make it out alive. That Easton would overpower the other men, that Dad would have made it to the police station before Victor found him. That Alex wouldn't be anywhere near the danger, either.

The concrete walls around me began to darken, the sound of Easton screaming my name fading.

Suddenly, my throat opened, and a flood of air rushed into my lungs so violently, I choked on it. A deep, barking cough so rough that I gagged.

My attacker was on the ground, and Easton was on top of him, punching the guy's nose, his cheek, his temple.

While Tooth-Gap Guy, the one Easton had been fighting, lay motionless twenty feet away. Dead or unconscious, I couldn't be sure. But Oily Hair, with his bloody hip, dragged himself into an army crawl toward his fallen gun, leaving a streak of blood painted along the concrete floor behind him like an artist had brushed a canvas.

My lungs burned, and my throat laced with metallic-tasting blood. I felt dizzy and light-headed, but I could not allow Oily Hair to reach the weapon. His eyes were trained on Easton, who continued to beat the hell out of the guy who'd tried to kill me.

I pushed my torso up and wobbled as I stood. Oily Hair was four feet away from the weapon and closing. The gun rested on the floor like it was sleeping peacefully, unaware that whoever grabbed it would likely win this battle and the others would lose their lives.

I took a step forward, hearing the flesh-on-flesh smacks and groans happening behind me as I stumbled closer to the injured man.

The floor rocked, but this time, I leaned into the fall and landed on Oily Hair's head. The sound of a turkey's wishbone cracking in half marked his nose breaking on the concrete.

He roared, but I leaned my shoulder into his neck more.

Out of the corner of my eye, I saw Easton stand up. With his fists covered in blood, he marched over to me and pulled me up.

"You okay?" Easton panted, his right eye already swelling and his lip bloody from the battle.

I nodded.

Easton grabbed Oily Hair's gun and tucked it into his waistband before the goon could reach it.

Spiderweb Tattoo Face and Tooth-Gap Guy remained lifeless on the ground, their weapons lying along the railroad track thirty feet away.

"I thought you were dying." Just the thought of it made me cry. "You were limp."

"The more injured I appeared, the more they'd let their guard down."

Easton bit into the edge of my tape and then ripped it open, unraveling the rest.

"So, you're okay?" I touched his arm.

"If it hit an organ, I'd be dead by now."

Tentative relief flooded my system.

But his brother wasn't okay; he lay on the ground, bleeding.

"Do you have your cell on you?" A rising wave of alarm rose through my core.

"No. They tossed it when they threw me in the van."

"We need to get Gavin help. And we need to get to my dad before Victor does."

Easton unleashed those ocean-colored eyes on me, scanning my body and then locking his gaze with mine until he seemed satisfied that I was as okay as I claimed.

But Gavin wouldn't be okay much longer. Easton and I rushed to where he'd fallen. He lay on his back, his breaths labored as blood oozed out of the bullet wound in his stomach.

I pressed my left palm against his wound, feeling his warm blood pool beneath my skin. I added my right hand on top, so I could press harder, but the blood merely slowed.

"Hold on, Gavin." I tried to sound strong, but time felt like an enemy, flying by too fast to save him.

Gavin's rounded eyes locked with mine as crimson stained the concrete beneath him. "Why are you helping me?" His voice was weak.

"You're Easton's brother."

A crease appeared between Gavin's brows. "But I turned you over to Victor."

No matter what mistakes Gavin made... "You're the only family Easton has, and I won't let him lose you."

Like Gavin, Dad had strayed and made choices that had hurt those he loved. He'd almost died before we could make amends, but he'd survived, giving us the time we needed to finally talk things out, mend our wounds, and start a new chapter in our relationship.

Easton deserved that same opportunity with his brother—to get him back and heal their hurts.

I couldn't let Gavin die before they had that chance.

Gavin's chest rose and fell quicker.

"Go get help," I said to Easton.

"I'm not leaving you alone down here." Easton eyed the darkened tunnels.

"I need to keep pressure on the wound."

"*I'll* put pressure on it."

But before either of us said anything else, a sound silenced us.

Footsteps, echoing off the murky tunnel. The steps of a single person were slow and methodical, almost as if they knew we could hear them approaching and wanted to drag it out.

I wanted to believe it could be a police officer coming down here to rescue us. After all, surely, my dad had called the police by now, and maybe they'd tracked down the van, found it parked outside that door. But my instincts told me the steps didn't belong to an ally.

Whoever was down here with us wasn't here to help.

"Zoey, run," Easton whispered.

But before I could process his demand, a silhouette emerged into the light.

Pointing a semiautomatic at us.

"Don't move."

## 41

Victor glanced at his fallen men before turning his attention back on us.

Easton positioned his body in front of mine.

"We could've made one hell of a team." Irritation laced Victor's words, making me wonder if anyone had ever turned him down before.

"I would never team up with you," Easton growled.

"You rob places for a living. You really think a complication wouldn't come up eventually?"

"That's the difference between me and you," Easton said in disgust. "I don't view people as complications."

Victor licked his teeth. "You never had the balls to be on my crew."

"I never had any interest in joining your crew. My brother fell for your lies, but I didn't."

Victor's gaze fell to Gavin, whose breaths were so light that I feared he'd die at any second.

"He saw my vision. Bigger heists. More money. I don't let things like witnesses or cops scare me out of taking what I want."

I could only pray that if we didn't make it out of here alive, Hernandez would not stop hunting until he found Victor and locked him up forever. Because Victor was willing to kill whoever was in his way. And someday, a witness might not just be any innocent person; it might be a child.

Victor shrank the distance between us to fifteen feet, and when he pointed his gun at me, Easton lunged and knocked Victor to the ground. The gun scraped across the concrete as it slid away while Easton punched Victor in his jaw. Which cracked like a twig. Victor bucked Easton off of him and kicked Easton's bloodstained stomach. Right where he'd been shot.

Easton howled and grabbed his abdomen as he crumpled to the ground, where Victor began beating him.

"Help him," Gavin pleaded.

I glanced at the gun, which was a few feet away, then back at Gavin. A bloodstain the size of a pumpkin pooled beneath him. I'd finally gotten the hemorrhaging to slow down, but if I let go, the faucet would turn back on, and I had to assume any further bleeding would be fatal.

If I didn't go for the gun, though, Victor would kill Easton.

"Help him," Gavin repeated.

My eyes stung. I said it out loud to make sure he understood what he was asking me to do. "If I let go, you'll probably die."

Victor punched Easton in the ear so hard, his head swiveled and his eyes started to roll into the back of his head.

Gavin locked his fading eyes with mine. "Save my brother," he pleaded.

I glanced at Gavin for one more second before jumping up.

I bolted to the gun, grabbed it, took aim, and pulled the trigger.

The gun didn't fire.

As Victor continued to whap Easton's temple, I looked at the gun, trying to figure out why it wasn't shooting. The trigger itself gave no indication. The gun didn't look damaged.

Maybe it was out of bullets. It was one of those guns that packed the bullets in a magazine, and I didn't know how to release it to check the bullet count.

With Victor's cracking fists making Easton's eyes close, I frantically glanced at the weapon in my hands.

A little silver lever sat at the base of the barrel. A safety?

I pushed the lever.

Lined up my shot at Victor's head again.

And pulled the trigger.

Another blast echoed off the concrete as Victor stilled, then fell to his right.

"Easton!" I screamed and ran to his side.

But his eyes didn't open.

## 42

E *aston has a heartbeat. Thank God.*
      I raced to Gavin's side, tears streaming down my cheeks as I pressed my hands against his wound again. Gavin groaned, but he lost so much blood, his skin was vampire-level pale. I needed to get him medical attention, but if I let go of his wound, by the time I ran out into the street and flagged down help and came back, I was confident he would be dead.

Easton might be, too.

*I'm alone in a darkened hell beneath the city and watching the love of my life die right in front of my eyes.*

"Hold on." I pressed my trembling hands down as hard as I could.

Gavin's eyes locked with mine again. Only this time, his eyes looked like his soul was connected to a dimmer, fading.

"I'm sorry," he whispered.

His eyelids slowly descended. I willed them to stop, to not close, for if they closed, they might never open again. And I couldn't tell Easton his only family was gone.

Gavin's eyes did close though, and he stopped moving, just as a new sound appeared.

The sound of hope.

As a symphony of footsteps grew louder, I couldn't tell if his chest was moving up or down anymore.

"Police!" a voice barked from the end of the tunnel I'd come in through.

"Over here!" I shouted. "We need help!"

A few seconds later, three police officers, wearing bulletproof vests, advanced toward me with their guns drawn atop powerful flashlights that swept the area for any sign of danger.

While the other two officers kicked the fallen weapons further to the side, one of the officers approached me and put his gun back into its holster.

Hernandez.

"Got a 10-52," Hernandez shouted to the end of the tunnel. Then, he walked to Easton, put his fingers on his neck.

What if it had stopped beating?

Hernandez was silent as his fingers felt for the heartbeat that was connected to my own.

"Is he okay?" I yelped.

"He's alive," Hernandez said.

I blew out a breath. But that didn't mean Easton was out of the woods. Blunt force trauma to the head, bullet wound to the stomach, and who knew what was going on inside his body?

One of the officers came to me and took over putting pressure on the wound, allowing me to rush to Easton's side. I wanted to cup his face but was terrified to move him, worried one wrong bump could damage his spinal cord or something.

His skin was pale, making me fear that he'd bled more than I realized. Possibly internally. And parts of his face were beginning to swell and darken from the assault.

If he hadn't fought Victor, I'd be dead. Easton had taken this beating to save my life.

And it might have cost him his own.

He was a protector for those he loved. A protector of his brother, of me, willing to lay down his life for us.

How many people would literally die to protect someone? How many would do it *after* that person had hurt them the way Gavin had?

Hernandez moved around to the other fallen men, checking their pulses. "This one's gone," he said, referring to Victor. "The others have a pulse."

"My dad. Victor was going to kill him. Is he—"

"He's at the station," Hernandez said. "Safe. So is Alex. Your dad called it in right away. Was smart enough to get the plate number. Put out an APB. Didn't take long for an officer to spot the van parked outside the tunnel entrance."

"He's really okay? Because when they shot Easton, my dad fell—"

"He's fine," Hernandez assured. "But we'd better get these guys to the hospital."

## 43

I stared at the crimson remnants on the tips of Easton's hair. The nurses had done an excellent job, cleaning the rest of the blood off, but dried fragments remained on some of his longer pieces. The skin around Easton's right eye was so swollen that only a millimeter of his sapphire iris was exposed, and his cheeks and jaw were covered in purple, as if someone had dabbed his face with a violet paintbrush.

Easton lay on a white hospital bed after undergoing surgery while a jumble of voices blended into the background of beeps and sneakers on the linoleum floor. It smelled like bleach. And fear.

"Hey," I whispered, taking Easton's hand when he stirred. "The doctor said you're going to be just fine."

Easton's medicated gaze landed on my face, inciting a smile. Which made him grimace from the pain. And then he frowned with concern.

After I'd been examined in the ER, I'd washed the blood off my skin, but I still had it on my clothes.

"Are you okay?" His voice was scratchy, like the beating must have roughed up his throat.

"I'm fine. But you seriously scared me," I said. "You weren't moving."

Easton looked down at his hospital gown, at the medical equipment surrounding him. "Fill me in on what happened. Last thing I remember, I was fighting Victor."

I squeezed his hand and picked up where his concussion had left off, Easton absorbing every word.

"My brother's alive?" Easton's face pinched in relieved disbelief.

"He was when they brought him in, but he lost a lot of blood. They took him up to surgery, too, but his is taking a lot longer. They said the doctor will be down soon to give us an update."

Easton's azure eyes looked down, a line appearing between his eyebrows. He cleared his throat and then held my gaze again.

"You saved my brother," he said. His tone was tight, as if fighting back tears. "Why? He was trying to get you killed."

"He's the only family you have." My chin quivered. "He may or may not continue to make terrible choices, but if he lives, at least he has the chance to turn his life around. The chance to love you again, the way you deserve to be loved by him, before it's too late."

*Everyone deserves a chance to atone for their mistakes. Do they not?*

Easton let out an incredulous breath, and he looked at me with a ghost of a smile.

"Just when I thought I couldn't admire you more," he whispered with a slight shake to his head.

Meeting Easton taught me that there are many different layers to people. Some good, some bad. Which is why it's so important to peel back all those layers to see what is truly underneath before we hastily rush to judgment.

We are not the sum total of our mistakes, but a sum total of what's in our hearts. We are all just a complicated array of good and bad choices, and I learned the importance of looking beyond our human frailties.

"You were worried that the lightness inside of Gavin was gone." I held his stare. "But when he saw you were losing the fight with Victor, do you know what Gavin did?" I asked. "He told me to let him go. Even though keeping pressure on his wound was the only thing keeping him alive, he said, 'Save my brother.'"

Easton's eyes welled with tears.

"No matter what he did before then, in that moment, he was willing to sacrifice his own life to save you." That was the layer I wanted Easton to hold on to.

Easton's lips quivered, and he cleared his throat. As he looked down at the floor, I wondered if he was replaying the erosion of Gavin's love for him, only to realize it had been there all along, buried beneath his bad choices.

A doctor emerged from the hallway. She had short red hair that swept up a little higher in the front and vintage brown-rimmed glasses. "Easton Wells?"

Easton nodded.

"I'm Doctor Morrison." She rubbed her hands together, as if they were cold. "I performed surgery on your brother."

"Is he…"

"He's in recovery," she said. "We removed a .22 caliber bullet from his abdominal cavity, repaired a perforation of his small bowel, and gave him a blood transfusion."

"Is he going to be okay?" Easton's voice rose with hope.

"He got lucky. If he'd lost more blood…" She paused. "His vitals are stable. At this point, the biggest risk for him is a post-op inter-abdominal abscess. It only happens in about 3 percent of patients, though, so I'm optimistic he'll make a full recovery."

Easton's chest deflated in relief. "Can I see him?"

"Once he's out of recovery, he'll be moved into a room. Medically, he'll be cleared for visitors, but you'll have to ask law enforcement."

Right. Gavin was a wanted criminal, now in custody.

So was Easton, who looked down at his right hand, which was cuffed to the bed's rail.

"I'll keep you posted on your brother." The doctor offered a sympathetic smile.

And then she left us alone.

With Easton staring at the handcuff, each second that passed, all the hope he'd felt appeared to drain from his body as reality grew unwanted weeds over his heart.

Easton didn't look at me as he spoke in a pained voice. "I really wish you'd listen to me; I don't want you to wait for me while I'm in prison. I don't want you to throw your life away on me."

"You *are* my life."

"Zoey—"

"And I'm not going to let you take that away from me."

"Zoey—"

"I've accepted your choices, Easton. And now, you need to accept mine."

He pursed his lips together.

"I'll wait for you, no matter what you say or do about it. I'll visit you every chance I get even if you refuse to see me. And the day that you get released? I'll be there to drive you home."

I could see by the furrowing of Easton's brows and the tears that broke over his battered cheeks that Easton never allowed himself to imagine a future with me in it.

"I've never had anyone love me like this before," he whispered.

I tried to act like his declaration hadn't bruised my soul.

Easton squeezed my hand. "You saved me, Zoey. In every way a man can be saved."

I stood up and leaned over his bed so my face dangled in front of his. And then I slowly and incredibly gently pressed my lips against his.

My growing love for Easton was as if every cell in my body had been awakened from a deep hibernation, emerging into the light of a forest.

I kept my lips on his for several seconds before pulling back and staring at the sapphire speckles in his eyes. They were darker on the outside and grew lighter toward the iris in a gorgeous gradient of blues and greens.

"Is your dad okay?" Easton brushed my cheek with the backs of his fingers.

I nodded. "He's in the waiting room."

Easton looked from my left eye to my right. "Do you think they were telling the truth? That your dad organized the heist?"

I took a deep breath and ran a hand through my hair. "I don't know. But I need to talk to him."

"Hey." I walked up to my dad in the waiting room. He'd parked his chair next to Alex, who'd come here to make sure I was okay.

"How is he?" Dad's voice was tense, like his concern for Easton only existed because Easton mattered to me.

"Easton's okay. They think his brother will be okay, too."

Dad nodded.

"Can we talk?" I asked him.

Alex looked from me to my dad. "I think I'll head home." He stood up and stared at me for a long moment. "I'm glad you're okay, Zoey."

All his earlier anger dissipated with the softening of his shoulders. I was sure he didn't understand how I could fall for a criminal who'd held me hostage, but Alex had been friends with me long enough to know there was a reason. He might not agree with it, might forever hold on to the belief Easton was a terrible person, but based on the soft smile he gave, clearly, he wasn't going to stay mad at me over it.

Something I greatly appreciated.

"Thank you, Alex. For everything. Seriously, you're a really good friend, and I don't know what we would have done without you."

I felt bad for having ever suspected him of being involved in the robbery. He really had hired the PI to help find who did this to me.

Alex offered me another weak smile and then ambled out the front doors to give me and my father some privacy.

The waiting room was busy, though. The conversation I wanted to have with him wasn't something I cared to do in public.

"Let's go for a walk," I suggested, "so we can talk in private."

Dad followed me outside the automatic doors and wheeled himself next to me as I lumbered down the sidewalk.

It was twilight, just after the sunset, and skyscrapers already had their lights on, bracing for the coming darkness that would soon swallow the city. The storm had passed a bit ago, and the pavement was still glistening from its brief rain. Vehicles hummed along the road in a stream of white headlights and red taillights while a scattering of pedestrians walked along the sidewalks. A light breeze blew my hair into my face as I looked down at my father.

"I'm sorry for keeping Easton's identity a secret from you." I looked away, a pang hitting my ribs.

Dad's wheelchair bumped over a sidewalk crack. "Wish you had been honest with me."

"It was complicated."

Dad pursed his lips. "Complicated?"

"I didn't think you'd understand." I shrugged. "But there's no excuse for lying. I'm sorry."

A block away, the metallic scraping pierced the air as the "L" train tunneled through the buildings.

"Dad, when they'd grabbed me and put me in the van, they recognized you."

Dad clenched his eyes shut and stopped rolling his wheelchair. An ambulance's siren wailed somewhere close by.

"So, it's true, then."

Dad blew out a breath so deep, he must've been holding it in since before the robbery.

"You hired them," I said through blurry eyes. "Why?"

Dad pinched the bridge of his nose. "Zoey…"

The ambulance came around the corner, its siren so loud that it stabbed my ears, and then it parked outside the doors of the hospital. Thankfully turning off the siren.

"I need to hear you say it. Because otherwise, it doesn't feel real."

Dad regarded me, his rounded eyes full of sorrow. "I couldn't watch you suffer the financial burden of taking care of me anymore. I spent weeks making phone calls, trying to get myself into an inpatient rehab, trying to apply for government assistance to get out of your way so you could have a normal life, but none of it panned out. I had even called friends, distant relatives, asking for help."

I put my hand over my aching stomach.

"And in the meantime," he continued, "I would see you come home so stressed over money, no matter how much you tried to hide it. And it was just getting worse." Dad shook his head. "I failed to get out of your hair."

*Out of my hair.* The ache spread up to my ribs.

"But I swear, sometimes, it's like once you're down on your luck, you're a plague that no one wants to touch. They don't want to get involved, like they're worried your bad luck will rub off on them. Or maybe they assume that once they open that door, I'll just keep walking through it, asking for more, and you know what?"

Dad scrubbed the side of his face. "It's not their responsibility to save me," he said. "But it's not your responsibility, either. This entire situation spiraled out of control. When you first took me in, I thought it would be for a few weeks. I never imagined that all the bills would be put onto your shoulders. It's not right. I'm the parent; you're the child. I'm supposed to enrich your life, not poison it."

Up ahead, a father and his little girl walked down the sidewalk, holding hands, while she licked an ice cream cone. The sight of it made my chest clench at the innocence of it all.

"I felt helpless, Zoey. You were drowning in financial pressure, and I couldn't work, and none of the government assistance was coming through, and hospitals and rehab places wouldn't touch me with a ten-foot pole because I had filed for bankruptcy. I could go on and on about all the other things I tried to do to help, but I didn't care what it took. I was going to find a way to help you, come hell or high water."

The farther we got from the hospital, the stronger the smell of fried pastries grew. Somewhere nearby must be a sweet shop of baked goods.

"But a robbery? Dad, you've never broken the law before."

"The robberies were all over the news. And I saw how they would target affluent houses when no one was home. When you would go to work, I started taking rolls through the neighborhood. Started talking to people on the streets and asking questions. Wasn't long before a guy introduced me to another guy who could arrange the whole thing."

The guy had introduced him to Gavin.

"Did they know it was your condo?"

"Just told them it was empty." Dad pinched his nose again. "If I'd had any idea you were ever planning to go back to that condo, I never would've done it, Zoey. I thought you wouldn't go back until it sold."

The traffic on the road slowed down as a stoplight turned red.

"Why didn't you tell me after?" I demanded, anger and betrayal boiling my blood.

"At first, I was in shock. I couldn't believe you had gone there that night and had almost been killed. The guilt ate me alive. I was disgusted with myself that I had once again found a way to hurt you."

My throat stung.

"Seemed like the harder I tried to help you, the more I hurt you, and I was so angry with myself, I couldn't bear admitting what I had done. It was pathetic and weak, but I was scared, too. I was afraid if you found out, you would never forgive me."

Dad looked down in shame. "And yet, I couldn't let it go, either. As angry as I was at myself, I was seething at the men who'd laid their hands on you. I was promised that no one would ever get hurt. They were willing to kill you over this, and I was not about to let that go."

He looked at me again. "That's why I was so obsessive in finding out who had done this. When you'd go to work, I would go back and try to find the original man I had talked to, but he was nowhere to be found."

*I wonder if Victor took care of him.*

"So, you hired a private investigator." I rubbed my forehead. "And when you found them, what were you going to do?"

Dad looked up at the sky before looking back to me. "I told myself I was going to turn them into the police. But I don't know if I would've had the willpower to do that. I might have taken justice into my own hands."

This was too much to process. Dad and I had finally reached a place where we were moving forward with our relationship. And that whole time? He knew that there was this big secret that he was keeping from me.

I thought the biggest thing I had to get past was Easton's prior offenses, but now, my dad's behavior confronted me. It felt like the universe was testing me, to see if I'd really get over my biases and forgive people for their bad choices.

"Why didn't you tell me about this sooner?" I clenched my hand. "We had that heart-to-heart, and you never even mentioned any of this."

"I was scared it would put you in more danger. I was concerned that if they found out you were the daughter of the man that had hired them, they'd try even harder to eliminate you because I could ID one of them. I was going to tell you once they were behind bars. I just wasn't going to do it when it might put you in danger, Zoey. I'm sorry."

This was unreal.

A man on a cell phone walked around us on the sidewalk. I waited until he was for sure out of earshot before I spoke again.

"And the police? They know what you did?"

"I confessed right after the heist. I was fully transparent and gave Hernandez every piece of information I had. What the middleman and the burglar he connected me with looked like, where I met them, everything. I turned over every piece of information, so they could try to find these people."

"And you didn't get arrested?"

"Was told charges would be forthcoming, but at the time, they were trying to find the suspects, and I think they were hoping the burglars might try to contact me. Maybe to find out who you were."

"And the police didn't think I had a right to know this?"

"I pleaded with them not to tell you until this was all over. You had been through a tremendous trauma, and the last thing you needed was more heartbreak." He dropped his tone lower. "I'm so sorry, Zoey. I hope you can find it in your heart to forgive me."

I looked at the father walking with his little girl up ahead. She was crying, staring at her ice cream cone, which had fallen on the sidewalk, while the dad knelt before her, wiping away her tears.

It would take time for my anger and disappointment to subside, but I wasn't going to turn my back on Dad. Because even though I was upset right now, he needed to know that, "I do forgive you, Dad. But you have to promise me that from now on, we'll always talk everything out. And no matter what happens, you'll never do something like this again."

"I can't believe I did it in the first place." He shook his head and pursed his lips. "I wish I could go back in time and take it all back."

I scrubbed my face with my hands. "I don't want you to move out, Dad. Not until you're physically and financially independent."

"Zoey—"

"This is my life, and I get to make the decisions for myself. And I want to help my father get back on his feet. And I want time with you, too, Dad. To have that second chance with each other that we've both wanted."

Dad's lower lip quivered, and a sadness cut through his eyes. It took him several seconds to find his voice. "How could you want to help me after what I've done?"

"Because you're my father. And what you did was really stupid, but I still love you. And I always will. And there's nothing you could ever do to make me love you any less."

Dad's Adam's apple bobbed.

"I might be going to jail." He cast his eyes down.

"Then, I'll visit you there. Someone's got to make sure you're doing your PT."

A ghost of a grin stretched over his lips.

"Maybe you'll share a cell with Easton."

Dad's smile fell, and he looked back up at me. "Suppose you wouldn't listen to me if I said you deserve better?"

"You kind of lost the upper hand, Dad. Besides, you both orchestrated that robbery."

Dad frowned. I could see his eyes searching for the building blocks of an argument of how his sins weren't as bad as Easton's, but he must have seen the determination in my posture and knew it was a lost cause. Leaving him with two options: alienate his daughter after all of this or accept her choices. Even if he didn't agree with them.

"Come on." I nodded toward the hospital. "You guys never had a formal introduction."

"You want me to meet the criminal that held you hostage?" Dad licked his teeth. "And not kill him?"

"I want you to meet my boyfriend. And, yes, non-murder would be great."

## 45

D ad wheeled himself over to the side of Easton's hospital bed. Gave him the don't-mess-with-my-daughter glare.

"Sir." Easton straightened himself up.

"You're a criminal."

"Dad…"

"Was," Easton said. "I'm giving up that lifestyle."

"You're dating my daughter."

"Yes, sir."

"She deserves better."

"Dad!"

Dad pursed his lips. Clearly, accepting my choices was harder for him than he imagined.

"You're right." Easton broke eye contact. "I've told her repeatedly to let me go, but Zoey's…"

"Stubborn?" I arched a brow.

"Headstrong." Easton's mouth curled slightly on one side. "And after everything she's been through, I won't break her heart by cutting her out of my life unless that's what she wants."

"And if she changes her mind? And does want you out of her life?"

"I'll support that one hundred percent. And be here for her in whatever capacity she desires."

Dad's chest inflated, but I could still see him struggling with this. "Why are...*were*," he corrected, "you a burglar?"

Easton explained his life story to my father—his parents dying, living on the street, stealing at first to stay alive and then allowing it to escalate from there. What I loved about it was that Easton made no excuses for his choices. He simply laid out the sequence of events and decisions he had made that brought him to this point.

"The condo burglary changed everything," Easton continued.

"Why?" my dad pressed.

Easton exchanged a quick look with me and then cleared his throat. "Ever since my parents died, my life had gone on this crooked track, heading toward a cliff. But then Zoey was like an electrical surge that jolted the train and made me look up for the first time."

My dad folded his hands in his lap.

"For years, I've been merely existing. Going on that broken track. Waking up each day and never thinking beyond it. Never having a reason to change. But then I met Zoey, and she made me realize how much more my life could be."

My throat swelled.

"After that, my only focus was protecting Zoey. And things just... evolved from there."

My dad rubbed his cheek. "You'll be going to prison," Dad grumbled.

"I told Zoey I didn't want her to wait for me."

"And I reminded him no one controls my decisions, except me."

Dad gave me a look with tight eyes, like he was about to go into the whole why-would-you-wait-for-him-while-he's-in-prison debate. But I shot him the I'm-a-grown-woman-and-this-is-my-decision look that shut it down.

After a few more seconds, Dad returned his stare to Easton. "Even if you don't spend an eternity in prison, how can I trust you won't go back to breaking the law?"

"I'll never do anything that could bring her harm."

"If you ever hurt my daughter—" Dad flexed his fingers.

"I'd never."

Dad blew out an exasperated breath. I could tell he didn't like this. A felon wasn't his dream match for his daughter. But he also knew this wasn't his call to make. I was an adult, and Easton had my heart. In time, I trusted Dad would grow to love Easton as much as I did. Or at least not despise him.

"Some people are not bad in nature, Dad. They just make mistakes."

## 46

TWO YEARS, SIX MONTHS, AND THIRTEEN DAYS LATER

I jumped out of bed and looked at the clock, then danced to the shower.

I loved my new bathroom with the tiled floor that looked like wood, the white vanity, and the updated trim. But then I loved everything about my new apartment, especially its location. I loved that it was closer to the heart of Chicago and that it was only one block from the "L" train, so getting to work was super quick. I loved that I had my own balcony, where I could sit and watch the stars at night. But most of all, I loved that it was mine.

I missed living with Dad, but it was a wonderful new chapter for both of us when he'd moved out a couple years ago. Besides, he visited me. A lot. And we'd become closer than ever.

I hummed the entire time I washed my hair, the hot water cascading over my skin. I sang as I put my makeup on and glanced at the framed photograph hanging on the wall. Taken a year ago, the photo was me, sitting on the South Rim of the Grand Canyon, watching the sun set.

One moment of that trip stood out above the rest.

*I hold up the dandelions I picked in honor of my deceased boyfriend.*

*I'd read that the dandelion is a symbol of resilience, hope, and the rebirth of life. The dandelion is able to survive in some of the harshest conditions, and can bounce back from adversity, and continue to grow. The bright yellow petals represent joy, and the black seeds carry wishes for new beginnings with them as they fly into the air.*

*I have a mixture of yellow ones and some that have already turned into white puffballs.*

*"It took me a while to get here," I say. "And I still miss you every single day. I always will. But from this moment on, I vow I will never break my promise to you again. I finally found the happiness I promised you I would, and this time, I'll never let it go."*

*I blow the little white puff balls off their base and watch them float off into the pastel sky.*

*And inside my heart, the past finally releases and floats into my future.*

I glanced at the smaller picture that I'd hung on the side wall—of me holding Anthony's baby for the first time—and my heart warmed with memories from that day, when he'd flown to Chicago and Dad and I got to meet my niece.

I continued smiling as I got dressed, irrationally looking at the clock every two minutes.

I would not be late. Not for this. I wanted to hit the road within the next twenty minutes.

A knock on my front door made me grin.

I opened it, and there, standing on the other side—yep, standing—was Dad. He'd made a full recovery.

"I brought bagels." He held up a brown bag.

Dad gave me a quick kiss on the cheek as he walked inside and set breakfast down on my kitchen table. "Alex sends his regards."

"How does he like his new clinic?"

"Loves it. We'll have to go out to celebrate," Dad said.

We had a lot to celebrate these days. Including my much-improved financial situation. I never collected the reward money. Even if they would have given it to me, when I found out my brother had put a second mortgage on his house to fund it, I refused to take it.

Instead, I got a second job tending bar, collected a tidy little bonus from my primary job after another year of outperforming my targets, and slowly climbed out of that hole. I'd have to say, though, the biggest financial swing came when Dad's situation rebounded and that financial burden evaporated.

It allowed me to start classes at college to pursue my degree in veterinarian science. Would it take a while to get the degree? Yep. But time was going to pass anyway, so why not pursue a job working with animals, like I'd always wanted?

Dad pleaded guilty to conspiracy to commit burglary. He avoided more serious charges, thanks to his immediate confession and cooperation with the case. I also suspected that his physical condition and mental state at the time of the burglary played a role in the DA agreeing to lowering the charges and commuting his sentence, but I couldn't be sure. In any case, Dad was only sentenced to thirty days in jail with two years of probation and two hundred hours of community service.

Meanwhile, before and after Dad's stint in jail, Alex continued giving my dad physical therapy at a majorly discounted rate and let me pay off my debt to him over time. He kept fighting me on taking the money, but I insisted. Dad regained his independence, moved into his own apartment, and started his own company.

I didn't think starting his own company was his original goal, but getting hired back into his old position with a criminal record hadn't panned out, so he opened up a consulting agency. Without start-up capital, he built it on his sweat equity, slowly building it from the ground up. He was still doing corporate strategy work, but not for one company. Rather many different companies, on his own terms, charging his own rates, freelance.

It would take him several years before he was pocketing more than basic living expenses, but he was on the road to financial freedom and was thrilled about it.

The best part was seeing how happy he was. He and I had never been closer, and his independence had eradicated the remaining sadness inside of him.

These days, we hung out at least two times a week. Sometimes, we'd go out to dinner or take in a museum. Sometimes, we'd just sit and talk. To put a word on it, it was...wonderful. A fresh new chapter, full of joy.

Joy that was about to get a hella lot bigger.

"You nervous?" Dad met my gaze.

"Excited."

"Sure you don't want me to drive with you?"

"Positive. I want it to be just him and me on the drive home."

Dad took out a bagel, spread cream cheese on it, and took a bite.

"You worried it'll be different now that you'll be with him all the time?"

I checked myself out in the mirror, wanting to look perfect today. I kept my hair long, in waves, and had a brand-new white T-shirt and jeans on.

"I've visited him every week for the past two and a half years. We talk on the phone every single day, and we write letters to each other every day, too, so, no, I'm not nervous. I'm excited."

Beyond excited.

If a child had to wait ten years for Christmas? That was what this felt like, times a thousand.

Dad cream-cheesed a bagel for me and set it on the table. "Eat."

"I'm too excited."

"Eat. Your blood sugar might fall. Last thing you need to do is faint when you see him."

I sighed heavily, pretending to be annoyed, but he had a point.

I begrudgingly downed half a bagel and looked at the clock again.

"It's time."

I smiled so wide, I thought my lips might crack.

I kissed my dad on the cheek. "Lock up when you leave, yeah?"

"I'm heading out, too. I didn't take the day off work like you did."

"So, your offer to drive with me was kind of rhetorical then." I smiled.

Dad rolled his eyes.

"Drive safe, and, Zoey?" Dad paused. "He'd better be worth the wait."

I almost skipped all the way to my car—yep, I had my very own car now!—waving at Dad as he pulled away in his own. I blasted pop music all the way to the prison, and when I parked, my hands were shaking.

I wish Easton had let me come inside, but he'd insisted I stay out here.

"God knows how long they are going to take, and I don't want you getting exposed to something when I'm not there to protect you," he'd said.

I didn't fight much because honestly, it didn't matter to me where we reunited. Just that we did.

I chewed on my thumbnail, pacing near my car. It was cold out today. A fresh inch of snow blanketed the parking lot, and my breath came out in puffs of white clouds as the icy wind stabbed my cheeks. But I didn't care. I had my coat, I had my gloves, and my heart kept me warm.

I glanced at the time on my phone. Easton was supposed to be released twenty minutes ago. He'd warned me not to worry if it was a little late, but I was officially worrying. What if they'd somehow retracted his plea deal? The one that allowed him to only be convicted for five years, only serving half for good behavior?

If they did that, it would be complete bullshit. Easton followed through with every one of his conditions. He'd avoided kidnapping and attempted murder charges with my testimony that Easton never went along with the plan to kill me—in fact, he'd helped me escape and protected me from Victor and his crew. I mean, yeah, it got a little dicey there for a moment, given that Easton was the leader of those Robin Hood Thieves burglaries, but no one had been hurt in them. And Easton's information allowed police to take down Victor's crew, who'd moved here from Philly—where, evidently, their burglaries often resulted in murders.

Easton even convinced his brother, Gavin, to accept a plea deal in exchange for more information for the investigation. His brother had another few years to serve, thanks to some of his more serious charges, but the point was, Easton did everything they'd asked, and his testimony had been vital to keeping people safe from Victor's crew.

The officers stopped all the burglaries and publicly claimed a victory in front of the city. It would be a really crappy thing to do to wait until the last day of his sentence and take back his plea deal. And it would look really bad to do that.

Plus, I didn't think that was legal. But I chewed another millimeter off my thumbnail, wondering if it was possible.

No. Hernandez would have called me if that happened. Right? He'd been a fantastic detective, staying in touch with me the entire time.

I paced left, then right, staring at the prison for any sign of life. Barbed wire rested along the top of the beige stone walls, a 360° lookout tower positioned only twenty feet from the iron gate, whose copper coloring had faded through the years.

A gate that still hadn't opened.

Thirty minutes late.

I pulled my cell phone out to call the prison to confirm nothing had delayed Easton's release when a metallic groan alerted me to movement.

The gate slid open slowly, sounding like an ancient garage door struggling to maintain control.

Easton emerged in a white shirt and jeans, his brown jacket open in the front despite the frigid air.

Damn, he looked fine.

It felt like he walked toward me in slow motion, his brown hair with caramel highlights swaying in the breeze. With his fists shoved inside his coat pockets, Easton scanned his surroundings, searching for me. And when he found me, he smiled so wide, I could see his teeth.

I froze. I'd dreamed of this moment every night, and here I was, not running and jumping into his body, wrapping my legs around him like I thought I would. It was as if all the happiness I felt had paralyzed me.

Closing the distance between us, Easton kept his eyes fixed on mine with such severe focus that a car could've hit him and he'd have still kept his gaze on me. A hungry determination, patience losing its last edge, flashed through his stare as he finally reached me. Grabbed my waist and slammed his lips against mine.

We hadn't kissed for over two and a half years, and I swore it was like a drug exploding passion through my entire body. I had fantasized about having his lips on mine so many times, but this was more intensely better than I had ever imagined.

Easton's hands were in my hair, and mine were around his neck, pulling his ripped body against mine. We kissed and kissed and groped until we realized we could do more—so much more—as soon as we got home. Only the promise of *more* gave us the power to pause.

"I love you." He looked down at me with his sapphire eyes.

"I love you." I grinned. "Now, let's go home."

Easton smiled and opened my car door for me.

As we drove away from the prison, I knew that we could handle whatever life threw our way after everything we'd overcome.

Two lost souls leaving the ugly past behind and embracing the beauty of the future.

# EPILOGUE

## WILLOW

I did not have a sixth sense that something dark and twisted was about to happen. Or that I'd soon be fighting for my life. I was simply focused on grabbing a quick drink with some friends at a nearby restaurant.

As I walked over to the table where Zoey, Emily, and Jenna were already seated, I reminded myself not to stare at the scar slashed across Jenna's face. My friends were with another woman who I struggled to place.

"Willow!" Zoey jumped up and gave me a hug, then motioned toward the unfamiliar face. "Have you met Fallon?"

"I don't think so," I said.

"Fallon and I used to work out at the same gym," Zoey explained. "Before it burned to the ground, that is."

Right. The fire. Zoey had seriously been through the wringer.

"Good to meet you." Fallon shook my hand. "I hope you don't mind me crashing. I was just finishing up dinner with a friend and saw Zoey here. Thought I'd say hi."

"It's always nice to meet someone new." I smiled.

That was when I spotted him.

Shane Hernandez.

Walking toward the front of the restaurant from the men's room, he didn't seem to notice all the women's eyes in the place being pulled in his direction. He didn't seem to notice them salivating over his ripped body that tried to break free of his emerald button-down shirt and deliciously tight black pants. His black hair looked effortlessly styled, complementing the olive skin that stretched across his stubbled jaw—a jaw I'd fantasized kissing on more than one occasion.

I wondered if he ever sensed my attraction to him. It had been there since the moment he moved into the apartment next door to mine, but maybe he just saw me as a friend. A person he held the building's door open for, a person he exchanged mail with whenever the mailman swapped some parcels in the wrong box, and on a really great day, a person he stopped and talked to.

Maybe *friend* was even too generous of a term.

After all, he knew very little about me.

But that was all about to change.

Because as a detective, he'd soon work my case, determined to uncover the secret of how I'd fallen from a bridge into the deadly river below.

Was it an accident? Was I thrown? If so, who would want me dead?

And would they try again?

Working to uncover the shocking truth about that fateful evening, we had no idea what was about to happen to us both...

THANK YOU FOR READING LETHAL JUSTICE! I HOPE YOU LOVED EASTON and Zoey's story as much as I do. **Shane Hernandez gets his HEA in GRAVE DECEPTION, which continues next.**

BUT FIRST, WHAT **SHOCKING PLAN DID EASTON HAVE AS HE WALKED along the lakefront the fateful day he met Zoey?** As a THANK YOU

TO READERS, delve into this **exclusive FREE chapter from Easton's POV** (https://kathylockheart.com/easton-pov-the-truths-we-hide/). It will leave you breathless...

# GRAVE DECEPTION

# GRAVE DECEPTION BLURB

My new neighbor is a scorching hot police detective—one I have a massive crush on, but I never wanted to get his attention like this: as the apparent victim of an attempted murder.

After rescuing me from the icy waters of the Chicago River, Shane begins investigating the people closest to me, and to my horror, discovers several of them have a motive to want me dead.

Worse, he firmly believes they will try again.

The more time Shane spends with me trying to unravel how I plummeted from that bridge, the more protective he becomes, and the harder we fall for each other. But I can tell Shane is hiding something from me—something that has the power to destroy our happily ever after.

All I want is to solve the case so we can put this entire nightmare behind us.

**But I never imagined the shocking truth about that fateful evening... or what's about to happen to us both...**

*For the readers who embraced this series. I hope you love Shane's happily ever after.*

# AUTHOR'S NOTE

Grave Deception is an emotional, tension-filled romance. This love story contains violence and other content that may be triggering for some readers. I prefer you go into a story without spoilers, but if you would like **a list of detailed triggers**, you can find it posted on my website at KathyLockheart dot com.

## 1

*Surrendering to death is different than I imagined.*

I assumed the final seconds of life would feel quick, but as I plummeted from a bridge toward the glacial water of the Chicago River, my body felt like it was suspended in midair, the winds pushing against me, shoving against the sands of time.

Tonight, a thin layer of fog snaked around steel skyscrapers, their windows glowing against the onyx sky—as if the city's mythical beauty was trying to veil this grisly tragedy. Arctic gusts stung my cheeks and hardened the ashen chunks floating in the coal-colored water beneath me.

*I wonder if they'll find my body. Or if I'll sink and Mom will never know what happened to me.*

My heart bled for her. The poor woman didn't deserve to suffer yet another loss—this time, her twenty-nine-year-old daughter. Her grief from Dad's death had cloaked her soul with so much darkness that even the sun could not penetrate it. Her heart so fractured, it had hardened her skin into an impenetrable shield, emotionally shutting everyone out for years.

It was only recently, after she'd started therapy, that Mom had made the progress I'd always hoped for, and she was finally on the cusp of turning things around. If I didn't make it, all her progress would drown with me. She'd sail into the empty sea of loneliness, destined to die alone.

I didn't want that for her, and it felt unfair, to lose my life before I'd had the chance to experience some of life's most profound milestones. I would never walk down the aisle or know the joys of motherhood. The closest I'd come to having kids was the stray cat I fed every day. If I died, who would take care of her? I'd been feeding her for months, and now, she had grown to depend on me. Adopting her was my ultimate goal, but my landlord didn't allow pets, so for now, I put out food every morning and night, gave her medication to prevent fleas, and put a cat shelter full of blankets outside to keep her warm. If I never returned, would she survive?

I wished I'd told Shane about the cat; maybe he could have taken over where I left off.

Shane Hernandez. The guy I'd had a crush on ever since he moved in as my next-door neighbor. He was the complete package. Tall, sexy as hell, with eyes that could make you forget about everything going on around you. He was kind, too, always making the effort to stop and ask how I was doing when we bumped into each other in the hallway, and as if that weren't hot enough, he was a detective with the Chicago Police Department, sporting a gun and badge hanging from his belt that hugged his incredible physique. Insert swoon-fest.

I could see flashes of our first encounter.

"LEAVE ME ALONE, EZRA," I SNAP, YANKING MY ARM AWAY.

*I walk along the sidewalk toward the double doors of my apartment complex.*

*"I'm just trying to help you get inside, Willow."*

*"I don't need your help."*

*"You've had too much to drink."*

*Not typical and not intentional. I tried a new mixed drink that was dangerous, how its strength snuck up on you.*

*But I'm not drunk. I'm buzzed. Big difference. He wants me to be drunk so he can play the part of the noble guy who helps a vulnerable woman get home safely. As if behaving like a gentleman can make up for what he did to me.*

"It's over between us," I remind him. "How many times do I have to say it?"

*Ezra ignores me and grabs my elbow. Like I need his help to walk.*

Asshat.

*When I yank my arm away, I lose my center of gravity, and I fall to the ground.*

*Ezra manhandles me again because it isn't enough that he invaded my girls' night and jumped into my Uber.*

"Let me go!" *I snap.*

*But Ezra uses both hands to grab me now.*

"She said let her go," *a deep voice warns.*

*Ezra whips his gaze to the figure standing ten feet from us. It's dark outside, the only light coming from two exterior bulbs that cast an orange haze around the mystery man.*

"Mind your own damn business." *Ezra pulls me.*

"Stop!" *I say.*

*Seriously, I'm not a violent person, but so help me, if Ezra doesn't leave me alone, I'm going to slam my heel into his crotch.*

"Chicago PD." *The shadowy figure flashes a badge that reflects the light from the building.* "Step away from her right now, or I'll arrest you for assault."

*Ezra pauses.* "I'm not hurting her. I'm helping her because she's drunk."

"She told you to stop. Step away from her. Now."

"You can't arrest me for helping her."

"If you don't leave her alone? I sure as hell can."

*Ezra glares at the guy, his fingers flexing at his sides.*

"But you don't step away right this second?" *the guy growls.* "Maybe I'll rearrange your face instead."

*I have no idea if the cop is being serious or sarcastic, but hallelujah, it works. Ezra moves away from me.*

"I was just trying to help," *Ezra says before slinking away into the night.*

"You okay?" *the cop asks.*

*I stand up slowly. In the dark, I can only make out his muscular body, which is encased in dark pants, a button-down shirt, and a gray wool jacket. He tucks his badge back into his pocket and straightens his tie.*

"I'm fine. Thank you," I say, but I can't stop myself from adding, "You didn't need to do that. I had it under control."

*I start to walk, losing the upper hand when my high heel hits a crack. Before gravity makes me another victim, a hand catches me by the hip, and I'm pressed against a firm side, a stern face looking down at me.*

*Holy crap. That chiseled jaw, those steely blue eyes. The guy holding me against his unfairly gorgeous body is my new next-door neighbor. His palm sends a flash of heat through my hip as he holds my gaze for five heartbeats. Five slow, belly-warming heartbeats.*

"I've seen you around but haven't introduced myself yet."

*He's noticed me. My hormones begin a glee fest, but the blood beneath my cheeks is too busy worrying he might've noticed me drooling over him.*

"I'm Shane," he says.

"Willow," I say, adding, "You're a cop?"

"A detective," he says. "I wouldn't be a good one if I didn't say this..." *His voice is warm and caring, no hint of animosity.* "Gettin' this drunk is dangerous, Willow. You don't know how many girls in this city get assaulted every day."

*I step away from him to make it clear I can stand on my own, that my clumsiness is merely from dangerous footwear.*

*High heels are weapons of mass destruction.*

"I'm not that drunk," I say, motioning to where Ezra walked off. "He's just using my slight overindulgence as an excuse to try to weasel his way back into my life. Which will never work."

*Shane raises his eyebrows. Seems to consider this with a ghost of a smile, which he quickly drops.*

"The guy. Does he normally get that handsy with you?"

"No. He's harmless." *Overbearing and a class-A dickwad. But harmless.*

"Didn't look harmless," he says.

*My neck burns in embarrassment of this scene. Of all the ways I wanted to meet my hot neighbor, this was not one of them.*

"I'm sorry I bothered you," I say.

*The tone of his voice lowers an octave. "You're never a bother, Willow."*

THAT ENCOUNTER SPARKED THE FIRE OF MY GROWING ATTRACTION TO him, yet in our subsequent run-ins, I kept getting mixed signals. On the one hand, it seemed like he looked for excuses to stop and make small talk with me, and when he did, he studied me intently, like my every word fascinated him. During those talks, I'd catch him staring at my mouth with this wanton look in his eyes, and other times, his hungry gaze would comb over my body. But sometimes, we'd be in the middle of talking, and he'd suddenly clear his throat and excuse himself, leaving me with the impression he was intentionally cutting the conversation short.

Maybe he was attracted to me but thought dating a neighbor was a bad idea. After all, if we broke up, that would be seriously awkward, running into each other, but still. I wished I could have explored something with him, because as the foreboding water rushed toward me, I realized I'd never have another chance.

No.

I wasn't going to die.

The bridge was only three stories above the river—people survived higher falls than that. The bigger danger was the water, which, in winter, was a hair above freezing. So cold, it would lock up your muscles, making it virtually impossible to swim. Causing death within minutes, if not sooner. And it would endanger anyone else that might try to rescue me.

But so help me, even if the landing broke my bones, I'd fight with everything I had and make it to the shore.

I could do it.

I had to.

I braced myself as the river slammed into me.

And everything went black.

Pain pierced through my body like a thousand daggers stabbing me—each dagger ice, slicing up my skin with their arctic blades. I tried to scream, but I couldn't open my mouth, couldn't open my eyes, either. In a sea of darkness, the only thing that existed was muffled sounds.

Splashes.

Yelling.

Something hard clenched my torso.

"Hold on!"

Something else pressed to the back of my neck, lifting my face above the waterline.

"Willow?" The voice echoed its shock through my ears.

The voice knew my name. How did the voice know my name? Why did the voice seem familiar to me?

My body shifted and jerked, water splashing on my face and going up my nose, dripping a freezing path into my throat. Whoever it was seemed to struggle with my weight—my winter coat and jeans anchoring me down.

I could hear the mystery man breathing heavily, and I could feel his arm loosening its grip around me, undoubtedly weakening from the beginnings of hypothermia.

"Hold on, Willow." There was an urgency to his voice, as if he knew I needed to actively fight against falling asleep. Because it wasn't just falling asleep…

Flirting with the border between life and death, fighting to live was exhausting. My body hurt, my lungs hurt, and trying to stay alive was as tiring as fighting against a violent rip current. How easy it would be to just let go and get carried toward death.

"Grab her beneath her shoulders!" the voice barked. "But be careful. Support her spine!"

Something locked beneath my armpits, and then my back scraped across something as the water receded from my torso, then my legs.

With my body now still, I tried to open my eyes again.

*Why can't I open my eyes? Why can't I scream?*

*I'm so cold. It feels like every cell, every vein, every bone in my body is freezing into pure ice.*

I wanted a blanket, to be curled up by a warm fire—anything to get warm.

I tried to take a breath, but I couldn't, and my lungs screamed with death's grip squeezing them.

*Help.*

"Her pulse is weak," the voice growled, panting. "I don't think she's breathing. Check the ETA on the ambulance. We have less than four minutes before permanent brain damage sets in, another minute or so until she's dead."

Fingers tilted my chin, opened my mouth, and then something warm draped over it. A thrust of heated air burst into my throat. The relief was only temporary though, because the wind whipped against my neck and carved a tunnel into my body, all the way to my bones.

"Coats!" the voice barked. "Give me your fuckin' coats!"

As his mouth returned to mine, blowing another deep rush of oxygen into my lungs, I could hear zippers. And then layers of clothing shielded my body from the assaulting wind.

As the mouth blew another gust of air into me. And another. And another.

In the distance, a siren wailed.

"Come on, Willow. Fight!"

I sensed something just above my mouth.

Then, his lips returned.

Suddenly, I gasped, and my eyes flew open, taking in the scene before me.

I was lying on a snowy embankment with several fuzzy silhouettes of people standing around me. But only one person was drenched, only one had jumped into the ice water to pull me out, risking his own life in the process.

Shane Hernandez.

"Willow." He cupped my cheek and stared down at me, his relief giving way to vengeance. "Who did this to you?"

2

I opened my eyes to a white-tiled ceiling that butted up against stark walls. Colorless and empty, mirroring how I was feeling right now—trapped in a hospital bed with ivory railings that would make it harder to escape this nightmare.

After a few moments, a face hovered over me. And not just any face.

Shane Hernandez.

Making me momentarily forget everything else, except his beauty.

Shane was a gorgeous blend of rugged strength and soft charm. Blue eyes that reminded you of the sky on a warm summer day, black hair that you longed to run your fingers through, a strong jaw that accentuated his full lips—lips you wished you could feel pressed against your own—and tan skin that sheathed his sculpted muscles.

Which bulged against his…teal *scrubs*?

He must have noticed my confusion, because he glanced down at his attire.

"Was soaked when I came in. They took mercy on me and gave me something dry to wear."

Which had the bonus of showing off his arm tattoos.

When he returned his focus to me, the fluorescents illuminated the relief in his eyes that I was awake and the nervous uncertainty that was likely reflected in my own.

"How are you feelin'?" His deep voice drifted across my skin like the welcome heat of a bonfire on a crisp autumn night. His azure eyes held mine so intensely, it felt like they had seized me, shackled me to him while his energy scorched the air between us.

So overwhelming that I had to look away.

"My head is pounding, and I feel exhausted." But not bad, considering what happened. And what could have happened, if it hadn't been for Shane.

"You pulled me from the river." *You saved me.* And risked his life doing it.

I allowed myself to become engulfed in his gaze again, surrendering to the heat this time. Welcoming it, savoring it, even as the walls of the hospital seemed to burn to ash around us. His eyes met my cheek, and he looked as if he wanted to reach out and brush it.

"You scared me." In Shane's eyes, flames of worry became eclipsed by a wildfire of vengeance. "I heard you scream a bloodcurdling scream—the kind you hear when someone's being..." His lips tightened into a line. "I saw you hit the water, but I didn't know it was you until I got to you. What the hell happened, Willow?"

His iron gaze searched my face, trying to pull answers out of my eyes—like if he looked close enough, he'd find them.

I had to break Shane's stare again to have any shot at thinking straight, but when I tried to spur my memories of what happened on that bridge, it felt like an ice pick burrowed into my skull. I couldn't remember what happened before the fall—only fragments of what came after.

"What were you doing there?" I asked.

Shane placed his hand on mine like he needed to feel for himself that I was actually here. Alive. Although his grasp was tender, it torched my skin, crackling embers up my arm and into my ribs.

"Was going for a run," Shane said.

"At night?" I asked.

"I jog whenever I can squeeze it in. Was running on the pathway along the river"—so, he was on the ground level, not above it on the bridge—"when I heard you scream."

What were the odds? Of all the times and all the places for us to be in the same space together in a city that houses three million people. A freak coincidence? Or serendipity?

"How did you fall from that bridge, Willow?"

"Good. You're awake." A nurse in teal scrubs, identical to the ones Shane was wearing, smiled as she entered the room. "Doctor's on his way."

She pumped hand sanitizer into her palms and then checked my IV bag.

"Ms. Johnson." A man with hair as white as Santa's entered the room. Wearing a blue button-down beneath a lab coat, he approached the opposite side of my bed as Shane and pulled a pencil-sized flashlight out of his pocket, shining it in my left eye, then my right.

The assault of light was one of the only things that could break the spell cast by Shane's energy.

"How long have I been here?" I asked.

"Three hours or so," the doctor said. "Can you follow my finger, please?" He held his index finger up and watched my eyes as he shifted it from side to side.

"When can I go home?"

Because that's all I wanted to do—go back to my apartment, crawl under my covers, and sleep until my head didn't hurt anymore. And then maybe spend some time figuring out how I fell from that bridge and why Shane was affecting me *this* much—because the energy I felt from his gaze, his touch, was beyond powerful.

"We're keeping you overnight for observation," the doctor said. "You got lucky. Fractured wrist. Based on the clinical exam, a concussion. Could have been a lot worse."

*My wrist is broken?* I looked down at my left arm, and that's when I noticed the cast.

"Is she going to be okay?" Shane's brows crinkled into worry again.

"She'll be released tomorrow with a list of things to watch for with a concussion. But she seems to be doing just fine. Once the pain meds wear off fully, you'll probably feel like you were in a car accident, though. Pretty banged up and bruised. I recommend taking it easy for a few days."

"My memory of last night is fuzzy," I said.

"Short-term memory loss is not uncommon with concussions," the doctor said.

"Will she get it back?"

Shane's wary eyes fixed on to the doctor's face as he removed his stethoscope from around his neck and pressed it to my chest.

"Hard to say. Some patients do; some don't."

"What if I take her to the bridge where she fell, have her look around?" Shane asked. "Might that trigger her memory of what happened to return?"

"If there was a prescription to heal post-traumatic amnesia, I'd write one, but unfortunately, many patients never regain their memories. I'm not saying it's not possible, but we need to be patient. Her best chance of recovering them is from rest and time to let her body heal."

"My head is pounding," I said.

"I'll increase your dose of pain medication and have the nurse come in with it. It won't be a full dose this time, since you already had some three hours ago, but it'll help. Meanwhile, a police officer is waiting outside to take your statement," the doctor said. "I'll send him in."

"I'd prefer to do it another time." Not only was I exhausted, but also, my memories were missing. Maybe if I went home and slept for a little while, I could actually give the cops something to work with and not waste their time.

"I'm afraid he's on his way."

*Great.*

The doctor left the room, but Shane remained on the side of my bed, as he'd evidently done for the past three hours.

"You didn't need to stay here." Though he'd always been friendly in the past, flirty even, staying here was a burden. "I'm sure you have better things to do with your time than to babysit your clumsy neighbor."

Especially since the clock on the wall said it was past one in the morning. A detective needed sleep to be at his sharpest.

Unless...was Shane here on official business? Was the cop waiting outside here with him?

"Is my fall part of an ongoing case of yours or something?" I asked.

That would be just my luck. Fall victim to some serial bridge-thrower.

"No," Shane said.

Then, why?

His ocean-colored gems latched on to my eyes and didn't let go as he placed his hand on top of mine. Again, it torched my skin and crackled heat through my chest.

"I needed to make sure you're okay."

It felt like Shane was looking directly into my soul, wrapping me in the warm embrace of his genuine concern for my well-being. No, more than concern. The haunting shadow in his eyes hinted at an agony he'd suffered when he'd been waiting to find out if I was going to be all right.

But surely, the rest of his appearance—looking like he'd been through hell with dark circles under his eyes and a mop of messy hair that he'd been running his hands through—wasn't from worrying about me. Right? Surely, that level of stress was from physically jumping into the water.

A uniformed police officer dragged me from my thoughts when he entered the room.

"Ms. Johnson."

The guy was in his late twenties, I guessed, and resembled the actor Joe Pesci. Dark brown eyes set in an oval face, thin lips. A slight overbite to his upper teeth. He was short, a broad chest that told me he hit the gym a lot, but his legs were thin, like he often skipped leg day.

As soon as Shane's eyes landed on him, Shane's jaw tensed.

The officer's face tightened when he spotted Shane by my bedside, too.

"Detective," the cop said in a clipped tone.

"Officer De Luca." Shane nodded.

For a second, I seriously wondered if they were about to arm wrestle, but the cop cleared his throat.

"Mind if I ask what you're doing here?" De Luca asked him in a curt tone.

"As I told you in my statement, she's my next-door neighbor," Shane said. "And I pulled her from the river."

De Luca's eyes snapped back to Shane's hand wrapped around mine.

Shane didn't need to say anything for the tension to roll off his body.

Meanwhile, drumsticks performed an evil ritual on my skull.

"I need to ask her some questions, so you know the drill." The cop dismissed Shane with a wave of his hand toward the door.

I pressed my fingers to my temple, willing the ache to subside.

"Would it be okay if I got some sleep first?" I couldn't imagine his interview would be brief—a woman mysteriously landing in the Chicago River. Plus, "My memory is fuzzy. I think it's the pain meds, so I'd prefer to let them wear off first."

"I'm here now," De Luca said in annoyance, as if wasting his drive time here was a bigger offense than collecting more accurate information.

"That's not what she asked," Shane said. "It might be better to wait for her head to clear. Take her statement tomorrow."

De Luca's nostrils flared.

Shane saw his nostril flare and raised him a chest puff.

*I wonder if two police officers would get into a fistfight.*

*In a hospital no less.*

"You need to leave, Detective." De Luca glowered at Shane.

"Since I already gave you my statement, I don't. Unless that's what Willow wants."

De Luca licked his teeth and cut his eyes to mine, silently

demanding I kick Shane out, but all I wanted was for De Luca to come back another time.

"I'm hoping my head will be clearer tomorrow," I reiterated.

"Do you know how you came to fall from that bridge?"

"No."

"Did you jump?" De Luca asked point-blank.

"What? No."

I couldn't believe he'd asked me so bluntly, with no empathy in his voice.

Tonight, I wound up in a river and almost died, for crying out loud. Equally disturbing, I had no recollection of how it happened. Could he at least try to imagine how awful this felt? This was a lot for me to process, and I was doing my best to not let the anxiety of it all consume me. A little compassion would be appreciated.

"You said you have no memory of it," De Luca said.

Shane stiffened at his tone.

"I don't, but I know I didn't try to kill myself."

"How do you know for sure?"

"I…"

"Been depressed lately?"

Down? A little. But depressed? "No. And I would never kill myself; I wouldn't do that to my family. Plus, I'm terrified of drowning. When I was a kid, I fell into the community pool for a few seconds, and I've had a fear of drowning ever since. If I *were* depressed enough to off myself, it would be something gentle, like taking a bottle of pills or something. I'd never jump into icy water to drown myself. It must have been an accident."

"I walked the bridge before I came here," De Luca said. "No holes in the railing or any other visible signs of a defect. Bridges are built with a safe pedestrian pathway. But if you were drunk, or being reckless, done it on a dare, climbing around or something, that might be another story."

"No. I'd never do that. I told you, I have a fear of drowning."

"I didn't smell alcohol on her breath when I did mouth-to-mouth," Shane said. "Surely, the hospital did a tox screen."

De Luca glowered at Shane, as if to say, *I don't need you to tell me how to do my job.*

My head's pounding got worse. I pressed a finger to my forehead.

"I didn't see blood or any signs of a struggle," De Luca said to me. "I'll walk the bridge again in the daylight, but there wasn't anything to suggest there was a violent confrontation."

"She has fresh bruises on her upper arms," Shane said. *I do?* He lifted the sleeves of my hospital gown slightly to expose the tops of them. "Looks like someone grabbed her."

"You said you and some pedestrian pulled her from the water," De Luca countered.

"Under her shoulders. We didn't grab her upper arms. Someone else did. Which means there was a confrontation *before* she went over."

"None of the witnesses along the river saw anything until they heard her screaming when she fell, and there were no witnesses on the bridge."

"Someone did this to her," Shane said.

"We don't know that."

"You heard her; she's terrified of drowning, so she didn't do this to herself, and she has bruising."

"She could have bruised her arms, hitting the ice chunks in the water, or it could have been from earlier in the evening or yesterday."

"*Or* someone grabbed her and threw her off the bridge."

I couldn't tell if De Luca was trying to be unbiased or if he was offended at Shane's insistence.

"It's also possible she was intoxicated enough to do something reckless. You know better than anyone the dangers of getting tunnel vision on a case, Detective. Let me do my job."

"Then, do it. Find out who the hell did this to her."

De Luca inhaled an angry breath and pulled up a screen on his phone.

"Let's start from the beginning," he said. "What were you doing before you were on that bridge?"

The nurse walked into the room, carrying a syringe, which she pierced into my IV. "This will make her drowsy," she warned.

I loved her for not asking the cops for permission to administer it first; evidently, leaving a patient in pain for longer than necessary wasn't going to happen on her watch.

I could feel heat radiating down my body, the stabbing pain in my head subsiding as my eyelids went to war, fighting to stay open.

"Get some rest, honey."

Once the nurse left, I tried to answer the officer's question.

"I don't…" I shut my eyes, and it took concerted effort to open them again. "I don't remember what…"

As I yawned long and deep, Shane frowned, his worried eyes pinned on me as he said, "Maybe you should finish her statement tomorrow."

De Luca opened his mouth, as if about to argue his case, but perhaps he saw the exhaustion in my face and he took pity on me. Or maybe my eyes were glassy from the narcotics and he realized he'd be wasting his time, trying now. Because after a deep breath, he cleared his throat.

"Fine. We'll finish tomorrow," he said.

De Luca glared at Shane for several long moments before ambling out of the room.

"Okay, is he your childhood nemesis or something?" I smirked, because, well, *pain meds*.

"I'm goin' to make some calls," he said. "See if I can get someone else assigned to your case."

"So, he *is* your childhood nemesis."

"You almost died tonight." Shane's lips flattened into a tight line. "You need a cop that'll go the extra mile, not someone who'll do the bare minimum."

Bare minimum. Yikes. There was a story there for sure, and if he disliked De Luca so much…

"Why can't you work the case?" I yawned. My eyelids didn't care that a sex god was in the room.

"Conflict of interest, since I know you." With his eyes scouring my face, he looked haunted by something, something he seemingly couldn't leave without asking. "Willow, can you think of anyone who might've done this to you?"

I laughed. Because *narcotics*.

I couldn't remember how I'd come to fall off that bridge, but one thing I knew for certain: "No. No one in my life would ever hurt me."

His face got all disapproval-ish.

"You'd be damn surprised what people are capable of, Willow. You should be careful not to see people through such rose-colored glasses. We need to find out what happened to you as quickly as possible. Because if someone did this to you, they might try again."

3

I woke when light warmed my eyelids, the sun streaming through the blinds of the hospital room. Muffled voices of what I presumed to be a nearby nurses' station rumbled outside of my closed door, shoes squeaking along the hallway—probably hospital staff making their rounds. In here, it smelled like disinfectant that stung my nostrils.

"Morning," Shane said.

My eyes snapped to the chair next to my bed. In it sat Shane, now wearing a blue T-shirt that clung to his biceps for dear life, jeans, and a Cubs baseball hat that framed his sultry eyes.

I once again found myself struck by his beauty and the heat that radiated off him like he was a walking fireplace.

"How's your head?" Shane asked.

I shifted, trying to sit up a little, but immediately groaned. Whatever pain medicine they gave me last night must have worn off because, now, parts of my body felt like they'd been on the receiving end of a baseball bat.

"I didn't expect to see you this morning," I said.

Shane might've felt some sense of obligation to stay last night until

I had woken up, given he had been at the scene of the bridge incident. But after that? I'd have thought he would've gone home.

"I got you some things." Shane opened up a plastic bag and set a toothbrush, toothpaste, and some face soap on the nightstand next to my bed.

"You went to the store for me?"

"Pharmacy is close by."

Still, he didn't need to do that. Surely, the hospital supplied necessities.

When he looked at me, my gaze surrendered to his, electricity firing currents beneath my skin.

"I got you your favorite coffee." Shane pointed to a cup with the logo of my favorite coffee shop, Angie's Coffeeteria. "Might be lukewarm by now, but I can see if I can find a microwave to zap it for you."

"How did you know Angie's Coffeeteria is my favorite coffee place?"

Shane scrubbed his jaw as he stared at me. "Anytime I've bumped into you in the mornings, you're always carrying a cup from it."

My cheeks became an inferno, competing with my chest for which body part was hotter right now.

"I'm not sure if I got the right drink," he hedged. "Maybe you get one of those fancy drinks. This is just black coffee. Cream and sugar on the side."

I wondered if I could hide the surprise on my face that he had gone so far out of his way for me. Not only saving my life, but trying to make the aftermath of this dreadful experience as comfortable as possible.

No one had ever done something this nice for me.

Mom had done her best, raising us girls after my dad died, but she was lost in pain with nothing left over to give to a child in their most vulnerable years. I liked to believe that it made me more independent, thickened my skin, even, and that I was stronger because of it. But in moments like this, it reminded me that, growing up, affection was as absent as my father was.

"I also grabbed you some clothes since they cut yours off in the

ER." Shane motioned toward a bag on the other side of the room. "They're mine. They'll be way too big for you, but it'll just be for the drive home."

I looked down at my hands, trying to contain the swelling tenderness I was feeling for Shane.

"You have someone you want me to call, Willow?"

I thought about this. All things considered, I was okay. The injuries I'd sustained weren't life-threatening, and they would soon discharge me from the hospital. So, there was no need to bother my friends with a hospital run for a non-life-threatening emergency. Not even Emily. Coming to a hospital in downtown Chicago was a massive ordeal with traffic and parking, and I'd be waiting around awhile for paperwork. Monopolizing most of her day when she was just getting over a cold no less. Something this intrusive was better suited for immediate family.

But I would not burden Mom with this. If I called her to the hospital, I'd have to tell her what happened, and she would discover I could've died. I tried to avoid the cruelties of breaking down the walls she'd built around her grief; it escaped its prison enough on its own.

Which left me with my sister, Hayley. Calling her was a bad idea— the last time we were supposed to meet, she didn't even show up.

*I SIT AT THE TABLE, HOPING THIS IS FINALLY THE TURNING POINT IN MY relationship with my sister—a turning point I've longed for, for as long as I can remember. We were close when I was younger, but since Hayley was older when Dad died, it had a bigger impact on her, and as the years passed, Hayley pulled away from everyone—her addiction creating an even bigger divide between us. I never gave up hope that I could get her back, though—a good person doesn't give up on a family member. Even if that family member isn't always treating you perfectly, you keep making the effort with them.*

*Case in point, tonight, I invited her to have dinner with me on my birthday—just the two of us. I booked us a table at a restaurant with a view of the city. White tablecloths. Candlelight. Dinner plates so shiny, I can see the candlelight reflection dancing across them. And dang it if excitement doesn't ignore my warnings to not get my hopes up too high and buzz inside of me.*

*I sip my water and stare at the skyscrapers outside the window, imagining all the people getting together right now. How many of them were years in the making?*

*I check my watch.*

Maybe she's stuck in traffic.

*I wait another few minutes and then text Hayley.*

*Me: Are you having trouble finding the place?*

*I drink another half glass of water.*

*I call her, but it goes right to voice mail. I leave her a quick message and then text her again.*

*Me: Are you okay?*

*No answer, not even after another five minutes.*

*She's over an hour late. The waiter keeps glaring at me, a line of people near the hostess booth waiting for tables to open up.*

*Me: Are you still coming?*

*No reply.*

*Worry pits in my stomach, and I feel guilty for wondering if she's using again because what does that say about me as a sister? I should have more confidence in her sobriety. That's what a supportive person would do, but the thought isn't coming from a place of anger, but from concern.*

*Because, now, I'm worried that something's happened to her.*

*I call her ten more times, I send her more texts, and then finally, after two hours of waiting, my cell buzzes.*

*Hayley: So sorry. I can't make it. Happy birthday!*

*How is it possible that a heart can rejoice and sink, all at the same time? Rejoice that she's okay—or at least seems to be—but sink because she blew me off. Again. And somehow, for reasons I don't understand, this time hurts even more than when she didn't show up to either my high school or college graduation.*

*Tonight would've been just me and her, and it would have gone a long way to healing the wounds created by years of her flaking out on me.*

*I grit my teeth.*

*Me: I hope whatever it is, is important.*

*I feel like a fool for thinking this would turn out any differently, and I flag down the waiter to let him know someone else can have the table—leaving him the money I would have spent on my meal as a tip. As starving as I now am, I'm too humiliated and angry to order food and eat it alone.*

*I walk home, seesawing between wiping tears from my cheeks and clenching my hands into balls. This is stupid. Yes, it hurts, but I'm fine. This isn't a new development that she didn't show up tonight. In fact, I shouldn't have planned for anything else.*

*The next day she pops over—an exceedingly rare occurrence. I normally try to bite my tongue, take the high road when she's hurt my feelings. After all, when we were kids, Hayley played a big role in raising me. But enough is enough.*

*I stand in my doorway, not allowing her inside as she says hello and gets to her point.*

*"I thought we could go grab lunch."*

*Seriously? I wasted my entire night getting ready, sitting and waiting at a restaurant just for her to no-show. With no actual explanation, mind you, and she thinks I'll follow her to lunch now, like a puppy begging for scraps?*

*"What came up last night?" I cross my arms over my chest.*

*"Oh, uh..." Hayley runs a hand through her hair. "Just, like, a thing with a friend of mine."*

*"A thing."*

*"Yeah. I was totally planning on coming, but, you know."*

*"I don't know, actually," I said. "That's why I'm asking. Why did I sit there for two hours, waiting for you? And why didn't you text me sooner to let me know you couldn't make it?"*

*"Jeez, Willow. If you're trying to make me feel like crap, I already do."*

*"You could have fooled me." She hadn't even responded to my text last night.*

*"You shouldn't feel so upset."*

*I shake my head in disbelief. "Thanks for telling me how I should feel," I say. "If you don't mind, I have to go."*

*I shut the door and press my back to it, telling my erratic breathing to calm the hell down, that this is progress—me pushing back on her. Staying silent all these years hasn't changed anything, so establishing firmer bound-*

*aries with her—telling her that her behavior, at times, is unacceptable—is an important step to getting our relationship back on track, and our foundation will be stronger for it.*

WE'D EXCHANGED A COUPLE OF BRIEF TEXTS AFTER THAT INCIDENT, BUT not much more.

Shane's fierce gaze blasted right through me, as if he could obliterate the bricks I'd built around myself, uncovering every truth about me.

"Okay, we're goin' to talk about why you have this hesitation to call someone, but for right now? I'll be the one to drive you home."

Butterflies launched in my stomach. "You don't need to do that."

Maybe I should at least try to see if Hayley would show up. As thrilled as I might be to have more unprecedented time with Shane, I didn't want to be a burden. And almost dying last night reignited my desire to get close to my sister, once and for all.

I looked at the nightstand. "Where's my phone?"

"At the bottom of the river, would be my guess."

Damn. I couldn't call anybody even if I wanted to; I had everybody's phone number saved in my phone, not memorized.

"Your keys survived though. They were tightly packed into your jean pocket, I guess."

Well, at least there was that. One less hoop I had to jump through to get home and into my bed.

"Why did you stay here last night?" *Why are you doing so much for me?*

All those years I'd fought for scraps of affection from my family, and Shane was handing it out like it was no big deal.

"I witnessed you fall from a bridge, Willow. You weren't breathing. You think I'm just going to leave and go run errands today?"

*Well, yeah.*

My answer must've been written all over my face because Shane's lips tightened.

"It's pretty damn obvious that you're not used to people being kind to you."

My face flushed so hot, I had to look down at my hands. Which was silly. I was stronger than this.

"That's not true." My friends were nice. My family was kind even if it wasn't consistent and even if sizable gaps of hurt interrupted the kindness.

"We just don't know each other well enough for an overnight-stay-in-the-hospital kind of thing."

I wasn't sure if Shane believed me.

He stood up, came to my side of the bed, shoved his hands into his pockets, and said, "I want to make sure you're okay. And, until we figure out who did this to you, I don't think it's a good idea for you to be alone."

Now was not the time for my heart to be dissecting all of his words, looking for clues about possible romantic intentions. It was inappropriate. And yet, that's exactly what that traitor was doing right now.

"Which brings me to my next point." He looked down at me for several seconds before speaking. "Until this all gets sorted out, I'd like you to stay at my place."

My hormones elicited a dance squad in perfect formation, cheering, *Yes, yes, yes.* But my pride took over. I was an adult, capable of taking care of myself.

"I appreciate the offer, but no."

"Willow…"

"Look, I'm sure, in your line of work, every incident seems suspicious to you, but there is no killer after me. No one in my life would've done this."

Shane thinned his lips in obvious disagreement.

"Would you have gone to meet a stranger at ten o'clock at night, alone?"

"Maybe I wasn't alone?"

"If you were with someone, they might have been responsible for your fall. And if they weren't, they would've called for help or, at a minimum, run down to the bystanders when I pulled you from the water."

Fair point. But that didn't change the facts: I trusted everyone in my life implicitly, and while it was beyond disturbing that I'd almost died—*I must be in shock, because it still doesn't feel real*—I wasn't going to let Shane get himself all worked up over a non-crime.

"Then, I must've been alone. I must have somehow fallen off the bridge by accident."

Did an accident sound slam-dunk obvious? No. You don't hear about people falling off bridges very often for a reason, but I knew no one in my life would ever try to kill me, and I wasn't suicidal, so it was the only logical conclusion.

I hoped the cops would figure out how the accident could have occurred. Was there a fault in the bridge they'd initially overlooked? Was it one of those bridges that opens like the top of a box when tall boats come along the river, and for some reason, it was slightly open at the top when I happened to walk over it? Because if it happened to me, it could happen to someone else. And they might not make it...

"Willow." A nurse poked her head in. "I'll be in with your discharge papers in a few minutes."

I nodded.

Shane appeared to debate on asking me more questions, but he glanced at the skin beneath my eyes. The makeup concealer industry made a fortune off girls like me, whose skin darkened like crazy on anything less than six hours of sleep.

"We should get you home so you can take a nap before De Luca shows up to take your statement."

"I thought you didn't want him on the case."

Shane's jaw tightened. "I should've known I'd need somethin' tangible to get him reassigned. But he's not a detective, so as soon as he determines a crime has been committed, detectives will open an official investigation."

"The only way to get De Luca off the case is if he's convinced that someone tried to kill me?"

When Shane nodded, I frowned.

*He thinks I'm some weak victim, just lying here, waiting for other people to help. But he doesn't know how strong I really am, and maybe he needs to see that.*

I threw the covers off my lap, trying to hide my wince. With strain, I reached back to make sure my hospital gown was all sorts of tied up —have an ass-flash would totally hamper my demonstration of strength.

When I dangled my feet off the bed, Shane tensed, looking at me like a baby about to take her first steps.

"What do you have against him?" I asked.

"That's a long story."

My goal was to grab the bag of clothes and change in the adjoining bathroom, but as soon as I tried to stand up, the room started to go black from the drop in blood pressure. I was going down like a sack of potatoes—and not in a cute, romantic dancing-dip way. More like a puppet-that-got-her-strings-cut kind of way, but before I hit the ground, Shane's arm crashed around my back and pulled me upright, slamming my chest to his.

It was just reflex on his part, the way he'd pulled me against him— the guy hadn't had time to plan it out, for crying out loud—but now, we both stilled.

He looked down at me, his worry giving way to something else as his eyes raked over my face, landing on my lips. He smelled like the ocean that shared its color with his eyes, framed by those dark, serious eyebrows that pulled down slightly.

"Easy," he whispered.

He held me for several seconds before setting me down on the bed.

"I stood up too fast," I said to ensure he didn't misread this as me being frail.

"Maybe it's too soon for you to go home."

"No. I hate hospitals."

Now that I was safely sitting on the bed, Shane took a couple steps back and evaluated me.

"Bad experience in one?" he asked.

"My dad," I said, surprised how natural it felt, talking to Shane. "He died when I was little."

Pivotal memories of him flashed through my mind.

*I'm four, and Daddy is holding my hand, walking me to the field behind our house to pick wildflowers. My favorites are the purple ones—those are way harder to find than dandelions. I love them so much that he's helped me dig a big rectangle in our backyard for a garden we're going to build, and he's going to let me fill it with them.*

*"Will you always love me, Daddy?" I ask as we walk.*

*Daddy looks down at me. His hair glows orange from the sun behind him. "Always."*

*"Even when you die?"*

*His eyebrows crinkle.*

*"Mommy said her grandpa died. Will you still love me when you die?"*

*"I'll always love you, Willow. Even when I'm gone."*

*Daddy squeezes my hand.*

*"But you don't have to worry about that. I won't die for a long, long, long time."*

*A couple months later, I place wildflowers on top of Daddy's shiny black casket. It took me a half hour to find purple ones hidden in the weeds, and I had to walk through thorny bushes that scraped my legs to get them, but Daddy deserves the good wildflowers. Especially since they'll be the last ones I can ever pick for him.*

*"You lied," I whisper over my tears. I don't think I'll ever stop crying. I think I'll cry every single day for the rest of my life.*

*I'm eight, holding the pink flyer with purple letters that the school sent home with us about the father-daughter dance. It has three yellow bubbles with pictures of girls dancing with their daddies with big smiles. My friend Julie said her daddy is taking her shopping for a fluffy purple dress, and he's going to take her out to dinner before the dance, and they'll pick their favorite song and dance to it, and when she gets married someday, they are going to dance to that song again.*

*A drop splats on the paper from a tear as I stare out the window at the rectangle of overgrowth that was supposed to be my and Daddy's special garden.*

*I'm a terrible person for wishing somebody else's daddy could've died instead of mine.*

*I crumple the page and bury it in the trash can, so Mommy doesn't see it and get sad again. Maybe Mommy would be happy if I didn't keep making her sad by leaving these things out.*

I NEVER WANTED ANY OTHER FAMILY TO GO THROUGH WHAT WE DID, lost in the emotional and financial damage created by grief's aftershocks.

That's why I wanted to open up my own business to help families in distress. Organizing counseling and taking the business skills I'd learned to help them shape their résumés, search for work, and find loans to get a down payment on housing. I'd had this dream for years, and though I had volunteered my time at various organizations, I'd never had the courage to take the leap. Wrapped in the sanctuary of a steady paycheck, 401(k), and good health insurance, I kept postponing. And now, here I was, having almost missed the chance of making my dreams come true.

"I don't remember much," I continued, "but I do remember being in a hospital when they told me the news."

I saw pain flash through his eyes. Pity, empathy would make sense. But not pain.

*Why did he look hurt?*

Shane cleared his throat, recalibrating back to the task at hand.

"Let me get a nurse to stay in here while you change," he said.

I allowed it, only so I wouldn't break my skull in half and have to stay in here another night.

The nurse was nice, and a few minutes later, I was dressed in Shane's ocean-scented outfit.

As he warned, they were much too big. His T-shirt went down to the middle of my thighs, and his light-gray sweatpants were so baggy, I had to roll the bottom several times and cinch the drawstring tightly.

"I'll go get your boyfriend," the nurse said.

"He's not my boyfriend."

She gave me a smirk, the she-devil, and then vanished into the hall.

Shane returned, pushing a freaking wheelchair into the room.

I glared at him. "I'm not sitting in that."

"Hospital policy. Come on." He patted the seat. "Maybe I can pop a wheelie."

I reluctantly—and I mean, *reluctantly*—let him help me into the wheelchair, only because I was a rule follower. And again, I needed my skull in one piece to escape this jail.

A few minutes later, I got into his car, because, fine, we were heading to the same place, and it made no sense to disturb my friends when I had a ride.

Gray clouds—the thick snowstorm type—lingered in the sky, casting the charcoal skyscrapers in shades of silver and blue. Icy winds beat against the side of the car, and a nearby ambulance wailed, drowning out the vehicle engines that purred near a traffic light.

"Thank you," I said. "For"—saving my life, bringing clean clothes— "everything. And for driving me home."

Shane allowed his eyes to wander from the road for a few seconds, his face softening as he studied me.

"I'm glad you're okay, Willow." He gripped the steering wheel tighter. "When I pulled your head above the water and realized it was *you* who'd fallen from the bridge..."

He didn't finish his thought. Instead, his forearms tightened, and his knuckles whitened.

Having someone care about me this much was, pathetically, a foreign experience. I didn't know where to cram all these strange emotions mixing together, so I settled for avoiding eye contact and glancing around his car, searching for any excuse to change the subject.

"You have a siren." I noticed.

He said nothing.

"Do you ever use it for non-work purposes?"

Shane furrowed his eyebrows, looking at me. "Why would I do that?"

"The usual. Beat traffic, get through red lights, scare people for fun."

He cast his gaze back to the road, his lips twitching up. "Of course not."

"Ever use it to pull over someone you know?"

Again, a sideways glance. "No."

"Would you?"

"Not unless I wanted to be a dick."

I smiled and watched the buildings pass in silence until, finally, we arrived at our apartment complex.

Shane and I lived on the first floor of the ten-story building.

Despite my insistence that I could do it alone, Shane kept a steady hand wrapped around my arm—I swear I could feel its heat through his coat he'd made me wear—as we walked into the building and ambled down the hallway leading to my front door.

When we reached it, I stopped in my tracks, a shiver of unrest drifting through my bones. At first glance, my front door looked as it always did—shut tightly—but when you approach the same door every day, some part of your mind picks up on small discrepancies before you're fully aware of what seems off. Whatever it was, was so small, I stood there, inches away from it, studying the door closely to identify what made me pause. And that's when I realized what it was.

The door was shut, but not fully—a centimeter or so not butting up against the outside frame.

Shane must have sensed my anxiety and seen my eyes wandering over my door, because he stepped closer, scrutinizing it himself.

And then, without a word, he pulled me down the hall, unlocked and opened *his* apartment door, and shoved me inside. *Shoved*, even though it hurt a little.

"What are you—"

He covered my mouth with his hand, a silent warning firing from his eyes.

If I wasn't so startled by it, this might be sexy as sin.

He held his index finger over his lips and flattened his palm, motioning for me to stay. Then, he vanished into his bedroom, brandishing a gun when he returned.

He punched 911 into his phone and handed it to me.

"Stay here," he whispered. "Tell them there's a possible break-in."

Then, he was gone.

4

I stood motionless as a squeak alerted me to my front door opening.

*Shane's going inside.*

*With a gun.*

Obviously, Shane thought someone might be in there, so why risk going inside? Why not wait for backup? If he interrupted a burglary or something, Shane might not be the only one wielding a weapon...

I pushed the green button on the phone and alerted the operator to what was going on—a possible break-in—as quietly as possible.

All the while chewing my fingernail.

The level of worry I had for him right now surprised me. Of course I'd be worried about *anyone* in a dangerous situation, but this wasn't anyone. It was Shane, and that's what had me chewing my nail so hard, it hurt.

An eternity later, I could hear sirens growing louder, and Shane's front door opened.

He held the weapon at his side, his muscles relaxed compared to the rigid balls of steel they were when he had left.

"Place is empty," he said.

"So, it was a false alarm?"

"I didn't say that."

"So, someone *had* been inside my place?"

Shane opened a drawer in his kitchen, pulled out a leather holster, and strapped it to his belt. Then shoved the gun inside.

"I don't know," he said. But his tone gave away his lie. He very much thought someone had been inside. "Let's wait for the uniformed officers to do a more thorough search."

And that's precisely what they did. Responding officers swept my apartment from top to bottom and found no evidence that an intruder had been inside. No overturned furniture, no evidence of a scuffle, no evidence that someone had jimmied the door. They concluded I had likely forgotten to lock it on my way out and it just hadn't latched fully.

Which was strange. Living in a big city, I *never* left without locking up. Ever.

But at least that meant there was no break-in.

Not that Shane agreed with that. When the officers left, he ran a hand through his black locks—his biceps trying to distract me by bulging from his shirt—and he repeated to me what he'd said to the officers.

"My gut is tellin' me this is related to what happened to you. You never leave your apartment unlocked," Shane said, "let alone with the door ajar."

*He's been more observant of me than I've given him credit for. But I guess that's what makes a good detective—always noticing things.*

"And this all happens around the same time you fall from a bridge?" He shook his head. "Until we sort this out, you're staying at my place."

I almost smiled—I did find his protectiveness sexy—but squared my shoulders. I knew he meant well. But I wasn't some victim in perpetual danger, and no matter how good his intentions might be, my independence was something I guarded fiercely.

After growing up without a father, having an emotionally absent mother, and an older sister who'd become more isolating with each year, I'd learned to take care of myself at a very young age. It was my comfort zone, and now, I didn't like to depend on anyone.

*The only person in this life you can fully rely on is yourself.*

Plus, I'd just been released from the hospital, had a splitting headache, and wanted to lie down and take a nap in the comfort of my bed.

"Sorry. No can do."

"Willow…"

"You heard what the officers said. No forced entry. Nothing missing."

"That they saw."

"No shred of evidence anyone was even inside my apartment."

"No evidence someone *wasn't*."

And based on the stern look on his face, he expected me to accept his hypothesis as fact.

At work, Shane was probably used to being a boss and telling people what to do. He had a commanding aura about him that likely compelled most into obedience, but I wasn't in his jurisdiction.

I pinched my temples, trying to thwart a growing migraine.

"I'm going to lie down now."

When I stepped forward to leave his apartment, he blocked my path by pressing his palm against the wall to my left, his forearm muscles flexing as he caged me in.

I raised my chin, challenging the air between us, but he matched my determination with a stubborn-ass look of his own.

"Willow, I'm not letting you back in your apartment when we don't know what the hell is going on."

"*Letting* me?" I threw my hand up and immediately regretted it because of the stabbing pain in my shoulder that must've been a torn muscle. Pain Shane must have picked up on, because he glared at my arm with that fiery vengeance again, as if counting down the moments until he could get revenge against whoever had hurt me.

"This isn't your call." I tried to step around him on the other side, but he mirrored my movements and blocked my path. "Isn't holding someone against their will illegal?"

"You were almost killed last night. If you think I'm letting you out of my sight, you have another thing coming."

I glowered at him. "I can't decide if I find your overprotectiveness" —*sexy as hell*—"sweet or mind-blowingly annoying."

His lips curled up on one side. And as if his sort of smile wasn't distractingly scintillating enough, after a few seconds, his gaze traveled down my face and landed on my lips. Standing only inches away, he kept me trapped with his muscular arm, and his mouth parted slightly.

The energy around us shifted. A mixture of anger, and possessiveness, and passion.

I'd never had anyone inspire this reaction inside of me before. I could feel my every nerve stand on end, tempting my lips toward his while he dared me to fight against it.

But if he thought standing here like a panty-melting sex god would make me surrender to his every command, well…my hormones might be completely on board with that, but I wasn't.

I shoved the heat from my chest down to my toes.

"Look, I appreciate everything you've done for me, but I'm a grown woman. I don't feel well. I have a headache. And I'm going into *my* home and crawling into *my* bed and going to sleep."

He said nothing.

Good.

Point made.

I stepped toward his door, surprised he didn't stop me. He didn't stop me when I reached the hallway, and he didn't stop me when I reached my front door, opened it, and shuffled inside. But once I went to shut said door?

He stormed inside, locked the dead bolt, and flopped down on my couch with his feet up.

Like someone who'd been lying on my worn-out cushions so often that he knew how the sliding glass door stuck, knew some of the drawers in the painted-too-many-times kitchen cabinets didn't fully close, and knew that my coffee table hid a small chocolate stain on my carpet from when I fell asleep, bingeing the

Twilight series. And the thing was, he looked like he belonged in my place.

Not that I'd tell him that. He wouldn't hear me anyway, what with all his non-listening to my boundaries.

"What are you doing?" I snapped.

"Mind if I watch a movie?" He picked up my remote.

"Um, yes. I mind. A lot. As I said, I want to sleep."

"I'll keep the volume low."

In my old fantasies, he'd been in my living room, shirtless. In my new fantasies, I was whacking his bossy head with a frying pan.

"Leave," I said.

"Fine." He rolled his eyes. "I'll keep the volume off." He added to himself in an annoyed tone, "I hate captions."

"You'll keep the *TV* off, because you're going back to your place."

"If you think I'd leave you alone after someone tried to kill you, you clearly don't know me very well."

Ugh! I hoped after a long nap, my memory would suddenly come back so I could say this with complete certainty.

"No one tried to kill me. Bridges get caked with ice this time of year, so I must have somehow slipped and fallen. And clearly, I don't know you because I never pegged you for breaking and entering or whatever this is. Please leave."

I crossed my arms over my chest, and we entered a stare-down. In corner one, a female with stick-straight brown hair and chocolate-colored eyes. At five foot five, weighing a mere one hundred and twenty-four pounds, she faced the competitive disadvantage of having arms as thin as twigs. In corner two, we had the most stubborn male specimen to ever walk the earth. A muscular guy well above six feet tall, he could probably throw said girl across the room, using nothing but a deltoid muscle. He could even use his eyeballs as weapons, for God's sake, what with those light-blue specks on the inside—simply winking me into submission.

"I've made my decision," I snapped. "Mind-blowingly annoying."

His lips curled up, and he clicked the button on the remote, the television blaring to life.

"Shane!"

His eyes snapped to me, all humor gone as tension strangled his words.

"Willow, if I go next door, I won't be able to focus on anything because I'll be worried that whoever broke in the apartment is comin' back."

"No one broke in." If they had, there'd have been signs of a robbery. *At least, I think so.*

"I'll keep checking on you if I hear any noise, which'll make it harder for you to rest. Just let me stay here and watch something. I promise you I will be quiet."

It was getting harder to hold on to my irritation when he said sweet things like that and looked all innocently at me, as if unaware that part of me savored the idea of him staying a little longer…

"And if I say no?"

To this, Shane held my gaze intensely. "Let's not cross that bridge, shall we?"

I cocked my head. "Was that pun supposed to be funny?"

"Is that a yes?"

For all the loving things holy.

"Whatever. If you so much as sneeze, I'm kicking you out."

Shane's mouth tugged up again, and he looked at the television. "Do you get HBO?"

I rolled my eyes and wandered into my bedroom, where I shut the door, changed into my pajamas—ignoring the part of my brain that said Shane's clothes smelled sexy—and lay down in my bed, trying to ignore my hot, sexy, stubborn-ass savior who was guarding me with a loaded gun.

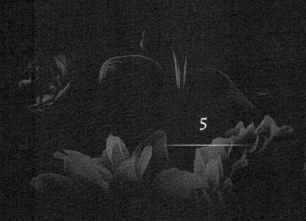

5

I thought I would sleep longer—certainly make it past four o'clock in the afternoon—but the doctor wasn't kidding. With the painkillers worn off, my body was sore in more places than it wasn't. I needed a heavy dose of Tylenol.

I ambled out of my bedroom and froze.

*Sweet baby Jessica, Shane Hernandez is sprawled out on my couch. Asleep.*

In my sleep-deprived haze, I'd forgotten he was here.

The poor guy probably got no sleep last night, running around, grabbing me clothes and supplies. He was still wearing the same jeans, T-shirt, and baseball cap that he'd had on at the hospital, his gun's holster fastened to his right hip. His head was tilted slightly to the left, angled toward the back of my couch, and his T-shirt had lifted up a few inches, exposing the tan ridges of his defined stomach. As if that wasn't sexy enough, his arms were crossed over his chest, his biceps gorging over the pressure from his underlying fists—swelling the tattoos that wrapped around his arms.

I remembered the first time I'd seen those tattoos.

·  ·  ·

LAUNDRY DAYS SHOULD BE OUTLAWED. NO ONE LIKES THEM. AND LAUNDRY
days in an apartment complex with one shared room?

The seventh circle of hell.

I gather up the laundry I normally did on Sunday afternoons. I hadn't
gotten to it this past weekend, so here I am, doing it during the week.

As I exit my apartment, my eyes wander to my next-door neighbor's
door. I've seen him several times since tipsy-mageddon, and not once did he
make me feel bad for what had happened. If anything, he's been overly
kind, asking if I am okay. Asking if I'd like him to walk me to and from
my car each day. I've declined his offers, but I can't stop thinking
about him.

My ears become all nosy, listening, curious what he is doing right now. Is
he home?

As I make my way down the hallway, I'm not hoping to see him.

I'm not.

I'm just...being a courteous neighbor, making sure I'll say hi if I pass him.
That's all.

But his door doesn't open.

My shoulders do not sag with disappointment. This basket is just heavy.

I walk down the long corridor. The laundry room is near the front doors,
to the left if you're coming from my place. Guess they put it there for convenience or whatever, but the entire building has only ten washing machines.

So, they're a hot commodity. At least, on the weekends they are. During
the week, I have no idea how often they are used, but when I enter the room, I
discover the answer is not many.

In fact, only one person is in this room, at the far end, with his back
to me.

The splashing grind of a washing machine echoes off the white walls,
filling the space with the fresh-linen scent of laundry detergent. If I wasn't
wearing socks, you would hear the click of my feet against the yellow-stained
tiled flooring, but apparently, the guy doesn't hear me.

He grabs his shirt from between his shoulder blades and tugs it up and
over his head, revealing an intricately woven system of tattoos along his back
and arms. The guy has some serious muscles, one competing with the next for
first place in deliciousness. Muscles that bulge and flex as the guy places the

shirt into the washing machine with the rest of his laundry and begins stabbing at the buttons.

God, even his stabbing finger is sexy. I bet his face is smolderingly fine.

My estrogen begs me to throw all my morals out the window and become an instant porn star, party of two. The guy still hasn't noticed that I'm here. Does he always do his laundry in nothing but a pair of workout shorts? If I had known that, I totally would've stalked the laundry room.

My salivary glands activate into overdrive, and I literally have to wipe a piece of spit off my lip.

The guy grabs his laundry basket and turns around.

Ho-ly shit.

The tattoo god is Shane Hernandez, my new next-door neighbor.

Shane has tattoos?

Shane is a laundry room god that will forever invade my sexual fantasies?

Daaaaaaaaamnnnnnn.

"Hey." He walks up to me like he's unaware he's the spitting image of a model for Tattoos Ink Magazine. Its slogan would read, Men so sexy, they'll destroy all other men for you. He means his smile to be friendly, but the way those inviting lips curl up is seductive.

"Oh, hi."

It's the best my brain can come up with because all the blood has abandoned my head in favor of my lower belly. If this is what the police detective next door looks like, I will need to start robbing banks. Like, now.

"The one in the corner is broken," he warns, pointing to the machine with its lid open.

And when he twists around? His stomach muscles clench slightly, deepening their lines.

I open my mouth to respond, but nothing comes out. He hasn't told me I have the right to remain silent, but evidently, I no longer have the capacity to speak.

I've been attracted to Shane for a while. But this Shane? This Shane elicits stay-up-all-night-fantasizing-about-what-he-is-doing-on-the-other-side-of-that-wall attraction. This is straight-up imagining-what-he's-like-in-bed attraction.

*"I was just doing laundry,"* I say.

Brilliant.

A trained detective would have never guessed that, Willow. Being that you're holding a pair of rotting clothes, shoved into a laundry basket, standing in a laundry room. What else you got to win him over?

*Shane smiles. Like he isn't holding his own laundry basket against the side of his thousand-pack abs. Smart. Sexy. Does laundry. Call 1-800-every-woman-wants-me.*

*"Most of 'em are free. That's why I prefer doing laundry during the week,"* he says.

*Smart detective. Probably worked recon to find the best day and time of the week to do laundry.*

*Mental note. My laundry day has officially changed to Tuesdays, 6:34 p.m.*

*"Cool."*

Cool? What the heck, Willow? Cool? You have a college degree. You're independent, and smart, and hardworking, and you have a better vocabulary than cool.

*Damn that chest.*

*His tattoos are a labyrinth of objects woven together, forming an artful blanket across his skin—all of them black, high contrast, giving off a sinister vibe. In my quick glance, I make out a bird with its wings sprawled, a clock with Roman numerals, roses, the sun. They're as fascinating as they are gorgeous.*

*I'd love to stare at them as he throws that basket down, grabs me by the hips, hoists me up and onto one of these washers, and then...tells me anything I say can and will be used against me. Hard.*

*"I'll wait for you,"* he says.

*I blink. And I have to remind myself I've come here to do something. What was it again?*

*"Do you want me to throw it in for you?" Shane's eyebrows pull together.*

*"What?"*

*He grins. "Your laundry. You want me to put it in the washing machine?"*

*I have laundry?*

*Oh. Right.*

*Yep. Holding it.*

"I use the machines," *I blurt out.*

*My cheeks suffer third-degree burns.*

*Shane's lips twitch like he's trying not to laugh at me.*

*I clear my throat and force my eyes away from the candy they crave.*

*Oh my gosh, say something intelligent.*

"I do laundry on Sundays normally."

*Ugh. That's the opposite of intelligent.*

*Shane raises the smirk even further and says,* "Well, maybe I'll have to start doing laundry on Sundays then."

*My heart thumps so loudly in my chest, I bet his super-trained detective ears can hear it.*

"I'll just get this started," *I say.*

*I don't look at him as I walk to the washing machine; if I do, I'll forget how to use it.*

*How has Shane been hiding all of that underneath his shirt? I mean, sure, anyone can have tattoos, but Shane seems so straitlaced. His pants are always crisp, his button-down shirt wrinkle-free. He isn't just a rule follower; he's a rule enforcer. And even though he'd made that,* "Maybe I'll rearrange your face," *threat to Ezra, I'd assumed he wouldn't go through with it, so I had still pegged him as all rules. These tats don't fit the mold that I'd formed of him in my head—a mold that I already thought was beyond sexy.*

*But this?*

*This was next-hemisphere sexy.*

SHANE HAD WALKED ME BACK TO MY APARTMENT DOOR THAT DAY.

And now, here he was—again.

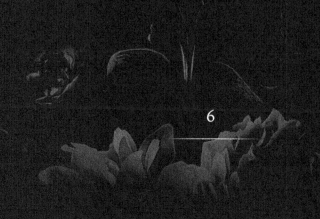

6

*You're staring at him. Stop being all creepy.*

I tiptoed into the kitchen, hoping I could retrieve the Tylenol without waking him, but the cabinet must've wanted a good show because it squeaked, stirring Shane.

He made that stretching sound that people make when they're first waking up. I had never heard anyone make it sound sexy before.

*I wonder what noises he makes when he's in bed with a woman.*

"Willow?" He pushed himself up into a seated position and rubbed his eyes.

"I didn't mean to wake you."

Shane looked at his watch. "We have to get ready for your statement with De Luca. Starts in an hour."

Right. I still had to finish my statement.

"Thank you for staying," I said. "But I've got the rest of the day covered."

I was attracted to Shane. Completely. But right now, I wanted him to leave. I didn't like people seeing me in pain or weak. It was too intimate—made me feel too vulnerable, I guess—and anything that resembled someone trying to take care of me made me uncomfortable.

Later this week, when things normalized, maybe I'd get the courage to ask him out for a cup of coffee. I had the perfect excuse: thanking him for everything he'd done last night. Most importantly, saving my life.

I reached up on tiptoe, stretching my arm up to reach the Tylenol that I had stupidly put on the third shelf, but my shoulder cried out in pain from a torn muscle.

Shane walked over and pressed a hand to my lower back.

"Sit down."

"I need—"

"Tylenol." His eyes were on the container I'd been trying to reach. "I know. Sit down. I'll bring it to you."

"That's not necessary."

"Do you want to get back to normal as fast as possible?"

I frowned. How did he know which buttons to push?

*Buttons.* My hormones relived that moment in the laundry room again. This time, in slow motion. The traitors.

"You need to take it easy and let your body heal. Sit down." He nodded his chin toward the couch.

I debated arguing with him, but I didn't want to reinjure myself on the basis of being stubborn.

Instead of walking over to the couch, however, while Shane busied himself opening the bottle and rooting around for a glass, I went to the sliding glass door.

I unlocked it and jerked it up and to the left like I always did each morning. This time, I yiped.

"Willow!" Shane barked.

I grabbed my shoulder, my cheeks flooding with embarrassment.

"I just hit it at the wrong angle."

"Yeah. No shit. Sit. Down."

Shane's hand pressed against my hip, and he guided me over to the couch, waiting until I sat. "Don't move."

I pursed my lips at him.

He saw my pursed lips and raised me a glower.

"Stop trying to be a freakin' hero and rest," he growled.

"I'm just trying to go about my daily life because that's exactly what I'm going to do."

"You're going to do two things today. Give your statement to De Luca and follow the doctor's orders and rest."

I glared at him as he walked into my kitchen and retrieved the glass of water and Tylenol he'd prepared before I almost ripped my arm off my body.

"Here," he said.

I downed the pills and the water he handed me.

"I assure you, I can take care of myself." I had taken care of myself for a long time. When I was a kid, my mom was emotionally and sometimes physically absent for large chunks of my life, so my sister and I had learned to cook, clean, and take care of ourselves sooner than most people do.

I could certainly handle a broken wrist, sore shoulder, and banged-up body.

"How's your head?" Shane asked, ignoring my statement and taking the empty glass back.

*Feels like a little maniac is inside of it, shooting a BB gun through my brain.*

"Fine."

Shane regarded me with his ocean-colored eyes that were darker around the outside, lighter blue on the inside. I bet he was used to flashing those gems at women and getting them to obey his every command with the sexual spell they cast over them.

"I'd like to rest until De Luca gets here," I said. Polite code for, *Please leave.*

Shane didn't acknowledge my passive request. Instead, he went back into my kitchen, opening up every single cabinet door, one at a time.

"What are you looking for?"

"Ah," he said to himself.

When he pulled out the bag, my mouth fell open.

"What are you doing?"

"You need to rest," was all he said.

He rooted around until he found a bowl, poured the dry pebbles into it, and walked over to the sliding glass door. Evidently expecting it to open like a normal door.

He yanked at the door handle, checking to ensure it was unlocked.

A better person wouldn't have smirked at his frustration. Too bad I wasn't a better person. Because watching him yank it harder and harder while mumbling things like, "What the hell?" and, "What is wrong with this freaking thing?" gave me all sorts of satisfaction.

"You have to pull it up and to the left. Jerk it at an angle," I said.

Shane frowned. "That's a fire hazard."

*Duh.*

"I'm going to call the landlord today," he announced.

Like I hadn't thought to do it myself. "I already did. Three times, they came out here and fiddled around with it and left, saying the building has shifted and there is nothing they could do about it."

"That's bull. I'll call again."

I rolled my eyes. His sapphires might be capable of putting women under magical spells, but our landlord? Good luck.

Shane jerked the door the way I had told him, and it opened. Icy air drifted into the living room as he stepped outside and set the bowl on the four-foot concrete slab that had been advertised as a "patio" when I'd first rented the place.

Patio, my ass. It was big enough to fit one folding chair. Two, if you didn't mind your thigh fondling the person's sitting next to you.

"How do you know I feed Snowflake?" I asked.

Shane stepped back inside and shut the door with a lot more ease. Locked it.

"You named a stray cat?"

"It's not her fault she's a stray. Maybe someone gave up on her. Didn't give her enough chances to show what a good kitty she is."

Shane gave me a look like he wasn't sure if I was being serious.

"Why *Snowflake?*"

"Because she's one of a kind."

*Obviously.*

A hint of amusement flickered across his face.

"How do you know I feed her?" I repeated.

"I've seen you do it plenty of times."

*He did?*

I knew Shane was a detective, trained in the art of observation, but still. My stupid chest warmed at the thought of him being all observant of me.

My chest didn't get the memo that De-*sex*-tive Shane Hernandez was bossy as hell and was sort of in my apartment against my will. So, this was basically a break-in situation. Maybe even a hostage scenario.

"Look, I appreciate everything you've done. But it's time for you to go back to your place."

"We already discussed this. Someone might have broken into your apartment."

*This again.* If cops *hadn't* swept the place up and down, if they *had* found a single clue that someone had been inside, I'd agree with his concern. But the reality was, while I made it my habit to lock up when I left, I was only human, capable of making mistakes. Like forgetting to lock my door.

"No one broke in; no one stole anything. So, if you don't mind," I said, shooing him with my hand, "I have things to do."

"So, do them. I prefer for you to follow the doctor's orders, but don't let me stop you if there's somethin' more pressing than trying to figure out who tried to kill you last night."

I scoffed, and when he didn't move, I stood up and walked across the room until I was in front of him. I wished I were taller so I didn't have to look up at him like this. I wished my stupid stomach weren't coming to life with flutters with him being this close, and I wished my eyes hadn't betrayed me by appreciating the artful lines of muscles on his forearms as he crossed his arms over his chest.

"Let me rephrase," I said. "Leave my apartment."

He had the nerve to step forward. "I'm not leaving you alone, unprotected."

"You're being ridiculous."

"Agree to disagree."

"This is MY apartment!"

"Which I'll leave once I know you're safe."

"I *am* safe!"

"Agree to disagree."

Images of karate-chopping his windpipe flashed through my mind. "Are you always this infuriating?" I asked.

"Are you always this stubborn?"

"Why the hell do you care so much if some random neighbor gets killed?"

"Because you're not random! I care if YOU get killed!"

Shane's Adam's apple bobbed, and I swear a look of embarrassment washed over his face, as if he slipped and said something he never intended to.

But that something was everything.

My damn nerves sparked to life, longing to feel his mouth on mine, to taste his tongue, feel his hands in my hair. Because I realized in this moment that even though I didn't *want* to rely on anyone, having someone *want* to protect me felt incredible. Especially when that someone was Shane.

I couldn't remember the last time anyone had done something like that for me. Or if anyone ever had for that matter.

People love you the best way they know how, but in my life, love had always fallen short of feeding my soul the way it was supposed to. Shane's affection and concern for me was the first time I'd felt like the holes in my soul had the potential of filling in.

It exhilarated me, but also terrified me.

I wasn't sure what just happened or if he wanted to kiss me as badly as I wanted to kiss him, but before I could feel what his lips felt like on mine, a meow broke the silence.

Snowflake was on the patio, walking in circles by the glass.

She was a gorgeous cat. Mostly white with black patches and olive-colored eyes.

"I normally pick her up and hold her," I said.

I froze in place, struggling to free myself from the sexual tension.

But she was meowing so loudly, she must be worried; I'd never left her alone for an entire night before. She always got some snuggles.

I walked toward the door, but Shane beat me to it, opening it for me so I didn't have to tear a ligament this time.

I stepped outside, barefoot. The half inch of snow on the concrete hadn't melted yet, and it hurt my skin more than it should have—almost as if the insides of my bones were still defrosting from being in the icy waters of the river.

"Hey there," I cooed, petting Snowflake's head. "I bet you were so hungry this morning. I'm sorry."

She rubbed her back on my leg. I hated that she was stuck outside in this cold. Sometimes, I snuck her into my apartment for an hour or two at a time, knowing that I was risking my lease. I petted her for as long as my bare feet would allow in the snow and then came back inside and sat on the couch.

After closing the door and locking it, Shane took a position in the kitchen, his back resting against my countertop.

"I'm sorry for being rude," I said. "I'm overly tired. I'm in pain, and I'm not used to people trying to take care of me."

I had never admitted that to anyone.

"You have nothin' to be sorry for, Willow. I'm trying to help. Even if it doesn't come across the right way."

I sighed and groaned when I shifted my ribs. "I need to get a new phone today."

"I can take you after your meeting with De Luca," Shane said.

I wasn't going to argue with him anymore. Maybe after De Luca determined no one had done this to me, Shane would go back to normal, and we could spend time with each other in a typical way. Because I was even more attracted to him than ever. While I'd normally break out in a rash if anyone helped me like this, for some reason, with him, I didn't hate it. If anything, it felt nice, having Shane look out and care for me. But I preferred we get to know each other better on equal footing.

"You need to push De Luca to open an official investigation. He needs to be shoved. Hard," Shane said.

"Isn't he going to want to talk to you? You were at the scene."

"He already took my statement at the hospital."

Oh, right. Shane mentioned that when De Luca first came in.

"Why can't you work the case?" Not that I wanted him to. He'd be a dog with a bone without the objectivity needed to prove I wasn't pushed.

"Because you're a friend," Shane said. "And I was at the scene. Could jeopardize the prosecution."

*Friend.* What a callous word to exist in the English dictionary.

"Tell me you're going to push De Luca."

"I'm going to answer his questions and let him do his job."

"Willow, I'm tellin' you, this guy wants to file his report and go home and watch the game. You need to push him because the person responsible for last night might be someone close to you. And they might try again."

"It's winter. The ground is full of ice and snow, and bridges are prone to icy conditions—particularly bridges over water. I've slipped on ice countless times since moving to Chicago."

I was a normal girl, not a woman from one of those *Dateline* episodes. Did I have some relationships in my life that were less than perfect? Yep. But did that mean someone would have tried to hunt me down and kill me? No. Not even close. As I told him before, if I fell off a bridge, it had to be some sort of an accident. Period.

Shane frowned. "Can you think of any disagreements you've had with anyone lately? Friends? Family? Work colleagues? Neighbors?"

I shot him a look.

"I thought you can't get involved in the case."

"This isn't the detective in me asking; this is a friend asking."

I gave him an incredulous stare. "I'm not discussing all of my relationships with you."

Because some of them were complicated and embarrassing. When you have to fight for people's love, you often feel unwanted, and when you feel unwanted, you sometimes wonder if it's *you*. If there's something wrong with *you* that makes you disposable.

"We don't have to get into relationships. Just tell me a little about yourself."

I wasn't stupid enough to think he wasn't fishing around for suspects, but there was no need to be rude to him. He'd saved my life, and maybe he needed to get some questions out of his system to see there wasn't a sinister cesspool of killers in my world.

"I have a mother and a sister. I went to the University of Illinois and moved to Chicago when I graduated with a degree in business."

"Do you have a lot of friends?"

"I have a few close friends. Most of them live in the city. Some of them I haven't talked to in a while, but when we do talk, it's like no time has passed at all."

"Do you have a boyfriend?"

"No."

We stared at each other, a moment passing between us, as if an unspoken line in the sand had just been wiped away.

Shane cleared his throat and, based on his long sigh, appeared to recalibrate with a new line of questioning.

"And your family. What are the dynamics like?"

I bit my lip. "As normal as you'd expect after my dad died."

Shane held my gaze, his voice softening. "You said he died when you were a kid?"

I nodded.

"Do you mind if I ask what happened to him?"

This was one subject I never discussed with people—it was too intimate. But strangely, I didn't run into the shadows of my heart with Shane. Maybe it was because he had been with me in a moment of life or death, so talking about death wasn't as jarring as it normally was. Or maybe it had shoved our bonding into fast-forward. Whatever the reason, I felt comfortable answering him.

"All I know is that someone killed him, but I'm not sure of the details."

I knew how crazy that had to sound to a detective skilled at getting every one of his questions answered, but when I was twelve—

after a particularly brutal encounter with my mom—I stopped trying to actively find out what happened to him.

After years of my mother refusing to answer questions about my father, I'd decided to take matters into my own hands and googled my dad's name. Up popped a screen with dozens of people with that same name—Johnson is the second most common last name in this country, and Michael is an extremely common first name, too. Sifting through the pages of results, I managed to come across his obituary, but the only thing it confirmed for me was that he had in fact died. If I wanted to learn any more about *how* he died, I realized I needed to narrow my search by combining his name with the date of his death or city, but before I had the chance, my mom stormed into my room.

Turned out, all the parental software and apps she had on our electronic devices that safeguarded us against internet dangers also alerted her to my sleuthing.

It wasn't her screaming in my face, or grounding me for two months, or even her physical outburst, throwing things around my room, that broke me; it was the look in her eyes, of deep pain and betrayal, that made me feel like an awful person for hurting her by looking into the one thing that had the power to break her. Especially when Mom spiraled out of control for weeks after that. Realizing how badly my curiosity had hurt my mom, I decided to let it lie until she was ready to discuss it with me.

Especially since my devices were so closely monitored.

Over the years, I became conditioned to just accept that my dad was dead, and with all the other drama Mom and Hayley created, sadly, it was only every now and then that I'd get the urge to know how Dad died again.

Each time I did, paranoia swept through me that even without electronic monitoring, Mom would somehow find out if I went sleuthing again, and this time, her anger would be so bad, our relationship would be destroyed. I reminded myself I had one parent left —one—and nothing was worth jeopardizing that.

Plus, I trusted that, someday, she *would* tell me what happened.

"His death has always been very painful for my mom, and I didn't have the heart to keep pressing her for what happened to him."

But after almost dying, how could I go to my grave, not knowing the truth? Not only of what happened, but why Mom had kept it such a big secret. Was it really the right thing to do, to drop it?

Shane scrubbed the side of his face. "Yeah, I can relate to that."

I looked up at him. "You can?"

Shane grabbed the countertop with both hands and crossed one foot in front of the other. "I don't talk about this with anyone." He met my gaze, and something passed between us as the wall he kept up around others collapsed, flooding my heart with affection that he'd trust me with whatever he was about to divulge. "But my dad died when I was little, too. He was a police officer and was shot in the line of duty when I was four."

*Holy crap.*

I never would've guessed he had endured such a violent loss in his past. That took some major courage to join law enforcement after that. I mean, anyone that joined the force knew the dangers, but when your own father lost his life...I guess I was surprised Shane still took that risk.

"This might be a completely inappropriate question," I said. "But did that ever make you not want to become a police officer?"

I wondered if my question was too intimate, but Shane didn't hesitate.

"The opposite. My dad was a hero, who dedicated his life to protecting others. If I could be half as good as he was, I knew I'd do a lot of good in this world."

My insides came alive with butterflies. Shane Hernandez wasn't just ruggedly handsome or kind. He had a heart of gold. The kind of heart I had searched for, but never found in any other guy.

As we stared at each other in silence for several heartbeats, I wondered if he felt this too, this connection expanding like a fast-growing sunflower. For me, the feeling was unprecedented.

I could have stared at him like this for hours, but a loud knock made me jerk.

Shane clutched the gun strapped to his hip and held his hand up to me, motioning for me to stay put. He pulled his weapon from its holster and approached the door slowly, looking out the peephole, his eyebrows scrunched together.

"Identify yourself," Shane commanded.

It took a second for the person on the other end to answer.

"Uh...Mike? With 1-800-Flowers?"

"Leave them by the door," Shane said. "And walk away."

Oh my God. The poor flower deliverer was probably so confused right now.

Shane stared through that peephole forever before unlocking and opening the door.

Gun drawn.

He stepped into the hallway, weapon first, sweeping from left to right.

I guess he was satisfied that there wasn't some serial killer waiting for me in the hallway because he put his gun back in its holster, picked up a vase of red roses, and came inside, kicking the door closed behind him. Which he locked right after he'd set the bouquet on the counter.

"I wonder if someone knows I was in the hospital last night."

How, though? I pulled the little card from the roses as Shane put both of his hands on the countertop, glaring at the flowers as I read the note.

*I miss you. I hope you'll reconsider giving me another chance.*

*~ Ezra*

"Who are they from?" Shane asked.

"My ex-boyfriend."

Shane didn't blink. "Was that the prick who got handsy with you the night we met?"

I nodded, and Shane's face set into stone.

"How long ago did you guys break up?"

"A few months."

"Mind if I ask why things ended?"

Normally, I wouldn't answer this question—it was humiliating— but Shane needed to know that Ezra wasn't abusive or anything.

"I caught him kissing another woman."

And son of a brat if I hadn't let it momentarily lower my self-esteem. I'd been ashamed that I had let *his* behavior impact *my* self-worth, but for a hot minute, it had.

Shane raised an eyebrow.

"I forgave him at first. Tried to work it out."

"You took him back?"

"You don't need to sound so judgy. Sometimes, you have to work at things in life, and I thought it was worth giving our relationship a second chance."

"But it didn't work?"

I bit my lip. "I found text messages with another woman, and that was it; broke it off."

"How'd he take it?"

I shrugged. "How does any breakup go?"

"Did he accept it was over?" Shane asked.

*"I'M GOING TO DO WHATEVER IT TAKES TO WIN YOU BACK, WILLOW," EZRA declares.*

"I'M SURE HE'LL MOVE ON, EVENTUALLY."

Shane said nothing.

"He's tried to get me back before, so these flowers are just par for the course," I assured.

Shane pinched the bridge of his nose.

"What?" I asked.

Shane stared at me for several seconds, keeping his voice gentle. "In my line of work, I've come to see that far too often, our feelings for someone stifle our instincts, and our heart dismisses red flags before our brain has a chance to think."

"Meaning?"

"I know this is hard for you to accept, but I believe someone tried to kill you. And the statistics say it's someone close to you."

I bit my lip, telling my heartbeat to calm down. Just because Shane was a detective didn't mean he was right.

Shane glanced at the flowers, then back at me. "Tell me you see what I'm seeing."

I swallowed.

"That your ex-boyfriend isn't letting you go, isn't accepting no for an answer, and sends you flowers after you were almost killed."

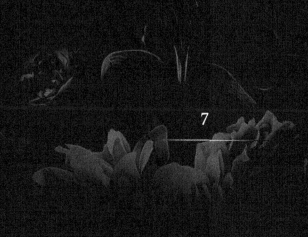

## 7

"What are *you* doing here?" De Luca asked.

Maybe letting Shane answer my door was a mistake.

"I told you, she's my neighbor," Shane said. "And a friend."

Blech—that word again.

De Luca glared at Shane for a few seconds before spitting out a question. "You think I wouldn't find out?"

"It's not personal," Shane said.

"Trying to have me removed from the case isn't personal?"

"I'm trying to do what's best for Willow."

They exchanged another look before De Luca strolled past Shane into my living room.

My TV was off, its black screen reflecting De Luca's rigid posture as he took a seat on the other end of my couch, which jolted from the weight shift. Outside my sliding glass door, snow flurries drifted to the ground without a care in the world while, in here, my apartment's air thickened with tension.

Tension that was brimming from De Luca's dark brown eyes— eyes so dark, I could barely discern the black pupil from the surrounding color.

"Afternoon."

As De Luca pulled open his phone, presumably to a screen where he took notes, I wondered, *Would De Luca agree with Shane's suspicions?* Because the more I thought about it—even after I tried to open myself up to what Shane had said—I just could not imagine someone having tried to kill me. There had to be another explanation for how I'd fallen from that bridge.

"Do you want me to leave?" Shane asked me.

Ironic. Before, I'd been trying to do just that, but now, when I had the perfect excuse—finishing my statement—something didn't sit right in doing it.

I think it was because De Luca's tone of voice was so rude, his body language screaming he'd rather be anywhere but here. I suppose his simmering animosity could be from whatever was going on between him and Shane, but if that were true, he shouldn't be glowering at *me* right now.

Shane never did. Not even when I disagreed with his theory. He was warmth and compassion, whereas De Luca was cold and hard—and about to probe into my private life. I could handle it alone, but for the first time in my life, I didn't have to.

"I'd rather you stay," I said.

De Luca scowled at me, scratched his cheek so roughly that thin streaks of pink painted his skin, and then started with the basics. Confirming my date of birth, that kind of stuff. And then he got to the questions.

"What were you doing on the bridge?" De Luca asked.

"I don't remember."

"Where were you coming from before you got to the bridge?"

I pinched the bridge of my nose. "I don't remember. I think home maybe?"

"Where were you headed?"

"I don't know."

"Were you with anyone?" he asked.

"I don't remember."

De Luca tugged his earlobe. "Were you drinking or otherwise under the influence?"

"Not that I recall. Didn't the hospital do a test?"

"Initial screens were negative, but I'm asking what you *recall*. You drink a lot?"

"No," I said.

"Use drugs?"

"Never."

"In the hospital, you said you hadn't been depressed lately. But do you have a history of depression?"

I twisted my hands together, my face burning.

"I would remember if I was depressed enough to want to kill myself."

"You said you don't remember."

"That night. But I remember everything before yesterday, and I wasn't depressed."

"She was screaming when she fell," Shane said defensively.

De Luca's stare snapped to the ground and took a few seconds to return to me.

"Anyone threaten you?" he asked.

"Not exactly."

"Not exactly?"

"I'm a human resources manager. My company recently let seven people go. A couple of them got angry. Said some things that they shouldn't have."

Shane's gaze became so severe, I felt like it could snap my spine.

"Like what?" De Luca asked in an ambivalent tone.

"*You're making a mistake, how dare you*—that type of thing."

"But they didn't make a specific threat against you?"

"No."

"Was it your decision to fire them?"

"No. It was management's. I'm the HR manager who has to facilitate the process."

*Not soul-crushing at all.*

"Were they under the impression it was your decision?"

"No. They knew it was management."

De Luca typed something. "You part of any organizations, sports teams, that sort of thing?"

"I volunteer at a few places that help feed the hungry, give business skills to folks who are out of work."

"Anything unusual occur?"

"No."

"Anything else unusual happen recently? Notice anyone following you or find a tire slashed or anything like that?"

"No. I get some weird DMs sometimes on my social media accounts," I admitted. "But I'm sure that happens to every person online."

"Any of them particularly alarming?" De Luca asked.

"No."

"Anything else out of the ordinary happen?"

"Someone may have broken into my apartment last night," I said.

"May have?"

"The front door wasn't fully shut when I got home."

"Anything missing?"

"No."

"Did you call the police?" he asked.

"Yes."

"What did the responding officer say?"

"There was no evidence of a break-in."

De Luca nodded.

"My, uh…" Ugh, I knew this was going to sound bad, but as much as I believed no one had done this, I couldn't be a stubborn fool, either. "My ex, Ezra, sent me flowers this morning."

"Flowers."

"He wants me back."

"Ezra ever get violent with you?" De Luca asked.

"He got a little handsy with me when I was drunk one time, but I wouldn't classify it as violent."

Another thought crossed my mind—something Shane would pounce on as a motive, but it was too far-fetched to be related to this. And it had nothing to do with Ezra.

"You should subpoena her phone records," Shane said.

De Luca sucked his lower lip between his teeth, biting down harshly.

"Normally takes weeks to get the data back," Shane said. "But it can be a lot quicker if you show exigency."

De Luca's chest inflated.

"What's exigency?" I asked.

Shane was kind enough to answer me, much to the obvious frustration of De Luca.

"A life-threatening emergency, where we need the information to prevent a crime that could result in death or serious bodily injury. For example, if we think your life is in imminent danger from a killer. Phone records don't have pictures or text messages though; you have to physically download that information from the phone. Do you know if you have messages in iCloud enabled?"

"Detective..."

I shrugged.

"If you have it backed up," Shane said, "and it synced that night, we could see if anyone texted you." Shane turned his attention back to De Luca. "You should have her sign a consent to search so you can look into it."

De Luca snapped his head around to Shane, the two men scowling at each other.

That's when I realized that whatever was going on between them was bigger than I first sensed.

After a few moments, De Luca turned back to me. "One last question. Do you think anyone in your life is capable of doing this to you?"

And there it was, point-blank. I felt like this was some sort of loyalty test between De Luca and Shane, which was silly. The question was about what happened last night, not some macho posturing between the two.

Still, after everything Shane had done for me, it felt like a little bit of a betrayal when I answered honestly. "No. I don't think anyone did this to me."

De Luca nodded and stood from the couch.

"This needs to get kicked up to detectives," Shane insisted.

"We have no witnesses that saw someone with her on that bridge. No physical evidence of a struggle. No witness statement suggesting she was attacked. No threats, nothing."

"She can't remember."

"There is no evidence of foul play. Thus, no justification to kick this up to detectives. Probably a reckless mishap or failed suicide attempt." His tone was so ambivalent, you'd think he hadn't just detonated a bomb in my psyche. "I'll see if any video surveillance points to that bridge, but I wouldn't hold my breath."

"So, you're not goin' to open an investigation then?" Shane snapped. "Not even so they can talk to her goddamn ex?"

De Luca glowered at Shane.

"As a witness and a friend of the victim, you know you need to stay away from this case," De Luca said in a calm tone. "It would be a shame for your career to go down the drain over this."

8

"Fuck." Shane shoved his hands through his hair and paced in my living room. The veins in his arms pulsed like little snakes winding around his skin, and his chest remained permanently inflated. "De Luca is going to close the report. No one will be lookin' into this, Willow."

Shane was trying to protect me, but I needed to protect him by convincing him to stand down.

"De Luca *is* looking into this. Maybe he doesn't do things your way, but he said he's going to look at camera footage."

"Even if we get lucky enough to have a camera pointed at the exact location you went over, do you know how long that might take him? Meanwhile, whoever did this is still out there, and he doesn't appear the least bit concerned by that."

"What is with you two? Because I can tell whatever's going on is not about this case. There's clearly a history there."

"It doesn't matter." Shane pinched the bridge of his nose.

"It does to me," I said, making it clear I'd wait.

Shane stilled for a moment before taking a deep breath. "De Luca and I used to work together, and he frequently cut corners. I reported him for it. And later, it was because of that report that he lost out on a promotion."

Cut corners. No wonder Shane was so worried about De Luca's competence on this. Had De Luca learned his lesson and straightened out, or should I also be worried he might cut corners on my case, too? Even if I was worried, there wasn't anything I could do about it, other than ask De Luca questions and ensure he was following up about it; if Shane couldn't get De Luca reassigned with his weight in the department, I certainly couldn't either.

Not that I'd express my concerns to Shane; I didn't want to fan the flames when he looked on edge enough. His body was so tense, it looked like it was carved out of stone, and his eyes looked darker than I'd ever seen them—a haunted midnight blue.

"Let me see your phone records," Shane said.

"What?"

"You would have access to all your phone records with your carrier."

"Do you *want* to piss De Luca off?"

Shane walked up to me with his hands at his sides, his pupils dilated. "Let me see them."

"Shane..."

"Tell me what's been happening in your life over the last few weeks."

See? I'd made the right call, not telling Shane about that fleeting thought I'd had when De Luca was here. Shane wouldn't see it as a far-fetched motive; he'd probably get spun up about it, and it was going to be hard enough to get him to stand down from this investigation without adding to his concern.

"You cannot get involved in this," I insisted. "I heard what De Luca said."

"To hell with what De Luca said."

"You're a witness and a friend of..." I couldn't mutter the word *victim*. "He made it sound like if you step one foot into this case, your career could be damaged." It must break a substantial policy that law enforcement has in place. "And after you tried to get him taken off the case, he sounded like he'd jump at the chance to get you into trouble. You have to let this go."

"Willow." Shane took a step forward. "I believe you that you wouldn't have jumped on your own. And I believe you when you said you're afraid of the water, so you wouldn't be reckless enough to be balancing on the railing or some stupid shit like that. But where we disagree is your accident theory. There's no evidence that supports someone being able to go off that bridge on accident. And you have those bruises on your upper arms, which leaves one possibility —*someone* did this to you."

Even if De Luca wasn't the most thorough police officer, there would either be camera footage of what happened or there wouldn't be. Shane stepping on De Luca's toes wasn't going to make any of this go faster. It would just get Shane into more trouble, and I couldn't let that happen.

"Even if your career wasn't on the line," I said, "the price tag of your curiosity is my sense of security. It's disturbing enough to know this is being investigated, and for my own sanity, I'd prefer to have De Luca look into this out there"—I pointed toward my sliding glass door —"so it's not in my face every moment of the day."

"I told you, if someone did try to kill you and failed, they could try it again. Especially if they think you might tell the cops who did this to you."

"I have no memory of it."

"But whoever did this doesn't know that. And even if they did, they can't take the chance that your memory might someday come back. Whatever the hell their motivation was for tryin' to kill you before, you can add to that them facing life behind bars if you open your mouth. They have more motivation than ever to finish what they started." His eyes tightened, demanding I acknowledge the danger he thought I was in. "You seriously just want to walk away and not look into it?"

I wasn't walking away or not having it looked into.

"I know you're used to working cases and looking for suspects, but I'm not a case. I'm a human being with a normal life. And trying to convince me over and over and over again that somebody that I love and care about might've tried to end me? It's unfathomable."

"Willow—"

"I'm not being naive," I interrupted. "I'm just being honest. I truly do not believe that anyone I know is capable of physically harming me. Okay?"

*I hope I'm not wrong.*

Shane's jaw set into frustrated granite as he stared down at me. "What about people you don't know?"

If someone did this to me, it would have to be a stranger, but I'd never meet a stranger alone in the dark, so I couldn't see how that was possible, either. Unless…maybe I was walking and became the victim of a random act of street violence or something. I didn't know, but Shane needed to back off for his own sake.

"If it was a stranger, then they don't know who I am, so they wouldn't be able to come after me again," I said, trying to calm Shane down. "I'm still hoping my memories will come back, but in the meantime, please, let it go."

Shane grabbed the back of his neck and held it for several seconds. "After what I saw outside the apartment that night with your ex…I should've asked more questions."

Was that why he was so upset? He blamed himself for not preventing it?

"We don't know if Ezra was involved in this, and even if he was, this isn't your fault, Shane. So, if that's why you're so obsessed over this—"

"It's not. I just…" His cerulean eyes combed over my face as he dropped his arms back at his sides. "I won't stand back and allow something else to happen to you, Willow. You're too"—he stopped himself, finishing with a whisper—"important to me."

But how could that be?

"You barely know me." I regretted it the second the words vomited from my mouth because it might come across as ungrateful. I wasn't. I was just surprised. While I'd always sensed a mutual attraction between us, his almost profession was bigger than that.

"I've noticed everything about you from the first time I laid eyes on you," he declared.

I swallowed under the intensity of his gaze as he took a step closer, challenging my space and my assumptions, staring down at me for several breathless moments.

"Your beauty took my breath away." Shane's voice was low, almost a growl, as he studied my eyes, my cheeks, my lips. My heart began to beat so hard, I wondered if he could hear it. "And I loved how you'd always walk with your chin held high with this stoic look on your face, like you were determined to make each day a success."

Shane brought his arm up tentatively, so slowly that it was as if he was unsure I'd allow him to touch me like this. But of course I was okay with it. I *longed* for his hand to complete its agonizing journey to my face, and when his palm pressed to my cheek, my mouth parted in ecstasy. The warmth of his skin washed over me like the shimmering rain of a summer storm.

I'd never felt this immense energy with anyone before, like my body was full of magnets, activated and pulling to his every caress.

"Every once in a while," he continued, "I got to hear you laugh, and its melody would..."

He bit his lip, his chest only two feet from my own, expanding with faster breaths as he swallowed, seemingly struggling to continue talking through this haze that had come over him. It was like watching someone become lost in a memory, only this memory was us. Here. Now.

"I craved that laugh so damn bad," he said. "And I kept finding excuses to run into you."

He brushed his thumb along my cheekbone, leaving a trail of heat over my skin.

"I'd rush over and hold the complex's door open for you." A sad smile tugged his lips up in the corner. "Or I'd collect my mail if I saw you in the mail room—anything to steal a few moments with you."

Something was changing between us right in front of my eyes, something expanding past the boundaries of the romance we'd been dancing around for months.

He studied my mouth with a hunger I'd only seen flashes of before. Now, that flash illuminated into an all-out spotlight as his tone dropped another octave, a need pulsing through his words.

"I kept having to remind myself to keep my distance because…"

*Because what?*

I hated the way he swallowed harshly—it looked painful—but I savored the way his gaze swept over my face, his eyebrows pulling together, like he couldn't stand keeping his distance from me anymore. He stared at my mouth as if fighting against a desire he'd had since the moment he first saw me—the desire to feel my lips against his own.

My mouth moistened, hoping he'd surrender to whatever internal battle waged in his mind because, my God, I could tell his lips would feel amazing on mine. His tongue would, too. I wanted to feel his hands in my hair, dragging his palms down my back as he kissed me the way I'd only daydreamed of.

Shane trailed his thumb slowly down my cheek and began to trace my lower lip.

Holy mother of erotica, the sensation caused my breath to catch. How could a touch so simple feel more sensual than anything I'd ever felt with a man before? I wanted to lick his thumb, suck it even, and grab the back of his neck and end this agony by pulling his mouth to mine.

Every skin cell on my body heightened, aching to be touched.

I rested my hands on his shoulders, feeling the curves of strength beneath my palms—rock-hard muscles banding together, stretching over his iron torso.

It was surreal, getting to touch him like this, but even more surreal was that I was about to feel his lips on mine. Shane tilted his head, staring at my mouth as he moved his knuckle beneath my chin and tilted it up.

His phone's chime burst through the silence and immediately became my enemy because it ruptured whatever spell had made him abandon his mysterious reservations. He took a step back, and his features rearranged into regret, like he'd gotten lost in urges he shouldn't have allowed himself to act on.

I knew this attraction might feel complicated to him, especially since he was a police detective who became inadvertently caught up in the aftermath of my fall after saving my life. The fact that he also happened to be my next-door neighbor just added another layer of complication on top of everything else.

But why did I get the sense his step back was because of something else? Something bigger and more complex?

"I should order us some food," he said.

Food.

Dinner.

"Crap!"

I almost forgot, and since this was the first time I'd see my sister after the birthday debacle, I was not going to miss this. I needed to hurry, or I'd be late, and that was a major pet peeve of my mom's.

"I'm meeting my family for dinner." Mom, Grandma, and Hayley. "It's my mom's birthday, and we're going to her favorite restaurant."

I hurried toward my bathroom, forcing my mind to put whatever just happened between us behind me for the moment. Later, I could wonder about it all I wanted, but for right now, I needed to focus on getting to dinner on time.

"I don't think—"

"Look, I know you're worried about me, and I appreciate it. But you're treating me like I have a gun to my head. We don't know for sure if anyone did this to me, and even if they did, they're not waiting outside my door with a loaded pistol, ready to take me out."

Shane appeared in my bathroom doorway, watching me frantically start my shower.

"I'm going to the dinner," I said. "I have to get showered and changed."

And brush my teeth because, gross, I hadn't done that since I'd fallen from the bridge.

Maybe it was a good thing we hadn't kissed. I probably tasted like a meerkat.

"Willow…"

"Shane."

He opened his mouth to argue but closed it when I held up my palm, letting him know this wasn't up for debate. As I held my other hand under the shower water, waiting for it to turn warm, Shane's shoulders rose and fell while he appeared to evaluate me.

After another moment, he asked, "Can I please come with you?"

My dang heart did jumping jacks at the thought of spending more time with him. Maybe if we spent more time together, I'd find out the rest of his confession—why he'd been keeping his distance before. More importantly, had that changed?

"Fine. But for right now, I have to get in the shower."

Shane bit his lip but reluctantly exited my apartment, presumably so he could get cleaned up and dressed. He waited to hear the lock of my dead bolt, though, before the door to his apartment opened.

It took me a minute to get undressed with the aches and pains, but I managed to do it alone this time. The hot shower took longer than I wanted it to, thanks to having to wash myself with only one hand, my cast safely outside the shower curtain. The plastic shield thing the hospital gave me, which would protect the cast from water, looked like it'd take a few minutes to put on, and I just wanted to hurry.

When I stepped out, I dried off, wiped the fog off the bathroom mirror, and reached for my toothbrush.

But it wasn't there. Confused, I swept my eyes over my bathroom, and there, on the white porcelain back of the toilet, was my toothbrush.

*What in the world?*

I always kept my toothbrush on the right side of my sink, next to the toothpaste. Always. And even if I'd absentmindedly put it somewhere else, I would never put it on the back of the toilet. Because *gross.*

Did someone move my toothbrush? Maybe Shane had moved it when he'd swept my apartment to make sure no one was in here? No. That made no sense. But it made no sense that my toothbrush would magically transport itself to the back of my toilet, either.

For a second, I actually considered the possibility that someone *had* broken into my apartment. But if they were looking to rob me, first of all, they would not have been looking on my bathroom counter, and second, even if they were, they'd knock things around so they would fall on the floor, not neatly place them on the toilet ledge.

Maybe they had knocked it on the floor and then set it back there?

No. It was a stupid thought. They'd have set it back on the counter, not the toilet.

Still, I hurried through my apartment to ensure nothing else seemed out of place before returning to the bathroom.

I must've been brushing my teeth while on the phone or something and had to set it down for a second and then forgot about it...

## 9

"I can't believe I let you talk me into you coming," I said.

Now that I thought about it—without the almost kiss clouding my mind—this was a huge mistake. There was a reason I kept my family life private, and tonight might be a complete shit show.

In fact, I had this nagging gut feeling that something bad was going to happen, and I really didn't want Shane to witness whatever it was.

I had a thick skin when it came to my family—a thick skin that diluted the hurts caused by Mom's emotional swings and Hayley's rejection—but sometimes, I forgot that others weren't used to or prepared to face the unpredictable chaos a family get-together brought.

"I'm surprised you're even goin', to be honest. After what happened last night."

I chewed on my fingernail.

"Your determination to make this dinner, which arguably falls on one of the worst possible days to fulfill social obligations…this have anything to do with your hesitation about calling your family at the hospital?"

I picked at my nail.

"Yeah, I thought so."

An empty pit opened in my stomach. "It might be a cluster."

Shane watched me straighten my coat. "Tell me what role to play."

"What?"

He rested one elbow on the Uber's door, angling his body to see me better. "You're clearly goin' through some crap with your family. It's not my business, so I won't pry. Or I'll do my best not to pry, so long as I don't think whatever's goin' on with your family could escalate to pushing you off a bridge. But I can at least try to make this night easier on you. Tell me what role to play."

Knots of tension unwound in my chest, replaced with appreciation. He didn't know how much his offer meant to me.

"Just a friend is great," I said.

Shane placed his hand on mine—a gesture he probably meant to calm me, but it did so much more.

"I'll make an excellent dinner date."

I was sure he would, but it felt terribly intimate, allowing Shane to see the dysfunction that might be on display tonight.

"I'm warning you, it might be awkward," I said. "My mom's hit or miss with her moods at these things, even though she's the one that insists on them. And my sister is...unpredictable."

"I'm well versed in what grief can do to family dynamics," Shane said.

I met his empathetic gaze, which seemed to wrap around me and pull me into an embrace.

"Sometimes, it's easy to forget that other families go through this," I said.

"Death has so much collateral damage that no one really thinks about. You think about the kids growing up without a dad or the widow struggling to make ends meet. But you don't think about the fractures it can create in relationships."

He truly understood.

Shane continued, "My dad's death destroyed the relationship with an entire side of our family."

That, I was not expecting.

"How?"

"From what I've gathered, my mom was stuck in the anger phase. She blamed the guy who shot my dad, of course. But he was dead, and when your loss is that big, I think your pain branches out to find a home where it can fester. To look for someone to blame—anyone—and when blamin' his killer didn't fill the void, she blamed my dad's father."

"His father?"

"I come from a long line of cops," Shane explained. "My dad's dad was a cop, and so was his dad. When my father was killed in the line of duty, this tension between my mom and his side of the family started to percolate. I think, deep down, my mom blamed them for pressurin' him to go into law enforcement in the first place."

I couldn't imagine losing my child and then having their spouse blame *me* for it.

Shane's poor grandpa. But his poor mom, too, because she was rocking in a sea of agony, probably not intending to create waves of anguish.

Shane's tone deepened. "You would think that people who share the same loss would draw closer together, but sometimes, it's the opposite. Like maybe you see them as walking reminders of everything you lost or something. I don't know. But instead of strengthening the bond between my mom and my father's side of the family, it weakened it."

Weakened a family bond.

As heartbreaking as it was, it felt reassuring to know it wasn't just my family that had gone through this. It made me feel less rejected by my family—a reminder to myself that their rejection had nothing to do with *me*, but rather the aftershocks of grief.

Grief was such an isolating monster. Hurting people so devastatingly that they pulled inward, away from some, while lashing out at others. Eating away at relationships one at a time until we felt lost in the shadows, all alone. Hoping our remaining loved ones would return to us one day.

Maybe if we talked about loss the way Shane and I were now, healing could begin, but it seemed everyone avoided the topic of loss at all costs.

Except for Shane. He was the first person who talked about it so openly, and in doing so, he cast a light into my darkness and held out a hand so I was no longer alone.

"I'm sure my grandfather sensed her misplaced blame," Shane continued, "and probably resented it. The tension between them grew until, eventually, we stopped seeing my dad's side of the family altogether. My grandpa would still send us birthday cards and Christmas presents; he still let us know he cared about us, but we didn't get to see him anymore."

I couldn't even imagine how Shane's dad would feel about that. I bet he'd have wanted everyone to wrap their arms around each other. Not break up.

"How did that make you feel?" I asked.

My question surprised me; it was a thinking-out-loud moment, but even more surprising was when Shane scrubbed his jaw and answered. He tried to keep his tone neutral, but I could hear the pain breaking through his words.

"Let down. I wished they had put their own feelings aside and made the kids the priority, you know?"

Yeah. Grief not only ate relationships; it devoured childhood innocence.

"Because with my dad dying, holidays were tough enough. The last thing we needed was being estranged from loved ones."

My ribs ached; I knew how that felt.

"I've never met anyone that understands these kinds of family complexities like you do," I said.

Shane regarded me, a shared pain etched across his features. "I've never talked about it like...*this* with anyone before."

In all his years, the guy had never opened up like this to anyone, just as I had never opened up to anyone, either—as close as I'd been to Ezra, I'd never gone deep into my family dynamics. I felt sorry for

Shane, knowing how isolated he must have felt as he watched other guys clanking beer mugs and playing poker without a care, but I also felt privileged that he'd trusted me with something so intimate.

"Your mom must have hated you becoming a cop," I said.

Shane raised his eyebrows. "More than you can imagine. She threatened to not come to my graduation over it."

Ouch.

"My life felt like a constant tug-of-war," Shane continued. "Because of my dad's death, what I wanted more than anything was to lock up people like my dad's killer. To protect people, so hopefully, their fathers would never get shot. And I wanted to carry on the legacy of our family, to not let it die with him, because letting the line of cops end with him just felt like another death to me. A death I could prevent from happening. Yet, at the same time, I worried me becoming a cop would put a tremendous stress on my mom. She'd already suffered enough, and the last thing I wanted to do was to drag her back into that hell."

Jeez. Whenever I had seen Shane before, he always looked so put together and peaceful. There was a calmness about him, and I never would've suspected that beneath the surface, there had ever been such a storm in his past.

Once again, Shane's words made me feel less alone in my suffering. By unveiling his personal, intimate experiences with loss, Shane unlocked my cage of shame—shame over the hurt I'd felt by my own family's dynamics.

The Uber stopped in front of the restaurant, and Shane held the door open for me so I could escape the bitter cold and walk into the heat of the restaurant.

Where I spotted my mom and grandma, sitting at a four-top.

Shane followed me as we wove around the tables, my wrist still aching despite the Tylenol.

"Do not tell them what happened to me," I said. "My mom misses my dad a lot around her birthday, and I don't want to worry her about your...hypothesis."

"As soon as you take your coat off, they're going to see your cast. What are you going to tell them?"

"I don't know..."

## 10

To everyone else, the restaurant's ambiance was romantic—charcoal walls with a scattering of pastel-pink flower arrangements; dimmed lighting; white tablecloths with sparkling wineglasses; the smell of rich chocolate desserts, mingling with tomato-rich dishes; and soft violin music, designed to hush the surrounding conversations. But to me, it was like a gorgeously designed cover for an unpredictable book. You had no idea what you were getting into until you turned that first page.

When Mom spotted me, she smiled. A good sign that she was in a decent mood tonight—that it wouldn't be a repeat of last year, when she'd been sullen and had barely talked during dinner.

My shoulders relaxed a little.

Hopefully, Hayley would be in a good mood, too. I wasn't sure what to expect, given we hadn't seen each other since the day after the birthday blowoff, but I intended to talk to her tonight to see if we could put my birthday debacle behind us and take a new step forward.

Mom's gaze shifted to Shane, not hiding her surprise.

"Hey, Mom." I bent down to give her a quick kiss on the cheek. Then Grandma's. "I hope it's okay that I brought a friend of mine. This is Shane. Shane, this is my mom, Laura."

"Ma'am," Shane said, shaking her hand. "It's good to meet you."

"And this is my grandma, Kathleen," I said.

"Ma'am." Shane shook my grandma's hand too.

Grandma's eyes combed over Shane's handsome appearance—his dark hair, polished with product; his turquoise eyes, reflecting the candle's flames, accentuating his strong jaw. His black pants, light-blue button-down, and navy tie showed off the curves of his rugged body. To say he was the hottest guy in the restaurant wasn't an understatement.

Women were watching him, but he didn't seem to notice.

Shane placed his hands on the neckline of my coat, locking eyes with me—a secret moment passing between us as he silently asked me if I was ready for this.

When I nodded, he slid the coat off my body.

Pain seared through my shoulder with my arm's movement, but I hid it from my facial expression.

"What happened to your arm?" Mom's brows furrowed in alarm.

I kept my face nonchalant. "I fell."

Shane glanced between me and my mother as he draped both our coats on the backs of our chairs.

"When did this happen?"

"Last night. Shane got me to the ER, where they put a cast on it." All true. So far, only lies by omission, and I wanted to keep it that way. Telling an outright lie to my mom would only hurt her when she eventually learned the truth. Even if I was trying to protect her.

A waiter interrupted my mom's incredulous stare, and when he found out we had an extra person, a fifth chair was added. Chairs were adjusted, and after a minute, the four of us were seated with one empty chair remaining.

"Where is Hayley?" I asked.

"Late." My mom's lips flattened into a line.

Not a good sign.

"Is she doing okay?" I asked. Code for, *Has she fallen off the wagon?*

Mom busied herself with straightening the silverware.

"I've been trying to call you," she said. Code for, *Change the subject*. Which she'd do even if Shane wasn't here.

Mom's only coping mechanism in life was her giant broom, shoving anything difficult under the rug. And Hayley's issues were no exception.

The broom gave Hayley a lot of free passes in life. That, and the bond she and Hayley shared, cemented in tragedy, was a connection I was never invited to be a part of. Hayley was fourteen when Dad died, and since I was only four, I guess I wasn't old enough to share in their grief. Making me feel like a bit of an outsider in a family already deficient in affection.

"I lost my phone. I'm going to get a new one tomorrow."

Because by the time I got done with this dinner, it would be cutting it too close to get to the store before they closed today.

I braced myself for follow-up questions about how I lost my phone and where and how I had fallen hard enough to break my arm. Most moms would ask follow-up questions.

But not mine.

She went with, "So, how's work going?"

*Small talk, then.*

"Honestly? It hasn't gotten better."

When I had chosen human resources as a profession, I thought I would be spending my days hiring new people, developing strategies to retain talent, helping coach the company on ways we could better support our employees. And at first, I was. But for the last two years, it was the opposite. The company I worked for laid people off every quarter. And guess who had to take part in all the *planning* meetings of how many lives to ruin and whose lives those would be? No matter how well they were all performing.

And that was just the tip of the iceberg. The real heartbreak was when I'd have to sit in on the meetings where we let them go. And then there were the follow-up meetings with the people who'd lost the income for their family, seeing them in tears, terrified of how they'd pay their mortgage. They'd show me pictures of their kids and beg me to help, not knowing I lacked the power to do so. My orders were given by management, and, yes, I'd tried to advocate for people. And, yes, I'd laid out plans and other strategies that we could try instead of letting people go, but it always fell on deaf ears.

Increasingly, those situations became harder for me to handle emotionally. It was draining and, candidly, toxic for me. I didn't want to go into work to fire people all the time.

My boss kept assuring me the business was going through a cycle and that it wouldn't always be this way. I'd already researched other companies and discovered that moving would not solve that underlying issue, so I was just trying to hold on for dear life until this "cycle" was over.

"I'm sure it will get better," Mom said.

Six words that summed up Mom's parenting advice to me over the years. *I'm sure it will get better.* Ironic, since Mom's grief never seemed to get better. She didn't know how to help someone navigate a path toward making things better. To her, life was about accepting the gunshot wound and letting it bleed out for whatever remained of your life.

At least she'd started to turn things around by seeing a therapist this past year, and that was a huge win—offering up more hope than ever that we could finally get close. Hell, when I'd been falling from that bridge, that's all I wanted—more than anything else in my life. So, why was all this hurt and anger and frustration bubbling up now? I guess a year of limited progress hadn't overcome twenty-four years of all these suppressed, unresolved feelings that continued to batter me.

"I've always wanted to start my own business, helping people find jobs and get back on their feet," I said. "I'm going to start researching what that would entail."

Shane's lips curled into an impressed smile.

"What about your current job?" Mom asked.

"It's just some research," I said. "I'd have to learn more before making anything official." Maybe I could start a business on the side and grow it into something full-time. My goal wasn't to get rich; it was just to pay my bills and help people.

A waiter stopped by to top off our waters and to ask if we had any questions about the menu before walking off.

"Have you spoken to Hayley lately?" Mom asked.

Sweep. Under the carpet went my career crisis.

"Just texts."

"You should call her."

"*I* should call *her*?"

"She feels terrible for missing your birthday."

"Does she?"

"You're too hard on her."

I took a drink of my water, refraining from snapping back with what I really wanted to say—*You're too soft on her.*

"If she wanted to spend my birthday with me, she would have been there."

My needs in life probably sounded weak. Needing to be *wanted* by my sister and closer to my mother weren't the goals of superheroes, but they were human, and I knew if I had those two things, everything in my life would feel more stable—relationships, my anxiety, everything.

But I swear, some days, it felt like the harder I fought for it, the farther it slipped through my grasp.

"How'd you lose your phone?" Grandma asked, trying to change the subject to safe waters. Unaware that it launched an anchor in the choppy ones.

As frustrated as I felt toward my mom right now, I never wanted her to find out about my almost dying.

I locked eyes with Shane. He appeared to measure my nervousness and placed his hand over mine.

"Ma'am," he said, "can I just say, I think it's amazing that you guys get together like this? Not all families make the effort with each other these days."

My eyes stung. With a soothing tone, Shane took out his own broom and swept the rising tension away.

"When my husband died, I vowed I'd always make my girls a priority," Mom said with pride.

I was shocked she mentioned Dad's death. Dad was basically the Voldemort of the house—don't ask, don't tell, just exist silently in the shadow of his ghost—and it was selfish to feel the pang of hurt, hearing the word *priority* with the word *girls*. Plural.

I wasn't this needy. I was independent, and I shouldn't fixate on the hope that, one day, Mom would come to love me as much as she loved my sister.

I was just emotional from almost drowning—that's all. When you almost die, it has a funny way of cleaning the lens you see life through. The relationships that aren't as strong as you want them to be feel even more important to fix.

I'd kept my face neutral—I could tell I did—because Mom and Grandma didn't waver in their expression.

But Shane must have sensed the shift in my body language because he gave me a look that would have gone unnoticed by anyone else and placed a hand gently on my knee, where no one would witness his reassuring affection.

Suddenly, his presence here felt like an asset—an asset I was grateful to have.

"I lost my father when I was a child, too," he said.

My mom presumed the comment was meant for her, but I could tell it was meant for me. It was him saying I wasn't alone in this twisted web of pain that comes after the death of the family's patriarch.

"I'm so sorry to hear you lost your father." Mom's brows furrowed into empathy. "They say time heals all wounds, but it never does, does it?"

"No, ma'am."

"Please. Call me Laura."

Translation: Shane just won my mom over.

"What do you do for a living, Shane?" My mom folded her hands.

"I'm a detective with the Chicago Police Department."

My mom's smile no longer reached her eyes. In fact, she dropped her gaze from his completely, fidgeting with her nails the way she always did when extremely nervous. I wasn't sure Shane noticed it, but I did.

And a bolt of hurt shot up my spine because that slight gesture told me more than I'd learned in the last twenty-plus years.

I chugged half of my water, trying to convince myself her wariness over Shane's profession could be due to Hayley. Her addiction with drugs and alcohol had landed her in hot water sometimes, and maybe Mom got nervous, having law enforcement so close. But I knew better. Shane was here as a guest, not here to bust Hayley, if she ever even showed up.

And it's not like Hayley would do something illegal in front of him.

No. My instincts confirmed this had nothing to do with my sister. Mom had just mentioned Dad's death before asking Shane about his profession—Dad's death, which she'd always claimed was too painful to discuss the circumstances of.

And I'd bought that, slinking into shame whenever my curiosity had surfaced.

But clearly, I'd been a fool.

It wasn't until this very moment that I realized she had a much different reason for not sharing the details behind his death.

*She's hiding something.* Keeping me in the dark as to who killed him. *And has been my whole life.* I could tell by the way she was now avoiding eye contact with me.

Clearly, the reason she'd tensed when she learned Shane's profession was because a trained detective—particularly one emotionally unbiased from the situation—would be able to see past her excuses and omissions if the topic of Dad came up.

It was shocking to realize someone I'd pegged as timid had actively kept this from me my entire life. And beyond hurtful. I was so respectful of *her* wishes and her needs, and evidently, she'd never cared about mine. All those years she'd played the role of *it hurts too much to talk about.* What a crock of shit.

Why would she keep the details surrounding Dad's death from me?

Almost dying had stiffened my resolve; I wouldn't sit back and allow her to lie to me any longer. It might be selfish to do this at her birthday dinner, but after over two decades, I needed to strike now, before I lost my nerve because I knew myself—I'd leave here and talk myself out of this anger, and we'd go back to the spin cycle of dysfunctional secrets, possibly for the rest of our lives.

With my mouth dry, I interrupted Shane's conversation with my grandmother.

"I remember being in the hospital that day," I said to my mom.

Mom couldn't even hide the grimace.

I could feel Shane's stare on the side of my face.

"I remember having blood on me. I remember people talking in hushed whispers. And I remember feeling scared and confused because I was so little, and I remember you refusing to tell me what happened."

"Willow, we're in mixed company," my mom said.

"Mom—"

"Drop it. If you want to have a conversation, we can do it later. In private." Code for, *Yes, there's a ton I haven't told you, but I never will.*

My chest was heaving now at the betrayal, at her lies. Beneath the fancy white tablecloth cloaking my family in normalcy, Shane squeezed my thigh in a gesture of comfort.

It felt like I was at a table of enemies, and Shane was my only ally. I placed my hand on top of his, savoring the solace of his palm flipping over and locking fingers with mine. His embrace was my safe haven in this dinner from hell.

"Who killed Dad?" I pressed. "And why?"

"Drop it," Mom snapped.

The feeble woman had summoned her inner lioness. She glared at me, like I was a horrible person for wanting to know how my father died.

I hadn't thought about the details for a long damn time, but now, I wanted to know, and if last night taught me anything, it was that I didn't have forever to get answers. I pushed aside my inner panic, ignored the fear that I was pushing Mom too far.

"I deserve to know." I even kept my chin up, no matter how fast my heart was hammering.

"You can either drop it or leave."

Look at her, suddenly all strong. Where was this strength when she prioritized her own needs over her small, heartbroken kids all those years ago? I couldn't sit at this table and stare at my mom's lying face for another moment. If I did, I'd start crying—I could already feel it coming—and I prided myself in having a thick enough skin to not break down. Especially not in front of anyone.

I shot up from my chair. "If you'll excuse me, I need to go to the ladies' room."

I wove through the tables and escaped into the women's restroom, where the sobs broke through the dam I'd built to hold them in—cracking open the wound of my father's death.

How could I ever trust my mother again? Was I the only person she was lying to? Did everybody else in my family know the truth and I was the only fool in the dark?

Why would she lie about Dad's death?

Strong people wouldn't let her get away with this, and I was going to be a strong woman. Clearly, she wouldn't answer in mixed company, but so help me, I'd confront her alone another day, and when I did, I would not leave without answers. She would not get away with lying to me for over twenty years.

I stared at myself in the mirror, wiping the stream of vulnerability from my cheeks before emerging from the women's restroom.

Shane stood with his back pressed against the wall, arms crossed over his chest, his shirt now rolled up to his elbows.

"You okay?" he asked.

"I'm fine."

His steely blue eyes grabbed me in their hold as he stepped closer, placing his hands on my upper arms.

"It's okay if you're not."

Those simple words—*it's okay if you're not*—unleashed the tears I normally held back from everyone, flooding my cheeks.

Shane wrapped his arms around me, and in the silent comfort of his embrace, I allowed myself to be weak in front of him. Only, it strangely didn't feel weak, doing this. I felt simply...human, allowing myself to have an understandable reaction to such a life-altering betrayal.

He seemed to know there was nothing he could say to ease my pain. He seemed to know that the only thing I needed right now was the comforting reminder I wasn't alone.

Because I felt so very alone right now.

"Do you want to go?" he whispered.

I did. I wanted to leave, but I also knew if I ruined this dinner, Mom would never forgive me. And with our relationship fractured, I was too scared to allow it to crumble to dust.

After all, she was still my mother. My only parent.

"No," I managed. "Let's just get through the main course and then make up an excuse?"

As I pulled away, Shane reached up and swiped a fallen tear from my cheek with his thumb.

"You okay?"

I would not lie to him. "No."

He nodded, his jaw tightening with concern. "Tell me what I can do to help."

"Being here helps," I admitted. "Being a buffer."

"A buffer." He chewed the inside of his cheek. "I can be a buffer."

He reached down and took my hand in his, as if it were no big deal, but to me, it was everything. His palm was warm, affection seeping up my arm and into my chest, calming the hurts that were stabbing me from the inside.

And then he guided me back to the table.

Mom didn't look up from her menu.

I refused to let that sting.

Shane pulled my chair out for me and gently lured me into it by holding my elbow. Then, he sat down, opened his menu, and put his hand back on my knee.

Again reminding me I wasn't alone in this.

We sat in silence for one full minute. People nearby chatted. The waiter walked by without stopping at our table. The violin music began a new song.

I couldn't take any more of this.

Maybe I'd just leave. She was the one lying, not me, and if she was willing to end our relationship because I couldn't suffer through this? Well…

Shane leaned over and put his mouth next to my ear, whispering, "Breathe."

Then, he pulled back and asked, "So, what do you do for a living, Laura?"

Man, he was good. His tone had no trace of animosity, yet was not overly bubbly, either. The perfect blend of politeness, intrigue, and respect. Even for someone who didn't deserve it.

"I'm an insurance agent." The return of her fake smile told me she was relieved Shane had changed the subject.

"What type of insurance do you work in?" Shane asked.

"I started out my career in homeowners and vehicle insurance, but I now specialize in life insurance. It's never too early to get it, you know." She waggled her finger. "Most people don't think about life insurance until they're much older, but everyone should have a policy."

How did she not realize that talking about life insurance flirted dangerously close to talking about the death of someone you loved? I took a huge gulp of water, trying to swallow my frustration.

"Do you have a policy, Shane?"

"I don't. My grandparents on my mother's side did, though, and they left us quite a nest egg."

"Still, you should get your own policy. I've ensured everyone in my family has life insurance."

*Yeah, because that makes up for lying and hiding the truth for years.*

"If you ever want to discuss it"—Mom fished a business card out of her purse, then handed it to him—"call me."

*Unbelievable. Drumming up business after dismissing my feelings.*

I took another angry gulp of water.

A motion that didn't go unnoticed by Shane, who offered me a look of empathy before returning to his role of Friend of the Year.

"Thank you," Shane said, tucking the card into his pants. "If someone younger and unmarried wanted to get a life insurance policy, how would you recommend choosing a beneficiary?"

Shane was beyond kind, keeping my mom talking like this.

"I recommend choosing someone your age. But if you don't have anyone you trust, you can choose a family member, like Willow did."

Shane took a tight sip of water. "Willow has life insurance?"

"As I said, everyone in my family has life insurance."

Yes, but based on Shane straightening the silverware unnecessarily, he probably assumed she'd been referring to everyone her age.

"How big of a policy would you recommend for someone my age?"

I stared at him, but he avoided my eye contact.

"The bigger, the better," Mom said. "The price of life insurance increases as you get older, so while you might not need a big policy right now, it's advantageous to lock in a larger policy today at the lower rates, and that way, you'll have it later in life, when you're married with children."

"That makes sense," Shane said. "Do you think ten thousand is adequate?"

I side-eyed him.

Mom laughed. "Oh dear, no. You want something that can take care of your future family. I recommend estimating the full value of the home that you want to have someday, plus money for your future kids' college funds, as well as living expenses for your entire family for upward of twenty years, just in case."

"Sounds expensive."

"It's very reasonable. Depending on the type of policy you get, you'd be surprised. Willow only pays thirty-five dollars a month for a million-dollar policy."

Shane was the one with the smile not reaching his eyes now as he shifted his gaze to me. "You have a million-dollar life insurance policy?"

*Crap.* Mom was oblivious to his sudden rigid posture.

"Who's the beneficiary?"

As if tensionville couldn't get any worse, Hayley showed up to the table, looking even more disheveled than usual. Her long hair was stringy with oil at the roots, as if it hadn't been washed for a couple of weeks. Her dress had a purple stain on it that looked like wine, and her eyes looked dilated.

As if she'd just taken a hit of something before she arrived.

My chest ached, realizing she must be off the wagon again. Maybe that's why she didn't show up to my birthday, and then I go and lay into her as if she did it to be intentionally hurtful.

I should have known substance abuse was likely the cause.

I hated Hayley's struggle with addiction; I felt helpless, watching her suffer.

Hayley plopped down at the empty chair and stared at Shane, her eyes tight, looking like she was trying to place him. Hard to do when she'd never met him before, but sadly, she was too high to remember that.

"Who's this?" she asked.

*Please do not tell me Shane has ever arrested my sister...*

In a city this large, the odds of that had to be low. Right? Maybe she'd hoped to talk to me tonight, just as I'd hoped to talk to her. A talk that would have to wait—I wouldn't have it with her when she was high.

"Hayley, this is my friend, Shane."

"Nice to meet you," Shane said.

After staring at him for a couple more seconds, Hayley moved her gaze to my cast. "What happened to your arm?"

"I fell," I said.

She looked like she was about to ask more questions, but Shane interjected with his own, still fixated on the conversation we'd been having before she'd arrived.

"Who's her beneficiary?" he asked.

"Most people choose their spouse, of course," Mom droned on. "Willow's will change later, but for now, it's me."

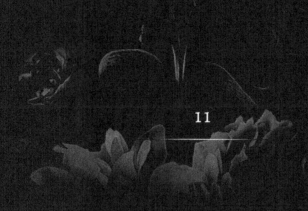

## 11

"Why didn't you tell me?" Shane asked. He'd been silent on the Uber ride back to my apartment, like he was so upset, he needed time to calm down. He waited until we were inside, alone, before he ambushed me with his frustration.

"Because I knew what you would think."

"You didn't tell De Luca."

"It didn't even cross my mind until I was in the middle of the interview with him, and when it did, I thought he'd become fixated on someone I know for a fact would never hurt me. But you're right; I need to tell him. I'll do it the next time we talk."

Shane rubbed both hands over his face. "I hate to say this," Shane sighed. "But…I picked up on a lot of tension between you and your mom."

"She would never hurt me." Physically. Emotionally? That was another story.

"Tryin' to be diplomatic here, but it sounds like she has a million reasons to hurt you."

"Shane…"

"I'm not sayin' she did," he clarified. "I'm sayin' it's a big policy,

Willow."

"My mom's not a killer."

"The two of you have palpable tension."

"I'm sure all families do," I said.

"She always that dismissive of you?" Shane asked with an edge.

My neck flushed, embarrassed by our dysfunctional relationship yet flattered by his fierce protection over me.

"She doesn't like talking about painful subjects."

Shane rubbed his thumb along his eyebrow, his tone cautious. "Like Hayley's drug use?"

Guess it was obvious.

"I sensed some animosity between you two."

I sighed. "She didn't show up to my birthday," I said. "I called her out on it, but she wasn't mad at me. It was the other way around."

"But you're not on good terms with her?" Shane asked.

"I'm not on bad terms with her. Our relationship has always been complicated, but she did a lot for me when we were kids."

I could still remember the times when Mom wasn't there, when Hayley took it upon herself to brush my hair in the mornings and walk me all the way to my elementary school. She was a teenager; she didn't have to do that, especially when she was struggling with her own problems—like being in and out of rehab.

"Does your mom support your sister financially?" Shane asked.

"Not exactly."

Which made Shane inflate his chest again. "Drugs are an expensive habit. Doubt she's contributing to any of the bills, then. Supporting two people instead of one isn't cheap. Is your mom struggling financially because of it?"

"Stop." Being mad at my mom was one thing. Accusing her of the most heinous crime one could commit was another.

"Do you know how many cases I've worked where people have been killed over small amounts of money? A million-dollar policy doesn't strike you as a red flag?"

I glared at him.

"I'm not sayin' this is easy. But, Willow"—he shoved a hand

through his hair—"the cops are not looking into this enough. You have to be diligent to protect yourself."

"And how do you suggest I do that? Stay in my apartment forever? I have a job. I have friends. I have a life."

"Maybe you should avoid your mom for the time being."

I laughed. "Wow. And who else is on that list?"

"I would like to make a list," Shane said.

"I was being angrily sarcastic."

"If you'd allow it."

"No. I won't allow it. You'd put everyone in my life on that list."

"Only people that have somethin' to gain. Or have an issue with you. Do you and your mom normally get along?"

"I'm not talking about this."

"I'll take that as a no."

"We don't have some deep hate for each other, Shane. It's complicated."

"You and her have any issues recently?"

"My mom is not a killer. And even if I played a ludicrous twilight-zone game of pretend for a moment, if she was a killer, she'd never kill one of her kids."

"Would your sister benefit from the policy?"

"No. My mom lets her crash at her place—that's it. And Hayley might assume I have a policy, but she knows that Mom would never give her a single penny; Mom refuses to fuel Hayley's drug habit. Only reason she lets her crash there is so she won't be homeless."

Shane appeared to consider this. "Has your mom had any recent financial pressures?"

"I'm not getting into this."

"What about her rent or mortgage? People on the cusp of eviction can get desperate."

"Look." I sighed. "I'm beyond grateful that you were at that dinner. Seriously, it was the only way I could get through it, but I'm not doing this. I am not going through my life and dissecting everyone as a possible suspect. Maybe some families could withstand that kind of suspicion, but mine can't. Mine is fragile. You poke around with questions, they'll take them as *accusations*. You went to dinner with me, so now, they'll think I'm behind it, and I don't want my mom to stop talking to me. I don't want to lose my family, Shane. It's my biggest fear. We might not be one of those close-knit families, but I love them and want them in my life. I already made my mom upset enough by asking her about my dad."

And, yes, I still planned to ask her about it again in private and demand to know why she'd kept it a secret all these years. If she still didn't answer me, I'd resort to doing my own research or hire someone to look into it deeper than I'd be able to.

But asking direct questions about my dad was a family thing. Accusing her or others of murder? I might as well walk away now and never call them again. I'd be shunned forever.

"Please. Drop this. For my sake. I can't stop De Luca from doing what he needs to do, but I can stop you from making it a thousand times worse."

Shane scrubbed his face with both hands. "Willow, all due respect, don't you think you're diggin' your heels in too deep?"

Stubborn. He thought I was being stubborn.

Maybe I was being too stubborn in this situation. But here was the thing: I'd always given people a lot of chances because I believed in forgiveness and redemption and all of that—and no human was perfect. But the thing about taking the high road all the time? Some days, it can make you feel like a doormat, so there was this constant seesaw—of forgiving someone versus standing up to them—that I tried to balance at all times. Did I get it right all the time? No.

But now, everything was different.

Feeling my mom pull away like that at dinner made me realize that there may have been something else obstructing our relationship this whole time—not grief, as I thought, but lies. I needed to get answers from her, the truth and why she kept it from me. Maybe then I could finally feel the connection with her I'd been chasing my whole life.

After almost dying, I wanted that connection more than ever with both her *and* Hayley.

I could tell Shane was about to say something, but he never got the chance because someone knocked on my door.

My heart pathetically swelled, hoping it was my mother, coming here to apologize—I deserved an apology, and I'd insist we go somewhere to talk in private—but my hope died when I looked through the peephole.

*Shit.*

Shane had despised Ezra since meeting him that night I'd had too much to drink, and now, Shane was convinced Ezra was his prime suspect. As if that wasn't tense enough, Ezra had been trying to get me back for months, and if he saw Shane inside my apartment, he'd jump to all sorts of conclusions.

Allowing the two to see each other felt like a ticking bomb.

I stepped away from the door, deciding I wouldn't open it, but Ezra knocked louder.

"Why aren't you answering it?" Shane whispered.

"I'm not in the mood for company."

Based on Shane's frown, he didn't buy that.

"I'll get rid of them." Shane stepped toward the door.

"No!" I grabbed the handle. "I'll do it."

At least I had a chance of getting Ezra to go away without losing my temper.

In theory…

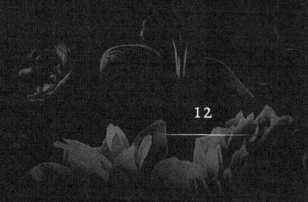

12

"Babe." Ezra's gray eyes rounded slightly when he saw my cast. "What happened?"

His blond hair flowed around his face in staggered lengths that rested on his shoulders, but the most pronounced facial feature was his thin nose, which had a bump in the center from when he'd broken it playing hockey as a kid. Like his cheeks, it was slightly reddened on account of having just been outside in the winter cold.

"It's a long story." One I had no interest in getting into right now. "What are you doing here?"

Ezra's puffy winter coat shifted open when he tucked his hands into his jeans, his eyes soft, just as they were the first time he had bruised my heart.

"Can we talk?"

"Now's not a good time."

"Please?"

"She said now's not a good time." Shane stepped out from behind the door and stood at my side.

A look of hurt washed over Ezra's face as he looked from Shane to me. Then anger when he must've recognized him as the cop who'd threatened to arrest him that night I'd had too much to drink.

Shane took a step even closer to me, his hip practically touching mine.

*If I were a fire hydrant, I'd be covered in urine.*

"Ezra, this is Shane. Shane, this is my ex-boyfriend, Ezra."

With obvious bitterness in his eyes, Ezra held his hand out—undoubtedly trying to be a bigger person to prove to me that he had changed, but Shane crossed his arms over his chest, leaving Ezra hanging.

Ezra dropped his arm and snapped his eyes to me. "Can I talk to you for a minute?"

"I told you, it's not a good time," I repeated.

"It's important." There was a desperation permeating from him that I had never seen before.

"Please," Ezra said. "It took me a half hour to get here. Just give me five minutes?"

"Ezra…"

"Two minutes," he said.

Option A: I could continue arguing with Ezra, but he was clearly determined to get something off his chest, and every moment Ezra refused to leave, the vein on Shane's forehead looked closer to exploding.

Option B: let Ezra say whatever the hell he'd come here to avoid this escalating.

I sighed, stepped back, and motioned for Ezra to come inside. Much to the disapproval of Shane, who tried to annihilate my ex with the world's most powerful glower.

Ezra walked into my living room and flicked his eyes to Shane.

"Alone?" Ezra said. This time with an edge.

"Hell no," Shane said.

"Shane—"

"I'm not leaving you alone with this guy."

"This guy?" Ezra stepped into Shane's space. "Who the hell are you again?"

Shane matched Ezra's movements, closing the distance between them until they could probably smell each other's breaths. I had to shove my hand against Shane's chest and push *hard* to get him to move.

"Shane, it's fine."

"Willow—"

"I'm fine. Please give us a minute."

Shane's chest rose and fell faster beneath my palm.

"You're right on the other side of that wall," I reminded him.

Shane clenched his jaw and glared at my ex-boyfriend as he put his hand on his *gun holster*.

"Fine. I'll be right outside," Shane said.

I refrained from rolling my eyes.

Ezra looked irritated as F at Shane's posturing and watched him with guarded eyes as Shane slowly left my apartment.

I didn't hear him go inside his own place, though. Must be out in the hallway.

"The hell was that about?" Ezra asked.

"It's a long story."

"Just like your broken wrist is?"

It clearly bothered him, being out of the loop when Ezra probably suspected Shane knew exactly what happened to my wrist. Going from knowing every detail of someone's life to finding her with another man in her apartment, with a mysteriously broken arm, shone a spotlight on the intimacy that had vanished between us.

"Ezra, I really don't have the time for this."

He looked over at my kitchen countertop, his lips curling down. "So, you got my flowers."

"I did."

"You didn't answer my text this morning."

A chill crawled up my spine. For the briefest of moments, Shane got into my head. My potential killer would know my cell phone was missing or ruined from the water, so was this an attempt to divert suspicion away from himself?

I pushed a finger to my forehead, refusing to allow this situation to mind-F me.

"I didn't see it," I said.

"Did you see the note?" Ezra motioned toward the flowers.

"I did."

"And?"

"And what?" I asked.

Ezra regarded me, softening his tone when he spoke next. "I miss you."

He took a step toward me, but I held up my hand, silently warning him to give me my space. A flicker of resentment washed over his face, but he extinguished it and kept his tone gentle.

"I promise if you give me another chance, nothing like that will ever happen again."

"Ezra—"

"Please, Willow. What more do I have to do for you to take me back?"

"I did take you back," I reminded him. "I gave you a second chance, and it still didn't work."

His lips tightened. "You gave up too soon."

"*I* gave up? I'm not the one who was kissing someone else when their girlfriend was in the ladies' room or texting other women behind her back."

He balled his hands into fists. "Willow—"

"Please just go."

"Willow—"

"Go!"

Ezra's eyes darkened, and his jaw ticced.

"How long are you going to make me pay for my mistake? I told you I was drunk. As for those texts you found, I told you, those women texted me, not the other way around. It was just a little harmless flirting. It didn't mean anything. *You* mean everything to me. I want to be with you, Willow, no one else. Does that mean nothing to you?"

"You will not bait me into another argument, Ezra! I don't know how many times I have to say this to you before you will understand. Stop with the flowers. Stop with the phone calls and texts."

He took a frustrated step toward me. "When will you stop punishing me?"

"I'm not punishing you! Relationships end when there's no trust. I don't trust you. I will never trust you, and I want you to leave."

I don't know why he expected this conversation to finally be the one that changed my mind, but I could see a wave of frustration break into outrage with the way he glared at me, his chest heaving. He stomped over to the kitchen, grabbed the flowers, and chucked them against the wall.

The vase exploded like a bomb, shards of glass and water thrown through the air like shrapnel.

I'd thrown my hands up to protect my face out of instinct. My muscles ached from the sudden movement, but I was too shocked to focus on it.

Ezra had never acted like this before. Ever. Not once had I ever seen him lose his temper, let alone throw something that could have hit me. Before I could process it for more than half of a second, my front door burst open. Shane's eyes met mine—relief flaring in them that I was unharmed—before absorbing the broken glass and spilled flowers. He curled his lips and charged Ezra.

Shoving him up against the wall with his forearm pinned to his throat.

## 13

"I cannot believe Ezra did that." Emily leaned forward, her gorgeous red hair falling like curtains around her ivory cheeks.

Emily, Tracey, Amelia, and I sat at a café by my apartment because ever since Shane left for work this morning—I'd stayed home to nurse my sore body one more day—my anxiety about the last three days, the bridge, Ezra, my family—trapped me in a pressure cooker, and if I didn't escape, I felt like I'd combust.

Seeing my friends would help. Particularly Emily, whom I met after graduating college and moving to Chicago. I'd been drawn to her confidence—envying it, if I were being honest.

Tracey and Amelia, I'd met a little later—Tracey from a different department at my office (she'd since moved companies) and Amelia at my grandma's church function, where her grandma was on the same committee as mine.

The church's bake sale had nothing on this café, though. This place had muffins you would donate a kidney to taste; Costa Rican coffee, freshly ground and roasted on the hour; and ambiance that smoothed away any wrinkles of apprehension going on in your life. Amber lighting enveloped the tables that were spaced several feet apart—a rare commodity in downtown Chicago—affording you privacy to think or chat with your friends.

"I know," I agreed. "I've never seen him like that before. It was scary."

"I can't believe he sent flowers to begin with," Amelia said with a bite to her tone. "It's been over for you guys for months."

Tracey made no effort to hide the bewilderment on her face. Couldn't blame her; it was an odd thing for Amelia to fixate on, given everything else we'd just talked about—how I'd fallen from a bridge, how cops were looking into it, and how Ezra pulled this stunt with the flowers.

"I don't know how you're being so brave," Tracey said. "I would be beyond freaked out if I almost died and had no memory of how it happened."

I sighed. "I am. I'm trying to hide how much it upsets me, especially when I don't remember what happened because it'll only make Shane more upset. But how the hell did I wind up in that river? I mean, no scenario makes any sense."

I pinched the bridge of my nose.

"They'll figure it out." Tracey placed her hand on my arm.

"Totally," Emily agreed.

Amelia said nothing, and we sat in silence while I tried to stop this unhelpful anxiety that stirred every time I thought about almost dying.

Emily looked like it pained her, not being able to make me feel better. But she must have decided snapping my thoughts back to something else would pull me out of my despair, if only temporarily, because she cleared her throat.

"What happened after Shane pinned him to the wall?" she asked.

"Shane called the cops. Tried to get him arrested for vandalism."

"But he's not in jail?" Emily asked.

"No."

The responding officer disagreed a broken vase met the threshold for vandalism or attempted assault, since it hadn't hit me, and he didn't succumb to Shane's pressure otherwise.

"Did you file a restraining order?" Emily asked.

Amelia pursed her lips, and her chest inflated slowly.

"I didn't." Much to Shane's dismay. "Ezra was out of line, and he deserves to feel like an asshole for what he did, but I don't want to ruin his political career by filing one." That kind of record would follow him everywhere.

Ezra was a lobbyist for a major pharmaceutical company. Honestly, when I met him, I expressed moral concern over it—was he lobbying for bigger profits rather than expanding medicines to save lives? He assured me that wasn't the case and also pointed out this job was a "stepping stone" in his political career—allowing him to frequently travel to Washington and meet key leaders. His endgame was a high-ranking role in politics, and a restraining order could severely hamper his chances at achieving it.

Was I being too soft by not filing one? Hopefully not. I was trying to do what I felt was *necessary* to protect myself without ruining people's lives, careers, or damaging my relationships with family in the process. It was a seriously hard juggling act.

"Is everyone in your life going to be a suspect?" Amelia kept her tone gentle, but I swore offense flashed through her eyes. "I talked to you on Saturday. Does that mean the cops will want to talk to me?"

My palms began to sweat, and the dull ache that persisted in my wrist intensified. This was precisely what I was afraid of—offending the people I cared about. I'd just had a blowout with my family, and the last thing I wanted to do was have a blowout with my friends over this.

"They might."

"I talked to you, too, and I *hope* the cops talk to me," Tracey said. "The sooner they rule out innocent people, the sooner they can focus on who did this to you and lock them up."

"You heard what Willow said. They don't even know someone did this to her. For all we know, she could've done this to herself—" Amelia caught herself. Eyes wide. Full of remorse.

Tracey and Emily were too busy throwing daggers at her to make eye contact with me, but if they had, they'd see my entire neck swelling in red.

Her words cut deep inside me, filleting my stomach until it bled.

"I'm sorry. I didn't mean it," Amelia said. "Even though you've been down lately, I don't think you *actually* did it to yourself." *Actually?*

Down lately? Yes, that last round of layoffs at work had broken my heart—one of the people who lost their jobs was a single mother with three kids, who had no savings, and the hurt from watching each person suffer through job loss accumulated one on top of the other. And, yes, my sister missing my birthday had drudged up the pain of that whole thing too, but was I down in the dumps enough that even my own friends thought there was a chance I'd done this to myself?

"You think I tried to kill myself?" I couldn't hide the shock on my face.

"Of course not," Emily said, glaring at Amelia.

"Then, why did you say it, Amelia?" I demanded.

"I just would hate for cops to accuse an innocent person of something that they didn't do. That's all."

Her words continued to whip my bleeding wound until the pain was so intense, I had to look away.

Right behind it was anger that surged through my veins, wrapping around my throat until the air tasted like poison. Amelia seemed more concerned with the potential blowout toward the people in my life than my almost dying.

Before anyone could say anything else, Emily's eyes settled on something behind me.

Two hands appeared on the table, a set of male arms caging me in.

"A word?" his voice grumbled near my ear.

He smelled like the ocean. How could someone so assertive smell so gentle?

Emily and Tracey looked like they didn't know what to make of his anger while Amelia looked at him with guarded eyes.

"Sure," I said. "I'll stop by when I'm done here."

His fingers tightened.

"Now, please." He said it like a command and walked to the side of the room, apparently confident I would obey.

The only reason I walked over to Shane was because I knew he would probably create a scene if I didn't. I needed to get him to leave so I could get back to my friends and smooth things over.

Also, Shane needed to remember that no matter his good intentions, I didn't take orders from him.

He leaned against the wall, committing a crime of looking gorgeous. With his black coat hanging open in the front, he wore a pair of fitted black slacks and a blue button-down that kissed his muscles—making him look like a sinfully hot action star playing the role of a detective in a movie.

I'd venture to say every set of women's eyes was on him right now.

"What the hell are you doin' here?" he asked.

"Conversing with friends. You?" I asked.

Shane pursed his lips. "I told you it would be safer for you to stay home."

"I know."

Shane's chest inflated so much, I wondered if it was going to pop.

"Did you go to the cell phone store without me?"

As a detective, surely, he knew there were other ways to contact friends.

"No. I messaged my friends through social media on my computer."

Shane rubbed his jaw, as if trying to massage away his frustration over my having not followed his advice to become a hermit. "We need to talk."

"I'll stop by after—"

"It's important."

I studied him. He seemed a lot tenser than he had this morning when he'd checked on me before heading to work. Which was saying something.

"About?"

Shane eyed my friends. "Let's talk at home."

"Just say it," I insisted.

He scrubbed his cheek. His poor face would get rug burn if he kept that up.

"Your ex," he said, looking back at me. "Did you know he has a history of violence?"

My lungs stopped pumping air through my body.

"What are you talking about?"

Ezra didn't have a violent history. I'd never once seen him get into a fistfight with a guy, he'd never been arrested, and he'd never been in trouble with the law. The vase was the only time I'd seen him act like that.

"Last night didn't sit well with me, so I dug around a little today."

"You dug around?" I tilted my head. "Are you *trying* to get yourself fired?"

"Ezra has a probable criminal past."

"Probable? What in the hell does that mean?"

"When he was a minor, he was a suspect, questioned in a violent crime, but he was never charged or arrested. Nothin' that would pop up in a basic background check. I had to reach out to the investigating jurisdiction to find out the details of the offense."

"Which was?"

Shane studied me, allowing several seconds to pass, as if he thought my oxygen level needed to rise before I could handle whatever he was about to say.

"Assault and battery."

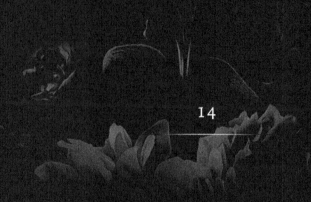

14

"Assault and battery of who?" I asked.

"Can we talk about this in private?"

I looked over at my friends. Amelia's hurt feelings would have to take a backseat to this development; I needed to hear whatever Shane had uncovered.

"Let me say goodbye."

Shane glanced at them. "Who's the girl in the black shirt?"

I looked at the table. "Amelia. Why?"

His gaze fixed on something specific, and his eyebrows furrowed slightly.

"No reason," he claimed.

But he wouldn't look at me.

"I'll wait for you outside," he said.

And then he walked off, as if he thought I'd let him off the hook that easy. Fat chance. I'd circle back to that one, for sure, but for now, I said goodbye to my friends, explaining there was a development in the case I had to talk about with Shane.

When I left the café, I found Shane standing outside in the crisp winter air.

Gray clouds loomed over the skyscrapers like an ominous warning. The buildings stood so tall, they looked like they were standing up against the imposing threat of snow, as if refusing to accept the reality around them.

"So, who did Ezra hurt? And why wasn't he arrested?"

When we began walking, it took Shane a minute to explain.

"Off the record, the detective on the case knew in his gut it was Ezra based on what information he had. Especially when Ezra showed up with a broken nose."

Ezra said he'd broken his nose playing hockey as a kid. Not in high school.

"But knowin' something and having enough evidence to arrest and charge someone are two different things. Especially when the victim clammed up and wouldn't ID him. Said he'd get beat up even worse if he snitched. On the record, Ezra was just a minor who *allegedly witnessed* a fight that put the kid in the hospital with a concussion."

"Who was the victim?" I asked.

"Ezra's best friend in high school, evidently."

If it was true, I couldn't believe he'd kept this from me. We'd dated for six months, and I thought I knew everything about him.

And while it was possible he was innocent, I found it very hard to believe Ezra wouldn't even mention witnessing his best friend from high school getting beat up, let alone that he'd been called in as a suspect on the assault. Especially since he intentionally lied to me about how he'd broken his nose.

It felt like another betrayal by him. Another thing someone had hidden from me.

"So, you think he's capable of hurting me," I deduced.

"Someone close to you has a hidden, violent past," Shane said.

"We should take it to De Luca."

"I did." Shane's teeth clenched. "Didn't change his mind."

I guess that shouldn't surprise me. Someone in my life being called in for questioning over a teenage fight a decade ago didn't change the fact that there was no evidence a crime had even been committed on the bridge.

"I can't let this go now," Shane said. "Not now. Now that I know about your life insurance and your ex...I need to look into this."

"I'm not going to let you compromise your career over a hunch."

"It's not just a hunch. You have people in your life with real motives, Willow."

I pursed my lips.

"I still can't *imagine* someone I know having tried to hurt me," I said. No matter how logical Shane laid out the evidence, my heart just could not accept this as a possibility. "And I cannot have you tear down relationships with people when I'm working so hard to build them back up."

"Okay, look." Shane stopped walking and scratched his temple. "Let's say, for a moment of pure hypothesis, someone you know did this to you."

I opened my mouth to argue, but he held up his palm before I could talk. Then put his hands into his pockets, as if his relaxed posture could make what he was saying sound less shocking.

"You owe it to yourself to look into this, Willow. Sounds like you're overly considerate of other people, and maybe it's about time they return that favor."

He studied my eyes.

"Besides, if they love you, won't they want you to be safe?"

I opened up my mouth, but, dammit, a good rebuttal to that didn't appear—especially since Tracey had said something similar.

"I will be very delicate," he promised. "I'll never ask any questions in a way that implies I'm accusin' them. But your family loves you. Your friends care about you. If someone did try to kill you, all of them would want you to do whatever it took to keep yourself safe."

Logically, he was right. The people who cared about me would want me to take the steps necessary to stay safe, and Shane understood what was at stake, that he couldn't ask accusing questions without risking the very relationships I was trying to protect. If there was anyone I trusted to handle this delicately, it was Shane.

But still, this was difficult to accept. And no matter how delicate he would be, there was no guarantee that his probing questions regarding their whereabouts at the time of the incident wouldn't offend or hurt the people I cared about. I mean, look at how Amelia had reacted.

"I will be very careful," Shane assured.

I wanted to say no, but even I had to admit that Ezra's behavior yesterday was alarming. And the life insurance policy? That could be a big motive for anyone, I guess—after all, money is a universal motivating factor.

I hoped Shane was wrong. Hopefully, the incident *was* an accident, like I thought, but if someone *had* been with me that night, who was it, and why hadn't they come forward? Was it possible they panicked when I fell, and they ran and then became worried that it would make them look guilty? It would give me peace of mind to at least have Shane explore this with his expertise.

How could I possibly move forward in my life, not knowing for sure?

Damn, if only my memories of the fall would return, it would answer all these questions.

"I'll let you work on this on three conditions," I decided.

"*Three?*"

"First, I'm not living like a hostage. I'm going about my daily life, and this includes meeting up with my friends, going out to dinners, going to work. I'm not going to sit in my apartment every minute of the day with your overprotectiveness suffocating me."

I bet he wanted to dispute this condition, but if he was right and someone in my life wished me harm, the only way to protect me was if I agreed to let him investigate.

Still, his chest swelled, and he held off saying anything for several seconds.

"And the second condition?"

"We work this *together*. I'm not giving you the keys to go investigate my life without being ingrained in what you're doing."

This one looked easier for him to swallow. Probably because he'd need my help anyway.

"Third, you don't do anything that could threaten your job. De

Luca warned you to stay away from this case, and he seems to have a stick up his butt about you. So, that means no pulling any official information using police resources."

"Willow—"

"I will not let you jeopardize your career over this."

"I'm not going to stand by and let you get killed."

Someone trying to kill me once was a stretch. Twice? I wasn't on board with that fear.

"No police resources."

His jaw set tight. "You're tyin' both hands behind my back."

"I'm protecting you from yourself."

Shane swiped his thumb along his nose. "I'd like to renegotiate using police resources."

I shook my head. "Best and final offer."

Shane shoved his hands into his pockets. Stared at the ground as if it could help him plead his case.

"Fine," he grumbled.

A wave of panic flooded through me at the turning point this meant in my life.

I hid the tremble in my voice and squared my shoulders. "How do you propose we start?"

Shane eyed my hands, which were flexing nervously in and out of balls, and then offered a gentle smile, like he wanted to ease my anxiety.

"How about I ask you some questions over dinner?"

Shane Hernandez had noticed so many things about me over the past few months, but now, I'd given him permission to dig deep into my life, my relationships. My heart thundered as I wondered...

*What question will he ask first?*

*More importantly, what will he uncover?*

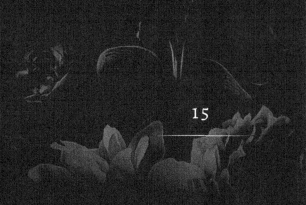

15

"Tell me about Ezra." Shane adjusted his shirtsleeves, which were rolled up to his elbows. As if readying himself for some kind of a mental battle.

We had walked to a diner a half block from our apartment that sat about fifty people. Crimson tables rested between a perimeter of olive-colored booths, sitting atop black-and-white checkered flooring. A busy front door chimed every couple of minutes, it seemed, with another person picking up a to-go order from the counter, the activity producing a draft that frosted my skin. Chicago's favorite rock station played on the speakers positioned in the ceiling while the smell of fried potatoes mingled with grilled beef.

A very unassuming backdrop for deep-diving into a possible attempted murder.

I stirred the cubes in my water glass with a straw. "What do you want to know?"

"For starters, give me more specifics about how you ended things."

The memory came back as if it happened only moments ago.

. . .

I'M AT A GET-TOGETHER, AND I'M WATCHING EZRA FROM ACROSS THE ROOM, *talking to a girl I don't know. He's throwing his head back and laughing at something she said.*

*My body tenses.*

*I study the girl and wonder if she's his type. Long black hair down to her waist, so straight, it looks like it has been ironed. Her hair is prettier than mine. Shiny, fluid like water. Her body is thinner, too. I bet she can put any outfit on and make it look good. She looks so effortless, talking to Ezra, as if her life has absolutely no complications and she's just drifting from one fun experience to another.*

*I take a sip of my drink to wash down my jealousy. My mistrust.*

*To my knowledge, Ezra has not kissed another woman since that night a month ago. When he begged me—begged, begged, begged me—to give him one more chance, he vowed he'd never ever hurt me again like that.*

*Because it had nearly destroyed me.*

*His phone buzzes; he left it on the table next to me, and I find my eyes wandering to it. Then widening when I see a text.*

*Bianca: U have the sexiest eyes I've ever seen.*

*Bianca? Who the hell is Bianca?*

*I glare at Ezra, who is full-on flirting with the woman now. Right in front of me. Too bad for him I know the password to his phone.*

*Yep. Look at me. I'm that girlfriend, dammit.*

*I pull open the text and feel my stomach drop. They've been texting for days. The words* sexy, gorgeous, cute laugh, when can we meet *all pop out at me. I continue reading. Looks like they met in a club two weeks ago and have been texting ever since, talking about getting together soon.*

*Anger pierces my heart. It isn't the first time some random woman has texted him, but I can't believe Ezra is doing it again after I confronted him about it before, and I can't believe he has the audacity to make plans to meet up with this Bianca after swearing his faithfulness to me. How naive I'd been.*

*Cheating is like an iceberg. Cheaters are skilled at hiding their deception below the waterline; if you see anything, it's likely just the tip of how deeply their betrayal actually runs.*

*His betrayal has turned me into a person I hate—a jealous, mistrustful woman. I've become that girl who watches her boyfriend at parties like he's on some visual leash. Dissecting his every move and word for any clues he might stray.*

*I'm all for giving people second chances and the benefit of the doubt, but I'm also not a moron, and when my boyfriend is repeatedly behaving inappropriately with other women, it's time to pull the plug.*

*I walk up to Ezra.*

*"I need to talk to you," I say.*

*"Babe"—he looks between me and Ms. Gorgeous—"I'm in the middle of a conversation."*

*"It's important," I say.*

*Ezra flashes an annoyed look at me, and his annoyance grows when the gorgeous girl walks away.*

*He wraps his hand under my elbow and guides me to the other side of the room, where no one can hear him.*

"HE GRABBED YOUR ARM?" SHANE'S JAW TICCED.

"The word *grabbed* implies something threatening."

"Did his grasp bother you?" he challenged.

"Of course."

Shane's stare bores a hole through my skull.

"Then, that's all that matters. He's lucky I wasn't there that night."

I wasn't sure what to say to that, so I continued with what happened.

*"YOU EMBARRASSED ME," EZRA SNAPS.*

*"I can't do this anymore," I say.*

*Ezra releases my elbow and searches the room for the hot girl. "Do what?"*

*"This. Us. I can't be with you anymore."*

*Ezra's eyes snap back to mine, and he flicks his fingernails at his sides, like he does when he's angry.*

*"The hell are you talking about?"*

*"I thought I could get past your infidelity, but I can't. Especially when you keep doing it."*

*"My infidelity? Are you fucking kidding me? I didn't sleep with anyone, Willow. I kissed one girl. Kissed—that's it. And what the hell do you mean, keep doing it?"*

*"Who's Bianca?"*

*His eyes narrow. "You went through my phone?"*

*"She says she's planning to meet up with you."*

*"I can't control what people send me."*

*"You can control talking to other women behind my back. Inappropriately."*

*"So, I can't talk to anyone if they're female?"*

*He's goading me into a fight, where he'll try to break down my every objection until he gaslights me into thinking I'm overreacting. Just like he did last time.*

*"I'm not doing the back-and-forth game. I don't trust you anymore, and when there's no trust, there's no relationship."*

*Ezra glares at me. I assume he's going to try to talk me into staying with him again, but unlike last time, he must see the unwavering decision in my eyes because he looks furious. He licks his bottom lip and eventually shakes his head as he looks me up and down in disgust.*

*"You're going to regret this."*

"He threatened you?"

"I took it more as his ego talking—like I'd let the best catch in the sea slip away. But looking back on it now, maybe I gave him too much benefit of the doubt. Especially after seeing how he behaved with that vase."

Shane massaged his hands and stared at my elbow with a look of vengeance.

"I pride myself on maintaining control. Carrying the badge means I can't give in to the rage I sometimes feel." Shane snapped his eyes to mine, holding them for several heartbeats before continuing, "But last night, when I heard that crash? When I realized he'd thrown that vase that could have hit you?" Shane cracked his knuckles. "You have no idea what I almost did to him."

What if there was another risk to Shane's career that I hadn't considered? What if Ezra did something stupid again, and next time, Shane crossed a line that police are not allowed to cross?

Surely, it was arrogant of me to worry that might happen. Shane had been a cop for years, probably had complete self-control over his emotions.

Right?

"I don't want to cause you any problems," I said.

To this, Shane's eyes once again met mine, only this time, the anger in them melted as he set his hand on the table, a mere inch from my own. I stared at his hand, wondering what it'd feel like on my body, twisting through my hair, touching me in places I'd only fantasized about. As if sensing my desire, Shane allowed his thumb to graze my pinkie, surging an electric current up my arm.

In a low rumble, he said, "Willow, you're the farthest thing from a problem."

My heart responded to his words, to his caress, stretching through my chest toward him, longing for him to slide his fingers up my arm and stroke my cheek instead of my hand.

Based on the parting of his lips as his blue eyes gripped mine, he wanted to do more than just touch my hand, too.

"You give people too many chances." Shane's voice was tender. "Giving that asshole ex another chance after how he treated you. Makin' the effort over and over with your family when even I can see they're not treating you right. As Maya Angelou once said, 'When people show you who they are, believe them.' Think you need to heed her warning."

My stomach stilled under the adoration of his gaze, the thrilling shiver from his fingertips skating across the back of my hand. The touch was so simple yet incredibly intimate.

"You deserve better than that, Willow. You deserve to be somebody's first priority."

He had no clue what his words did to my soul, extinguishing the flames of hurt that I never believed would be snuffed out. I'd assumed the only person capable of healing those wounds was the one who'd inflicted the blisters. But Shane was the salve to my burns, soaking the pain away in his tenderness.

He made me feel like the person I never knew I could be despite not having known him very long.

Some people come into your life like a whisper of a breeze. Others a tornado, their impact immediate and severe.

It felt like my heartbeat was dancing to his movements as he gently rolled my hand over and began tracing little circles on my palm.

"Why do you think that is?" Shane asked. "You givin' too many chances?"

This was a question I had asked myself countless times throughout the years. It took me several seconds to emerge from this sensual fog to offer the hypothesis I had come up with—one I hadn't shared with anyone else.

"Growing up, when my mom was around, she could be so much fun. She'd keep me home from school just so we could make chocolate chip cookies together and watch a movie marathon. She would laugh and put on music so we could dance on the coffee table. I think she was trying to make up for the other times, because in those other times, her grief was like a flu that would affect her every so often, and when it did, she would get sadder and sadder, and it would snowball. When it got really bad, she'd leave and disappear for days."

My vision blurred with the memory.

*I'm seven, and I'm clutching my teddy bear—the one Daddy got for me before he died. On accident, I had cut Teddy's foot open, but Mommy had stitched it up with purple string. I liked the purple string; it shows you don't have to give up on something you love just because it isn't perfect.*

*Like Mom. She's not perfect, but I'll never give up on her.*

*I stare out the window. I have to go to the bathroom so bad, but I only leave my post when I can't hold it anymore. She's been gone six days, and she's never been gone that long, and I feel like the only way her car will come down the road is if I'm watching for it.*

*I watch the rain wash across the asphalt like it's cleaning a path for*

*Mommy. Headlights appear. I tense and stare at the car coming toward our house.*

*My heart beats even harder as the lights get brighter and the windshield wipers shove aside the rain. It's as if the car is racing toward me so Mommy can jump out and run into my arms, promising she'll never leave me again.*

*But the car keeps going.*

*And my heart sinks even deeper.*

*I wonder how far it can drop before it stops beating.*

*"She's not coming back," Hayley snarls.*

*"Yes, she is!" I say through my tears, even though inside, I'm terrified it's not true. I clutch Teddy tighter. "She's coming back," I whisper. "She's coming back."*

"I NEVER GAVE UP HOPE THAT SHE'D RETURN. GIVING UP HOPE MEANT giving up on Mom; it meant giving up on the person I wanted in my life more than anyone. And even if she wasn't treating me the way a child should be treated, I still wanted her. I guess a child still wants her parent, no matter what." I did, at least.

Some people dream of wealth. Some power. I dreamed of love— the unconditional and everlasting love of a mother. Many have it. Some even take it for granted, but for those of us that have never experienced it, its absence becomes a crater in our chest that we'd give anything to fill.

For the first time, the empty ache had started to dull, which shocked me because it was Shane's tenderness trickling into the chasm rather than my mother's—whose everlasting affection still eluded me.

Sometimes, I felt ungrateful for being hurt because I was lucky. I wasn't abused or abandoned forever, and compared to my sister, I'd come out virtually unscathed by it all. But I guess it was only human to long for a mother's love.

"The void in my life without her would've been bigger than the void she created when she'd withdraw. So, I always waited," I said. "And when her car would come rolling back up that driveway, I would rush out the door and jump into her arms. Convinced that if I had given up on her, she would've never come back."

And thus began my pattern of holding out hope that people and circumstances would always get better if you held on long enough. Every time my mother returned, that belief further solidified into cement.

"Plus, after losing my dad, I guess I don't want to risk losing anyone else," I admitted.

"Sounds like your reason for holding on to things for too long is a fear of abandonment," Shane said. "Your dad died. Your mom emotionally abandoned you. Your sister's addiction probably makes you feel abandoned by her, too, choosing substances over you."

I hated that my eyes shimmered. I hated that I'd always wondered if it was me—the reason I wasn't close to my family. That I was lacking somehow. I mean, what kind of person gets rejected by their own family? But then I'd chide myself for having woe-is-me thoughts like that.

"So, you keep making the effort," he continued. "Settling for unhealthy relationships and situations where you deserve better."

*I deserve better.* I didn't want my eyes to sting even harder because I had a lot of good things in my life, and I refused to let a few less than ideal variables define me. Yet…a soft spot in my heart clung to his declaration and encouraged me to change my ways.

I wish I could say I'd broken up with Ezra because I'd decided to no longer give people too many chances, but the truth was, I'd broken up with him because his lies and betrayals made me fall out of love with him.

"I talked to people over the years about my dad." Shane cleared his throat and shifted in his seat. "Guy that shot him had been a problem for months."

I blinked, taken off guard by the abrupt change in conversation. Confused as to how it connected to what we just talked about.

Shane shifted his fingertips to the back of my hand again, rubbing soft circles over my knuckles as he stared so deeply into my eyes, it felt like he was looking into the hidden crevices of my soul.

"Cops were frequently called on him for a bunch of minor infractions," Shane said. "But from what I've been told, while the rest of the cops became fed up with the guy, my dad saw a desperate guy who was at a fork in the road."

Shane added two more fingers to circle the skin on my hand. I wanted to close my eyes and savor his touch; it affected me so much, it was all I wanted. Like a warm blanket after being pulled from those frigid waters, offering a solace I've never felt from anyone before.

"After years on the force, my dad saw what he believed was a pattern with career criminals, putting them into two buckets—those that had been causin' problems since they were born and those that came to a crossroads in their lives and caused problems after."

His fingers drifted up to my wrist, making it harder to focus on his words.

"I guess a mass school shooting that took place in his hometown heavily influenced my dad. He wasn't a part of it, but hearin' about the twenty-year-old that stormed into that elementary school and started shooting really got to him. And while there's a lot of factors that contributed to it," Shane continued, "my dad fixated on one in particular—how preventable it was. Guess the guy that did it had a bunch of red flags in the days leading up to it that should have been caught. But the guy hadn't shown violent tendencies until those last six months of his life. Evidently, a string of bad stuff happened to him, and when he started becomin' bitter, everyone in his life just walked away. His life continued to spiral, and he got angrier and angrier with the world until he finally..."

Got a gun and killed innocent children.

Shane sighed heavily and pinched the bridge of his nose. "Point being, my dad was convinced that if someone had shown some compassion to that guy when all that shit was goin' down, maybe he wouldn't have turned into a mass murderer. Maybe those kids wouldn't have died."

If I put myself in his dad's shoes, if I swore an oath to protect people, I'm sure I'd be looking for ways to protect people *before* they committed a crime, too.

"So, this guy loses his job and starts gettin' into trouble. Earns himself a few nights in jail on several occasions. Dad sees a guy down on his luck and heading toward a psychological cliff, so to speak, and tries to talk to him. Tries to help redirect his anger, provides him with support groups, things like that."

Shane's jaw tensed.

"My dad picked the wrong guy to try to help. Because the next time he gets called in, this guy was gettin' evicted. My dad went in to try to talk to him, and that's how he ended up getting shot. Tryin' to give someone a second chance that was never going to change."

My stomach rolled. No wonder he was so cynical about what people were capable of. No wonder he believed once someone squandered their second chance, you should walk away.

"I know you want to see the best in people, Willow. But always trying to see the best in people can sometimes cost you everything."

I wanted to believe that he was wrong, that the worst wasn't yet to come...

## 16

"Mind if we stop in my apartment first?" Shane asked. After the heavy conversation at the diner, we'd gotten my new cell phone and had just walked into our apartment complex. "I'd like to get a notebook for this."

"Sure." I stood behind him as he unlocked his door, opened it, and switched the light on as I stepped in.

Aside from the couple of minutes I had been in his apartment when he thought my place had been broken into, I had never been inside his place.

The inside was absolutely pristine and so free of clutter, it was almost bare. A black leather couch faced a flat screen TV, but there were no decorations hanging on the walls, no plants. Nothing to give the place life, really. The space smelled like Shane's cologne—an ocean scent I wished I could bathe in.

"I'll be right back."

Shane disappeared into his bedroom while I stepped into his kitchen, curious about his morning routine. This whole time, he'd been in here, living in an apartment with an identical layout to mine. The gray countertop contained a blender, a coffeepot, and a compact air fryer. All of them black, all of them so clean, they could pass for being brand-new, straight out of the box.

"Okay." Shane reappeared with a notebook, Post-it Notes, and pens of various colors.

"I would've assumed you would take notes electronically," I said.

"I do. But I like a visual map when I'm lookin' into stuff. Helps me think."

How eerie that, soon, those pages would be filled with details about my life, the people in it, and any issues I'd had with anyone.

My throat ran dry, and I had to tell myself again that this needed to be done. Because each time we stepped closer to this, I wanted to run away.

Shane must have read the look on my face because he set the materials down and stepped closer to me, putting his hands on my shoulders, as if knowing his touch sedated my anxiety.

"This won't be easy, but I'll be here with you every step of the way. Okay?"

I genuinely hoped we'd discover no one had done this to me because I wasn't sure how to move forward in my life if I'd let a killer into my inner circle. How do you ever trust another human being again? How do you ever feel safe again? How long do you have to be with someone before you let down your guard, if you ever do?

"I have one question before we start," I said. "Our goal is to find a good enough clue so De Luca can kick this up to detectives, right?"

Shane released my shoulders. "I'm worried De Luca is going to drop the ball on this one—either to spite me or out of sheer laziness or possibly both. I don't trust him to take the situation seriously."

"But if we find something big enough to show De Luca, won't he realize you've been poking around the case?"

"You let me worry about that."

"No. That guy is just looking for a reason to get you into trouble, and I'm not going to hand it to him on a silver platter."

Shane grabbed the supplies.

"How are we going to hand this over to De Luca without him throwing you under the bus?" I repeated.

But I could see Shane wasn't worried about that; all he cared about was getting to the bottom of whatever happened to me, so he was putting his blinders on, allowing his emotions to get the better of him.

I squared my shoulders. "I'll turn it over to him," I said.

"What?"

"We find something? I'm turning it over to him. And I'm leaving you out of it. Nonnegotiable."

Shane's face tightened. "Fine. Whatever. Now, can we get on with it?"

I took a deep breath and nodded.

"Good. I was going to suggest—"

Shane was interrupted with three knocks that vibrated his front door.

"I know you're home," a female voice said.

Shane dropped his head. Tossed the papers back onto the counter.

"Your car is out front, so whatever case you've been buried in can wait," she shouted.

Shane cocked his head back with a look that said, *You've got to be kidding me.*

Which immediately piqued my interest. I'd never seen a woman at his apartment before.

Shane grumbled his way to the front door and opened it.

"Three voice mails, no answer," she said. "I brought beer. Thought you could use a break from—" Her voice halted, and her eyes widened when her gaze landed on me.

I recognized that face. I had met her once before when I went out with some of my girlfriends for a quick drink. Though I couldn't remember her name.

"Hell hath frozen over." She grinned and slammed a six-pack into Shane's chest so hard, the bottles clanked as she marched past him, looking me up and down with her hands on her hips. "I've met you before," she realized. "You're Emily's friend."

"Willow." I reached my hand out to shake hers.

She shook it right away. Looked so damn gleeful, I wondered if she was mistaking me for someone else.

"Fallon." Shane's voice was clipped. "If you don't mind."

She motioned toward me, her smile somehow growing even wider. "You have a girl in your apartment!"

Shane rolled his eyes.

"When did this happen?" she asked.

"Fallon—"

"Shane has never once had a girl over," she said. "He's like Batman. Keeps his place all locked up and secretive. But you …" she said, looking me up and down again. "You breached his moat."

"For the love of…" Shane set the six-pack of beer down onto the counter with more force than necessary.

I bit back a smile.

"Okay." Fallon looped her arm through my elbow and guided me to the couch, grabbing two of the beers on her way. "Tell. Me. Everything."

She opened the beers and handed me one.

"Fallon, we're workin' a case."

She scrunched her eyebrows. "I don't remember Emily telling me you're a cop. Are you a cop?"

"No."

She flashed a smirk at Shane. "Nice try. Okay, so when did you two meet?"

I took a sip of the beer, which prickled my throat.

"She's my neighbor," Shane said. "If you don't mind, we have a lot of work—"

"If you think I'm going to leave without asking questions, you're insane." She waved a dismissive hand at him without even looking his way.

I had to bite my lip harder to contain my amusement.

Meanwhile, Shane snapped the top off a beer and took a huge sip.

"Are you his ex-girlfriend?" My cheeks immediately warmed, embarrassed that the question had popped out of my mouth.

Fallon cocked her head back and laughed. "God, no. He's like my brother. I'm married." She wiggled her ring finger at me. "I've been friends with Shane forever, and in all these years I've known him, he's never had a girlfriend."

He hadn't? Never?

A rush of unease swept through me.

He was handsome, sexy as F. Successful. Caring. Kind. How would a guy like that never have a girlfriend?

He didn't strike me as a player with a rotating door of one-night stands, but maybe I'd misjudged him? And had missed all the girls coming and going? He didn't strike me as preferring men with the chemistry I'd felt between us, either.

"I have *never* seen him with a woman. He has never let anyone in his apartment before. Even to 'work a case.' " She used air quotes on that last part.

He didn't? Not even once, not even for a minute?

"He was just grabbing a notebook."

"Girl, this is his Batcave. No one is allowed in. No one. Only reason I get in is because—"

"You basically break and enter," Shane interrupted, annoyance dripping from his words.

"He loves me so much. Now, enough about me. Let's talk all about Willow."

"You're makin' her uncomfortable," Shane chided.

"Am I?" She legit looked worried.

I bit my lip and shook my head. Truthfully? I loved this girl and her easy banter with Shane.

"See? Stop being all alpha protective of her and tell me all about your girlfriend."

"She's not my girlfriend."

"Don't let him get under your skin. He gets all grumpy when he's tired. I can tell he likes you A LOT just by the way he looks at you."

"Fallon."

"I've never seen him look at anyone like he looks at you."

"Fallon!" Shane yanked the beer from her hand and motioned toward the front door. "If you don't mind."

She stood up, and Shane took steps toward her, physically encouraging her to back up to the front door.

"But I haven't even gotten her number yet!" Fallon said.

"Goodbye, Fallon." Shane opened the door.

She stepped out into the hallway. "But I want to invite her out for a drink!"

"Goodbye, Fallon." Shane shut the door.

"You know, she might not appreciate your broody mood, Shane!" Fallon yelled from the other side.

Shane rolled his eyes and walked over to me, rubbing the back of his neck. "I'm sorry about that."

"She's nice."

"She can be"—Shane cocked his head—"a bit headstrong."

"She's cheery."

"Didn't use to be," he said, frowning at the door. "Some days, I miss her old moody personality."

"What changed?"

To this, Shane met my eyes. "She fell in love."

Something swirled around inside my chest.

"How long have you guys been friends?"

"Since we were kids." Shane picked up the notebook, the pens, and the Post-it Notes and set them down on the coffee table.

When he sat on the couch next to me, his leg brushed mine.

Even through fabric, the heat of his skin slowed the oxygen flow to my lungs.

This energy between us was always there, lingering like a flammable gas in the air around us, and when he touched me, it would ignite, the explosion rendering me breathless.

Shane must've felt it, too, because his sapphire eyes met mine and lingered as his mouth parted, his tongue swiping along his lower lip. As the seconds ticked on, Shane looked down to my mouth, his breathing quickening, as if wondering what it would be like to cave in to his desires and pull my mouth to his.

The painful furrow of his eyebrows looked like fighting his desires was hard, doing what he believed was the right thing by not crossing this line with the subject of an open case. And based on how long he lingered like that, it seemed like it took every ounce of his willpower to shift his leg away from mine and recalibrate.

"What I'd like to do," he started, his voice a little shaky, "is make a list of the people closest to you. We'll start with them and go from there."

"The people closest to me?"

"Statistically, most murders are committed by somebody close to that person. What I'd like to do is discuss your relationship with each of these people and understand what the events were leading up to Saturday night. Any arguments, or disagreements, or tension, that sort of thing."

All the saliva evaporated in my mouth, leaving it a desert that stretched down my throat. My heartbeat quickened, and that hamburger that I had eaten no longer agreed with my stomach.

"I don't know if I can do this." Agreeing to it was one thing. Lifting up the hood on all of the relationships closest to me and looking for broken parts was an entirely different situation. This was like giving someone cancer drugs just to be on the safe side when those drugs cause catastrophic side effects.

"I'll be with you through this." Shane's voice was tender, his expression encouraging.

After a few moments, I hesitantly nodded. "Okay. Let's get this over with."

"List the people closest to you."

I took a sip of encouragement from my beer.

"Start with family," Shane suggested.

"I talk to my mom the most, though we're not as close as most families. My sister and I talk off and on, but not nearly as often as I'd like. I see my grandma at family get-togethers."

Shane nodded. He wrote *Mother: Laura* and *Sister: Hayley* on two separate Post-it Notes and placed them on the front page of his notebook.

It was jarring to see it in ink like that, listing them as official suspects in his research. Mom. Hayley.

"Friends. Boyfriends. Coworkers?"

"Ezra was in my inner circle but hasn't been for a while."

Ezra's name was already on a Post-it before I finished my sentence, pinned to the top of his page.

"My best friend is Emily. Second best friends would be Tracey and Amelia."

"Any issues with Emily?"

"No."

"Tracey?"

"No."

"Tell me about Amelia."

Why'd he ask it that way? Different from the way he'd asked about Tracey and Emily?

"Amelia?"

Shane held my gaze firmly.

"Um...we became friends a couple of years ago and our families know each other."

"She looked upset in that café."

"I think she was offended we'd be looking at people in my life as possible suspects."

"You told her we were?"

"No. I told them I fell off the bridge and it was being investigated."

Shane sat back, rolling the pen between his fingers. "Why do you think she would get upset?"

"I suppose because it's offensive to accuse anybody of something that heinous."

Shane didn't look convinced. He scrubbed his jaw, looking down silently.

"You're keeping something from me," I accused. "You asked about Amelia at the café, too."

Shane's eyes snapped to mine, his silence a loud confirmation.

"Condition number two," I reminded him. "We work this together. You tell me what you know."

"I don't know anything for certain," Shane hedged.

"Semantics. Spit it out."

"I'll have a lot of thoughts cross my mind throughout this investigation. Some of them may lead to something, but most of them won't. You sure you want me to share them with you?"

"You already know the answer to that."

Resigned, Shane offered up a slow nod of his head. Like, *Okay. Don't say I didn't warn you.* "Did you notice those scratches on her arms?"

I blinked. "Amelia's?"

Shane nodded again, measuring my reaction.

"What scratches?"

He cleared his throat. "She rolled up her sleeves for a second. Only a second," Shane clarified, as if that were an important clue. "And when she did, she had fresh scratches on her forearms that looked to be consistent with fingernails."

I didn't see them. But then I'd been so distracted, worrying about upsetting everyone, I hadn't been paying attention.

"She mention where she got them?"

I shook my head.

"Okay. That's a question we need to ask."

Amelia had acted shady that day, but, "She'd have no reason to hurt me."

"It's probably nothin'." But Shane's eyes gave away his deceit. He put her name on a Post-it Note and pinned it to the first page of his notebook.

"Okay. Let's talk about your job."

I felt like I was in a tornado, a fresh batch of debris slapping my face with each rotation.

"My company did a fresh round of layoffs last month."

"Anyone seem upset?"

"Everyone is upset when they get laid off."

"Any chance I could get a list of those names?"

"Not without a warrant; it's confidential company information. I'd get fired for giving it to you."

Shane pursed his lips. "Okay, we'll start with people closest to you first. See where that takes us."

No matter how many times we talked about this, I couldn't get past the shock of it. Would it ever go away?

"You really think someone did this to me," I said.

"I do."

"What makes you so sure?"

Shane twisted the pen in his hand. Leaned back against the couch and spoke in a cautious tone. "I visited the bridge today."

Okay, I didn't expect that.

"That bridge is *not* easy to fall off of. I can't imagine a scenario where someone fell over it by accident. Even if someone was being extremely reckless."

Today, I had the whole day off, and I could've gone to the bridge to look around. Maybe the doctor was wrong. Maybe seeing it would spark some kind of memory.

"I'd like to see the bridge."

Shane blinked. "Now?"

"Now."

## 17

The rust-colored bridge stretched across the Chicago River for the length of thirty cars, connecting a road that snaked between sixty-story buildings whose windows twinkled against the fabric of night. It was hard to imagine something this beautiful playing a role in the grim disaster that unfolded on an evening just like this one.

Tonight, orange construction cones blocked vehicles from entering the bridge, and based on the guy wearing a fluorescent-orange vest, waving his hands at us, pedestrians weren't supposed to be on it either.

"You can't go on there," he said as Shane and I approached it.

Shane flashed his badge. "Police business. We won't be long. Bridge safe to walk on?"

The guy working the bridge looked annoyed as he nodded.

"Were you working here Saturday night?" Shane asked.

The guy shook his head. "No, sir. This job doesn't have activity Friday or Saturday nights."

I guess that would explain the lack of eyewitnesses, but it didn't explain why I would wind up on a bridge that I wasn't supposed to be on.

"We won't be long," Shane said.

As soon as my first step landed on the narrow walking path that flanked the road, my throat went dry. Walking along the same path I must have taken on Saturday, each haunting clink of my footsteps seemed to echo off the surrounding skyscrapers, like a clock ticking down to an ominous end. Adrenaline flooded my limbs, weakening my stomach, as if my body's cells remembered what I could not—how this path had almost cost me my life.

Once we reached the center, Shane positioned himself next to me, but remained silent, as if he knew I needed the solitude of taking this all in.

A scattering of ice sheathed the gray water, which sat stagnant, like it was too cold to move.

I couldn't believe I had fallen into that water. Looking at it now, I was certain that if Shane had not jumped in and saved me, I would not have made it.

I glanced toward the bank of the river, to a void in the snow. *That must be where Shane pulled me out.* The bravery and selflessness it would have required to jump into the dark, deadly waters made my eyes sting.

"You can see what I'm talkin' about." Shane put his hand on the bridge's railing. Which stood up to our chest, and between it and the ground, a crisscross of beams inches apart. Not enough room for a tiny child to fall through, let alone an adult. And the height of the railing made it impossible for someone to get over it without intent. Further, the top of the railing was a cylinder shape, not flat, which made the idea that I'd been recklessly trying to walk on it even more implausible. Also, this was *not* one of those bridges that opened when big boats crossed, so my thought that maybe it'd opened wide enough to fall through was also shot to hell.

"You're right," I said. "There's no way I could've fallen off by accident."

I didn't want this revelation to breach my chest, but it gusted through me like a typhoon, ravaging my fragile insides. My hands became clammy, and my legs wobbled—all while my heart rebelled against it, beating so quickly, it felt like it was spasming.

"I think I'm going to be sick," I said.

"Sit down," Shane commanded.

I did as he asked, the iron's coolness breaching the seat of my jeans, as Shane squatted next to me, putting a calming hand on my shoulder.

"I agreed to work with you on this, but deep down, I didn't truly believe that someone had done this to me."

"I know."

"But someone must have."

"Yes."

"You think they meant for me to die? Not just get hurt?" Even I knew how ridiculous that sounded, but when one faces a reality so shocking and heartbreaking that it will blow up your entire world, one grasps on to straws.

"You don't throw someone off a bridge into deadly, icy water unless you're trying to kill them."

*I will not cry. I survived, and I am okay. Just because I don't feel like it, I am. I am okay. I'm okay.*

"De Luca visited the bridge," I said. "If he still doesn't think this is foul play, he must think I tried to kill myself."

But I wouldn't have done that, certainly not like this.

Shane sucked the energy from around him to feed his swelling anger while I focused on getting my erratic breathing under control. After a couple of minutes, I stood up, squared my shoulders, and looked decisively into Shane's cobalt eyes as he stood, too.

Strange that I didn't feel embarrassed that Shane had witnessed my moment of weakness with that mild panic attack. With anyone else, I would have because it made me look vulnerable, but with Shane, I felt safe enough to expose the most flawed parts of myself.

"I want to find out who did this." I gritted my teeth. "And I want to put them in prison."

With a gust of wind ravaging his hair, Shane glared at the railing.

"I'm going to find who did this," he said in a low, even tone. "And make them pay."

He stilled in the hollow space of vengeance before placing his hand on my lower back. "Come on. I should get you home before you freeze to death."

The walk back to our apartment complex was poisoned with the drug of truth. I could no longer stay high in the safety of denial, crashing down into the treacherous reality of having been attacked.

When we reached my apartment, Shane looked into each of my rooms, each closet, even the bathtub, before returning to the front door—prepared to give me the time I needed to process this.

He studied me, and even the trained detective in him couldn't hide his worry. "You okay?"

*No. It feels like my entire existence has crumbled around me.* Who would've done this? Who did I invite into my life that hated me so much, they threw me off that bridge to die? Like an unwanted, disposable piece of trash.

And most terrifyingly, what if Shane was right? What if they might try again?

"I will be," I lied.

Shane's lips pursed. "I'd like to look at your cell phone records. Look at who you spoke to that day."

I nodded, the shock of it all casting me in a daze.

"Can you log in to your account with your cell phone carrier for me? I can start to look over that tonight."

I took his outstretched phone, opened my carrier's web page, logged in, and handed it back to him.

Shane studied me for several seconds, his chest swelling before he finally released a sigh. "You sure you won't let me stay on the couch?"

Part of me wanted him to—the part that felt afraid. But fear was weak, and I needed to stay strong if I had any hope of enduring this.

"I need to process everything."

Shane took a step closer to me.

"You were strong tonight. Going to that bridge could not have been easy."

"I don't feel strong. I feel stupid and naive." And so fragile, it felt like all of my hope, my happiness in life, drowned in that river.

He slowly brought his hand up and cupped my cheek. In his embrace, my fear melted away, surrendering to his calming force. I wished he'd hold my face forever.

"You're not naive. No one can accept that someone tried to kill them without resistance. You're a kindhearted person who sees the best in people, Willow. It's one of your best features that made me start to—" He stopped himself, and I sensed whatever he almost said would've potentially changed things between us. But he kept whatever it was bottled up and settled for stroking my cheek with his thumb as he whispered, "Don't let the asshole that did this take that from you."

I focused on the warmth of his hand, the only part of my body not screaming in hurt. His words washed over me like a sedative, silencing the pain radiating through my bones.

"Thank you," I said. "For forcing me to see the truth."

His gaze turned severe. "How could anyone ever want to hurt you?"

My stomach came alive with butterflies. I didn't think I'd be able to feel anything other than shock and hurt right now, but Shane had a way of making me feel things I never thought possible.

His gaze flickered to my mouth, igniting that energy around us once more.

How could I feel so unlucky, having let someone in my life that wanted to kill me, and yet so lucky, having found Shane? A person who made me feel important, wanted, desired, and like I mattered more to him than anything else.

Shane's chest rose and fell quicker, a fresh look of torment ripping across his features as he parted his lips.

I wanted him to kiss me. I wanted to feel his words and compassion rush down my throat and into my chest. I wanted every part of him, his body and mind, to escape into passion, to feel him on top of me.

He lowered his face closer to mine. One agonizing inch at a time, exploding my greedy need with every beat of my heart. I stared at his mouth drawing painfully closer to my own, and then, so gently that it was almost a whisper, Shane pressed his lips to mine.

*Oh my God.*

I had imagined this moment many times after Shane had moved in next door, but this was better than any of those daydreams. His lips were warm and gentle as they opened slightly and took my upper lip between them. He stepped closer to me and allowed his mouth to open wider, just enough for his tongue to breach our lips and connect with my own.

He pulled my head to get more of me, and I grabbed his shoulders, pressing my chest against his. I groaned as his tongue connected with mine again. And again.

I wanted him to touch my body, to get carried away with this current of passion.

But suddenly, Shane pulled back like my kiss had burned him.

His eyes were shut tightly, his jaw set in tension. If I didn't know better, I would think he looked angry. Especially since his hands were now at his sides, balled into fists.

My heart spasmed at the look on his face.

"I should let you rest," Shane said.

I didn't know what just happened, but it left me frozen in the ice of confusion and hurt. I knew he probably didn't want to get involved with the subject of an active investigation, but his reaction seemed to go deeper than that...

"Good night, Willow." He didn't look at me as he walked out the door and shut it behind him.

"Lock the door," he insisted from the other side.

It took me a minute to move my feet. I dragged them through the anchor of fresh pain until I reached the dead bolt and latched it shut.

Only once it latched did Shane's apartment door open and close.

The wall separating us felt like it just got thicker.

My whole life, I had felt rejected by my family—be it emotionally or in favor of substances. With Shane, I had only felt acceptance and compassion and even desire. Until now.

Now, I felt rejected by him, too. And with him, I never saw it coming.

I lay on my bed and stared at my ceiling, trying to convince myself he wasn't rejecting me; he was just trying to maintain a professional relationship until the case was closed. When that didn't work, I tried to convince myself that my growing feelings for him weren't strong enough to warrant this mental purgatory. And when that didn't work, I decided to try and force my mind into escaping turmoil.

Researching what it would take to open up my own company seemed like the perfect distraction. First, I searched online for what legal steps were required to set up a small business and what the legal and tax implications were to do so. I took notes on the different corporations you could form, how to handle the funding and money, and what paperwork needed to be filled out.

And then I opened up an online form and filed to open an LLC.

I smiled at having taken the first official step forward in my dream.

But when my escapism ended, my mind went right back to spinning with thoughts of Shane, so I decided to still it with a book.

I retrieved the current novel I was reading from my nightstand, but within the first two paragraphs, I was confused. Some character named Quincy was ranting to the main character. Only...Quincy hadn't been introduced yet.

I flipped back a couple of pages, thinking maybe the author did this surprise on purpose, but no. His name peppered the pages of the last chapter and the one before it.

Come to think of it, I distinctly remembered leaving off on chapter fifteen, when the main character had just adopted that cat—who reminded me of Snowflake—yet my bookmark was now on chapter twenty.

Maybe I'd read the next five chapters and forgot? Maybe this was part of my short-term memory loss. But so far, my short-term memory loss was confined to the bridge incident. Not other random details, like completely forgetting portions of a book I had read.

Or moving my toothbrush…

But then I didn't remember leaving my apartment that night

either, so there were at least a few minutes before the bridge I didn't remember. If not more. Maybe I'd been reading this book before I left?

*Yeah*, I tried to tell myself.

That's what it had to be.

*Right?*

## 18

"And he just pulled away? Just like that?" Emily asked.

I nodded.

Emily made her *yikes* face.

I knew it. I knew I wasn't overreacting.

I nursed my glass of wine while confiding in my best friend as we sat at a secluded table in a pub three blocks from my apartment, where I'd met Emily after work. The place was dark—leather seats and black walls—with somber music playing in the background that matched my current mood. After what happened last night with Shane, I needed somebody to help sift through this confusion because I didn't trust myself to read into this situation with Shane correctly. After all, my mind was mostly churning through the bridge incident. My heart, on the other hand, wouldn't stop obsessing over what happened between us.

"You think he regrets it," I deduced.

Emily took a sip of her drink, which was not a good sign. She only did that when she was trying to be very careful with her words, and she was only very careful with her words when she was trying not to hurt somebody's feelings.

My heart put a seat belt on and said, *Buckle up; this is going to suck.*

"He's a protective alpha, right? Typical cop that's out there, trying to protect everybody? Maybe he sees you as a damsel in distress and got carried away."

*Ouch. My heart just crashed into the windshield.*

I didn't want anyone to see me as a damsel in distress, and I didn't want Shane to have some kind of hero complex where he felt the need to rescue me. *Again.*

Emily must've read the pain in my face because she quickly tried to backpedal.

"Maybe you're wrong," she said. "Maybe it's all in your head. I mean, boys can be totally moody sometimes. Maybe he just doesn't want to get involved with you while he's investigating the case?"

"A friend of his—you've met Fallon before, right?"

Emily nodded. To the best of my recollection, she'd only met her once or twice as part of a broader friend group.

"She showed up unexpectedly and admitted that he's never had a girlfriend. He's never even had a girl over to his apartment before."

To this, Emily raised her sculpted eyebrows. "Never?"

"Never."

Another sip of wine. Another look, like she was choosing her words carefully. "Any idea why?"

"Nope."

"Did you see him this morning?"

"He stopped by briefly before he left for work to let me know he was leaving."

"What did he say?"

"Nothing. He was running late, so he had to hurry."

"So, he was rushed. Possibly too rushed to talk about what happened," she mused.

Emily took two slow sips of her drink and then set it down.

"Okay, here's what you do," Emily said. "The next time you see him, he'll either pick up the romance where it left off or he won't. If he acts like it didn't happen or if he acts weird at all with no explanation, then you know that, in his eyes, the kiss was a mistake, and he doesn't want to take it any further."

My heart lodged in my chest. Why did I care this much? It shouldn't hurt this bad, the prospect of him not wanting me.

If he didn't, where would we go from here? As much as I appreciated him investigating my fall, how uncomfortable would it be to work with a guy that I was completely into if he rejected me like that?

"Okay." I nodded. "I'll feel him out the next time I see him."

I could do this. I had to do this.

A waiter interrupted us, offering a refill we didn't need yet. When he was gone, I geared up for the second question I'd come here to ask Emily.

"What was up with you the other day?"

Emily shifted in her seat. "What do you mean?"

"You were staring at Amelia like something was bothering you."

Did she notice the scratches, too? I wouldn't bring them up myself —doing so would imply I was suspicious of Amelia, and it didn't feel concrete enough to make those kinds of implied accusations.

Emily looked like she considered denying it, probably not wanting to add to my worry.

"I'm sure it's nothing."

"What's nothing?"

A pause.

"Amelia. She's been acting off lately. I thought it was weird how perturbed she'd been that Ezra had sent you flowers and how defensive she was being. And then, ever since we met you that day, she's been up in arms that Ezra might get blamed for your fall."

"She's worried about *Ezra*? Why?"

Emily shrugged. "I don't know. When I asked her about it, she bit my head off."

I frowned.

"I'm sure it's nothing," Emily said, though I wasn't sure of her sincerity. "I mean, Tracey just left town all of a sudden, and I know *she'd* never hurt you."

Okay, this was beyond disturbing that Emily was having to *convince* herself that Amelia would never be capable of something like that.

"I'm sorry. I shouldn't have said anything," Emily said, seemingly reading into how much it bothered me.

"Don't be."

"I just hate that any of this happened to you. I've had bad dreams ever since you told me."

"Em..."

She bit her lip. "You deserve to get your happily ever after, Willow. You've been through so much in your life, and you don't deserve to be going through any of this."

Her eyes shimmered.

"I bet that cop is totally into you. I mean, look how protective he's been," she said.

"You're just saying that to cheer me up."

"Speak of the devil." She nodded her chin toward the door.

*You have got to be kidding me.*

I purposefully didn't go home after work, and I purposefully didn't tell Shane where I was going so I wouldn't have to talk to him before Emily and I had a chance to fully dissect every word from last night and properly catalog it in our own case file.

The mysterious case of Shane rejects Willow.

"Willow, can I have a word?" he asked.

Emily flashed a look at me that said, *Good luck.*

I stepped with Shane to the side of the room and wrapped my arms around my stomach, like it could hide the bruises on my heart.

"How did you find me?"

"You mean, when you didn't answer my calls?"

My face heated. He couldn't be this dense—to reject a girl and expect her not to need a second to process it.

"Process of elimination," Shane answered. "Walked a direct route from our place to your work. Got lucky on stop number six. What are you doing here?"

"We talked about this," I said. "I'm going to live my life like normal."

Shane shoved his hands in his pockets. "I know. Doesn't mean I won't worry, though."

But he wasn't worried enough last night to stay in my apartment for more than thirty seconds after he kissed me.

"I want to talk to you about what I discovered today with the phone records," he said.

So, this was just about the case, then. He wasn't here to say he thought about it all day and wanted to clarify why he had acted so weird last night. Or wanted to kiss me again.

"What did you find?" I begrudgingly asked.

He looked over at Emily, then back at me. "I'd like to talk alone."

But I didn't want to be alone with him. Not until I knew where we stood. Once I knew where we stood, I would know how to act around him, but right now, I might misinterpret everything and humiliate myself again.

Speaking of interpreting things, I studied Shane's face, which was hardened. That had to be a bad sign. Right? Yet he had come all the way here, just to check on me. A good sign?

Ugh. This was impossible. I wished Emily could come over here and give me her opinion, but if I wanted to understand where I stood with Shane, I would have to do something different.

*Don't wait for him to clarify things. Clarify them yourself.*

With my heart pounding, I kept my gaze fixed on his as I tested the energy between us, taking a step forward, bringing our faces closer. Shane appeared to assess my movement, frustration cascading through his features.

He broke eye contact.

And took a step back.

Point. Clarified.

How stupid of me to think he'd felt the same way for me as I did him. And he wasn't just pushing me away because of his career; if that were true, he would've said as much in order to spare my feelings and humiliation. This wasn't about his career; it was about me. He wasn't interested. As for yesterday's kiss, Shane must've gotten caught up in the heat of the moment. I had misread everything going on between us.

His affection for me was cruel. It had given my heart false hope—

that, for once, someone's care for me would be unending. My mom's affection came and went. My sister's was a faucet that cranked down to zero, and then someone, evidently, despised me so much, they wanted me dead.

Shane's rejection ripped my chest open, flooding it with hurt and humiliation. And anger, because I was stronger than this—than craving affection in the first place.

The worst part was, I didn't understand why he'd changed his tune —from cupping my cheek yesterday to avoiding eye contact today.

Maybe the bridge incident made him look at me with nothing but pity. Maybe he would never get involved with someone that needed so much help. Maybe he saw me as a victim and would never see me as the strong, independent woman that I actually was. Or maybe, after saving my life, he felt a sense of responsibility for me.

Whatever his reasons, I didn't know how I'd ever look Shane in the eyes again, let alone work with him to find the answers we needed so we could both move on with our lives.

"I'll text you later," I said.

After I had time to process this new, uncomfortable reality.

It was my turn to not meet Shane's eyes.

"Willow, wait," he said. "We need to discuss this. Now."

I was grateful for the plans I'd made; they afforded me a perfect excuse to delay spending time with him.

"I can't. My mom gets off work in a few minutes, and I'm heading there after this."

Maybe Mom wasn't willing to talk to me in front of Grandma and Shane. But if I confronted her and didn't let her off the hook, she would have to answer my questions.

"Postpone," Shane said.

"I can't."

When I'd reached out to her, I told her it was important. If I rescheduled or showed up late, she would use it as ammunition to wiggle out of my answers. Because how important could it be if I didn't even show up on time?

"What I found is alarming," Shane said.

*Alarming?* "Then, tell me what it is."

Shane glanced at Emily, then back to me. "It's not somethin' I'm going to talk about in a hallway conversation like this, pressured for time."

"So, give me the CliffsNotes."

"When can you meet?"

I evaluated him. The hurt side of me wanted to keep putting him off, but the sooner we found something that we could hand over to De Luca, the sooner Shane could get off this case, and I wouldn't have to interact with a guy who'd rejected me.

"Give me an hour," I said. "I'll swing by when I'm done."

"Let me come with you."

"No."

Mom would never talk if Shane was there, and I needed space from him.

"I'll swing by as soon as I'm done," I repeated. "I have to get back to Emily."

"Willow…" Shane said.

But I didn't listen to him. I walked back to the table and sat down. It was irresponsible of my heart to fixate on his rejection more than whatever he had found with my cell phone records. But there it was. I couldn't even glance in Shane's direction because if I looked at him, I might start to cry, and I was not about to cry over some guy who didn't want me. Let alone let him see just how much his rejection had affected me.

Based on Emily's eye movements, Shane must have lingered by the wall for a minute before walking out of the bar.

"Okay, he's gone. I take it, it didn't go well?"

"Is it that obvious?"

Emily pursed her lips. "Screw him. You're a total catch, and if he doesn't want you? That's his loss."

His loss. That's what people said to me when Ezra messed around on me. When my sister blew me off. Her loss. Funny how everyone around me was losing out on so much.

"We're next-door neighbors that share a wall. Do you know how uncomfortable this is going to be now? He probably thinks I'm a pathetic puppy that fell for him."

I pinched the bridge of my nose. This was the last complication I needed in my life.

"Give me your phone," Emily said.

"What?"

She didn't wait for me to comply; she grabbed my phone and flipped it over so my face unlocked the screen and then began typing.

"Don't you dare text him!" I tried to grab my phone, but she held it away.

"I'm not texting Shane."

"Then, who are you texting?"

But she didn't answer me. A slow smile curled up on her lips as she continued texting. After a minute, she said, "There."

She set the phone back on the table.

"Remember the doctor that you met in the bar last week? And you guys totally hit it off and exchanged numbers?"

"Yeah?"

"You guys finally have that date you planned to go on."

I glared at her. "Seriously, Emily? Now is not the time for—"

"You want to coexist with Shane and not have it awkward, right?"

I pursed my lips.

"If you go on a date with this doctor, it'll make it very clear to Shane you've moved on."

I frowned. "Shane wouldn't even know about the date." Because I wouldn't tell him.

"Oh, I'm betting he will." She smirked. "He seems to find you every other time you're away from him."

"Why do you have such a mischievous gleam in your eyes?"

"Because based on the way he looks at you? I think he *is* into you. And I can't wait to find out what his reaction is going to be when he finds you out with another man."

## 19

"How did Dad die?" I asked, my tone a bit curt.

It wasn't fair to her that Shane's rejection compounded my frustration toward my mom and her deceptions. It was weak to wonder why no one wanted me, and it was pathetic to feel like no one ever would.

Evidently, I couldn't make people love me, but I sure as hell could —and would—get answers I deserved.

My mom blanched. "It's nice to see you too, Willow."

I kept my shoulders square, pretending I wasn't terrified inside.

I had never confronted my mother like this, but after thinking about it more, I knew this was my last shot to get *her* to be the one to tell me. Once Shane started asking his questions, she might be so offended, she would refuse to share with me again. I could never forgive her if I had to learn about this by researching it on my own or from a stranger, like a private investigator, and since playing softly over the past two decades had not worked, I decided on a stronger approach.

Especially since the fate of our relationship hung in the balance of her honesty. There was no way to get closer to her until we obliterated the lie standing between us.

"How did he die?" I repeated.

We sat in the living room of my mother's twelve-hundred-square-foot bungalow outside the city. This was the bungalow that we had moved into after Dad's death. Her living room was full of muted blues and grays, like she wanted to be surrounded by colors that made her sad. The pictures on the walls were from decades ago —all snapshots of happier times with Dad in them. It was like Mom's life had frozen in place the day Dad died, and she never moved forward.

Her body had, though. She looked like she'd aged four decades, not two. Deep lines ground into the skin around her sunken eyes, her cheeks hollow from being too thin. Her skin was unnaturally pale, even by Chicago winter standards, and her shoulder-length dark hair had spouted grays and had started to thin.

She sat in Dad's old recliner, stirring the cup of tea she'd made herself when I'd first arrived. Staring at me as I tried not to show any trace of anxiety.

"I know this isn't easy to talk about," I said. "But he was my father. And I want to know what happened."

Mom's voice was a whisper. "What difference does it make?"

"Closure, Mom. So I can move forward with my life."

She regarded me, her face softening slightly. "And you can't move forward with your life without dredging up the past?"

"I remember having blood on me," I said. "Were we in a car accident?" Was he drinking and driving?

She took a long sip of her tea.

I clenched my fingers, trying to find my patience. "I haven't pressed you enough over the years because I've been tiptoeing around *your* feelings. But you've never considered mine."

"That's not true."

"You talk about Dad like he's a superhero. I would always listen to your stories, and I would believe every word of it."

"Your father was a loving husband and father. Nothing I told you was a lie."

"If he was so perfect, then why won't you tell me what happened to him?!" I pressed my hands together to keep them from shaking, chiding myself for letting the tone in my voice escalate.

She set her tea on the side table. "Your father was an extraordinary dad to you girls."

*Keep pressing, Willow. Now or never. Don't recede back into submissive habits. You've spent your whole life letting people walk all over you. Stand up for your needs.*

"Maybe he was. Or maybe he was…" I started.

"He was what?"

"Why are you hiding the details of how he died?"

"Because I don't want to taint your memories of him, okay?"

"Taint my memories. How would knowing the details taint my memories?"

"Willow, please…drop it." With every word, my mother receded into her pain.

"Did he hurt me?"

"I'm not ruining your father's memory over one bad day."

*One bad day…*

"I was in the hospital when he died. Was I hurt?"

"No human is perfect."

"Was Hayley hurt?"

"I'm not erasing all his wonderful memories, so if that's what you want, please…just go."

"Did I kill him?" I knew I was small, but did I pick up a gun or something?

"No, of course not!" she replied incredulously.

"I'm not leaving until you answer me."

Now, Mom's chin went up. "I'm not talking about this."

My heart pounded harder.

"If you won't give me answers, I'll look into it on my own. I'll even hire someone to get them for me if I have to."

Her eyes welled with tears, and she shot out of her chair. I bit back the apologies and desperate words trying to escape, to smooth over the wrinkles of pain.

*Now or never, Willow.*

If she refused to be honest with me, I wasn't sure how I could ever talk to her again. Ironic that all I wanted was to feel close with my mom, but all the lies she'd swept under her rug stood between us now.

Mom started pacing, a nervous energy radiating from her steps.

"How did he die?"

She added finger flexing to her pacing.

"Did he hurt you?" I asked.

No answer.

"What happened?"

"Stop."

"Why?"

"I don't want the circumstances of your father's death to define you."

"What does that mean?"

The muscles in her face softened, and her lower lip quivered. "Why can't you just let this go?"

"I'll find out what happened with or without your help. I can either hear your side of the story or not."

Her lip quivered harder, beating my anger down. I hated seeing Mom so sad. I hated that it was affecting me right now because she deserved to feel sad after keeping all of this from me for so long. I hated that I thought she deserved it.

This was all such a mess.

Mom swiped a tear from her cheek. I allowed the silence to tick on as she chewed her lip until, finally, she cleared her throat.

"He was a good person," she said, "who made a mistake."

Mom collapsed into the chair and wouldn't look me in the eye when she finally answered the question I had been waiting for my whole life.

"Your father was stressed out over finances and had too much to drink. He got into a verbal altercation that escalated to the point of getting himself killed. He was shot once in the head. And I couldn't stop it."

Mom shoved her face into her hands, and her shoulders shook.

She had to know that wasn't even close enough to being a full explanation, but I tried to bite my tongue to allow her words to come at her own pace.

"I kept it from you to protect you," Mom said. "I couldn't save your father. And in the aftermath of his death, I have been so self-centered with my grief that I failed both of you girls. I failed Hayley and allowed her to become addicted to drugs and alcohol. You were the only one in the family who wasn't living under this dark cloud, and I was not going to rob you of that. You still had the chance to go after your dreams, so why would I take all of that away from you?"

"It's not your fault that Hayley is an addict."

Tears ran down her cheeks. "Of course it is. I emotionally checked out, and I left Hayley holding the bag. She would have to step in and take care of you whenever I had a breakdown and left for days at a time. Days! Even though she was also in the throes of extreme grief. What kind of horrible mother does that to her own children?"

Mom wiped away tears of shame.

"It's not a question of *why* she started doing drugs," she said. "But why wouldn't she have? I was the one person who could've and should've protected her, and I never did."

That's why Mom had always been Hayley's enabler. She didn't favor Hayley, as it often felt to me throughout the years, but in reality, her actions toward Hayley stemmed from guilt.

And that's why they seemed so close and why I always felt as though I were on the outside, looking in. Mom had built this impenetrable wall meant to protect me, both from the truth and from the toxicity that she and Hayley lived. Undoubtedly, she thought I deserved more than a mother and sister who were broken by the events of the past.

"Who killed him, Mom? And how did I end up with blood all over me?"

## 20

'Okay, after you logged in to your cell phone carrier's account for me, I obtained the last three months of cell phone records," Shane said.

He sat on my living room couch while I tried hard to listen to him, but my mind kept wandering to what had just happened with my mom.

Over the years, I had always assumed my dad had simply been in the wrong place at the wrong time. After all, this was a man who had picked wildflowers with his little girls and doted on his wife. Who could've hated him enough to kill him intentionally? In the absence of information from my mom, I had even spun multiple tales of what may have happened. The most probable, I had decided, was when I had seen news stories about a series of armed robberies at gas stations nearby. I had imagined that maybe similar robberies had happened years before, and maybe my father had been paying for gas and had become a victim to an armed robbery gone wrong.

But with the few details she'd provided, my mom just repainted the entire picture of the circumstances surrounding his death.

Dad had been stressed about finances. Dad had been drinking. Just that one day? Or in general, had he been using alcohol excessively?

He'd gotten into a verbal altercation and, in her words, "gotten himself killed."

Gotten himself killed.

And Mom "couldn't stop it."

"I started with the day of…" Shane continued.

That was not a picture of a wrong place, wrong time. It was a picture of a man becoming unraveled.

Did Mom sell insurance back then? Was there insurance on her life? If so, might he have attacked her in a desperate attempt to get that money?

And how did I get blood on me? Was that why she shut down in the middle of our conversation, refusing to divulge anything else?

"…and compare the list of all incoming and outgoing phone calls to the contact list you provided me."

Did my sister know what really happened? In my shell-shocked state, I hadn't even thought to ask Mom that question.

"I paid particular attention to the hours leadin' up to your fall."

Grandma had to know, too, didn't she? She was, after all, helping to keep the details of his death a secret.

"Three calls in particular were of interest."

In fact, everyone in our family would have had to have been in on it.

"The first was from your friend Tracey. You called her an hour before your fall. That call lasted for six minutes."

How could they all do that? What were they hiding that was so bad? Because that's what they were doing—hiding it.

"The second was an incoming call from Amelia. Shortly after Tracey's. That call only lasted three minutes."

Who had killed him? When I pushed Mom for an answer, she had shut down.

"But the third call," Shane said, pointing to a piece of paper, "was an incoming call from Ezra."

Which meant she knew the killer.

"Which means the last person you spoke with that night was Ezra."

You don't keep that kind of information a secret unless the killer is someone in the family. Right?

"Willow, are you listening to me?"

I blinked and snapped myself out of my trance. "Yes. Ezra. Last person I talked to."

Shane studied me. "Are you okay? You haven't been yourself since you got back from your mom's."

I didn't answer.

"What happened?"

With the pain of Shane's rejection anchored into my stomach, the need to talk through this shocking twist in my life swam to the surface. And broke through.

"I confronted her about how my dad died."

Shane pierced me with his indigo eyes. "Did you finally get some answers?"

It would be easier to stay angry at Shane if he wasn't so sincerely compassionate.

"Sort of."

"What happened?" Shane set the papers down on my coffee table.

My pride wanted to tell him nothing—if he cared so much about me, he shouldn't have pushed me away. But my heart chided me; Shane not wanting me did not take away from how kindhearted he was.

"My dad was murdered. Evidently, he'd been drinking and stressed about money, and he got into an altercation."

Shane's eyes raked over my face, and the familiar pang of hurt jolted. If he made me feel this cared about, some girl would be so lucky to become the object of his everything.

*I wish I could've been her.*

"Did she say who killed him?" Shane asked.

"No. I tried to ask her more questions, but she shut down again. Like she always does."

"I'm sorry."

I rubbed my eyes. "I thought finding out how my dad died would give me some kind of closure. But it just ripped the wound open and left me with more questions than answers."

I hated how my eyes welled with tears, and I hated that, out of all the people I could talk to about this, I was most comfortable doing it with Shane. It would be easier to keep my feelings at bay if that weren't the case, but he was the only person in my life who could understand what this felt like. And the way he was looking at me—his eyes soft, a line creasing between his brows—I could tell that he not only understood, but he also cared deeply about how hard this was for me to process.

"I don't understand why she kept it from me all this time."

Shane paused. "It wasn't right, lying to you. You deserve the truth. I'm sure, in her own way, your mom was probably tryin' to protect you."

I slouched my shoulders and tried to hold on to the anger I felt toward my mom.

"Aren't you supposed to be the cynical one here?" I asked.

Shane was changing a little, wasn't he? From the cynic who didn't believe in second chances to someone encouraging me to cut my mom some slack.

"You're making it hard to stay mad at her," I said.

Shane's lips tugged up on one side. He stared at me, grabbing hold of me with those azure eyes.

"I'm sorry she's kept this from you for your whole life. That must be overwhelming."

What a great way to put it. Overwhelming.

He put his hand on my knee the same way he had the night we'd had dinner with my family, when he didn't want me to feel alone in that mess. I wish my pulse didn't react to his touch, or his gaze, which slowly trailed to my lips. I wish my lower belly didn't heat up when his thumb brushed light strokes against my thigh. If he wanted a platonic friendship, he shouldn't touch me like this or stare at me with that wanton desire, his tongue wetting his lower lip as he studied my mouth.

This was real, wasn't it? He was attracted to me. And if he cared about me and wanted me, maybe I'd misunderstood. Maybe he did have feelings for me. My heart stretched through the barbed wire surrounding it, reaching for Shane—never needing him more than I did right then.

But suddenly, Shane dropped his hand. He cleared his throat and moved over another two feet from me. Two feet that might as well have been a mile.

It felt like I had been shot in the chest. Not only losing out on the physical feeling of his mouth on mine, caving in to my desires, making me forget all about my hurts, but also, pushing me away after we'd shared such an intimate profession.

What was wrong with me? Was this romance all in my head?

Shane's rejection was the last thing I should care about. There were much bigger priorities in my life right now, like getting to the bottom of what happened on that bridge and processing everything I had learned about my dad. It was juvenile to feel hurt right now, to have my eyes once again burning, but I couldn't stomach him looking at me with pity, a needy girl with unfulfilled feelings for him.

As if the universe wanted to side with Emily, my phone buzzed with a text from the doctor she'd set me up with.

"Tell me that's not Ezra," Shane said, trying to eye my screen.

"No. It's a guy I have a date with."

Shane's eyes snapped to mine. I swore I saw a flash of jealousy, but you can't be jealous of something you don't want.

"I don't think it's the best time for you to be dating."

Well, I was certainly not going to sit around here and feel sorry for myself that Detective Rejection wanted nothing to do with me. And I did not know how long it was going to take to solve this case, so even if I wasn't into this date, at least it would make it clear to Shane that I was moving on.

Because you know what? I didn't *want* Shane anymore. I refused to chase after someone again. Screw him.

"So, the phone records," I said, "we should turn these over to De Luca."

Shane stared at my phone, his chest inflating and deflating before he shook his head. "They aren't evidence of anything."

"Ezra was the last person to talk to me, and he had a conniption fit in my apartment, where the cops were called."

"It's not enough evidence to prove foul play. We need somethin' more than an angry ex."

Dammit. What else did we have to do to get detectives to take over? Because I couldn't keep working with Shane; it stung too much.

"Okay, so Ezra," I said. "He's the first person we talk to, then?"

Shane scrubbed his jaw. "Yes."

I nodded.

Normally, I wouldn't rush Shane out of my apartment so quickly, but our business for the evening had concluded, and I needed to be alone to strengthen my walls for when I was around him next. Plus, I wanted to stop my mind from spinning.

But even after he left, I couldn't relax. I tried reading, again perturbed about what in the world happened with my bookmark. I tried watching a show, but when none of that worked, I resorted to cleaning my kitchen.

With everything going on, I hadn't used my kitchen much. A handful of dishes sat in the sink, so I began rinsing them off.

Only…

The water wasn't draining. It was filling up so quickly; there was obviously some sort of clog. I began scooping water out of one side of the sink with a cup, and only when I reached the bottom did I discover what the culprit was.

It wasn't leftover bites of food; it was hair.

A wad of my hair the size of a golf ball.

I had never had a clog like this before. Not in my entire life. How did this much hair get into my drain?

*It's probably just from…natural shedding of hair, I guess?*

But that made no sense. First of all, I hadn't noticed any hair loss. Second, why would it be in a clump like this? And third, why would it be in the kitchen sink? Why not the shower drain, where most hair naturally falls out?

I set it on the counter and looked at it. It looked like a drowned hamster, and it smelled like curdled milk.

Something about it didn't sit well with me, made my blood pump faster through my body. I didn't brush my hair near the sink, and even if I did, I wouldn't allow my hair to pile into the drain. I would wipe it up. It would take *a lot* of hair to create a clog this big, so why hadn't I noticed any issues with my drain before? It should've drained slower before stopping completely.

It was almost as if this clog had appeared suddenly.

Come to think of it, I hadn't washed dishes since I'd gotten home from the hospital. Since I'd found my apartment unlocked...since I'd found my toothbrush on the back of the toilet, my bookmark in the wrong location.

I seriously thought about calling Shane over, but my bruised ego was tired of turning to *him* for everything. Plus, it sounded so crazy. Even if I called the responding officers from the possible break-in, I could just imagine my conversation with them.

*"Yes, sir, I'm worried someone may have broken into my apartment and moved my toothbrush, moved my bookmark, and shoved a wad of my hair into my sink. Can you come dust for prints?"*

*"Any sign of a break-in, Ms. Johnson?"*

*"An unlocked door."*

*"So, the only things are this toothbrush in a different spot from where you thought you left it, a bookmark, and a clogged drain?"*

*"Yes."*

*A cutting stab of a glower. "Yes, Ms. Johnson, we'll escalate this to the top of the crime lab immediately."*

I rolled my eyes.

Maybe the sink had been draining slower lately, and I hadn't noticed it. Maybe I'd knocked one of my brushes into it, and hair had accumulated or something.

After all, if a burglar had broken in here, they'd have taken something. Not taking the risk or time to shove my hair into a drain. What possible reason would they have to do that?

It made no sense.

Yet…it was getting harder to assure myself someone wasn't responsible for this. If I told Shane, he'd go ballistic and probably insist on staying at my place from now on.

The next time I talked to De Luca, I should at least mention it…

## 21

"Do you know how upset you made Mom?" Hayley stormed into my living room. "She's been in bed all day, Willow. What the hell?"

It had shocked me when I answered the door to find my sister here. But I guess I should've seen this coming.

"I never meant to upset her," I said. "I was just trying to get some answers."

"You know when she gets like this, she can spiral. What the hell were you thinking?"

"I'm trying to get closure."

"By making my life a living hell? In case you forgot, I'm stuck living with Mom at the moment. So, when she yells at me? I just have to sit there and take it, and as usual, you never have to deal with any of it."

"What does that mean?"

"Mom will never yell at *you*; she never has. She has always sheltered you from everything, just like she did with Dad's death. You got to go on and have a happy life while *I'm* the one that paid the price by dealing with Mom's heartbreak."

"I was four," I reminded her.

"You've grown up. Happy, unlike me."

Happy? Did she think family secrets made me happy?

"Do you know who killed Dad?" I asked.

Hayley narrowed her eyes, a flash of resentment breaking through her gaze. She looked like she was struggling between the orders our mother had always given her and her apparent jealousy toward me.

"I should say so. Seeing as how I was there when it happened."

I rocked back on my heels.

"You *saw* him get killed?"

She stood there for what felt like an eternity and said nothing, just like Mom had said nothing for all of these years.

"Mom should have told me the truth a long time ago," I said.

"Stop blaming Mom. She's not the one who killed Dad and ruined our lives. You want someone to blame for our screwed-up family? Blame the son of a bitch that killed him! He's the one you should hate! He did this; he took everything from us, so stop blaming Mom!"

"So, it was a man?"

Hayley looked like she debated answering my question, if only to throw it in my face, but Mom had worked hard to keep me from finding out the truth. And Hayley was at the mercy of Mom, who was allowing my sister to stay in her house. She couldn't stray too far from Mom's wishes or else she'd be homeless.

*That's it. I'm hiring a private investigator to find all the answers to this mystery, including how much my family members knew all these years.*

As if she could read the intent in my eyes, Hayley said, "Stop digging up the past. You won't like what you find."

"The hell is that supposed to mean?"

"I had to pick up the pieces the last time Mom broke down, but I'm done being left holding the bag. Go back to your fucking fairy-tale life and stop ruining what's left of ours."

Hayley stormed out.

No wonder she'd struggled her entire life. Everything made sense now, and a flood of compassion and empathy opened up in my heart for her. Hayley had been suffering with these demons for so long. No wonder she turned to drugs and alcohol.

In addition to the pain of witnessing Dad's death, she'd been left alone at times to care for her younger sister in the wake of tragedy. Mom was an adult and didn't even pull that off. Instead, she left it on the shoulders of a teenager.

It should come as no surprise that Hayley had seeds of resentment toward her. And as if that wasn't bad enough, she'd watched Mom shelter and protect me from the truth for years when she was never there to protect Hayley from the horrible reality.

Maybe that was another reason Mom didn't want to talk about that fateful day, not only because of her grief over Dad, but also, because it would bring back horrible memories for Hayley.

Maybe it was Mom's way of trying to protect Hayley from at least part of it all.

If I had known any of this, I would have been more compassionate toward Hayley all these years.

Maybe this secret stood between me and Hayley, too.

## 22

This was a mistake. I seriously wanted to cancel this date, but here I was. Wearing a light-blue dress with a neckline so low, I couldn't wear a bra with it. The dress came to my thighs, showing off that muscular line in my legs that I'd worked hard to get. I kept my hair stick straight versus styling it up and put minimal makeup on my face—a little color on my lips and thicker eyeliner on my eyes, but otherwise going for the more natural look. I finished it off with a pair of stud earrings and black stiletto heels.

A totally inappropriate outfit to wear in Chicago's rigid winter temperatures, but I had bigger problems in life.

When the knock came, I grabbed my dressy coat, my purse, and opened my front door.

Clay was holding a bouquet of pink roses.

His eyebrows shot up, and a smile etched across his face. "You look...wow."

"You do, too."

And he did, wearing fitted dress pants, a gray shirt that showed off his muscles beneath his black coat, and his blond hair styled with gel.

"These are for you." He handed me the bouquet.

Luckily, it was already in a vase, so I didn't have to scrounge around, looking for one.

"Thank you." I smiled and set the flowers on my table.

"What happened to your arm?" he asked.

"I fell."

"What type of fracture?" His tone was curious. "Hairline? Transverse? Oblique?"

"Hairline."

He smiled. "Glad it wasn't compound. Those are incredibly painful."

This wasn't exactly a cake walk either, but the ache had faded a little more each day.

"Shall we go?" He motioned with his arm.

I was surprised he merely asked for a medical clarification rather than how I'd broken it, but hopefully, his lack of curiosity would continue through dinner—I didn't want to get into it.

I stepped out into the hallway and locked my door.

At the precise moment Shane's door opened. Wearing his running gear—a fitted black shirt and pants that hugged his hips—he froze when he saw us.

His gaze gradually descended my dress and back up.

Then, he glared at us.

Glared.

Leaning in his doorframe with his arms crossed like some kind of possessive alpha.

Clay shot me a WTF look, but I just smiled as if Shane's behavior were totally normal. Did I want this date? No, not with this timing, but if I had any hope of enduring my lease, I needed to do this.

I reached down and took Clay's hand.

Which snapped Clay out of his WTF trance and put a smile on his face.

"Clay, this is my neighbor, Shane. Shane, Clay. We were just leaving." I tugged Clay down the hall. "Where do we have reservations?"

"You're going to love this place," Clay said. "Best Italian food in the city."

"She hates Italian food," Shane said in an annoyed tone as he locked his door and followed us down the hallway.

"No one hates Italian food," Clay said.

"She does."

"How do you know?" I challenged.

"Couple months back, you and one of your friends were walking down the hall, heading out to dinner, tryin' to decide where to go. You told her no Italian. You hate Italian."

My cheeks flushed. Did detectives catalog every word you ever said?

"We can go somewhere else," Clay said.

"No. I can find a salad or something."

I shot Shane a shut-up look.

"You sure?" Clay asked.

"Yeah."

"Okay, great, because this place is supposed to have killer chicken Parm."

"You're really goin' to take her somewhere you know she doesn't like just so you can get the dinner *you* want?"

"Shane—"

"What's your problem, man?" Clay asked.

"If you invite her out to dinner, you should take her somewhere she can actually eat."

"Shane!" I snapped.

Shane's eyes landed on me, his jaw set in frustration. And when Clay helped me slip my coat on, his fingers brushing my neck, Shane looked at Clay's hands as if they were the enemy.

I pretended not to notice as I stepped outside, eager to put Clay at ease.

"Is that the car you were telling me about?" I asked.

A red Corvette sat a few spaces down, so shiny that it looked like it had just been driven off a car lot. Its angles looked like something from the future; the slope of the roof slanted down toward the rounded trunk with a spoiler on it.

"You like it?"

"It's gorgeous."

Shane glared at Clay, then at his car, and I could tell by the look on Shane's face that he was about to say something to get under Clay's skin. Why? Why was he acting like this? Before Shane had the chance to mutter whatever rude grenade he'd prepared, I pulled him off to the side.

"What is your problem?" I whisper-demanded.

"I don't like him."

"You don't know him."

"He cares more about himself than you."

"And you know this after meeting him for what, ten seconds?"

"All I needed to see. You deserve better."

"You know nothing about Clay."

"Do you?" Shane challenged.

"Why are you out here, anyway?"

"I was about to go for a run."

"Well, be on your way, Hernandez. I have a date to get to."

Spoiler alert: the date was boring as hell. Dr. Arrogant would not stop talking about himself. I don't think he asked me a single question about me or my life. I couldn't wait to get home.

Not that I would ever admit any of this to Shane. I hated that he had been right, but he was a seasoned detective and had spotted Clay's selfishness quicker than me. But in fairness, Shane's magnetism had distracted me in the hallway.

Thankfully, the dinner was finally over. We sat in his ostentatious Corvette, ambling along a road in downtown Chicago, while Clay droned on again about all the cadavers he'd dissected in medical school.

*Just what every girl longs to hear.*

Suddenly, red and blue lights cut through the evening's darkness through the rear window.

I looked at the speedometer, but Clay wasn't speeding.

"What the hell?" Clay pulled off to the shoulder.

I looked behind us, and when I realized the lights came from an unmarked squad car, my hands clenched.

*He'd. Better. Not.*

The unmarked squad car's door opened, and a silhouette emerged.

*It can't be him. So help me, if it is...*

The blue and reds shone behind the man as he walked toward our car. Painfully slow. And when he reached the car? He came to *my* side rather than Clay's and tapped on my window.

It took me a second to figure out how to roll it down on account of my immense irritation.

"A word?" Shane said.

"What the hell, Hernandez?" I asked.

He opened the door, as if he were being chivalrous instead of a level-ten dick.

"Step out of the car."

"No." I tried to shut the door, but Detective Dick kept it pried open with his ridiculous forearm strength.

"I'll repeat myself one more time. Step out of the car."

"Or what? You going to drag me out?"

Shane's eyes flared with anger. "Don't tempt me."

"Go ahead. I double dog dare you."

While Shane and I entered a glaring competition, Clay stirred to life.

"What's your deal, dude?"

"Shut up," Shane snapped.

That's all Clay needed. Dr. Arrogant apparently would not tolerate being spoken to like that. He shoved his door open and launched himself out of the driver's seat.

Shane put his hand on his weapon, because, yeah, he was wearing the damn holster on his belt.

"Back in the car." Shane held up his palm.

"Screw you." Clay walked around the hood of his car and approached Shane.

"Clay, stop!" I demanded.

Clay took another step toward Shane. "Get away from my car and away from her."

I lunged out of my seat. *The last thing we need is a shoot-out over egos.*

"Take one step closer to me," Shane said in a tone that added, *I dare you.*

Clay did.

But before Shane could manhandle him, I jumped between them, shoving my hands against Shane's chest until he backed up to the rear of the Corvette.

Clay stood at the side, then ambled toward the front of the vehicle. Thank goodness.

"What the hell are you doing?" I demanded.

"You know who that guy is?"

"You're acting like a lunatic! How did you even find us?"

"When he picked you up, I got his plates. And I ran them while you were at dinner."

"Is that even legal?" I asked.

Traffic slowed as vehicles drove past us, looking at the lights and the scene we were making on the side of the road.

"He's got unpaid child support in three states."

Wow. Clay told me he didn't have kids. But this was a moot point; I'd already decided I wasn't going on a second date with him.

"Well, thanks for the warning. If you don't mind, I'll get back to it then."

But when I took a step forward, Shane moved in front of me, blocking my path. "Get in my car. I'm takin' you home."

"News flash: I don't need you to protect me from him."

"Get in the car, Willow." Shane nodded toward his sedan.

"Is that what this is? You see me as some sort of perpetual, helpless victim that needs your protection?" I stepped closer to him and got in his space. "I'm a big girl. Pulling us over tonight was completely out of line."

"You deserve better."

Even though I didn't think Clay could hear what we were saying, he must have lost patience with this whole thing because he walked up to me and gripped my elbow.

"Come on." He tugged me toward my open door, but in a flash, Shane grabbed him and pinned him to his shiny Corvette trunk—his hands behind his back.

"Touch her again, I'll fuckin' pummel you."

"Shane!" I said. "Stop!"

What had gotten into him?

"What the hell, man?!" Clay snapped.

"Let him go!"

Shane and I locked eyes. His chest heaved with fury, and when he looked back at Clay, his lips curled in disgust. But he pushed off him.

Clay spun around. Stood nose to nose with Shane, both men huffing white puffs out of their nostrils as the blue and reds flashed across their skin. Car tires crunched against snow salt as vehicles chugged between skyscrapers, watching a standoff between two men.

"Get back in the car," Clay snapped to me.

"Talk to her like that again…" Shane warned.

Clay looked at Shane's hand, positioned on his gun's holster, then at the unmarked sedan's police lights, then at me. His lips curled as he stood there, glowering.

"You're not worth this hassle."

I had to launch myself in front of Shane, both palms on his chest to stop him from whatever vengeance he was about to carry out. "Stop."

I could feel his heart beating, even beneath his coat, as he watched Clay slam the passenger door, walk around the hood, climb inside, and drive off.

"What has gotten into you?" I demanded.

Around us, snowflakes drifted lazily from the black sky, streetlights illuminating them as they shimmered to the ground, creating a magical scene that was straight out of some fairy-tale romance. Unfortunately, it wasn't.

"You can't keep acting like this," I said. "It makes me think you actually want me when you don't."

I tried to push past him, prepared to walk home in my ridiculous heels, but he blocked my path and looked down at me with angry eyes.

"You think I don't want you?" he snarled.

"I know you don't."

Shane's jaw set with frustration. "I've never wanted another woman more in my life." He took a step forward, and I took a step back, moving toward the hood of his car, mirroring his movements. "You're all I think about." Another step from him. Another from me. "All I want to do right now"—another step—"is pin you to the car and show you what I've been imaginin' doing since I first laid eyes on you."

I swallowed, the puffs of white fog coming from my mouth, quickening.

He stood there. Glaring at my parted lips as if they were the enemy. Glaring at me like I'd committed a felony for even thinking that his feelings for me weren't mutual. Based on the look on his face, I'd say his feelings were stronger than I'd ever imagined.

"I don't understand. You pushed me away..." I said.

"To protect you, Willow! I've never felt this way about *anyone*." He pinned me with his fierce stare. "With other girls, it'd be easy to avoid feelin' anything for them, but the connection I have with you isn't just physical. As soon as I started kissing you, I knew if I let it go any further, it would mean so much more than I could handle. My heart would want to go all in with you, so I've been struggling to hold back. To protect you."

I had seen Shane come unglued—pinning Ezra against the wall of my apartment and just now, in the way he'd handled Clay—but suddenly, I was witnessing the fabric of his heart unthreading.

Mine opened from its wilted hurt to blossom.

He cared about me. Deep enough to do what was best for me, even if it hurt him.

Seeing the look in his eyes, I felt like a fool for having ever questioned it in the first place. I guess when you experience as much rejection as I have, when something feels too good to be true, it doesn't surprise you when that person walks away.

"Protect me from what?"

I was trembling now, not from fear of his aggressive pursuit, but from the winter winds whipping around my bare legs.

A movement Shane noticed with furrowed eyes.

"Get in the car," Shane said. "We can talk in the heat."

## 23

*S*hane Hernandez *has never wanted another woman more than me.*

As I sat in his passenger seat, Shane's words danced around in my head like joyful music while my heart replayed the encounters we'd had over the past several months. Every stolen glance in the hallway, every time he'd held a door open for me, my attraction toward him had grown. And now, to hear confirmation that it *had* been mutual...

It felt like my heart was jumping out of my chest.

When your heart leans toward someone, all you want is for their heart to lean back.

"What did you mean, you pushed me away to protect me?" I asked.

Shane pulled his sedan out into traffic and tightened his lips. "I'd rather talk about this when we get back home."

I blinked. "Why?"

His gaze met mine. "Because I want to be able to look you in the eyes."

*Holy romantic mother of moments.* His stare was so hot and sexy, it could melt an iceberg.

This *must* have to do with getting involved with me during an active case. Right? Or what if...

What if Shane sensed something about our situation that I never considered before? While he might be good for *me*, what if I wasn't good for *him*? My life was so chaotic right now, and I seemed to draw him into situations that brought out the worst in him.

"I feel like I'm a bad influence on you," I said.

Shane cocked an eyebrow and looked at me before returning his steely eyes to the road. "How so?"

"I feel like whenever I'm around you, chaos ensues. With Ezra. Clay. I feel like I'm drawing you over to the dark side or something."

Shane's lips twitched in amusement, as if the very idea of *me* turning him bad was ludicrous. "There's a lot you don't know about me."

I blinked. "Meaning?"

"I've always had a darker side to me, Willow. It's something I have to actively keep in check. This isn't the first time it's been tested."

Did he seriously think I was going to let *that* go without an explanation? Nope. Not even waiting until we get back to the apartment on that one. I stared at him, making it clear I'd wait.

He sighed and shifted in his seat.

"When I was a kid, after my dad died, we lived in a trailer park for part of my life. A shitty one," he said. "There was this family that lived next door with a girl my age. Wasn't long before I suspected somethin' ugly was happening in that house."

Shane sucked his bottom lip into his teeth, as if fighting against the undertow of a terrible memory.

"The girl went to school with me. She never had enough to eat. I could tell she was being neglected, but the first time I heard her scream…"

Shane chewed the inside of his cheek.

"There were these drug dealers going to that house all the time. I got in the habit of watching when they would come, keepin' my ears open. Sometimes, there would be no noise. Other times, I could hear her scream like someone was hurting her. I called the cops, of course, but by the time they got there, the drug dealers were gone, and no one was ever hauled away in handcuffs. I kept tryin', but the guys were too slippery to get caught. Meanwhile, those awful screams kept coming."

As if Shane hadn't suffered enough, losing his dad, he was an earwitness to some horrific abuse happening to that girl...

"Did your mom ever hear?" I asked.

Shane shook his head. "My mom was always workin' two, three jobs at a time, trying to keep us afloat. I told her about it more than once, but she told me to mind my own business and stay out of it. That interfering might put me in danger."

My chest sank.

"Lookin' back on it, I know she was just protecting me, but I wish she had done something more."

I thought it was bad enough when I felt helpless to make my mom feel better, to help Hayley get out of her spiral. I couldn't even imagine hearing abuse and feeling powerless to stop it.

"Anyway, this goes on for a while, and I felt so damn helpless since I was just a kid. Still, I tried. I had gone to my mother, and I had gone to the police on multiple occasions. They took me seriously, especially being the son of a fallen officer, but the dealers seemed to know every trick in the book to evade them. Seemed like they were always one step ahead. If I'd been more patient, maybe they would have eventually caught them, but at the time, it felt like that wasn't going to happen until someone died or something. I even stormed over there one time."

"What happened?"

"The front door swung open, and this dude tried to run me off with a semiautomatic. I almost fought him. But I got scared because he was twice as big as me, and if I lost, I worried he would shoot her and her family."

My heart ached for Shane. He was such a kind soul, always wanting to help people, even when he was grieving himself. He was stronger than I would have been. It was hard enough for me to get through the days when Mom was struggling with her grief. I couldn't imagine coping with her incapacitating sadness, enduring my own, and taking on the trauma of a next-door neighbor.

"She and I are still great friends, but she doesn't know that, to this day, I still have nightmares about her screams. And when I'm in those nightmares, that helpless feeling creeps back in."

My eyes burned. Admitting something that vulnerable couldn't have been easy.

"I should've snuck her in to stay at our place instead of leaving her in that trailer to fend for herself. In hindsight, there was more I could have done. And I have to live with the guilt of having failed her."

My eyes blurred with tears.

"You didn't fail her, Shane. By the sounds of it, you were the only person trying to throw her a life raft."

He cleared his throat and took a few moments to gather his thoughts.

"When I joined the police force, I took an oath to serve and protect. And I promised myself one thing: if anything like that ever happened again, now that I was in a position of power, I'd do whatever I could to help that person."

And his next-door neighbor had survived what he believed to be an attempted murder. Now, it all made sense. Even if he had not been attracted to me, Shane would've stepped in and done everything that he had done, anyway.

Shane had to be the most selfless, kindest person I had ever met. It took strength to reach out and help someone, especially when that someone battles your efforts every step of the way, as I had. Despite my pushing back, Shane never faltered, and that took a level of heroics, if you ask me.

In fact, that's what Shane was. A real-life hero.

When his dad died on the police force, Shane would've had every reason not to risk the same fate by putting his own life on the line in order to protect other people. And yet, he did the opposite. He dedicated his life to helping others, just as his dad did. He sacrificed relationships, time, and probably a tremendous amount of emotions, just so he could wake up every day and help protect those in need.

My heart bled for him.

It swelled for him.

It longed for him.

Shane Hernandez had just captured every last fragment of my heart.

"You don't have to answer this," I clarified. "But was that girl Fallon?"

His friend—the only friend I'd ever seen, come to think of it—that had found me in his apartment.

Shane's chest inflated slowly. And then he nodded.

"I never told her this." His voice dropped lower, pulsing with an ominous tone. "In fact, I've never told anyone this. But one day, she confided in me that the guy beat both her and her mom." His jaw locked. "That was it. The next time I saw the guy, I did something…"

Shane made a right turn and waited until the car straightened out before continuing.

I leaned forward, eager to hear his next words.

"Our trailer park was surrounded by open fields, and there was this one field that you had to walk past in order to leave. The field must've been abandoned because no one ever did anything with it. No farming, no mowing. The grass and weeds were as tall as my shoulders."

We came to a red light and stopped, the windshield wipers trying to combat the growing snow.

"It was the perfect hiding place for anyone who wanted to ambush someone."

Ho-ly crap.

"The guy was alone. Like always. I stayed hidden in the weeds so he couldn't see me, and then I jumped him. I took him by surprise, so his weapons were useless to him, and I landed a couple of good blows before he even realized what was goin' on. Which helped. It stunned him long enough to let me finish what I'd set out to do."

My mouth was dry. My throat a desert. "Did you kill him?"

Shane's jaw tensed. "I wanted to. But I left him alive."

Good God. I never imagined law-enforcing Shane would've attacked someone like that. That must be the darkness he said he had to work to keep at bay. Being a police detective, witnessing what heinous criminals were capable of, had to have challenged his calm resolve throughout the years.

"Have you ever been tempted to do something like that again?" I asked.

His eyes pierced mine. "Yes," he said. "With you."

My breath caught in my throat.

"When I find out who tried to kill you..." Shane's knuckles whitened as he looked back out the windshield.

The cold violence cutting through his eyes sent a shiver of fear through me, warmed only with desire.

I didn't know what to say to that, didn't know exactly what he meant. Did he mean he was fighting the temptation to get vengeance? Or was it a threat?

"Is that why you wouldn't date me? You're trying to keep your rage under control?"

It made sense. The closer he'd let himself get to me, the harder it might be to control his fury.

"No."

"Then, why? How does not dating me protect me?"

"It's because of what happened after my dad died."

## 24

Wwe parked, then went into my apartment, where I took off my coat and shoes and leaned against the living room wall.

Shane put his hands in his pockets and finally settled into what he wanted to say. "My mom struggled. A lot. Obviously, she struggled financially to support two small kids on her own when she had been a stay-at-home mom before that. But the bigger part…"

Shane walked over to the sliding glass door and watched the snow fall to the ground from the beginning of a winter storm.

"They didn't have a lot of money, but they loved the hell out of each other. You could see it in all the family photo albums and feel it through all the stories that were told. You know, you see these relationships where the love fades; people even wind up in divorce. But every once in a blue moon, there's a love like no other. My mom used to describe it as the kind of love that could make the moon shine brighter." Shane looked up at the sky.

His tone was somber as he continued, "When my dad died, it gutted her. She thought she was hiding it from us. She would wait until she thought we were asleep. Or wait until she was in the shower. But my sister and I could hear her cryin'. It was the kind of crying that

I had never heard before. This deep, visceral wail, like her heart was literally bleeding."

My throat swelled. I knew that kind of crying; I'd heard my mom cry like that, and years later, I would come to understand that I had been going through two different types of grief—the grief of losing my father and the grief of watching my family suffer from his loss.

"With each of my milestones in life, there was this black cloud cover. Like my high school graduation. All the other parties I'd gone to had these brightly colored balloons and music playin'. Dancing. And we did celebrate," Shane caveated. "It wasn't like my mom wasn't capable of being happy. It just…"

His breathing shallowed, and for a minute, I didn't think he was going to continue.

"The elephant in the room was that he was missing it. When my mom thought I wasn't looking, I could see how sad she was. I'd catch her crying in the corner. It wasn't just the grief of losin' him; it was losing out on him being part of every experience we'd had. Seein' her kids growing up without a father."

Shane walked over to my refrigerator, opened it, and pulled a beer out. He held it up. "May I?"

I nodded.

"Do you want one?"

"No." I rubbed my arms, this conversation chilling my bones.

Shane took a long pull from his beer, then set it down and grabbed the countertop.

"My dad's death devastated my family. Financially. Emotionally. I was only four when he passed, so I never had a father in the Little League stands, cheerin' me on. My mom couldn't be there because she was busy workin' her ass off. Yet she was still struggling to keep the heat on. Christmas mornings…Thanksgivings…birthdays…were all other kids' dreams; for me, holidays and special occasions of any kind were so painful, they became my nightmares."

My chest tightened as Shane looked at the floor, his voice low.

"I wanted to be happy because I thought if I could just find a way to be happy, then maybe Mom might be happy again too."

My stomach ached, remembering how I'd had those same thoughts when my dad died. When I hid the invitations to father-daughter dances and Father's Day crafts. Thinking I was the one making Mom unhappy by reminding her of what she'd lost.

"But those first years, every Christmas mornin'...I'd check under the tree to see if Santa brought me the only thing I wanted in the entire world."

My eyes welled with tears, picturing a desperate little boy in pajamas, running to the Christmas tree. His heart destroyed when, once again, his naive hope to ever see his father again was shattered.

He sighed and scrubbed his face with both hands. "It was even harder on my sister and my mom. And to watch them suffer like that?"

He took a sip of beer. "I will never allow myself to be in a position where I could leave behind a wife and kids the way my dad did. Never. It's my biggest fear in life."

A tear escaped my eye.

"I'm in law enforcement, and that will never change. I work every day to try to chip away at making this world a little safer for everyone else. But, when I decided to become a police officer, it was with the condition that I'd never get seriously involved with *anyone*, Willow."

I silently gasped.

"I will never leave behind a woman I love, and I'll never leave behind children to suffer the hell of not having a father." His tone was as firm as concrete, making it clear he would never change his mind on this.

My chest literally hurt, like it was burning from the inside.

"That's why I never allowed myself to act on my feelings for you, Willow." Holding my stare, he added, "And I never will."

Every remaining fragment of my heart fell for Shane at that moment. Yet it shattered at the sacrifice he was making. Shane would spend his entire life alone. He'd never be showered in daily love, would never wake up on Christmas morning to his own kids jumping on him in bed. He'd never watch them unwrap birthday gifts, or watch their first Little League game, or attend their school play. He would never hold his own child in his arms or kiss his bride on their wedding day.

He'd dedicate his life to making the world a safer place and retreat to his empty apartment, alone, every night.

Watching as the rest of the world fell in love and got their happily ever after.

I didn't want that for him. Selfishly, I wanted to be with him or else my heart would never be whole. But even if he didn't choose me, I wanted him to be happy.

"Shane..."

"I'm sorry I gave you mixed messages." He chewed his lip. "Candidly, I've never had to fight this hard before to keep my distance from someone."

But then I fell from the bridge. And his long-standing promise to help someone going through anything like his neighbor had us spending a lot of time together.

"I don't think you should shut yourself off like this, Shane. I think you deserve your happily ever after. And you wanting to dedicate your life to protect people..." My lower lip quivered. "The right woman won't look at that as a liability. She will look at it for what it is —heroic."

"This isn't about convincin' her to take this risk," Shane said. "I won't allow it."

"But I don't think you should make that decision for her. That's a decision that you make as a couple together."

"This is about protecting her," Shane said. "Before it ever gets to that stage. There's no point in having a relationship if I'm unwilling to let it become serious."

That's why he never allowed women over to his apartment; he didn't date, because why bother? He wouldn't allow a relationship to get serious, let alone lead to marriage, and he was too much of a gentleman to lead a woman on.

"Shane—"

"I know you want to talk me out of this, but I'm not changing my mind, Willow. And for the record? It's not because my feelings for you aren't strong enough. It's the opposite. If there is one person I want to ensure I never hurt, it's you."

My chest warmed at his loving comment, then froze from the consequence it left behind.

"But pushing me away hurts." Spending the rest of my life searching for a man half as remarkable as Shane hurt.

"I'm sorry, but I'll never put you in that position." Shane held my gaze. "Friendship is all I can ever offer you, Willow, if that's something you'd be willing to accept." His voice was low, like he feared my answer.

It took me a second to respond—not that I'd ever say no; it was just a lot to process. Something I would have to continue to process for who knows how long. But in the meantime, I didn't want him thinking I didn't care about him enough to keep him in my life in whatever capacity he could handle.

I offered a sad smile. "Of course."

He looked like he wanted to pull me against his chest and hug me. But instead, he let a few seconds pass and then cleared his throat.

"I guess we should talk about the next step in our investigation." His tone was tense, like he had to force himself to change the subject.

I nodded. Pretending my heart wasn't on fire. Maybe it would've been easier to go through life, assuming he didn't want me. Because if we both wanted each other...knowing nothing could ever come of it was as painful as being dipped in acid.

"Why don't you call Ezra and see if he'd be willin' to talk in person?"

"I already did," I said.

Shane stilled.

"I'm meeting him for coffee in the morning."

Shane set his beer down. "The hell you are."

"He's not going to talk to you, Shane. The last time he saw you, you had your forearm on his throat."

"If you think I'm going to let you meet with a guy that may have already tried to kill you once, you obviously know nothin' about me."

"I have an idea how I can meet him and still keep myself safe..."

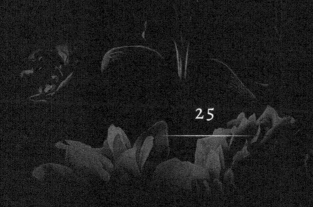

## 25

G oose bumps erupted all over my skin and exploded up my neck to my scalp. My heart joined the party, thumping against my ribs.

*I feel like someone's watching me.*

But that was stupid. I was inside my apartment, alone, the door locked. Safe. And if need be, Shane was on the other side of my apartment wall, having left less than an hour ago. There was absolutely no reason for this alarm circulating through my bloodstream.

To prove my point, I hoisted myself up off the couch and went into the kitchen, grabbing a small bag of popcorn out of the cabinet.

I tried to eat a kernel, but my stomach was too busy pleading with me to *run.*

I slammed the popcorn down.

This was moronic. Maybe this case reminded me that out there, other people did get hurt. Other people were in danger.

That's probably all this was. My body in some sort of heightened sense of alarm, even though it was unwarranted.

I moved back to the couch and flipped through the channels until I got to the comedy station.

But something drew my eye to my sliding glass door, which

looked out over the space between two buildings. In the summer, it contained a small garden area intended to be a gathering place between the surrounding apartment buildings—one of the features I loved, because it reminded me of the garden my dad and I had started to build. In the winter, the space was a barren chamber of concrete—dark, the only light coming from the surrounding windows.

It was out there, forty feet away—a figure.

A human figure.

*They're staring right at me.*

All the saliva in my mouth evaporated, and my heart started pounding.

They weren't staring at me. This was in my head. I couldn't even see their face—heck, I couldn't even see if it was a man or a woman. Just because they were facing this way didn't mean they were staring at me. There were tons of first-floor apartments, and they could be staring at any one of them. They were probably just out there, smoking or something, since you couldn't do that inside.

But my sixth sense wouldn't stop screaming at me.

*They aren't staring at anyone else, Willow.*

*They're staring at you.*

*Run.*

Despite my trembling limbs, I got up and stood in front of the glass. Staring right back. And when I did, the figure walked into the night, swallowed by its darkness.

"I EMAILED YOU A WORD DOCUMENT A FEW MINUTES AGO," I SAID.

Shane eyed me. "Come right in."

My cheeks heated. I'd stormed into his apartment without knocking. *What is wrong with me? I never do this kind of stuff.*

And Shane was in his boxer briefs, his hair messy—how did messy hair look even sexier, by the way?—sitting on his couch, sipping a cup of coffee. His tattoos wove around his skin, trying to distract me from my mission. Trying to make my eyes wander to all the curves of his muscles and his airbrushed-looking stomach.

Being only friends with him was going to be seriously hard.

Rule number one: I needed to avoid ever seeing this much of his skin again.

"I'm sorry for barging in." And now that I was thinking of it, "Don't you lock your door?"

"Not since you were almost killed, no." He set his mug down on the coffee table and looked at me with those ridiculously sexy sapphires of his.

"Why?" Chicago was a major city with the crime rate to prove it. Not a safe small town.

Shane's steely gaze remained on me. "Because if you're ever in trouble, I'm not wasting precious seconds getting to you."

My neck blazed now, and my stomach warmed.

Rule number two: He couldn't say things like that.

"You think someone might come after me again?" I asked.

"You know the answer to that."

Last night's figure flashed through my mind. There one minute, gone the next. So swiftly, I'd questioned if I'd seen anything at all. Plus, seeing a figure outside a huge apartment complex didn't mean someone was stalking me. But with the toothbrush, bookmark, and clogged drain, I'd feel safer if Shane looked into this.

"I know we're looking at my inner circle or whatever, but that's a list of every guy that's DM'd me on social media in the past six months," I said, referring to the email I'd sent. "Thought we should look into them, just in case."

I wished I could get my hands on company records without a warrant—and without risking my job—so we could look into the people who'd been recently fired. But one step at a time…

Shane stared at his phone, then glared at me. "This is a huge freakin' list."

"Noted. Where do we begin?"

Shane scrolled along the document on his phone, then sat back on the couch and evaluated me. "What brought this on?"

"Just...being cautious," I said.

Shane eyed me skeptically. "You're gettin' scared."

"No."

Even more skepticism oozed from that perfect face.

"You sort it in any specific order?" Shane asked.

I nodded. "Yes. From creepiest and most persistent to the least."

Shane frowned. "You get *any* sleep?"

Not really. "How long will it take?"

Shane stood up, and my inappropriate eyes wandered down his ripped stomach. When I met his gaze again, he smirked.

Rule number three: I had to stop fantasizing about what he looked like with no boxers on, and he had to stop liking my obvious enjoyment of his eye candy.

Damn saliva in my mouth.

He stepped toward the kitchen, but stopped and put his hand on my hip. Kissing the top of my head.

Damn heart. How long would it take to get the memo I wasn't allowed to feel sparks from his affection?

"I'll get started on it later this morning, but first, you need to convince me again to go through with your suicidal plan."

M y potential killer walked through the front door of the café, his eyes scanning the place for me.

I waved, trying to get his attention before he spotted Shane, who was sitting six tables to my right. It took forever to convince Shane to sit that far away from me after losing the battle to have him stay outside, but at least he wasn't parked right next to me. Still, it was too damn close if you wanted my opinion. Because if Ezra saw him, he wouldn't be answering any of our questions.

And I had a lot of questions. I wanted to ask about his past with the assault and battery accusation. And most urgently, about being the last person who talked to me before I plunged into the icy Chicago River.

I felt safe, meeting Ezra here, since it was a public coffee shop and I was sitting at a table along a wall of windows facing a public side- walk. The place was fairly busy, morning rush hour in full swing with a line of ten people at the counter, ordering coffee to go, while a few others had the luxury of camping out at the tables. Some talking to another person, most staring at their cell phone screens as they downed a cup of caffeine. The smell of freshly ground coffee mixed with the sweet scent of chocolate pastries while the hum of cappuccino makers blended with people's voices. All very mundane. Safe.

But what I didn't feel great about was Shane, who glared at Ezra like he was reconsidering this entire setup. And the tight look on his face? Made me wonder...

*Will Shane control his emotions long enough for me to get the answers we need?*

Ezra spotted me, smiled, and walked over, carrying a fresh bouquet. Wildflowers this time.

My heart ached at the memory of putting wildflowers on my dad's casket. I had to shove it aside to focus on the task in front of me.

"Morning." Ezra had styled his blond hair with fresh product and wore black slacks and a gray shirt beneath his wool coat.

He handed me the flowers and, right before he sat down, kissed my cheek.

A loud clank drew my eyes toward Shane, who was glaring at Ezra.

"I got you your usual," I said, nodding to the coffee on the table.

He didn't take a sip right away, instead clearing his throat.

"Listen, I'm sorry for how I behaved the last time we talked. I don't know what came over me when I threw that vase."

His tone seemed sincere, and he looked at my hand like he wanted to take it in his, but he forced himself to give me space.

"I've never seen you act like that before."

Ezra wiped his lips. "Yeah. I'm not sure what happened. I guess I just..." He squeezed his lower lip. "When we first broke up, I convinced myself you just needed some time and that you would eventually come back to me. But now, we're coming up on the sixth-month mark, and that feels like a milestone. If I don't get you back soon, too much time will have passed for you to give me another chance. And..."

Ezra stared at me as his lips fell into a somber grimace.

"Willow, I keep trying, but I just cannot imagine my life without you in it."

I kept the tone of my voice calm, careful with my word choice.

"If you wanted me in your life, why haven't you been completely honest with me?"

Ezra blinked. "What do you mean?"

"I know about you being a suspect in an assault when you were a teen."

Ezra's brows started with shock but then settled on anger.

"Let me guess. That neighbor cop looked into me."

*That's not a denial.*

"Why did you keep it from me?" I asked.

"Why is this guy poking around in my damn business?"

"The whole time we were together, you never once mentioned it."

"Because I threw a vase at your wall? He's what, trying to convince you I'm some violent felon?"

Out of the corner of my eye, I saw Shane tense at the tone of Ezra's voice. I doubted Shane could make out all our words, but Ezra's body language spoke volumes about how pissed he was.

"Why did you hurt that guy?" I asked.

"Why is he looking into me? Does he want to get into your pants or something?"

"Why did you hide it from me?"

"That's it, isn't it? He wants you, and he knows I might win you back, so he's trying to discredit me."

"He doesn't want to get into my pants, Ezra. You keep asking me to trust you, but to do that, I need you to be honest with me. Tell me what happened."

Ezra was clearly struggling to let go of his anger over my neighbor poking around in his business, but eventually, he must've realized that if his plan was to convince me to give him another chance, he couldn't do that with a big secret standing between us.

"I was at a party and walked in on my buddy taking advantage of a girl. So, I beat the crap out of him."

I blinked. "Why would they name you a *suspect* if you were just protecting someone?"

"Because cops don't take too kindly to vigilante justice."

I wasn't sure I believed him. What a noble version of events to explain a criminal past. The old Willow would have accepted his explanation at face value, but the new Willow had come here to see the look on his face, his demeanor, to try to sort out fact from fiction.

"Why didn't you tell me?" I challenged.

"It isn't something I'm proud of, Willow. And you know I'm working toward a career in politics. If I want to get elected to a senior role, like governor or senator, being a suspect in a violent attack isn't something I can have out in the open. So, I keep it to myself."

Ezra's boss was well connected in this city—and Washington—so with one phone call, he could drastically cut down, if not eliminate, Ezra's career.

"Is that why you asked me here?" Ezra's brows furrowed in offense. "Because your neighbor dug up dirt on me?"

"No," I said. At least, not fully. "There's something I want to ask you."

Ezra waited.

"Saturday night, you called me. But I don't remember what we talked about."

Ezra chuckled lightly. "I barely remember it myself. Drunk dial. I was at a club with my boys, talking about how much I wanted you back."

My cheeks heated.

"And I do want you back. I've changed, Willow, I swear."

"Is that what you said when you called me on Saturday night?"

He smiled. "I think so? Honestly, I don't remember a lot about that call. Ended up passing out at three a.m., so the bouncer tossed me into an Uber."

He was at a club all night? Until he passed out? That would be something we could prove.

"Who paid for the Uber?" I asked.

Ezra looked confused. "Me. Why?"

"Can I see your app?"

"Why?"

I didn't answer him.

"Is this a trust test?" Ezra asked. "To see if you can trust me again?

Because I swear I was not with a girl. Look." He pulled out his phone, opened up the app, and showed me the ride data from Saturday night.

Uber arrived at the club at 2:58 a.m. and dropped Ezra off at his apartment twelve minutes later.

His story was checking out, but...

"Did we see each other Saturday night?"

A line appeared between Ezra's eyebrows. "No. Why?"

Was it possible that sometime between the phone call and his three a.m. ride home, he had seen me?

"What happened Saturday night?" Ezra asked.

I took a sip of my coffee, unsure how to answer this.

Ezra's eyes landed on my broken wrist. "Did that happen to you on Saturday night?"

"I should go."

His voice hitched in alarm. "Willow, did someone do that to you?"

"It doesn't matter."

"To hell it doesn't. If someone did that to you, so help me, I'll..." Ezra composed himself before finishing his threat.

That look in his eyes seemed completely genuine. Was it real? Or was that old, gullible me resurfacing?

"What happened?" he pressed.

I sucked my bottom lip between my teeth, debating how to answer this.

"I fell off a bridge."

Ezra sat back in his seat. "You *what?*"

"Shane pulled me out of the water."

It took several seconds for Ezra to digest that, like my proclamation had punched him in the chest.

"Your neighbor?"

I nodded.

"How did you fall?"

"Police are trying to figure that out."

"You don't remember it?"

I shook my head.

Ezra looked down and to the side, putting the pieces together.

"Wait, are you asking me if *I* had something to do with it?"

I said nothing.

His jaw settled into offense.

"In a city of three million people, your neighbor happened to be at the exact time and place you went off a bridge, and you ask *me*? You should ask him these questions."

"What did you mean, I'd regret it?" I pressed.

"This is un-freaking-believable," Ezra snarled. "I didn't push you off some goddamn bridge. Maybe no one pushed you. Maybe you did this to yourself."

"What is that supposed to mean?"

"I heard you've been depressed lately."

"From who?" I asked.

"The anniversary of your dad's death. All that crap going on at work. Plus, all the stuff going on with your family."

I raised my chin and pretended his words hadn't penetrated my confidence. He was the third person to suggest I may have done this to myself—De Luca, Amelia, now him. If three independent people thought it might be true, could it be?

Was it possible I was so down, I was suicidal?

"When we broke up, you said I would regret it. What did you mean by that?"

"*That's* why you're asking me this?"

I waited.

Ezra sighed and rubbed his eyes, but thankfully, the anger from his voice dissipated as he answered, "I was angry, and I thought you'd eventually see what I did—that we're meant to be together."

I pressed my fingers against my temples, feeling so damn confused. Everything Ezra was saying made complete sense. He'd shown me his receipts. He answered all of my intrusive questions. If another failed attempt to win me back had resulted in some explosive fight where he had tried to kill me, why would he send me flowers and show up at my apartment soon after? For all he knew, I would remember who had done it. So, why risk it? It made no sense.

"Thank you for coming." I stood up next to the booth. I needed time to digest all of this and figure out my next steps. If it wasn't Ezra, who else could it be?

Ezra mirrored my movements, looking desperate to get his point across before I walked away.

"Willow, please. I swear to you, I did not hurt you." He brought his palm to my shoulder. "I would never hurt you. I want you back."

"Take your fuckin' hands off her." Shane yanked Ezra's hand away from me, twisting his arm.

"Dude, what the fuck?" Ezra cried out rather than fighting back. Smart move for a future politician to *not* fight with a law enforcement officer in public.

"Let him go," I said.

Ezra could fight back, this could escalate, and since Ezra's touch hadn't been violent, Shane would be the one in trouble.

Shane shoved off of Ezra, who rubbed his forearm, glaring at him.

"What the hell is he doing here?" Ezra looked from me to Shane, betrayal locking his jaw. "He was here the whole time?"

"I..."

"What was this, some kind of attempt to set me up?" His question was dark and laced with warning.

"No." Not exactly.

Ezra glanced between me and Shane one final time.

"You'd better be careful trusting him, Willow. He's getting into your head, making you suspect everyone in your life, but from what you told me? There's only one person in your life that was anywhere near your fall on Saturday."

## 27

"So, he offered no proof as to his whereabouts at ten o'clock Saturday night," Shane argued.

I could feel my blood pressure spiking, and I jogged faster through the crosswalk. We'd left the café only minutes ago, after Ezra had stormed out.

The city was like a breathing organism. The "L" train roared overhead as vehicles crowded together in morning rush-hour traffic, their tires careening past us with no regard for human life. Wind cut through the buildings like a turbine, burning our noses and cheeks, not caring that it hurt. Seventy-story buildings cut any hope of the sun warming our skin.

"He showed me the Uber receipt." I clenched my fists. "He got picked up from a club and went directly home."

"*I was too drunk to remember what happened Saturday night* is not an alibi, Willow. It's a red flag."

A red flag.

I gritted my teeth, my head pounding as hard as my heart. How many goddamn red flags had we uncovered lately? Yet we never ruled out any of them! None of them. Ezra looked like a suspect, then he didn't—no, wait, he still did. I thought meeting him would get some answers, but no. Just more questions. Just like everything else in my life—the closer I got to the truth, the further it seemed to slip from my grasp.

I couldn't take it anymore. I pinched the bridge of my nose, fighting back tears. Fragments of conversations and implications bouncing through my thoughts.

*Your ex-boyfriend isn't letting you go, Willow.*

*Your mom has a million reasons to hurt you.*

*Will your sister benefit from your life insurance policy?*

*Can I get a list of the people who were fired from your work?*

*That list of guys who've sent DMs is freaking long.*

*Amelia has scratches on her arms. She tell you how they got there?*

And then the ones others had pointed out.

*You've sounded really down lately.*

*The anniversary of your dad's death. All that crap going on at work. Plus, all the stuff going on with your family.*

I had been feeling sad. Ezra had broken my heart a few months ago. Grief always surrounded the anniversary of my dad's death. I felt more alone than ever, my family and I on the outs again. How much can one person be pushed before they snap? Was it possible...

Was it possible I had done this to myself?

If I was depressed enough to end my life, would I have blocked that out too? Just like I blocked out the fall itself and blocked out whatever happened to my dad that left me covered in blood?

Ezra's words echoed through my head.

*In a city of three million people, your neighbor happened to be at the exact time and place you went off a bridge?*

*There's only one person in your life that was anywhere near your accident on Saturday—Shane.*

"We need to look closer at the timeline," Shane urged.

"Enough!" I ceased walking.

He rocked back on his heels and must've noticed my hands trembling because he softened his expression.

"I'm not tryin' to make your life difficult."

"But you are!" I said. "I know you don't mean to, but you are!"

Anger coursed through my veins at how much my life had been upended. And I knew it wasn't fair for me to feel this way, but instantly, all my anger was directed at Shane. He was the one that had been in my ear since this all started. He was the one making me look at everyone in my life like a murder suspect. Tearing my life to shreds along with any semblance of peace and normalcy.

I didn't know who I could trust anymore, and I couldn't continue living in this never-ending nightmare. I felt like I was going crazy. Looking at every person in my life through the lens of a police detective—it was just too much to take.

"You keep planting these seeds of doubt in my head with everyone!"

"Willow…"

"No, listen to me! Do you know what this feels like?" I said, taking a step toward him. "Imagine someone putting the most painful moments of *your* relationships under a microscope."

Shane put his palms up in surrender. "Look, I—"

"You know what that does? It makes you feel crazy! I don't trust anyone anymore! I don't trust Ezra, I don't trust my mom, or Amelia, or people at my work, or strangers who've DM'd me. I don't even trust *you!*"

Shane stilled, and his eyes hardened. "What are you talkin' about?"

"You were with me that day by the bridge! In a city of three million people, that's pretty coincidental."

His understanding evaporated, his eyes tightening in offense. "You think I would hurt you?"

"According to you, someone did. If we're throwing everyone else I care about into the mix, why not you?"

Shane's face darkened, and he took a hostile step closer to me. "You actually think, after everything I've done, that I would harm a hair on your head?"

I don't know why I took a step back, but I did. Repeatedly. Until my back pressed against the skyscraper behind me. If pedestrians were gawking at us, I'd be none the wiser. Right now, it was like Shane and I were alone, angry energy swirling together in a toxic bubble.

But if he thought putting one palm against the wall next to my head was going to intimidate me into shutting up, he had another thing coming.

"I don't know what to think anymore! That's the whole point. I don't even trust myself! Because you know what? I've been sad lately. Ezra's been trying to get me back, which has made all the pain of him breaking my heart resurface, reminding me of just how damn lonely I feel! I also hate my job, but I've been stuck without a plan for so long, it feels near impossible to move forward. And then...there's my family...who have been lying to me about my dad for years! I might've only recently confirmed this, but in my heart, I think I knew it all along. So, yeah, I've been down. And I never thought I was the type of person who would plunge to my death willingly, but maybe I was wrong. They say every human has a breaking point. Maybe I reached mine."

"You were screamin' bloody murder when you went off that bridge."

"Out of terror, I'm sure."

"If you wanted to kill yourself, you wouldn't have screamed like that."

"Says who? I watched a documentary one time about suicide off the Golden Gate Bridge. Do you know what they found when they interviewed the handful of people that survived?"

Shane's jaw tensed.

"Over ninety percent of people regretted it the instant they jumped. Even if I was screaming because I didn't want to die, it doesn't mean I didn't jump."

"You're terrified of drowning."

"But maybe I hadn't woken up that morning, intending to kill myself. Maybe something made me snap, and the bridge was right there when it happened."

"You don't remember the fall itself, but you remember the days and weeks leading up to it. If you were depressed enough to want to end your life, you would have remembered that, Willow. I really don't think you did this to yourself."

"Well, maybe you don't want to hear this because it would make you think less of me."

Anger punched through his eyes. "That's insulting."

"Maybe you don't want to admit to yourself that, deep down, you do wonder. Maybe you have some distorted image of me that doesn't quite jive with this hot mess of a girl who was so desperate to escape it all that she jumped from a bridge? Maybe you'd want to have nothing to do with that girl. And you want to prove to yourself that I'm not the type of girl who'd do something like that."

"How can you think so little of me?"

"Maybe the real reason you don't want to be with me is because you think it's true; you think I did this to myself."

Shane's jaw clenched. "Which is it, Willow? You think I'm a homicidal lunatic?" He paused. "Or a guy who is such a piece of shit that he would reject someone if they were hurting inside?"

My throat burned. "I..."

"Listen to my words carefully." His angry eyes captured mine as he rested his other palm next to my head, caging me. "I would never harm a hair on your head. And if you were hurting so badly that you would consider ending your life, I would spend every waking second proving to you that life is worth living."

"Shane..."

"I've always been honest with you, so hear me when I say this: There is *nothing* you could ever do or say that would make me think less of you. And there's nothin' you could do to make me want you less."

My lip quivered. He needed to keep those things to himself if we had any hope of keeping our emotions in check.

"What if you're wrong? What if you're seeing danger where there isn't any because of what you went through with Fallon? What if you're projecting those fears onto me?"

I hated myself the instant the words left my mouth. The instant I saw the look on his face. I felt ashamed, sickened by it. What was I turning into?

And how selfish was I being, allowing this—whatever this relationship was—to continue? Because it wasn't just my sense of stability that was on the line.

Shane was coming unglued. Even if he didn't jeopardize his career by getting involved in the case, he pinned Ezra up against the wall by his throat. And then nearly broke his wrist in the coffee shop. Not to mention, he pulled Clay over without due cause. I was not an expert in law enforcement, but none of this could be good. Shane was unraveling, and it was all my fault.

"Listen to me very carefully." Shane's voice was low and even. "My instincts are crisp as hell, and they are not contaminated by what happened with Fallon. Everything in my gut tells me someone did this to you, and I will not stop until we find out who it is. And make them pay."

"But if it's not because of what happened in your past, why are you this obsessed with it?"

"Because I'm falling in love with you, dammit!"

My breath snagged at the base of my throat as I studied his eyes—indigo yet burning red. I was pinned between him and the wall, his massive forearm muscles caging me in next to my ears. And all the vehicle engines faded until all I could hear was the beating of my heart.

As it thumped for Shane.

Shane looked at my mouth one final time, then claimed my lips with his. Silencing my fears and worries. Channeling his frustration into passion.

My chest pressed against his, expanding with each stolen breath. I wished we'd had this argument somewhere else, somewhere we could rip each other's clothes off and take our frustrations out.

His tongue assaulted mine in the best possible way while I greedily surrendered to it. Pulling his body tighter against mine. Grasping for the strength to not rip his clothes off and take him in public.

My cell phone's ring invaded our slice of heaven.

I ignored it. And welcomed Shane's fingers breaching the hem of my shirt.

My cell phone rang again.

I wanted to smash my back pocket against the wall, if only to make it shut up. But it didn't stop our hands from wandering, our mouths from dancing, pedestrians hooting and hollering at us as they passed.

When my cell phone rang for the third time in a row, Shane stepped back.

"You should get it," he growled breathlessly. "It must be important."

No. Nothing was important. Nothing but Shane, and his profession, and his mouth on mine. But evidently, he would not continue kissing me until I stopped whoever the hell was calling me from interrupting us again.

"Hello?" I couldn't hide my annoyance.

"Willow. Officer De Luca here. Got a minute?"

"I…"

"I'll make it brief. Remember I told you I'd pull the cameras near the bridge?"

Shane was looking at me, obviously concerned about whatever my face was telling him.

"Yeah?"

"Reviewed them. Only one camera had the angle of where you went over, and the quality is shit. It's dark, and you can't make out much, but you can see what happened right before you went into the water."

My heart raced in my chest.

"And?" I pressed.

"I'm sorry for not believing you, Willow. Shows *two* people on the bridge that night. Can't tell if the other person was male or female, but we can see a confrontation."

Shane's eyes grazed down to my free hand, and his brows furrowed when he noticed it trembling.

"We can see that in the scuffle, you're pushed over the railing."

## 28

"Do you recognize anything?" Detective Rosse, who was now in charge of my case, asked.

De Luca, Rosse, and I sat in a conference room at the Chicago Police station while Shane stood against the wall with his arms crossed so tightly, I worried his body would suffer vascular damage. Like the place wasn't already tense enough with its metal chairs, dramatically long rectangular table, and a mirror that was undoubtedly two-way glass.

A minute ago, they'd lowered the lights so I could see the flat screen hanging on the wall better. Not that it helped. I squinted at the footage.

"Can you play it again?"

The video rewound and started from the beginning.

"Why is the quality so bad?"

It was so grainy, I could see pixels. While I could make out two dark figures, if the footage wasn't time-stamped and the location confirmed by the police, I wouldn't even know one of them was me.

"Camera is a half block from the bridge. Only caught the incident in the upper right corner of the footage." And they'd zoomed in as best they could. "Do you recognize anything about the other person?"

I watched it again. Two figures appeared to face each other. Arm gestures suggested we were arguing—an argument that led to a wrestling match. And in that wrestling match, I went up over the railing. The other person stood on the bridge, watching as I fell into the deadly waters of the river below.

They crouched down, watching the water—presumably watching me get rescued by Shane—before they took off running.

"I can't make out anything," I said. "I can't even tell if it's a man or a woman."

"I don't see a lot of hair," Shane said. "Might indicate male. Although it could be a female with a short haircut or her hair pulled back."

I squinted at the footage again; Shane was right.

No long hair.

Rosse asked, "Know any women who have short hair?"

"No."

Rosse noted that in the digital notebook on his iPad. "We'll prioritize questioning men first, but we won't rule out a female."

We had already gone over everything else with him, filling him in on the life insurance policy, Ezra wanting me back and him calling me that night, the scratches on Amelia's arms, everything.

"I want to circle back to something you said," Rosse added. "You mentioned your company recently let several people go, and two of them were particularly disgruntled?"

"They'd put in over ten years with excellent performance evaluations and were panicked about losing their income," I said.

"Would you have met them outside of work?"

"No. I don't think so," I amended. "I mean, if they were crying and asked me to meet them somewhere public, there's a slight chance I might have, but I don't think anybody from work would've done this."

"Why's that?"

"I'm not the one who makes head-count targets. Executive management makes those. My job in HR is to help facilitate the head-count reductions, as directed by management. So, they would know this wasn't my fault."

Rosse evaluated me. He had bushy eyebrows and a square jaw that looked as if working Chicago's darkest cases had turned his face to stone.

"Sometimes, people misplace blame," he said.

I guess that was possible, but, "I didn't know them well, and I wouldn't meet a stranger late at night. Alone."

"Now that we have proof of foul play, I'll be contacting your company to get a list of those names."

He went silent for a moment, typing into his iPad.

"Anything else that you can think of that you haven't already mentioned?"

I was about to say no, but shut my mouth. A gesture Rosse surely noticed because he set his iPad down and stared at me.

"It's probably nothing." I hoped.

A line appeared between Shane's eyebrows.

"But right after that night, I noticed that my toothbrush had been moved."

Shane pushed off the wall.

"And later, I discovered that my bookmark was in the wrong spot. And then…"

Shane's body was a statue, his unblinking eyes fixed on me.

"I found this…lump of hair in my kitchen sink. Each of these things seemed strange at the time and made me feel uneasy. I even wondered if someone was playing mind games with me, but since nothing was missing, I thought I must be projecting my fear onto the situation."

"And you didn't mention this to the police?"

"Because I probably put the toothbrush in the wrong location and forgot which chapter I was on in my book. As for the hair, I don't know. Maybe I knocked my hairbrush in the sink one day and didn't realize it or something."

"You notice anything else in your apartment that's off?"

"No."

"*When* did you notice these items were out of place?"

"The first time I used them after getting released from the hospital. First time I brushed my teeth, the first time I read that book, and the first time I washed dishes."

Rosse poked at his iPad screen. "Let me ask you this: when you got home from the hospital, you found the door unsecure, correct?"

I nodded.

"Let's say someone *is* responsible for the items. Could all three have happened when your apartment was open?"

I nodded. "But why would anybody move those things around?"

Rosse captured me in his hardened gaze. "Just collecting facts at the moment, Ms. Johnson."

He set his iPad down again, as if that were all he needed.

"There's one other thing," I said.

*Shane's going to have an aneurysm over this.*

"There's a chance I saw someone watching me the other night."

*Yep, Shane's forehead vein is about to explode.*

"Outside my sliding glass door, I saw a figure, but I couldn't see well, so it might have been nothing."

Kaboom. The vein in Shane's neck exploded, too.

I twisted my fingers together as Rosse gathered the details—the date, the time. The whole while, Shane clenched his hands into fists and paced.

"I think I have what I need to get started."

I looked from Rosse, to De Luca, to Shane.

"Where does this leave us?"

"I'll be in touch when I know more. Meantime, take precautions to keep yourself safe, Ms. Johnson. Lock your doors. Don't walk at night alone. Don't meet anyone alone. Whoever did this to you is likely about to get formally questioned by law enforcement. Psychologically, they can feel backed into a corner. Turning up the heat on them, so to speak."

Yeah, but, "If the police are looking at them, they'd be risking their neck, trying something again. More likely to get caught." Right?

"When people who've committed a crime are backed into a corner, they don't always think rationally. And, in their mind, there's only one person who can identify them as your attempted killer."

Ice shot through my limbs.

"So, things are about to get a lot worse," I said. "More dangerous."

Rosse offered me an empathetic look. "I'd vary your routine if I were you. Just to be safe."

## 29

"**P**ack a bag," Shane said.

"Just slow down for a minute," I said. "This changes nothing."

"It changes everything." His eyes snapped to mine, his stare so intense, it almost cracked me in half.

He was right. It did change everything.

Rationally, I had been going along with Shane's investigation because it was the responsible thing to do. But deep down, I guess I never fully believed it. Until now.

Now, any fragment of hope that there was some alternative explanation we hadn't thought of yet had been obliterated. Blown up, the ashes of the life I thought I had falling around me until my once-colorful existence became entombed in gray.

I couldn't even cling to the hope that this person was a stranger anymore. Not only because of the statistics that it was likely someone I knew, but also because I would never meet a stranger alone, let alone in the dark of night like that. And I would never go for a walk late at night by myself—to bump into a stranger who happened to be a killer.

Which meant it had to be somebody I knew.

My lungs began to spasm, causing my fingers to tremble. Shane's gaze locked on my hands, and he stopped pacing.

"You okay?" His tone was deep with concern.

I shook my head.

*I don't think I'll ever feel okay again.*

"Someone in my life hates me enough to want me dead."

I wasn't one of those people that had dozens of friends. I had a small group of close friends; I had my family. And once, Ezra. Even though we had our ups and downs, these were all people that I trusted with my whole heart to never wish me harm. I never imagined that someone I invited into my inner circle could hate me so much, they would want me dead.

I felt completely and utterly shocked. Scared of what was going to come next. But I also felt angry.

What had I ever done to someone to warrant them throwing me off a bridge into the icy river? No matter what disagreements or arguments we might've ever had, nothing escalated to the point of murder. How dare they try to rob me of my life and all the things that I wanted to do.

I clenched my hands into balls. "My whole life, I've taken the high road when people have hurt my feelings or made mistakes," I said. "I'd forgive them and move forward. I forgave Ezra the first few times I saw problems with him. Long before I saw him kissing that other girl, I'd seen his eyes wander and caught him flirting. And every time my sister rejected me, I reminded myself she was going through a hard time, and I needed to be there to support her. I kept inviting Mom back into my life each time she abandoned me. I kept my friendship with Amelia, even though she'd gotten snarky with me for no reason frequently. And Tracey, who became selfish at times, breaking plans whenever a hot date asked her out."

Shane stepped closer to me.

"I always hold on to hope that things will get better, the same way I held on to hope when I was a kid, believing my mom would return whenever she left us. But how long do you hold on to things that are not good for you?"

Because reflecting on it, allowing people to mistreat you repeatedly isn't taking the high road or being a kindhearted person; it's just giving them a free pass to treat you like a doormat. And sends the message that you're okay with it. I held on to toxic relationships for far too long.

This tendency bled into other areas of my life as well. My job, for instance, which I'd continued to hold on to long after I'd grown to hate it.

I was angry at myself for having allowed this pattern of holding on to unhealthy things for so long that it almost cost me my life.

Whoever did this to me was probably someone who'd thrown up red flags along the way, someone I should have cut out of my life long ago. It was time to sift through these people, not only to find out who my killer was, but to also weed out the toxic relationships from those that lift me up rather than bring me down.

"I need to stand up to people, stand up for myself. All the time. Not just once in a while. And I need to decide what boundaries I'm comfortable with."

"Starting with me," Shane said.

I eyed him, confused by what he meant. Confused why that look of desire washed across his features as he unleashed that stare at me— the one he'd had before he kissed me against that skyscraper.

"When I saw that footage tonight, something changed for me, too. Seeing someone try to kill you, seeing you almost taken from me..." Shane paused. "I know this contradicts everything I told you before," he started. "And if you're not comfortable with it, you need to tell me."

His eyes pierced mine, and he took a step closer, studying my face, my eyes, my lips, my jaw. And he shook his head slowly, speaking in a soft tone this time. "I've been falling for you for a while," he admitted. "From the first moment I laid eyes on you and your beauty, I felt something. And when I met you, I was mesmerized by you. Most people would have been sheepish after a stranger witnessed their ex getting handsy with them, but you squared your shoulders to me and said Ezra was using your *slight overindulgence as an excuse to try to weasel his way back into your life.* Right then and there, I knew you were special, and I found myself wanting to learn everything I could about you. You might think I notice things like what coffee shop is your favorite or that you feed a stray cat because I'm a detective, but that's not it. I notice you, only you, Willow, because everything about you intrigues me. And all this time, I've been falling for you. Fought it with everything I had, but it was like fighting a rip current. A losing battle. And the more time I've spent with you, the faster that rip current shot me out to sea. And now, my heart is completely invested in you. And there's no goin' back."

"But you said—"

"I don't know what the future holds for us. I can't even think about that right now. All I can think about is you and how damn angry I am that someone did this to you. You don't deserve it. You're sweet and kind and would never hurt anyone, and whoever this Goddamn monster is that threw you over that bridge?" Shane's jaw ticced. "They deserve to suffer. When we find them, I want five minutes alone with them."

His affection, laced with vengeance, took a minute to digest.

"I don't want you to feel this angry." I wanted him to be happy. Always, because the truth was, I'd been falling for him, too.

"You know what's buried beneath the anger?" Shane asked. "Fear. I can't remember the last time that I've felt afraid. Because being in a dangerous job is a different fear—survival. But there's a fear far worse than dying."

He stepped even closer, so close that I could feel the heat coming off his chest, and looked down at my lips.

"Having someone you care deeply for die and not being able to stop it."

I sucked in a breath.

"I'm not going to die," I assured.

Shane stretched his fingers at his sides, the blue in his eyes darkening as he stared at me. "I lost my mom. When my dad died, part of her died too, and she was never the same again. I lost my sister when he died, because she changed. She went from being this hopeful, cheery person to the sullen version of herself who doesn't seem to be as happy as she once was. Over time, I lost my dad's entire side of the family because of the dynamics created in the aftermath of his death."

Shane tentatively traced my lower lip with his thumb, staring at my mouth, as if unable to imagine living without it pressed to his. His touch felt so incredible, I had to actively focus on his next words.

"I've lost enough in my life, Willow, and I will not lose you."

He began breathing heavily, his eyes glued to my lips, his hand sliding up my face, cupping my cheek.

"Are you still in pain?" He took another angry step toward me.

"What?"

"From the fall," he growled impatiently. "Are you still in pain?"

*What? "No?" Not really. Why?*

"Good." He pushed me against the wall.

Not gently.

And crashed his mouth to mine.

Oh. My. Word.

He stroked the side of my face with his knuckles as I opened my mouth, surrendering to Shane's tongue as it slid inside me. A flash of heat radiated down my throat, rippling over my chest, and engulfed the sensitive flesh between my legs. Flesh that came alive like electricity that had been turned on, now begging to be touched. Especially when he grabbed my hip and raised my arm above my head.

It was all like magic pixie dust that activated a hibernated part of my passion that entirely surrendered to the heat of his mouth on mine. Erasing any space between us, he pressed me harder against the wall, taking out all his anger and frustration out on my body.

We'd kissed before, but this... this was different. He'd professed his feelings for me, and though I didn't know where we'd go from here—feeling didn't mean he'd changed his stance on marriage—fighting to resist this wasn't working.

I pressed my tongue harder against his, making him groan into my mouth.

I wanted to swallow that groan; I wanted to eat it and feel it reverberate throughout my entire body as I pulled him on top of me. I wanted to see all of him and feel all of him. Inside me. Tasting me. Looking me in the eye as he made me his own.

He grazed his teeth along my jaw and kissed down my neck, thrusting his hips against me, pressing his excitement between my thighs.

"You feel what you do to me?" he asked.

"Yes," I whispered, breathlessly, my chest heaving.

When his mouth reclaimed mine, his hand breached the fabric of my shirt and slid up my belly, sending a spark of electricity to my chest as he moved his hands slowly over my skin, one agonizing inch at a time until finally, he palmed my breast.

And possessively squeezed it so hard, I cried out. A good cry. A please-do-it-again cry.

If this was angry Shane, I wanted to make him angry every day. I'd find reasons to pick fights with him, just so he'd throw me up against the wall and have his way with me. I would secretly pray that someone would cut him off in traffic or piss him off so he could come home and release his frustrations like this.

My nipple hardened even more as Shane pinched it between his thumb and finger, sending a shockwave of heat between my thighs. I pressed my breast harder against his hand.

"Don't stop," I whispered.

He grumbled a grouchy laugh and slipped his tongue deeper into my mouth, silently assuring me he had no plans to stop anytime soon.

He robbed my mouth of his, an icy need abandoning my lips as he looked me in the eye.

"You like this?" he asked, moving his hand to my other breast. And squeezing it.

"Yes," I managed.

"Tell me what you want, Willow."

He squeezed my other nipple, making my head fall against the wall, my back arching.

"I want you," I said.

He pulled my flesh against his, all my soft parts pressing up against all his hard ones, as I glided my hands over the contours of his shoulder muscles, feeling them tense beneath my palms.

Shane shot two hands around my thighs and lifted me up, wrapping my legs around his waist. Not breaking the kiss, he walked us a few steps to my kitchen.

And set me down on my table.

This time gently.

Standing between my knees, he guided me backward until I was lying down, him hovering over me, kissing me. Then inching my shirt up so he could move his kisses to my stomach. And continued to travel upward.

He moved my bra up, groaning at the sight of my exposed breasts, and when his mouth reached my nipple, I sucked in a breath. He swirled his tongue around and around my sensitive bud, sucking on me, tasting my skin, engulfing the fire between my legs into an inferno.

I locked eyes with him, his tongue firm and tight, then soft and tender as it spread its love to my nipple, around and around until my head fell back against the table. I could feel his groan of approval against my skin, and every inch of my body begged for his attention.

His mouth moved from one breast to the other, his tongue dancing over my skin, my nipples, while he'd palm the other side as he worked his ecstasy.

All the while, the heat between my legs was becoming unbearable.

He continued kissing, sucking me, nipping at me, though, as if he enjoyed making this wanton need grow until I couldn't take it anymore. I shoved my fingers into his hair, tugging it, until finally, his lips moved away from my breasts, leaving my skin lined with frosted goose bumps from the wetness.

He kissed up my neck, my jaw, and then my mouth again.

But his hands… his hands began to move. He was strong enough to hover over me, pressing his lips against mine while he unbuttoned my pants and slipped his hand beneath my panties.

Shane held my gaze as he slowly slipped one finger between my folds, a groan escaping my lips as he growled.

"You're so wet for me."

My body heated even more at the praise in his tone, and I didn't dare take my eyes off his as he slid his middle finger down, breaching my entrance.

"Shane," I whispered.

"I'm just getting started, Willow."

I grabbed his shoulders, and when he thrust two fingers inside of me, I arched my back. He moved his thumb to the sensitive bundle of tissue at the top of my center, knowing explicitly how to move his hand. The right pressure, the rhythm and cadence of his touch.

"You like that?" he asked.

I nodded, licking my lower lip.

He curled his fingers inside of me, hitting a delicate patch of nerves that made my eyes roll back as he pulled his fingers back slightly, then in. Over and over.

It felt so good the rest of the universe collapsed into nothing. The only thing that existed were his fingers stretching me, filling me as he worked the bundle of nerves on the inside, and circled the sensitive bud on the outside with his thumb. His eyes, watching me, his mouth falling open in lust as I began to move my hips against his palm. The sounds of my moans, his breathing, the smell of arousal electrifying the space around our bodies.

Shane moved his fingers softer at first, then harder, knowing my body better than my own, his jaw locking as he watched my facial expressions.

I liked that he watched me. I cherished how he'd notice when he'd hit me at the right pressure, and then do it again and again until he could see the wave inside of me building.

Desperate for its release, I pressed one of my hands on top of his and pushed down harder. He swirled his thumb over the apex of my center, making me start to come unglued.

He brought his mouth back to mine and whispered against my lips, "You feel so good, Willow."

That was all I needed to hear. I collapsed under the pleasure of his words, biting his lip and squeezing my legs so hard, I wondered if it hurt him.

"Willow," Shane groaned as I shuddered.

He continued to work my body until the last of my trembles subsided, and then he kissed my jaw, my neck.

I pushed his chest so I could sit up, and then I rubbed my hand on his engorged jeans, watching as his eyes shut, and his head fell back with a groan.

I wanted to taste him. Lick him. Feel him inside my mouth, and return the pleasure he'd just given me. And then I wanted him to pin me down and claim me.

Because if my orgasm was that strong with just his hand, I couldn't imagine how hard I'd come undone with him inside of me.

I unbuttoned his pants.

But suddenly, a harsh pounding on my door thwarted our passion session.

Three knocks.

With a fist, by the sound of it.

Shane looked at me with despair.

"I won't answer it," I whispered.

I unzipped his pants and began to pull his jeans down.

*Bam. Bam. Bam.*

"Ignore it," I whispered.

Shane looked less sure this time, glancing at my front door before letting me pull his pants down another couple of inches.

*Bam. Bam. Bam.*

"Willow, it's me. We need to talk right away."

## 30

"Why are you harassing Ezra?" Amelia snapped.

She didn't wait for me to invite her inside, just stormed past me into my apartment. Like it wasn't irritating enough that she'd interrupted Shane and me. Also, what was with the word *harassing*?

"He told me about your little coffee shop ambush." She glared at Shane. Who remained a statue against the far wall with his wrists crossed over his engorged pants. If she wasn't so self-centered, maybe she would see she'd interrupted something *intimate* with her incessant pounding.

"Since when do you and Ezra talk?" I crossed my arms over my chest.

Shane's eyes hardened as he looked at her hair. Which was in a bun. Amelia normally wore her hair down, but if someone had styled their hair in an updo that night, it might match the silhouette on that video.

"You're pretty upset that I questioned him," I said.

"Because he's a good guy and he doesn't deserve this. His boss has connections and might even fire him."

I eyed her. "How do *you* know that?" I'd never mentioned it.

Amelia's eyes twitched, and understanding etched into my bones.

How could I have been so blind?

A memory fired the clue I'd dismissed a while back. It was one of those things where, at the time, your instincts weren't *screaming* at you. But it was more of a gentle *huh-that's-odd* type of whisper.

*I WALK INTO THE CLUB WHERE I'M MEETING EZRA AND SEVERAL OF MY friends.*

*I arrive fifteen minutes early, so I assume I'm going to be the first one here, but I'm not. Sitting at the bar with their stools facing each other, Ezra and Amelia are talking. They're leaning forward, likely so they can hear each other over the noise of the music, but their faces are only a foot apart. And the way they're smiling at each other, it makes me uncomfortable.*

*How are they already halfway through a drink?*

*"Hey." Ezra smiles when he sees me. He stands up and gives me a kiss.*

*Amelia smiles too. But it doesn't meet her eyes.*

*"Why are you here so early?" I ask.*

*"Finished work a half hour ago," Ezra said. "Either had to go all the way home and then run late or just come directly here."*

*I look at Amelia.*

*"Got lucky with the 'L' train," she says. "Normally have to wait several minutes, but when I showed up to the platform, one showed up right away."*

*I guess that tracks.*

*Of course it does. Amelia is my friend. Why would I feel suspicious?*

BUT WHAT IF I HAD BEEN WRONG BACK THEN? EZRA KISS-CHEATED ON me one time and text-cheated another. Did it not stand a reason he might've been capable of full-blown cheating? Maybe even with one of my friends?

"You need to tell the detectives that Ezra wasn't involved with that bridge incident."

"I don't know that," I said.

"Ezra would never hurt anyone."

"He hurt me when he cheated on me."

"He didn't full-blown cheat."

Interesting. If she hadn't had sex with him, would she consider that not cheating, then?

"So, there are degrees to cheating now?"

"Ezra's boss has connections with politicians in Chicago."

"You said that already," I reminded her. "How exactly do you know that?"

"If those cops show up and ask him questions, one phone call, and Ezra won't be able to pursue a political career in this city. He could even lose his job."

"If someone had feelings for him, losing his job would be unfortunate. Since he might have to move."

I was testing her, and sure enough, her lips hardened.

"He doesn't have enough savings to weather that. How can you not care?"

I did care. But that wasn't the point of our conversation.

"How do you know all that about him?" I challenged.

"Tell the detectives to back off."

"How long have you two been close?" I asked.

Amelia huffed. "You're ridiculous."

"So, it doesn't bother you then? That he's been trying to get me back ever since I broke up with him?"

There. Right there. That flash of anger in her eyes confirmed it. She did have feelings for Ezra, and, yep, it bothered her that he wanted me back. A lot. That was why she was so fixated on him sending me flowers; it hurt her feelings.

I remembered something Ezra said about that night, how he'd called me to beg me for another chance.

I knew I shouldn't ask her questions about the case, but now that I could see the look in her eyes, I couldn't stop myself.

"Were you with Ezra the night I fell?"

She looked disgusted. "We're done here."

Amelia tried to walk past me, but I blocked her path.

Shane pushed off the wall and came closer.

"Did you know he called me that night?"

"You know, if you go around, treating everyone in your life like some psychopathic killer, whenever they figure out what happened, none of us will be here for you when you come crawling back to apologize."

"How did you get the scratches on your arms?"

"Go to hell, Willow."

Amelia walked around me and stormed out of my apartment.

31

"You okay?" Shane asked.

I didn't know what level Amelia and Ezra may have betrayed me, but something else she said formed a pit in my stomach because it reminded me of the fear I'd had since day one.

"She's right," I said. "Once Rosse starts questioning everyone, people are going to be so offended, they may shut me out of their lives."

"That's not true."

"Maybe not for everyone, but my family? Our relationship isn't strong enough to have someone poking around like that."

Look how upset I'd made my mother when I confronted her about lying to me my whole life. My questions had already driven a wedge in our relationship, and now, Rosse was going to probe her about my life insurance policy, her whereabouts, and probably ask her point-blank if she'd tried to hurt me. Mom would feel attacked by me. Again. This time pegged as an awful human whose own daughter sent cops to her house, accusing her of attempted murder.

She might never talk to me again. And when Hayley found out about it, she would probably never talk to me again, either.

I scrubbed my hands over my face.

"Willow." Shane walked up to me, has dark hair accenting his blue eyes as he brought his palm to my cheek—brushing my skin with this thumb, as if he knew his touch was what I needed. And when he spoke, he kept his tone cautious. "Have you ever seen Amelia get violent?"

"No."

Relief did not flood Shane's face. I could see the wheels turning in his head, undoubtedly thinking about her hairstyle, the scratches on her arms, and whatever mysterious relationship she and Ezra obviously had.

"I need to talk to my mom and sister," I said. "I need to talk to them before it's too late."

Shane's lips tightened. "I don't think that's such a good idea."

"The last time I talked to them, I upset them. I can't risk ending things like that. I need a chance to mend things—or at the very least, get better closure."

"I still don't think it's a good idea."

"Rosse agrees the hair points toward a guy."

Shane frowned. Looked at the front door Amelia and her bun had walked through. "It's not concrete enough to risk your life."

"I'm sorry, but I'm doing this with or without your approval."

Shane bit his lip and then placed both of his hands on my upper arms. "I'm going to say somethin', and you're not going to freak out."

"Prefacing anything with that sentence will make anyone freak out."

"I made some calls. Put a…contingency plan in place, just in case things went south."

"A contingency plan."

"With Amelia showin' up here and Rosse about to question people, I think it's time. I arranged for us to stay in a cabin. Couple hours northwest. Wooded area, near a lake. It'll be beautiful this time of year."

"I have to work. So do you."

"The place has internet. You won't have to take full vacation weeks if you work remotely."

"Weeks?" My mouth gaped. "Are you crazy?"

"Hopefully, it won't be that long, but even if it is, I have plenty of vacation time built up."

"No. And in case you forgot, I've already missed work, and I don't want to ask the company for exceptions to be made for me to work remotely."

His jaw tightened. "I'd like you to pack a bag."

"No."

Shane glared at me.

I guess we weren't going to get back to making love right now.

"You're not safe here."

"Most everyone in my life knows that I live next door to a law enforcement officer. Even if they did want to hurt me again, they wouldn't be stupid enough to come to my place."

This was so surreal, plotting out possible attack points.

No, I wasn't planning them out. Shane and Rosse had to be wrong. Whoever did this was counting their lucky stars that they had gotten away with it, and they would never come back and try again.

The real question was, would I ever figure out who did it?

If I didn't, I could see two scenarios playing out. Either I would cut almost everybody out of my life out of fear or I wouldn't, and my attempted killer would remain in my life forever. I could sit across the dinner table with them someday and have no idea that they tried to end my life.

The thought made me sick. Neither scenario was acceptable. The only acceptable solution was to find out who did this.

And in the meantime, for me to talk to my mom and sister before it was too late.

"I'm heading to my mother's house. You're welcome to come, but you'll have to stay in the car."

## 32

"I'm sorry I upset you," I said.

I held the photo frame, staring into the eyes of a man I would never know. He had his arms around me and Hayley, Mom standing next to him with a smile on her face wider than I'd ever seen it. Mom's smiles never reached her eyes like that anymore, and her eyes didn't sparkle with optimism.

She sat in her rocking chair, clutching a glass of amber liquid. She had taken up smoking again, evidently, blowing out a long puff of poison as she stared at me with impassive eyes. Mascara clumped in the corners, her eyeliner smudged, like her cherry lipstick.

Shane sat parked out front, unwilling to leave me alone until they identified that person on the bridge. He even made me come up with a signal "just in case" something happened and I couldn't get to my phone—to flicker the lights. Even then, it was nearly impossible to get my bodyguard to stand down.

But he understood what was at stake with my coming here.

My goal was simple. I needed to put my family's past behind me once and for all. Because if I didn't let go of it, resentment would spread its weeds and strangle my soul. I'd become a bitter version of myself, filled with the heavy anger from my past anchoring my heart, preventing me from sailing into the clear skies of my future.

And after experiencing the joy I felt anytime I was with Shane, I was choosing a different destiny. I was choosing happiness over hurt.

To do that, I would no longer fight against the current of trying to morph my relationships with my mother and sister into something that they weren't. I would try one last time to learn whatever Mom was willing to share with me, and then I would accept these relationships for what they were.

Only then would I be free.

I sat on Mom's couch, her living room reeking of stale smoke.

She tapped her cigarette above an ashtray, its ashes flaking off and joining a little mountain of old ones.

"I still don't understand why you lied to me." I kept my voice low and even. Sad, not accusatory.

"I told you, I was trying to protect you."

"But how?" I pressed. "How does keeping me in the dark protect me?"

My mom pursed her lips. "Remember what you told me when you and Ezra broke up?"

I stilled; I'd been vulnerable at that time in my life and shared what Ezra had done. Not typical with the lack of depth in our relationship.

"Remember how it affected your self-esteem? Even though *his* offensive actions had no bearing on your beauty or talent?"

My hit to my self-worth only lasted a week, and, yes, I was aware of how pathetic it sounded to let him affect me.

"Imagine if that was something dark that would haunt you and you'd question your self-worth for the rest of your life, not just after a breakup. I didn't want that for you, Willow. I wanted you to feel the sun on your face."

My stomach ached with an open pit expanding.

"Does everyone else know what happened to Dad, except me?"

She took a long drag of her smoke, not making eye contact. With each second that passed, my body grew colder, lacking the warmth I craved.

"Why did you single me out?" I asked.

"I didn't single you out," Mom said. "I tried to protect your sister, too, but she—" Mom tightened her lips, which were surrounded by premature wrinkles, caked with makeup.

"She what?"

"When someone dies, you don't talk about the bad parts of them, Willow. You talk about the good parts. Especially with their children. I was honestly trying to protect you," she repeated. And this time, pain seeped through every syllable.

"I thought if you knew everything, it would hold you back. You'd see yourself as less than worthy, preventing you from getting into healthy relationships or pursuing your dreams."

My *dreams*. Mental note: I needed to check the status of my LLC filing and set up bank accounts for it once I got my ID number from the state of Illinois.

"Why would Dad getting killed make me feel less than worthy?"

Mom took another long drag. The cloud of smoke billowed from her mouth as she looked up at the ceiling—or maybe up to the heavens—as if willing them to give her the right answers.

"Dad did something to get himself killed." I deduced. "He hurt someone, didn't he?"

"I didn't want the weight of this on you. I wanted you to be free of it. And," she added, "I suppose we all want our loved ones to be remembered by their best qualities, not their worst."

"Was it a child?" That would explain the hushed whispers echoing through my nightmares.

Her eyes snapped to mine.

"Did Dad do something to a kid?"

"No." Mom's eyes shimmered with tears.

I had to remind myself this wasn't just about me. Mom lost the love of her life, the father to her children, and in her own way, she was trying to honor his memory—at least through the eyes of his daughters.

"Then, why are you *still* keeping it from me?" I whispered.

She'd warned me loud and clear, but I kept asking.

I wiped my tear.

Mom took another long drag of her cigarette and flipped it into the ashtray.

"Because of *who* killed him," she said.

Who?

Who had killed him? Keeping this a secret from me my whole life was because of *who* had killed him? Who was it? That meant it wasn't a stranger, then. It had to be someone close to us. Someone she was protecting, then.

But who? Were they in jail? And who, in her eyes, would be worthy of a lifelong cover-up for the sake of her daughter?

Hayley said it was a *he*. But Gramps was dead before Dad died, Mom and Dad had no brothers, and there were no other men in our lives—at least none I was aware of. And once I called Hayley on it, she gave me that strange look that I had interpreted as guilt for having let a detail slip. But what if it wasn't guilt? What if she'd said it to steer me away from the actual killer?

Suddenly, a hypothesis crashed into my head, as if it had been there all along. My mom's suffocating grief...had it been heightened with guilt? Not wanting to sully his name—was it because he was doing something terrible behind closed doors? Domestic violence turns deadly every day. Had my mom and dad had a relationship that, at times, turned violent, and in one of my dad's outbursts, Mom had killed him? And hadn't been charged because it was self-defense?

It would explain her extreme emotional swings that I'd chalked up to grief—leaving the house and kids that she felt she'd destroyed. If she took a life—the life of the father of her children—she'd only be able to reassure herself so many times that it was necessary.

But it would only be human to replay that horrifying event repeatedly, thinking, *If I had done this or that, perhaps I could've gotten away, and he'd still be alive. And my daughters would still have their father.*

Was that the dark family secret?

Mom flicked her cigarette over the ashtray four more times, even though it didn't need it.

"Who killed him?" I whispered.

Mom took a long drag, as if summoning the courage for something. Her eyebrows pulled together, deepening the wrinkle between them as she shook her head.

"Willow, sometimes, the past is best left in the past. I can assure you, he loved you girls more than anything."

My chest ached, and seeing the torment in her eyes made me feel terrible for having asked her so many times for answers. Because now that I wondered if my mother might have taken Dad's life in self-defense, I realized my every word was a shovel, digging up pain.

No matter how curious I might be about what happened, I would never confront my mom about this again. I would allow her the space to heal. These were her boundaries—talking about Dad's death was off-limits—and I needed to accept it once and for all. Did that mean I'd give up on getting answers? No. I'd hire a private investigator and leave her out of it so she and I could move forward in whatever space this left us. Would I feel as close to her as I could if she had been honest with me? No. But again, I needed to accept this version of the relationship we *did* have rather than trying to hope it would change.

And accepting that made me feel the first wave of peace I'd had in a long time.

My cell phone buzzed.

*Shane: Rosse just texted me. He has an update and is going to call you about it.*

*Me: What is it?*

*Shane. He didn't say. When your phone rings, answer it.*

I didn't know how long I had before Rosse called, but I felt a small measure of closure with my mother to put this portion of our relationship—where I inundated her about our past—behind me. And now, I had one more person to clear the runway with.

Hayley, who just walked into the house.

It was time to find out if she had any desire to have a relationship with me or if I was about to close this door forever…

## 33

"What are you doing here?" Hayley spat when she spotted me.
"Hello to you too," I said.

"You know, your *boyfriend* is sitting outside in a car, not looking conspicuous at all."

"He drove me here."

Mom extinguished her cigarette, flipped the footrest down on her recliner with force, and marched over to my sister. Holding her head between her hands as she stared into her eyes.

"I'm not high, Mom. Thanks for the vote of confidence, by the way." Hayley kicked her shoes off and dumped her coat on the floor.

"I want to talk to you," I said to Hayley.

"Now's not a good time."

"It's never a good time."

Hayley went to the refrigerator, pulled out a bottle of water, and walked toward the hallway that led to the back bedrooms.

I blocked her path.

"Well, I don't want to talk to you right now, so move."

I kept my face neutral, as if her words hadn't blasted another hole in my heart. Why did this still affect me? Her constant rejection was the only common thread in the fabric of our relationship.

But something had changed.

Me.

Did she even want a relationship with me? I would no longer pursue one if she didn't, and before I closed the door forever, I'd get some things off my chest.

"It's important," I said, keeping my tone strong when I added, "Please."

Hayley glared at me.

"Hayley, you could spend a few minutes talking to your sister," Mom said.

As if we were kids and not grown adults. Hayley was ten years older than me. You'd think out of the two of us, she wouldn't need Mom to step in and referee.

"Five minutes," Hayley said. "I have plans."

Hayley plopped into the chair Mom had been sitting in.

"I'll give you girls some privacy," Mom said. "But when you're done, there's something important I want to tell you girls."

Interesting. Mom hadn't sat us both down and talked to us for years. I could tell by the nervousness dancing across her face that it was something she wasn't expecting we'd react positively to.

Mom disappeared into the back hallway.

I took a breath, focusing on what I wanted to ask her, nerves sweeping through me. Deep down, I'd felt fairly confident I would always have a relationship with my mother. My sister, on the other hand...our relationship felt like a rock dangling precariously over a cliff—one that, for years, had taken all my energy to keep it from falling into the cavern, where I'd never see it again.

"What do you want?" Hayley looked at her watch.

"I want to know what I ever did to make you so angry."

She glared at me. My sister hated talking about anything emotional—collateral damage from our dad dying.

"Do you have to be so freaking dramatic all the time?"

"You rarely answer my calls or texts, and if you do agree to hang out with me, you don't show up half the time."

"I'm busy."

"That was an excuse I swallowed for years, but it doesn't work anymore."

"Willow, for God's sake, not everything is about you."

"If you don't want things to change between us, that's fine. I'll stop trying and leave you alone." I wasn't going to beg to be in someone's life that didn't want me there; I deserved better than that. "But I deserve to know the reason why. What did I do to make you hate me so much?"

My sister's eyes rounded slightly. Our whole life, I'd chased after her, and I had never thought about it before, but maybe a part of her found some comfort in that chase—having someone work that hard to want to spend time with her. And now, I was ending it.

I wouldn't feel guilty about it, either. She could look hurt all she wanted, but it was nothing compared to the hurt that she had caused me throughout our lives. I was simply accepting this for what it was and hoping to understand what got us here.

Hayley looked down and began cracking her knuckles—something that she did whenever she felt anxious. I wondered if she was processing this—the official end of our relationship as we knew it.

"I don't hate you," she whispered. It was the gentlest tone I think she had ever taken with me. "I envy you."

She wouldn't—or couldn't—make eye contact with me, as if embarrassed by her confession.

"Envy what?"

"You got to live a normal life," she said. "I never did. You were only four when Dad died, so you didn't know what you lost. But I did."

I wanted to tell her she was wrong, that I had more memories and heartbreak than she gave me credit for. But I said, "I've envied you all of these years because you had more time with Dad than I did."

My sister's lip quivered, as if pain wrapped around her and squeezed until she could no longer breathe.

"He didn't deserve to die," she whispered.

If I asked her if Mom killed him, would she tell me? Would that be a betrayal to Mom, who'd made it clear she wanted to close that door forever? Was it my secret to uncover?

When Hayley's eyes met mine, they were shimmering.

"He died in front of us."

My stomach dropped like the anchor of a big ship.

That's why I had blood on me that day in the hospital. They must have checked me over to make sure I hadn't been hurt, too.

"But you don't remember it because you were young enough to block it out. You got to move on with your life without knowing what happened to Dad."

Hayley's eyes filled with tears, and it stunned me. I'd seen a lot of sides to Hayley in our years, but I'd never seen her vulnerable.

"I didn't get that." She cleared her throat and swiped angrily at her cheek. "Any time I felt Dad's loss, whether it was a holiday or just a random day where I really missed him...I didn't have the luxury of not knowing why he wasn't there."

Hayley curled her lips, her tone venomous. "Someone killed my father and took him from me."

Was that why Mom and Hayley had such an up-and-down relationship? Up, because Mom supported Hayley through everything. But down, because if Mom was the one who killed him, maybe Hayley knew that and held on to that blame.

Hayley picked at her fingernails harshly.

"Every time Dad wasn't there, every event that he didn't get to come to, that's all I could think about—that someone murdered him."

I kept my voice soft, not wanting to sound accusing. Just wanting to understand her better.

"That's why you started doing drugs," I realized.

She wrapped her arms around her chest. Hayley had always seemed so powerful to me, but right now, she looked frail, her shoulder bones poking out of her too-thin frame.

"It was the only way to escape this...anger inside of me."

Good Lord, poor Hayley.

"Who killed him, Hayley?"

To this, her features fell into vengeance, and she cracked her knuckles so loudly, they sounded like bones snapping. Her tight eyes were lost in a sea of rage, her jaw clenched. Any mention of the person who murdered our father flipped a switch, transforming her from a broken soul to an enraged human who'd give anything to annihilate the person who stole our father from us.

Looking at her now, I could see how much anger had been festering inside of her this whole time, destroying all of her relationships in its path, and maybe, as the only act of love I'd now get from her, she wanted to protect me from planting its seed inside of me. Because she shook her head, making it clear she would not answer.

Instead of feeling frustrated, though, I felt protected by her because maybe she thought the answer would make me just as bitter as she was. And she cared enough about me to not sentence me to that fate.

"Do you resent me for not knowing?" I asked.

Hayley took a few seconds to answer. "Sometimes."

I pretended my stomach didn't clench. At least this was a major healing moment between us, though—one we might finally move forward from.

But if Shane were here, I know the exact question he'd ask. I was confident I knew the answer, and the old me would bite my tongue, for fear of rocking the boat. Especially at such a perilous moment in our relationship.

But I needed to square my shoulders and protect myself. Uncover the truth, no matter how uncomfortable this was going to be.

"How badly do you resent me?" I asked.

Hayley swiped her cheek. "What, you want a number from one to a hundred?"

"Have you ever wanted to hurt me?"

Her eyebrows slammed together in confusion. "Why would I want to hurt you? You're not the one that killed him."

I studied her, scrutinized even, until I was confident I believed her. Hayley was a mess and always blowing me off, but she'd never been violent with anyone. The only person she ever hurt was herself.

"Why did you ask me that?" Hayley wiped both cheeks.

"It doesn't matter."

"Bullshit. Why'd you ask me that?"

I said nothing.

"I might be envious that you got to live without this fucking burden, but I would never hurt you, so why the hell would you ask it?"

Shit. *She's furious at me.* I'd gotten my answer. There was no need to do more damage by telling her why I'd asked it.

"I should go."

"Answer the question."

I stood up.

"Answer the question!"

My heart began pumping harder, like my blood was so thick, it had to work in overdrive. Hayley and I had just had the most intimate moment of our entire relationship, exposing hidden truths behind emotions that had confused me for years. It was the first time I felt true hope that we could grow closer together after this.

Answering her question would make the waters of our relationship even more turbulent, yet she'd never let it go.

She couldn't blame me for asking it, either. If I had to stomach people like Mom being a suspect, Hayley had to be in that mix, too.

The old Willow would have run out the door without replying, but I resolved to be open and honest, even though others hadn't always extended that same courtesy to me.

"I didn't just break my arm," I said. "I was pushed from a bridge."

Hayley's eyes rounded into full-on alarm. "Someone attacked you?"

I hated the shock on her face, worried it would drudge up feelings about Dad's death, worried it might make her go out and drink.

"Are you okay?" she asked.

I gave a gentle shrug.

"Who did it?" she asked.

"I don't know."

She seemed to digest this all.

"Wait." Her eyebrows furrowed, obviously piecing together my earlier question. "You think *I* had something to do with it?"

"I'm asking everyone if they had reason to hurt me."

Hayley stood up. "You see me as such a lowlife, you think I'm some cold-blooded killer?"

"Hayley—"

"What, because I'm an addict, I'm a killer too?"

"No, I—"

"How dare you accuse me of something like that?"

I'd had to ask, but there was no way I would've been meeting up with Hayley that night and not remembered. Getting to meet up with Hayley would've been a tremendous deal to me, and she was so hard to get ahold of, it would've been something we planned for days, if not weeks, in advance.

"I didn't mean to offend y—" I started.

"You don't matter enough to consume me with hate, let alone be worthy of murder."

She stormed off down the hallway, away from my interrogation. Away from my re-shattered heart and any hope I had to glue our relationship back together.

All these years, I had longed for the emotional breakthrough my sister and I had just had. And then I ruined it.

Long ago, I'd come to terms with the probability Hayley and I may never have a relationship. But that was when the crumbling of our relationship was due to her drug use and lack of effort. If our relationship ended as a result of the question I had asked—one she perceived as a heinous accusation—how could I ever live with that? Because this time, it wouldn't be Hayley's fault; it would be mine.

My cell phone rang, dragging me from the depths of my mental hell.

"Hello?" I choked out.

"Willow. Detective Rosse. I have a development and need you to come down to the station."

## 34

Once again, we were in the conference room at the Chicago Police station.

"Whatever it is, it must be substantial for them to bring us in," Shane said.

He squeezed my hand, probably assuming my anxiety was from this case. And not from ruining any hope of fixing things with my sister.

"You okay?" he asked for the fifth time since we'd left my mom's house.

"I'm fine," I lied. "Let's just hear what the detective has to say."

The conference room was cold, royal-blue walls with fake wood flooring. A flat screen hanging on one side, a whiteboard on the other. I wondered how many other lives were ruined in this room and how many victories from solving crimes. At least this room seemed to experience the lows and highs; my mom's home seemed to only encase the lows.

"Ms. Johnson." Rosse stepped in, holding his tie from swaying as he sat down, holding a gray folder. "Appreciate you coming in on such short notice."

"Of course."

Rosse's eyes settled on Shane. "I need to speak to her in private," Rosse said. "I'm sure you understand."

This piqued my interest. He had let Shane in the room when we first reviewed the surveillance footage, so why not now?

"I'll wait for you in the lobby." Shane squeezed my knee.

"It might be a little while." Rosse took out a pair of bifocals from his pocket and opened the folder. "I'll be happy to drop her off when we're done here."

Hope swelled in my chest that they'd cracked the case.

Shane looked reluctant, maybe even downright stubborn, about leaving me at the station.

"I'll call you when I leave here," I said.

Shane pursed his lips. "Yeah, okay. I'll grab some case files and meet you at home."

Case files. Code for the ability to work from home—or actually, the cabin—if whatever Rosse was going to say was about to heat up this case.

Shane gave me one last look of worry before leaving the room.

Rosse cleared his throat. "I'd like you to review the footage again."

"Why?"

He fired up the flat screen and fast-forwarded to a section of the footage that gave us the best view of the suspect. Still grainy, still a dark silhouette of a figure.

"Are you sure you don't recognize this person?"

Seriously? He called me all the way down to the station to ask me a question we had already covered?

A little annoyed, I stared at the image all the same, willing something to come to me.

"No."

Rosse nodded, as if unsurprised.

"Have you had any contact with Ezra lately?"

"Not since the coffee shop." Which I'd already filled Rosse in on when I'd met with him the first time.

"Anyone else?"

I told him about Amelia and how she was pissed that Ezra might be considered a suspect and answered his follow-up questions. Then, I told him about my conversation with Hayley.

When we finished the entire exchange, he glowered at me.

"You shouldn't be talking about this investigation with anyone," Rosse chided. "It could undermine the case."

I twisted my hands in my lap. "I'm sorry. It won't happen again."

Rosse pursed his lips and looked at his file. "I wanted to give you an update on the investigation. We formally interviewed Ezra, and he has no alibi."

"I saw the Uber app," I reminded him. "It showed he got a ride home at three in the morning from that club."

"Yes. However, I talked to the owners of that club and got a list of names of people that were there. The people that were hanging out with Ezra couldn't account for his whereabouts for over an hour that night."

"Ezra said he got drunk and passed out."

"Then, I asked the owner if I could see the security footage. They have one security camera at the front of the club and one in the back. One of them shows Ezra leaving the club at 9:23 p.m. You were pushed off the bridge at 10:01 p.m. He returned to the club at 10:28 p.m."

My stomach swirled with bile. "Did anyone see where he went?"

"No."

"Did he tell them where he was going?"

"He didn't notify anyone he was leaving. You remember what time his call came into you that night?"

I shook my head. I had willingly handed over my phone records to expedite this.

Rosse looked at the paper in front of him. "He called you at 9:14 p.m. That call lasted five minutes and thirty-three seconds. Four minutes after that call ended, he left the bar."

My heart started beating faster.

"I went to the club and made the walk myself," he said.

He made me wait for it—confirmation of Ezra's likely guilt or innocence arriving with whatever words Rosse spoke next.

"I could walk to the bridge and get back in time."

"But how would he have gotten me to meet him there? I would never go meet Ezra at some random bridge."

Rosse folded his hands on the table. "What if he told you he was suicidal? And he was going to jump? Would you have gone to try to stop him?"

Yes. Yes, I would. But...

"That's a huge hypothetical," I said.

"Maybe," Rosse agreed. "But my point remains. Ezra would know what to say to you to lure you to that bridge."

I felt like I was going to be sick.

"So, Ezra's the primary person of interest," I deduced.

A mixture of relief and heartbreak washed through my veins—relief that we were close to the end of this, but heartbreak because I had blown up my relationship with my sister for nothing. I should've kept my mouth shut. I should've let the investigation unfold naturally and not been so impatient to get answers.

Rosse asked me a million questions related to my relationship with Ezra in much more depth than our first meeting. It took over an hour to wrap it up.

When we finished, Rosse stood up. "Come on. I'll drive you home."

Twenty minutes later, I stepped out of Rosse's car.

"Thank you," I said.

"I'll be in touch, Willow."

He waited until I was inside the double doors of my apartment complex before I heard his engine rumble away.

I stepped into the hallway with my head in such a fog; I didn't notice the figure until it was too late.

## 35

He stepped out of the laundry room.

"Do you know what you did?"

I startled and glanced past his shoulder, down the long corridor of doors that led to mine. In my fog, I hadn't looked to see if Shane's car was in the parking lot yet. When I texted Shane after leaving the station, he said he was on his way home. Did that mean he'd beaten me here? Or was he still on his way, imminently about to walk through the complex's front doors behind me and stumble onto this scene?

If he saw Ezra here, Shane would lose his shit. And not only would Shane get in trouble for that, but the entire case could be jeopardized because of it.

And if Ezra was guilty, I wanted to do everything in my power to make sure he could never hurt anyone again.

"A detective showed up at my work today." Ezra took a step toward me. "A *detective*. People saw that, Willow. They heard they were asking questions about an attempted homicide!"

"They're interviewing everyone in my life." I kept my voice calm and neutral, and I clenched my hands so he wouldn't see them trembling. Because the look Ezra was casting was one I had never seen before.

His eyes were wide, his lips curled.

"I've been questioned before for assault and battery. Those charges were never filed, but if you add that to getting questioned on an attempted murder? If they name me as a person of interest? The combination of those two will end *any* chance of a political career."

"They're just trying to figure out what happened."

He stepped forward. "And I'm trying to protect my goddamn career!"

I glanced around quickly. If things got heated, I'd run out the front door or grab the fire extinguisher hanging on the wall and smash him with it.

"Don't you get it? This could ruin everything for me! Everything!"

"If you didn't get arrested or charged for anything, I'm sure it'll be fine."

"Oh, well, as long as you're sure, that's all that matters. Are you fucking naive?"

Even though he took another step into my space, I stood my ground and raised my chin.

"Do not take that tone with me."

"My boss has been looking at me sideways ever since that detective left. He'll probably fire me over this regardless!"

"Guidelines issued by the Equal Employment Opportunity Commission say you can only lose your job if—"

"Stop spouting HR crap at me. We both know how the real world works, Willow. If he wants to fire me, he will find a way."

"Well, you can't blame me for that. It's the Chicago Police Department investigating a potential crime. So, if you have a problem, take it up with them."

I tried to walk past him, but his arm shot out and stopped me, blocking my path.

"They'd better back off."

"Let me get past."

"If you cost me my political career, so help me…"

I glared at him. "Is that a threat?"

He licked his teeth. "That detective is making a big freaking deal out of me going for a walk."

I said nothing. Heeding Rosse's warning to not discuss this case.

"After I talked to you, I was too upset to sit there, so I went for a walk to clear my head."

That's why he was here. He thought if he could convince me, I could what, assure Rosse that Ezra would never do this and get him to back down? Ezra wasn't just reckless or a liar; he was desperate.

"Thanks for clearing that up," I snarled. "Now, move out of my way."

His jaw tightened. This wasn't going how he planned.

"I was upset because I love you and want you back."

I laughed out loud at how ludicrous this was. Him blocking me so I couldn't move yet declaring his love for me.

My laugh probably wasn't smart. It seemed to enrage him, based on the tightening of his face.

"See? This is the same goddamn attitude you were giving me that night when I called you. But would you meet me? No. Would you even listen to a damn word I said? That's why I called you a bitch."

I flinched. He'd never called me a name once in the entire time we'd been together, but I could see it playing out. Him, after one too many drinks, calling to try to get me back and getting angry when my answer hadn't changed.

"And then I went for a walk because I was afraid I'd screwed everything up. But I never saw you, Willow. And I meant it when I said I'd never hurt you."

But he just admitted to sabotaging everything with me. He knew I would never tolerate anyone talking to me like that, abusing me by calling me a name. By his account, he was drunk, angry—plenty of motive to fall off the deep end. He had the opportunity and an immense hole in his alibi. And he had lied about it all.

Not that I was going to tell him any of this. I'd call Rosse and tell him everything that Ezra was doing right now.

"That's why I sent you flowers the next day. I felt bad for calling you a name, Willow. But think about it. If I thought you were dead, I wouldn't send you flowers."

I reached into my bag, digging around for my cell.

When I said nothing, Ezra's voice hardened. "I would never hurt you, Willow."

I looked at him, deadpan. "I don't believe you anymore."

Wrong. Thing. To. Say.

His eyes flashed with fury.

He stepped even closer to me.

"You're being a bitch, you know that?" he growled.

"Move, or I'll kick you in the balls so hard, your voice will permanently sound like Mickey Mouse."

"Back off, Willow, and get it through your thick head—I didn't hurt you."

"Yeah, you seem like a harmless bunny rabbit." I glared at his arm, caging me into the hallway.

I tried to push past it, but he stepped forward until his face was inches from my own.

I shot my knee up to kick in between his legs, but he twisted his hips to block it, and when he did, it threw my center of gravity off.

I landed on my back with a yelp, and Ezra towered over me, his fists clenched at both sides.

Evidently, my yelp had been rather loud because a door swung open, footsteps ran toward us, and Ezra was slammed against the wall, his cheek smooshed against it as his arms were twisted behind his back.

"You ever lay a hand on her, I'll rip your heart out with my bare hands!" Shane barked.

36

"You okay?" Shane cupped my jaw, looking into my eyes, as if decoding my every movement.

"I'm fine."

But Shane could see past my lie.

How could I be fine? I knew Shane was right; it was the right thing to do to file the restraining order, but that didn't make it any easier. If Ezra didn't turn out to be the person who'd pushed me from the bridge, that order of protection would have a detrimental impact on his political career.

I wasn't even sure the judge would grant the emergency order of protection, but after learning that Ezra was the primary person of interest in my attempted murder case, he granted it. In twenty-one days, there would be a full hearing, but for now, an interim order was in effect.

Shane stroked my skin and lowered his voice, as if it could soften the blow of what he said next. "Don't get mad."

"Worst way to start a sentence."

"But I grabbed some things from the store for you. Toiletries, so you don't have to pack so much."

I pulled his hand away from my face and kissed his palm. "I'm not going to the cabin."

"Willow..."

"They took Ezra away in cuffs, so he's locked up."

"For a few hours. Maybe the night. But since he didn't technically lay hands on you, it's unlikely it'll be much longer than that. If we could file charges for being an asshole, he'd be locked up forever."

"Rosse's getting close," I assured.

"Charging someone with attempted homicide requires a thorough investigation. It could be days, weeks, or even longer before charges officially come."

"Exactly. Going away right now helps nothing."

Shane moved closer, our noses only inches apart. "It keeps you safe."

"I ruined my relationship with my sister, and I had that huge blowout with Amelia. This has done enough damage to my life. We both know this won't be over until whoever did this to me is in jail anyway, and God only knows how long that could take. I have a life, Shane. I can't just run away with you and stay locked up in that cabin forever."

Something flashed through Shane's eyes. Something with heat and fire.

He brought his hand to my hip, his voice dragging low through his words.

"What if you don't think of it as running? What if you think of it as somethin' else?"

I tried to hide the fire rippling beneath my skin at his touch. With one look, he had the power to bring me to my knees. Literally. And he was unleashing it right now, beneath those dark eyebrows and matching black hair that I was now fantasizing running my fingers through.

"Meaning?"

"No part of you wants to get away with me for a few days?"

I swallowed. Of course I did.

"Don't you think that's a little manipulative, Detective Hernandez?"

His mouth curled up on one side. "I'll do whatever it takes to protect you."

And then he did. As he moved his lips to the base of my throat, leaving a trail of kisses up my neck, my greedy need to feel him performed a hostile takeover of my thoughts.

He kissed me until I couldn't take it anymore, and then, as final evidence he was trying to use every tactic to get me to change my mind, he stopped.

The tease.

"Sleep on it," he said. Obviously relieved we had a few safe hours with Ezra locked up. "We can leave in the morning."

## 37

Outside, a crashing sound preceded Snowflake's scream. I launched from my couch, yanked at the sliding glass door—damn, my shoulder still hurt a little when I did that—and jumped out onto my patio.

"Snowflake!"

The little house I had put outside for her had crashed against the door in the whipping winds and momentarily pinned her. Scaring the crap out of her. But thankfully, it did not appear to injure her.

She rubbed her back against my bare calf. My freezing calf.

"It's okay. It's just another winter storm." I picked her up and cradled her against my chest. "Come on. You can watch TV with me."

But my sliding glass door was closed.

I'd shut it out of habit, protecting my apartment from the subzero temperatures outside. The subzero temperatures that assaulted my skin, lining my entire body with goose bumps. Without my big, fluffy blanket on the couch, my T-shirt and thong might as well have been a death suit.

I yanked the handle, but the door didn't move.

Crap.

I hated this door. I hated how it stuck and how the landlord could never figure it out, because Shane was right. This was a hazard. I had mastered the art of opening it from the inside, but not from the outside. I tried to repeat my movements on the outside, but the door acted like it was nailed shut.

My body trembled harder.

In this weather, frostbite would set in crazy fast.

When I put Snowflake down, she scurried into her little house as I battled with the door. I pulled horizontally, I jerked vertically, I jerked at angles. But it wasn't budging, all while a winter wind whipped against my skin, freezing me all the way to my bones.

My teeth chattered as I looked around, trying to decide my next step. It was the middle of the night. I could walk around the entire building to the lobby, but that path would take me through snow with bare feet. Not to mention, I'd risk someone seeing me nearly naked.

Humiliation would kill me before hypothermia.

I walked to the patio next to mine and banged on the glass.

No lights were on inside. No movement.

Now that I thought about it, I didn't even know if Shane was home. I hadn't heard him in a long time. Was he asleep?

"Shane!" I knocked.

Maybe he would let me bring Snowflake inside. I reached down to pick up the cat, but she ran off and out of sight.

*Dammit.*

I was convulsing from the cold.

"Shane!" I knocked again, louder this time.

His light came on.

Hallelujah.

The blinds covering the door opened a crack, revealing Shane standing there in nothing but a pair of boxer briefs. His hair disheveled.

He opened the door quickly and pulled me inside, shutting the door and blinds behind me. If I wasn't damn near hypothermic, this might have been sexy with me standing here in nothing but a T-shirt.

But sexy goes out the window when you can't talk straight because your jaw is frozen half shut.

"What are you doin' out there?"

"Th…the…c…cat…g…got…s…scared."

"Jesus, you're shaking."

Shane grabbed a blanket from the back of his couch and wrapped it around me, then pulled me to his chest. His skin felt like an inferno, so I could only imagine I felt like an icicle.

"How long were you out there?"

He rubbed his hands up and down my back.

"N…not…l…long…"

"Why did you go outside in nothin' but a T-shirt?"

"Th…the…c…cattttt."

He smirked down at me. "Stop talking." He pulled me tighter, my cheek pressing against his wonderfully warm chest.

"You're like an ice cube," he groaned. "I would offer you hot chocolate, but all I have is coffee or beer."

"I…I'm f…fine."

"You're not fine."

He pulled the blanket tighter around me.

"I'm…s…sorry I w…woke you."

"You're far more important than sleep, Willow."

He held me close, the warmth of his body eclipsed by the warmth of his heart, which shimmered a glistening path to mine.

Shane stared at me with an intensity that promised to melt the ice away, his throat rolling with a swallow. His eyes combed over my face. Gravitating to my lips. Threatening to burn them with one scorching kiss.

Every cell in my body came alive, and a shiver ran down my spine, only this one wasn't from the cold. The skin on my back sizzled with his every stroke, my chest swelling as it pressed against his muscles.

My lower belly warmed at the sight of him—layers of muscles entrenched in ink, all of them flexing with desire.

Sucked into his gaze like I'd surrendered to hypnosis, I licked my bottom lip and savored the way Shane's eyes dilated at the sight of it, his chest rising and falling faster as he stared at my mouth.

I wanted his lips on mine.

I wanted his hands to touch more than just my back.

I wanted Shane. All of him. His heart, his body, his soul. But even though he'd professed feelings for me, he'd been uncertain about what it all meant for us—hadn't committed to being with me. Feelings didn't change his biggest fear, his decision to never get serious with anyone. And for that reason, I should walk back to my place now before I let this go any further because, unlike the frenzied rush of hormones with the kitchen table incident, this was something I could feel all the way to my core. If I went through with this, Shane walking away later would be a sledgehammer to my heart.

But if all I could have was his body, then tonight, I'd take whatever he was willing to give.

Shane moved his hand to my face, cupping my cheek and stroking my cheekbone with his thumb.

"Let me run you a warm bath," he whispered.

But I wasn't shaking anymore. And I couldn't stand being away from him for another minute.

I shrugged the blanket from my shoulders, took a step back, and pulled my T-shirt up over my head, standing in nothing but a thong.

Shane's eyes glided down my shoulders, chest, abs, legs, and back up again.

Meeting my eyes with a hungry need pulsing through his gaze.

"You're gorgeous."

When I stepped out of my panties and kicked them to the side, Shane stood frozen.

Here I was, giving myself to him. Waiting for him to claim me.

His eyes fixated on the space between my legs, and then he walked up to me and crashed his mouth to mine.

Oh. My. Word.

His lips were an ember, igniting everything throughout my body, his hand on my jaw scorching my skin. Heating the space between my thighs.

It wasn't enough. No amount of kissing this man would ever be enough. And when he opened his mouth and allowed his tongue to lightly press against mine, I groaned. I reached my hands up to his shoulders, our kiss gaining in momentum as I nibbled his lower lip and pressed my mouth harder to his.

I loved every thrash of his tongue, every growl from his throat as his hands wandered down my body, until he pinched a nipple between the pad of his thumb and finger.

Making me yipe.

"Tell me what you want," he demanded.

I swallowed. "I want to feel you inside me."

He groaned, and trailed his fingertips down my breasts, down my stomach, and then slipped a finger past my folds and into my entrance. Making my back arch with pleasure.

He looked like a hungry man as he began to curl and move his finger, watching me, kissing my jaw, my neck. Sucking on my nipple.

And then, he dropped to his knees and threw my right thigh over his shoulder.

Looking up at me, he licked my folds.

I groaned, shoving my hands into his hair as he worked his tongue slowly up to the apex of my sex, and began to suck.

I jerked from the overwhelming sensation and pulled his hair in approval when he began circling the bundle of nerves with his tongue. Groaning, hungry to feast on me.

Shane Hernandez was a powerful man, one who could command most people to do what he said, but right now, he was on his knees. Pleasuring me. Listening to the tempo of my moans as he dipped his tongue inside me, and then trailed it upward again. Sucking on me. Circling. Over and over.

I could feel the wave building. Especially when he teased my entrance with his finger and plunged it inside.

"You're so wet for me," he growled, his voice vibrating against the sensitive skin.

His praise was making my wave rise higher and higher and I

pulled his head harder against me, inviting a nip of his teeth—a brief glint of pain followed by an avalanche of ecstasy.

And then I crashed. Hard, as he savored every drop of my orgasm, leaving me spent.

I gasped when he stood up and spun me around, pressing my chest against the wall.

Roughly.

He positioned himself behind me.

Holy crap. This was so hot. So damn hot, the kind of passion that's too big for gentle lovemaking.

"Are you on the pill?" he asked in a hungry, impatient tone.

He ran his hand along the base of my back, lower and lower, until he reached around and met my center.

I cried out, "Yes."

I was surprised he started touching me again, but I liked that there was an anger to it, as if making him wait for it since we'd first met had made him suffer. I liked his anger. I liked feeling the pressure of his fingers as he dipped two of them inside of me from behind. I liked that with his free hand, he grabbed my breast as he stared into my eyes, watching my mouth fall open, my body squirm beneath his movements.

His hand was magic, like a key to the lock of my ecstasy. I tried to hold still, especially when he held my back in place, but he was bringing me to the cusp again.

"Shane..."

"Not yet."

He stopped, pulling his hand back, making me whimper. He stepped out of his boxers, my eyes glued to the pleasure waiting for me as he coated his shaft with my arousal. Before he grabbed my hips roughly and tugged them back a bit.

"Grab the wall," Shane growled.

I gladly obeyed and gasped when he filled me in one angry movement.

Then, he started to move.

With one hand on my hip, Shane's other hand grabbed my neck

and twisted my head until his lips claimed mine. His tongue in my mouth. His movements were frenzied, an explosion of pent-up sexual tension that demanded release between us.

"You make me crazy," he groaned into my mouth. Licked my tongue.

He pulled my hips back and pressed my torso down lower, keeping a hand on the nape of my neck.

"You don't know how long I've wanted you," he growled.

Angrier and angrier, he thrust his hips, as if the months of waiting for this were unfair—an injustice that deserved an extraordinary vindication.

I could feel a wave building with him hitting just the right spot, moving at just the right tempo, just the right beat. He cupped my breast, moving so perfectly against me.

"Shane..." I groaned.

"Not yet," he demanded.

I clawed at his wall as the wave rose even higher. I couldn't hold on much longer. I couldn't.

I turned my head and looked up at him, locking my eyes with his. He looked wild with pleasure, his jaw tight, his fingers claiming my hips with such force, they might leave marks tomorrow. Marks I would savor.

Keeping his gaze fixed on me, he moved faster and faster until...

"Shane..." My fingernails dug into the paint.

"Now," he growled.

His sapphire eyes looked darkened with sensuality as we both hit our release, riding each other's waves until every last tremble and moan subsided. Leaving me quivering, spent from the most sensual experience I'd ever had in my life. Locked in each other's gaze the entire time.

I pressed my temple to the wall, panting.

Shane stepped back, spun me around, and crashed his lips to mine. He grabbed the backs of my legs and hoisted my legs around his waist as he kissed me, walking me to his bedroom.

Clutching me with a possessive, desperate hold.

"That wasn't enough." He threw me onto his bed. "Give me five minutes, and I want to go again."

I smiled. Especially when I realized how he planned to spend the five minutes while we waited for him to be ready again.

Shane fell to his knees and sank his mouth to my center.

## 38

I woke up to morning sunlight streaming through Shane's blinds, stretching across his tattoo-covered torso. His eyes were still closed, and his chest rose and fell lazily with each of his hypnotic breaths. He looked so peaceful with his black hair tousled, his tan skin stretched over bands of muscles.

But as soon as he woke up, he wouldn't feel peaceful anymore. Reality would come crashing back, and we'd have a very hard conversation in front of us.

One that was going to hurt like hell.

Last night, after making love three times and falling asleep in each other's arms, it felt like the gaps in my soul had been filled with his affection. And now, lying naked in his bed, I never felt like I belonged anywhere else but right here, with Shane.

It was strange to think how many years I spent fighting for a sense of belonging within my own family. Maybe I'd been searching for this feeling in the wrong place all along.

And now that I had it, the thought of ever letting it go incinerated my heart.

It was like spending your entire life alone, in the center of a ballroom dance floor, watching other couples dance while you stand there, feeling like an outcast. And then suddenly, the dance floor clears, and a prince's eyes land on you. In a sea of people, he wants you, only you, and he motions for you to join him.

You glide your way into his outstretched arms, your heart pounding, and as soon as you start to dance, you've never felt happier or more wanted in your entire life. In that moment, you never want the music to end. Because once the music stops playing, reality will bring you right back to your lonely little spot, surrounded by other happy couples dancing. Only this time, you will be painfully aware of what you are missing out on.

And you know that no matter how many more princes come into the room, none of them will hold a candle to how that one special prince made you feel.

But Shane made it very clear early on that he would not allow himself to be in a serious relationship with anyone. Yes, he'd developed feelings for me, but that wouldn't change his position. It would just prolong this heaven and plunge me deeper into hell when it ended.

How could I ever be with another guy after Shane? Shane, who jumped into a freezing river, risking death to save me. Shane, whose protection for me extended to how I allowed myself to be treated by others.

I knew what the answer was. I would search for a man who would make me feel a fraction of what Shane had made me feel, and I would spend the next twenty years searching for that feeling, just like I had spent the last twenty years searching for that emotional connection that I was craving from my family.

I was stronger now, after everything I had overcome and learned, but I would continue to go through life like a leaf blowing through the air, unanchored and never belonging to anyone. Just as I'd always been.

My throat swelled painfully. I swallowed and forced down the emotions as I looked past him to a photograph sitting on his dresser of a man holding what appeared to be Shane when he was a toddler. The guy had Shane's eyes, the same hair.

"It's my dad," he said.

Damn, Shane looked sexy when he opened his eyes. The gradients of light and blue speckles mixed together in a harmony of color, pulling me closer with a simple look.

"Do you remember him?"

"Not as well as I want to," he admitted, running his fingers through my hair.

It felt like a clock was ticking down toward the end of our time together and closing my window of opportunity of getting to know him better. Soon, the fragments of his soul he'd be willing to share with me would go back into their lockbox. And I'd no longer have its key.

"What do you remember?" I asked.

Shane trailed his fingertips along my bare back, looking up at the ceiling as he considered this.

"One of the best memories I have was when I was four, shortly before he died. Whenever he would leave for work, I would sit on the front porch, and he would get in a squad car and turn the lights on for me as he drove away. It was this ritual, I guess you could call it, that he had started to say goodbye to me. He'd do the same thing when he got home."

"Sounds sweet." I kissed his chest.

Shane stroked my arm as his voice faded with the memory. "It was. Until the day I was waiting on the porch for him to come home and his squad car pulled up with no lights on. And it wasn't my dad that got out. It was two uniforms." He cleared his throat. "I never saw my dad again."

My stomach walls ached at the image of a little boy waiting for his daddy, who would never return.

"It was one of the worst moments of my life." Shane's voice was a whisper. "Seein' my mom collapse like that. Because when you're a little kid, your parents are like superheroes. They're indestructible. So, when my mom collapsed, I remember it made me feel unsafe. Like she was vulnerable, and if she was vulnerable, how was she supposed to protect us? And then, when I learned the reason she collapsed was because my dad had been killed, I think it just took away my entire sense of security."

What a great way to put it...your sense of security. How very true. Seeing parents weak or vulnerable has the power to make you feel unsafe when you're a kid.

Shane continued to stroke my hair, his voice sounding lost in the past. "Remember feeling like...when you have a nightmare and you wake up, you're so relieved that it wasn't real? Because the nightmare was dark and all you felt was terror and sadness and despair and hopelessness. Your heart is pounding, and you're sobbing, and you're runnin' away from this monster that's chasing you, but he's gaining on you." He paused. "It kind of felt like, one day, I was playin' with my soccer ball in the backyard, and the next day, I was in that nightmare that I never woke up from. It became my life, and I had to learn to live in the darkness with that monster."

My eyes stung. Because it was the perfect analogy to describe what it felt like.

"That's awful," I whispered.

Shane swept my hair over my shoulder.

"It came in waves," he said. "The first was shock, of course. It didn't feel real. Every time I would see a police car, I would look inside and think maybe my dad was in that one and that's why they couldn't find him—he'd gotten into the wrong car. Or maybe he was out fighting crime and had lost track of time and hadn't come home yet."

How heartbreaking. I could imagine an innocent little boy grasping at all sorts of explanations as to why his dad was suddenly gone.

"When it finally did sink in, I never knew sadness could be so debilitating. I couldn't think straight. I wasn't eating very much. I couldn't sleep. That lasted for a long time. A long damn time."

When little boys were supposed to be playing T-ball and making lists for Santa, Shane had been drowning in grief. I wished I could go back in time and hug that little boy, to tell him it was okay to be sad, to miss his dad. To cry.

"After a while, sadness turned into rage. I was so angry that he had been killed. When I was ten, I used to draw these superhero costumes, where I planned to find anyone who'd ever killed a police officer and beat them up." Shane's lips curled. "I even talked my mom into makin' me the costume for Halloween, though she had no clue what it was actually for. It was blue and red, because those were my dad's favorite colors, and it had a letter *J* stitched on with black felt. *J* for justice."

My stomach rolled, imagining a ten-year-old child enduring all of that.

"I eventually realized it would never work. I was too small to beat up adults, and I had no way of tracking all those bad guys down. So, after a while, I just felt...lost, I guess. Kind of existing without feelin' much. I didn't have a lot of friends because I wasn't very fun to be around."

I kissed his chest and looked at him intensely in his eyes.

"I admire you even more because of what you've overcome." Because he'd overcome his adversity far better than I ever had.

Shane brushed my collarbone, looking at me with a ghost of a smile, as if I were the remarkable one. But he was. Strong and brave and honorable. His life could've gone a million different ways with all of that trauma and pain, and I was impressed he hadn't allowed it to ruin his life.

"After the first few years passed, I remember feelin' like I had this responsibility to be the man of the house. I tried to never show my emotions."

In some ways, I could relate to that. I tried to keep my emotions locked down so that I wouldn't upset my mother. I wondered if Shane ever failed the way I had.

"Were you able to *always* hide your feelings?" I asked.

Strangely, I wanted to hear that someone else had cracked like I had. Because when I was younger and I let the grief upset me in front of my mother, the only way I got past the guilt was to convince myself it was only human. That any human under the same circumstances would sometimes crack under the pain.

"There was this one day I couldn't hold it in because it was the hardest day I'd had after he died," he said.

I wondered if Shane understood how intimate I felt with him sharing this with me. Even more intimate than what we'd shared last night.

"The day we left our house to move into that trailer park gutted me because leaving that house was like leaving my dad behind. That home housed the only memories I had with him. The kitchen counter he had set me on when he'd put a Band-Aid on my knee. The back-yard, where he used to play catch with me. The front porch, where we used to sit and watch him go to and from work each day. Leavin' it all behind was like leaving him behind all over again. And I was terrified his memory would fade without being surrounded by the only place I'd ever shared with him."

My lip quivered.

"I couldn't hold it together that day. And the worst part was, me breaking down made it even harder on my mom. It's not like she wanted to leave that house. She had no choice. We couldn't afford it. We could barely afford the trailer we moved into."

He continued to stroke my back, lost in thought.

"Thank you for sharing that with me," I said. He'd been an integral part of my life at one of my lowest points. It was touching to be let so deeply into his.

But my bliss was pierced with barbed wire that wrapped around my chest because we might feel happy right now—and maybe that would go on for a while—but eventually, he would remember the heartbreaking reason he'd pushed me away in the first place.

When Shane professed his feelings for me, he said he didn't know what the future held for us—that he couldn't even think about that right now. Then, he kissed me and got lost in passion.

But now, I did need to think about that because passion with Shane only made my feelings for him grow deeper. And I knew deep down, no matter how much he may care for me, his biggest fear in life—leaving behind someone he loved—would rear its ugly head and steal him from me. Maybe it would happen on the anniversary of his dad's death, or maybe he'd have a close call with a suspect at work, but inevitably, something would pull him from this bliss. And when that happened, when he did the noble thing and walked away...

I would be destroyed.

Each day I spent with him would be like giving him another fragment of my heart, and the longer we were together, the less of my heart would remain when he left me.

"You okay?" he asked.

I tried to wash away the sadness inside of me, unsure how to approach this conversation. I mustered a fake smile, pretending my chest wasn't burning.

When everything you've ever wanted is right in front of you but still just outside your reach...was it truly better to have loved and lost than to have never loved at all? Because I was pretty sure I was falling in love with Shane. Maybe already had. And I wasn't so sure the aftershock of losing this with him was worth the earthquake of bliss we'd gotten to share.

Maybe it was. Maybe, someday, I'd wake up and decide it was all worth it. But not right now. Not when I was about to tell him I couldn't do this.

"I think it's best if I go," I said.

At the tone of my voice, Shane lay on his side and propped himself up on his elbow, brushing the backs of his fingers along my jawline.

"What's wrong?" His eyebrows furrowed.

I brushed his hair with my fingertips, trying to sound strong. "Last night was fun, but we both know this is a mistake."

Shane's head jerked back. "Since when?"

"We both know how this is going to end."

"And how is that?" Shane asked.

"With you leaving me."

Based on the tightening of his eyes, he was offended. "I told you, I can't stay away from you."

For now. Later though...

"We're caught up in infatuation," I started.

"Infatuation?" he choked out.

"But once that fades..."

"Is that all this is to you?"

"I'll be left out in the storm to pick up the pieces."

I was a coward. A braver person would take whatever time she could get with him—a day, a month, a year. But as much as I wished I'd convinced Shane to not live his life alone, one night of lovemaking didn't erase the last twenty years. If anything, the closer he got to me, the more he'd probably be afraid of leaving loved ones behind, and the more likely he'd be to end it.

This wasn't fear talking. It was me trying to protect my heart.

Shane's face tightened into shocked anger. He swallowed, as if I had just told him his puppy died.

"I didn't realize you were afraid of..." He paused, pinched the bridge of his nose, and clenched his eyes shut. "You lost your dad. Of course that would...what was I thinking?"

Shane shoved the covers off, shot out of bed, and slammed boxer briefs on.

Moments ago, I'd been entwined in his arms, closer to him than... well, than I'd ever been with anyone in my life, really. And now, he wouldn't even look at me; he was so disgusted. His every movement, every lack of eye contact, pulled him further away—like he'd been swept into a current, stealing him from me.

I felt panicked. I wanted to pull him back and accept him for as long as he'd let me. Yet my heart would never survive that in the long run.

"I just don't want to be left," I managed over the lump in my throat. "My mom left every time I felt safe, and—"

He held up his palm. "You don't have to explain. And for the record, I'm not mad at you. I'm furious with myself." He licked his bottom lip. "What the hell was I thinking?"

Shane left his room. Left me. Alone, naked, and heartbroken.

## 39

I wasn't sure what to do. I sat on Shane's bed, covering my nude body with a sheet while I held my hand to my mouth, trying to contain my sob.

In the kitchen, I heard cabinets opening and closing harder than necessary. The refrigerator door opened and closed. And then eerie silence haunted the space.

I was stronger than this. I didn't need to cower in his bedroom. I could lick my wounds later, when I was alone, and I could scream into a pillow and sob in my bathtub, but right now, I needed to face this.

I stood up and realized my panties and T-shirt were still in the living room. Talk about a walk of shame, humbling to have to walk out there in the nude.

Metaphorical for how naked I felt with my feelings.

Before I had the chance to walk out there, though, Shane appeared, leaning against the doorframe. He had his arms crossed over his bare chest, the tattoos strangling his torso, and clutched in his right hand were my clothes.

"I'm sorry for getting angry," he said.

"I'm sorry for making you angry."

"I've been selfish."

I chuckled and shook my head. "If you think putting your entire life on hold to protect me is selfish, we have different definitions of that word."

"If you'd allow it, I'd lock you in my bedroom forever to protect you from this world."

My heart thumped in my ears.

"But that's not what I'm talking about. I was so caught up in *my* fear," Shane said. "I failed to stop and think about yours. Because you're right. If I'm killed in the line of duty, you would be left to pick up the pieces by yourself."

I blanched. "That's not what I was talking about."

Shane's blue eyes looked so deeply into mine; it was like they were fishing for answers. An explanation.

No wonder he got so upset. Of course I'd always be worried about something happening to Shane, especially in his line of work. But I wasn't talking about him dying.

"I was talking about you leaving me. Breaking up with me," I said.

Shane's head jerked back an inch. "Why would I break up with you?"

"Because your biggest fear is to leave someone behind, and you're a cop, and..."

Understanding softened Shane's face. His lips even tugged up into a half smile as he pinched the bridge of his nose again and shook his head. "I thought you were breaking up with me."

"I am breaking up with you. As a preemptive strike."

"No"—he locked eyes with me—"you're not."

"I know we're not officially together, but put whatever term you want on this. I'm breaking up with you before you choose to break up with me later."

He sat down next to my hip and ran his fingertips up my arm, smiling wider. "No."

"I am."

"I don't accept."

"Shane..."

"Willow." He brought his face inches from my own. "I've made my decision. If you want to leave me because I'm a jackass or something, I'll accept it. But not because of this."

"You said you never wanted to be in a relationship if you were a cop."

He grabbed hold of my gaze so tightly, I didn't think I could ever wiggle out of it.

"That was before I met you," he said. "Before, that was an acceptable sacrifice to make. But once I met you? It was an impossible sacrifice to make. Meeting you changed everything."

My heart had the audacity to feel hopeful. But I couldn't let it all the way in. Just like I couldn't let every car that passed by my childhood window completely flood me with hope.

"I know this might sound sudden." His thumb moved to my collarbone. "But I won't fight it anymore, Willow. Because after gettin' to know you, I can't imagine not being with you."

"But your biggest fear—"

"None of us is guaranteed a tomorrow. Is my job more dangerous than most? Yes. But no one knows what the future holds. You could have died when you were pushed off that bridge, and the very idea of losin' you completely guts me. So, I've realized that I need to grab ahold of happiness when I can and not let fear hold me back. Because I refuse to live a life without you in it, to live a life filled with nothing but emptiness and regret. You, Willow, are worth the risk. The real question is whether I'm worth that risk for you."

Which was everything I'd ever wanted to hear. But was I okay with him making that sacrifice?

Was allowing himself to be in a loving relationship really a sacrifice, though? Wasn't a bigger sacrifice spending his life alone?

"What if you change your mind?" I asked. "If you go to work one day and there's a shooting or something and there's a close call, you might start to think differently."

I adored Shane. And nothing would make me happier than surrendering to my feelings for him. But I was not one of those women willing to surrender my control. If any circumstance existed that might change his mind, I would not choose to dive into this.

"I won't lie and say the fear isn't there anymore," he said. "It is. But I refuse to let that fear dictate my life to the point I can't be happy, and I won't be happy without you, Willow. Because of you, I'm finally ready and willing to take a risk. The only question is…will you give me the chance to make you fall in love with me?"

I didn't realize how fast I was breathing until now. But there it was, my chest rising and falling so quickly that I wondered if I might faint.

"I'm already falling," I admitted. Like him, I think I had been for a while. Slowly, like the leaves of a tree beginning to turn color. A handful at first. And then it spreads until the entire tree is blazing red.

Shane's lips curled up on both sides. Illuminating the entire room with his joy. Then, he crashed his mouth to mine.

And pinned me to the bed.

THREE HOURS LATER, I FINISHED THE DELICIOUS BREAKFAST SHANE made, and I decided it was time to go home and shower.

Shane gave me clothes and shoes to temporarily wear and then walked me to my door and made sure I got in safe. Especially since I had to go back in through the patio door, not having my key on me. It took him only two yanks before the damn thing opened.

*Mental note: I need to work on upper body strength.*

I stumbled inside with frozen feet, laughing with Shane behind me.

"Did you do this?" I looked over my shoulder at him as I walked to the giant bouquet of flowers sitting on my kitchen counter. Blue and red roses.

Shane's smile fell. "No."

He glanced at the front door. Right. Delivery guys leave flowers at your doorstep; they don't enter and leave them inside. And my dead bolt was still locked.

From the inside.

Whoever brought these must've come in through the sliding glass door because there'd be no way to lock the dead bolt behind them without the key.

Which was beyond creepy. And odd. Wouldn't they have struggled with the door, like we had?

Shane motioned for me to hold still as he advanced into my bedroom, then my bathroom, checking each closet, the bathtub, even under the sink cabinets.

All the while, I inched toward the flowers—a moth to the mysterious flame that was a little card with my name on it, dread filling me as I reached for it.

"Willow, don't—" Shane started.

But it was too late. I'd plucked it from the tightly packed flowers—their scent wafting through my apartment like some kind of ominous warning.

Inside was a handwritten poem.

*Willow,*

*Roses are red.*

*Violets are blue.*

*Drop the investigation,*

***or I'll fucking end you.***

## 40

"Where the hell is he?" Shane demanded.

"You need to calm down," Rosse insisted.

"You kidding me?" Shane shoved a hand through his hair. "The front door was dead-bolted."

"I'm aware."

"He broke into the apartment."

"We don't know the perp is male," Rosse reminded him.

"Bullshit we don't."

"We're dusting for prints."

"You know what it'll tell you. So, answer the question. Where the hell is he?" Shane snarled.

Rosse joined the two uniformed police officers processing this probable break-in with its suspicious, creepy threat—since it obviously had something to do with his case.

"Maybe someone has been breaking in all along, and I didn't know," I said. "Remember the toothbrush, the bookmark, the hair in the sink?"

"When you came home from the hospital, was the sliding glass door locked?"

"I think so." It had to be. Even though I hadn't checked it myself, surely, between Shane and all the officers, somebody confirmed it had been locked when we first walked in. "But even if I didn't, it gets stuck, so it's super hard to open; I couldn't even open it myself last night, so I'm not sure how they'd get inside."

Was it possible the jammed door made the lock unreliable?

"Tony, step outside." Rosse gestured with his arm.

One of the uniformed officers opened the sliding door after three yanks and stepped outside. Rosse closed it behind him and flipped the lock.

"Try to open it." He motioned to the handle.

The uniform grabbed the handle. Tugged it. Hard. Multiple times, but the door wouldn't open. Rosse unlocked the latch, and the officer tried again. The door stuck, just like it had for me last night, but with enough force, the officer got it open on his fourth attempt.

"Thing's a bitch." The cop frowned at the track.

"Carpet's wet from melted snow," the cop noted. "Could all of it be from you?"

I looked at the spots, remembering my path to the kitchen, Shane's to the other rooms.

"No," I said, pointing to a path neither of us had taken. "That wasn't from us."

"Whoever was in here came through this door," the cop said. "But their footsteps outside are long gone."

Four inches of snow had fallen in the last hour with whipping winds covering up any shoe imprints.

"Was Ezra still being held last night or not?" Shane asked.

Rosse stared at Shane.

"I can find out on my own," Shane reminded him.

Rosse scratched the side of his face. "He was released late last night."

"Son of a bitch," Shane said. "Plenty of time for him to pull this stunt."

"There's a restraining order," Rosse said. "So, if it's him, we'll be able to bring him in and charge him with breaking it. We'll process the scene for prints. Look into the source of the flowers," Rosse said.

"But for your own safety, I'd be careful to assume it's him. Assumptions can be dangerous; you could let your guard down with someone else."

Had he changed his mind from the last time we spoke? Was Ezra no longer suspect number one?

"Who *do* you think did this?" I asked.

The detective regarded me. We both knew we were not just talking about the flowers. We were talking about the bridge case because, obviously, the flowers were from whoever had tried to hurt me.

"Unfortunately, it's too soon to say."

"Just run down what you know," I said, putting my hands on my hips.

Shane stood to my left, his eyes watching me, as if worrying I'd fall over from fear.

Fat. Chance. I was angry. Beyond angry. Whoever the hell did this, I wanted them locked up, put in jail, end of discussion.

"The ex-boyfriend obviously has a motive. One man we spoke to, who sent you direct messages on social media, has a record, but so far, his wife is maintaining his alibi."

First, gross that the guy was married and messaging some stranger online. Second, after everything we had uncovered, I was still skeptical that a stranger had pushed me.

"We'll pull surveillance cameras and knock on some doors. See if any neighbors saw anything."

"Perfect. I'll wait here and hope the killer doesn't return," I said sarcastically.

"We're working as fast as we can."

"I know. I'm sorry." My nerves were converting me into a class-A witch. "I just want to move on with my life, and every time I turn around…" I gestured toward the flowers.

Rosse gave a pity nod.

"Can I ask you something off the record?" I inquired.

I wanted Rosse to tell me if this was Ezra or not. As Shane told me, knowing something and gathering enough evidence to prosecute were two different things.

"Do you think it's Ezra or not?" I asked.

The detective shoved his phone back into his pocket and kept his eyes on the floor for several seconds before looking up at me. He glanced at Shane, then back at me, and I wondered if he would normally not answer this question but for Shane standing there.

"Just tell her," Shane said. "She won't hold you to it if it doesn't pan out."

Rosse let a deep breath out of his nose. "Your ex made some innuendos to his jail mate last night."

"Innuendos?"

"Not enough to be a threat and hold him. But enough that if it were my daughter?" Rosse's ominous eyes stabbed at mine. "I'd tell her to pack a bag and get out of town until we catch the son of a bitch."

## 41

It was after sunset when the winding road turned into the half-mile-long driveway. Night canopied the dense forest that surrounded the quaint cabin. With its outdoor lanterns creating an amber glow along its wooden exterior, the wraparound porch, and the chimney already blowing smoke above the snow-covered pine trees, the place was picturesque. Like something out of a postcard.

Not the safe haven for a dangerous hideaway.

"Guy on the force is lettin' me use this place. Had his uncle, who lives in town, set everything up for us already." Shane put the car into park.

I followed him inside, where a log fire already crackled in the living room.

"Had him stock up on a few days of food, if you're hungry," Shane said, locking the dead bolt behind me.

I shook my head, and then, while Shane checked each window, ensuring everything was locked up and secure, I took in my surroundings.

The living room contained a two-seater royal-blue sofa facing an oversize window, the fireplace in the corner, and a worn oval-shaped coffee table with a crescent-shaped dent on it. They had painted the kitchen cabinets white with fake marble countertops. All of it glowing orange from the gorgeous fire warming the space.

I walked up to it and held my palms out.

"Not bad, right?" Shane appeared behind me, slipping my coat from my shoulders.

"Still feels like overkill."

I couldn't believe it had come to this, and I couldn't stop questioning if these precautions were too extreme. I mean, if the person wanted to kill me, why leave me a threatening note? Why not hide in the corner of my apartment and off me right there? But the fact that I was debating the likelihood of my death was what sealed my decision to go to this cabin with Shane. And it was only temporary.

I tried to look at the positive. The good thing about the flowers was that it presumably left a trail of evidence pointing to the person who bought them, and the person who bought them was most likely the person who had pushed me off that bridge. Which meant we were far closer to catching them than ever before.

"Thank you," I said. "For arranging all of this."

Even though I hoped it wasn't necessary, it was kind all the same. Another example of Shane's fierce protection over me.

Shane stood behind me, holding my hips as he brushed his lips against my neck. It was just a whisper of a kiss, yet it shouted throughout my entire body, echoing throughout my chest and awakening every inch of my skin, which now begged to be touched by his rough hands. He pressed his chest harder into my back, and as he dragged his lips upward to my jaw, I shut my eyes, feeling the worry and disappointment over being driven from my home wash away with the waves of pleasure now dancing across my body.

"And I promise I'll make this stay memorable," Shane whispered, allowing his tongue to briefly caress my neck.

"You're trying to get my mind off of it," I managed, struggling to think coherently with my lower belly warming to a boil.

"Is it working?"

Part of me wanted to hold on to my anger over this situation, but I'd already allowed this person to dominate my life and rob me of any sense of security. I didn't want to give them the power to control every aspect of my life—namely, the good fortune of being alone in a cabin with Shane. I would not squander this and pout.

Even if I wanted to be upset right now, I couldn't be—not with Shane's fingers breaching the hem of my shirt, kindling flames along my belly, my chest, which he grabbed as I turned my head and surrendered my mouth to his.

I ran my fingers through his silky black hair, feeling his excitement grow as he pressed his hips against my lower back. His tongue was gentle and sweet as it danced with my own, my desire to feel him swelling in my thighs.

Shane turned me around so we faced each other. Damn, the amber glow made him so much sexier, the way it bronzed his skin and the flames reflected in his blue eyes. I could stare at those eyes forever, memorize every pixel as he tilted his head and pressed his mouth to mine again.

With the pops of firewood crackling, the smell of its burning wood billowing into the room, I opened my lips and welcomed Shane's tongue against mine, groaning as I ran my hands up through his hair. Each time I'd kissed him, it had felt like the first—that urgent, desperate need for his mouth to never leave mine overwhelming my thoughts. Especially when he trailed his fingertips down my back, pulling at the hem of my shirt.

He broke our kiss and pulled it over my head, allowing himself a hungry gaze of my body, before I helped him get his shirt off— marveling at his tattoos, which appeared to be engraved even deeper into the ridges of his muscles. I placed my palms against his firm chest, feeling the beat of his heart. He let me study his celestial body for only a moment before he grabbed the back of my head and pulled my mouth to his.

Though gentle, his kiss was needy and urgent. He walked me backward, and when the backs of my legs hit the couch, he relinquished his hold on me long enough to strip me out of my shoes and remaining clothes. Followed by his own.

Last time, he'd claimed me. It was my turn to claim him.

When I pushed *him* down onto the couch in a seated position and climbed on top of him, I could tell by the slight rounding of his eyes and smile that I'd surprised him. I buried my fingers in his hair as I kissed him harder, relishing his groan as I rocked my hips along his lower stomach. He grabbed my breasts as I lifted my hips up slightly and then sank down on top of him, connecting our bodies.

Shane growled and grabbed my hips as I began to move. Slow at first, trailing kisses along his sharp jaw, holding his shoulders, but then I picked up my pace and leaned back, staring right into his sapphire eyes. Watching his every reaction as I tilted and moved on top of him, finding the spot that made his eyes roll into the back of his head.

I could feel a wave of my own building, too, grinding that delicate spot against him.

Shane kissed my nipples, crashing that wave closer to the shore.

"Don't stop," I whispered, pulling at the back of his head.

He gladly obeyed, tasting and sucking as he stared up at me with hungry eyes, our bodies working together in an artful dance.

And then…then the wave began to crash, so powerfully that my body started to lock up. Shane kept his eyes on mine, listening to my every moan as he grabbed my hips and pulled at them to keep our dance going.

And just as the last trembles of my wave began to subside, Shane pulled my lips to his and growled into my mouth.

Before stilling beneath me.

We made love again and again the next night.

And the night after. As the days strung together, I existed on the seesaw of elation—for getting so much exclusive time with Shane—and hopelessness that they would ever close this case.

42

"What is taking so long?" I asked.

"I know it's difficult to maintain patience," Detective Rosse said on the other end of the phone.

"I thought between the flowers and the fingerprints, there would've been an arrest by now."

"Attempted murder is a significant charge, one that the district attorney requires sound evidence for."

"I can't wait here forever," I said. "I have to get back to my job in person. The Wi-Fi here is terrible."

He said nothing.

"How much more time do you need?" I pressed. "Ballpark."

If it was longer than a few more days, we needed to go back.

He sighed and spoke in a low tone, like he was answering me reluctantly. "Give me another twenty-four hours."

I sat up. In the week and a half we'd been here, I'd talked to Rosse every day for updates. Every day was more of the same. *We're working on it, crime scene results, questioning, yada yada.* Never once had he given me a timeline. Let alone one so short.

"There's been a development," I surmised.

Shane was spread out on the couch with his feet up, glancing at me with questions in his eyes. The poor guy was so damn worried they'd never get enough evidence to put my attempted killer behind bars. Ironically, being a detective gave him a front-row seat to how many people got away with crimes. Shane had been trying to hide his worry, but he frequently cracked his knuckles as he glared at my un-ringing phone.

Sensing they might be close was thrilling. But what if it wasn't the ending we hoped for? What if the DA reviewed all the evidence and declined to press charges? I didn't want to burst into tears in front of Shane while I was on the phone, upsetting him by finding out that way. If this was bad news, I'd find a gentle way to break it to him.

First step: privacy, so I could find out what was going on.

I opened the door of the cabin and stepped out onto the snow-lined porch.

Nestled deep into the woods of northern Illinois, the cabin was surrounded by emerald pine trees, dusted with snow. Occasional deer walked by, often in the early morning hours or at sunset, when the orange light softened the forest into an amber glow. Right now, that glow was fading to black—just like the probable conclusion of Rosse's investigation.

I brushed the snow off the antique rocking chair with my palm, cursing when a sharp pain sliced into my skin.

*Even the chair wants me to leave this place and get back to my life.*

I sat down, squeezing my now-bleeding palm.

"We confirmed the flowers were from Ezra. He was released with enough time to buy them and go to your apartment. The flower shop employee remembers him."

Holy shit.

I waited for him to say more.

"So, that's the development? He's been the one who threatened me?"

*That's it?* After days, all we had was confirmation my ex-moron sent me threatening flowers? Surely, they'd figured that out days ago and just hadn't been willing to share it with me until now.

"No." The detective took a deep breath. "You sitting down?"

A blood drop splattered onto the snow from the wood that had pierced my palm. I quickly studied the wound, relieved it didn't look deep enough to warrant an emergency room trip.

"I've got the warrant in my hands, Willow. We're going to arrest Ezra for your attempted murder."

A tornado of emotions blew through me. Relief that they had found the person responsible and were going to arrest him. That this was finally over and I could put it behind me. But also shock.

How could I have been in a serious relationship with someone and never suspected they were capable of violence like this? It hurt to realize Ezra willingly and purposely tried to end my life. And for what? Because I wouldn't take him back? Because he had called me a bitch that night and panicked and thought it was all over? I had no idea what he must have done or said to lure me to that bridge—likely threatened suicide or something. But even more bizarre than shock, staying well past its expiration date, was pity.

I couldn't believe I felt a little sorry for Ezra. I shouldn't. A normal person would feel nothing but disgusting hatred for him, and I did feel those things. But Ezra was likely going to spend years in prison. And a small fragment of my heart wilted at the end of this tragic love story.

"So, it's over," I said.

The detective was silent.

"It's over, right?" I repeated.

"Ezra's not at his apartment. He's been fired from his job, so coworkers haven't seen him for days."

"So, you can't find him?"

"With how many cops we have looking for him, I can't imagine he'll last more than a day. We'll pick him up."

Relief pumped through the blood that oozed from my cut, but sometimes, relief makes you let your guard down.

## 43

The shape outside looked like nothing at first. It sat among a sea of forty-foot-tall pine trees, whose limbs appeared black in the early evening sky.

I gazed out the kitchen window as I washed fresh blood from the stupid cut on my palm. It wasn't that bad; Shane didn't need to curse himself for not bringing a first aid kit, and he certainly didn't need to rush into town to get bandages.

I glanced out the window again, only this time, the shape moved.

My heart launched a cannon of needles through my body.

Because now that it had moved, I could see it wasn't just any shape.

*It's human.*

I had never seen another person out here. This cabin was ten acres away from the next one and three miles from the main road that led into a town with one convenience store–slash–gas station–slash–grocery store.

I darted to the living room and looked out the front window, thinking maybe Shane was back already. But his car wasn't there.

I ran to the kitchen window.

*I'm overreacting.*

*I'm just being paranoid.*

I squinted to get a better look at the person, but it was dark outside, and all I could make out was a shape. A man, I think?

He walked into the woods and vanished.

*Probably just a neighbor. Probably out for a walk at sunset and had walked too far.*

I yanked the kitchen drawer open and grabbed a butcher knife just to be safe.

The figure came back out of the woods. He stood next to an ancient pine tree and stopped.

*He's staring right at me.*

I ducked down beneath the window so he couldn't see me. Which was stupid. He already saw me. And he likely noticed there was no car outside—that I was in here all alone.

There was no way Ezra would have been able to track us up here, right?

I needed to call Shane.

I crawled out of the kitchen toward the bedroom, where my cell phone was charging on the nightstand, but I didn't make it that far.

Because the figure walked right by the bedroom window. All I could see was his shadowed profile, so I couldn't see his face to confirm it was Ezra.

If it were an innocent neighbor, he wouldn't walk past a bedroom window in the back of the cabin like this, and if he needed something, he could've knocked on the front door.

I needed to grab my cell phone, hide in the closet, and call the police. And Shane. But this cabin was so tiny, it wouldn't take that unknown figure long to find me. A minute, maybe two, if I was lucky. And we were out deep in the forest. Lord knew how far away we were from the closest police station. I might have a knife, but he could knock it out of my hand or overpower me or have a gun or some other weapon.

But if this guy did wish me harm, my only hope was to get as much distance between me and him as possible.

Hide.

Or run.

I looked at the nightstand, ten feet to my right. At the front door…
and then I shot up like a missile, unlocked the dead bolt, and ran into
the sanctuary of trees, not looking back.

I didn't need to run all the way to town. I just needed to be deep
enough in the forest to get away from whoever that was and wait until
I heard Shane's car pull up so we could call the police.

I wove through a blanket of trees so fast, my lungs burned. It felt
like icicles were piercing them from the inside with each breath I
took, and now, my feet were screaming in agony. Even through the
adrenaline, the snow attacked my skin.

The butcher's knife trembled in my hand as my body shivered. A
blanket of goose bumps erupted, failing to keep me warm as I risked a
look back at the cabin. Behind a curtain of trees, I couldn't see it
anymore, which was good. If I couldn't see it, whoever that was probably couldn't see me.

But what if he followed my footprints?

My bare feet screamed in agony from the cold snow. It felt like
being stabbed by a thousand needles, yet I couldn't go back to the
cabin. Not until I saw Shane's headlights approach.

I could only hope it wouldn't be long because I was wearing
nothing but a thin layer of cotton pajamas.

I glanced up at the surrounding trees, spotting an empty oak in the
middle of pines. Its branches offered an escape from the snow and a
better view to watch for headlights.

I ran ten feet to it and grabbed the first branch, my injured palm
yipping in protest. The bark was as thick as a baseball bat, and it
scraped my arms as I tried to pull myself up.

Two hands grabbed my hips.

I screamed and spun around, pressing my knife's tip against the
chest of a dark figure, who threw his hands into surrender.

"Easy!" he said.

Chest heaving, standing in the snow, I kept the blade of the knife
against his chest until my eyes adjusted to the blackness. Only then
did I lower my weapon.

"Hey." Shane pulled me to his chest. "It's okay. You're safe."

"S…someone's w…w…walking around tt…th…the cab…bin."

"It was me." Shane shrugged off his coat, wrapped it around my shoulders. "I was getting logs for the fire so you can lie down after I bandage your hand."

"No. Y…your c…car wasn't out f…front. You w…weren't back y…yet."

"I parked on the side this time, sheltered behind two pines."

I melted into Shane's chest and savored the way his arms tightened around my body.

"Jesus, you're not wearing shoes?"

He picked me up, one arm under my legs, the other beneath my back.

"I can walk," my ego assured. But my icicle feet told my ego to shut the hell up.

His steps punched through the snow.

"Next time, call me instead of confronting a stalker in the dark, okay?"

I pressed my cheek against his shoulder as he carried me through the icy forest and back into the warmth of the cabin. Once inside, Shane wrapped me in two blankets and added three more logs to the fireplace before bandaging my palm.

"Thaw," he said, kissing my forehead.

But I only warmed up for a few minutes before my cell phone rang. Shane brought it to me from the bedroom and looked at me with anxious eyes.

It was Detective Rosse's number.

## 44

"I have news," the detective said. No *hello*. No *how are you*. Just straight and to the point.

"Good news or bad news?"

"You sitting down?"

Shane sat by my feet and pulled them onto his lap, pretending not to be apprehensive over whatever the detective was about to say.

But failing.

"I am," I said.

"We got him," Rosse said. "Ezra's in lockup."

I closed my eyes and let out a breath that felt like I had been holding since I hit the water.

"He is?"

"Caught him at O'Hare with a one-way ticket to Mexico."

I set my hot chocolate down on the coffee table. "He was going to flee the country?"

"Appears so. But we got him."

All the anxiety that had been swirling around inside of me released its grip on my ribs, and I could finally relax for the first time in a long time.

I smiled, and at the sight of my smile, Shane's muscles loosened. He put his elbow on the armrest of the couch and pressed his thumb and middle finger to his closed eyes. I wondered if he was fighting back tears.

"How long ago did this happen?" I asked.

" 'Bout an hour ago. He's in Cook County Jail right now."

"So, it's over?"

"No judge will grant him bail after trying to flee."

It was over. Ezra was behind bars.

It felt like I had been trapped under the weight of a boulder that had just been lifted off my body, and I was finally free to stand up, brush myself off, and walk away.

My hypothesis over *why* Ezra had tried to kill me bugged me, though, because it was incomplete. He'd been trying to get me back for six months, so what happened that night that culminated in murder? And if he had tried to kill me, why was he so stupid to leave a threatening note in my apartment that would put a target on his back? He hadn't even covered his financial tracks of having bought the flowers.

Would I ever find out the answers to these questions?

"I'll be in touch, Willow."

"Okay."

"Have a good night."

"Detective Rosse?" I took a deep breath. "Thank you."

"I'm glad we caught him, Willow. I'll be in touch soon with next steps."

I hung up.

"They got him."

Shane's smile stretched so wide, I could see his teeth. He jumped on top of me and kissed me like we'd been separated by war—his lips firm and urgent, his fingers twisting through my hair.

I couldn't believe that it was finally over. This nightmare had consumed less than a month of my life, and yet it felt like it had transformed everything.

"I adore you," Shane whispered against my lips.

We only kissed for a minute before my cell phone chimed with a text.

"It's from my mom." I squinted, confused. "She said she has something important to tell me."

45

"I'm moving to Texas," Mom said.

I literally froze in place, as if her words harnessed the power of immobilization.

When I had arrived at my mother's place, the first thing that struck me was how gorgeous she looked. She had a fresh haircut, her hair styled with loose waves around her face, her makeup was pristine with a rosy glow to her cheeks, and she wore a silk black shirt with fitted jeans. In all our years together, I couldn't remember her taking such good care of herself. She looked amazing. Ten years younger, at least.

Last time, she'd been smoking—something she only did when she was anxious. Like, say…telling us big news.

"What?" I asked.

"This is what I'd wanted to share with you and Hayley a couple weeks ago, but you left before I had the chance," Mom explained. "There's a large insurance firm looking to open up a branch in Texas. I would be the leader of it with expansion possibilities across the southwest. I interviewed for it and got the job."

"I thought you liked your job?"

And I didn't want her to move. Texas was what, a three-hour flight away? Our relationship might not have been *Brady Bunch* perfect, but if she moved away, we would never get a chance to have the type of relationship I had been trying to build for the last twenty years.

But she was a grown woman, entitled to live her life however she wanted.

"I do," she said. "But…"

Mom motioned for me to take a seat on her couch.

"The truth is, I've been thinking about leaving Chicago for a long time," Mom admitted, looking down at her hands. "Everywhere I look, there are reminders of your father."

Looking back on it, this should not have surprised me. Mom had said things throughout the years about how nice it would be to move to another state and get a fresh start. At the time, I had chalked it up to her daydreaming, but I shouldn't have.

Of course Mom would want a fresh start. Chicago was where her love story ended in tragedy. Chicago was where she stayed to raise her two little children, but having Grandma nearby to help might have been the main reason. But now, we were both grown.

"I've been wanting to do this for years, but I felt I couldn't go because your sister was so reliant on me."

Reliant. That was a kind word. And given that Hayley's problems were rooted in the trauma of Dad's death, I could see why Mom had never put her foot down as much as I thought she should've.

"I…" The selfish part of me wanted to say, *Don't leave. Especially because I'd learned this morning that my life is about to change forever…*

But I had never seen her look so peaceful. While her moving away from me might hurt, it was surely something that was going to make her very happy.

And you know what?

It was time for me to make a different decision. For over twenty years, I had tried to change the relationships with my mom and sister into something that it never became. How long do you hold on to a relationship that only exists in your hopeful wishes? How long does it take to accept things for what they are rather than what you want them to be?

Asking her to stay would not only be selfish; it would repeat the same cycle.

It was time to let go and accept things the way they were.

"I'll miss you," I said.

Relief flooded my mom's face, and her eyes welled with tears.

"I'm sorry for not being the mother you deserved," she said.

My throat swelled. Funny how a simple acknowledgment and apology were especially healing to a complex wound.

"Your sister told me what happened to you. That you'd almost died."

I wasn't sure what to say.

"I wish you had told me."

"I didn't want to worry you," I said.

Ironic, how she'd spent years keeping things from me to protect my heart, and I'd done the same to her.

"I hope you know how much I love you," she said.

My turn to cry. I knew this moment of adoration was born in a goodbye rather than a genuine change in our relationship, but I appreciated it all the same.

"I'm glad you're finding your happiness, Mom. You deserve to be happy."

Every human deserves happiness, no matter how hard we have to fight to claim it.

"I started seeing a therapist who helped me process some of my feelings. I should have handled the birthday dinner with you better and when you came to me afterward to talk about your dad."

Wow. The apologies continued unraveling resentments tied around my bones.

"She helped me realize I wasn't just processing grief. Or guilt over Hayley's issues. The biggest obstacle I've had in my life is shame. Shame that Hayley is struggling with addiction. Shame that I wasn't a better mother to you when I should've been. Shame that your dad died and I wasn't there to stop it, and shame in how it all went down, what he—"

Mom shook her head, unable to finish.

"I think a fresh start will do me good."

Footsteps came up the front walkway.

"Where will Hayley go?" I whispered.

My mom pursed her lips. "We're figuring that out."

Translation: no idea. But it was time for Hayley to leave the nest. Once and for all.

The front door burst open, and Hayley looked at me and Mom. At our hands, at the closeness between us. Which may have been upsetting to my sister to see Mom being so kind to me after I'd hurt Hayley with my questions over the bridge incident.

"You told her?" Hayley asked.

Mom nodded.

"When do you leave?" I asked Mom.

"They want me to start right away. I fly out tomorrow."

"Tomorrow?" I choked out.

"I'll still have to come back to pack up my stuff."

Yeah, but if she was starting a new job tomorrow, packing would be a weekend trip at best. I wish I'd had more notice to talk to Mom.

I hoped Hayley had more notice than I did—or at least was given some kind of grace period to find alternate housing. Because she looked damn stressed. She fidgeted by the front door, scratching the side of her face with her fingernails.

Hayley rarely answered my calls as it was, and after I offended her? Once my mom left, there would be nothing forcing us to talk again. Hopefully Hayley would get her life together, but if not, she might jump from house to house, couch hopping, and if she wasn't able to pay her cell bill, there'd be no easy way to stay in touch with her.

No matter how justified my questions might have been, I wanted to apologize to Hayley for offending her. And now might be my last chance to do it.

"Can I talk to you?" I asked her.

She bit her lip, looking unsure.

"I won't take long," I said.

Hayley's defeated shoulders showed a subdued version of the angry girl who had stormed off the other day. My heart flickered with hope that she didn't want to leave things on bad terms with me before Mom moved away, either.

"Sure. There's something I want to show you, anyway," Hayley said. "Can I borrow your car, Mom?"

Show me? What in the world would she want to show me? And why was she acting so off? Not looking me in the eyes?

I followed her to Mom's car and tried to put her odd behavior aside; Hayley's world was getting turned upside down. Perhaps she was going to ask me for help and felt embarrassed to do it in front of Mom.

"I want to apologize for our fight," I said.

"It's fine."

Clearly, she was still upset by it, though. Hayley scraped the skin of her palm with her nails and wouldn't look at me.

"I should have known better than to ask you if you'd want to hurt me."

Hayley looked out over the steering wheel as she turned onto a side street. We hadn't been driving long, but we'd entered a neighborhood I didn't recognize.

"I guess if I were in your shoes, I would have asked the same thing," she said absently, as if only half listening.

She pulled in front of an abandoned house. With the sun tilting in the horizon, its disheveled appearance had nowhere to hide. It was a tiny box house with a flat roof and plywood nailed over the windows, the front lawn littered with beer cans, broken glass, and Styrofoam containers.

"Is this where you're moving to?"

Maybe Mom had given her some money to help find a place to fix up.

"No," Hayley said. "Come inside with me?"

A man with a matted beard and puffy red coat stood on the corner, staring at me.

"I want to show you something," she said when I hadn't moved.

"This place is clearly abandoned; we have no business walking in."

Hayley's eyes tightened. "You don't recognize it?"

"Why would I?"

"Because it's where Dad died."

## 46

The house smelled like urine had soaked into its baseboards for years. The walls had been spray-painted with black, orange, and bright green paints. Numbers, symbols. Gang signs perhaps. But thankfully, the place was empty.

I took timid steps across the kitchen floor, the linoleum peeling up in the corners and stained yellow. The air was cold and stuffy, no circulation or heat, but Hayley didn't seem to mind.

"Maybe we should go." I didn't like the idea of getting in trouble for trespassing.

"This is where he died." Hayley pointed to the kitchen floor. "You were right there." She pointed to the hallway. "And I was right there." She pointed to the adjoining living room. "Mom was at the store."

*We lived here?*

A haunting chill seized my muscles.

My dad had felt like a ghost my whole life. And now, here I was, standing in the very spot where he took his last breath.

I wished I could remember more. The kitchen felt vaguely familiar to me. So did the living room. It was as if some brain cells still remembered the layout of the house, but none of the horror that happened inside.

"Why did you bring me here?" I asked.

Hayley opened a drawer in the kitchen and pulled out newspapers, spread them across the countertop, as if she knew I'd be unable to resist finding answers about his death.

"You can read it for yourself."

Some part of me screamed that I should run. Hayley was staring at me, her eyes slightly widened, frame tilted toward mine. After twenty-four years, the answers to the questions that had haunted me my whole life were only a few steps away.

My version of a drug I could not resist.

I inched toward the countertop, toward the words that could forever alter my life.

My past. My present. And my future.

The first thing that I noticed was Dad's picture. The second thing I noticed was the headline.

TWO KILLED WHEN FATHER PULLS GUN ON COP.

*Police say Michael Johnson turned violent after police served him an eviction notice. The suspect pulled a gun on a police officer, turning a routine visit into a deadly shoot-out. Residents could hear shouting as tension escalated, culminating in both men firing one round. Both fatal.*

I staggered away from the kitchen counter.

Away from the new reality before me.

An eviction notice.

A standoff.

Why did this sound so familiar?

Was it ingrained in my brain? Buried somewhere deep in my psyche?

It all made sense now, why mom was so ashamed—because Dad had murdered a police officer.

This was the deep family secret they had tried to keep from me. This explained why Mom didn't tell me everything, why she thought I would live under the shame of what had happened that awful day. Because being the daughter of a man who killed a police officer? That was quite the dark cloud to live under, and I wasn't so sure I would've been able to crawl out from underneath its horror.

This was why Mom had taken on the burden of carrying this immense secret—to give me the best life possible.

All the while, Hayley had lived with this darkness. All her anger, all these years—I now understood her better than I ever had and why her suffering had transformed her into a toxic person.

I remembered the conversation Shane and I had about grief. Grief wasn't just a monster, eating relationships in its path. It was a cancer, spreading into every infected orifice it could find.

"That cop killed him," she said. "Came into our home with a loaded gun and shot our father dead."

I've had a challenging time accepting our dysfunctional family dynamics. But this whole time, Hayley and Mom must've struggled to accept the reality surrounding Dad's death. Their hearts having twisted the facts. Yes, technically, Dad had been shot by someone, but he'd been the one to pull the gun on an armed police officer. Even if the police officer had fired first, it would've been in self-defense, not murder.

Grief had warped their perception of those events.

I turned around and looked at my fallen sister. At her hollowed-out cheeks, her stringy blonde hair that looked light brown with all its oil at the roots, and her clothes that were too baggy for her body.

I knew nothing I could say now could unravel the twenty-plus years of brainwashing she had done to herself.

"Is any of this ringing a bell?" She rocked from her left foot to her right.

"I was only four," I reminded her. "I don't remember what happened."

"Yeah. Don't remind me," she said.

And then she pulled a gun from her coat pocket.

And pointed it at my face.

## 47

"What the hell are you doing?" I put my hands up. "Give me your phone."

"Hayley…"

"Phone! Now!"

When I pulled it from my back pocket, she yanked it from my hand and held it up to my face to unlock the screen.

"Hayley, I don't know what you think—"

"Shane…" she spat.

My blood thinned.

"I figured you were the pick-up-on-the-first-ring kind of guy. Do you know who this is?"

Silence.

"A man who remembers voices. Impressive. Listen, I've got your girlfriend here with a gun pointed at her head. If you like her better with her brains inside of her body, you should come to the address I'm about to text you. Oh, and don't bring or notify a single cop."

Nausea lurched bile up my esophagus.

"Now, that's no way to talk to a lady, Detective. You'd better hurry. I'm running out of patience, and if anyone comes by to check on us, boom."

Hayley hung up the phone and threw it on the floor.

"What are you doing?" I asked.

"How does it feel?"

"How does what feel?"

She rocked from side to side and swiped her nose with the back of her free hand. "Knowing the truth about Dad?"

"Why did you call Shane?"

"Answer the question. How does it feel?"

I needed to tread lightly. I didn't know what might set her off and make her pull that trigger.

I had no right to be this shocked, witnessing Hayley going off the deep end. For years, she'd constantly leaned over the cliff of disaster.

"It's awful. I wish I had known all of these years. Why didn't you tell me sooner? This isn't a burden you had to bear alone."

Hayley's eyes filled with tears, and her lip quivered.

"Oh, because *Willow was so little* and *she's so lucky she doesn't remember.* Let's all tap-dance around Willow and make sure she has a perfect life while the rest of us live in hell."

Even with a gun pointed at my head, I hated hearing her suffer like this.

"Please put the gun down, Hayley."

"Screw you."

"If you wanted me to know so badly, why didn't you just tell me before? You know I kept asking Mom about it when we were kids until she shut the topic down."

"If you cared half as much as you said you did"—she sobbed, shaking with violent tears—"you could've figured this out a long time ago. There's Dad's name in black and white in a newspaper article. You could've put the pieces together if you actually gave two shits."

"I do care. I didn't dig into it because Mom begged me a long time ago to let it go, and if I went against her wishes—even if I did it on my own and tried to be discreet—there was a chance she'd find out and would be so upset that I might've lost her, too! I chose to let it go so I could keep the one parent I had left, Hayley, but of course I care about what happened to Dad!"

"You do *not!*" She stepped closer, the gun now only three feet from my forehead. "You claim you wanted the truth, but deep down, you knew you didn't want to hear it! You just wanted to look like the concerned sister that wanted to find out what happened to her family. You were playing a role, but you were never one of us."

"Hayley, please. Put the gun down."

"And now, Mom's moving away, and everything's just going to keep getting worse."

"Killing me will not solve anything. You don't want to spend the rest of your life in prison, Hayley."

She laughed this ominous, heartbroken cry and rubbed her runny nose with the back of her wrist. "I won't be here anymore."

At first, I thought she meant she'd flee, but I could see something else in her eyes…something disastrous.

*Is she going to kill me and then herself? Why call Shane then?*

"Hayley, you don't want to do this."

"Shut up!" she screamed so loud, spit sprayed across the room.

"Mom will be destroyed if you do this."

"Serves her right for abandoning us to go start her happy life. I mean, what the hell? What kind of mom makes one daughter live in hell and lets the other one live in a fairy tale? And just when the one daughter can't take it anymore, she up and moves to Texas, leaving her behind. Nobody cares about me. Nobody ever cared about me, except Dad!"

"That's not true. Mom has always taken you in when you needed help."

"While threatening to kick me out on the streets! Just like the day you had your fucking fall."

I stepped back, my hips hitting the counter.

"What are you talking about?"

"You want to hear what *caring* sounds like? Mom told me if I got arrested one more time for possession, she was throwing me out for good. And when I asked her for money for groceries, she said she'd buy them for us herself from now on. But I needed cash. I owed money to my dealer, and she wouldn't give me any. And then what do *you* do, Willow? When I go to you, asking for a little money to help, do you give it to me? No. You lecture me about spending money on drugs."

"You came over that night?"

"And when I turned and walked away from you, you kept lecturing me. You followed me on your high horse, yelling at me for giving Mom a hard time when *she* was the one giving *me* a hard time! *She* was the one holding me back in life, making me live with this secret. And the daughter that got everything handed to her wouldn't even give me fifty bucks."

"The night I went over the bridge, I was with you?"

"I told you to back off. But did you listen? No. You grabbed my arm and started searching my pockets. And when you found a *tiny* pack of powder, you said you were calling the cops. You gave me some damn speech about how time in jail would sober me up."

"You tried to kill me."

"I was just trying to get my drugs back! *You're* the one that wouldn't let it go and turned it into a wrestling match! You're the one that threatened me! You told me you lived next door to a cop. If you turned me in, I'd be homeless!"

Betrayal ate through my veins like acid.

Hayley had *long* hair, but we knew it was possible the person in that grainy video might've had longer hair pulled back into a bun or something.

"You swore you hadn't hurt me," I said. "You made me feel bad for even asking it."

"What did you expect? That I'd confess and get arrested for that?"

I had expected I could see through her if she'd been lying, but I was wrong.

My stomach churned. I could picture it all. Her showing up at my apartment unexpectedly, begging for money, looking high—like she'd fallen off the wagon. Me following her to talk some sense into her. That's why my apartment door wasn't locked. I must've run out in a hurry after her and chased her down before we had a confrontation that climaxed on that bridge.

"After you threw me over the bridge, did you stay to make sure I made it out alive? Or did you just walk away without even looking back?"

"I saw you get pulled from the river and saw you moving when they loaded you into the ambulance, so I knew you were alive. Figured you'd tell people what I'd done, so I needed to run, and to do that, I needed cash. Mom would never give me any, so I went back to your place to look for some. But when I couldn't find any, I panicked. I paced in your apartment for a while, trying to think of how to leave town with no money."

My heart clenched at her treason. I had to grab the counter to keep my weak knees from failing.

"I couldn't tell Mom what I'd done—she'd kick me out for good. So, I called a few hospitals until I found the one you were at and asked if they'd allow you visitors. I was going to beg you not to press charges. When the nurse found out I was family, she gave me the update that you were fine but had no memory of what had happened."

Giving her the chance to get away.

"When I saw you at Mom's birthday dinner," she said, "I was petrified you'd remember it all once you saw me."

That's why she'd looked so off.

But if she'd been in my apartment, looking for cash, she must have been careful to leave everything in place or I would have noticed. Except for…

"Why did you move my stuff?" My toothbrush. My bookmark. "And clog my drain with my hair?" Hair she must have gathered from all my combs and brushes.

Her face darkened.

"Because once again, everything was going to work out just fine for you. Just like it always has! It was all going to go back to the way it was before—with you living in your happy little bubble and with me trapped in a dark nightmare, reliving Dad's murder over and over again. It wasn't fair, especially after how mean you were to me that night, so I wanted you to crawl out of your skin, like I always have."

Emotions can be the strangest thing. The realization that my sister threw me off that bridge was the only thing I should be fixated on. And, yes, of course, that hurt immensely. But, while I'd never forgive it, an unplanned confrontation that turned violent was bad enough.

Going into my apartment and trying to *purposefully* mess with me psychologically? Somehow, that was an even harder pill to swallow. Imagining her moving my stuff and gathering my hair from my brushes and shoving it into my drain while I was being treated at the hospital. The betrayal stung so deep, it was like my heart shattered and fell to pieces at my feet.

*I will not cry. Not for her. Not anymore.*

My sister never loved me the way I loved her.

"Were you spying on me?" Was that figure I'd seen outside my apartment Hayley?

She glared at me. "Spying? Get over yourself. I checked on you outside your apartment a couple of times."

"Why?" I asked.

"I wanted to see if you were with the traitor."

"What does *that* mean?"

"You didn't read far enough." She pointed at the newspaper article.

I was scared to move, scared it was a ploy to shoot me in the back. Still, I turned my eyes to look at the newspaper article again.

I read beneath the fold, where the article went deeper into what led up to the eviction notice. Evidently, my dad had fallen on hard times financially, and after being laid off, he fell behind on his rent. My heart spasmed at that, thinking of all the people in my job I had to help lay off. It went on to say that as Dad's stress level rose, he'd started to get into verbal altercations with people, the police being called on a few occasions for it. Until, finally, the eviction notice pushed him past his breaking point.

In a confrontation with an officer, Dad insisted everyone leave him and his family alone. That he wasn't going to raise his kids homeless. The tension escalated until he drew a gun, the officer responding in like. Escalating voices and crying kids in the background, and then shots fired.

To the right of the article was a picture of the fallen officer.

My stomach sank to the earth's center.

*I recognize him. Those same eyes, that same jaw and smile.*

It matched the photo Shane had in his bedroom of his fallen father —the police officer shot in the line of duty.

*Oh my God.*

My father killed Shane's dad.

## 48

I threw up in the sink. It burned my esophagus even worse than my eyes burned from tears.

I remembered the blood on me in that hospital room after Dad had died. Only…it might not have even been his blood. It might have been the blood of Shane's father. Who was I closest to when the shots rang out? Whose blood had splattered onto me?

While I was a four-year-old girl, standing in this bloodstained kitchen, Shane was a small boy, sitting on the front porch. Waiting for his dad to come home from work. Having no idea his father was a corpse, lying on this floor.

The hurt was so overwhelming, I thought I might pass out.

So was the realization of how deep my sister's resentment ran. Grief had planted seeds of anger inside of her, weeds infesting her feelings until they'd grown into vengeance.

"You ran to the officer," Hayley snarled. "Dad told you to stand still, but you didn't listen. You ran to the officer and got in between them, and that's when the officer must have thought Dad was about to shoot you, so he fired his gun, killing Dad. If you'd just stayed put, Dad would still be alive."

I'd run into the middle of the standoff? Causing gunfire to ensue?

I felt faint. Like the room was spinning.

Logically, I knew I'd only been a four-year-old. But my heart didn't seem to care, flooding my veins with the poison of guilt. If I hadn't done that, maybe Dad would still be here.

Maybe Shane's dad would be, too.

I took deep breaths, trying to force those thoughts into the back of my mind because, right now, I needed to focus completely on convincing my sister to put the gun down.

"When did you find out it was *Shane's* father who shot Dad?"

She glared at me. "When I saw Shane at dinner, he looked familiar. It took me a couple of days to place him."

If I hadn't let Shane tag along to that birthday dinner, could this all have been avoided?

"Don't do this," I said.

"Put your hands behind your back."

"Hayley, I know we had a fight on my birthday, but I love you more than you know."

"Oh, you do? You love me so much, you wouldn't even give me money when I needed it. You love me so much that when I tried to leave your house, you followed me and threatened to turn me into the police."

"I'm sure I was doing what I thought was best for you."

"Bullshit. You've always done what is best for yourself. Hands behind your back. Now."

"If you kill me, I'm not the only one who will die," I said. "I'm pregnant."

## 49

Hayley's eyes widened in shock for several seconds before tightening into disgust.

"How could you have a baby with that man?" she spat.

"Hayley."

"How could you?! His dad killed our father!"

"Shane's a good person."

And it's not like I had any idea that his family was connected to ours; this was another price tag I was paying for the secrets that were kept from me. Not that I'd provoke her right now by pointing that out. Or pointing out that our dad was the one at fault for this, not Shane's.

Hayley paced with the gun still pointed at me, a wild look in her eyes as she struggled to process this.

"This could be good," she eventually mumbled to herself. "He'll be more cooperative then."

Good? She viewed my unborn child as a pawn in her twisted game? And what did she mean, more cooperative?

*How am I supposed to talk her down if she's lost it that bad?*

The scary thing was, Shane would do whatever it took to save me, but not because of the pregnancy. I'd just found out a few hours ago. Hadn't even told Shane yet.

I couldn't believe I was pregnant. It was reckless of me to assume missing *one* pill wouldn't be a big deal. I always took my pill with my morning coffee, but I had spent that Sunday morning in the hospital. I didn't realize I had missed a pill until Monday and then thought nothing of it.

"You're going to kill me." This shock wouldn't relent.

"Only if I have to," Hayley said.

What did that mean? What would constitute her having to kill me? What was her endgame here?

My mind raced, feeling like the answer was right in front of me. *Think, Willow.*

She lured Shane here and insisted he come alone. Why? And why *here*? In the kitchen where our dad and Shane's dad had died all those years ago. Two guns drawn, two bullets, two heartbeats that stopped.

She had to know that Shane would come here armed and would be prepared to fire at the person threatening my life. Was this some sort of test to see if he loved me? It made no sense. And even if he didn't love me, he'd absolutely fire his gun if Hayley turned her gun on him, giving him no other choice. Any threatened person would.

And that's when it clicked. The significance of the location. Shane, the son of the officer who'd killed Dad. Her comment about her not being here anymore. My sister's resentment that I'd had a life of happiness while she'd lived "in hell" all these years, and her bitter hatred toward Shane's father that now extended to Shane.

What she had planned was far worse than my death.

Hayley would pull a gun on Shane, knowing he'd pull one too. Maybe her goal was to kill him before he could pull his weapon—revenge against the son of our dad's killer. But the more probable outcome was that Shane would fire, too.

She was going to force me to watch her and Shane kill each other.

And make me live in the hellish aftermath, just like she had after Dad died.

I felt dizzy, a hostage to a haunting tragedy mirroring the one from over twenty years ago.

I should never have come here with Hayley. I should never have gotten in that car with her or given her the benefit of the doubt. I should have cut her out of my life long ago. I'd given Hayley too many chances.

Just like Shane's dad had given my father too many chances.

My breaths started coming so quickly, I couldn't get enough oxygen, but I needed to snap out of it and focus. Any minute, Shane would show up, walk through that door, and she was going to kill him. As some sick, twisted revenge against his father.

And if it didn't go according to her perfect plan? She'd kill me and my unborn child.

I was not about to let that happen.

I waited until Hayley turned her head to see what sounded like an engine approaching.

And then I lunged.

I grabbed her wrist and bit her hand that held the weapon.

Hayley shrieked as I slammed my body into hers, and we both crashed to the floor—me on my left side, her on her right.

She gripped the pistol even tighter, straining to control its aim.

I tried to twist the gun away from me, but Hayley now held it with two hands, and with her adrenaline pumping, she was strong. So damn strong.

I couldn't twist the weapon, so I released it and grabbed the barrel, pushing it away from me as my sister growled over tightened lips— her discolored teeth covered in spit and hatred.

Hayley slammed her elbow into my temple.

For a second, the pain was so intense, I thought I had been shot, but Hayley pushed herself up off the floor.

I rolled onto my knees and sprinted out the front door.

I made it across the front lawn.

I made it to the sidewalk.

I locked eyes with the man I had seen standing on the corner with a big, fluffy red coat.

"Help!" I screamed.

*Pop, pop, pop.*

My right leg gave out, and I collapsed onto the concrete sidewalk.

"Holy shit!" the man yelled and dropped to the ground on his belly.

At first, all I felt was a tight pressure in my thigh, followed by the warmth of my blood streaming inside my jeans. But then...a burning pain seared through my leg.

I tried to get back up.

*Run, Willow.*

*Run, or you're dead.*

*And your baby is, too.*

I took one step and fell down again.

I got up and glanced over my shoulder.

Four houses away, Hayley was walking toward me slowly, her right hand casually gripping the weapon that had tried to end my life. It was pointed to the ground, as if she knew she had already killed me and was just waiting for the blood loss to do its work.

Because my leg was bleeding crazy fast. It already pooled beneath my knee and spread down my calf, and I could feel its warmth dripping down my ankle as I hobbled away from her.

I limped across the snow-covered lawn, blood leaving a bright red streak behind me, giving away any hiding spot I might find.

I had to keep going. I hobbled between the houses, around the air-conditioning units, and moved to the back of the house to my left, my footsteps straddling the line between the tiny backyard and a field behind it.

That's when a brief recognition hit me of where I was—a memory buried in my mind, just as this field was buried beneath the snow.

*This is the field where Dad and I used to pick wildflowers.*

Each step felt like someone was taking an axe to my thigh, and the blood now soaked my lower leg. I looked over my shoulder and saw my sister following.

"Hayley, stop," I said.

But my voice was weak. Not that it would've mattered. If there was anything I could've said to her to get her to stop, I would've said it by now.

I made it one more house down before my leg gave out.

Even then, I kept going.

For the sake of my baby, I crawled on my hands and knees through the snow, praying someone lived in one of these houses. Praying they'd be courageous enough to come outside and help me. Praying something would slow Hayley down so I could find a hiding spot to stop the bleeding.

Time was the biggest weapon. If I didn't stop to slow the bleeding down, I'd die. But if I stopped, Hayley would shoot me again, and I would die, anyway.

Despite using every ounce of adrenaline my body gifted me with, I was moving so slowly, I could hear the crunch of Hayley's steps behind me, growing closer and closer.

*Crunch.*

My elbows wobbled from fatigue.

*Crunch.*

I kept crawling.

*Crunch.*

My vision blackened along the edges, and I fell to my side.

My body landed across the line that separated the backyard and the snow-covered field. Some part of my heart recognized this exact spot in the field, where my father used to hold my hand.

*Crunch. Crunch.*

I reached down to my belt buckle and loosened the leather strap, pulled out the metal tooth, and then slid the belt from around my waist.

*Crunch. Crunch. Crunch.*

It wasn't easy. I barely had enough strength to get it out, and each of my tugs was echoed with a louder crunch of snow as my sister stepped toward me.

I wondered why she hadn't finished me already. She had hit my leg from much farther away than she was right now. But I couldn't think about that.

I slid the belt under my thigh and fastened it through its loop. Then, I yanked as hard as I could, screaming in pain as the tourniquet cut off the blood supply to the bullet wound.

*Crunch. Crunch.*

I was panting and fairly confident I was about to vomit.

Hayley stood over me and looked down at the mess beneath her. My hands were sticky, the white snow stained in crimson.

"Hayley, please," I whispered.

"It wasn't supposed to go this way," she said. As if that made being murdered by my sister less heartbreaking.

I loved her. Even as she stood above me, even after all her years of pushing me away, I loved her. I hated that she'd become so broken inside that she'd turned into this.

Hate had infected her soul, spreading until it extinguished the light of the Hayley she once was.

My life didn't flash before my eyes, but a happier memory of her did.

*I'm holding Hayley's hand as we run through this field behind our house, jumping over yellow wildflowers and giggling as Daddy chases us.*

*I love Hayley. I hope we stay best friends forever.*

HAYLEY RAISED THE GUN AND AIMED IT AT MY CHEST.

I placed my hand over my unborn child. "I'm sorry," I whispered to him or her. "For not protecting you."

I shut my eyes, wishing my last moments on earth weren't as a failing mother.

"Put your fucking hands up!"

My eyes snapped open to see Hayley's eyes widen as he approached her.

Shane emerged to my right, walking between two houses with his gun drawn, pointed directly at my sister—his arms straight as tree branches, his eyes fixed on the woman about to kill me.

Hayley stared blankly ahead of her as Shane took another step, closing the distance between them.

She allowed Shane to take two more steps.

"This one's for you, Dad," she whispered.

"Hayley, no!"

Like on the bridge, time surrendered to an almost standstill. I lay on the alabaster snow, crimson pooling around me as the orange glow of the setting sun wrapped around my sister who stood over me, arm raised, her finger on the trigger.

Shane wasn't wearing a coat. He was in black slacks, his button-down rolled to his elbows, as if he'd left a meeting when he'd gotten Hayley's call and hadn't bothered to do anything but grab his keys. His forearm muscles clenched as he gripped the weapon, looking over its barrel as a revolver swung toward him.

Shane's eyes widened slightly as she turned. I could see a moment of hesitation on his face, but when her aim landed on his chest, two pops echoed off the nearby houses.

Hayley and Shane both stilled.

They dropped their arms.

And collapsed to the ground.

50

"Shane!" I tried to shout.

Another surge of adrenaline must have coursed through my body because I gained enough energy to crawl over to him.

He was lying on his back, his eyes open. And I could hear a wetness in his lungs as he fought for air. His chest heaved up and down with each desperate gasp.

In the distance, I could see that guy in the red coat on his phone, advancing slowly toward us, probably uncertain if the gunfire was for sure over.

"Call 911!" I shouted. I wasn't sure he would hear me, though. My voice was so weak, and I was so tired, but maybe he was calling for help already.

"Shane," I cried.

I collapsed onto my right side next to him, and with my last ounce of strength, I pressed my left hand against the wound on his chest. Trying to slow the bleeding.

Shane's cerulean eyes locked with mine, only the color seemed to drain from his. They weren't bright anymore, more like a bluish gray.

"I"—he gasped for air—"didn't get to you"—gasp—"in time."

My eyes welled. "Shh. Save your strength."

"I'm"—gasp—"sorry."

The tears broke over my cheeks.

I wasn't a doctor, but even I could see his life fading away. I could hear it in the wet rasps that were supposed to be his breaths. I could see it in the way his lips were losing their color, along with his skin. And I could see it in the way his eyelids began to sink.

"Don't close your eyes," I cried.

Shane's breaths sounded like snoring, his chest caving in and out. His blood oozed outward beneath my hand.

*No, he can't go like this. Not like this.*

He lay helpless, watching me die, too, after all he'd done to protect me. Shane kept his eyes on me, but they were only half open now.

"No! You will not leave us, you hear me? You need to fight...fight for me. Fight for us. Fight for the family we're going to have. I'm pregnant, Shane."

I regretted the words the minute they left my mouth because I shouldn't have told him that his deepest, darkest fear was coming true. His words echoed through the broken chambers of my heart.

*My worst fear is dying and leaving behind a woman I love. Children raised without a father.*

Shane's fading eyes filled with tears. He dragged his arm over to me and placed his hand on my lower belly.

"Tell our child"—gasp—"about me." His voice had lost all its strength, a mere whisper. "Tell him or her"—gasp—"I love them."

A single tear breached the rim of his eye and slid down his cheek.

"You can tell our child yourself," I cried. "Don't leave me. Don't leave us."

"I'm"—gasp—"sorry."

Then, his eyes closed.

## 51

A sharp poke on the top of my hand woke me.

I struggled to open my eyes, my body feeling as though it were weighed down with lead. A faint beeping mixed with the sound of someone clearing their throat.

A sharp pain seared again.

And again.

I tried to open my mouth, but it was sandpaper, and I had an unpleasant taste on my tongue, like I hadn't brushed my teeth for a couple of days. The air smelled faintly of commercial bleach, but at least I was warm.

After a fourth poke, I dragged my eyelids open.

"Sorry, honey," a female voice said.

My blurry vision sharpened into focus to see a nurse standing over me. Wearing royal-blue scrubs with her graying hair pulled into a messy bun, she had a mole on her cheek the size of a pencil eraser.

"You must have shifted in your sleep," she said. "Had to restart your IV."

She stabbed the needle in the top of my hand again.

And that's when everything came flooding back to me. The shooting. My blood loss. Shane. The baby…

"My baby," I said. "Did the baby survive?" My throat was so dry, I had laryngitis.

The nurse taped the needle with white bandaging and looked down at me with pity. "You're still pregnant, as far as we can tell. But it might be a couple of weeks before we know for sure."

My eyes burned. How could I feel heartbroken at the thought of losing a child I didn't even know existed until this morning? Was it still this morning?

"And Sh…" Shane. Did Shane survive? I swallowed the lump in my throat. "Did…" My eyes welled with tears.

"Get some rest." The nurse used one of those voices that people use when they don't want to give you bad news.

"Please, just tell me," I begged.

The nurse looked at me and must have seen the desperation on my face because she sighed and took pity on me.

"I'm sorry for your loss," she said.

This couldn't be real.

Shane's worst nightmare had come true.

*Shane is dead.*

Shane, my protector, my lover.

The most honorable man I'd ever met, the best human I'd ever met.

Shane, who had sacrificed his own happiness just to protect the possible heartbreak a woman might go through if she lost him. Shane, who reluctantly surrendered to his feelings, lost his happily ever after before it even started.

Shane couldn't be dead. He couldn't be.

There was no way he was dead.

The nurse was wrong.

Shane had to have opened his eyes again. He was alive, somewhere. We were going to go home in a few days and feed Snowflake, hold on to each other even tighter, thankful to have survived. We'd have ultrasounds, and we'd feel the baby kick and grow. We'd buy a crib and laugh when we'd struggle with the assembly. We'd hear the first cry of our newborn as both our eyes filled with tears, and we'd have sleepless nights and bottles and little hands to hold. And there'd be zoo trips, and date nights, and lots of smaller moments too, like washing dishes and kissing under the mistletoe, and a million more experiences to be shared.

And his little boy or girl would wait on our front porch for Shane's car to pull up to our driveway each night. And run into his arms.

Shane wasn't gone. He would not miss out on all of that. He would not miss out on life.

"I'll let the doctor know you're awake," the nurse said.

And then she left me in this room, all alone in my nightmare.

He was alive.

He had to be.

There couldn't be a scenario where he was dead.

Maybe if I said it to myself enough, it would be true.

It felt like my insides were on fire, and I clenched my stomach, hoping that our unborn baby would survive so I could hold on to a piece of Shane forever.

I rolled onto my right side, not even caring that my thigh was in pain from the bullet wound they must have repaired, and I stared at the large, empty space.

Behind me, the door to the room opened, followed by voices guiding in something on wheels.

I couldn't imagine having to share this room with anyone; they should have put me in a private room, where I could grieve alone, without a stranger witnessing my despair.

I closed my eyes and whimpered in my hands, trying to stop my sobbing.

The wheels rolled louder along the floor.

"Closer," a hoarse voice whispered.

What if the pain from my heartbreak was enough to kill the baby? How could I possibly put one foot in front of the other? How could I get discharged from this hospital and go back to that apartment with all its memories? Yet how could I ever leave it?

I appreciated that story Shane told me so much more now. About how one of the hardest moments of his life was having to leave his house behind, the only place that held all his memories with his dad.

That's all I would have with Shane now. Memories. Memories of those days in the rustic cabin in the woods that I'd been so impatient to leave behind. Memories of us falling in love. My heart ached at the thought of never seeing him again. I would never get to touch him again or feel his heartbeat beneath my palm.

I felt like my insides were on fire as I sobbed harder, my head throbbing from crying so hard.

A warm hand lay on top of mine and squeezed.

I didn't want the comfort of a stranger. I just wanted to be left alone.

I tugged at my hand, but the person kept their grip around mine.

I opened my eyes and followed the guy's hand up his arm—an arm covered in tattoos. My heart lurched in my chest as my gaze cascaded over his hospital gown. And I met two sapphire gems staring back at me.

## 52

"Shane!"

I lunged off my bed and onto the little space between his body and the hospital bed's railing. Not the smartest move I ever made, considering my right arm jerked back and my IV almost came out. The one the nurse had poked me six thousand times to get situated.

"Easy!" one nurse yelled. "He has a chest injury, honey. You need to be careful."

"You're alive!" My eyes were so blurred with tears, I could barely make out his smile. But I could feel his palm when he brought it up to my face and stroked my skin.

"I was so damn worried about you," he whispered.

"I thought you were dead," I cried. "The nurse. She said, 'I'm sorry for your loss,' and I thought—"

I couldn't even finish the sentence. Even knowing he was okay, it hurt too badly to say something so devastating out loud.

I wiped the tears from my cheeks and noted his heartbroken expression.

"It was your sister." Shane grimaced. "She didn't make it. I'm so sorry."

Hayley was dead. My sister, my only sibling. I knew she might be —I'd heard the gunshots—but it was still a shock to hear the finality of it.

A normal person would fixate on her being nothing but a villain, especially since she'd almost killed me, Shane, and our unborn baby. But she was still my sister—the one who stayed with me when Mom had gone off for days at a time—and it would take a while to mend the laceration in my heart from knowing I'd never see her again.

But Shane had nothing to be sorry for. She'd tried to murder him, tried to murder me, and consequently, she died in the process. Of course I did not wish this terrible fate upon my sister. I wished she could've had a happy life, but Shane did not need to apologize for saving our lives.

"Hayley's the one who pushed me off the bridge," I said. "Evidently, we'd gotten into an argument, and I'd followed her there."

Shane's eyes absorbed my every word, and I could see his mind racing.

"She confessed it all, right before she shot me," I said.

Shane's chest rose and fell quicker, perhaps remembering the bloody scene he'd stumbled across.

He brought his hand down and placed it on my lower stomach.

"Did the baby…" He couldn't finish his thought.

"It'll take a couple more weeks to be sure, but it seems I'm still pregnant."

The blue in Shane's eyes was back in full force, gorgeous sapphires sparkling as he smiled at me.

"When did you find out you're pregnant?" he whispered.

"A few hours before—" I paused. "I'm sorry. I *am* on the pill. I missed one, and I'm so sorry for being so negligent. I should've—"

Shane's finger pressed against my lips.

"Willow"—he grinned—"you're having my child. I'm not upset. Surprised? Yes. But upset?" His mouth curled higher. "Not even close."

Warmth rushed around my chest. I hadn't thought about it until this very moment, but if anything was going to sway Shane into changing his mind about being in a relationship, this would have been it. Seeing him so happy that I was pregnant...it obliterated any lingering fear that, someday, he might regret his decision and leave me.

"It's funny how, sometimes, you don't realize exactly what you want until you have it and then almost lose it," he said. "I want you, Willow. I want this baby. It's all I want."

But I wouldn't let hope take flight yet because there was one more obstacle in front of us, one large enough to make Shane change his mind and never want to be with me again. I was the daughter of the man who had killed his father.

"Shane, there's something I need to tell you."

How would I even begin to explain this?

"Before you came, my sister showed me a newspaper article."

Shane's palm remained on my lower abdomen, on the baby that would suffer if Shane didn't want to talk to me again once he *knew*.

"The article was about when my dad died. Evidently, he—"

"Willow!" Mom burst into the room.

Her hands were on my face, her lips kissing my cheek.

"I've been so worried," she cried. "They weren't sure with the blood loss..."

Mom had dark circles under her eyes, which were swollen, as if she had been crying.

"I'm so sorry," she said. "I had no idea what Hayley had planned."

"Mom."

"I swear, if I had known, I would've stopped her."

"Mom."

Shane looked between me and my mom, but he didn't have time to ask any questions because the door swung open and another woman entered the room. This woman was more composed, her hair slicked back into a ponytail, wearing jeans and a blue sweatshirt with white sneakers. She looked familiar, though I couldn't place her until she came around the other side of Shane's bed and took his hand.

"You're out of recovery," the woman said to Shane. "They said surgery went well."

Disapproval flashed through her eyes that I was intruding on Shane's bed. But to her credit, she put on a smile.

"This is Willow, I presume? I'm Penny, Shane's mother."

His widowed mother.

The woman who had suffered unimaginable loss at the hands of my father. My mom was a ticking time bomb, verbal diarrhea about to erupt from her volcano of guilt for having not seen this coming, and I couldn't imagine a more insensitive or heartbreaking way for Shane or his mother to find out who I really was.

I needed to get Shane alone. He deserved to hear this in privacy and have time to process it before he broke the news to his mother.

"It's nice to meet you." I smiled.

"I'm so sorry," Mom said to her. "I never would have suspected my daughter would have done anything like this."

Shane's mom forced a tight smile.

"Shane, can I talk to you in private?" I asked.

"I think she just flew off the deep end," Mom continued.

"Mom."

"She's struggled ever since she was fourteen years old. Ever since—"

"Mom! Now's not the time."

My voice wasn't terribly powerful, but it was jarring enough that everyone in the room looked at me.

"Please," I said. "I have something important I need to talk about with Shane, and it's urgent."

My mom and Shane's mom looked at each other in confusion while Shane stared at me, his brow furrowed in concern.

"Can we have a minute?" Shane asked.

Everyone lingered, seemingly unsure what to make of my outburst, but the room cleared, and Shane and I were alone once more.

"What's wrong?" he asked. "Is the baby—"

"I have something to tell you, and I don't know how to say it."

He cupped my cheek.

When a long silence passed, he said, "It's just me. You can tell me anything."

"I mean, I just don't even understand the odds of this. It's…" My lip quivered.

"Hey," he whispered and waited until I looked him directly in his eyes. "It's going to be okay, Willow."

I opened my mouth, willing the words to come out. But evidently, I was a coward. They lodged behind the lump in my throat.

I allowed myself five more seconds to absorb Shane's affectionate gaze, knowing this was the last time he would ever look at me the same way again.

And then I spoke the words that would change everything.

"Shane…my dad's the one that killed your father."

## 53

S hane shut his eyes tightly, letting several long seconds pass.

"You knew?" I whispered.

He shook his head. "No. But I..." Shane took a deep breath, one that didn't look pain-free based on his wincing. "When I was a kid, I wanted to hunt down the guy who'd killed my dad and get revenge."

Right. The superhero phase.

"I convinced myself that my mom had lied when she said my dad's killer was dead to spare me heartbreak, so I went into her room where she kept this box of important paperwork to see what she really knew. Found a report about his death, which had the name of his killer on it, but there weren't many other details—but the report did confirm my dad's killer was also dead. So, I couldn't beat him up or do anything else I'd fantasized about."

Shane swallowed.

"I'd seen his name on that report, but once I found out he was dead, my interest in him was over, and I didn't look into him further. I shifted my focus to learn more about my dad's life and started asking people to tell me stories about him."

His chest swelled slightly.

"I knew your last name was Johnson, too, but Johnson is one of the most common last names in the country. Never imagined you'd be connected to him in any way, but..." Shane pressed his lips together. "When you told me your dad was killed and your mom was being all secretive about it, there was a moment I wondered if...but then I thought it was statistically improbable. Millions of people live in this city alone. I mean, the odds of something like that..."

My mouth ran dry, drinking his every word.

"Told myself it was a crazy thought and that once we solved your case and I knew you were safe, I'd dig up the old files and prove to myself that thought was ludicrous. Because honestly"—he shook his head—"I never truly believed it could be linked. The statistics of it are..."

He sighed deeply, again wincing from the pain of it.

My heart somehow found room to beat even faster, terrified he'd push me away and never talk to me again. Because how could he ever be with someone whose family destroyed his? How could he ever look at me, the daughter of his dad's killer, with anything but disgust?

What were the odds that our families were interconnected, anyway?

Shane licked his lower lip, lost in the abyss of his own thoughts. I'm sure thinking the same thing I was. My dad was the troubled man who Shane's father had tried to help multiple times. A man evidently spiraling in financial distress until he got the eviction notice. Which must have pushed him past his breaking point.

Shane's father must've been trying to reason with him. Maybe he sensed my dad had truly snapped this time, but the honorable police officer would not leave two children in the home with an unstable man. Especially not one with a loaded gun. I could picture the entire scenario playing out, escalating to guns drawn, shots fired.

Two souls stuffed into black body bags and hauled away, leaving the remains of fractured families behind.

"I'm sorry," I whispered. "I didn't know until my sister brought me to our old house. Where it happened. She showed me a newspaper article."

It felt like tragic karma to me, learning that this newspaper article existed and then discovering it held all the answers to years of unanswered questions pertaining to my father's death.

Shane still had said nothing, hadn't looked at me in the eyes again. I don't know why I had hoped that this would have a different outcome. Selfishness, I guess.

We would have such a complicated future, co-parenting a child from two opposing families. And on top of it, if his mom blamed his dad's death on her father-in-law simply for her husband taking the same career path, how would she ever accept the daughter of her husband's killer as Shane's girlfriend? Or the mother of his baby?

But that was all wishful thinking, presumptuous to even consider that Shane would ever speak to me again.

I had no right to think about my destroyed heart in all of this. Shane and his family were the victims here, the victims of my dad's violence. My sister's violence.

I needed to give Shane his space. He deserved as much time as necessary to let this all sink in before deciding what the future held. Maybe I could even ask to be moved to another room while we both recovered.

I rolled to my side so I could hoist myself up over his bedrail again, but Shane's hand gripped my shoulder.

"Hey," he whispered. "That's a lot to process, but it doesn't change how I feel about you."

On my left side, my back was to him. I froze, too scared to grasp the hope he'd just given me.

"How could it not? My family is responsible for all of this."

"Look at me," he said.

I hesitated but rolled back over and shifted onto my right side again. So I could stare him in the eyes.

He cupped my head. "Your father is responsible for his actions, not you. You were a child when this happened. A victim to it, not a party to it."

My eyes welled with tears.

"But my sister tried to kill you."

"And you. I'm sorry that I let my hatred for Ezra blind me to the facts that might have pointed me in Hayley's direction. Maybe De Luca was right; I was too close to this case to see things clearly. And because of that, I put you in danger. I could have lost you and the baby forever."

"You have nothing to apologize for. Even Detective Rosse zeroed in on Ezra." All the evidence, both circumstantial and physical—including the flowers—pointed to him.

"*You* have nothing to apologize for," he countered.

I frowned. "You might feel this way now, but down the road, you might feel resentful toward me."

"I won't."

"How can you be so sure?"

"Because my feelings for you will never change, Willow."

How could that be? How could at least a fragment of his soul not wilt toward me?

"No matter what they did," Shane continued, "no matter what *you* might ever do, it won't change how I feel about you. My feelings for you are unconditional."

I bit my lip, trying to tame the hope swelling inside of me. I didn't want to jump onto its wave and ride it to the top, because if it vanished from beneath me, the crash would hurt too much.

"I don't understand how you could ever look at me the same again."

"Willow, when I look at you, all I see is the other half of my heart."

I studied his eyes for any hint of doubt, and when I saw none, I rested my forehead against his shoulder and wept.

All those years, the emotional rejection from my family created a hole in my chest that throbbed with a dull, constant ache. At times, that ache heightened, and it felt like someone had wrapped my chest in nails. And at other times, the pain felt dimmer, like a metronome in the background. Always there. Always hurting, varying its tempo and volume.

Shane wanted me. Shane accepted me for exactly who I was. Of all the people in the world to accept me, having it come from the one person who had every right to hate me made it all the more powerful.

All the more healing. Because it meant he accepted *every* part of me, adored those parts even, so much so that he could look past the dark monster that used to chase him in his dreams.

"I'm so sorry," I cried.

He kissed the top of my head.

"This isn't yours to apologize for, Willow. I will not let the grief from my dad's death take another relationship from me. Especially not one with you."

## 54

Snowflakes drifted from the sky, dusting people's dark coats and the shiny black casket in what looked like powdered sugar. There was no wind in the open field of headstones, as if the gray sky was giving us a moment of silence to digest the finality of a life cut short. Around me, sniffles and whispers overshadowed the soft voice of the pastor, who stood at the front, reading from the Bible.

I thought I would appreciate the closure the ceremony gave me, but evidently, the goal of a funeral was to take whatever sadness burned inside of you and add flames to the fire.

It didn't help that Shane wasn't here to calm my nerves. While he was doing a lot better, he had at least another week in the hospital before he'd be released. Which meant my mom and I had to come here alone. Without him.

It also didn't help that Hayley had become the villain in the news articles. The girl who'd once tucked me in on the nights Mom left would only be remembered for her demons.

Finally, the pastor stopped talking and motioned for me and my mom to come to the front.

My throat battled against the swelling as I walked along the snow-covered grass. Mom placed her hand on the coffin, sobbing so hard that I couldn't make out what she was saying. I put my hand on her back, knowing nothing had the power to make her feel better, but wanting to comfort her all the same.

And then it was my turn.

I hadn't been able to pick the wildflowers myself, given it was winter, but I'd gone to four different stores until I found the exact wildflowers that used to grow in the field behind our house. The same wildflowers I had placed on dad's casket all those years ago.

I set them gently atop her casket, noting how beautiful it was—the lilac and emerald greens on top of the thin layer of snow. As if it wasn't tragically heartbreaking.

"I'm sorry," I whispered to Hayley. "I'm sorry you were in so much pain. I wish I could've helped you."

To think of all those times I'd fixated on whether she showed up for *me*. My graduations, my special events. I'd interpreted all those moments as rejections, but maybe they were cries for help.

Maybe she was isolating herself, drawing herself deeper and deeper into her abyss of suffering until there was nothing left but pain.

Until, like our father, Hayley had reached her breaking point.

I stared at the coffin, picturing my sister lying there.

And a memory stabbed my heart.

AFTER I PUT WILDFLOWERS ON DADDY'S COFFIN, I HUG HAYLEY. *"I MISS him."*

*"Me too," Hayley cries.*

*Mommy spent a lot of time sobbing in her bedroom these last few days. I'm scared she'll never come back out.*

*A fresh stream of tears falls down my cheeks. "I don't understand why he had to die."*

*Hayley hugs me tighter. "Me neither."*

*"He promised me we'd go pick flowers," I say.*

*"I'll take you." Hayley runs her fingers through my hair. "I'll help you pick all the wildflowers you want."*

. . .

WHEN THE FUNERAL CONCLUDED, MOM AND I ACCEPTED WELL WISHES from those in attendance.

One of them was Tracey.

"Hey." She gently hugged me, the scent of her strawberry body wash wrapping around her hair. "I'm so sorry for your loss."

"Thanks, Tracey."

I hadn't seen her since she'd mysteriously left town.

"Emily said you left for a few days?"

Tracey pulled back and nodded. "I had a minor family emergency. Our family dog was dying, and I raced home to say goodbye before it was too late."

"Why didn't you say something?"

She shrugged. "After everything that happened with you, it was so inconsequential in comparison."

I frowned. "It's not inconsequential, Tracey. I know how much Max meant to you. I'm sorry for *your* loss, too."

The tremble of her lower lip told me she appreciated that more than I could imagine, but our moment together was cut short when a figure approached me.

"I'll talk to you later," Tracey said before walking away.

My spine stiffened.

"Hey," Amelia said. "I'm sorry for your loss."

I offered a weak smile, unsure what to say as she stood there, fidgeting.

"You haven't answered any of my calls," she mumbled.

I wished I had texted her back so she didn't resort to talking to me here.

"I think it's best if we...take a break," I said.

With a slow bob of her head, she released a sigh of resignation, as if anticipating this would be my answer.

"I have a question," I said.

Amelia rounded her eyes, as if she'd assumed this entire exchange was going to be one-sided.

"Where'd you get the scratches on your arms?"

The ones that put her on Shane's short list of suspects.

Amelia looked down. "It's embarrassing."

I waited until she blew out a breath and ran her fingers through her hair.

"I saw Ezra flirting with a girl," Amelia said. "This was the night before you fell, and I thought Ezra and I were getting closer. I got super pissed, and I confronted the other woman and went off on her."

Ezra was a nonstop flirt. Even in the beginning of our relationship and evidently even when his goal was to get me back, he was still flirting.

"The girl shoved me," Amelia said. "I shoved her back, and it just... it was stupid, and I was too humiliated to tell you about it."

Especially because telling me would mean confessing her feelings for Ezra.

"I know this isn't the appropriate time to say this," she started, "but just in case it's the last time we ever—" She looked down, unable to meet my eye for a moment. "I'm sorry for betraying you. Ezra was so charming, and I think I let my feelings get all confused, like it was a forbidden romance or something."

I said nothing.

"If it makes you feel any better, I don't think he ever cared about me like I thought he did. I think he was using me to get back at you."

Maybe. I wondered what Ezra's side of the story was. And why I wanted to hear it, along with some other things, before I could officially put this all behind me.

"Do you think we can ever be friends again?" Amelia asked.

I wasn't against forgiveness, but the reality is that we sometimes hold on to things for far too long instead of accepting that some relationships are unhealthy, toxic, or unfulfilling. And those dynamics may never change. We need to learn to identify when to keep fighting and when to lay down our sword.

"I'm sure we'll see each other at social gatherings." And I'd be cordial. "But I think it's best if our friendship took a break."

Amelia nodded in response, as if she'd expected this. "I really am sorry."

Clearly not knowing what else to say, she ambled away.

"How are you holding up?" Emily asked, the next to approach me.

I shrugged. "Numb at the moment."

She frowned. "How's Shane?"

"Improving."

To this, she gave a sad smile. "I'm glad. Sounds like you found yourself a really good guy."

I did.

"I hope to find that one day, too." She smiled. "Are you still planning to see Ezra?"

I nodded.

"Do you think he'll be honest with you?"

I sighed. "I guess I'll find out."

## 55

I sat on the silver barstool, one of ten lined up in a row. Each with its own portion of glass in front of it, encased with a small tan divide, as if that afforded us privacy. A rumbling of voices punched through the stuffy space that smelled of unwashed sneakers.

I could feel the nausea swelling again and popped one of my mints. A pregnancy trick I'd learned to manage my morning sickness.

Ezra walked in, wearing beige khaki pants and a short-sleeved pullover shirt, a prison guard escorting him to his seat opposite of me.

His blond hair didn't look polished anymore. It looked messy, and his eyes had hints of purple beneath them.

He glared at me, and when I picked up the black phone, he made me wait for fifteen seconds before doing the same, as if he was considering never talking to me again.

"What?" he snapped.

"How are you holding up?"

"Like you give a shit."

"I do."

Ezra glowered off to his side before leaning his elbows on the small counter in front of him. "What the hell do you want, Willow?"

*Closure.*

"I know it wasn't you that pushed me off that bridge."

"No shit. I told you that all along, but you wouldn't listen."

"But you sent me that threat. You broke into my apartment to leave it there. Why?"

"What does it matter now?"

"It matters to me. Those flowers are what drove their investigation over the edge, Ezra. Your threats, combined with all of the other circumstantial evidence, is what made them think that you're the one that pushed me off the bridge."

"Know what I don't get?" he snarled. "Only thing I ever did to you was kiss and text some other chicks. And you ruined my life over it. You got it in your head that I'm capable of murder when your lunatic sister has been going off the deep end for, like, two decades."

I hid my grimace.

"Word gets out fast, Willow. I know she's the one that pushed you over the bridge and then attacked you again. But you blamed me."

"I didn't suspect you until you started acting unhinged."

"Go to hell." Ezra shifted, as if he was about to leave.

"Wait," I pleaded.

He was so mad at me; it was doubtful he'd have stayed to talk for another couple of minutes if not for his immense boredom. Anything had to be better than staring at those walls all day.

I squared my shoulders. "I know that you and Amelia dated."

Ezra's jaw set tighter.

"Was it when we were together?"

I should have clarified this with Amelia, but on the day of the funeral, I'd been unprepared and preoccupied to have that conversation with her.

He tossed his angry eyes to the side, obviously debating whether or not to grace me with an answer.

"No. We flirted a little while you and I were still dating, but nothing happened until after we broke up."

It was strange that this provided me comfort. I guess I needed our love to have been real for it to have been worth the pain that came after.

"For the record," I started, "I didn't think anyone had done this to me at first. But once they realized someone *had* pushed me off the bridge, I looked at *everyone* in my life with suspicion, not just you."

Ezra's hardened gaze softened. Just a smidgen.

"And then everything escalated, and you sent those flowers. Why'd you use your own credit card to buy them? You knew they'd get traced back to you."

"It shouldn't have mattered; I didn't try to kill you, so if the cops had done their job, they would've known I wasn't your killer."

"The cops follow the evidence. And you let it all point to you. Threats can constitute a crime, Ezra. Especially when you violate a restraining order to deliver them. Not to mention, breaking and entering. So, why'd you do it?"

"Because I was pissed! You were ruining my life *again*. I'd lost my job, I got brought in for questioning, and I was sick of feeling power-less. I wanted to tell you off, but I had to settle for the card instead."

"You wanted to tell me off."

His look said, *Obviously.*

"So, you bought me flowers?"

His lips pursed. "Thought the only way you'd open the door was if you thought I was there to apologize."

"Why break in to leave them?"

"The hell does it matter now?"

"It matters to me," I said.

"I don't have time for this." Ezra stood up.

"Wait," I said.

If I didn't get all the answers, I would never have the closure I needed. Could I accept that? Yes. I'd learned acceptance through all of this, but it was worth asking him one last time.

"You tell me honestly, and I'll put in a good word with the district attorney. That's a pretty generous offer, considering everything you've done."

Ezra sat back down, his eyes filled with anger. "A generous offer? How about you drop all the goddamn charges?"

In addition to violating the restraining order, Ezra was being charged with felony breaking and entering, since he'd entered my home, intending to threaten me. If I spoke on his behalf, there was a possibility it could get bumped down to a misdemeanor.

"You intimidated me and threatened my life. Are you going to answer the question or not? Because if not? I will not put in a good word for you. The district attorney wants to make an example out of you. Trying to interfere with the investigation by showing up in the hallway and demanding I have them back down? Then threatening the victim? They're going for the maximum sentence allowed, Ezra. Your only hope of getting the charges knocked down is if the victim puts in a good word with the DA. And you know it. So, it's your choice."

Ezra licked his teeth, looked down at the ground. And eventually met my eyes.

"I came with the flowers, but you weren't home. Thought maybe you were in the shower or were feeding that stupid cat, so I went around back. Found the sliding glass door unlocked."

So, he helped himself into my apartment and left a death threat?

"You threatened to end me, Ezra."

He said nothing.

"No matter how angry you might have been, you threatened to kill me."

My heart pounded, and I asked the question I'd come here to ask. Finally.

"Would you have?"

Ezra rolled his eyes in annoyance. "I'm a lot of things, Willow. But I'm not a killer."

Some part of me relaxed. I guess the part that feared there might be more than one person in my life willing and able to hurt me.

While I felt sorry that Ezra got tangled up in all of this, it was his own poor decisions and behavior that drew the police's attention to him. And now, he had to be held accountable for the mistakes that he had made.

Sad, how I'd struggled to accept things in my life. And he'd almost lost everything because *he* couldn't accept the end of a relationship.

"Goodbye, Ezra."

I hoped he'd find peace one day.

## 56

The Garden of the Phoenix in Chicago was located just south of the Museum of Science and Industry. With the thirty-foot-tall trees surrounding the small body of water that snaked through emerald lawns, it didn't feel like we were anywhere near a large city. I could see buildings, of course, behind the oak trees, but it was as if they were peeking over them, trying to see the magic inside this park.

At its center, flanked by wide trees, condensed green bushes, and uneven boulders, was a fifteen-foot iron bridge that arched over the narrowest passage of water, which reflected the bright blue sky and overhanging branches of trees like an oil painting.

I'd never been here but had always wanted to come—especially now, in the spring, when more than a hundred cherry blossom trees transformed the grounds into a pink fairyland. I'd read that cherry blossoms symbolized both birth and death, beauty and violence. Fitting for everything Shane and I had been through in the past few months.

I was glad Mom moved to Texas, like she had planned; I think if she had stayed here, the grief would've devoured what was left of her heart. We talked more often than I had assumed we would, and so far, she had already flown back three times just to visit me.

Shane's mother, on the other hand, had a harder time adjusting to it all. Understandably, when your son finally brings someone home to meet you and that someone is pregnant with your grandchild, it's devastating to find out her father was your husband's killer. That's not something you can get past quickly or easily. But to her credit, she made the effort to get to know me. I wouldn't say that it was easy, because it wasn't. I could still see a flash of pain pass through her eyes from time to time, but I could also tell she didn't hold me personally responsible for what happened in the past. She wanted her son to be happy, and she wanted to be part of her grandchild's life.

Shane held my hand as we walked toward the bridge. A different bridge than the one that had started everything all those months ago. I put a hand on my swelling stomach, delighted that we'd decided to wait to find out the baby's gender until his or her birth. I loved having things to look forward to these days. I loved our new apartment that we recently moved into together and our new pet, Snowflake, who we'd adopted two months ago.

But most of all, I loved Shane.

I'd left my HR job to open my dream company, which currently focuses on helping unemployed people get back on their feet. I had to take out a loan for it, living off that debt for a bit, but according to my cash flow projections, I'd break even shortly after the baby was born and pull in enough money to pay the bills. These days, I used all my mad HR skills to help people write the perfect résumé, to get them proper training that would make them more attractive in the workforce, and I worked with companies in the Chicagoland area to match hardworking people with open roles. I loved every second of it.

I actually looked *forward* to working rather than dreading it.

"Is your mom having fun, planning the baby shower?" I asked.

"You kidding? She's going overboard." Shane rubbed his eyebrow. "Yesterday, she said something about storks. I hope to God she meant cardboard cutouts, not the real thing."

I laughed.

"Fallon's eggin' her on." Shane rolled his eyes. "Keeps sending her more ideas on some shared Pinterest board. Last I heard, they were up to thirty games planned for the event."

"God help us." I smiled.

"I know. She invited a bunch of my coworkers, too, thanks to Fallon's contacts. Sounds like half the force'll be there."

I was relieved Shane had made peace with being a police officer despite being in a relationship. I would never want him to give up who he was out of fear.

Life is short. Denying yourself experiences or relationships, fearing it will end in heartbreak, will only lead to a life of loneliness and sadness. You have to go for what you want in life—fully and completely.

Just like Shane had chosen to do.

I was proud of him.

"My mom has her flight booked for it," I said. "It'll be"—interesting?—"nice having everyone together."

Shane squeezed my hand, his knowing eyes meeting mine. "The past is the past, Willow. My mom doesn't blame you guys for it."

"I know, but...you have to admit, that's a big matzo ball."

"I think it gave my mom a new perspective."

I eyed him skeptically. "How so?"

"My mom had her walls up at first, but she's thrilled because she's never seen me happier. She sees what a kind person you are. And once she let you into her heart, I think it healed her in ways it might not have otherwise. I think she realized she had misplaced her grief for a long time."

"Maybe you're seeing what you wish to see."

Shane's mouth curled up on one side. "She invited my dad's side of the family to the baby shower."

Holy cow, a two-decade-long family rift mending? My eyes exploded with tears. *Dammit.*

"I blame the hormones." I wiped them.

Shane chuckled as he swiped my cheeks.

"Enough with the heavy," he said. "We didn't come here to talk about all this. We came here to see some cherry blossoms."

Shane took my hand, and as we continued walking along the grounds, I felt like the luckiest woman in the world. To find such a remarkable guy, to have so much to look forward to.

We walked to the top of the bridge and stopped to look down at the water, pink cherry blossoms rippling through its reflection.

"Check out that one," Shane said, pointing to my right.

"It's beautiful."

I turned back around to find him on bended knee. In one hand, he held a little white box, opened with a sparkling diamond ring in its center. In the other, a couple of purple wildflowers he'd grabbed along the way—the kind I'd told him reminded me of my father.

"Willow, a long time ago, I shut the door to my heart. I told myself it was because I didn't want to risk someone losin' me. Like my dad. And that was part of it, but it wasn't the whole part."

I studied the speckles in his eyes, which shimmered.

"I'd spent so many years in a dark place, isolating myself, and I forgot what happiness felt like. What it would be like to fall in love. And the longer I spent in that cave, the harder it became to find my way out. But when I met you, that all changed. You were like my compass, showing me the way, makin' me *want* to come out for the first time in my life. I went from not wanting to get close to anyone to not being able to *exist* without you by my side. If it wasn't for you, I would have stayed in that cave forever. Alone, going through the motions of life instead of living."

His eyes shimmered more.

As did mine.

"I can't imagine spending a single moment without you by my side. I love you, Willow. I want to spend the rest of my life with you. Will you marry me?"

I nodded, the tears rolling down my cheeks. "Yes."

Shane smiled and took the ring out of its holder, placed it on my ring finger. Then, he stood up and took my face between his hands.

"I love you," I whispered.

Shane brought his lips to mine.

Our love had healed so many old hurts and taught us to let go of the things we couldn't change and embrace the happiness within our reach.

~

THANK YOU FOR READING GRAVE DECEPTION! I HOPE YOU ENJOYED THE story that readers participated in writing (more on that in a minute).

IF YOU HAVEN'T READ THE FIRST TWO BOOKS IN THE SERIES, GRAB YOUR copy today with **THE LIES WE TELL**—a collection of the first two **stand-alone romances** in the Secrets and the City series, Deadly Illusion and Fatal Cure—**where we meet Shane and Zoey for the first time. The beginning of their story is something you don't want to miss.**

**WHAT HAPPENED WHEN SHANE GOT THAT PHONE CALL FROM HAYLEY and he rushed to save Willow?** Find out in this **exclusive FREE chapter from Shane's POV** (https://kathylockheart.com/shane-pov-the-truths-we-hide/).

*P.S. IF YOU LOVED THE TRUTHS WE HIDE, I'D BE HONORED IF YOU'D consider posting a 2-word review on amazon.*

~

DID YOU KNOW READERS PARTICIPATED IN THE WRITING OF THIS STORY? **As a reminder, here are some of the ways you PARTICIPATED in writing Grave Deception.**

🖤 YOU VOTED FOR YOUR FAVORITE TROPES. WINNERS WERE AS follows, and yep, all of them are in Grave Deception!

☑ Friends-to-lovers
☑ Touch-her-and-perish
☑ Forced Proximity.

♥ You voted for the STORY you wanted to read, and the winning story became Grave Deception.

♥ I NAMED A CHARACTER, TRACEY, AFTER A READER (I DID THIS IN Lethal Justice, too, with Katy, and it was so fun I might have to do it in every book.)

♥ YOU NAMED WILLOW'S FAVORITE COFFEE SHOP ANGIE'S Coffeeteria. :-)

# ACKNOWLEDGMENTS FOR LETHAL JUSTICE

First, **I'd like to thank you, the reader.** Your time is incredibly valuable, and I strive to give you an immersive reading experience that you will love. You have a ton of options when it comes to books, and you gave me and my books a chance. THANK YOU. Readers mean the world to me, and I'd love to connect with you. Please find my social media links at www.KathyLockheart.com.

Thank you to my husband for believing in me more than I believe in myself. We celebrated a milestone anniversary during the writing of this, and I love you more than you will ever understand.

Thank you to my children for bringing immense joy into my life. Getting to be with you and watch you as you grow is the most rewarding, wonderful experience of my life. I don't know how I got so lucky to have you both. I love you.

To my family for loving and encouraging me every step of the way. For my mother, who is a walking embodiment of kindness, your spirit has inspired me to be the best version of myself possible. To my dad, watching your inspirational fight to reclaim your life motivates me to keep pushing, even when times are hard. And to my sister, your love and kindness are felt more than you know.

To the rest of my family, thank you for cheering me on and being such a vital part of my life! Your love is the fuel that keeps me going on the hard days.

To my friends, Kristin and Sharon, for your incredible support. For cheering me on when I was taking a huge swing in life, and never showing a trace of doubt along the way. You guys are amazing, and I'm so blessed to have you in my life.

To my official beta readers and early ARC readers: Amy, Kristen, Katy, Alyson, Kayla, Terry, and Tracey! Thank you for reading this long before it was done and for all your valuable insights that made Lethal Justice even better!

To my editors—Susan Staudinger. Your brainstorming sessions and multiple rounds of editing made this story remarkably better than it would have been without you! And Jovana Shirley with Unforeseen Editing, and Judy's Proofreading—who ensured this novel was in fantastic shape. To my cover artist, Hang Le, for bringing such beauty to this novel!

To all the people who bring kindness and joy into the world. Thank you for making this world a better place!

# ACKNOWLEDGMENTS FOR GRAVE DECEPTION

First, **I'd like to thank you, the reader.** You have a ton of options when it comes to books, your time is incredibly precious, and you gave *me* a chance. From the bottom of my heart, THANK YOU. <u>Readers mean the world to me</u>, and I'd love to connect with you! Please find my social media links at www.KathyLockheart.com.

Thank you to Susan Staudinger. Your developmental and content editing, combining with our amazing virtual sessions made Grave Deception far better than it ever would have been without you.

Thank you to my early ARC readers: Katy, Kayla, Shay, Kim, Kate, Alyson, Sam, Sara, Kim, and Sandy. It means the world that you'd take the time to read this story, and provide insight back to me!

Thank you to my husband for showing me the beauty of true love and being my biggest cheerleader. Thank you to my children for giving me a love I didn't know existed until you were born and for inspiring me to be the best *me* I can be. Always go after your dreams.

To my family for enveloping me with love, encouraging me, and embracing my idea to become a writer.

To my friends, for your never-ending support.

To Amy and Kristen, my formal beta readers. Thank you for helping make this story even better.

To my editor Jovana, your attention to details polished this story and made it the best it could be! To my cover artist, Hang Le, for bringing such beauty to this novel!

To all the authors who came before me—your success paves the road for new writers to do what they love. Thank you.

*~ Kathy*

# LET'S CONNECT!

The easiest way to connect with me is to go to my website, www.
KathyLockheart.com, and find my social media links. I interact with
readers, so don't be surprised if you see me reply to your post or
invite you to join a reader team!

*Xoxo*

*Kathy*

- amazon.com/Kathy-Lockheart/e/B08XY5F2XG
- bookbub.com/profile/kathy-lockheart
- facebook.com/KathyLockheartAuthor
- tiktok.com/@kathylockheart_author
- instagram.com/kathy_lockheart
- twitter.com/Kathy_Lockheart
- pinterest.com/kathylockheart

Printed in Great Britain
by Amazon